Anonymous

Sea and Sail

Marvelous adventures on the ocean. Being interesting, instructive and graphic

accounts of the most popular voyages on record, remarkable shipwrecks,

hair-breadth escapes, naval adventures, the whale fishery, etc.

Anonymous

Sea and Sail

Marvelous adventures on the ocean. Being interesting, instructive and graphic accounts of the most popular voyages on record, remarkable shipwrecks, hair-breadth escapes, naval adventures, the whale fishery, etc.

ISBN/EAN: 9783337316631

Printed in Europe, USA, Canada, Australia, Japan

Cover: Foto ©Andreas Hilbeck / pixelio.de

More available books at **www.hansebooks.com**

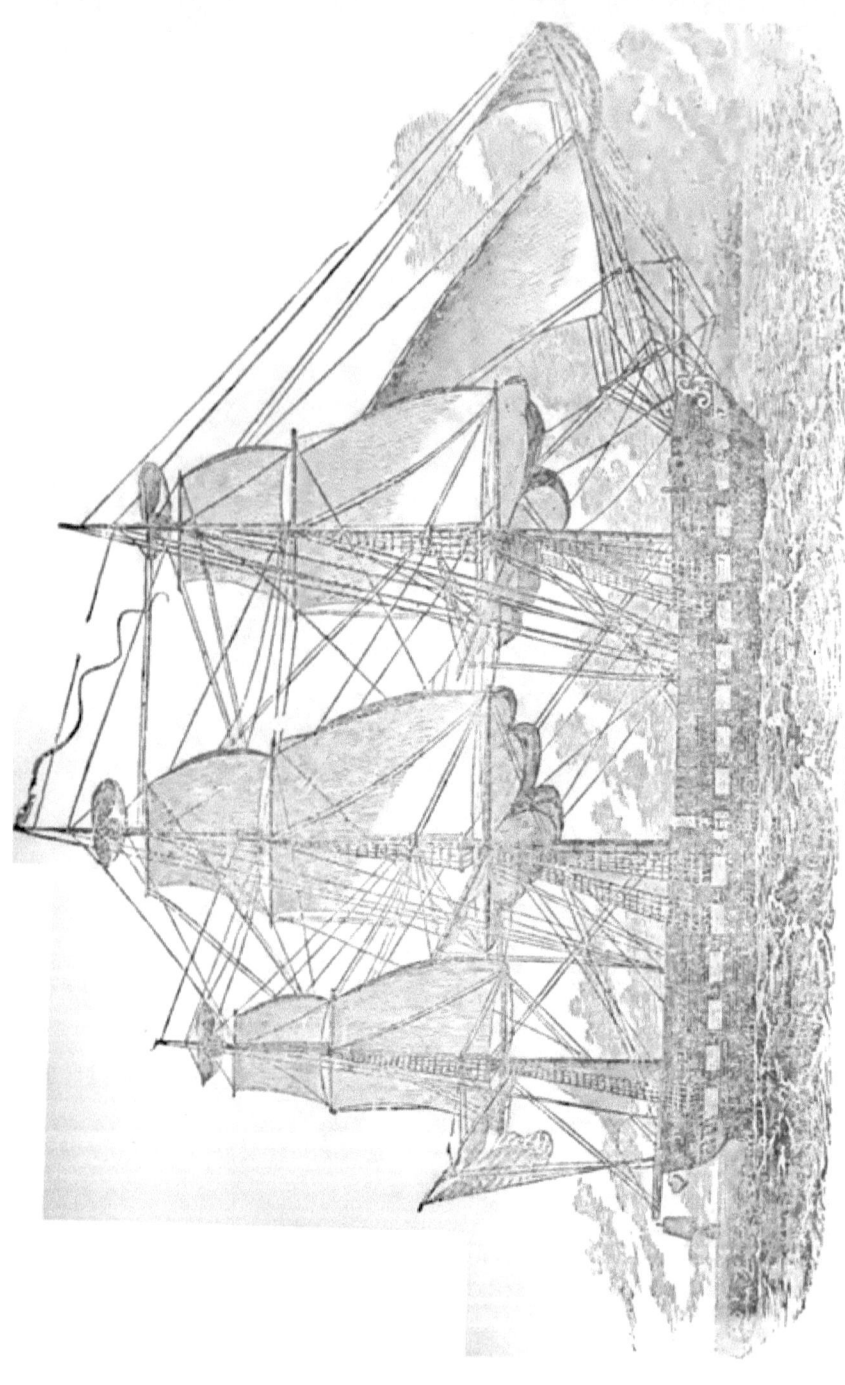

FRIGATE CONSTITUTION

SEA AND SAIL;

OR,

MARVELOUS ADVENTURES

ON THE

OCEAN

BEING

INTERESTING, INSTRUCTIVE AND GRAPHIC ACCOUNTS OF THE
MOST POPULAR VOYAGES ON RECORD, REMARKABLE SHIP-
WRECKS, HAIR-BREADTH ESCAPES, NAVAL ADVENT-
URES, THE WHALE FISHERY, ETC., ETC.,

*Illustrating the Advantages of Decision of Character,
Perseverance and Unwavering Hope in Time of Peril.*

ILLUSTRATED.

NEW YORK:
WORLD PUBLISHING HOUSE,
139 EIGHTH STREET.
1876.

PREFACE.

THE object of the present volume has been to afford a series of brief but graphic sketches, illustrating the pleasures, perils and beauties of the great highway of nations, which might prove both interesting and instructive. It was believed that a miscellany of the kind, which by its variety might not readily tire, and which might be laid down and resumed at frequent intervals, without losing its interest, would be acceptable to both young and old alike.

It embraces nearly every subject of importance in the history of navigation and maritime discoveries, while the sketches of nautical manners and adventure are from the most authentic sources. From the examples presented, it will be seen of what astonishing advantage are the virtues of decision, temperance, perseverance, and unwavering hope, in moments of extreme peril and despair. It is the coward only, who at such times deserts his post; bids defiance to orders, and surrenders himself to unmanly fear.

CONTENTS

CONTENTS.

POETRY.

ENGRAVINGS

SEA AND SAIL.

EARLY MARITIME DISCOVERIES

The Portuguese were among the first to signalize themselves in the career of geographical discovery. At the beginning of the fifteenth century, Prince Henry, son of John I. was at the head of the marine of Portugal. Under his immediate direction, several voyages were undertaken to the coast of Africa; in one of which the voyagers were driven by a storm out of their usual course along shore, and for the first time the terrified mariners found themselves in the boundless ocean. When the storm abated, they were in sight of an island, to which, in their thankfulness to Heaven for the succor it afforded, they gave the name of Puerto Sancto, or the Holy Haven—the least of the Madeiras. The voyages of the Portuguese now succeeded each other rapidly; and other navigators of this nation, either grown bolder, or again driven off the coast, discovered the Azores. In 1433, the Portuguese passed Cape Nun, hitherto the limit of their courses, and arrived at a cape, which presenting a frightful barrier to the still timid seamen, in the terrible surf that broke on the shoals near it, they named Bojador, signifying its projection into the sea and the consequent circuit it required to double it.

In succeeding expeditions, Cape Verd was reached, and the Senegal arrived at, and Lisbon saw with astonishment a different race from the Moors. Cape Mesurado was the limit of the Portuguese discoveries at the death of Prince Henry in 1463, which damping the ardor of discovery, it was not until 1471 that the Equator was crossed, and the islands in the gulf of Guinea were discovered.

The terrors of the burning zone, and the belief of the union of Africa and Asia being dissipated by these successive voyages, the passage to India round Africa was no longer deemed impossible, and a fleet was fitted out under Bartholomew Diaz for the express purpose of attempting it. The captain coasted Africa to within sight of its southern point, to which he gave the name of Cape of all Torments from the violent storms he experienced off it, and which, as well as the want of provisions, obliged him to return to Lisbon, after an absence of sixteen months. The name of the Cape of all Torments was changed by the king to that of Good Hope, from the prospect it afforded of accomplishing the passage to India

2

Ten years however elapsed after the discovery of the Cape before this passage was again attempted; and Vasco de Gama had the honor of doubling the promontory the 20th of November, 1497. Sailing along the east coast of Africa, he passed through the Mosambique Channel to Mombaze and thence to Melinda, where he procured pilots, and crossing the Arabian sea, arrived at Callicut the 22d of May, 1498. It is thought that the ridiculous ceremony of ducking, &c. on crossing the line was first practised in this voyage.

COLUMBUS.

While the Portuguese were attempting to arrive at India by the east, Columbus conceived the idea of reaching it by the west, which produced a discovery that was totally to alter the face of Europe by inundating it with the treasures of a new world.— Christopher Columbus was a native of Genoa. He seems to have been accustomed, in a degree, from his youth, to a sea-life, and once commanded a ship in an engagement with a Venitian galley, when both vessels having grappled took fire, and he saved himself by swimming nearly two leagues to the shore.

Columbus had formed an opinion, after much reflection, that by sailing across the Atlantic towards the west, new countries, probably forming a part of India, must be discovered. Fired with this project, he first proposed his plans to the king of Portugal, but that monarch not readily complying with his terms, Columbus concluded to resort to the court of Ferdinand and Isabella, who then ruled the united kingdoms of Castile and Arragon. His proposals were listened to with respect, and an assembly of all the learned men of the realm was called to listen to his reasoning, and weigh his arguments. He rose before this learned body, and explained to them his project and the probabilities of its success. But his propositions were rejected as absurd. One of their assertions was, that if a man should sail away westward as far as Columbus proposed, he would not be able to return on account of the roundness of the globe. They said it would be going down; and that coming back would be like climbing a hill, which a vessel could not do without the strongest gale!

But though baffled by these prejudiced men, he finally found an advocate in the Queen Isabella, who promised her assistance to the undertaking. After much delay and difficulty, an expedition was fitted out, and Columbus appointed admiral. He sailed with his companions from the bar of Saltes, a small is and in front of the town of Huelva, on the morning of the third of August, 1492. They steered their course in a S. W. direction for the Canary Islands. The day after their departure, the rudder of one of the caravels was unshipped. This was supposed to have been done through the contrivance of two men on board, who disliked the voyage. Her captain however repaired the rudder by means of ropes, so as to be able to keep on their course as far as the Grand Canary. Here three or four weeks were spent in repairing the vessel, and in taking in supplies of wood and water; after which, on the sixth of September, they departed in a westerly direction. On the fifteenth of the same month, at night, they saw a wonderful flash of fire fall into the sea. On the next day they fell in with a large quantity of green weeds, among which they found a live crab; and soon after great flocks of birds were seen flying towards the west. The sailors watched, with the greatest anxiety, for every sign of land. But being often disappointed they began to murmur and grow afraid.

Towards the night of the 22d, two or three land-birds came singing on board the vessels, and flew away at daybreak. One thing that terrified the sailors was that the wind always blew directly in their stern. They believed that in those seas they should never have a wind to carry them back again. It fortunately happened however, that about this time the wind started up freshly from another quarter, with a rolling sea. The signs of land having continually failed, the crews grew more incensed against the admiral. Provisions were falling short, and the general wish seemed to be to turn back. Some of them even proposed to throw Columbus into the sea, and give out on their return that he had fallen overboard, while engaged in taking some observations.

On the eleventh of October they experienced signs of land, which could not be mistaken. A cane and a log were picked up, and a branch of thorn full of red berries was likewise found. Convinced, by these tokens, of the vicinity of land, Columbus after evening prayers, made an address to his crew, reminding them of the mercy of God in bringing them so far, and encouraging them to continue. About ten o'clock that evening, while keeping an anxious look-out from the top of the cabin, the admiral thought he beheld a light glimmering at a great distance; and at two in the morning the signal of land was given by a sailor named Rodrigo de Triana. When the day dawned they beheld before them a large island, quite love, full of green trees and delicious springs, and apparently well inhabited. The ships immediately came to anchor. The admiral went ashore in his boat, well-armed, and bearing the royal standard. After formally taking possession of the island, he named it San Salvador. It is now called Cat Island, and belongs to the group of the Bahamas.

He also discovered Cuba, Hispaniola, and several other small

islands, and having left a colony in a fort at Hispaniola returned
'o Spain in March, 1493. In September following, he set out
on his second voyage, and sailed by the Leeward Islands to Hispaniola; in a third voyage undertaken in 1498, he discovered the
continent of America, but in consequence of some envious charges made against him, was sent in fetters to Europe. He was
instantly liberated on his arrival, but so deeply did the injury sink
into his mind, that he always carried about him the chains he had
worn, and ordered that they should be buried with him. He sailed
from Cadiz, in May, 1502, on his fourth voyage. On arriving off

Columbus.

St. Domingo he found eighteen loaded ships preparing to depart
for Europe. As from certain tokens he discerned the approach
of a hurricane, he requested permission to enter the harbour, and
at the same time warned the fleet not to sail. Both his request
and warning were disregarded. The hurricane came on. By
proper precautions he escaped its fury; but it fell with such destructive violence on the fleet, that only two or three ships were
saved, and the rest perished with all their wealth.

Columbus proceeded on his voyage and traced all the coast
about the isthmus of Darien. Sailing homewards he was wrecked on the island of Jamaica. Here he underwent great distress
from the mutiny and desertion of his men, and the suspicions of the
natives, who withheld their supplies of provisions, till, by the pre-
diction of an eclipse, he obtained an irresistible authority over
their minds. At length he was delivered by a squadron sent from
Hispaniola; and after a short stay at St. Domingo, he embarked
with two ships for Spain. One of these was obliged by storms

to return, and in the other with great difficulty and dangei, he reached St Lucar in December, 1504, and thus finished his last disastrous voyage. On his return he had the mortification of finding his best friend, Isabella, dead. He was worn down by anxiety and disease; his services were neglected, and his hopes miserably disappointed. He finally died at Valladolid, on the 20th of May, 1506, in the fifty-ninth year of his age; passing through the last scene with that piety and composure, which he had displayed in all the trying emergencies of life. In 1536, his remains were removed to Hispaniola, and interred in the city of St. Domingo. But in 1795, they were again disinterred and conveyed to Havanna, in Cuba.

.

MAGELLAN.

Ferdinand Magellan was by birth a Portuguese, descended from a good family, and born towards the end of the fifteenth century. In consequence of certain services in the Indian Seas, he applied to the government for some recompense; but being treated with neglect, he left his own country to seek employment in a foreign land. In company with Ruy Falero, an eminent astronomer, and one of his associates, he travelled into Spain, and explained to Charles V. the reigning monarch, his project of making discoveries in distant seas. The court listened to the adventurers with favor, and consented to fit out an expedition.

Magellan's little squadron consisted of five ships, manned with 237 men, and supplied with provisions, ammunition and stores, for two years. On the 1st of August, 1519, they left Seville, and on the 27th of September sailed from Saulucar, steering for the Canaries. They refreshed at Teneriffe, and early in October passed the Cape de Verd Islands. Holding on their course, they bore along the coast of Africa, till they crossed the line, seventy days after their departure. In the beginning of December they, came to that part of Brazil which is now called the Bay of St. Lucia. They subsequently anchored at the mouth of a large river, supposed to be the Rio Janeiro, where they continued a fortnight. On their first landing, the inhabitants flocked to the beach in great numbers, beholding, as they imagined, five sea-monsters approaching the shore. When the boats put out from the ships, the natives set up a great shout, conceiving them to be young sea-monsters, the offspring of the others.

Proceeding along the South American Coast, the squadron arrived in April, 1520, at a large bay, now called by the name of

2*

St. Julian. Here they saw a wild, gigantic race, of great size and fierceness who made a roaring not unlike that of bulls. One of them came on board the admiral's ship, and was well pleased with his reception; but happening to cast his eyes on a looking-glass, he was so terrified, that starting backwards, he beat to the ground

Straits of Magellan.

two men who stood behind him. Others subsequently came on board, and their behavior afforded great entertainment to the officers. One of these savages, ate a basket full of ship-biscuits, and drank a cask of water at a meal. They wore sandals, or a kind of shoes, made of skins, and this caused their feet to appear like those of an animal. Magellan named them Patagonians, from the Spanish word *pata*, signifying a hoof, or paw.

Magellan determined to continue here till the return of spring, as it is winter in the southern hemisphere during our summer. He had ordered the allowance of provisions to be shortened, to meet this exigence, which caused much discontent among the crews. A mutiny soon followed, which was not quelled till one of the officers was hanged, and some others were sent on shore to be left among the Patagonians. Five dreary months were passed in the harbor of St. Julian, during which, every exertion was made to insure the successful prosecution of the voyage. On the 24th of August, the squadron again set sail, the weather being fine, and proceeded southward, till a violent gale from the east drove one of the vessels on shore, but the crew was happily saved. Coasting south with the four remaining ships, they approached a cape, near which an opening was discovered which was found afterwards to be a strait. Upon this, Magellan gave orders that all the other ships should carefully examine the strait, promising to wait for them a certain number of days. While the three vessels were employed in this expedition, one of them was driven out of the strait by the reflux of the tide, when the crew, dissatisfied with their situation, rose on their captain, made him prisoner, and again set sail for Europe. After waiting several days beyond the time he had fixed, Magellan entered the strait or arm of the sea, which has ever since retained his name. The entrance lies in 52 degrees south latitude, and the strait, which is about 110 leagues in length, is very wide in some places, and in others not more than half a league from shore to shore. On both sides the land was high, and the mountains were covered with snow, on advancing about 50 leagues west from the entrance.

In about six weeks they found themselves again in an open sea, the coast terminating westward in a cape, and the shore of the continent taking a northerly direction. The sight of the Pacific Ocean gave Magellan the utmost joy, he being the first European who sailed upon it. Proceeding W. N. W. he arrived at the Ladrone Islands, to which he gave that name on account of the thievish disposition of the natives.

They sailed from the Ladrones on the 10th of March, 1524, and after visiting a number of islands, entered the port of Lebu on the 7th of April. From Lebu they sailed to the island of Mathan, which being governed by two kings, and one of them refusing to pay tribute to the king of Spain, Magellan prepared to reduce him. He marched into the interior of the island accompanied by sixty Europeans. Here he was attacked by three distinct bodies of the islanders, whose united force amounted to upwards of six thousand. The battle was for some time doubtful, till Magellan's impetuosity carrying him too far, he was killed, by being wounded in the leg with a poisoned arrow and stabbed through the body by a spear. Eight or nine of the Spaniards and fifteen of the Indians were also slain. After the death of the admiral, new commanders were chosen from among the surviving officers, and as the ships were now in a very bad condition, it was found necessary to make use of one to repair the other two.

Sailing W. S. W. they came to the rich island of Borneo. From this place they sailed to Cimbubon, where they were detained forty days in repairing their ships and taking in wood and water Bending their course hence S. E. for the Moluccas, they came to anchor in the port of Tidore on the 8th of November After remaining here sometime, they set sail in one ship alone and with fifty-nine persons on board, for Europe. To double the Cape of Good Hope with the greater safety, they sailed as low as 42 degrees S. latitude, where they were obliged to wait seven weeks for a wind On doubling the cape they were much distressed by hunger and sickness. For two months they held on their course to the N. W. without touching at any port, during which

time they lost twenty-one persons, and the rest were on the point
of starving

In this situation they arrived at St Jago, one of the Cape de
Verd Islands. Finally on the 7th of September, they entered St.
Lucar in Spain, with their number reduced to about eighteen persons According to their reckoning, they had sailed 14,000 leagues,
and crossed the equator six times, having been absent three years
wanting fourteen days. This was the first voyage round the
world that had ever been made

SIR FRANCIS DRAKE.

Mr. Drake was first apprenticed to the master of a small vessel trading to France and Zealand; at the age of eighteen he went
purser of a ship to the Bay of Biscay, and at twenty made a voyage to the coast of Guinea. Having obtained Queen Elizabeth's
permission for an expedition against the Spaniards, five ships were
fitted out, having on board 164 able men and a large quantity of
provisions. This fleet sailed out of Plymouth Sound on the 5th
of November 1577; but meeting with a violent storm, they were
obliged to put back and refit. On the 13th of December they
sailed again, and on the 25th passed Cape Cantin, on the coast
of Barbary. After visiting numerous islands and meeting with
various adventures, having passed the line, they at length discovered the coast of Brazil on the 5th of April, it being fifty-four
days since they saw land. As soon as the people on shore saw the
ships, they made large fires in different parts, and performed ceremonies to prevail on the gods to sink the vessels, or at least to
prevent their landing. Sailing southward they anchored in fort
St. Julian, where the admiral going on shore with six men, some
of the natives slew the gunner, whose death was revenged by the
commander, who killed the murderer with his own hand. At
this place Magellan having executed one of his company who
conspired against his life, Drake caused one of the crew named
Doughty to be tried for the same offence against himself; and
xecuted him on the same gibbet.

On the 20th of August, they fell in with the strait of Magellan, which they entered, but found so full of intricate windings,
that the same wind which was sometimes in their favor, was at
others against them. After several difficulties they entered the
South Sea on the 6th of September, and on the next day a violent storm drove them 200 leagues south of the strait, where they
anchored among some islands, abounding in herbs and water

Being now arrived at the other mouth of the strait, they steered for the coast of Chili. On their course they met an Indian in a canoe, who informed them that at St. Jago there was a large ship laden for Peru. The admiral rewarded him for this information, whereupon he conducted them to the place where the ship lay at anchor. There were only eight Spaniards and three negroes on board, who mistaking them for friends, welcomed them and invited them to drink Chili wine. Drake accepted the invitation, and going on board, put them under hatches; arriving on shore he rifled the town and chapel, from which he took great quantities of silver and gold. Proceeding to sea, they arrived at the port of Tarapaxa, where some of them going on shore found a Spaniard asleep, with eighteen bars of silver laying by his side, which they took without waking him.

Entering the port of Lima on the 13th of February, they found twelve sail of ships at anchor unguarded, the crews being all on shore. Examining these vessels they found much plate, together with rich silks and linens, which they took away; but having learned that a rich ship called the Cacafuego had lately sailed from that harbor for Taila, the admiral determined to follow her. Having come up with the chase, they gave her three shots, which brought away the mizzen-mast, whereupon they boarded her, and found thirteen chests full of rials of plate, eighty pounds weight of gold, a quantity of jewels, and twenty-six tons of silver in bars.

They subsequently took several other rich prizes, and Drake having now revenged himself on the Spaniards, began to think of the best way of returning to England. To return by the strait of Magellan would be to throw himself into the hands of the Spaniards; he therefore determined to sail westward to the East Indies, and return by the Cape of Good Hope. But wanting wind, he sailed towards the north, and in 38 degrees N. latitude, discovered a country, which from its white cliffs he called New Albion, though it is now known by the name of California. Here they were received with much hospitality by the natives, and the king made Drake a solemn tender of his whole kingdom. Sailing hence, they saw the Ladrones on the 13th of October. The admiral held on his course without delay, and on the 4th of November, fell in with the Moluccas. Having arrived at a little island south of Celebes, they staid twenty-six days, in order to repair the ships. Setting sail hence, they ran among a number of small islands, and the wind shifting about suddenly, drove them upon a rock, on the evening of the 9th of January, 1579, where they stuck fast, till four in the afternoon of the next day. In this extremity they lightened the vessel, by taking out eight pieces of ordnance and three tons of cloves. On the 18th of June, they doubled the Cape of Good Hope, and on the 22nd of July arrived at Sierra Leone, where they found a great number of elephants. They staid

here two days, and holding on their course for Plymouth, arrived
there on Monday, the 26th of September, 1580; but according to
their own reckoning, on Sunday the 25th, having gone round the
world in two years, ten months, and a few days. The honor of
knighthood was conferred on Drake, and a chair was made from
his ship which is still shown as a curiosity at Oxford

THE BEACON-LIGHT.

Darkness was deep'ning o'er the seas,
    And still the hulk drove on;
No sail to answer to the breeze,
    Her masts and cordage gone:
Gloomy and drear her course of fear,
    Each looked but for a grave,
When full in sight, the Beacon-light
    Came streaming o'er the wave!   .

Then wildly rose the gladd'ning shout
    Of all that hardy crew—
Boldly they put the helm about,
    And through the surf they flew,
Storm was forgot, toil heeded not,
    And loud the cheer they gave,
As full in sight, the Beacon-light
    Came streaming o'er the wave!

And gaily oft the tale they told,
    When they were safe on shore,
How hearts had sunk, and hope grown cold
    Amid the billows' roar;
That not a star had shone afar,
    By its pale beam to save,
When full in sight, the Beacon-light,
    Came streaming o'er the wave!

THE SPANISH WRECK.

About the year 1683, Sir William Phips, afterwards celebrated for his attempts to take Quebec, in 1690, applied to the English Government for aid and permission to fit out a suitable vessel for the purpose of searching for the wreck of a Spanish ship which had been lost near one of the West India Islands, richly laden with silver. His request, after some delay, was granted and a frigate called Algier Rose, carrying eighteen guns and manned with ninety five men, was placed under his command. He arrived in New England the same year and proceeded forthwith to the place where the treasure was reported to have been lost. He encountered many difficulties in his voyage and came nigh, more than once, losing his life by the mutiny of his crew. It is reported of him that while his ship lay by an island, for the purpose of enabling his men to take on board a fresh supply of wood and water, they agreed among themselves to take the ship into their own hands, and make a piratical expedition into the South Seas. They were all on the island with the exception of Captain Phips and eight or ten of the crew. Among these was the carpenter, whose services they could not well dispense with, and they accordingly sent to the ship, requesting him to come to them, as they had something for him to do. No sooner had he come among them, than they disclosed to him the cruel project, which was to set the Captain, and the above named eight or ten men upon the island, and then leave them to perish, while they would take the ship into their own hands and perform the proposed voyage. They gave the carpenter half an hour to consider of the subject, whether he would join with them or not, and sent him back accompanied by a seaman to prevent any interview between him and the Captain, by which a disclosure could be made. While at work on the ship, he suddenly feigned an attack of the cholic, and rushed into the cabin for the purpose of obtaining relief, and while there, gave the Captain an account of the determination of his crew. He directed the carpenter to return upon the island, and give his consent to join the conspiracy.

When the carpenter had left the ship, the Captain ordered the men on board, to prepare the pieces for action, removed the plank by which a landing had been effected, and ordered them not to permit any one of those, save the carpenter, to approach the ship. A quantity of provisions had been carried on shore and covered with a tent, and two or three guns placed near to protect them from the Spaniards who might be passing that way: these guns were all charged, ready to be made use of in the event of an attack from the conspirators. The disaffected part of the crew now returned to the ship for the purpose of executing their plans

No sooner had they come in sight, than the captain ordered them
not to approach, saying to them that their intentions had been
discovered, and that they were to be left upon the island, there to
remain and perish. Seeing how hopeless their condition was
become, they gathered courage from despair, and resolved to
rescue the provisions from the ship, and began to make a bold
push. As soon as they began to approach, the captain in a resolute manner, cried out, "stand off, ye wretches, at your peril!"
—They quietly relinquished their determination to attack, and
fell upon their knees, imploring pardon, and offered to comply
with any disposal he might make of them, provided he would receive them on board. After having kept them on their knees
long enough, he granted their petition and received them into
the ship, and sailed immediately for the island of Jamaica, there
put them on shore, and employed other seamen in their place.

He now commenced an examination for the wreck, and after
spending a long time in an almost fruitless search, sailed for England. By the advice, however, of an old Spaniard, he had satisfied himself of the prospect of succeeding in accomplishing his object, and determined to return again and prosecute his plan. His
crew being composed of strangers, made him think it advisable to
change them for others in whom he could have greater confidence
in the event his labors should be crowned with success.

On his return to England, his conduct gained the royal approbation, and the applause of the nobles, and many distinguished
men encouraged him to engage in a second expedition and under
more favorable and promising circumstances.

His project was opposed, however, by many powerful enemies.
but, promoted by the proverb, *he who can wait, hath what he de
sireth*, he overcame every obstacle and disappointment, and, under
the patronage of the Duke of Albemarle, had a new ship fitted
out with a more honest crew, furnished with instruments and conveniences suited to the nature of the expedition. Arriving at
Port de la Plata, he made a large canoe from the cotton tree sufficient to carry eight men, and with the old Spaniard for a guide,
again commenced examination for the wreck. There 'hey floated about, fishing for their treasure among dangerous reefs and
shoals for many weeks without success. So fruitless was the
search that more than once had he, as well as his men, determined to abandon the work. At length, when returning to the ship,
discouraged by repeated disappointment, and the hopelessness of
a successful issue of the project, one of the men looking into the
water discovered a feather, as he thought, growing out of a rock.
Thinking that they would not go back to the Captain without
something to present him, they ordered an Indian to dive down
and bring it up, which having done, he gave an account of many
large guns which he saw in his descent. The diver again went
down, and, to the joy and astonishment of the men, returned with

a sow or lump of silver, which turned out to be worth from ten to twelve hundred dollars. They buoyed the place and returned to the Captain overjoyed with their good fortune, as it was well known that the wreck was one of the ships belonging to the king of Spain, which had been lost on a returning voyage from South America richly laden with silver bullion. The loss of the ship is supposed to have happened about the year 1637, and the immense treasures which were reported to have been sunk with her were often made the subject of ingenious speculation, and many had sunk their own fortunes and efforts to find it. It was reserved, however, in the silent depths, that Capt. Phips might be the fortunate finder of it at so late a period after its loss. He now found in the bullion brought to him full assurance that destiny had allotted to him to *suck of the abundance of the seas and of treasures hid in the sand.*

Having prepared his instruments for fishing up the contents of the wreck, all hands were now busily employed in the work, and in a short time they succeeded in procuring the astonishing amount of *thirty-two tons of silver.* In addition to this Captain Adderly, an adventurer from Providence, and particular friend of Captain Phips, obtained six tons more from the same wreck at the same time. It was by an agreement that Adderly met Phips at the place of the wreck with a small vessel. He was so overjoyed with the extent of his riches and so elated at such unlooked for acquisitions, that he lived but a little while to enjoy them. It is said that he went to the island of Bermudas where he became insane and died about two years after the six tons of silver came into his hands. Phips, however, made a more profitable account of the expedition, and lived to enjoy the proceeds of it without prejudice to his health or destruction of his mind. In a few weeks after leaving the wreck, he arrived safe in London, in 1687, with a cargo valued at near FIFTEEN HUNDRED THOUSAND DOLLARS. He made an honest distribution of it among those who aided him in fitting him out with a vessel and proper conveniences, and received about seventy-five thousand dollars for his share of the profit. The Duke of Albemarle, out of respect to his honesty and fidelity, presented his wife, who was then in New England, a gold cup worth "near a thousand pounds." And King James as a reward for his important services in bringing such amount of property into the country conferred on him the honor of Knighthood.

Sir William Phips was born February 2, 1650, at a despicable plantation on the river Kennebeck. He removed to Boston where he married a daughter of Roger Spencer, and pursued the busi ness of a smith, which was the occupation of his father. It is said that he frequently promised his wife that he would one day *command a King's ship* and be the *owner of a fair brick house in the Green lane of North Boston,* all which proved true, for after the discovery of the wreck, he returned into New England, in the summer of the year 1688, "able after five year's absence, to

3

entertain his lady with some accomplishment of his predictions; and then built himself a fair house in the very place which he foretold."

Sir William Phips was industrious, courageous, and persevering: his principal fault was, occasionally indulging his temper. This failing he did not overcome until late in life. It is this day said by the very aged people living at the north part of Boston, where he resided, that when he was governor of Massachusetts, he had a quarrel with a truckman, at which time he was in so great a passion, that he threw off his coat and dared the man to fight. After this, however, he became very serious and devout, when he joined the Church, made a written acknowledgement of his past errors, and in terms of deep humility, gave evidence of a pious mind.

Phips was made "Captain General and Commander-in-Chief of Massachusetts Bay," in 1690.

The Brick House which he built stands in Salem Street, and is improved as an asylum for orphan boys.

DAMPIER

William Dampier was born in Somersetshire, England, in the year 1652. He lost both his parents when very young, and was bound apprentice to the master of a ship at Weymouth, with whom he made a voyage to France and another to New England In 1673, he served in the Dutch war, and was afterwards an over seer to a plantation in Jamaica. He next visited the bay of Campeachy as a logwood cutter, and, after once more visiting England engaged in a band of Buccaneers, as they called themselves, although in reality pirates, with whom he roved on the Peruvian coasts. He next visited Virginia, and engaged in an expedition against the Spanish settlements in the South Seas. They accordingly sailed in August, 1683, and, after taking several prizes on the coasts of Peru and Chili, the party experienced various fortune but no very signal success. Dampier, wishing to obtain some knowledge of the northen coast of Mexico, joined the crew of a captain Swan, who cruised in the hopes of meeting the annual royal Manilla ship, which, however, escaped them. Swan and Dampier were resolved to steer for the East Indies, and they accordingly sailed to the Piscadores, to Bouton island, to New Holland and to Nicobar, where Dampier and others were left ashore to recover their health. Their numbers gave them hopes of being able to navigate a canoe to Achin, in which they succeeded, after encountering a tremendous storm, which threatened them with unavoidable destruction. After making several trading voyages with a Captain Weldon, Dampier entered, as a gunner, the English factory at Bencoolen. Upon this coast he remained until 1691, when he found means to return home, and, being in want of money, sold his property in a curiously painted or tattoed Indian prince, who was shown as a curiosity, and who ultimately died of the small pox at Oxford. Dampier is next heard of as a commander, in the king's service, of a sloop of war of twelve guns and fifty men, probably fitted out for a voyage of discovery. After experiencing a variety of adventures with a discontented crew, this vessel foundered off the Isle of Ascension, his men with difficulty reaching land. They were released from this island by an East India ship, in which Dampier came to England. He afterwards commanded a ship in the South Seas, and accompanied the expedition of Captain Woodes Rogers as pilot.

A MAN OVERBOARD.

Sailors are men of rough habits, but their feelings are not by any means so coarse; if they possess little prudence or worldly consideration, they are likewise very free from selfishness; generally speaking, too, they are much attached to one another, and will make great sacrifices to their messmates or shipmates when opportunities occur.

I remember once, when crusing off Terceira in the Endymion, that a man fell overboard and was drowned. After the usual confusion, and long search in vain, the boats were hoisted up, and the hands called to make sail. I was officer of the forecastle and on looking about to see if all the men were at their station, missed one of the foretop men. Just at that moment I observed some one curled up, and apparently hiding himself under the bow of the barge, between the boat and the booms. 'Hillo!' I said, 'who are you? What are you doing there, you skulker? Why are you not at your station?'

'I am not skulking, sir,' said the poor fellow, the furrows in whose bronzed and weatherbeaten cheek were running down with tears. The man we had just lost had been his messmate and friend, he told me, for ten years. I begged his pardon, in full sincerity, for having used such harsh words to him at such a moment, and bid him go below to his birth for the rest of the day. —'Never mind, sir, never mind,' said the kind hearted seaman, 'it can't be helped. You meant no harm, sir. I am as well on deck as below. Bill's gone sir, but I must do my duty.' So saying, he drew the sleeve of his jacket twice or thrice across his eyes, and

mustering his grief within his breast, walked to his station as if
nothing had happened.

In the same ship and nearly about the same time, the people
were bathing along side in a calm at sea.   It is customary on such
occasions to spread a studding-sail on the water, by means of
lines from the fore and main yard arms, for the use of those who
either cannot swim, or who are not expert in this art, so very
important to all seafaring people. Half a dozen of the ship's boys
were floundering about in the sails, and sometimes even venturing
beyond the leech rope.   One of the least of these urchins, but
not the least courageous of their number, when taunted by his
more skilful companions with being afraid, struck out boldly beyond the prescribed bounds.   He had not gone much farther than
his own length, however, along the surface of the fathomless sea,
when his heart failed him, poor little man; and long with his confidence away also went his power of keeping his head above the
water.   So down he sank rapidly, to the speechless horror of the
other boys, who of course, could lend the drowning child no help.

The captain of the forecastle, a tall, fine-looking, hard-a-weath-
er fellow, was standing on the shank of the sheet anchor with
his arms across, and his well varnished canvass hat drawn so
much over his eyes that it was difficult to tell whether he was
awake or merely dozing in the sun, as he leaned his back against
the fore-topmast backstay.   The seaman, however, had been attentively watching the young party all the time, and rather fearing that mischief might ensue from their rashness, he had grunted
out a warning to them from time to time, to which they paid no
sort of attention.   At last he desisted, saying they might drown
themselves if they had a mind, for never a bit would he help
them; but no sooner did the sinking figure of the adventurous
little boy catch his eye, than, diver fashion, he joined the palms of
his hands over his head, inverted his position in one instant, and
urging himself into swifter motion by a smart push with his feet
against the anchor, shot head foremost into the water.   The poor
lad sank so rapidly that he was at least a couple of fathoms under
the surface before he was arrested by the grip of the sailor, who
soon rose again, bearing the bewildered boy in his hand, and calling to the other youngsters to take better care of their companion,
chucked him right into the belly of the sail in the midst of the
party   The fore-sheet was hanging in the calm, nearly into the
water, and by it the dripping seaman scrambled up again to his
old birth on the anchor, shook himself like a great Newfoundland
dog, and then jumping on the deck, proceeded across the forecastle
to shift himself.

At the top of the ladder he was stopped by the marine officer,
who had witnessed the whole transaction, as he sat across the
gangway hammocks, watching the swimmers, and trying to get
his own consent to undergo the labor of undressing. Said the soldier

to the sailor " That was very well done of you, my man, and right well deserves a glass of grog. Say so to the gun-room steward as you pass; and tell him it is my orders to fill you out a stiff nor'-wester." The soldier's offer was kindly meant, but rather clumsily timid, at least so thought Jack: for though he inclined his head in acknowledgment of the attention, and instinctively touched his hat when spoken to by an officer, he made no reply till out of the marine's hearing, when he laughed, or rather chuckled out to the people near him, " Does the good gentleman suppose I 'll take a glass of grog for saving a boy's life."—*Capt. Hall*

CAPTAIN WOODES ROGERS.

This voyage was undertaken chiefly by the merchants of Bristol. Captain Woodes Rogers was appointed commander in chief, and William Dampier first pilot of the expedition. They sailed from King-road, Bristol, on the 1st of August, 1708, their force consisting of the Duke, a ship of three hundred tons burden, thirty guns, and one hundred and seventy men, commanded by Rogers; and the Duchess of two hundred and seventy tons, twenty-six guns, and one hundred and fifty-one men, under the command of captain Courtney. They entered the harbor of Cork on the 6th of August, where they enlisted a number of seamen in the room of about forty fellows who had ran away. They set sail on the 1st of September, with a very mixed crew, and on the morning of the 10th discovered a sail, to which they immediately gave chase. On coming up with her she proved to be a Swedish ship, and was permitted to proceed unmolested on her way. During the time the ship was in custody, a design had been privately formed on board the Duke, by four inferior officers, to make a prize of her; and when they found she was given up, they began to mutiny; but the boatsman, being displaced, and, with ten others, put in irons, and a severe whipping given to some of the leaders of the disturbance, all was quiet again. On the 14th, however, some of the ship's company, headed by a daring fellow, came up to captain Rogers at the steerage-door, and demanded the boatswain out of irons. The captain gave them good words, and having taken the ringleader, as if to speak with him on the quarter-deck, had him suddenly seized by the help of the officers, and lashed by one of his own followers. On the 16th the captain released the prisoners from irons on their acknowledging their sorrow for what they had done.

On the 17th, gained sight of the peak of Teneriffe, and the next day took a Spanish bark of twenty-five tons. On the 25th of September passed the tropic, when about sixty of the crew, who

had never been this course before, were ducked three times,
by hoisting them up halfway the main-yard, with a rope to which
they were made fast, and sousing them into the water. After
visiting the Cape de Verd islands, where they took in water and
provisions, the ships again set sail on the 8th of October, in the
evening. On the 14th, they came within sight of Brazil, and soon
after came to anchor before the island of Grande, in eleven fathoms water. While they lay here another quarrel arose on board
the Duchess, and eight of the ringleaders were put in irons. On
the 25th, two men deserted and made their escape into the woods;
but, in the night, were so terrified by the noise made by the baboons
and monkeys, that they ran back, plunged into the water, and prayed to be taken on board again

Peak of Teneriffe.

The ships sailed out of the bay of Grande on the first of De
cember, steering for Juan Fernandez, and on the 5th of January,
encountered a violent storm, which drove such a quantity of
water into the Duchess, that they expected she would sink every
moment. As the men were going to supper about nine o'clock
at night, she shipped a sea at the poop, which beat in the bulk-
head and all the cabin windows. On deck the yawl was staved in
pieces and one or two of the men severely hurt. On the 17th,
took an observation, by which they found they had got round
Cape Horn and were to the northward of Cape Victoria. About
this time the scurvy began to make great havoc among the crews.
They now bore away for the island of Juan Fernandez, which
appeared in sight on the last day of January. On going on shore
here they discovered a man clothed in goat-skins, whose name

was. Alexander Selkirk. His story will be found at the end of this narrative. They remained at this island till the 14th of February having fully refreshed themselves, when they weighed anchor, with a fair gale at south-east.

After taking a number of valuable prizes, on the 23d of April, captain Rogers with some of his men made a descent in boats and barks upon the town of Guiaquil, which they took with but little resistance and plundered of great quantities of money, jewels, and provisions. He then marched out of the town, and returned on board his own ship, where he was heartily greeted by those of his people whom he had left behind. They afterwards obtained a considerable sum as a ransom for the town, and bore away for the Galapagos islands, with a strong gale at S. S. W.; discovered land on the 17th of May, but found it barren and destitute of water. Continuing on their voyage, they took several rich prizes, visited Gorgona and the Gallapagos, and sailing for the East Indies arrived at the islands of Serpana and Guam. They left the latter place on the 21st of March, and on the 25th of May, made Bouton. They sailed from this island on the 8th of June, and on the 23d of July, they hove down upon Horn Island to careen their vessels. Having supplied themselves with such necessaries as they wanted, they left Batavia on the 12th of October, and sailed for the Cape of Good Hope.

They came to anchor in the Cape harbor, on the 28th of December. The English saluted the Dutch fort with nine guns; which compliment was returned with seven. At this place they waited for the convoy of the Dutch fleet till April, on the 5th of which month the Dutch admiral hoisted a blue flag, and loosed his fore-top-sail, as a signal to unmoor; and the next day the whole fleet sailed with a fresh breeze at S. S. E. On the 23d of July they arrived in the Texel, and sailing hence with seven prizes came to the moorings in the Downs on the 2d of October, 1711.

STORY OF ALEXANDER SELKIRK.

Mr. Selkirk, whose adventures gave rise to the celebrated story of Robinson Crusoe, was a native of Scotland, and bred a sailor from his youth. He was left on the island of Juan Fernandez, on account of a difference between him and his captain, which, together with the ship's being leaky, made him at first willing to stay there; but afterwards wishing to go on board, the captain would not receive him. Selkirk had with him his clothes and bedding, also a firelock, a little powder, some bullets and tobacco; a hatchet, a kettle, a knife, a bible, and a few mathematical in-

struments and books. He diverted and provided for himself as well
as he could, but for the first eight months he was extremely melan
choly, and could hardly support the terror of being alone in such
a desolate place. He built two huts with pimento trees, covered
them with long grass, and lined them with the skins of goats, which
he killed with his gun, as he wanted, so long as his powder, of
which there was but a pound, lasted. He procured fire, by rubbing two sticks of pimento wood upon his knee.

In the smaller hut, which was at some distance from the other,
he dressed his victuals; and in the larger he slept, and employed
himself in reading and praying; so that he said he was a better
christian while in this solitude than he ever was before, or than,
he feared, he should ever be again.

The pimento wood, which burnt very clear, served him both
for fire and candle, and refreshed him with its fragrant smell. He
could have procured fish enough, but would not eat them for want
of salt; except a sort of cray-fish, which were very good, and as
large as our lobsters. Of the goat's-flesh he made excellent broth.
He kept an account of five hundred of these animals which he
had killed, and as many more which he caught; and, having mark.
ed them on the ear, let them go again. When his powder was
gone, he took them by outrunning them. His agility in pursuing
a goat had once like to have cost him his life; he pursued it with
so much eagerness, that he caught hold of it on the brink of a
precipice, of which he was not aware, as the bushes concealed it
from his sight; so that he fell with the goat down the precipice,
a prodigious height, and was so stunned and bruised with the fall
that he lay there insensible about twenty-four hours, and when he
came to his senses, he found the goat dead under him. He was
so hurt that he was hardly able to crawl to his hut, which was
about a mile distant, nor was he able to go abroad again in less
than ten days. He came at length to relish his meat without salt
or bread, and found plenty of good turnips, which had been sowed
there by captain Dampier's men, and had now overspread some
acres of ground. He soon wore out his shoes as well as his
clothes by running in the woods, and at length his feet became
so hard that he ran every where without difficulty.

After he had recovered his cheerfulness, he diverted himself
sometimes with cutting his name on the trees, together with the
time of his being left, and continuance there. He was at first
much pestered with rats, which had bred in great numbers, from
some which had got on shore from ships which put in there for
water. The rats gnawed his feet and clothes while he slept, so
that he was obliged to cherish some cats, which had also bred
from some that had got ashore from different ships; these he fed
with goat's-flesh, by which many of them became so tame, that
they would lie about him in hundreds, and soon delivered him from
the rats. He likewise tamed some kids; and, to divert himself

would frequently sing and dance with them and his cats, so that he at length overcame all the weariness of his solitude, and became quite easy. When his clothes were worn out he made a coat and a cap of goat's skin sewed together with little thongs of the same, which he cut with his knife. He had no other needle than a nail, and when his knife was worn out he made others as well as he could of some iron hoops that were left ashore, which he beat straight and thin and ground upon stones. Having some linen cloth, he cut out some shirts, which he sewed with the worsted of his old stockings; and he had his last shirt on when he was found.

Selkirk had been on the island four years and four months, when one day beholding a ship at a distance, he kindled a fire, and the next morning saw a yawl containing eight men well-armed approach the shore. It proved to be from the Duke, under the command of captain Rogers, who had seen the fire and supposed it to be from the crew of some enemy's ships, who had landed on the island. Next day, while still under apprehensions of an enemy, they stood in for the shore, from which blew such sudden and frequent gusts of wind, that they were forced to reef their topsail, and stand by the masts, lest they should go by the board. Seeing no ships, they conjectured that some had been there and left on seeing their approach.

At first going on board the Duke, Selkirk seemed much rejoiced, but had so far forgot his native language, for want of use, that he could not speak plainly or connectedly. A dram was offered him but he would not taste it, having drank nothing but water for so long a time, and it was a good while before he could relish the victuals on board.

Selkirk saw no venomous creature on the island, nor any sort of beast but goats, which had originally been put on shore by Juan Fernando, who settled here with some families and gave name to the place. He afterwards left it, and it was entirely deserted when Selkirk took up his abode there.*

* The island of Juan Fernandez is now used by the Chilian government as a place for the transportation of convicts, and a garrison is stationed there. About one hundred of these criminals lately formed a plot, seized the garrison, took possession of an American brig just arrived from New York, and sailed for Copiapo, in Chili, where they landed. At the last advices they had not yet been taken

THE OCEAN

The ocean hath its silent caves,
 Deep, quiet, and alone;
Though there be fury in the waves,
 Beneath them there is none.

The awful spirits of the deep,
 Hold their communion there;
And there are those for whom we weep,—
 The young, the bright, the fair.

Calmly the weary seamen rest,
 Beneath their own blue sea;
The ocean solitudes are blessed,
 For there is purity.

The earth has guilt, the earth has care,
 Unquiet are its graves;
But peaceful sleep is ever there,
 Beneath its dark blue waves.

A SCENE OFF BERMUDA.

The evening was closing in dark and rainy, with every appearance
of a gale from the westward, and the weather had become so thick
and boisterous, that the lieutenant of the watch had ordered the
lookout at the mast-head down on the deck. The man on his way
down, had gone into the main-top to bring away some things he
had left in going aloft, and was in the act of leaving it, when he
sung out, "A sail on the weather-bow!" "What does she look
like?" "Can't rightly say, sir; she is in the middle of the thick
weather to windward." "Stay where you are a little. Jenkins,
jump forward, and see what you can make of her from the foreyard." Whilst the topman was obeying his instructions, the look-
out again hailed. "She is a ship, sir, close-hauled on the same
tack; the weather clears and I can see her now."

The wind ever since noon had been blowing in heavy squalls,
with appalling lulls between them. One of these gusts had been
so violent as to bury in the sea the lee-guns in the waist, although
the brig had nothing set but her close-reefed main-topsail, and reef-

ed foresail. It was now spending its fury, and she was beginning
to roll heavily, when, with a suddenness almost incredible to one
unacquainted with these latitudes, the veil of mist that had hung
to the windward the whole day was rent and drawn aside, and the
red and level rays of the setting sun flushed at once, through a
long arch of glowing clouds, on the black hull and tall spars of
his Britanic majesty's sloop Torch. And, true enough, we were
not the only spectators of this gloomy splendor; for, right in the
wake of the moonlike sun, now half sunk in the sea, at the distance
of a mile or more, lay a long warlike-looking craft, apparently a
frigate or heavy corvette, rolling heavily and silently in the trough
of the sea, with her masts, yards, and the scanty sail she had set,
in strong relief against the glorious horizon.

Jenkins now hailed from the foreyard, "The strange sail is
bearing up, sir." As he spoke, a flash was seen, followed, after
what seemed a long interval, by the deadened report of the gun,
as if it had been an echo, and the sharp half-ringing, half-hissing
sound of the shot. It fell short, but close to us, and was evidently
thrown from a heavy cannon, from the length of the range. Mr.
Splinter, the first lieutenant, jumped from the gun he stood on
"Quartermaster, keep her away a bit," and dived into the cabin
to make his report.

Captain Deadeye was a staid, stiff-rumped, wall-eyed, old first
lieutenantish-looking veteran, with his coat of a regular Rodney-
cut, broad skirts, long waist, and standing-up collar, over which
dangled either a queue, or a marlinspike with a tuft of oakum at
the end of it, it would have puzzled Old Nick to say which.
His lower spars were cased in tight unmentionables, of what
had once been white kerseymere, and long boots, the coal scuttle
tops of which served as scuppers to carry off the drainings
from his coat-flaps in bad weather; he was, in fact, the "last of
the sea-monsters," but like all his tribe, as brave as steel; when
put to it, as alert as a cat. He had no sooner heard Splinter's
report than he sprung up the ladder. "My glass, Wilson," to
his steward.

"She is close to, sir; you can see her plainly without it," said
Mr. Treenail, the second Lieutenant, from the weather nettings,
where he was reconnoitering. After a long look through his star
board blinker, (his other sky-light had been shut up ever since
Aboukir,) Deadeye gave orders to "clear away the weather-bow
gun;" and as it was now getting too dark for flags to be seen
distinctly, he desired that three lanterns might be got ready for
hoisting vertically in the main rigging.

"All ready forward there?" "All ready, sir." "Then hoist
away the lights, and throw a shot across her forefoot—fire!"
Bang went our carronade, but our friend to windward paid no
regard to the private signal; he had shaken a reef out of his top-
sails, and was coming down fast upon us.

The enemy, for such he evidently was, now all at once yawed, and indulged us with a sight of his teeth; and there he was, fifteen ports of a side on his main deck, with his due quantum of carronades on his quarter deck and forecastle; whilst his short lower masts, white canvass, and the tremendous hoist in his topsail, showed him to be a heavy American frigate; and it was equally certain that he had cleverly hooked us under his lee, within comfortable range of his long twenty-fours. To convince the most unbelieving, three jets of flame, amidst wreaths of white smoke, glanced from his main deck; but, in this instance, the sound of the cannon was followed by a sharp crackle and a shower of splinters from the foreyard.

It was clear that we had got an ugly customer; poor Jenkins now called to Treenail, who was standing forward near the gun which had been fired, " Och, sir, and its badly wounded we are here." The officer was a Patlander, as well as the seaman. " Which of you, my boy; you or the yard?" " Both of us, your honor; but the yard badliest." " Come down, then, or get into the top, and I will have you looked after presently." The poor fellow crawled off the yard into the foretop, as he was ordered, where he was found after the brush, badly wounded by a splinter in the breast.

Jonathan, no doubt, " calculated," as well he might, that this taste of his quality would be quite sufficient for a little eighteen-gun ship close under his lee: but the fight was not to be so easily taken out of Deadeye, although even to his optic it was now high time to be off.

" All hands make sail, Mr. Splinter; that chap is too heavy for us. Mr. Kelson," to the carpenter, " jump up and see what the foreyawl will carry. Keep her away my man," to the seamen at the helm; " Crack on, Mr. Splinter; shake all the reefs out; set the fore-topsail and loose top gallant sails; stand by a sheet home, and see all clear to rig the booms out, if the breeze lulls. '

In less than a minute we were bowling along before it; but the wind was breezing up again, and no one could say how long the wounded foreyard would carry the weight and drag the sails. To mend the matter, Jonathan was coming up, hand over hand, with the freshening breeze under a press of canvass; it was clear that escape was next to impossible.

" Clear away the larboard guns!" I absolutely jumped off the deck with astonishment; who could have spoken it? It appeared such downright madness to show fight under the very muzzles of the guns of an enemy, half of whose broadside was sufficient to sink us. It was the captain, however, and there was nothing for it.

In an instant was heard, through the whistling of the breeze, the creaking and screaming of the carronade slides, the rattling of the carriage of the long twelve pounder amidships, the thumping and punching of handspikes, and the dancing and jumping of Jack himself, as the guns were being shot and run out. In a few seconds all was still again, but the rushing sound of the vessel going through the water and of the rising gale amongst the rigging. The men stood clustered at their quarters; their cutlasses buckled round their waists, all without jackets and waistcoats, and many with nothing but their trousers on.

"Now, men, mind your aim; our only chance is to wing him. I will yaw the ship, and, as your guns come to bear, slap it right into his bows. Starboard your helm, my man, and bring her to the wind." As she came round, blaze went our carronades and long guns in succession, with good will and good aim, and down came his foretop-sail on the cap, with all the superincumbent spars and gear; the head of the topmast had been shot away The men instinctively cheered. "That will do; now knock off, my boys, and let us run for it. Keep her away again; make all sail."

Jonathan was for an instant paralysed by our impudence; but just as we were getting before the wind, he yawed, and let drive his whole broadside; and fearfully did it transmogrify us. Half an hour before we were as gay a little sloop as ever floated, with a crew of one hundred and twenty as fine fellows as ever manned a British man-of-war. The iron shower sped: ten of the hundred and twenty never saw the sun rise again; seventeen more were wounded, three mortally; we had eight shot between wind and water, our main-top-mast shot away as clean as a carrot, and our hull and rigging otherwise regularly cut to pieces. Another broadside succeeded; but, by this time, we had bore up, thanks to the loss of our after sail, we could do nothing else; and, what was better luck still, whilst the loss of our main-top-mast paid the brig off on the one hand, the loss of the head-sail in the frigate brought her as quickly to the wind on the other; thus most of her shot fell astern of us; and before she could bear up again in chase, the squall struck her and carried her main-top-mast overboard.

This gave us a start, crippled and bedevilled though we were; and, as the night fell, we contrived to lose sight of our large friend. With breathless anxiety did we carry on through that night, expecting every lurch to send our remaining top-mast by the board; but the weather moderated, and next morning the sun shone on our blood-stained decks, at anchor off the entrance to St. George's harbor.—*Scottish Magazine.*

CAPTAIN JOHN CLIPPERTON.

About the beginning of the year 1718, some English merchants, foreseeing war between England and Spain, resolved to fit out two ships for the South Seas. Two ships were accordingly provided, one called the Success, the other the Speedwell. The command of the former was given to captain Clipperton and captain Shelvock was appointed to command the latter. They sailed from Plymouth on the 13th of February, 1719, with a fair wind; but the whole stock of wine, brandy and other liquors, for the use of both ships, was still on board the Speedwell. On the 15th, had squally weather with rain; in the evening, unbent the best and small bowers in the Success, stowed their anchors, and found themselves often obliged to shorten sail for the Speedwell. Captain Shelvock came this day under the lee of the Success, and complained to Clipperton of the crankness of his ship, which proceeded from having too much weight aloft; and, therefore, desired him to send for his wine and brandy, which would give him an opportunity of striking down some of his guns into the hold This was never done.

About ten o'clock at night, on the 19th, there arose a fresh breeze, so as to oblige both ships to take in their topsails. The gale increasing, the Success made a signal for the Speedwell to bring to, and by seven o'clock both ships were under bare poles, nor able to bear a rag of canvass during the night. On the 20th, the storm abated, when Clipperton made sail, steering S. and by E., whereas Shelvock stood away to the N. W., so that from this day they never saw each other till they met by accident in the South Seas.

The Canaries being the first place appointed for a rendezvous, Clipperton sailed thither with such expedition as to arrive on the 5th of March. After waiting ten days he determined to continue his voyage, lest he should miss his consort at the next place of rendezvous, which was the Cape de Verd Islands. On the 21st, they saw St. Vincent, and next morning anchored in the bay They remained here ten days, but not meeting with their consort, proceeded on their voyage.

On the 29th of May, found themselves off the north point of the entrance of the straits of Magellan, and the next day entered the straits. They arrived in the South Seas on the 18th of August. and on the 7th of September cast anchor off the island of Juan Fernandez. They left this island on the 8th of October, leaving behind two deserters whom they had not been able to find. After taking a number of valuable prizes, the Success bore away for the Gallapages, in order to refresh; and anchored in York Road on the 9th of January, 1720. On the 11th of August anchored with a prize they had taken, at the island of Lobos de la Mar. While here a conspiracy among the crew was discovered and punished.

On he 1st of November, sailed for the Bay of Conception; and in the passage took a ship, laden with tobacco, sugar and cloth They made the Bay on the 6th in the afternoon, where they saw three men-of-war lying, with their topsails loose, who no sooner discovered them than they cut their cables, and stood in chase. At this time captain Clipperton had one prize with him, which, as well as the Success, hauled close upon a wind; on which the best sailer among the Spanish men-of-war, gave chase to the prize, which she soon came up with and took. The other ships crowded all the sail they could for sometime, till the largest, having her mizen-top-mast carried away, fired a gun, tacked, and stood in for the shore; which gave the Success an opportunity of making her escape. In the Spanish prize, Clipperton lost his third lieutenant and twelve of his men.

They continued cruising to the northward, and on the 4th of December found themselves very near the Gallapagos. On the 17th saw the island of Cocos, and most of the crew went on shore. On the 19th of January, 1721, sailed from this place, and on the 25th arrived on the coast of Mexico, where, discovering a sail, they sent their pinnace to give chase, to whom he struck. On the return of the pinnace they had the surprising account, that this was a Spanish ship, called the Jesu Maria, now commanded by captain Shelvock, who had lost his ship and most of his men, and taken this prize. These ships again parted, and on the 31th of May, Clipperton anchored in the road of Guam. On the 5th of July entered the port of Amoy, where the crew demanded that the prize-money should be shared. Clipperton not complying they applied to the chief mandarin of the place, requesting that he would do them justice against the captain. Clipperton was therefore summoned before him; and on the mandarin's demanding a reason why he refused to comply with the desires of the crew. he produced the articles, by which it appeared that the prize-money was not to be shared till their return to London. The mandarin decided that the shares should be settled, and this distribution was accordingly made on the 16th of September; 7,000l. sterling being set aside as belonging to the owners. This sum was immediately put on board a Portuguese East India man, which ship was afterwards burnt and the greater part of the money lost.

Clipperton afterwards took passage for England in a Dutch ship, and arrived there a bankrupt in health and fortune, after a long and disastrous voyage.

FEROCITY OF THE POLAR BEAR.

The annals of the north are filled with accounts of the most
perilous and fatal conflicts with the Polar Bear The first and one
of the most tragical, was sustained by Bareutz and Heemskerke,
in 1596, during their voyage for the discovery of the north-east
passage. Having anchored at an island near the strait of Way-
gatz, two of the sailors landed and were walking on shore, when
one of them felt himself closely hugged from behind. Thinking
this a frolic of one of his companions, he called out in a corres-
ponding tone, "Who's there? pray stand off." His comrade
looked, and screamed out, "A bear! A bear!" then running to
the ship, alarmed the crew with loud cries. The sailors ran to
the spot armed with spikes and muskets. On their approach the
bear very cooly quitted the mangled corpse, sprang upon another
sailor, carried him off, and plunging his teeth into his body, began
drinking his blood at long draughts. Hereupon the whole of
that stout crew, struck with terror, turned their backs, and fled
precipitately to the ship. On arriving there they began to look
at each other, unable to feel much satisfaction with their own
prowess. Three then stood forth, and undertook to avenge the
fate of their countrymen, and to secure for them the rights of
burial. They advanced, and fired at first from so respectful a
distance that they all missed. The purser then courageously proceeded in front of his companions, and taking closer aim, pierced
the monster's skull immediately below the eye. The bear, however, merely lifted up his head, and advanced upon them, holding
still in his mouth the victim whom he was devouring; but seeing him
soon stagger, the three rushed on with sabre and bayonet, and
soon despatched him. They collected and bestowed decent se-
pulture on the mangled limbs of their comrades, while the skin of
the animal, thirteen feet long, became the prize of the sailor who
had fired the successful shot.

The history of the whale-fishers records a number of remarkable
escapes from the bear. A Dutch captain, Jonge Kees, in 1668,
undertook with two canoes to attack one, and with a lance gave
him so dreadful a wound in the belly, that his immediate death
seemed inevitable. Anxious, therefore, not to injure the skin,
Kees merely followed the animal close, till he should drop down
dead. The bear, however, having climbed a little rock, made a
spring from the distance of twenty-four feet upon the captain, who,
taken completely by surprise, lost hold of the lance, and fell beneath the assailant, who, placing both paws on his breast, opened
two rows of tremendous teeth, and paused for a moment, as if to
show him all the horrors of his situation. At this critical instant, a
sailor rushed forward, and with only a scoop succeeded in alarming

the monster, who made off, leaving the captain without the slightest injury.

In 1788, Captain Cook of the Archangel, when near the coast of Spitzbergen, found himself suddenly between the paws of a bear. He instantly called on the surgeon, who accompanied him, to fire, which the latter did with such admirable promptitude and precision, that he shot the beast through the head, and delivered the captain. Mr. Hawkins of Everthorpe, in July 1818, having pursued and twice struck a large bear, had raised his lance for a third blow, when the animal sprang forward, seized him by the thigh, and threw him over its head into the water. Fortunately, it used this advantage only to effect its own escape.—Captain Scoresby mentions a boat's crew which attacked a bear in the Spitzbergen sea; but the animal having succeeded in climbing the sides of the boat, all the sailors threw themselves for safety, into the water, where they hung by the gunwale. The victor entered triumphantly, and took possession of the barge, where it sat quietly till it was shot by another party. The same writer mentions the ingenious contrivance of a sailor, who being pursued by one of these creatures, threw down successively his hat, jacket, handkerchief, and every other article in his possesion, when the brute pausing at each, gave the sailor always a certain advantage, and enabled him finally to regain the vessel.

Though the voracity of the bear is such, that he has been known to feed on his own species, yet maternal tenderness is as conspicuous in the female as in any other inhabitants of the frozen regions. There is no exertion which she will not make for the supply of her progeny. A she bear, with her two cubs, being pursued by some sailors across a field of ice, and finding that, neither by example, nor by a peculiar voice and action she could urge them to the requisite speed, applied her paws and pitched them alternately forward. The little creatures themselves as she came up, threw themselves before her to receive the impulse and thus both she and they effected their escape.

4*

LE MAIRE AND SCHOUTEN.

FIRST VOYAGE ROUND CAPE HORN.

A belief that to the south of the strait of Magellan there wou'' be found an open sea, or some other passage leading to the South Sea, had many years been gaining ground, when a company of Dutch merchants determined to make the experiment, which, if successful, would open to them, as they believed, the trade to India, by a new, instead of an interdicted passage, which the strait of Magellan then was.

Jacob le Maire was appointed principal merchant, and president of the ships; and Wilhelm Schouten, an able seaman, received the charge of patron or master mariner. The vessels fitted out were the Eendracht, a ship of three hundred and sixty tons, nineteen guns, and sixty five men, and a galliot, named the Horne, of one hundred and ten tons, eight guns and twenty two men. The president, Le Maire, and Patron Schouten, sailed in the former; the latter was commanded by Jan Schouten, brother to the patron, with Adrian Claesz as merchant.

June the 4th, 1615, they quitted the Texel, and in three days anchored in the Downs, where an English gunner was hired. On the 30th of August, dropped anchor in the road of Sierra Leone, where a stock of twenty five thousand lemons was purchased from the natives, for a few beads. On the 5th of October, were in latitude four degrees seventeen minutes N. when a great noise was heard on board the Eendracht, and immediately after the sea around it became red with blood. Afterwards a piece of the horn of some sea animal was found sticking in the bottom of the ship, seven feet below the water line, having penetrated through the planking, and into one of the ribs: about the same length remained without; it was similar in shape and size to the end of an elephant's tooth.

Having passed the line, they struck soundings in seventy-five fathoms depth, on the 4th of December, and two days after saw the American coast. On the 8th, anchored in Port Desire, where they took a large supply of birds, &c. On the 19th, the Horne caught fire, and was totally consumed. On the 13th of January, 1616, the Eendracht quitted Port Desire, and on the 20th, passed the latitude of the entrance of the straits of Magellan On the 24th saw Terra del Fuego to the right, not more than a league off, and on the 29th passed to the north of some rocky islets: Terra del Fuego appeared to the W. N. W. and W., all hilly land covered with snow, with a sharp point which they called Cape Horne, in honour of the vessel which they had lost. On D 30th, having passed to the south of the Cape, steered west encountering great waves with a current to the westward; and afterwards steered north. The ship continued to advance northward, and on the 1st of March, made the island of Juan Fernandez and caught two tons of fish, but could find no anchorage. Steering for the East Indies they visited a number of small islands, and on the 5th of August came to the Isle of Goley, subject to the King of Tidore. Sailed again next day; and, after being much delayed by calms, met, September the 7th, with a ship of their own country, anchoring the same day at the Island of Ternate. They were kindly received by the people in power: the Eendracht had

Cape Horn.

not lost one of her crew in her long cruisings, and they had discovered a new passage to the South Sea; yet these merits did not avail them, for on the arrival of the ship at Batavia, she was seized and condemned, on a supposed infringement of the rights of the Dutch East India Company, the officers and crew being put on board other ships to be conveyed to Europe

On the 31st of December, during the passage home, died the president, Jacob Le Maire, a victim to the unworthy treatmen. he had received—a worthy man and a skilful navigator; and on the 1st of July 1617, his companions arrived in Holland, by the way of Good Hope, having been absent two years and seventeen days

THE FLORIDA

Many of the vessels which formed the Spanish Armada, inten
ded for the conquest of England, perished on the north and west
coasts of Scotland. The ship Florida appeared to have been
more fortunate than any of her consorts; she found her way to the
bay of Tobermory, on the sound of Mull, one of the finest harbors
in the world. Scotland being then a neutral country under
James the Sixth, of that name, the Spaniards considered themselves perfectly secure, and remained long in that station, repairing the damages they had sustained, and refreshing the crew and
troops.

The Florida was, no doubt, an object of great interest and
curiosity in that remote situation, and all the principal families in
the neighboring country and islands were received on board as
visiters, where, tradition says, they were hospitably and splendidly
entertained. Elizabeth, the ever watchful and well-informed
Queen of England, had intelligence of the Florida through her
ambassador at the Scotch court, and it was ascertained that this
ship was extremely valuable: she had on board a large sum of
money intended for the pay of the army; she contained besides,
a great quantity of costly stores. The law of nations should have
protected the Florida from injury; but Elizabeth resolved on her
destruction; and it was accompanied by one of the most atrocious
acts, perhaps, ever recorded of any civilized government. The
English ambassador soon found an instrument suited to his purpose, and his name was Smollet. We regret to state, that he was
an ancestor of the celebrated writer of that name, who himself
alludes to this circumstance in one of his novels, apparently unconscious of the inference which followed. This agent of the
English Queen spoke the Gaelic language, and wore the High-
land dress. He went to Mull as a dealer in cattle, and easily
found his way on board the Florida, where he formed an intimacy,
and, along with other strangers, had frequent opportunities of
seeing every part of the ship. He at length found a convenient
time for his diabolical object, and placed some combustible substance in a situation where it was likely to produce the desired
effect. He immediately got ashore, and made the best of his way
southward.

He had travelled to a distance of six or eight miles, when he
heard the explosion of the Florida; and the spot where he stood
is still marked for the execration of mankind. The ship was
blown up, and nearly all on board perished. Together with the
crew and troops, many of the first men in the country were destroyed by this perfidious and bloody act, which reflects eternal

disgrace on the planners, and infamy on the perpetrator. Tradi
tion states, that the poop of the ship was blown to a great distance
with six men, whose lives were saved.

Some Spanish mares and horses had been landed, to pasture,
and these remained in the island of Mull. The breed of horses
in Mull has ever since been superior, and it still continues so,
probably from this cause.

The English ambassador at Madrid having procured information
of the precise amount of the treasure which had been on board
the Florida, a ship of war was sent by the English Government
to Tobermory in the beginning of the eighteenth century with
divers, for the purpose of recovering the specie. The wreck was
soon found, and many articles were raised, but no money was
acknowledged. The ship, however, never returned to England,
and it was suspected that she had taken refuge in France, for
evident reasons.

In the year 1787, the celebrated diver, Spalding, made an
attempt to recover this treasure, but he failed entirely as might
have been expected, the remains of the ship having sunk into the
clay, and totally disappeared.

COMMODORE ANSON.

The expedition under Commodore Anson was fitted out by the
English government in the year 1740, to attack the Spanish settlements in America. The squadron consisted of six vessels of
war and two victuallers. These were the

Ships.	Commanders.	Guns.	Men.
Centurion	George Anson	60	400
Gloucester	Richard Norris	50	300
Severn	Edward Legge	50	300
Pearl	Matt Mitchell	40	250
Wager	Dandy Kidd	28	160
Trial Sloop	John Murray	8	100

On the 18th of September, seventeen hundred and forty, the
squadron weighed from St. Helens, and reached Maderia the 25th
of October. Having sailed hence, they discovered the land of
Brazil, on the 16th of December, and on the evening of the 19th
cast anchor at the island of St Catharine's. Having repaired
their vessels, they quitted this place on the 18th of January, and
on the same day of the following month came to anchor in the bay
of St. Julian. The squadron again stood to sea on the 28th of
February, when the Gloucester not being able to purchase her
anchor, was obliged to cut her cable, and leave her best bower

behind. Having reached the southern extremity of the straits Le Maire, the wind shifted and blew in violent squalls, and the tide turned furiously against them, driving to the eastward with such rapidity, that the two sternmost vessels, the Wager, and the Anna Pink, with the utmost difficulty escaped being dashed in pieces on the shore of Staten Island.

For above three months, they struggled with severe gales and terrific waves, and on the 1st of April, the weather, after having been a little more moderate, returned to its former violence; the sky looked dark and gloomy, and the wind began to freshen and blow in squalls; and there were all the appearances of an approaching tempest. Accordingly, on the 3d, there came on a storm, which exceeded in violence and duration all they had hitherto encountered. On the 14th, in the morning, the weather clearing up a little and the moon shining out on a sudden, the Anna Pink made a signal for seeing land right a-head; and it being then only two miles distant, they were under great apprehensions of running on shore; and had not the wind suddenly shifted, or the moon shone out, every ship must have perished. They found this land, to their disappointment, to be Cape Noir, though they imagined they were ten degrees more to the west. On the evening of the 24th of April, the wind increased to a prodigious storm, and, about midnight, the weather became so thick that the whole squadron separated, nor met again till they reached the island of Juan Fernandez. To add to their misfortunes, the scurvy began to make such havoc, that on board the Centurion only, it carried off forty-three men in the month of April, and twice that number in May.

On the 22d of May the Centurion encountered the severest storm it had yet experienced. Almost all the sails were split; the rigging was destroyed, and a mountainous wave breaking over them on the starboard quarter, gave the vessel such a shock, that several of the shrouds were broke, and the ballast and stores so strangely shifted, that she lay on her larboard side. The wind at length abating a little, they began to exert themselves to stirrup the shrouds, reeve new lanyards, and mend the sails; during which they ran great risk of being driven on the island of Chiloe. After many difficulties they at length reached the island of Juan Fernandez, in a most desponding condition. Here many of the crew died of weariness and disease.

A few days after the Centurion had arrived, the Trial sloop appeared in sight, and on the 21st of June the Gloucester was discovered to leeward. The Anna Pink arrived about the middle of August, which, with the Trial and Gloucester, mentioned above, were the only vessels that ever joined the squadron; for the Severn and Pearl, having parted from the commodore off Cape Horn, with difficulty reached Brazil, whence they made the best of their way back to Europe; while the Wager was wrecked on the coast. The Anna Pink being judged unfit for service, was taken for the use of the squadron, and her men were sent on board the Gloucester.

About eleven in the morning of the 8th of September, they discovered a sail; when the Centurion, being in the greatest forwardness, made after her as fast as possible. Night coming on they lost sight of the chase. About three in the morning of the 12th, a brisk gale springing up at W. S. W. obliged them to lie upon a N. W tack, which, at break of day, brought them within sight of a sail, at about five leagues distant. She appeared to be a large vessel, and upon hoisting Spanish colors, and bearing towards the Centurion, the commodore ordered every thing ready for an engagement; but upon coming nearer, she appeared to be a merchantman, without a single tier of guns, and had mistaken the Centurion for her consort. She soon surrendered, and was found to be a valuable prize.

It appearing from letters on board the prize, that several other merchantmen were at sea, between Callao and Valparaiso, the commodore sent the Trial sloop, to cruise off the latter port; and ordered the Gloucester to cruise off the island of Paita, till she should be joined by the Centurion. The Centurion and her prize weighing from the bay of Juan Fernandez, on the 19th of September, took her course to the eastward, proposing to join the Trial off Valparaiso.

On the 24th, in the evening, they came up with the latter, having taken a prize of six hundred tons burden, laden with a rich cargo. On the 27th, the captain of the Trial came on board the Centurion, bringing with him an instrument, subscribed by himself and all his officers, setting forth that the vessel was so leaky and defective, that it was at the hazard of their lives they staid on board; upon which, the commodore having ordered the crew and every thing of value to be put on board the prize, the Trial was scuttled and sunk. It was now resolved to join the Gloucester off Paita. With this view they stood to the northward, and, on the 10th of November discovered a sail, which Lieutenant Brett was ordered to chase, with the Trial's pinnace and barge. They found her to be a Spanish vessel of two hundred and seventy tons burden. From the prisoners they learned that, a few days before, a vessel had entered Paita, the master of which told the governer he had been chased by a very large ship, which he imagined to be one of the English squadron, and that the governor had immediately sent an express to Lima, to carry the news to the viceroy, while the royal officer residing at Paita had been busily employed in removing both the king's treasure and his own to Piuza, a town fourteen leagues within land. It was at once conjectured that the ship which had chased the vessel into Paita was the Gloucester; and, as they were now discovered, and the coast would soon be alarmed, so as to prevent cruizing to any

advantage, the commodore resolved to endeavor to surprise the
place that very night.

When the ships were within five leagues of Paita, about ten
o'clock at night, Lieutenant Brett, with the boats under his command, put off, and arrived without being discovered, at the mouth
of the bay; though he had no sooner entered it, than some of the
people on board a vessel riding at anchor there, perceived him,
and immediately getting into their boat, rowed towards the shore,
crying out 'the English, the English dogs,' &c. by which the
town was alarmed and the attack disovered. The town was,
however, taken in less than a quarter of an hour from the first
landing of the boats; with the loss of one man killed and two
wounded.

They weighed anchor from the coast of Paita on the 16th of
November, the squadron being increased to six sail by the prizes
On the morning of the 18th, they discovered the Gloucester with
a small vessel in tow, which joined them about three in the afternoon, when they learned that captain Mitchell had taken two
prizes, one of which had a cargo consisting of wine, brandy and
olives, and about seven thousand pounds in specie; and the other
was a launch, the people on board which, when taken, were eating
their dinner from silver dishes. Notwithstanding this circum
stance, the prisoners alleged that they were very poor: having
nothing on board, but cotton made up in jars, which, being removed on board the Gloucester, were examined, when the whole
appeared to be an extraordinary piece of false package; there
being concealed among the cotton, doubloons and dollars, to the
amount of twelve thousand pounds.

The cargo and crews of the several vessels were afterwards
divided between the Centurion and Gloucester. Quitting the
coast of America, they stood for China, the 6th of May, 1742.
The Gloucester, which had become decayed, was cleared of every
thing by the 15th of August, and then set on fire. On the 27th
they arrived at the island of Tinian, where they remained some
time. On the night of the 22d of September, when it was excessively dark, the wind blew from the eastward with such fury,
that those on board despaired of riding out the storm. At this
time Mr. Anson, was ill of the scurvy, and most of the hands
were on shore, and all the hopes of safety of those on board seemed
to depend on immediately putting to sea; all communication between the ship and the island being destroyed.

About one o'clock a strong gust, attended with rain and lightning, drove them to sea, where, being unprepared to struggle
with the fury of the winds and waves, they expected each moment
to be their last. When at day-break, it was perceived by those
on shore that the ship was missing, they concluded her lost, and
many of them begged the commodore to send the boat round the
island to look for the wreck. In the midst of their gloomy reflec-

tions, the commodore formed a plan for extricating them from their present situation: which was by hauling the Spanish bark on shore, sawing her asunder, and lengthening her twelve feet; which would enlarge her to near forty tons burden, and enable her to carry them all to China.

But a discouraging circumstance now occured, which was, that they had neither compass nor quadrant on the island. At length, on rummaging a chest belonging to the Spanish bark, they found a small compass, which though not much superior to those made for the amusement of school-boys, was to them of the utmost importance.

When this obstacle was removed, and all things were ready for sailing, it happened on the afternoon of the 11th of October, that one of the Gloucester's men being upon a hill, saw the Centurion at a distance. She was soon visible to all, and the next day cast anchor in the road. On the 14th, a sudden gust of wind drove her to sea a second time, but in about five days, they returned again to anchor. On the 20th of October, they set fire to the bark and proa, hoisted in their boats, and got under sail, steering away towards the south end of the island of Macao.

About midnight, on the 5th of November, they made the mainland of China, and on the morning of the 9th, a Chinese pilot came on board, and told them that he would carry the ship into Macao for thirty dollars, which being paid him they proceeded, and on the 12th entered the harbor of Macao.

On the 6th of April, the Centurion again stood out to sea. On the last day of May they came in sight of Cape Espiritu Santo, where they continued to cruize till the 20th of June, when about sunrise the great Manilla ship came in sight, having the standard of Spain flying at the top-gallant-mast head, and to the commodore's surprise, bore down upon him. The engagement soon began, and lasted an hour and a half, when the galleon struck to the Centurion, after having had sixty-seven men killed and eighty-four wounded. The Centurion had only two men killed and seventeen wounded. The prize carried five hundred men and thirty-six guns, and her cargo was worth 400,000l. sterling. It is impossible to describe the transports on board, when, after all their reiterated disappointments, they at length, saw their wishes accomplished. But their joy was very near being suddenly damped by a very alarming accident; for no sooner had the galleon struck, than one of the lieutenants coming to Mr. Anson, whispered him, that the Centurion was dangerously on fire near the powder-room. The commodore received this shocking intelligence without any apparent emotion, and taking care not to alarm his people, gave the necessary orders for extinguishing the fire, which was done, though its first appearance threatened the ship with destruction.

On the 14th, the Centurion cast anchor off Bocca Tigris, forming the mouth of that river: and having got under sail on the 16th of October, 1743, came to anchor in the straits of Sunda on the 2d of January, and continued there till the eighth, taking in wood and water, when she weighed and stood for the Cape of Good Hope, where, on the 11th of March, she came to anchor in Table

St. Helena.

Bay. Mr. Anson continued here till the 3d of April, 1744, when he put to sea, and on the 19th of the month, was in sight of St. Helena, but did not touch at it.

On the 12th of June they got sight of the Lizard, and on the evening of the 15th, to their great joy, came safe to anchor at Spithead. On his arrival Mr. Anson learned, that under cover of a thick fog, he had run through a French fleet, which was at that time cruizing in the chops of the channel.

FISHING ON THE GRAND BANK

On crossing the banks of Newfoundland, the ship was hove to, for the purpose of sounding; and the quarter-master having tied a baited hook to the deep-sea lead, a noble cod was drawn to the surface, from the depth of ninety fathoms. Upon this hint, the captain, very considerately, agreed to lie by for an hour or two, and some fifty lines being put over, the decks were soon covered, fore

and aft, with such a display of fish as Billingsgate has rarely wit
nessed.

People who know nothing of a sea life fancy that fish is not a
rarity with us; but there is nothing of which we taste so little; so
that the greatest treat by far, when we come into port, is a dish
of fresh soles or mackerel; and even the commonest fish that
swims is looked upon as a treasure. It is only in soundings that
any are to be met with; for, in the open and bottomless ocean,
we meet nothing but whales, porpoises, dolphins, sharks, bonitas
and flying fish.

I never could conceive, or even form a probable conjecture,
how it is that some persons manage to catch fish, and others none
It is easy to understand, that in angling, a certain degree of skill,
or choice of situation, may determine the probable amount of
success. But when a line is let down to the depth of eighty or a
hundred fathoms, or even to twenty or thirty feet, quite out of
sight, what has skill to do there? And yet, in a ship, on the
banks of Newfoundland, or in a boat on the Thrumcap shoals in
Halifax harbor, I have seen one man hauling in cods or haddocks
as fast as he could bait his hooks; while others, similarly circum-
stanced in all apparent respects, might fret and fidget for half a
day without getting more than a nibble.

There can be no doubt, of course, that intellectual power must
be in operation at one end of the line, otherwise no fish will come
to the other; but the puzzle is, by what mysterious process can
human intelligence manage to find its way, like electricity, down
the line to the bottom of the sea? I have often asked successful
fishermen what they did to make the fish bite; but they could seldom give any available answer. Sometimes they said it depended
on the bait. "Well, then," I have answered, "let me take yours
and do you take mine." But in two minutes after we had changed places, my companion was pulling in his fish as fast as before
while not a twitch was given to my new line, though, just before,
the fish appeared to be jostling one another for the honor of my
friend's hook, to the total neglect of that which had been mine,
now in high vogue amongst them.

There is some trick, or sleight of hand, I suppose, by which a
certain kind of motion is given to the bait, so as to assimilate it
to that of the worms which the fishes most affect in their ordinary
researches for food. But, probably, this art is no more to be
taught by description, or to be learned without the drudgery of
practice, than the dexterity with which an artist represents nature,
or a dancer performs pirouettes. Uninstructed persons, therefore,
who, like myself, lose patience because they cannot catch fish at
the first cast of the line, had better turn their attention to something else.

Almost the only one I ever caught was during my first voyage
across the Atlantic, when, after my line had been down a whole

weary hour, I drew it up in despair. It felt so light, that I imagined the line must have been accidentally broken; but presently,
and greatly to my astonishment, I beheld a huge cod float to the
top, swollen to twice the usual dimensions by the expansion of
its sound, as the air-bag is called, which lies along the back-bone
At the depth of eighty or ninety fathoms, this singular apparatus
is compressed by the enormous addition of fifteen or sixteen atmos-
pheres. But when the air is relieved of this weight, by approaching the surface, the strength of the muscles proves inadequate to
retain it in its condensed form; and its consequent expansion not
only kills the fish, but often bursts it open as completely as if it had
been blown up with gunpowder.

BYRON.

In the year 1764, the Dolphin and Tamar ships-of-war, were
fitted out for the purpose of prosecuting discoveries in the South
Seas. Mr. Byron was commander-in-chief, and Captain Mouat
commanded under him.

On the 3d of July, the commodore hoisted his broad-pendant, and
they sailed in prosecution of the voyage. On the 13th of September they came to an anchor in the road of Rio de Janeiro, on the
coast of Brazil, when the commodore paid a visit to the governor,
who received him in state. They weighed anchor on the 16th of
October, steering for Cape Blanco, and on the 21st of November, entered the harbor of Port Desire, and the commodore in his
boat, attended by two other boats, went to sound it. He landed,
and they had a sight of four beasts, near thirteen hands high, and
in shape like a deer, which they took to be granicoes.

On the fifth of December the ships got under sail, and on the
20th, ran close in-shore to Cape Virgin Mary, and came to an anchor. The commodore observed a number of men on horseback
riding to and fro, opposite the ship, and waving something white
which he took to be an invitation to land; and as he was anxious to
know what people these were, he went in one boat with a party of
men well armed; the first lieutenant, with a separate party, following in another. When they came near the shore, the whole appeared to amount to five hundred persons, drawn up on a stony point
of land that ran far into the sea. Byron now advanced alone, but
as he approached, the Indians retreated: he therefore, made signs
that one of them should come forward, which was complied with.
_ _ advanced appeared to be chief, and was very
              height; round one of his eyes was a circle of

black paint, and a white circle round the other, the rest of his face was painted in streaks of various colors. He had the skin of a beast, with the hair inwards, thrown over his shoulders. The commodore and the Indian having complimented each other, in language equally unintelligible to either, they walked together towards the main body of the Indians, few of whom were shorter than the height abovementioned, and the women were large in proportion.

On the 21st of December they began sailing up the Strait of Magellan, with a view to take in a stock of wood and water. On the 26th, came to an anchor at Port Famine. In this place, they found drift-wood enough to have supplied a thousand vessels. The quantity of fish that was daily taken was equal to the supply of both the crews: and the commodore shot as many geese and ducks as furnished several tables besides his own. On the 4th of January 1765, they sailed in quest of Falkland's Islands.

On the 12th they saw land, and on the 14th a flat island, covered with tufts of grass as large as bushes. Soon after this they entered another harbor, to which Byron gave the name of Port Egmont. This harbor is represented to be the finest in the world, and capacious enough to contain the whole navy of England, in full security; there is plenty of fresh water in every part of it, and geese, ducks, snipes, and other edible birds, abound in such numbers, that the sailors were tired with eating them. The commodore was once unexpectedly attacked by a sea-lion, and extricated himself from the impending danger with great difficulty; they had many battles with this animal, the killing of one of which was frequently an hour's work for six men; one of them almost tore to pieces the commodore's mastiff-dog, by a single bite. The commodore took possession of the harbor, and all adjacent islands, by the name of FALKLAND'S ISLANDS.

On Sunday, January the 27th, they left Port Egmont. Next day the commodore gave the name of Berkley's Sound to a deep inlet between the islands. On the 6th of February stood in for Port Desire, at the mouth of which they came to an anchor, and had the pleasure of seeing the Florida, a store-ship, which they had expected from England. On the 20th, at Port Famine received orders to sail for England.

Having narrowly escaped the dreadful effects of a storm on the 3d of March, at length the Dolphin was moored in a little bay opposite Cape Quod; and the Tamar, about six miles to the eastward of it. On the 28th the Tamar narrowly escaped being dashed to pieces against the rocks, by the parting of the cable to her best bower-anchor. The Dolphin, therefore, stood again into the bay, and sent her proper assistance, after which they both anchored for the night; a night the most dreadful they had known. The winds were so violent as perfectly to tear up the sea, and carry it higher than the heads of the masts: a dreadful sea rolled

over them, and broke against the rocks, with a noise as loud as
thunder. Happily they did not part their cables, or they must
have been dashed in pieces against these rocks.

The ships came to anchor on the 4th of April, in a bay which
had been discovered, proposing to take in wood and water. While
they were here, several of the natives made a fire opposite the
ship, on which signals were made for them to come on board, but
as they would not, the commodore went on shore, and distributed
some trifles which gave great pleasure. Four were at length prevailed on to go on board; and the commodore, with a view to their
diversion, directed one of the midshipmen to play on the violin,
while some of the seamen danced; the poor Indians were extravagantly delighted; and one of them to testify his gratitude, took
his canoe, and fetching some red paint, rubbed it over the face of
the musician; nor could the commodore, but with the utmost difficulty, escape the like compliment.

They sailed from this bay on the 7th, and next day the wind
blew a hurricane. On the 9th, passed some dangerous rocks,
which in Narborough's Voyage are called the Judges. This day
a steady gale at south-west carried them at the rate of nine miles
an hour, so that by eight in the evening they were twenty leagues
from the coast. On the 26th, they sailed westward, and bore
away for the island of Massafuero and anchored at seven o'clock
on Sunday morning.

On the 30th of April they sailed, and on the 7th of June discovered land, being then in fourteen degrees five minutes south latitude,
and one hundred forty four degrees fifty eight minutes west longitude. The commodore steered for a small island, the appearance
of which was pleasing beyond expression. Several natives ran
along the beach, with long spears in their hands. The sailors
made every possible sign of friendship—but they retired to the
woods, dragging their canoes after them. The commodore proceeded to the other island, and brought to, at three-quarters of a
mile from the shore. The natives again ran to the beach, armed
with clubs and spears, using threatening gestures. The commodore fired a cannon-shot over their heads, on which they retreated
to the woods. This paradise in appearance, was named the
ISLAND OF DISAPPOINTMENT.

Quitting these on the 8th of June, they discovered an island on
the day following, low, and covered with various kinds of trees
among which was the cocoa-nut, and surrounded with a rock of
red coral. They now sailed to the westward, and soon discovered
another island, distant four leagues. The natives pursued them
in two large double canoes, in each of which were about thirty
armed men. At this time the boats were at a considerable way
to leeward of the ships, and were chased by the canoes; on which
the commodore making a signal, the boats turned towards the
Indians who instantly pulled down their sails and rowed away

with great rapidity. On the 12th of June, sailed to another
island, and as they coasted along it, the natives, armed as those
of the other islands, kept even with the ship for some leagues.
This island is situated in fourteen degrees and forty-one minutes
South Latitude, and one hundred and forty-nine degrees fifteen
minutes west longitude; and both the islands the commodore called
King George's Islands. The boats having returned on board, they
sailed westward the same day; and the next afternoon descried
another island, towards which they immediately sailed, and found
that it was well inhabited, and had a fine appearance of verdure;
but that a violent surf broke all along the coast. It lies in fifteen
degrees south, and one hundred fifty-one degrees fifty-three minutes west, and received the name of the Prince of Wales's Island.

On the 24th they discovered another island, which was named
the Duke of York's Island. A terrible sea breaks round the
coast, but the place itself had a pleasing appearance. On the
29th sailed northward, with a view to cross the equinoctial line,
and then sail for the Ladrone Islands. On the 2d of July they
discovered a low flat island, abounding with the cocoa-nut and
other trees, and affording a most agreeable prospect. A great
number of the natives were seen on the beach, many of whom,
in about sixty canoes or proas, sailed, and formed a circle round
the ships ; which having surveyed for a considerable time, one
of the Indians jumped out of his boat, swam to the ship, ran up
its side in a moment, sat down on the deck, and began laughing
most violently: he then ran about the ship, pilfering whatever he
could lay hands on, which was taken from him as fast as stolen.
This man having as many antic tricks as a monkey, was dressed
in a jacket and trowsers, and afforded exquisite diversion. He
devoured some biscuit with great eagerness, and having played
the buffoon some time, made prize of his new dress, by jumping
over the side of the ship, and swimming to his companions. These
Indians are of a bright copper, with regular and cheerful features,
and are tall and well made. One of them, who seemed to be of
some rank, wore a string of human teeth round his waist. Some
carried a long spear, the sides of which, for the length of three feet
were stuck with the teeth of the shark, which are as keen as a
razor. The officers named this place Byron's island, in honor
of the commodore. It lies in one degree eighteen minutes south
latitude, and one hundred and seventy-three degrees and forty-six
minutes east longitude. They sailed hence on the 3d of July,
and on the 28th had sight of the islands Saypan, Tinian, and
Aiguigan, which lie between two and three leagues from each
other. At noon, on the 31st, anchored at the south-west end of
Tinian. The water is so wonderfully clear at this place, that,
though one hundred and forty four feet deep, they could see the
ground. The commodore went on shore where he saw many huts
which had been left the preceding year by the Spaniards. The

commodore remained at Tinian till the 30th of September, by which time the sick being tolerably well recovered, he weighed anchor and stood to the northward.

On the 5th of November they came to an anchor off the island of Timoan on which Byron landed the day following. The inhabitants, who are Malays, no sooner saw the boat approaching the shore, than many of them came to the beach, each having a dagger by his side, a spear in one hand, and a long knife in the other. The boat's crew, however, made no hesitation to land, and bartered a few handkerchiefs for a goat, a kid, and a dozen of fowls.

Nothing worth notice happened till the 14th, when a sloop being seen at anchor in the harbor of an island, named Pulo Toupoa, Byron, having anchored in the same harbor, and observed that the vessel hoisted Dutch colors, sent an officer on board, who was received with great politeness. The commodore sailed the following day, and held his course till the 19th, when he spoke with an English snow, bound from Bencoolen to Malacca and Bengal, in the East India Company's service. At this time their biscuit was filled with worms, and rotten, and their beef and pork were unfit to eat. The master of the snow being apprized of the circumstance, sent Byron two gallons of arrack, a turtle, twelve fowls and a sheep. During their run hence to Prince's Island, in the Strait of Sunda, they were so abundantly supplied with turtle, by boats from the Java shore, that the common sailors subsisted wholly on that fish. They staid at Prince's island till the 19th, when they sailed for the Cape of Good Hope. On the 13th of February they came to anchor, and were treated with great politeness by the governor.

They sailed on the 7th of March, and, on the 25th, crossed the equinoctial line. About this time an accident happening to the rudder of the Tamar, and it being impossible to make a perfect repair of it at sea, the captain was ordered to bear away for Antigua; in consequence of which they parted company on the 1st of April; and the Dolphin, without meeting with any other material occurrence; came to an anchor in the Downs, on the 9th of May 1766, after having been rather above twenty-two months in the circumnavigation of the globe.

NAUTICAL PHILOSOPHY.

One night came on a hurricane—
  The sea was mountains rolling—
When Barney Buntline turned his quid,
  And cried to Billy Bowline—
" There 's a sou'-wester coming Billy,
  Don't ye hear it roar now ?
Lord help 'em, how I pities them
  Unhappy folks on shore now.

Fool-hardy chaps as lives in towns,
  What dangers they are all in—
At night lie quaking in their beds,
  For fear the roof will fall in—
Poor creatures, how they envies us,
  And wishes, I 've a notion,
For our good luck in such a storm,
  To be upon the ocean.

Now, as to them that 's out all day
  On business from their houses,
And late at night are walking home,
  To cheer their babes and spouses,
While you and I, upon the deck,
  Are comfortably lying,
My eyes ! what tiles and chimney tops,
  About their heads are flying !

You and I, Bill, have often heard,
  How folks are ruined and undone,
By overturns in carriages,
  By thieves and fires in London—
We've heard what risks all landsmen run,
  From noblemen to tailors,
Then Billy, let 's bless Providence
  That you and I are sailors."

A TALE OF THE SEA.

It was a bright moonlight evening, and so warm that our men
ay about the deck and in groups with hardly any covering; I
think I never saw so perfectly clear and brilliant a night.   Some of
the officers were reading, and with ease, by the light of the moon,
and the ocean as far as the sight could sketch was a glittering
mirror without a single ruffle or wave: we lay like a log on the
water, with all sails set, but not a breath of air to move them.

The crew were collected in small parties about the forecastle and main deck listening to the "long yarns" of some gray-headed seaman, about the "Flying Dutchman" of the "Black River of Gatand," while now and then some favorite sea song was bawled forth from the laughing crowd. The officers were walking about the quarter deck smoking and conversing, and occasionally extending their walk so far as to listen to the stories of the forecastle. This was my first voyage on the "wide, wide sea," and as I was the youngest of the mids I found particular favor with several of the oldest seamen, with whom by-the-by I liked to associate better than with my brother middys—I always loved to listen to their tales of murder and battles, and would sit for hours on the coils of rope. and hear old "Jack Transom" our second mate, an old man of sixty years relate his adventures and "hairbreadth escapes." We had left Port Royal on the south side of Jamaica the day before on our way to the mouth of the Amazon, and were at the time of this writing passing between the small islands of Monts-Errat and Guadaloupe: in the distance you could see the white moon beams playing on the fort and beach, and glistening on the low roofs and white walls of the little capital of Guadaloupe. I was standing on the capstan with a small night glass in my hand, looking at the opposite shore with its long low beach with here and there a small slave hut or mound of loose stones piled up as a covering over the grave of some drowned sailor whose body had been washed on shore. I dropped my glass and was getting down from my station when Jack Transom stepped up and asked for a squint, I handed the glass to him and after looking through it a moment he handed it back saying, "Ay, ay, there it stands with its creaking chains and dry bones rattling in the still air as if a ten knot breeze was ripping over it." "What's that?" said I, eagerly catching the glass and pointing it where 'old starboard' as he was familiarly called, directed me. It was some time before I saw what he meant. When I did, I was at no loss for his abrupt speech. A little north of the town on the white beach, stood a tall gibbet with its chains, and even as old Jack said, its white bones, for I plainly saw them even at that distance glimmering in the rays of the bright moon, and I almost fancied I heard them rattling and shaking against each other, although as I said before, there was not a breath of air, not enough to move a feather; I shuddered at the sight, for I was young and easily affected by any thing terrible or gloomy—we all knew that 'old starboard' was on one of his 'long yarn tacks,' and in a short time a group was formed around the old fellow, as anxious as the crowds of coffee drinkers in the saloons of Constantinople to listen to the wonderful adventures of the Caliph Haroun Alraschid or Sindbad the Sailor. "It's now forty years ago or thereabout," began 'old starboard,' stuffing a huge quid of the true Virginia into his left cheek, " since I first laid eyes on that same death telling gallows

I was then a mere fore-mast-man and perhaps rather green, seeing as how that was my first tack this way, and only the third time I had ever smelt salt water. It was a dark stormy night with a strong northwester blowing at the rate of ten knots an hour, and we were beating across this very channel under a heavy press with the hopes of clearing the shoals before morning; all hands were on deck clearing off and taking in some of our light canvass, for the gale kept on increasing and our main-mast creaked heavily with its load. When the watch ahead bawled out, helm-a-lee! sail a head! but before the words were scarcely out of his mouth we were upon the vessel; we struck her about mid ship. carrying away our bowsprit and dashing in the forecastle sails and knuckle timbers as if they had been glass; but it fared worse with the vessel we met; she was small, being about seven feet in the water, whereas we drew nearer fifteen—we passed slick over her as if she had been a mere boy's plaything. You may be sure there was no standing still, every thing was hauled up and we were before the wind in less than half a shake, the boats were lowered although there was such a sea running that it was almost impossible to live in a small boat—logs of wood and hen coops, were thrown overboard so that if any were alive they might save themselves—our first mate was standing on the quarter listening, when he declared that he heard a shout—we listened and then it came again and again, but fainter every time—at length our captain ordered a boat out, with directions to put in to the shore, and come off in the morning, as we should lay too. That night there was not an eye closed in the ship. We were all waiting for the morning, for many thought it sheer madness in our captain to send off a boat in such a sea, and so dark a night, and prophesied that she would be swamped in less than ten minutes. Though no one said so to the captain, for he was in one of his gloomy moods, and walked the deck nearly the whole night without opening his mouth. We stood off and on till morning, and by this time the wind had lulled considerably, and we had a moderate breeze—as soon as it was light we bore down to the little bay you see off yonder to the nor'-east, and having anchored, sent off a boat to the shore; I was in her, and I shall never forget my joy when I first saw our men standing on the beach and hallooing to us—we were soon among them and asking questions enough to sink a lighter. After leaving the ship they steered as near as they could tell, to where the cries came from; after running about ten minutes, they could hear them plainer, and at last got so near as to speak to the person—it was a man who was clinging to a large board, and was nearly exhausted—after a time they got him in, and finally reached the shore—the poor fellow was nearly gone, and could not speak a word, so they took him to a house, and after awhile by rolling and warming him, brought him to—it so happened that the house belonged to the governor or whatever they call him—and as soon as he clapt his eyes on the man he knew him, and had him taken to prison—and it turned out that after all our trouble we had only saved the poor wretch from being drowned that he might be hung—for as it was proved by many who knew him, having seen the fellow before, and by pieces of the wreck which floated ashore, that he was nothing better than a real pirate, (whose murders were so numerous they could'nt be counted) he had been taken twice before, but had escaped each time—the governor, to be sure of him now, ordered the execution to take place that day:—we had leave to stay on shore and see it—he looked pale and half dead when they brought him out, and for the soul of me I could'nt help pitying him, he stept so firm, and went so willingly to meet his death —he was led out to the gallows between two files of soldiers, our parson talked to him all the way, but he paid no attention and seemed to be thinking of something else. Mayhap the fine vessel he had lost, and all that—we saw the poor fellow swung off, and then went back to our ship, but here was no laughing or joking that day nor the next either—for we all felt as if we had some hand in it, and wished the poor devil had been food for the fishes, rather than to have fallen a prey to land-sharks. The body was taken down and then hung up in chains, and on our homeward voyage we saw them there rattling in the sea breeze and bleaching in the sun I have passed here often, but I have never forgotten to look for the gallows and the Pirate's remains, and I shall never forget that night while I live." All hands a hoy! shouted the boatswain, and in a moment I was left alone. Before I went to my birth I took one more look at the dreaded object, and determined if ever I found leisure to commit the story to paper

---

WALLIS.

In 1766, Capt. Wallis having been appointed to command the ship Dolphin, destined for a voyage round the world, received orders to take under his command the Swallow sloop, and Prince Frederick store-ship. They sailed on the 22d of August, and, on the 7th of September, came to anchor in the road of Madeira.

On the 12th, they sailed thence, and by the 12th of November, were in thirty degrees of south latitude, when they found the weather so cold as to have recourse to their thick jackets. On the 16th of December, being very near Cape Virgin Mary, they saw several men riding on the shore. The captain went ashore, and gave them combs, buttons, knives, scissors, beads, &c, and pleased the women greatly by the distribution of some ribbands. The tallest among these people was six feet seven inches; but the general height was from five feet ten to six feet. They were muscular and well made, but their hands and feet very small, in proportion to the rest of their bodies. The captain took eight of them into the boats: when they came into the ship, they expressed no surprise at the novelties they beheld, till a looking-glass being observed, they acted many antic gestures before it. The marines being exercised before them, they were terrified at the firing of the muskets, and one of them falling down, shut his eyes, and lay without motion, as if to intimate that he knew the destructive nature of these weapons.

On the 21st, they turned into the Strait of Magellan, and on the 26th, anchored in Port Famine Bay; and the sick were sent on shore. On the 28th, the empty water-casks were landed. When they arrived here, many of the people were very sick with the scurvy; but, by the plentiful use of vegetables, and bathing in the sea, they all recovered in a short time.

They sailed on the 18th and on the 3d of February, came to anchor in York Road. The next day, Captain Wallis, with a party, went on shore near Bachelor's River. There is a cataract near this river, the noise of which is tremendous, as it falls more than four hundred yards, partly over a very steep descent, and partly in a perpendicular line. On the 1st of March sailed again, and anchored in a place called Swallow harbor, whence they sailed the next morning; and, on the following day, the Swallow, being driven among breakers, made signals of distress; but was happily relieved by a breeze from the shore. On the 10th of April the two ships sailed in company; and, on the 11th, lost sight of each other, and did not meet again during the whole voyage.

This day the Dolphin cleared the Strait of Magellan, in which she had labored with innumerable difficulties, and escaped most imminent dangers, in a passage of almost four months, viz. from December the 17th, 1776, to the 11th of April following. The Spaniards, it seems, built a town here in 1531, which they named Phillipville, and left in it a colony of four hundred persons. They were all starved to death except twenty-four; and the place was called Port Famine, from the melancholy fate of these unfortunate men.

The long wished for relief was now fast approaching, for on Saturday, the 6th, the man at the mast-head cried, "Land in the west-north-west." As no anchorage was to be found, the captain steered for the other island, giving the name of Whitsun Island to this, because it was discovered on the eve of Whitsunday. Having approached the second, the lieutenant was sent on shore, with two boats, to take possession of the island and to call it Queen Charlotte's Island. The boats returned loaded with cocoa-nuts and scurvy-grass, after having found two wells of excellent water. Provisions for a week were now allotted for an officer and twenty men, who were left on shore to take in water; the sick were landed for the benefit of the air; and a number of hands were appointed to climb the cocoa-trees, and gather the nuts.

An adjoining island, lying in nineteen degrees twenty minutes south latitude, and one hundred thirty-eight degrees thirty minutes west longitude, received the name of Egmont Island. On the 11th, they observed about sixteen persons on an island, which was called Gloucester Island. This day they likewise discovered another, which was called Cumberland Island; and on the day following, a third, which received the name of Prince William Henry's Island. On the 17th, again discovered land, but could find no place in which the ship might anchor. This was named Osnaburgh Island, and having soon discovered high land, they came to anchor because the weather was foggy; but it no sooner cleared away, than they found the ship encompassed by hundreds of people. They sailed along the shore, while the canoes made towards the land On the 21st, the ship came to anchor.

The boats having been sent to sound along the coast, were followed by large double canoes, three of which ran at the cutter, staved in her quarter, and otherwise damaged her; the Indians, at the same time, armed with clubs, endeavoring to board her The crew now fired; and wounding one man dangerously, and killing another, they both fell into the sea. The ship made sail the following day, and was piloted round a reef, into a harbor, where she was moored. On the 24th, she sailed further up the harbor, followed by many canoes. In the evening, a number of very large canoes advanced, laden with stones; on which the captain ordered the strictest watch to be kept. Soon after a large canoe advanced, in which was an awning, on the top of which sat one of the natives, holding some yellow and red feathers in his hand. He delivered the feathers; and, while a present was preparing, he put back from the ship, and threw the branch of a cocoanut tree in the air. This appeared the signal for an onset, for the canoes, approaching the ship threw vollies of stones into every part of her. On this two guns, loaded with small shot, were fired, and the people on guard discharged their muskets. The number of Indians now round the ship was full two thousand; and though they were at first disconcerted, they soon recovered their spirits, and renewed the attack. Thousands were observed on shore, embarking as fast as the canoes could bring them off; orders were therefore given for firing the cannon, some of which were brought to bear upon the shore. The scattered canoes soon got together again, and threw stones of two pounds weight from slings by which a number of seamen were wounded. At this time several canoes approached the bow of the ship, in one of which was an Indian, who appeared to have an authority over the rest; a gun was therefore levelled at his canoe, the shot of which split it in two pieces, which

put an end to the contest; the canoes rowed off with the utmost
speed, and the people on shore ran and concealed themselves behind the hills. Next day a lieutenant was despatched, with all
the boats manned and armed, and having hoisted a pendant on a
staff, he took possession of the place by the name of King George
the Third's Island. Three days after this, the gunner conducted
to the ship a lady of a portly figure and agreeable face, whose age
seemed to be upwards of forty. Her whole behavior indicated
the woman of superior rank. The captain presented her with a
looking-glass and some toys, and gave her a handsome blue mantle, which he tied round her with ribbands. Having intimated
that she would be glad to see the Captain on shore, on Sunday,
the 12th, he landed, and was met by his fair friend, who was attended by a numerous retinue. As they advanced, great numbers
of Indians crowded to meet them. Many persons of both sexes
advanced to meet her, whom she caused to kiss the captain's hand,
while she signified that they were related to her. Her house was
above three hundred and twenty feet in length, and about forty
in breadth. The captain, lieutenant, and purser, who had been
ill, being seated, the lady helped four of her female attendants to
pull off their coats, shoes and stockings; which being performed,
the girls smoothed down the skin, and rubbed it lightly with their
hands for more than half an hour; and the gentlemen received
great benefit from the operation. Orders had been given that
the captain should be carried; but as he chose to walk, she took
hold of his arm, and when they came near any wet or dirty place,
she lifted him over, with as much ease as a man would a child. On
the 15th, a large party in all the boats rowed round the island.
The island was found to be every where very pleasant, and to
abound with various necessaries of life. On the 17th, Captain
Wallis received another visit from the lady whom he called his
queen. On the 21st, she repeated the visit, and presented him
with some hogs. The captain having sent a party on shore on the
25th, to examine the country minutely, caused a tent to be erected to observe an eclipse of the sun, and when it was ended, took
his telescope to the queen's house to show her the use of it; and
her surprise is not to be expressed, on her beholding several objects
which she was very familiar with, but which were too distant to
be seen by the naked eye. She made signs to be informed if he
held his resolution as to the time of his departure, and being answered in the affirmative, her tears witnessed the agitation of her
mind. The captain presented her with several articles of use and
ornament, which she received in silent sorrow. After some time
a breeze springing up, the queen and her attendants took their
final leave, with many tears.

   The place where the ship had lain was called Port Royal Harbor, and is situated in 17 degrees 30 minutes south latitude, and
150 degrees west longitude. The Dolphin sailed from Otaheite

on the 27th of July, 1767, and passed the Duke of York's Island
On the 28th, they discovered land, which was called Sir Charles
Saunder's Island. On the 30th again made land, which received
the name of Lord Howe's Island, on which smoke was seen, but
no inhabitants. Their next discovery was some dangerous shoals,
to which Captain Wallis gave the name of the Scilly Islands
They now steered westward till the 13th of August, when they
saw two small islands, one of which was named Keppel's Isle,
and the other Boscawen's Island. On the 16th they again discovered land, to which the officers gave the name of Wallis's
Island.

On the 18th of September they discovered the island of Saypan,
and soon afterwards that of Tinian, off which they anchored on
the day following. Tents were erected for the sick, who were
sent on shore with all expedition. By the 15th of October the
fruit and water were carried on board, and all the sick being recovered, on the next day they left the bay, and sailed to the west.

On the 3d of November they discovered three islands, which
were named Sandy Isle, Small Key, and Long Island; which
islands are in 10 degrees 20 minutes north latitude, and 247 degrees 30 minutes west longitude. They now altered their course,
and, on the 13th, saw the island of Timoun, Aros, and Pesang.
On the 16th they crossed the equinoctial line, and came again
into south latitude. The next day they saw the islands of Pulo
Toté, and Pulo Weste, and the seven islands. On the 22d saw
the coast of Sumatra; and came to an anchor in the road of Batavia, on the 30th of November, 1767. From this place they sailed
on the 8th of December, without losing a single man, and having
only two on the sick list.

On the 24th of January they encountered a dreadful storm,
which tore the sails to pieces, broke a rudder-chain, and carried
several of the booms overboard; yet during this storm they observed a number of birds and butterflies. On the 30th they saw
land; and came to anchor in Table Bay, at the Cape of Good Hope,
on the 4th of February. Sailed on the 25th, and on the 17th of
March, anchored in the bay of St. Helena. On the 28th crossed
the equinoctial line, and on the 24th of next month saw the Cape
of Pico. No material incident happened from this time to the
end of the voyage; and on the 20th of May, 1768, the Dolphin
came to anchor in the Downs.

VOYAGE FROM HALIFAX TO BERMUDA.

On the 6th of December, we sailed from Halifax, with a fresh
north-westerly wind, on a bitter cold day, so that the harbor was
covered with a vapor called " the barber," a sort of low fog, which

clings to the surface of the water, and sweeps along with these biting winter blasts, in such a manner as to cut one to the very bone.

As we shot past one of the lower wharfs of the town of Halifax, just before coming to the narrow passage between George's Island and the main land, on the south side of this magnificent harbor, a boat put off with a gentleman, who, by some accident, had missed his passage. They succeeded in getting alongside the ship; but, in seizing hold of a rope which was thrown to them from the mainchains, the boatmen, in their hurry, caught a turn with it round the afterthwart, instead of making it fast somewhere in the bow of the boat. The inevitable consequence of this proceeding was, to raise the stern of the boat out of the water, and, of course, to plunge her nose under the surface. Even a landsman will comprehend how this happened, when it is mentioned that the ship was running past at the rate of ten knots. In the twinkling of an eye, the whole party, officer, boatmen, and all, were seen floating about, grasping at the oars or striking out for the land, distant, fortunately, only a few yards from them; for the water thereabouts is so deep, that a ship, in sailing out or in, may safely graze the shore.

As the intensity of the cold was great, we were quite astonished to see the people swimming away so easily; but we afterwards learned from one of the party, that, owing to the water being between forty and fifty degrees warmer than the air, he felt, when plunged into it, as if he had been soused into a hot bath. The instant, however, he reached the pier, and was lugged out, like a half-drowned rat, he was literally enclosed in a firm case of ice from head to foot! This very awkward coat of mail was not removed without considerable difficulty; nor was it till he had been laid for some hours in a well-warmed bed, between two other persons, that he could move at all, and, for several months afterwards, he was not well enough to leave his room.

For us to stop, at such a time and place, was impossible; so away we shot like a spear— past Chebucto Head, Cape Sambro, and sundry other fierce-looking black capes of naked rock. The breeze rapidly rose to a hard gale, which split our main-topsail to threads, and sent the fragments thundering to leeward in the storm, in such grand style, that, to this hour, I can almost fancy I hear the noise in my ears. I know few things more impressive than the deep-toned sounds caused by the flapping of a wet sail, in such a fierce squall as this, when the sheets are carried away, and the unconfined sail is tugging and tearing to get clear of the yard, which bends and cracks so fearfully, that even the lower mast sometimes wags about like a reed. I certainly have heard thunder far louder than the sounds alluded to; but have seldom known it more effective or startling than those of a sail going to pieces in such a tempest of wind and rain

I was standing, where I had no business to be, on the weather side of the quarter-deck, holding on stoutly by one of the belaying pins, and wondering where this novel scene was to end, but having an obscure idea that the ship was going to the bottom. The admiral was looking up at the splitting sail as composedly as possible, after desiring that the main-top-men, whose exertions were quite useless, should be called down, out of the way of the ropes, which were cracking about their heads. Every now and then I could see the weather-wise glance of the veteran's eye directed to windward, in hopes that matters would mend. But they only became worse; and at last, when the fore-mast seemed to be really in danger, for it was bending like a cane, though the fore-sail had been reefed, he waited not to run through the usual round of etiquettes by which an admiral's commands generally reach the executive on board ship, but exclaimed with a voice so loud, that it made me start over to the lee side of the deck:—

" Man the fore-clue garnets!"

In the next minute the sail rose gradually to the yard, and the groaning old ship, by this time sorely strained to her innermost timber, seemed to be at once relieved from the pressure of the canvass which had borne her headlong, right into the seas, and made her tremble from stem to stern, almost as if she were going to pieces.

The next thing to be done was to get in the jib-boom, in order to ease the bowsprit. In effecting this rather troublesome operation, one of the primest seamen we had fell overboard. He was second captain of the forecastle, the steadiness of whose admirable skill as a steersman had, one day, elicited the complimentary remark from the captain, that he must surely have nailed the compass card to the binnacle. On this, and other accounts, he was so much esteemed in the ship, that more than the usual degree of regret was felt for his melancholy fate. I saw the poor fellow pitch into the water, and watched him as he floated past, buoyant as a cork, and breasting the waves most gallantly, with an imploring look towards us, which I shall never forget. In less than a minute he was out of sight. A boat could hardly have lived in such weather, and no further attempt was made, or could have been made, to save him, than to throw over ropes, which all fell short of their mark. Although we soon lost all traces of him, it 's probable he may have kept sight of us, as we drifted quickly to eeward under our bare poles, long after we had ceased to distinguish his figure in the yest of waves.

This gale, the first I ever saw, was also, I can recollect, one of the fiercest. It lasted for three days, totally dispersed our little squadron, well nigh foundered one of them, the Cambrian, and sent her hobbling into Bermuda some days after us, with the loss of her main-mast and all three top-masts.

The rock of the islands of Bermuda is of a very soft coarse

freestone, full of pores; so soft, indeed, that if it be required to make an additional window in a house, there is nothing to be done, we were told, but to hire a black fellow, who, with a saw, could speedily cut an opening in any part of the wall.

There is nothing more remarkable in this singular cluster of islands than the extensive coral reefs which fend off the sea on the northern side, and stretch out in a semi-circular belt, at the distance of two or three leagues from the land. On these treacherous reefs we saw many a poor vessel bilged, at moments when, from seeing the land at such a distance, they fancied themselves in perfect security.

They tell a story of a boatman who, it was said, lived by these disasters, once going off to an unlucky vessel, fairly caught among the coral reefs, like a fly in a cobweb, not far from the North Rock. The wrecker, as he was called, having boarded the bewildered ship, said to the master,

" What will you give me, now, to get you out of this place?"

" Oh, any thing you like—name your sum."

" Five hundred dollars?"

" Agreed! agreed!" cried the other. Upon which this treacherous pilot ' kept his promise truly to the ear, but broke it to the hope,' by taking the vessel out of an abominably bad place, only to fix her in one a great deal more intricate and perilous.

" Now," said the wrecker to the perplexed and doubly-cheated stranger, "there never was a vessel in this scrape, that was known to get out again; and, indeed, there is but one man alive who knows the passage, or could, by any possibility, extricate you—and that's me!"

" I suppose," drily remarked the captain, "that ' for a consideration' you would be the man to do me that good service What say you to another five hundred dollars to put me into clear water, beyond your infernal reefs?"

This hard bargain was soon made; and a winding passage, unseen before, being found, just wide enough, and barely deep enough, for the vessel to pass through, with only six inches to spare under her keel, in half an hour she was once more in blue water, out of soundings, and out of danger.

" Now, master rascallion of a wrecker," cried the disentangled mariner, "tit for tat is fair play all the world over; and, unless you hand me back again my thousand dollars, I'll cut the tow rope of your thievish-looking boat, and then, instead of returning evil for evil, as I ought by rights to do, I'll be more of a Christian, and do you a very great service, by carrying you away from one of the most infamous places in the world, to the finest country imaginable—I mean America. And as you seem to have a certain touch of black blood in your veins, I may chance to get good interest for my loan of these thousand dollars, by selling you as a slave in the Charleston negro market! What say you, my gay Mudian?"

DE BOUGAINVILLE.

A settlement having been commenced by the French on Falkland's Islands, in the month of February, 1764, the Spaniards demanded them as an appendage to the continent of South America; and France having allowed the propriety of the demand, Mons. de Bougainville was ordered to yield possession of the islands to the Spaniards.

On the 5th of December he sailed from the harbor of Brest, in the frigate La Boudeuse; having on board the Prince of Nassau Seighen, three gentlemen who went as volunteers, eleven officers in commission, and warrant-officers, seamen, soldiers, servants and boys, to the number of two hundred. On the evening of the 29th of January, they had sight of Rio-de-la-Plata, and on the morning of the 31st came to anchor in the Bay of Montevideo, where the two Spanish ships, which were to take possession of Falkland's Islands, had been at anchor for some weeks. They sailed with these ships on the 28th of February 1767; and, on the 1st of April, Bougainville, in the name of the French king, surrendered the islands to Don Puente, the Spanish governor, who received them for his most Catholic majesty, with the ceremony of hoisting the Spanish colors, and the firing of guns from the ships and on shore.

Falkland's Islands lie in about 52 deg. south latitude, and 60 deg. west longitude. From the entrance of the Straits of Magellan, and from the coast of Patagonia, their distance is about two hundred and fifty miles. The harbors are large, and well defended by small islands most happily disposed; and even the smallest vessels may ride in safety in the creeks, while fresh water is easily to be obtained. After waiting at these islands till the 2d of June, 1767, in expectation of the Etoile store-ship from Europe, Bougainville steered for Rio-Janeiro, at which place he had appointed the Etoille to join him. They had fine weather from the 2d till the 20th of June, on which day they had sight of the mountains on the main land of Brazil, and entered Rio-Janeiro the day following. At the same time a canoe was despatched from the captain of the Etoile, with information of the safe arrival of that vessel, which now lay in the port; and on the 14th July, both vessels sailed, and on the 31st came to anchor in the Bay of Montevideo. As it was necessary that Bougainville should remain in his present station till the equinox was passed, his first care was to build a hospital for the sick, and to take lodgings at Montevideo.

On the 14th of November, 1767, they sailed from Montevideo, with a fine gale of wind at north. On the 16th, and the five following days, the sea ran high, and the wind was contrary. The 2d of December they had sight of Cape Virgins, with a fair wind

They now saw a number of albatrosses and petrels, the last of which are said to be a sign of bad weather, whenever they are seen. They made their best efforts to reach the entrance of the Straits of Magellan; and Bougainville was seven weeks and three days in passing through it, the whole length of which, from Cape Virgin Mary to Cape Pillar, he computes at about three hundred and forty miles.

On the 22d of March, land was discovered, and when they had coasted one of the islands for about two miles, they had sight of three men, who advanced hastily towards the shore. They at first imagined that these were part of the crew of some European ship, which had been wrecked on the coast, but discovered their conjecture ill-founded, for the people retired to the woods, from which, in a short time, issued a number of them, supposed to be near twenty, with long staves in their hands, which they held up with an air of defiance. This done, they retreated to the woods. These islanders were of a copper complexion and very tall.

During the night between the 22d and 23d they had much rain accompanied with violent thunder, while the wind blew almost a tempest. At day-break land was discovered, which was called Harp Island, and in the evening a cluster of islands, eleven of which were seen, received the name of the Dangerous Archipelago. A steep mountain, which appeared to be encompassed by the sea, was discovered on the 2d of April, and received the name of Boudoir, or Boudeuse Peak, from Bougainville's ship. Bearing to the northward of this peak they had sight of land, which extended farther than the eye could reach.

As Bougainville coasted the island, he was charmed with the appearance of a noble cascade, which, falling immediately from the summit of a mountain into the sea, produced a most elegant effect. On the shores very near to the fall of this cascade, was a little town, and the coast appeared to be free from breakers. It was the wish of our adventurers to have cast their anchor within view of such an enchanting prospect; but, after repeated soundings, they found that the bottom consisted only of rocks, and they were, therefore, under a necessity of seeking another anchoring place, where the ships were safely moored.

They remained at Otaheite, until the 16th of April, when they departed, and in the beginning of May three islands were discovered. On the following day another island was seen to the west ward of the ship's course. To the islands the commodore gave the general name of the Archipelago of the Navigators. On the morning of the 11th, another island was discovered, which received the name of the Forlorn Hope.

The ships now steered a westerly course, and early on the morning of the 22d two islands were discovered, one of which received the name Aurora, from the early hour on which it was first seen, and the other that of Whitsuntide Isle, from the day which

gave birth to its being so named. In the afternoon, mountainous
lands, at thirty miles distance, were seen, appearing, as it were,
over and beyond the Island of Aurora. On the 23d it was discovered that this was a separate island, the appearance being lofty, its
descent steep, and the whole clothed with trees. From this time
to the 27th, they passed many islands, on one of which they observed a fine plantation of trees, between which there were regular walks, resembling those of an European garden. They now
quitted this great cluster of islands, which received the general
name of Archipelago of the great Cyclades, which, it is conjectured, occupies no less than three degrees of latitude, and five of
longitude.

From the 14th to the 18th of June, they discovered a number
of islands. On July the 2d a cape was discovered, which was
called Cape l'Averdi, on which were mountains of an astonishing
height. Two more islands were seen on the 5th, and, as the wood
and water were expended, and disease reigning aboard, the commodore resolved to land here, and, on the following afternoon,
the ships came to anchor.

In the afternoon of the 24th a favorable breeze enabled the ships
to get out to sea. On the 31st a number of Indian boats attacked
the Etoile with a volley of stones and arrows; but a single discharge
of the musketry got rid of these troublesome companions. On the
4th of August two islands were seen. On the 5th a third island
was seen, and then the northern point of New Britain, which lies
only forty one minutes south of the land. On the 7th a flat island
was seen, covered with trees, abounding with cocoa-nuts. Fishing-boats in multitudes surrounding the island; but the fishermen
took no notice of the ships. This received the name of the Island
of Anchorets. From this time till the end of the month innumerable small islands were observed every day.

Early in the morning of the 31st our voyagers had sight of the
island of Ceram, which runs in a parallel east and west, abounds in
lofty mountains, and is partly cleared, and partly in its original
state. At midnight a number of fires attracted their attention to
the island of Boero, where there is a Dutch factory, at the entrance of the Gulf of Cagei, which the French had sight of at
day-break. Their joy on this occasion is not to be expressed, for
at this time not half of the seamen were able to perform any
duty, and the scurvy had raged so violently, that no man on board
was perfectly clear of it.

They sailed on the 7th September and on the 13th the ships were
surrounded with Indian boats, bringing parroquets, cockatoos,
fowls, eggs, and bananas, which the natives sold for Dutch money,
or exchanged for knives. By day-light on the 19th they were
within about a league of the Coast of Celibes, which in this part
is described as one of the finest countries in the world. On the
morning of the 26th the coast of Java appeared with the rising

sun. Having come to an anchor for the night, the ships sailed early in the morning of the 27th and on the next day came to anchor in the port of Batavia.

The ships sailed thence on the 16th of October, 1768, and cleared the straits of Sunda on the 19th in the afternoon. By this time the crew were all perfectly recovered of the scurvy, but a few remained ill of the bloody flux. On the 20th the ships were in sight of the Isle of France, and, on the 8th of November, the Boudeuse anchored in the port of that island; the Etoile, which had been unavoidably left behind, anchoring in the same port on the following day.

They sailed from this the 12th of December, 1768, leaving the Etoile behind them to undergo some necessary repairs. Without encountering any singular accident they had sight of the Cape of Good Hope on the 18th of January, and came to anchor in Table Bay on the following morning. Bougainville quitted this on the 17th, anchored off St. Helena on the 4th of February, and on the 25th, joined the Swallow, commanded by Captain Cartert. Nothing material happened from this time till they had sight of the Isle of Ushant, where a violent squall of wind had nearly blasted the hopes of the voyage. On the 15th the commodore bore away for St. Maloes, which he entered on the following day, after an absence of two years and four months from his native country; during all which time he had buried only seven of his crew, a circumstance that will be deemed truly astonishing, when we reflect on the variety of dangers they had encountered and the amazing changes of climate they had experienced.

HISTORY OF THE BUCCANEERS.

The name Buccaneer, which originally signified one who dried or smoked flesh in the manner of the Indians, was given to the first French settlers of St. Domingo, who hunted wild boars and cattle, in order to sell the hides and flesh to their more settled neighbors. They lived in huts built on patches of cleared ground, just sufficiently large to admit of drying the skins. These spots were named Boucans, and the huts, which were commonly only temporary, Ajoupas, terms borrowed from the native Indians. With the more regular Spanish settlers of the same island they were continually at war, and therefore concealment was, in some degree, necessary: the motives of the Spaniards for this persecution being jealousy of the presence of all other Europeans.

The tenants of the Boucans, having neither women nor children, congregated in parties, each keeping a servant, who, being some adventurer from Europe, was obliged to bind himself for three years to an older Buccaneer, in order to gain a footing in the community; more a companion, however, than a servant, the fruits of their labors were enjoyed in common; and, in cases of death, the domestic regularly succeeded to the property of his master. In process of time, some, tired of this occupation, settled as planters in the little island of Tortuga, situated at a short distance from the north side of St. Domingo, to which they were, by degrees, driven by the repeated massacres of the Spaniards. Others commenced free-booters by sea, amply revenging upon that nation the injuries sustained by their companions on land. Success continually added to their confidence and to their numbers. They seldom at first, acted together; but in parties of from fifty to two hundred men each, embarked in small boats, ill adapted either to war or security from the elements, and would attack the largest vessels, overpowering them by a desperate bravery which nothing could withstand. Thus they fought their way to riches and power Every additional prize afforded increased means of capturing others; till, at length, the Spaniards, afraid of proceeding to sea, had their intercourse with the mother-country nearly annihilated.

Although their vengeance was directed against this, their wealthiest and bitterest enemy, other nations were not exempted from their depredations. When distressed for men, money, or ships, almost every stranger became an enemy. Thus far they were pirates. The booty was regularly divided into as many shares as there were men. None had a preference. The leader of an enterprise, commonly elected only for the occasion, among the most distinguished for skill and courage, enjoyed more honors, but had no claim to greater emoluments than his associates, except what the general voice chose to award when an enterprise proved profitable, and had been ably conducted.

No fixed laws guided their proceedings. These were made upon the spur of the occasion. But offences against the general good, such as peculation or treachery, were severely and summarily punished, either by death, or by leaving the culprit upon a desert island. Such was the certainty of punishment, or the sense of justice to each other, that few instances of this kind occurred. Their behavior verified the adage of—"Honesty among thieves;" for though robbers by profession, none were ever more equitable among themselves. Every share was chosen by lot. The wounded were provided for by a certain sum, and an allowance during cure. The companion, or servant of a member killed, received his share. If he had none, it was transmitted to his relations; or, if these were unknown, given to the poor, or to churches, to apologize for misdeeds neither repented of nor discontinued. They seldom went to sea except when in want of money, and, when gained, it was as quickly spent. Jamaica commonly formed the resort of the English, and St. Domingo of the French, where the fruits of their cruizes being soon dissipated in rioting and debauchery, necessity drove them to the same desperate undertakings for further supplies.

These associations continued, with but few intermissions, for nearly 150 years, peace or war in Europe being of no import in the eyes of their leaders. The principal of these were Morgan, Sammo Wilner, Towley, and others, among the English; Montbar, L'Olonois, Grognier, Picard, Le Sage, and Grammont, among the French; Van Horn, a Dutchman, and De Basco, a Portuguese.

Morgan, the most renowned of the English freebooters, after a variety of minor exploits, conceived the bold project of subduing Porto-Bello, which he accomplished with great skill and no loss, gaining a large booty from its plunder and ransom. Panama, however, a large town, situated across the isthmus of Darien, on the shore of the South Seas, promised still more wealth. Having reduced the island of St. Catharine's by a secret understanding with the Spanish governor, who wished to have the honor, though not the danger, of resisting the adventurers, he proceeded to the mouth of the river Chagres, leading part of the way to his ultimate destination. Here was a fort situated upon a rock; against which beat the waves of the sea; and defended by an officer and a garrison, worthy of the trust committed to their courage. The buccaneers attacked it with desperation, and were as vigorously resisted, but this resistance only stimulated the energy of men accustomed, not merely to expect, but almost to command success. For some time the contest continued doubtful, till a lucky shot killed the commander of the fort, while, at the same time, it took fire, when the besieged, losing courage, surrendered.

Morgan leaving his vessels at anchor under a guard, proceeded in canoes up the river, thirty-five miles, where, being no longer navigable, he disembarked, and marched towards Panama, about thirty miles distant. On a plain, without the town, a considerable army appeared drawn up to oppose his progress. This was no sooner attacked than dispersed. In the city, in boats, and in the neighboring forests, were found vast treasures concealed in caves and cellars, the inhabitants having had time to retire themselves, but not to carry off their wealth; added to these were immense quantities of valuable articles of commerce, which, being unable to remove, were, as well as the town, according to the barbarous practice of that age, set on fire by the adventurers, who regained their ships with a prodigious booty.

Among the French, who distinguished themselves as much for cruelty as bravery, was Montbar, a native of Languedoc. He had, in early life, conceived a strong prejudice against the Spaniards, on account of their cruelties to the Indians; this spirit increasing with his years, he embarked from Europe to join the buccaneers. In the passage out, a Spanish vessel being met with,

7

was attacked, boarded, and taken, Montbar leading the way to
the decks of the enemy, along which he carried wounds and death,
nothing being able to resist his desperate fury; and when submission terminated the engagement, his only pleasure seemed to be
to contemplate, not the treasures of the vessel, but the number
of dead and dying Spaniards, against whom he had vowed a deadly and eternal hatred. This inveterate enmity never subsided
His opponents suffered so much and so frequently from it, during
the whole of his life, that he acquired from them the name of the
Exterminator.

Another of the same nation, named L'Olonois, from the situation of bondsman, had raised himself to the command of two boats
and twenty-two men, with which he was bold enough to attack,
and fortunate enough to capture a small Spanish frigate on the
coast of Cuba.   With this vessel he succeeded in taking four ships
fitted out at Port-au-Prince to destroy him; but cruelly threw their
crews overboard, excepting one man, sent back to the governor
of the Havannah, with a message that all Spaniards who might
fall into his hands, not excepting even his excellency himself,
should experience a similar fate.   At Tortuga he met with Michael
de Basco, already celebrated for having taken a ship under the
guns of Porto Bello, valued at £220,000, and a variety of other
enterprises both daring and profitable.   Between them a new expedition was planned, supported by 450 men; in the bay of
Venezuela they reduced a fort, sinking the guns, and cruelly putting the garrison of 250 men to death.   Re-embarking, they
reached Maracaybo, built on the western shore of the lake of that
name, a city which had acquired wealth by its trade in skins,
cocoa, and tobacco.   The inhabitants, at the first alarm, fled with
their principal effects; enough, however, remained to keep the buccaneers in drunkenness and debauchery for some time; in the
mean while works were thrown up to impede their progress, which
they reduced at the expense of blood and labor, but without any
profit.   Maracaybo itself was ransomed; Gibraltar, situated near
the extremity of the lake, was burned, owing to the exasperation
of the adventurers at missing the expected plunder; and, at length
they retired laden with crosses, pictures, and bells, more than
with wealth.

Van Horne, in 1603, formed the design of an expedition, which
promised a rich harvest to his followers.   He himself was at once
their admiration and terror, being not only remarkable for intrepidity but for punishing the smallest want of it in others, often going round the decks during the heat of an engagement, and instantly shooting those who, in the smallest degree, flinched from their
guns.   In other respects he was equitable and generous, sharing
equally with his crew the produce of their courage, though sailing in a ship wholly his private property.

To aid in the present scheme, he took Gramont, Godfrey, Jon

qué, and De Graff, all commanders of approved skill and courage, with 1200 men, the largest force which had yet been mustered, and in six vessels sailed for Vera Cruz. Night, and ignorance of the armament, favoring their design, the buccaneers landed eight miles from the town, entered it undiscovered, and, before day-break, secured the governor, forts, barracks, and all the soldiers capable of making opposition. The inhabitants sought refuge in the churches, at the doors of which were placed barrels of gunpowder, guarded by the invaders with lighted matches, in order to destroy the whole in case of insurrection or tumult. The work of pillage, in the meantime, proceeded without interruption, nothing being left which it was possible or desirable to carry away. A proposal was likewise made to the imprisoned people, who had not tasted food for three days, to ransom their lives and freedom for a sum of £430,000. This, whether able or not, they were compelled to accede to, half the money being paid immediately, and the other half promised in a few days. Suddenly, however, a large armed force appeared before the town, and a fleet of seventeen ships from Europe before the port, which though sufficient to intimidate a regular army, if not to desert their plunder, had no other effect on the buccaneers than to induce them to retreat quietly with 1500 slaves, as an indemnification for the remaining half of the expected ransom, and to push deliberately through the Spanish fleet, which, instead of intercepting, was itself happy to escape from such terrible assailants.

For a long series of years these depredations continued Scarcely a town escaped, except such as were situated very far in the interior; forts and soldiers were of little use on the coast, for the former were soon reduced, and the latter, whenever they attempted a fair contest in the field, always conquered. Towards the decline of this predatory warfare, Gramont embarked with a considerable force for Campeachy, and landing without opposition, found 800 Spaniards drawn up to dispute the approach of the town, who were attacked, beaten, and pursued into it, with the invaders close behind, till stopped by the citadel. Against this all the cannon they could find was directed in vain. Fear, however, effected what force could not. The garrison dreading the name of the buccaneers, evacuated the place during the night, leaving only an Englishman in it, (a gunner,) who, with the spirit of a soldier, disdained to desert that which he had sworn to defend, and which, it appeared, was capable of being obstinately defended; and so highly did this principle of honor and courage operate upon the assailants, who were held together solely by the same feelings, that they received him with distinction, and rewarded him, not only with praises and liberty, but likewise with wealth.

For two months the conquerors kept possession of the city, searching not only every nook and corner in it for plunder, but the country, for thirty or forty miles round discovering what had

been hidden in the earth or in the woods, to the great loss of the
inhabitants, who vainly believed they had, by this means, secured
part of their property. The plunder, as soon as collected, was
deposited on ship-board. The governor of the province kept the
field with nearly a thousand men, but dared not interrupt men
who seemed as desperate, wherever booty was to be procured,
as they were insensible to danger and regardless of death. His
refusal to ransom the city caused its immediate destruction by
fire. The citadel, likewise, was levelled to the ground. A more
extraordinary sacrifice on the part of the free-booters was by a bon-
fire, made of logwood, valued at £1,000,000 and forming part of the
plunder, which, in celebrating the festival of St. Louis, on the
anniversary of the French king, whose subjects they principally
were, was given to the flames in the intoxication of folly rather
than of loyalty.

The last memorable attempt of the buccaneers, on a large scale,
in this part of the world, took place in 1697, when twelve hundred men joined a squadron of seven ships from Europe, in order
to attack the city of Carthagena. Their commander was named
Pointis, a man of little honor or generosity, but intent on aggran-
dizing himself. The enterprise was arduous; the place the strongest in the new world; the port difficult of approach to enemies;
and, if not immediately reduced, the climate so bad, that were the
Spaniards even to do nothing more than to contrive delays, it would
soon destroy the invaders. This, however, the latter knew. They,
therefore, proceeded vigorously to work, seconded by that zeal
accustomed to contend with and to conquer next to impossibilities;
of guns they had no want, and their men were prodigal of their
blood; each fought as if his individual honor and interest were
at stake, which, indeed, formed the life of these associations; and
their good fortune, as usual, prevailing, the city yielded to their
arms with a booty calculated at £1,750,000.

Of a great part of this they were deprived by the knavish rapacity of their commander. Exasperated at his tricks, a party
proceeded toward his ship, determined to inflict summary punishment on the offender, but recollecting this could be of no immediate service, cried out, "Brethren, why should we pollute
ourselves with the blood of this knave? He is unworthy the indignation of honorable men! Let him live to be despised and
hooted, rather than die lamented by any one who may hear of his
fate, without knowing his crimes. Our share of the booty is still
at Carthagena, and there alone must we look for it."

Returning to the city, which was re-entered without opposition,
the inhabitants were shut up in the churches till the sum of £220,
000 should be paid, the amount of the sum of which they believed
themselves defrauded. Possessed of this, they promised to retire
without molestation to property or person; without it they threatened the most frightful destruction to both. Unable, or unwilling

to satisfy men whose wants were as boundless as their conduct was daring and unprincipled, the poor people knew not what to do. A venerable priest, at length, mounted the pulpit, to aid, by the force of religious eloquence, the exactions of that rapacity which it was probably useless to refuse, and impossible to prevent, and which if ungratified, would terminate in more terrible and destructive consequences. This appeal not producing the sum expected, the city was ordered to be plundered. Sated, at length, with rioting and plunder; with money, merchandise, and moveables of all kinds, they quitted this unfortunate place; but, soon afterwards, falling in with an English and Dutch squadron, then in alliance with Spain, they were attacked and nearly destroyed; part being taken, part sunk, and part escaping to St. Domingo, a piece of due retributive justice for their extortionate and illegal deeds, which had now become, on many occasions, quite piratical, and unsanctioned by the practices of fair and honorable warfare.

From this time buccaneering rapidly declined, the majority becoming settlers in the different West Indian islands, to which they were induced by the European powers, sending out ships-of-war to clear those seas and establish perfect security in commerce, which had been, for a century, much interrupted, and so far as regarded Spain, often, for years together, quite destroyed. Those who persisted in illegal practices were executed as pirates; while others, more disposed to acquire wealth by honest means, received encouragement from the local governments in grants of land. The renewal of war with Spain occasionally drew forth some of the more turbulent spirits from their peaceful occupations, but the greater portion had acquired settled habits; and, in time, the name of buccaneer, as well as his practices, became gradually obliterated among all but the Spaniards, by whom they will never be forgotten.

It must also be admitted, that, these adventurers acted, in some measure, from principle. Many conscientiously detested the Spanish people on account of real or alleged cruelties towards the Indians. In plundering them, they believed they were only despoiling robbers of that to which they had no legal claim; and far from considering their actions as crimes, esteemed them not merely honorable but just.

THE WRECKERS.

"A storm! A storm!" the Wreckers cry,
As they look from the shore—yet no storm seems nigh;
But wind and billow, wreck and ship,
Along he main seem all asleep:

But where is the day?—'Tis gone! Not a trace
Of the sun! The cloud has taken his place,
And moves not—breaks not—hanging there,
As 't were fixed in the sultry, thick'ning air!

A flash!—Another!—sky and main
Begin to move!—a flash again!
Thunder—wind—the storm is come,
The sea 's a smoking sheet of foam!
Rain!—it pours in floods, as though
The clouds did mock the floods below!
And the Vessel, from her anchors torn,
Towards the shore by the raging billows is borne

Hurra!—Hurra!—a wreck—Hurra!
She strikes—by the board her tall masts go;
She reels—recoils, and strikes again!
They hoist the long-boat out—In vain—
'Tis swampt! She now beats broadside on—
Another sea—she sinks! she's gone!
Masts, cordage, planks, the breakers strew!
May heaven have mercy on her crew·

VOYAGE OF CAPTAIN JAMES,

FOR THE DISCOVERY OF A NORTH-WEST PASSAGE.

In the year 1630, several wealthy merchants of Bristol united
in fitting out a vessel for the purpose of accurately examining the
whole northen coast of America. The command of this vessel
which was small, only of seventy tons burden, but one of the
strongest ships of her size that had ever been built, was given to
Captain James. She was provisioned for eighteen months, and
manned with only twenty-two seamen, but these were all excellent
sailors.

His stores having been all shipped, and the men on board, Captain James left Bristol in the month of April, 1631. After passing the southern coast of Ireland, he sailed in a west-north-west-
erly direction, and on the fourth of June discovered the coast of
Greenland. Two days subsequently to this, his vessel was
encompassed with ice, many immense pieces of which beat so
violently against her that the captain was fearful she would have
been staved and sunk. The boat that accompanied her was crushed to atoms. In one instance he was obliged to order the ship
to be made fast to a great piece of the ice, and during a day and
night to employ men incessantly in pushing off such masses of ice
as floated against her; but in this labor all their poles were broken. The wind at length blew a perfect hurricane, and, though

the broken ice on almost all sides rose higher than the decks, and the vessel was beaten about in a most alarming manner, she suffered no injury.

On the morning of the tenth of June, these hardy adventurers passed some masses of ice that were as high as the topmast of their vessel, and left Cape Desolation, in Greenland, to the eastward. The weather was now so cold that at one time the sails and rigging were all frozen. On the twentieth, the ship reached the southern point of the island of Resolution, at the entrance of Hudson's Strait, but she was several times carried round by the current, and floating ice, and was in imminent danger of being crushed to pieces before she could be brought to anchor. It now began to snow heavily, and the wind blew a storm from the westward. This drove the ice from the sea into the harbor where the vessel was stationed, until it was choked up. For some time the ice seemed to be perfectly firm and immoveable, but it floated out again at the ebb of the tide. The various dangers to which the vessel was exposed in this harbor, of being thrown against the rocks, crushed to pieces in the ice, and sunk, were so great that the captain almost gave up all hope of being able to save her He describes the thundering noise of the masses of ice beating against each other, the rushing of the water, and the fury of the current to have been tremendous. After much difficulty and the most persevering exertions, however, she was navigated into a little cove or harbor, where, being made fast to the rocks, she was at length rendered tolerably secure.

Captain James landed on the island, but found that, although the summer was far advanced, the ponds were yet frozen. The ground was rocky and barren, and no traces of animals were visible in the snow, though it was evident from some hearths and remains of fire-wood which were seen, that human beings had not long before visited the place. Captain James continued here two days, and then sailed westward; but the masses of ice were still almost impenetrable. They grated the sides of the vessel with such violence that it was feared they would burst through the planks. On looking out from the mast-head scarcely an acre of open sea was visible: nothing was to be seen but a continued and irregular range of ice, towering in different places to an immense height. The ship was thus surrounded till the twenty-seventh of June, when, by a gale from the south-east, the ice opened, and she was enabled to make some way.

Though exposed to incessant danger by the immense masses of ice which floated on the surface of the ocean, Captain James and his associates proceeded still westward, and entered Hudson's Strait about the beginning of July. On the fifteenth of that month, they arrived betwixt Digg's Island and Nottingham Island, but the summer was so cold and unfavorable that it was now evident there would be no possibility of proceeding much further northward this year. About a fortnight afterwards, they were so fast enclosed in the ice, that, notwithstanding the ship had all her sails set, and it blew a strong breeze, she was immoveable and as firmly fixed, as if she had been in a dry dock. On this, the captain and many of the men walked out of her to amuse themselves upon the ice. Several of the crew now began to murmur, and to express great alarm, lest they should not be able either to proceed or return; and lest their provisions, which were beginning to fall short, would soon wholly fail. The captain encouraged them as well as he was able, and though he was aware their murmuring was not without reason, he affected to ridicule their fears. Among other contrivances to amuse them, he took a quantity of spirits upon the ice, and there drank the king's health, although there was not a single man in the ship, and though she was at that time under all her sails. This was the twenty-eighth of July. On the thirtieth, they made some little way through the ice, part of the crew leaving the vessel along with their shoulders, whilst others, at the same time, broke off the corners of the ice with mallets and iron crows, to clear the way. This labor was continued on the following day, and after much fatigue, they got the ship into thirty-five fathom water. All this time they were in latitude 58 deg. 45 minutes north, and a few days afterwards they were in an open sea free from ice. The captain and his crew now joined in devout thanksgiving for their deliverance from the dangers to which they had been exposed.

A few days subsequently to this, whilst the ship was under sail, she struck upon some rocks that were concealed by the water, and received three such terrible blows, that the captain was fearful her masts would have been shivered to pieces, and he had no doubt that a hole had been beaten through her sides. But such was the strength of her timbers that she received little injury, and in a short time, was again out of danger.

On the twentieth of August, and in latitude 57 deg. north, they came within sight of land, part of the continent of North America, which the captain named New South Wales, in honor of Charles, Prince of Wales, afterwards King Charles the second: and on the third of September they passed a cape, to which he gave the name of Cape Henrietta Maria, after the Queen. In the ensuing evening, they encountered such a tempest of thunder, snow, rain, and wind, as none of the crew had ever before been exposed to. The sea washed completely over the decks, and the vessel rolled so tremendously, that it was not without great difficulty all things could be kept fast in the hold, and betwixt the decks.

As the winter was now approaching, Captain James began to look out for some harbor, where he and his companions could pass that cheerless season, with as little discomfort, and in as much security, as possible. Landing, on the third of October, upon an island, in the bay that has since been called James's Bay, he found the tracks of deer, and saw some wild fowl; but not being able to discover a safe anchorage, he proceeded onward with the vessel, and two days afterwards moored the ship, in a place of tolerable security near the same island. It now snowed without intermission, and was so cold that the sails were frozen quite hard, and the cable was as thick with ice as a man's body.

Several men were sent ashore to cut wood for fuel, and they collected as much as, it was estimated, would last two or three months. It was found inconvenient, particularly for some of the crew who were sick, to continue entirely in the vessel; a kind of house was, therefore, erected on shore, under the direction of the carpenter. In the meantime the captain and some of the men went into the woods to see whether they could discover any traces of human beings, that, in case they found such, they might be on their guard against attack. None were found. The top-sails were now taken down from the vessel, thawed, and dried by great fires, and then folded up and secured from wet between the decks. The main-sail was carried on shore, to be used as a covering for the house. In about four days, the house was ready, and a portion of the crew slept in it every night, armed with muskets to defend themselves in case of attack, and guarded by two buckhounds, which had been brought from England, for the hunting of deer. Such of the other rigging of the vessel as could be taken down, was now removed, and placed under the decks.

On the fourteenth of October, six of the men set out with the dogs, in the hope of killing some deer, the tracks of which they had previously seen. They wandered more than twenty miles over the snow, and returned the next day with one small and lean animal; having passed a cold and miserable night in the woods. Others went out a few days afterwards, and to a still greater distance; these were not only unsuccessful, but they lost one of their companions, who, on attempting to cross a small frozen lake, fell in and was drowned. The captain consequently gave directions that hunting to such distances should be no more attempted.

The crew at first brought beer ashore from the ship; but this, even in their house, and close by the fire, was frozen and spoiled in one night. After this they drank water, which they obtained from a well that they sunk near the house. Their time was chiefly passed in setting traps and hunting for foxes and other animals, and in such occupations as were requisite for their own preservation.

The winter was now so far advanced, that the ship appeared, from the shore, like a piece of ice in the form of a ship. The snow was frozen on every part, and her decks and sides were covered with ice. The captain began to despair of ever again getting her off. Every day the men were employed in beating the ice from the cables, and digging it out of the hawsers with a calking iron; and in these operations the water would freeze on their clothes and hands, so as very soon to render them unequal to almost any exertion.

The ship was found to beat so much, that the captain could devise no other means of preventing her from being shattered to pieces and destroyed, than by directing holes to be bored through her sides, and sinking her in shallow water; where, in the ensuing spring, he might have a chance of again raising her. This was a fearful expedient; but, after all the provisions and things requisite for use on shore had been taken out of her, it was adopted; although it was the general opinion of the crew that she could never be floated again. They, however, had so strong an attachment for their captain, and so much confidence in him, that, even in the midst of despair, they obeyed implicitly all his commands. With true christian confidence, he exhorted them not to be dismayed. "If," said he, "we end our days here, we are as near heaven as in England; and we are much bound to God Almighty, for having given us so large a time for repentance, and having thus, as it were, daily called upon us to prepare our souls for a better life in heaven. He does not, in the meantime deny that we may use all proper means to save and prolong our lives; and in my judgment, we are not so far past hope of returning to our native country, but that I see a fair way by which we may effect it." He then said that there was timber enough in the island for them to build a pinnace or large boat, by which they might endeavor to effect their escape, in case their vessel should be destroyed. This was on the thirtieth of November.

The sufferings and the hardships which these brave men encountered for many successive months, it is impossible to describe. Happily, they had a tolerable store of provisions from their ship, and had not to depend upon the precarious subsistence to be obtained by hunting. Their liquids of every kind, wine, vinegar, oil, &c. were all frozen so hard, that they were obliged to cut them with hatchets, and then melt them over the fire for use.

In the beginning of January, the whole surface of the adjacent sea was so entirely frozen, that no water whatever was to be seen. Some of the men were obliged to be out of doors a considerable part of the day, in fetching timber, and in other necessary employments. Their shoes were all destroyed, except some that had been sunk in the ship, and which were now, of course inaccessible. They were, consequently, reduced to the necessity of binding up their feet, as well as they could, in pieces of cloth. Their noses, cheeks, and hands were sometimes frozen in blisters, which were as white as paper; and blisters as large as walnuts rose on different parts of their skin. Their mouths became sore, and their teeth loose.

Timber was cut down, according to the direction of the captain, and the carpenter and crew worked hard at the pinnace, till nearly the end of March, when the carpenter became so weak and ill, that it was necessary, to lead him to his labor.

Though they were in the midst of a wood, yet when their fuel began to fail, they had great difficulty in obtaining more. Almost all the axes had been broken in felling timber for the pinnace, and it was peculiarly requisite, that care should be taken of such cutting implements as remained, lest there would be none left for finishing it. And, in felling the timber now, the trees were so hard frozen, that it was first requisite 'o light large fires round such as were to be cut, in order to thaw he wood before the axes could make any impression upon them.

During all this season of distress, Captain James and his crew never omitted to perform their religious duties. They particularly solemnized Easter day, the twenty-sixth of April, 1632; and it was on this day, whilst they were sitting round their fire, that the captain proposed to attempt, on the first opening of the warm weather, to clear the ship of ice. This was considered by some of the crew impossible; because they believed her to be filled with one solid mass of ice. The attempt, however, was resolved upon; and the question was as to the implements with which it was to be made. These were brought into review, and were only two iron bars (one of which was broken), and four broken shovels, apparently very ineffectual instruments for such a labor.

The time passed miserably and slowly on, till the sixteenth of May, when they had a comfortable and sunny day. Some efforts were this day made to clear the decks of snow. From this period the vessel began to occupy much of the attention of the captain and his crew. The great cabin was found to be free both from ice and water, and a fire was lighted both to clear and dry it. One of the anchors, which was supposed to have been lost, they found under the ice, and recovered. The rudder, which had been torn off by the ice, they were not able to find. By the twenty-fourth of May, they had labored so hard in clearing the vessel, that they came to a cask, and could perceive that there was some water in the hold. They pierced the cask, and found it full of good beer; which was a cause of great joy to them.

Their next object was to dig through the ice on the outside of the vessel, to the holes that had been cut for the purpose of sinking her. They succeeded in this operation; and, through the lowest of these, a considerable quantity of water flowed out. The holes were then prevented from admitting any more water, by having strong boards nailed on the outside. Five days afterwards the weather became much warmer than it had been. The water in the hold of the vessel tended to thaw the ice; and, by means of pumps, it was gradually cleared. Several butts of beer, one of cider and another of wine, were found perfectly sound and

good; as well as many barrels of salt beef and pork. A considerable store of shoes and clothing was now also found. These,
when dried, were peculiarly acceptable. But it was a subject of
sincere rejoicing, that, on examination of the vessel, no defect
could be perceived in her; and sanguine hopes began to be entertained that she might still prove capable of performing the remainder of the voyage. Not long after this, the rudder was
discovered and got up from beneath the ice.

The carpenter now died. He had been a man beloved by the
whole crew, and, with the most exemplary patience, had endured
a long illness, in the course of which, with great exertion, he had
completed all the most difficult parts of the pinnace. Thus, although he was deeply lamented by his comrades, the loss of him
was not so severely felt as it might otherwise have been. At this
time nearly the whole of the crew were disabled, by illness, from
working; nor did any of them recover until after the commencement of the warm weather.

From the elevated parts of the land, the open water was first
seen on the nineteenth of June. Four days afterwards the provisions and other articles that were ashore, were carried on board.
A cross was next erected: the king and queen's picture were
tied to the top of it; and the island was named Charlton Island.
The rigging of the ship was now set. On the thirteenth, the sea
was clear of ice; and on the second of July, after the captain and
his crew had all devoutly paid thanksgiving to the Almighty for
their providential deliverance, they weighed anchor, and proceeded on their voyage.

Still, however, though in the open sea, they suffered great inconvenience from the beating of the floating ice against the ship.
On the twenty-second of July, they again passed Cape Henrietta
Maria. The ship had now become so leaky, that, for some time,
it was found difficult to keep her clear of water by the pumps.
After almost incredible exertions, they made their way northward,
according to their estimate, as far as 69 deg. 35 minutes, when at
length they came to an impenetrable mass of ice. It was the
opinion of the whole crew, that in the present condition of the ship,
the autumn now fast approaching, it would not only be imprudent,
but wholly impracticable, to make any further attempt to discover
the hoped for passage of the sea to the north-west. The captain,
therefore, with a sorrowful heart, consented to relinquish his object: and, on the twenty-sixth of August, determined on returning
to England. In his passage homeward, the vessel encountered
many difficulties from contrary winds and stormy weather; but, at
length, safely arrived at the mouth of the Severn, on the twenty-
second October, 1632.

THE PIRATE'S TREASURE.

AFTER many months of anxious and painful expectancy, I at length succeeded in obtaining my appointment to the situation I had so ardently wished for. Despairing at my apparent want of success, I had given up all hopes, and had engaged to go servant in the Clydesdale to the East Indies, when the favorable result of my friend's exertions changed the aspect of my affairs. My instructions set forth the necessity of my being at Surinam by a certain day, otherwise I should be too late to join the corps to which I was appointed, which, on the ceding up of the place to the Dutch, was to proceed to Canada. As it wanted only two months of that period, it became necessary to inquire for some vessel without loss of time. Giving up my engagement with the Clydesdale, I proceeded to the harbor, and after a toilsome search, succeeded in discovering a ship chartered by a Glasgow company lying ready at the west quay, and to sail with that evening's tide. While I stood examining the vessel from the pier, two sailors, who seemed to be roaming idly about, stopped, and began to converse by my side.

"Has the old Dart got all her hands, Tom!" said the one, "that she has her ensign up for sailing? They say she is sold to the lubberly Dutchmen now—what cheer to lend her a hand out, and get our sailing-penny for a glass of grog?" "No, no; bad cheer!" replied the other; "mayhap I didn't tell you that I made a trip in her four years ago; and a cleaner or livelier thing is not on the water! But there is a limb of the big devil in her that is enough to cause her to sink to the bottom. It was in our voyage out that he did for Bill Burnet with the pump sounding-rod, because the little fellow snivelled a bit, and was not handy to jump when he was ordered aloft to set the fore-royal. It was his first voyage, and the boy was mortal afraid to venture; but the Captain swore he would make him, and in his passion took him a rap with the iron-rod, and killed him. When he saw what he had done, he lifted, and hove him over the side; and many a long day the men wondered what had become of little Bill, for they were all below at dinner, and none but myself saw the transaction. It was needless for me to complain, and get him overhauled, as there were no witnesses; but I left the ship, and births would be scarce before I would sail with him again."

Knowing what tyrants shipmasters are in general, and how much their passengers' comfort depends on them, I was somewhat startled by this piece of information respecting the temper of the man I proposed to sail with. But necessity has no law! The circumstance probably was much misrepresented, and, from a simple

act of discipline exaggerated to an act of wanton cruelty. But be
that as it might—my affairs were urgent. There was no other
vessel for the same port—I must either take my passage, or run
the risk of being superseded. The thing was not to be thought
of; so I went and secured my birth. As my preparations were
few and trifling, I had every thing arranged, and on board, just as
the vessel was unmooring from the quay. During the night we
got down to the Clock light-house, and stood off and on, waiting
for the Captain, who had remained behind to get the ship cleared
out at the Custom house. Soon afterwards he joined us, and the
pilot leaving us in the return-boat, we stood down the Forth under
all our canvass.

For four weeks we had a quick and pleasant passage. The
Dart did not belie her name; for, being American-built, and originally a privateer, she sailed uncommonly fast, generally running
at the rate of twelve knots an hour.

As I had expected, Captain Mahone proved to be, in point of
acquirements, not at all above the common run of shipmasters.
He was haughty and overbearing, domineered over the crew with
a high hand; in return for which, he was evidently feared and detested by them all. He had been many years in the West Indies;
part of which time he had ranged as commander of a privateer, and
had, between the fervid suns of such high latitudes and the copious
use of grog, become of a rich mahogany color, or something between vermillion and the tint of a sheet of new copper. He was
a middle-sized man; square built, with a powerful muscular frame.
His aspect naturally harsh and forbidding, was rendered more so
by the sinister expression of his left eye, which had been nearly
forced out by some accident—and the lineaments of his countenance
expressed plainly that he was passionate and furious in the extreme. In consequence of this, I kept rather distant and aloof;
and, except at meals, we seldom exchanged more than ordinary
civilities.

By our reckoning, our ship had now got into the latitude of the
Bermudas, when one evening, at sun-set, the wind, which had
hitherto been favorable, fell at once into a dead calm. The day
had been clear and bright; but now, huge masses of dark and
conical-shaped clouds began to tower over each other in the western horizon, which, being tinged with the rays of the sun, displayed that lurid and deep brassy tint so well known to mariners
as the token of an approaching storm. All the sailors were of
opinion that we should have a coarse night; and every precaution
that good seamanship could suggest was taken to make the vessel
snug before the gale came on. The oldest boys were sent up to
hand and send down the royal and top-gallant sails, and strike the
masts, while the top-sails and stays were close-reefed. These
preparations were hardly accomplished, when the wind shifted,
and took us a-back with such violence as nearly to capsize the

vessel. The ship was put round as soon as possible, and brought too till the gale should fall: while all hands remained on deck in case of any emergency. About ten, in the interval of a squall, we heard a gun fired as a signal of distress. The night was as black as pitch: but the flash showed us that the stranger was not far to leeward: so, to avoid drifting on the wreck during the darkness, the main-top-sail was braced round, and filled, and the ship hauled to windward. In this manner we kept alternately beating and heaving-to as the gale rose or fell till the morning broke, when, through the haze, we perceived a small vessel with her masts carried away. As the wind had taken off, the Captain had gone to bed: so it was the mate's watch on deck. The steersman, an old gray-headed seaman, named James Gemmel, proposed to bear down and save the people, saying he had been twice wrecked himself, and knew what it was to be in such a situation. As the Captain was below, the mate was irresolute what to do; being aware that the success of the speculation depended on their getting to Surinam before it was given up: however, he was at length persuaded—the helm was put up, and the ship bore away.

As we neared the wreck, and were standing by the mizzen shrouds with our glasses, the Captain came up from the cabin. He looked up with astonishment to the sails, and the direction of the vessel's head, and, in a voice of suppressed passion, said, as he turned to the mate, "What is the meaning of this, Mr. Wyllie? Who has dared to alter the ship's course without my leave—when you know very well that we shall hardly be in time for the market, use what expedition we may?" The young man was confused by this unexpected challenge, and stammered out something about Gemmel having persuaded him. "It was me, sir!" respectfully interfered the old sailor, wishing to avert the storm from the mate; "I thought you wouldn't have the heart to leave the wreck and these people to perish, without lending a hand to save them. We should be neither Christians nor true seamen to desert her, and ——" "Damn you and the wreck, you old canting rascal! do you pretend to stand there and preach to me?" thundered the Captain, his fury breaking out, "I'll teach you to disobey my orders!— I'll give you something to think of!" and seizing a capstan-spar which lay near him, he hurled it at the steersman with all his might. The blow was effectual—one end of it struck him across the head with such force as to sweep him in an instant from his station at the wheel, and to dash him with violence against the lee-bulwarks, where he lay bleeding, and motionless. "Take that, and be damned!" exclaimed the wretch, as he took the helm, and sang out to the men,—"Stand by sheets, and braces—hard a-lee —let go!" In a twinkling the yards were braced round, and the Dart, laid within six points of the wind, was flying through the water.

Meanwhile Gemmel was lying without any one daring to assist

him; for the crew were so confounded that they seemed quite un
determined how to act.   I stepped to him, therefore, and the mate
following my example, we lifted him up.   As there was no appearance of respiration, I placed my hand on his heart—but pul-
sation had entirely ceased—the old man was dead.   The bar had
struck him directly on the temporal bone, and had completely fractured that part of the skull.

"He is a murdered man, Captain Mahone!" said I, laying down
the body, "murdered without cause or provocation."   "None of
your remarks, Sir!" he retorted; "what the devil have *you* to do
with it?   Do you mean to stir up my men to mutiny?   Or do you
call disobeying my orders no provocation?   I'll answer it to those
who have a right to ask; but till then, let me see the man who
dare open his mouth to me in this ship."   "I promise you," returned I, "that though you rule and tyrannise here at present, your
power shall have a termination, and you shall be called to account
for your conduct in this day's work—rest assured that *this* blood
shall be required at your hands, though you have hitherto escaped
punishment for what has stained them already."   This allusion to
the murder of little Bill Burnet seemed to stagger him considerably—he stopped short before me, and, while his face grew black
with suppressed wrath and fury, whispered, "I warn you again,
young man! to busy yourself with your own matters—meddle not
with what does not concern you; and belay your slack jaw, or, by
——! Rink Mahone will find a way to make it fast for you!"
He then turned round, and walked forward to the forecastle.

During this affray no attention had been paid to the wreck,
though the crew had set up a yell of despair on seeing us leave
them.   Signals and shouts were still repeated, and a voice, louder in agony than the rest, implored our help for the love of the
blessed Virgin; and offered riches and absolution to the whole
ship's company if they would but come back.   The Captain was
pacing fore and aft without appearing to mind them, when, as if
struck with some sudden thought, he lifted his glass to his eye—
seemed to hesitate—walked on—and then, all at once changing
his mind, he ordered the vessel again before the wind.

On speaking the wreck, she proved to be a Spanish felucca
from the island of Cuba, bound for Curacoa, on the coast of the
Caraccas.   As they had lost their boats in the storm, and could
not leave their vessel, our Captain lowered and manned our jolly-
boat, and went off to them.

After an absence of some hours he returned with the passengers,
consisting of an elderly person in the garb of a catholic priest, a sick
gentleman, a young lady, apparently daughter of the latter, and a
female black slave.   With the utmost difficulty, and writhing under
some excruciating pain, the invalid was got on board and carried
down to the cabin, where he was laid on a bed on the floor.   To
the tender of my professional services the invalid returned his

thanks, and would have declined them, expressing his conviction
of being past human aid, but the young lady, eagerly catching at
even a remote hope of success, implored him with tears to accept
my offer. On examination I found his fears were but too well
grounded. In his endeavors to assist the crew during the gale
he had been standing near the mast, part of which, or the rigging,
having fallen on him, had dislocated several of his ribs, and injured his spine beyond remedy. All that could now be done was
to afford a little temporary relief from pain, which I did; and
leaving him to the care of the young lady and the priest, I left
the cabin.

On deck I found all bustle and confusion. The ship was still
lying to, and the boats employed in bringing the goods out of the
felucca, both of which were the property of the wounded gentleman. The body of the old man, Gemmel, had been removed somewhere out of sight; no trace of blood was visible, and Captain
Mahone seemed desirous to banish all recollections both of our
quarrel and its origin.

As the invalid was lying in the cabin, and my state-room was occupied by the lady and her female attendant, I got a temporary birth
in the steerage made up for myself for the night. I had not long
thrown myself down on my cot, which was only divided from the
main-cabin by a bulk-head, when I was awakened by the deep
groans of the Spaniard. The violence of his pain had again returned, and between the spasms I heard the weeping and gentle
voice of the lady soothing his agony, and trying to impart hopes
and prospects to him, which her own hysterical sobs told plainly
she did not herself feel. The priest also frequently joined, and
urged him to confess. To this advice he remained silent for
awhile; but at length he addressed the lady: "The Padre says true,
Isabella! Time wears apace, and I feel that I shall soon be beyond its limits, and above its concerns! But ere I go, I would
say that which it would impart peace to my mind to disclose—I
would seek to leave you at least one human being to befriend and
protect you in your utter helplessness. Alas! that Diego di Montaldo's daughter should ever be thus destitute! Go! my love! I
would be alone a little while with the father." An agony of tears
and sobs was the only return made by the poor girl, while the
priest with gentle violence led her into the state-room.

"Now," continued the dying man, "listen to me while I have
strength. You have only known me as a merchant in Cuba; but
such I have not been always. Mine is an ancient and noble
family in Catalonia; though I unhappily disgraced it, and have
been estranged from it long. I had the misfortune to have weak
and indulgent parents, who idolized me as the heir of their house,
and did not possess resolution enough to thwart me in any of my
wishes or desires, however unreasonable. My boyhood being
thus spoiled, it is no matter of wonder that my youth should have

proved wild and dissolute. My companions were as dissipated
as myself, and much of our time was spent in gambling and other
extravagances. One evening at play, I quarrelled with a young
nobleman of high rank and influence; we were both of us hot and
passionate, so we drew on the spot and fought, and I had the
misfortune to run him through the heart and leave him dead. Not
daring to remain longer at home, I fled in disguise to Barcelona,
where I procured a passage in a vessel for the Spanish Main.
On our voyage we were taken by buccaneers; and, the roving
and venturous mode of life of these bold and daring men suiting
both my inclination and finances, I agreed to make one of their
number. For many months we were successful in our enterprises:
we ranged the whole of these seas, and made a number of prizes,
some of which were rich ships of our own colonies. In course
of time we amassed such a quantity of specie as to make us unwilling to venture it in one bottom; so we agreed to hide it ashore
and divide i. on our return from our next expedition. But our
good fortune forsook us this time. During a calm the boats of
the Guarda-costa came on us, overpowered the ship, and made
all the crew, except myself and two others, prisoners. We escaped with our boat, and succeeded in gaining the island of Cuba,
where both of my comrades died of their wounds. Subsequent
events induced me to settle at St. Juan de Buenavista, where I
married, and, as a merchant, prospered and became a rich man.
But my happiness lasted not! My wife caught the yellow fever and
died, leaving me only this one child. I now loathed the scene
of my departed happiness, and felt all the longings of an exile to
revisit my native country. For this purpose I converted all my
effects into money; and am thus far on my way to the hidden
treasure, with which I intended to return to Spain. But the
green hills of Catalonia will never more gladden mine eyes! My
hopes and wishes were only for my poor girl. Holy father! you
know not a parent's feelings—its anxieties and its fears! The
thoughts of leaving my child to the mercy of strangers; or, it may
be, to their barbarities, in this lawless country, is far more dreadful than the anguish of my personal sufferings. With you rests
my only hope. Promise me your protection towards her, and the
half of all my wealth is yours."

"Earthly treasures," replied the priest, "avail not with one
whose desires are fixed beyond the little handful of dust which
perisheth—my life is devoted to the service of my Creator; and
the conversion of ignorant men, men who have never heard of his
salvation. On an errand of mercy came I to this land; and if
the heathen receive it, how much more a daughter of our most
holy church? I, therefore, in behalf of our community, accept
of your offer, and swear on this blessed emblem to fulfil all your
wishes to the best of my poor abilities."

"Enough, enough!" said Montaldo, "I am satisfied' Among that archipelago of desert islands, known by the name of the Roccas, situated on the coast of the province of Venezuela, in New Granada, there is one called the Wolf-rock: it is the longest and most northern of the group, and lies the most to seaward. At the eastern point, which runs a little way into the sea, there stands an old vanilla, blasted and withered, and retaining but a single solitary branch. On the eve of the festival of St. Jago the moon will be at her full in the west. At twenty minutes past midnight she will attain to her highest latitude in the heavens, and then the shadow of the tree will be thrown due east. Watch till the branch and stem unite and form only one line of shade—mark its extremity—for there, ten feet below the surface, the cask containing the gold is buried. That gold, father, was sinfully got; but fasts and penances have been done, masses without number have been said, and I trust that the blessed Virgin has interceded for the forgiveness of that great wickedness! I have now confessed all, and confide in your promise; and as you perform your oath, so will the blessing or curse of a dying man abide with you. I feel faint, dying Oh! let me clasp my child once more to my heart before I——.'

Here the rest of the sentence became indistinct from the death-rattle in his throat. I leaped off my cot, and sprang up the hatch-way, and had my foot on the top of the companion-ladder, when a piercing shriek from below making me quicken my steps, I missed my hold, and fell on some person stationed on the outside of the cabin door. The person, without uttering a single word, rose and ascended the steps; but as he emerged into the faint light which still lingered in the horizon, I fancied that I could distinguish him to be the Captain. On my entering, I found the Spaniard dead, and his daughter lying in a state of insensibility by his side; while the female slave was howling and tearing her hair like one in a frenzy. The priest was entirely absorbed in his devotions; so, without disturbing him, I lifted the lady and bore her into the state-room. The greater part of the night was passed in trying to restore her to sensation. Fit after fit followed each other in such quick succession that I began to apprehend the result; but at length the hysterical paroxysm subsided, and tears coming to her relief, she became somewhat composed, when I left her in charge of her attendant.

The next day was spent in taking out the remainder of the felucca's cargo. There seemed now no anxiety on the captain's part to proceed on his voyage—he appeared to have forgot the necessity, expressed on a former occasion, of being in port within a limited time. He was often in a state of inebriety; for the wine and spirits of the Spaniards were lavishly served out to the whole ship's company, with whom he also mixed more; and banished hat haughtiness of bearing which had marked his conduct hitherto

In the evening the body of Don Diego was brought upon deck, where his crew, under the superintendence of the priest, prepared it for its commitment to the deep. The corpse was, as is usual in such cases, wrapped up in the blankets and sheets in which it had lain, and a white napkin was tied over the face and head. In its right hand, which was crossed over the breast, was placed a gold doubloon. Its left held a small bag containing a book, a hammer, and a candle, while on the bosom was laid the little crucifix worn by the deceased. It was next enveloped in a hammock, with a couple of eight-pound shots, and a bag of ballast at the feet to sink it. At midnight the vessel was hove-to, and all the ship's company assembled at the lee-gangway. The Spaniards and negroes bore each a burning torch in his hand; the blaze of which, as they held them elevated above their heads, cast a strange and fearful light through the deep darkness, and illumined the ocean far and wide with a supernatural refulgency. When all was ready, the priest, accompanied by Isabella, came up from the cabin, and the Spaniards lifting up the body, carried it forward to the waist, where one of the ship's gratings had been put projecting over the side, and on this the corpse was laid, and its feet to the water. Around this the torch-bearers formed a circle, and the priest, standing at the head, began the funeral service for the dead at sea. The wind had now subsided into a gentle breeze; and nothing disturbed the profound silence of the crew during mass, save the slight splashing of the waves against the windward side of the ship, and the deep drawn, convulsive sobs of the young lady as she stood, enveloped in the mantillo, in the obscurity of the main-rigging. Mass being concluded, the priest solemnly chanted the funeral anthem:—" May the angels conduct thee into Paradise; may the martyrs receive thee at thy coming; and mayest thou have eternal rest with Lazarus, who was formerly poor!" He then sprinkled the body with holy water and continued:—" As it hath pleased God to take the soul of our dear brother here departed unto himself, we therefore, commit his body to the deep, in the sure and certain hope of a joyful resurrection on that day when the sea shall give up its dead. Let him rest in peace!" The Spaniards responded "Amen!" and the priest repeating, "May his soul, and the souls of all the faithful departed, through the mercy of God, rest in peace—Amen!" made the sign of the cross; and the bow-chaser, which had been loaded and made ready for the occasion, firing, the end of the grating was gently elevated, and the corpse heavily plunged into the water. The waves parted, heaving and foaming round the body as it disappeared,—when to our horror and astonishment we beheld it, the next minute, slowly return to the surface, deprived of the canvass covering in which it had been sewed. The dead man came up as he had gone down, in an upright position, and floated a little time with his back to the vessel; but the motion of the water turned him round by degrees till we distinctly saw his face. The head was thrown back, and the eyes wide open; and under the strong stream of light poured on them from the torches, they seemed to glare ghastly and fearfully upwards His gray hairs, long and dishevelled, floated about his face, at times partially obscuring it; and one arm, stretched forth, and agitated by the action of the waves, appeared as if in the act of threatening us. When the first burst of horror had subsided, I caught hold of Isabella to prevent her seeing the body, and was leading her off, when some of the men, lowering their torches from the main-chains, whispered that it was the murdered man, old James Gemmel. The Captain had been hitherto looking on with the rest without having apparently recognised him; but when the name struck his ear, he shrunk back and involuntarily exclaimed, "it's a lie—it's an infamous lie! Who dares to say he was murdered? He went overboard two days ago? But don't let him come on board: for God's sake keep him down, or he'll take us all with him to the bottom. Will nobody keep him down? Will nobody shove him off? Helm a-lee!" he bawled out, waving to the steersman; but the man had deserted his post, eager to see what was going on; he, therefore, ran to the wheel himself, and again issued his commands, "Let go the main top-sail weather braces, and bring round the yard! Let them go, I say!" His orders were speedily executed. The vessel gathered way, and we quickly shot past the body of the old man.

For several days after this, we pursued our course with a favorable wind, which drove us swiftly forward on our voyage. The Captain now kept himself constantly intoxicated, seldom made his appearance in the cabin, but left us altogether to the care of the steward. All subordination was now at an end—his whole time was spent among the seamen, with whom he mixed familiarly, and was addressed by them without the slightest portion of that respect or deference commonly paid to the Captain of the vessel. The appearance of the men, also, was much altered. From the careless mirth and gaiety and the characteristic good humor of sailors, there was now a sullenness and gloom only visible. A constant whispering—a constant caballing was going on —a perpetual discussion, as if some design of moment was in agitation, or some step of deep importance was about to be taken. All sociality and confidence towards each other were banished. In place of conversing together in a body, as formerly, they now walked about in detached parties, and among them the boatswain and carpenter seemed to take an active lead. Yet, in the midst of all this disorder, a few of our own crew kept themselves separate, taking no share in the general consultation; but from the anxiety expressed in their countenances, as well as in that of the mate, I foresaw some storm was brooding, and about to burst on our heads.

Since Montaldo's death, Isabella had been in the habit of leaving her cabin after sun-set, to enjoy the coolness of the evening breeze; and in this she was sometimes joined by the priest, but more frequently was only attended by her slave. One evening she came up as usual, and after walking back and forward on deck till the dews began to fall, she turned to go below: but just as we approached the companion-way, one of the negroes, who now, in the absence of all discipline, lounged about the quarter-deck without rebuke, shut down the head, and throwing himself on it, declared that none should make him rise without the reward of a kiss. This piece of insolence was received with an encouraging laugh by his fellows, and several slang expressions of wit were uttered, which were loudly applauded by those around. Without a word of remonstrance, Isabella timidly stooped, and would have attempted getting down the ladder without disturbing the slave; when, burning with indignation, I siezed the rascal by the collar, and pitched him head foremast along the deck. In an instant he got on his legs, and pulling a long clasp-knife out of his pocket, with a loud imprecation he made towards me. All the other negroes likewise made a motion to assist him, and I expected to be assailed on all hands, when the mate interfered, and laying hold of the marlin-spike, which I had caught up to defend myself, pushed me back, as he whispered, "Are you mad, that you interfere? For heaven's sake, keep quiet, for I have no authority over the crew now!" And he spoke the truth; for the negro, brandishing his knife, and supported by his comrades, was again advancing, when the hoarse voice of the boatswain, as he ran to the scene of action, arrested his progress.

"Hallo! you there, what's the squall for? Avast, avast, Mingo off hands is fair play—ship that blade of yours, or I'll send my fist through your ribs, and make day-light shine through them in a minute." I related the behavior of the negro, and was requesting him to order the slaves forward, when I was cut short with—"There are no slaves here, young man! we are all alike free in a British ship. But damn his eyes for an insolent son of a ———; *he* pretend to kiss the pretty girl! I'll let him know she belongs to his betters! The black wench is good enough for him any day. Come, my dear!" he continued, turning to Isabella, "give me the same hire, and I'll undertake to clear the way for you myself." He made as if he meant to approach her, when, careless of what the consequences might be to myself, I hastily stepped forward, and lifting up the head of the companion, Isabella in an instant darted below. "This lady is no fit subject either for wit or insolence," said I, shutting the doors, "and he is less than man who would insult an unprotected female." For a little while he stood eyeing me as if hesitating whether he would resent my interference, or remain passive; at length he turned slowly and doggedy away as he uttered—"you ruffle big, and crow with a brisk note, my lad! But I've seen me do as wonderful a thing as twist your wind,pipe and send you over the side to cool yourself a bit; and so I would serve you in the turning of a wave, if it wasn't that we may have use for you yet! I see in what quarter the wind sets; but mind your eye! for sink me if I dont keep a sharp look out ahead over you."

I now saw that things had come to a crisis—that he crew meant to turn pirates; and I was to be detained among them for the sake of my professional services. I could not, without a shudder, reflect on what must be the fate of Isabella among such a gang of reckless villains: but I firmly resolved that, come what might, my protection and care over her should cease but with my life.

To be prepared for the worst, I immediately went below, loaded my pistols, and concealed them in my breast, securing at the same time all my money and papers about my person. While thus employed, one of the cabin-boys came down for a spy-glass, saying that a sail had hove in sight to windward. Upon this I followed him up, and found the crew collected together in clamorous consultation as to the course they should follow. Some were for lying to till she came down, and taking her, if a merchantman; and if not, they could easily sheer off—but this motion was overruled by the majority, who judged it best to keep clear for fear of accidents: accordingly all the spare canvas was set, and we were soon gaining large before the wind. But the Dart, though reckoned the first sailor out of Clyde when close hauled on a wind, was by no means so fleet when squared away and going free: she had now met with her match, for the stranger was evidently gaining rapidly on us, and in two hours we saw it was impossible for us to escape. The priest and I were ordered down with a threat of instant death if we offered to come on deck, or make any attempt to attract observation.

I now communicated to Isabella my apprehensions with respect to the crew, along with my resolution to leave the vessel if the other proved a man-of-war, and earnestly advised both her and the priest to take advantage of it also. She thanked me with a look and smile that told me how sensible she was of the interest I felt in her welfare, and expressed her willingness to be guided by me whatever way I thought best.

Shortly after this we heard a gun fired to bring us to, and the Dart hailed and questioned as to her port and destination. The answers, it appeared, were thought evasive and unsatisfactory, for we were ordered to come close under the lee-quarter of his Majesty's sloop of war Tartar, while they sent to examine our papers. This was now our only chance, and I resolved, that if the officer should not come below, I would force the companion-door and claim his protection. But I was not put to this alternative. As soon as he arrived, I heard him desire the hatches to be taken off, and order his men to examine the hold. The inspection did not

satisfy him; for he hailed the sloop, and reported that there were
Spanish goods on board which did not appear in the manifest:—
"Then remain on board, and keep your stern lights burning all
night, and take charge of the ship!" was the reply.   In a state of
irksome suspense we remained nearly two hours, expecting every
minute to hear the officer descending.   At length, to our relief,
the companion-doors were unlocked, and a young man, attended by
our captain, entered the cabin.   He looked surprised on seeing
us, and bowing to Isabella, apologized for intruding at such an
unreasonable hour.   "But I was not given to understand," he added, "that there were passengers in the ship—prisoners I should
rather pronounce it, Mr Mahone, for you seem to have had them
under lock and key, which is rather an unusual mode of treating
ladies at least.   No wine, sir!" he continued, motioning away the
bottles which the Captain was hastily placing on the table—"no
wine, but be pleased to show me your register and bill of lading."

He had not been long seated to inspect them when a shuffling
and hurried sound of feet was heard overhead, and a voice calling
on Mr. Duff for assistance, showed that some scuffle had taken
place above.   Instantaneously we all started to our feet, and the
lieutenant was in the act of drawing his sword, when, accidentally
looking round, I observed Mahone presenting a pistol behind.
With a cry of warning, I threw myself forward, and had just time
to strike the weapon slightly aside, when it went off.   The ball
narrowly missed the head of Duff, for whom it had been aimed,
but struck the priest immediately over the right eye, who, making
one desperate and convulsive leap as high as the ceiling, sunk
down dead, and before the Captain could pull out another, I
discharged the contents of mine into his breast.   We then rushed
upon deck; but it was only to find the boat's crew had been mastered, and to behold the last of the men tumbled overboard.   The
pirates then dispersed, and exerted themselves to get the ship
speedily under-way; while the boatswain sang out to extinguish
the lanterns, that the Tartar might not be guided by the lights.

"It's all over with us!" exclaimed my companion; "but follow
me—we have one chance for our lives yet.   Our boat is still towing astern; do you throw yourself over, and swim till I slide down
the painter, and cut her adrift.   Come, bear a hand, and jump!
don't you see them hastening aft?"   And in an instant he pitched
himself off the taffrel, slid down the rope which held the boat, and
cast her loose.   But this advice however judicious, it was impossible for me to follow—for, at the moment, repeated shrieks from
Isabella put to flight all thoughts for my own individual safety; I,
therefore, hurried back to the cabin, determined, that if I could
not rescue her along with myself, to remain, and protect her with
my life.   And in a happy time I arrived!   The candles were
still burning on the table; and through the smoke of the pistols,
which still filled the cabin, I beheld her struggling in the arms of

a negro—the identical slave who had displayed such insolence in
the early part of the evening. With one stroke of the butend of
my pistol I fractured the cursed villain's scull—caught up Isabella
in my arms—ran up the ladder, and had nearly gained the side
when the boatswain, attracted by her white garments, left the
helm to intercept me—and I saw the gleam of his uplifted cutlass
on the point of descending, when he was suddenly struck down
by some person from behind. I did not stop to discover who had
done me this good office, but hailing Duff, and clasping Isabella
firmly to my heart, I plunged into the water, followed by my unknown ally. With the aid of my companion, whom I now found
to be John Wyllie, the mate, we easily managed to support our
charge till the boat reached us; when we found that the greater
part of the men had been rescued in a similar manner.

When the morning dawned, we perceived the Dart, like a speck
in the horizon, and the sloop of war in close chase. Our attention was next turned to our own situation, which was by no means
enviable: we had escaped, it is true, with our lives, for the present;
but without a morsel of food, or a single drop of fresh water, with
us in the boat; we could, at best, only expect to protract existence
for a few days longer, and then yield it up ultimately in horror
and misery. By an observation taken the day before, on board of
the Tartar, Mr. Duff informed us we were to the north-east of the
Bahamas; and distant about one hundred and seventy miles from
Walling's Island, which was the nearest land. This was a long
distance; but, as despair never enters the breast of a British
sailor, even in situations of the utmost extremity, we cheered up
each other; and, as no other resource was left us, we manned our
oars, and pulled away with life, trusting in the chance of meeting
with some vessel, of which there was a strong probability, as this
was the common course of the leeward traders. And our hopes
were not disappointed! for next day we fortunately fell in with a
brig from the Azores, bound for Porto Rico, on board of which we
were received with much kindness; and, in five days, we found
ourselves safe moored in Porto-real harbor.

My first step on landing was to inquire for a boarding-house for
Isabella, and I had the good luck to be directed to one kept by a
respectable Scotch family, in Orange Terrace, and to this I conducted her. My next transaction was to charter a small cutter;
and to communicate to Duff the secret of the hidden treasure; at
the same time asking him to adventure himself and his men on its
recovery. I also gave him to understand the probability of a
renconter with the pirates, in the event of their having escaped
the sloop, for I was aware that Mahone had overheard the whole
confession, from my finding him listening at the cabin door.
Without hesitation, the lieutenant at once agreed to accompany
me, and engaging some hands out of a vessel newly arrived, we
soon mustered a party of fourteen men. As it wanted only six

days of the festival of St. Jago, and the distance across the Carib-
bean sea was great enough to require all our exertions to be there
in time, we embarked and sailed that very night.

Our cutter proved a prime sailer—and though the winds were
light and variable, by the help of our sweeps we made the Roccas
on the evening of the sixth day. As the Spaniard had foretold,
the moon was climbing the western sky, and pouring the fulness
of her splendor with a mild and beautiful effulgence on the un-
troubled deep, as we slowly drifted with the current between the
Wolf-rock and the adjacent isle. All was silent and calm over the
whole desert of the Archipelago and the vast surrounding waters,
save now and then the sudden flight of a sea-fowl awakening
from its slumbers as we passed; or the occasional roar of the
jaguar faintly wafted from the main land. We ran the cutter into
a deep and narrow creek; moored her safe, and proceeded, well
armed, to the eastern extremity. There we found the projecting
point of land, and the old vanilla tree exactly in the situation described—its huge, twisted trunk was still entire; and from the end
of its solitary branch, which was graced by a few scattered leaves,
the body of a man in the garb of a sailor hung suspended in irons.
The clothes had preserved the body from the birds of prey, but the
head was picked clean and bare, leaving the eyeless and bleached
skull to glitter white in the moonlight. In perfect silence, and
with something of awe in our spirits impressed by the solitude, and
dreariness of the scene, we seated ourselves on the rocks, and,
with my timepiece in my hand, I began to mark the progress of
the shadow. For nearly three hours we watched in this manner,
listening attentively for the slightest sound from sea-ward; but
every thing continued hushed and still, except the creaking of the
chain as the dead man swang to and fro in the breeze. Midnight
was now drawing near—the moon, radiant and full, was careering
high through the deep blue of heaven, and the shadows of the
branch and stem were approaching each other, and towards the
desired point. At length the hand of my timepiece pointed to
within one minute of the time. It passed over. The branch and
stem now merged into one, and threw their shadow due east; and
the first spade-full of earth had been thrown out, when the man
who had been stationed to keep a look out came running to inform
us that a boat was rapidly approaching from the east. We immediately concluded that they must be a part of the Dart's crew;
and their long and vigorous strokes, as they stretched out to the
full extent of their oars, showed that they knew the importance of
every minute that elapsed. Our implements for digging were
hastily laid aside, and we concealed ourselves among the rocks
till they should come within reach. In a short time the boat was
seen ashore, and eight armed men came forward, partly Spaniards
and partly the ship's crew; among whom I recognised the boat
swain, and, to my surprise, Mahone, whom I had shot and left for

dead in the cabin.   Without giving them time to prepare for the
assault, we quitted our shelter, and sprung among them at once,
laying about with our cutlasses.

For a little space the skirmish was toughly and hotly contested;
for the pirates were resolute and reckless, and fought with the
desperation of men who knew that the only chance for their lives
lay in their own exertions.   In the confusion of the fray I had
lost sight of Duff, and was closely engaged with one of the Spaniards, when the voice of the boatswain shouting forth a horrible
imprecation sounded immediately behind me.   I turned round,
and sprung aside from the sweep of his cutlass, and, as my pistols
were both empty, retreated, acting on the defensive; when he
pulled out his, fired, and hurled the weapon at my head.   The shot
passed without injuring me—but the pistol, aimed with better effect, struck me full in the forehead.   A thousand sparks of light
flashed from my eyes—I felt myself reeling, and on the point of
falling, when a cut across the shoulder stretched me at once on the
ground.   When I recovered from my stupor, and opened my eyes,
the morning was far advanced—the sun was shining bright over
head; and I found myself at sea, lying on the deck of the cutter;
and Duff busily engaged in examining my wounds.   From him I
learned that the pirates had been mastered after a severe conflict
—in which four had been slain, and left on the island; two had
escaped unobserved during the fight, and made off with their boat;
and two had been wounded, and were prisoners on board, one of
whom was Mahone.   On our arrival at Porto Rico, we delivered
them over to the civil power; and, soon afterwards, Mahone was

tried for the murder of the priest, when he was convicted on o··
evidence, condemned, and executed. Under good nursing, and
care, I gradually recovered.

Isabella is not now that destitute and unprotected orphan whom
I first saw on the middle of the western ocean—but the happy
mistress of a happy home, diffusing life and gladness on all around
her. My friend Duff has lately been placed on the list of post
captains, and is anxiously waiting for more bustling times, when
there will be more knocking about, and more hard blows got,
than what our present peace establishment admits of. John
Wyllie, too, has had advancement in his line, being now master
of one of the finest ships from Clyde; and I had the additional
satisfaction of knowing that none of the crew had reason to
regret their having jeopardized their lives in fighting for the
" Pirate's Treasure."

MISSIONARIES IN GREENLAND.

The hardships encountered by the early missionaries in Greenland were many and severe. The missionary Rudolph, in attempting to return to Europe after devoting twenty-six years of his life
to the cause of God in Greenland, experienced a very remarkable
and merciful deliverance. On the 18th of June, he quitted Lichtenau, in company with his wife, and in the evening embarked
on a vessel which was lying off the Danish factory of Julianenhaab.
The bay being nearly blocked up by drift-ice, they were detained
here for several weeks; but, some Greenlanders having stated that
the sea was open at a short distance, the captain weighed anchor
on the 22d of August, though the wind was contrary, and vast
bodies of ice were still within sight. For some time they advanced
with a roaring noise and a most uneasy motion, through immense
fields of ice; but, on the 25th, a storm arose from the south-west,
which drove the mountains of ice close upon the ship, and appeared
to menace immediate destruction. The scene was now truly tremendous, and it appeared that the vessel, with her sails closely
reefed, and driving before the wind must inevitably be dashed to
atoms. At one time she struck upon a small rock; but was got
off without receiving any particular damage; but soon afterwards,
she struck with such violence against an immense field of ice, that
several planks started at once, the water rushed in, and the vessel
filled so rapidly that the captain and the sailors had scarcely escaped with their boats to an adjacent field of ice, when nothing
more appeared above the surface of the water than the larboard
gunwale. Our missionary and his wife were the last who were

taken from the wreck; and, just before they quitted it, they were above their knees in water, and clinging firmly to the shrouds.

The mariners were now anxious to make toward the shore, which was only about a league distant; but the large boat was so heavily laden, and the wind was so high, that it was deemed more advisable to steer for the nearest island they could reach. This proved to be a rough pointed rock, and destitute of vegetation, except one small plot at a considerable height which was covered with short grass.—Here they attempted to land the provisions which had been saved from the wreck; but the waves beat with such fury against the rock, that the boats, with eight of the sailors on board, were driven to the opposite shore and appeared to be crushed in pieces. "All our hopes of being saved," says Mr. Rudolph, "now vanished; and the whole company gave vent to their feelings in loud and general cries and lamentations. In the evening we lay down to rest, close to each other, without either tent or covering, and, as it continued to rain heavily during the whole of the night, the water rushed down upon us in torrents from the summit of the rock, and we were completely soaked in wet, lying as it were, in the midst of a pool."

On the 27th the captain and most of the sailors determined to attempt to reach the shore, by walking across the ice; though, as it was frequently necessary to leap from one mass to another, and a fall into any of the intermediate chasms would have been instantly fatal, this undertaking was extremely dangerous. Rudolph and the partner of his affections would willingly have joined them, but they were too much weakened by fatigue and want of food to allow of such an exertion. They were, therefore, compelled to remain, together with the ship's cook, who was in the same enfeebled situation. The crew, however, promised that if they succeeded in reaching the shore, a boat should be sent to rescue them from their painful and perilous situation.

Time now passed heavily indeed, with our missionary and his companions, who, when the sun shone, employed themselves in drying the few articles which they had been enabled to save from the wreck; but they were, at last, so enfeebled by cold and hunger, that even this little exertion proved too much for their exhausted strength. Day after day they looked with inexpressible anxiety towards the land, with the hope of discovering some Greenlander hastening to their relief.

On the 2d of September, as they were lying down to sleep, the wife of Rudolph happened to raise herself, and discovered some Greenlanders, who had been rowing about in their kajaks the whole of the day without seeing any persons on the rock, and who were now proposing to return. From them the sufferers obtained a few herrings, but were obliged to remain on the rock another night, as the Greenlanders had no boat for their accommodation. The following evening however, they were safely conveyed to the

colony of Julianenhaaf, where they learned that the whole ship's
company, with the exception of one man, had been providentially
preserved; and on the 11th they proceeded to the settlement at
Lichtenau, where their miraculous deliverance afforded inexpressible pleasure to their fellow laborers and to the whole congregation.—Here they passed the winter; and in the course of the
following year they removed to Lichtenfels, whence they sailed
in one of the Danish vessels, to Copenhagen

DOLPHINS AND FLYING FISH.

Perhaps there is not any more characteristic evidence of our
being within the tropical regions,—one, I mean, which strikes the
imagination more forcibly,—than the company of those pictur-
esque little animals, the flying-fish. It is true, that a stray one
or two may sometimes be seen far north, making a few short skips
out of the water; and I even remember seeing several close to
the edge of the banks of Newfoundland, in latitude 45°. These,
however, had been swept out of their natural position by the huge
gulf-stream, an ocean in itself, which retains much of its temperature far into the northern regions, and possibly helps to modify
the climate over the Atlantic. But it is not until the voyager has
fairly reached the heart of the torrid zone that he sees the flying-
fish in perfection. No familiarity with the sight can ever render
us indifferent to the graceful flight of these most interesting of all
the finny, or, rather, winged tribe. On the contrary, like a bright
day, or a smiling countenance, or good company of any kind, the
more we see of them, the more we learn to value their presence.
I have, indeed, hardly ever observed a person so dull, or unimag-
inative, that his eye did not glisten as he watched a shoal, or, it
may well be called, a covey of flying-fish rise from the sea, and
skim along for several hundred yards. There is something in it
so very peculiar, so totally dissimilar to every thing else in other
parts of the world, that our wonder goes on increasing every time
we see even a single one take its flight. The incredulity, indeed,
of the old Scotch wife on this head is sufficiently excusable.
" You may hae seen rivers o' milk, and mountains o' sugar,"
said she to her son, returned from a voyage; " but you'll ne'er
gar me believe you hae seen a fish that could flee!"
We were once stealing along under the genial influence of a
light breeze, which was as yet confined to the upper sails, and
every one was looking open-mouthed to the eastward to catch a
gulp of cool air, when about a dozen flying-fish rose out of the

water just under the fore-chains, and skimmed away to windward at the height of ten or twelve feet above the surface.

A large dolphin, which had been keeping company with us abreast of the weather gangway, at the depth of two or three fathoms, and, as usual, glistening most beautifully in the sun, no sooner detected them take wing, than he turned his head towards them, and, darting to the surface, leaped from the water with a velocity little short, as it seemed, of a cannon ball. But although the impetus with which he shot himself into the air gave him an initial velocity greatly exceeding that of the flying-fish, the start which his fated prey had got, enabled them to keep ahead of him for a considerable time. The length of the dolphin's first spring could not be less than ten yards; and after he fell, we could see him gliding like lightning through the water for a moment, when he again rose and shot forwards with considerably greater velocity than at first, and, of course, to a still greater distance. In this manner the merciless pursuer seemed to stride along the sea with fearful rapidity, while his brilliant coat sparkled and flashed in the sun quite splendidly. As he fell headlong on the water at the end of each huge leap, a series of circles were sent far over the still surface, which lay as smooth as a mirror; for the breeze, although enough to set the royals and top-gallant studding-sails asleep, was hardly as yet felt below. The group of wretched flying-fish, thus hotly pursued, at length dropped into the sea; but we were rejoiced to observe that they merely touched the top of the swell, and scarcely sunk in it,- -at least they instantly set off again in a fresh and even more vigorous flight. It was particularly interesting to observe that the direction they now took was quite different from the one in which they had set out, implying but too obviously that they had detected their fierce enemy, who was following them with giant steps along the waves, and now gaining rapidly upon them. His terrific pace, indeed, was two or three times as swift as theirs—poor little things! and whenever they varied their flight in the smallest degree, he lost not the tenth part of a second in shaping a new course, so as to cut off the chase, while they, in a manner really not unlike that of the hare, doubled more than once upon their pursuer. But it was soon too plainly to be seen that their strength and confidence were fast ebbing. Their flights became shorter and shorter, and their course more fluttering and uncertain, while the enormous leaps of the dolphin appeared to grow only more vigorous at each bound. Eventually, indeed, we could see, or fancied we could see, that this skilful sea-sportsman arranged all his springs with such an assurance of success, that he contrived to fall, at the end of each, just under the very spot on which the exhausted flying-fish were about to drop! Sometimes this catastrophe took place at too great a distance for us to see from the deck exactly what happened; but on our mounting high into the rigging, we may be said to have been in at the death; for

then we could discover that the unfortunate little creatures, one
after another, either popped right into the dolphin's jaws as they
lighted on the water, or were snapped up instantly afterwards
It was impossible not to take an active part with our pretty little
friends of the weaker side, and accordingly we very speedily had
our revenge. The middies and the sailors, delighted with the
chance, rigged out a dozen or twenty lines from the jib-boom-end
and spritsail yard-arms, with hooks baited merely with bits of tin,
the glitter of which resembled so much that of the body and
wings of the flying fish, that many a proud dolphin, making sure
of a delicious morsel, leaped in rapture at the deceitful prize, and
in his turn became the prey of a successful enemy.

THE DYING DOLPHIN

The truth and beauty of the following description of a dying Dolphin by
Falconer, will be attested by those of our readers who may have witnessed a
similar scene.

And now, approaching near the lofty stern,
A shoal of sportive dolphins they discern.
From burnish'd scales they beam refulgent rays
Till all the glowing ocean seems to blaze.
Soon to the sport of death the crew repair,
Dart the long lance, or spread the baited snare.
One, in redoubling mazes, wheels along,
And glides, unhappy! near the triple prong.
RODMOND unerring o'er his head suspends
The barbed steel, and every turn attends.
Unerring aim'd, the missile weapon flew,
And, plunging, struck the fated victim through
Th' upturning points his ponderous bulk sustain,
On deck he struggles with convulsive pain—
But while his heart the fatal javelin thrills,
And flitting life escapes in sanguine rills,
What radiant changes strike th' astonish'd sight!
What glowing hues of mingled shade and light!
Not equal beauties gild the lucid west,
With parting beams all o'er profusely drest.
Not lovelier colors paint the vernal dawn,
When orient dews impearl th' enamel'd lawn,
Than from his sides in bright suffusion flow,
That now with gold imperial seem to glow:
Now in pellucid sapphires meet the view,
And emulate the soft celestial hue:
Now beam a flaming crimson on the eye;
And now assume the purple's deeper dye.
But here description clouds each shining ray.
What terms of art can nature's powers display?

HENRY HUDSON.

The distinguished English naval discoverer, Henry Hudson, sailed from London in the year 1607, in a small vessel, for the purpose of discovering a north-east passage to China and Japan, with a crew of only ten men and a boy besides himself; and, proceeding beyond the 80th degree of latitude, returned to England in September. In a second voyage, the next year, he landed at Nova Zembla, but could proceed no farther eastward. In 1609, he undertook a third voyage, under the patronage of the Dutch East India Company. Being unsuccessful in his attempt to find a north-east passage, he sailed for Davis's straits, but struck the continent of America in 41° N. lat., and holding a southerly course, discovered the mouth of the river Hudson, which he ascended about fifty leagues in a boat. His last voyage was undertaken in 1610. He sailed, April 17th, in a bark named the Discovery, with a crew of twenty-three men, and came within sight of Greenland, June 4th. Proceeding westward he reached, in latitude 60°, the strait bearing his name. Through this he advanced along the coast of Labrador, to which he gave the name of Nova Brittannia, until it issued into the vast bay, which is also called after him. He resolved to winter in the most southern part of it, and the crew drew up the ship in a small creek, and endeavored to sustain the severity of that dismal climate, in which attempt they endured severe privations. Hudson, however, fitted up his shallop for farther discoveries; but, not being able to establish any communication with the natives, or to revictual his ship, with tears in his eyes he distributed his little remaining bread to his men, and prepared to return. Having a dissatisfied and mutinous crew, he imprudently uttered some threats of setting some of them on shore; upon which a body of them entered his cabin at night, tied his arms behind him, and put him in his own shallop, at the west end of the straits, with his son, John Hudson, and seven of the most infirm of the crew. They were then turned adrift, and were never more heard of. A small part of the crew, after enduring incredible hardships, arrived at Plymouth, in September, 1611.

FAMINE ON BOARD THE FRENCH SHIP LE JACQUES.

Of all the disasters to which mariners are subject, the want of provisions is doubtless one of the most dreadful. In the history

of the return of the French ship Le Jacques from Brazil to France,
Jean de Lery gives an account of an extraordinary famine on
board that vessel, attended with the most appalling circumstances.

This ship, called St. Le Jacques, having completed her cargo
of dying-wood, pepper, cotton, monkeys, parrots, &c. at Brazil,
weighed anchor on the fourth of January, 1558. The whole
crew, seamen and passengers, consisted of forty-five men, exclusive of the captain. They had sailed seven or eight days, when
a leak in the hold was discovered, which induced five of the passengers to return in a bark offered them by the captain, in preference to continuing on the course to France.

We shall give in Lery's own words, the narrative of the remaining part of the voyage.

"On the third of February we found, that, in seven weeks, we
had not made more than one third of our way. As our provisions
diminished very fast, it was proposed to bear away for Cape St.
Roch, where some old seamen assured us that we should be able
to procure refreshments. But the majority advised that we should
eat the parrots and other birds, of which we had brought away
great numbers; and their opinion prevailed.

"Our misfortunes began with a quarrel between the mate and
the pilot; who, to aggravate each other, then went so far as to
neglect their duty. On the twenty-sixth of March, the pilot being
at the helm, in his turn, for three hours he kept all the sails set,
when a violent squall assailed the vessel with such force that she
was completely thrown on one side, so that the tops of the masts
were immersed in the water. The cables, the hen-coops, and all
the boxes which were not lashed fast, were swept overboard, and
the vessel was on the point of upsetting. The rigging, however,
being instantly cut away she righted again by degrees. The
danger, though extreme, tended so little to produce a reconcilia-
tion between the two enemies, that the moment it was past, they
attacked each other and fought with the most savage ferocity,
notwithstanding all the endeavors that were made to pacify them.

"This was only the beginning of a horrid series of calamities.
A few days afterwards, in a calm sea, the carpenter, and other
artisans, in the attempt to relieve those who were laboring at the
pumps, were so unfortunate as to remove, among others, a large
piece of wood in the ship's hold; upon which the water rushed in
with such impetuosity, that the affrighted workmen hurried breathless upon deck, unable to give an account of the danger. At
length they cried, in a lamentable voice: 'We are lost! We are
lost!' Upon this the captain, master, and pilot, not doubting of the
magnitude of the danger, and determined instantly to put the ship
about, ordered a great quantity of Brazil wood and other articles
to be thrown overboard, and concluding to abandon the vessel,
they first provided for their own safety. The pilot fearing lest
the boat should be overloaded by the numbers who demanded a

place in her, took his station, with a cutlass in his hand, and declared he would despatch the first who should endeavor to enter. Seeing ourselves thus left to the mercy of the sea, we who remained fell to work with all our strength, to pump out the water, and if possible to keep the ship from sinking. We had the satisfaction to find that the water did not gain upon us.

"But the most happy consequence of our resolution was, that it caused us to hear the voice of our carpenter, who, though small in stature, was a young man of great spirit, and had not, like the others, quitted the ship's hold. On the contrary, taking off his jacket he spread it over the largest leak, and stood upon it with both feet to prevent the entrance of the water, the violence of which, as he afterwards informed us, lifted him up several times. In this situation he shouted with all his might, desiring us to bring him clothes, cotton, and other things, to stop the leak, till he should be able to do it more effectually. I need not say that this demand was instantly complied with, and thus we were preserved from this danger.

"We continued steering, sometimes to the east and sometimes to the west, which was not our way; for our pilot, who did not perfectly understand his business, was no longer able to observe his route. In this uncertainty we proceeded till we came to the tropic of Cancer, where we sailed a fortnight on a sea covered with grass and marine plants. These were so thick and close that we were obliged to open a passage through them for the ship. Here we were near perishing by another accident. Our gunner being employed in drying some powder in an iron pot, left it so long upon the fire that the powder exploded, and the fire spread so rapidly from one end of the ship to the other that the sails and rigging were instantly in flames.

"They had nearly communicated to the wood, which being covered with pitch, would soon have taken fire, and have burned us alive in the midst of the ocean. Four men were much injured by the fire, and one of them died a few days afterwards. I should have experienced the same fate had I not covered my face with my hat, which defended me from its effects; so that I escaped with only the tips of my ears and my hair scorched."

This misfortune Lery reckons only among those which he calls the prelude.

"It was now, (he continues) the fifteenth of April, and we had still a run of five hundred leagues before us. Our provisions fell so short, that notwithstanding the retrenchment we had already made, it was resolved that we should be confined to only half of this reduced allowance. This measure, however, did not prevent our provisions from being exhausted by the end of the month. Our misfortune was occasioned by the ignorance of the pilot, who imagined that we were near Cape Finisterre, in Spain, while we were in the latitude of the Azores, at least three hundred leagues

distant from it.   This cruel error suddenly reduced us to the last
resource, which was, to sweep the storeroom where the biscuit
was kept.   These sweepings were distributed by spoonfuls, and
made a soup as black and more bitter than soot   Those who had
any parrots left (for most had eaten their's long before this time,)
resorted to this kind of food, at the beginning of May, when the
ordinary provisions failed.   Two seamen, who died of hunger,
were thrown overboard; and to prove the miserable state to which
we were reduced, one of our sailors, called Nargue, standing
reclined against the main-mast, after swallowing their eyes, which
he could not digest, I reproached him for not assisting the others
to set the sails; the poor man, in a low and lamentable voice, replied: 'alas, I cannot,' and instantly dropped down dead.

  "The horrors of this situation were augmented by the roughness of the sea, so that, either from want of skill, or strength to
manage the sails, they were obliged to reef the sails, and even to
lash the rudder fast.   Thus the vessel was left to the mercy of
the wind and waves.   The unfavorable weather likewise deprived
them of the only hope they had left, that of taking some fish.

  "Thus (continues Lery,) all on board were reduced to the
lowest degree of weakness and debility.   Necessity obliged us to
consider and contrive in what manner to appease our hunger.
Some cut in pieces the skins of an animal called *Tapirous sou*,
and boiled them in water, but this method was not approved of.
Others laid them on the coals, and when they were a little broiled, scraped them with a knife and eat them: this expedient proved so successful that we imagined it to be broiled sward of bacon.
After this experiment, those who had any of these skins, preserved
them with the greatest care; and being as hard as dried ox-hide,
they required to be cut with hatchets, and other iron instruments
Some even eat their leather stocks, and their shoes.   The cabin-
boys, pressed with hunger, devoured all the horn of the lanterns,
and as many candles as they could get at.   But notwithstanding
our feebleness and hunger, we were obliged, for fear of foundering, to stick to the pumps night and day.

  "About the twelfth of May our gunner, whom I had seen eating the intestines of a parrot quite raw, died of hunger.   We were
not much affected by this circumstance, for we were so far from
thinking of defending ourselves, if we were attacked, that we
rather wished to be taken by some pirate who would have given
us something to eat.   But we saw, on our return, only a single
vessel, which it was impossible for us to approach.

  "After devouring all the leather on boa.d, even to the coverings
of the boxes, we imagined that our last moments were at hand.
Necessity, however, inspired some one with the idea of catching
the rats and mice, and we hoped to be able to take them the more
easily as they no longer had any crumbs to subsist on, and ran
about the ship in great numbers, dying with hunger   They were

pursued with such assiduity, and so many kinds of snares were laid for them, that very few were left. Even at night the men watched for them like cats. A rat was of greater importance than a bullock on shore, and the common price of one was four crowns. They were boiled in water, with all their intestines, which were eaten with the rest of the body. Neither the paws nor any of the bones that could possibly be made soft, were thrown away.

"Our water likewise failed; we had nothing left to drink but a small barrel of cider, of which the captain and officers were extremely sparing. Whenever it rained, cloths were spread, with a bullet in the middle, to catch the water. They even caught that which ran off through the drains of the ship, though more muddy than the water in the kennels.

"We were at last reduced to such extremity that we had nothing left but Brazil wood; which, though more dry than any other, many, however, in their despair, gnawed between their teeth Our leader, Corguilleray Dupont, one day holding a piece in his mouth, said to me with a profound sigh: Alas! my friend Lery! the sum of four thousand francs is owing me in France, to which I would gladly resign my claim for a halfpenny roll and a single glass of wine.

"At length the Almighty, taking compassion on so many miserable wretches, extended almost motionless upon the deck, brought us on the twenty-fourth of May, 1558, within sight of the coast of Bretagne. We had been deceived so often by the pilot that we durst scarcely give credit to the first cries announcing this happy intelligence. We were, however, soon convinced, that we were within view of our native land. After returning thanks to heaven, the master of the ship publicly declared, that had our situation continued but another day, he had taken the resolution, not to draw lots as has sometimes been done in such cases, but, without informing any person of his design, to kill one of us for the rest to subsist upon.

"We found that we were very near Rochelle, where our seamen had wished to unload the ship and dispose of their Brazil wood. The master, after coming to an anchor two or three leagues from the shore, went in the boat, accompanied by Dupont and some others to purchase provisions at Hodierne, from which we were not far distant. Two of our companions who were of the party, no sooner set their feet on shore, than, impelled by the recollection of their distresses and the fear of being again involved in them, they betook themselves to flight without waiting for their baggage, at the same time protesting they would never return to the ship. The others immediately returned with all kinds of provisions recommending to their famished comrades to use them at first with moderation.

"We were now solicitous only to repair to Rochelle, when

French vessel passing within hail, informed us that the whole
coast was infested by pirates. On account of our feeble state
which would have rendered it impossible for us to make any defence, we unanimously agreed to follow the vessel from which
we had received this intelligence. Thus, without losing sight of
her we came to an anchor on the twenty-sixth in the port of
Blavet."

Many of the sailors on landing gorged themselves to such an
excess as to produce sudden death. All the passengers survived,
and after some suffering, were restored to health by adhering to
a temperate and regular course of diet.

THE LAW OF ARREST.

A TALE FROM FACTS.

Once upon a time there lived at Hamburgh, a certain merchant
of the name of Meyer. He was a good little man: charitable to
the poor, hospitable to his friends, and so rich that he was extremely respected, in spite of his good nature. Among that part
of his property vested in other people's hands, and called debts,
was the sum of £500, owed him by the captain of an English
vessel. This debt had been so long contracted, that the worthy
Meyer began to wish for a new investment of his property. He
accordingly resolved to take a trip to Portsmouth, in which town
Captain Jones was then residing, and take that liberty which, in
my opinion, should never be permitted in a free country, viz: that
of applying for his money.

Our worthy merchant one bright morning found himself at
Portsmouth. He was a stranger to that town, but not wholly
unacquainted with the English language. He lost no time in
calling on Captain Jones.

"And vat," said he to a man whom he asked to show him to the
Captain's house, "vat is dat fine veshell yondare."

"She is the Royal Sally," replied the man, "bound for Calcutta
—sails to-morrow: but here's Capt. Jones's house, sir, and he'll
tell you all about it."

The merchant bowed, and knocked at the door of a red brick
house—green door with a brass knocker. Capt. Gregory Jones
was a tall man. He wore a blue coat without skirts. He had
high cheek bones, small eyes, and his whole appearance was
eloquent of what is generally termed the bluff honesty of the seaman.

Captain Gregory seemed somewhat disconcerted at seeing his

friend He begged for a little further time. The merchant looked grave—three years had already elapsed. The captain demurred —the merchant pressed—the captain blustered—and the merchant growing angry, began to threaten. Suddenly Captain Jones's manner changed—he seemed to recollect himself, and begged pardon—said he could easily procure the money, desired the merchant to go back to his inn, and promised to call on him in the course of the day. Mynheer Meyer went home, and ordered an excellent dinner. Time passed, and his friend came not. Meyer grew impatient. He had just put on his hat, and was walking out, when the waiter threw open the door and announced two gentlemen.

"Ah, dere comes de monish," thought Mynheer Meyer. The gentleman approached—the taller one whiped out what seemed to Meyer a receipt. "Ah, ver well—I will sign—ver well."

"Signing, sir, is useless—you will be kind enough to accompany us. This is a warrant for debt, sir. My house is extremely comfortable—gentlemen of the first fashion go there—quite moderate, too, only a guinea a day—find your own wine."

"I do—no—understand, sare," said the merchant, smiling amiably. "I am ver vell off here, thank you."

"Come, come," said the other gentleman, speaking for the first time, "no parlavoo Monsoo, you are our prisoner—this is a warrant for the sum of £10,000, due to Capt. Gregory Jones."

The merchant stared—the merchant frowned—but so it was. Captain Gregory Jones, who owed Mynheer Meyer £500, had arrested Mynheer Meyer for £10,000; for, as every one knows, any man may arrest us, who has conscience enough to swear that we owe him money. Where was Mynheer Meyer in a strange town to procure bail? Mynheer Meyer went to prison.

"Dis be a strange vay of paying a man his monish!" said Mynheer Meyer.

In order to while away the time, our merchant, who was wonderfully social, scraped an acquaintance with some of his fellow prisoners. "Vat you be in prison for?" said he to a stout, respectable looking man, who seemed to be in a violent passion— "for vat crime?"

"I, sir—crime!" quoth the prisoner; "Sir, I was going to Liverpool to vote at the election, when a friend of the opposing candidate had me arrested for £2000; before I can get bail the election will be over."

"Vat's that you tell me? Arrest you to prevent your giving an honest vote? Is that justice?"

"Justice, no!" cried our friend, "it's the Law of Arrest."

"And vat be you in prishon for?" said the merchant pityingly, to a thin, cadaverous looking object, who ever and anon applied a handkerchief to eyes that were worn with weeping.

"An attorney offered a friend of mine to discount a bill, if he

could obtain a few names to endorse it. I, sir, endorsed it. T᠁ ᵇⁱˡˡ
bill became due--the next day the attorney arrested all whose
names were on the bill, eight in number. The law allows him to
charge two guineas each—there are sixteen guineas for the lawyer
—but I, sir, alas! my family will starve before I shall be released
Sir, there are a set of men called discounting attorneys, who live
upon the profits of entrapping and arresting us poor folks."

"Mine Got! but is dat justice?"

"Alas! no, sir, it is the Law of Arrest."

"But," said the merchant turning round to a lawyer, whom the
Devil had deserted, and who was now with the victims of his
profession, "dey tell me dat in Englant a man be called innoshent
till he be proved guilty; but here am I, who, because von carrion
of a shailor, who owesh me five hundred pounts, takes an oath
that I owe him ten thousand—here am I, on that schoundrel's
single oath, clapped up in a prishon. Is this a man's being innoshent till he is proved guilty, sare?"

"Sir," said the lawyer primly, "you are thinking of criminal
cases. But if a man be unfortunate enough to get into debt that
is quite a different thing—we are harder to poverty than we are to
crime."

"But, mine Got! is that justice?"

"Justice! pooh! it's the Law of Arrest," said the lawyer,
turning on his heel.

Our merchant was liberated: no one appeared to prove the debt.
He flew to a magistrate—he told his case—he implored justice
against Capt. Jones.

"Capt. Jones," said the magistrate taking snuff; "Capt Gregory Jones, you mean!"

"Ay, mine goot sare—yesh!"

"He set sail for Calcutta yesterday. He commands the Royal Sally. He must evidently have sworn this debt against you for
the purpose of getting rid of your claim, and silencing your mouth
till you could catch him no longer. He's a clever fellow this
Gregory Jones!"

"De teufel! but, sare, ish dare no remedy for de poor merchant?"

"Remedy! oh yes—indictment for perjury."

"But vat use is dat? You say he be gone—ten thousand miles
off —to Calcutta!"

"That's certainly against your indictment."

"And cannot I get my monish?"

"Not as I see."

"An I have been arreshted instead of him!"

"You have."

"Sare, I have only von vord to say—is dat justice?"

"That I can't say, Mynheer Meyer—but it is certainly the
Law of Arrest," answered the magistrate—and he bowed the
merchant out of the room

A SEA SONG

A wet sheet and a flowing sea,
　A wind that follows fast
And fills the white and rustling sail,
　And bends the gallant mast!
And bends the gallant mast, my boys,
　While like the eagle free,
Away the good ship flies, and leaves
　Columbia on the lea.

O for a soft and gentle wind!
　I heard a fair one cry;
But give to me the swelling breeze,
　And white waves heaving high;
And white waves heaving high, my lads,
　The good ship tight and free;
The world of waters is our home,
　And merry men are we.

There 's tempest in yon horned moon,
　And lightning in yon cloud;
And hark, the music, mariners!
　The wind is wakening loud;
The wind is wakening loud, my boys,
　The lightning flashes free;
The hollow oak our palace is,
　Our heritage the sea.

CAPTAIN COOK.

Mr. Banks, a gentleman of considerable fortune in Lincolnshire
England, was induced to undertake this voyage from curiosity,
and an invincible desire of attaining knowledge.   He engaged
his friend Dr. Solander, a Swede, to accompany him in this voyage.
Mr. Banks also took with him two draftsmen, and had besides
a secretary and four servants.   Lieutenant James Cook was to
command the expedition.

On the 26th of August, 1768, the Endeavour sailed from Plym
outh; the islands of Puerto Santo and Madeira were discovered
on the 12th of September, and the next day they anchored in
Fonchial Road.   The Endeavour sailed thence on the 19th.   On
the 22d, they saw the Islands of Salvages, northward of the Canaries   The 23d saw the Peak of Teneriffe, bearing west by
south.   This mountain is near 15,400 feet high.   On the 29th
perceived Bona Vista, one of the Cape de Verd Islands.   On
the 13th of November made sail for the harbor of Rio de Janeiro

Captain Cook went on shore on the 14th, and obtained leave to purchase provisions, and having requested that the gentlemen on board might remain on shore whilst they sojourned, and that Mr. Banks might go up the country to collect plants, these requests were peremptorily refused.

December the 8th, having procured all necessary supplies, they left Rio de Ja ciro. On the the 14th of January entered the Strait of Le Maire; but the tide being against them, were driven out with great violence; at length, however, they got anchorage at the entrance of a little cove, which Captain Cook called St. Vincent's Bay.

Mr. Banks and Dr. Solander set out from the ship on the 16th, with the design of going into the country, and returning in the evening. Having entered a wood, they ascended the hill through a pathless wilderness till the afternoon. The morning had been very fine, but the weather now became cold and disagreeable; the blasts of wind were very piercing, and a shower of snow fell. Mr. Buchan, one of the draughtsmen, fell into a fit. It was absolutely necessary to stop and kindle a fire, and such as were most fatigued remained to assist him; but Messrs. Banks, Solander, Green and Monkhouse, proceeded and attained the spot they had in view. Upon returning, they found Mr. Buchan much recovered. They had previously sent Mr. Monkhouse and Mr. Green back to him and the others, in order to bring them to a hill, which was conjectured to lie in a better track for returning to the wood. The whole party met there at eight in the evening. Dr. Solander having often passed mountains in cold countries, was sensible that extreme cold, when joined with fatigue, occasions a drowsiness, that is not easily resisted; he accordingly entreated his friends to keep in motion, however disagreeable it might be to them; his words were, "Whoever sits down, will sleep; and whoever sleeps, will wake no more." Every one seemed accordingly armed with resolution; but on a sudden the cold became so very intense, as to threaten the most direful effects. It was very remarkable that Dr. Solander himself, who had so forcibly admonished his party, should be the first who insisted upon being suffered to repose. In spite of the most earnest entreaties, he lay down amidst the snow, and it was with great difficulty they kept him awake. When a black servant was informed, that if he remained there he would be frozen to death; he replied, that he was so exhausted with fatigue, that death would be a relief to him. Doctor Solander said he was not unwilling to go, but that he must first take some sleep, notwithstanding what he had before declared to the company. Thus resolved, they both sat down, supported by bushes, and in a short time fell fast asleep. Intelligence now came from the advanced party, that a fire was kindled about a quarter of a mile farther on the way. Mr. Banks then waked the doctor, who had almost lost the use of his limbs already, though it was but a few minutes since he sat down. Every measure taken to relieve the black proved ineffectual; he remained motionless, and they were obliged to leave him to the care of the other black servant and a sailor, who appeared to have been the least hurt by the cold. Mr Banks and four others went forth at twelve o'clock and met the sailor, with just strength enough to walk; he was immediately sent to the fire, and they proceeded to seek for the two others. They found Richmond, one black servant, upon his legs, but incapable of moving them; the other black was lying senseless upon the ground. All endeavors to bring them to the fire were useless, nor was it possible to kindle one upon the spot, on account of the snow that had fallen, and was still falling, so that there was no alternative, but to leave the two unfortunate negroes to their fate, making them a bed of boughs of trees, and covering them very thick with the same. On the 17th in the morning, at day-break, nothing presented itself but snow. However, about six in the morning they were flattered with a dawn of hope of being delivered, by discovering the sun through the clouds, which gradually diminished. Previous to setting out, messengers were despatched to the unhappy negroes, who returned with the melancholy news of their death. In about three hours, to their great satisfaction, found themselves upon the shore, much nearer to the ship than their most sanguine expectation could have flattered them.

January the 26th, Captain Cook sailed from Cape Horn. The farthest southern latitude he made was 60 deg. 10 min. by 74 deg. 30 min. west. April the 4th, a servant to Mr. Banks discovered land. Captain Cook came within a mile on the north-side, but found no bottom nor anchorage. There appeared along the beach some of the inhabitants, with pikes or poles in their hands, twice the height of themselves. This Island was in latitude 18 deg south, longitude 139 deg. 28 min. west, and was named Lagoon Island. They saw another island in the afternoon, which was named Thrumb Cap. The 5th, continued their course, and discovered Bow Island.

From the 6th to the 10th, they passed several islands, and on the 13th, entered Port Royal Harbour, Otaheite, anchoring within half a mile of the shore. When the ship was properly secured, the captain went on shore with Mr. Banks, Dr. Solander, a party under arms, and an old Indian. They were received by some hundreds of the natives, who were struck with such awe, that the first who approached crept almost upon his hands and knees. He presented them branches of trees, the usual symptom of peace.

On the 15th, the captain, attended by Mr. Banks and others, went on shore to fix on a proper spot to erect a small fort for their defence. Before this party had gone much further, they were alarmed by the discharge of two pieces, fired by the tent-guard Upon their return, it appeared that an Indian had taken an or portunity to snatch away one of the sentinel's muskets; whereupon a young midshipman, ordered the marines to fire, which they did, when several Indians were wounded, but as the criminal did not fall, they pursued and shot him dead.

The fort began to be erected on the 18th. Mr. Banks's tent being got up, he, for the first time, slept on shore. On the 24th, Mr. Banks and Dr. Solander made an excursion into the country On the 25th, Mr. Molineux, master of the Endeavour, seeing a woman, whose name was Oberea, he declared she was the person he judged to be the queen of the island, when he came there in the Dolphin. She was soon conducted to the ship, and went on board, accompanied by some of her family. Many presents were made her, particularly a child's doll, which seemed the most to engross her attention. On the 5th, Mr. Banks and Dr. Solander set out in the pinnace and soon reached Eparre. Some Indians from a neighboring island, to which Captain Wallis gave the name of Duke of York's Island, informed them of more than twenty islands in the neighborhood of Otaheite.

They now began to make the necessary preparations for the transit of Venus, and on the first of June, the next Saturday, being the day of the transit, they sent the long-boat to Ermayo, having on board Mr. Gore, Mr. Monkhouse, and Mr. Sporing, a friend of Mr. Banks; each furnished with necessary instruments They were visited on the 21st at the fort by many of the natives, and among the rest Oamo, a chief of several districts on the island, who was very inquisitive with respect to the English, and by his questions appeared a man of understanding and penetration. June 26th, the Captain set out in the pinnace, accompanied by Mr. Banks, to circumnavigate the island. July 1st, returned to the fort at Port Royal Harbour; having discovered the island, both peninsulas included, to be about one hundred miles in circumference. They now began to make preparations for their departure. On the 10th, two marines being missing, an inquiry was made after them, when the Indians declared they did not propose returning, having each taken a wife. Mr. Hicks was immediately despatched in the long-boat, with several men, for them, and this party recovered the men without opposition.

July the 13th, after leaving the island of Otaheite, they sailed with a gentle breeze, and, on the 15th, discovered Huaheine. They found the people here nearly similar to those of Otaheite in almost every circumstance. This island is situated in the latitude of 16 deg. 43 min. south, longitude 150 deg. 52 min. west, distant from Otaheite about thirty leagues, and is about twenty miles in circumference. From Huaheine they sailed to Ulieta. Captain Cook took possession of this and the adjacent islands in the name of the king of Great Britain. On the 25th they were within a league or two of Otaha. On the 29th made sail to the northward, and at eight o'clock next morning were close under the high craggy peak of Bolabola; but, after giving the general name of the Society Islands to the Island of Huaheine, Ulietea, Bolabola, Otaha, and Maurua, which lie between the latitude of 16 deg 10 min. and 16 deg. 55 min. south, they pursued their course.

The Endeavour now passed a small island, white and high, and, as it appeared quite barren, was named Bare Island. On the 17th Captain Cook gave the name of Cape Turn-Again to a head-land, in latitude 40 deg. 34 min. south, longitude 182 deg 55 min. west. Before the Endeavour touched at New Zealand, which this was, it was not certainly known whether it was an island, or part of the continent. On the 20th anchored in a bay, about two leagues north of Gable End Foreland. Sailing to the northward, they fell in with a small island named East Island. In the evening of the 30th, Lieutenant Hicks discovered a bay, to which his name was given. On the 18th, the Endeavour steered between the main and an island which seemed very fertile, and as extensive as Ulietea.

The 26th, Captain Cook continued his course along shore to the north. On the 29th, having weathered Cape Bret, they bore away to leeward, and got into a large bay, where they anchored on the south-west side of several islands. On the 5th they weighed anchor. The Bay which they had left was called the Bay of Islands. On the 13th of March discovered a bay, which Captain Cook called Dusky-bay; and it is remarkable for having five high, peaked rocks, lying off it, which look like the thumb and four fingers of a man's hand; whence it was denominated Point Five Fingers. It was now resolved to return by the East Indies, and with that view to steer for the east coast of New Holland, and then follow the direction of that coast to the northward. They sailed March 31st and taking their departure from an eastern point, called it Cape Farewell. The bay from which they sailed was named Admiralty Bay, and the two capes thereof Cape Stephens and Cape Jackson.

They sailed from Cape Farewell on the 31st of March, 1770. On the 19th, they discovered land four or five leagues distant. The name of Botany Bay was given to this place, from the large number of plants collected by Messrs. Banks and Solander. They sailed hence the 6th of May, 1770; at noon were off a harbor which was called Port Jackson. Coasting this shore till the 10th of June, an accident had nearly terminated their voyage fatally The ship struck on a rock in the night, at some distance from the land, and made so much water as to threaten to sink every moment, which was only prevented by great exertions. After some little examination, they found a small harbor to look at the ship bottom, and there found, that the only thing which prevented her from sinking, was a large piece of a rock, broken off and sticking in the largest hole, which impeded the entrance of the water Here they procured some refreshments, landed the sick and stores,

made a variety of excursions by land and ater to the neigboring
places, and, for the first time, saw the animal now known as the
Kangaroo.

They sailed hence on the 13th of August, 1770, and got through
one of the channels in the reef; happy to be once more in an
open sea, after having been surrounded by dreadful shoals and
rocks for near three months, during all which run they had been
obliged to keep sounding without the intermission of a single
minute; a circumstance which, it is supposed, never happened to
any ship but the Endeavour. Previous to their leaving, Captain
Cook, took possession of all the eastern coast of the country, from
the 38th degree of south latitude to the present spot, by the name
of New South Wales. They were now at the northern extremity
of New Holland. The northeast entrance of the passage is formed by the main land of New Holland, and by a number of islands,
which took the name of the Prince of Wales's Islands.

They now held a northward course, within sight of land, till the
3d of September. On the 6th, passed two small islands, on the
9th, they saw what had the appearance of land, and the next
morning were convinced it was Timor Lavet. On the 16th, they
had sight of the little island called Rotte; and the same day saw
the island of Savu, at a distance to the southward of Timor. The
Endeavour sailed the 21st of September, 1770, and bent her course
westward. In the afternoon of this day a little flat island was
discovered in 10 deg. 47 min. south latitude, and 238 deg. 28 min.
west longitude. They made considerable way, till at length, by
the assistance of the sea-breezes, they came to anchor in the
road of Batavia. The town of Batavia is situated in 6 deg. 10
min. south latitude, and 106 deg. 50 min. east longitude. On the
27th of December, 1770, the Endeavour left the road of Batavia,
and on the 5th, came to anchor near Prince's Island. After a passage in which they lost twenty-three more officers and men, the
ship was brought to anchor off the Cape of Good Hope, on the
15th of March, 1771. Quitting the Cape, they came to anchor
off the island of St. Helena, on the 1st of May, from which place
they sailed on the 4th, and arrived in the'Downs, on the 12th of
June following.

CAPTAIN COOK'S SECOND VOYAGE.

A second voyage being resolved upon, Captain Cook was ap
pointed to the Resolution, and Captain Furneaux, to the Adventure;
and on the 13th of July, 1772, the two ships sailed from Plymouth
Sound; and, on the evening of the 29th, anchored in Funchia
Road, in the Island of Madeira.

On the 9th of August they made the Island of Bonavista, and on the 29th of October the land of the Cape of Good Hope. The 10th of December, saw an island of ice to the westward, being then in the latitude of 50 deg. 40 min. south, and longitude 2 deg. east of the Cape of Good Hope. On the 9th of February, found that the Adventure was not within the limits of the r horizon. At ten o'clock of the 25th of March, the land of New Zealand was seen from the mast-head. On Friday, the 26th, came to anchor, at three in the afternoon, after having been one hundred and seventeen days at sea, in which time they had sailed 3660 leagues, without having once sight of land.

On the 11th of April, weighed with a light breeze at south-east, and stood out to sea. After leaving Dusky Bay they directed their course along shore for Queen Charlotte's Sound, where they expected to find the Adventure. On the 18th, they appeared off the harbor, and discovered their consort the Adventure, by the signals she made. On the 7th of June, weighed and put to sea, with the Adventure in company, and on the 11th of August, land was seen to the south, which upon a nearer approach was found to be an island of about two leagues in extent. It lies in the latitude of 17 deg. 24 min. longitude 141 deg. 39 min. west, and was called Resolution Island. Steering the same course, they discovered several of these low or half-drowned islands, or rather a large coral shoal of about twenty leagues in circuit, which M. de Bourgainville very properly calls the cluster of low overflowed isles the Dangerous Archipelago. On the 15th, at five o'clock in the morning, saw Osnaburgh Island, or Maitea, discovered by Captain Wallis. At day-break found themselves not more than half a league from the reef of Otaheite.

Several of the inhabitants came off in canoes, most of whom knew Captain Cook again, and many inquired for Mr. Banks and others who were there before. On the 17th, they anchored in Ouiti-piha Bay, about two cable's length from the shore. On the 1st of September the ships unmoored, and made sale for Ulieta. Arriving off the harbor of Ohamaneno, at the close of the day, they spent the night in making short tacks. Captain Furneaux agreed to receive on board his ship a young man named Omai, a native of Ulieta, where he had some property, of which he had been dispossessed by the people of Bolabola. After leaving Ulieta, they steered to the west, inclining to the south, to get clear of the tracts of former navigators, and to get into the latitude of the islands of Middleburgh and Amsterdam. At two o'clock p. m on the 1st of October, made Middleburgh, bearing west-south-west; and then made sail down to Amsterdam. These islands were first discovered by Captain Tasman, in January, 1642—3, and by him called Amsterdam and Middleburgh. But the former is called by the natives Ton-ga-ta-bu, and the latter Ea-vo-wee Middleburgh or Eavowee, which is the southernmost, is abou ten leagues in circuit, and of a height sufficient to be seen twelve leagues. The anchorage, named English Road, is on the north-west side, in latitude 21 deg. 20 min. 30 sec. south. The island is shaped something like an isosceles triangle, the longest sides whereof are seven leagues each, and the shortest four.

On the 8th of October, made the Island of Pilstart. This island, which was also discovered by Tasman, is situated in the latitude of 22 deg. 26 min. south, longitude 175 deg. 59 min. west. On the 21st, made the land of New Zealand; at noon Table Cape bore west, distant eight or ten leagues. On the 25th, early in the morning, they weighed, with a small breeze, out of the cove. On the 26th, took their departure from Cape Palliser, and steered to the south, inclining to the east, having a favorable gale from the north-west and south-west. At 4 o'clock, 12th of Dec. being in the latitude of 62 deg. 10 min. south, longitude 172 deg. west, saw the first ice Island, $11\frac{1}{2}$ deg. farther south than the first ice seen the preceding year, after leaving the Cape of Good Hope.

On the 30th, at four o'clock in the morning, perceived the clouds, over the horizon to the south, to be of an unusual snow-white brightness, which they knew announced their approach to field-ice. Being at this time in the latitude of 71 deg. 10 min. south, longitude 106 deg. 54 min. west, they steered north from this time, and on the 11th of March, land was seen from the mast-head, bearing west. They made no doubt that this was Davis's Land, or Easter Island. After leaving Easter Island, they steer-ed north-west-by-north and north-north-west, with a fine easterly gale, intending to touch at the Marquesas. They continued to steer to the west till the 6th of April, at four in the afternoon, at which time, being in the latitude of 9 deg. 20 min. longitude 133 deg. 14 min. west, they discovered an Island, bearing west by south, distant about nine leagues. Two hours after saw another, bearing south-west-by-south, which appeared more extensive than the former. By this time, they were well assured that these were the Marquesas, discovered by Mendana in 1595.

The Marquesas are five in number, viz. La Magdalena, St. Pedro, La Dominica, Santa Christina, and Hood's Island, which is the northernmost, situated in latitude 9 deg. 26 min. south, and 13 deg. west, five leagues and a half distant from the east point of La Dominica, which is the largest of all the isles, extending east and west six leagues.

From the Marquesas, Captain Cook once more steered his course for Otaheite; and reached his former place of anchorage, Matavai Bay, on the twenty-second of April. During their resi-dence here, on this occasion, the voyagers were entertained with various exhibitions. One of these was a grand naval review. The vessels of war consisted of a hundred and sixty large double canoes, well equipped, manned and armed. They were decorated with flags and streamers; and the chiefs, together with all those

who were on the fighting stages, were dressed in their war habits
The whole fleet made a noble appearance; such as our voyagers
had never seen before. Besides the vessels of war, there were
a hundred and seventy smaller double canoes, which seemed to
be designed for transports and victuallers. Upon each of these
was a small house; and they were each rigged with a mast and
sail, which was not the case with the war canoes. Captain Cook
conjectured that there were no fewer than seven thousand seven
hundred and sixty men in the whole fleet. He was not able to
obtain full information concerning the design of this armament.

The refreshments that were obtained at Otaheite during this
visit were of great importance to the ship's company, for nearly
all the bread they had left was decayed and scarcely eatable; and
even of this, bad as it was, the quantity was so small that they
were reduced to a very scanty allowance.

After leaving Otaheite, the voyagers proceeded again to
Huaheine. During Captain Cook's stay at Huaheine, bread-
fruit, cocoa-nuts, and other vegetable productions, were procured
in abundance, but not a sufficiency of hogs to supply the daily
consumption of the ship's company. At Ulieta, to which the
captain next directed his course, the inhabitants expressed the
deepest concern at his departure, and anxiously importuned him
to return

After passing several other islands. he arrived, on the twentieth
of June, at an island which appeared to have a numerous population. The captain, with the other gentlemen went ashore; but
the natives were found to be fierce and untractable. All endeavors to bring them to a parley were to no purpose. They
approached with the ferocity of wild beasts, and instantly threw
their darts. Two or three muskets discharged in the air did not
prevent one of them from advancing still further, and throwing
another dart, which passed close over Captain Cook's shoulder.
The courage of this man had nearly cost him his life. When he
threw his dart, he was not five paces from the captain, who had
resolved to shoot him for his own preservation. it happened,
however, that his musket missed fire; a circumstance on which
he afterwards reflected with pleasure.

This island, from the disposition and behavior of the inhabitants, was called by our Commander Savage Island. It is about
eleven leagues in circuit; is of a round form and good height,
and has deep waters close to its shores. Among its other disadvantages, it is not furnished with a harbor.

In pursuing his course toward the west-south-west, Captain
Cook passed a number of small islands, and, on the twenty-sixth.
anchored on the north side of Anamooka, or Rotterdam. Here,
as in many former cases, the captain was put to some trouble, on
account of the thievish disposition of the people. It is one of a
numerous group to which Captain Cook gave the name of the

Friendly Isles, in consequence of the firm alliance and friendship which seemed to subsist among the inhabitants, and of their kind and hospitable behavior to strangers.

Pursuing their course westward, the navigators, on the sixteenth of July, discovered land, which they believed to be the same that M. de Bougainville, the French navigator, had named the Great Cyclades. After having explored the coast of this island for some days, they came to an anchor, in a harbor of the island of Mali-colo. The inhabitants of this island were in general the most ugly and ill-proportioned people that the voyagers had seen. They were dark-colored, somewhat diminutive in stature, and had long heads, flat faces, and countenances not much dissimilar to those of apes.

Proceeding hence in a south-westerly direction the Resolution passed several small islands. The harbor in one of them called Tauna, in which the ship was anchored, was only a little creek about three quarters of a mile in length, but no place could exceed it in convenience for obtaining both wood and water. After Captain Cook had finished his survey of the whole Archipelago, and had gained a knowledge of it infinitely superior to what he had attained before, he bestowed upon it the appellation of the New Hebrides.

Our voyagers sailed on the 1st of September, and on the 4th, land was discovered; in a harbor belonging to which the Resolution came to anchor the next day. As Captain Cook was unable to learn what the Island was called by the natives, he gave to it the name of New Caledonia. Excepting New Zealand, this is perhaps the largest island in the South Pacific Ocean. The inhabitants were strong, robust, active, and well made; and in their dispositions were courteous and obliging. They did not appear in the least addicted to pilfering.

On the 13th, the Resolution weighed anchor, and land was discovered, which was named Norfolk Isle. From this place our commander steered for New Zealand, in Queen Charlotte's Sound, where he shortly afterwards arrived. Several days elapsed before any of the natives made their appearance; but when they did so, and recognised Captain Cook and his friends, joy succeeded to fear. They hurried in numbers out of the woods, and embraced the English over and over again, leaping and skipping about like madmen. The whole intercourse with the New Zealanders, during this third visit, was peaceable and friendly.

In the prosecution of his voyage, our commander, on the 17th of December, reached the west coast of Terra del Fuego, and came to anchor in a place which he called Christmas Sound. Through the whole course of his various navigations, he had never seen so desolate a coast. But barren and dreary as the land was, it was not wholly destitute of accommodations. The country abounded with wild fowl, and particularly with geese;

which afforded a refreshment to the whole ship's crew, that was the more acceptable on account of the approaching festival. Had they not thus been happily provided for, their Christmas cheer must have been salt beef and pork. Some Madeira wine, the only article of provision that was mended by keeping, was still left. This, in conjunction with the geese, which were cooked in every variety of method, enabled the navigators to celebrate Christmas as cheerfully as perhaps was done by their friends in England.

Our commander soon afterwards proceeded through the Strait of Le Maire to Staten Island. About the end of February he crossed the line of the route he had taken when he left the Cape of Good Hope; having now made the circuit of the southern ocean in a high latitude, and traversed it in such a manner as to leave no room for the possibility of their being any continent in that part of the hemisphere, unless near the pole, and out of the reach of navigation. By twice visiting the tropical sea, he had not only ascertained the situation of some old discoveries, but had made many new ones; and, indeed, even in that part, had left little more to be accomplished. The intention of the voyage had in every respect been answered, and the southern hemisphere sufficiently explored. A complete termination was hereby put to the searching after a southern continent.

The great purpose of the navigation of Captain Cook round the globe being thus completed, he at length directed his views towards England, and determined to steer for the Cape of Good Hope; and on Wednesday, the twenty-second of March, according to his reckoning (who had sailed round the world), but on Tuesday, the twenty-first at the Cape, he anchored his ship in Table Bay. During the circumnavigation of the globe, from the period of our commander's leaving the Cape of Good Hope to his return to it again, he had sailed no less a distance than twenty thousand leagues. This was an extent of voyage nearly equal to three times the equatorial circumference of the earth, and such as had never been accomplished before, by any ship in the same compass of duration.

On the remainder of the voyage it is not necessary to enlarge. The repairs of the ship having been completed, and the necessary stores carried on board, together with a fresh supply of provisions and water, Captain Cook left the Cape of Good Hope on the 27th of April, and reached the island of St. Helena on the 15th of May. Here he remained till the 21st, when he sailed, and arrived in safety at Portsmouth, having been absent from England three years and eighteen days; in which time, and under all changes of climate, he had lost but four men, and only one of these by sickness.

CAPTAIN COOK'S THIRD VOYAGE

Although the Resolution and the Discovery were destined for the same service, they did not leave England at the same time. Captain Cook, in the former, sailed from Plymouth on the twelfth of July; and Captain Clerke, in the latter, on the 1st of August, 1776. The two ships joined at the Cape of Good Hope, about the beginning of November. Here Captain Cook made an addition to his stock of animals, by the purchase of cattle, horses, sheep, goats, rabbits, and poultry. All these, as well as most of the animals then on board the vessels, were intended for Otaheite, New Zealand, and other islands.

The ships sailed from the Cape about the beginning of December; and the navigators, pursuing their course towards the south-east, the weather soon became so cold that several of the goats and some of the sheep died. On the 12th, two islands were seen, the larger of which appeared to be about fifteen leagues in circuit. As no names had hitherto been assigned to these islands, our commander called them Prince Edward's Islands.

Though it was now the middle of summer in this hemisphere, the weather was not less severe than what is generally experienced in England in the very depth of winter. Instead, however, of being discouraged by this circumstance, the captain directed his course still further south, and on the 24th, reached the island called Kerguelen's Land; and the next day landed upon it. The weather was foggy during the whole time that the ships continued here. The island was so excessively barren, that perhaps no place, hitherto discovered, under the same parallel of latitude, affords so scanty a field for a natural historian as this. If our commander had not been unwilling to deprive M. de Kerguelen of the honor of this island bearing his name, he would have called it the island of Desolation.

Captain Cook next directed his course towards New Zealand, that he might obtain a further supply of water, take in wood, and make hay for his cattle. Nothing very remarkable occurred to the voyagers till the 24th of January, 1777, when they discovered the coast of Van Dieman's Land, and in two days after came to anchor. One day they were agreeably surprised by a visit from some of the natives. Every present which Captain Cook made them they received without the least appearance of satisfaction. During the few days that Captain Cook continued here, he neglected nothing that could promote the knowledge of science or navigation.

He sailed from Van Dieman's land on the 30th of January, 1777, and about a fortnight afterwards came to anchor at his old station of Queen Charlotte's Sound, in New Zealand. Operations for refitting the ships, and for obtaining provisions, were carried on with great vigor. So healthy were the crews, that at this time there were only two invalids upon the sick lists of both ships. Captain Cook, in this his last visit to New Zealand, gave to one chief two goats, a male and female, with a kid; and to another two pigs, a boar and a sow. It had been his intention to have left other animals than these; but he was unable to find a chief who was powerful enough to protect them, and he therefore gave up all thought of it.

On the 24th of February Captain Cook proceeded on his voyage, in a north-easterly direction and, about five weeks afterwards, arrived at an island situated in about twenty degrees of south latitude, and called by the natives Watecoo. This island, which is about six leagues in circuit, is a very beautiful spot, having a surface composed of hills and plains, covered with a verdure rendered extremely pleasant by the diversity of its hues. Its inhabitants were very numerous, and many of them were elegantly formed. Their whole behavior, whilst on board, showed that they were perfectly at ease, and that they felt no apprehension, either that they should be detained or ill used.

It has been stated that it was a principal object of this voyage to examine the Pacific Ocean in the high northern latitudes. But, hitherto, the progress of the vessels had been so unavoidably retarded by unfavorable winds, and other adverse circumstances, that it was become impossible for the commander, this year, to think of proceeding towards those latitudes. The rainy season soon afterwards commenced; and the united heat and moisture of the weather, in addition to the impossibility of keeping the ships dry, threatened to be very injurious to the health of his people. So great, and so judicious, however, were the attentions which he paid to their health, that there was not as yet one sick man on board either ship.

On the 1st of May, the vessels arrived at Anamooka. A friendly intercourse was immediately opened with the natives. The only interruption to the friendship which had been established, arose from the thievish disposition of the inhabitants of Anamooka. Numerous opportunities were here afforded, of remarking how expert these people were in the business of stealing. Even some of the chiefs did not think the profession unbecoming their dignity. One of them was detected in carrying a bolt out of the ship, concealed under his clothes. For this offence Captain Cook sentenced him to receive a dozen lashes, and kept him confined till he had paid a hog for his liberty; and afterwards the navigators were no longer troubled with thieves of rank. Their servants, or slaves, however, were still employed; and upon them a flogging seemed to make no greater impression, than it would have done upon the mainmast. At length, Captain Clerke invented a mode

of treatment, which was thought to be of good effect. He put
the thieves into the hands of the barber, and completely shaved
their heads. In consequence of this operation, they became
objects of ridicule to their own countrymen; and our people, by
immediately knowing them, and keeping them at a distance, were
enabled to deprive them of future opportunities for a repetition of
their rogueries.

Captain Cook now proceeded to the Friendly Islands, and was
received in the most friendly manner imaginable by the inhabitants.
Besides the immediate benefits that were derived by the ships
from the friendly intercourse which had been established, so extensive an addition was now made to the geographical knowledge of
this part of the Pacific Ocean, as may render no small service to
future navigators. From the information which our commander
received, this Archipelago is very extensive. More than one
hundred and fifty islands were reckoned by the natives, who made
use of bits of leaves of different size for designating their number,
and their relative dimensions.

On the 17th of July, our commander took his final leave of the
Friendly Islands; and in about three weeks, he reached Otaheite.
Omai's first reception among his countrymen was not entirely of
a flattering nature. Captain Cook found that since he was last at
Otaheite, in 1774, two Spanish vessels had been there, and had
left some hogs, dogs, goats, one bull, and a ram. The officers
and crews of these vessels had behaved so well, that the inhabitants spoke of them in the strongest expressions of esteem and
veneration. On the present visit, the navigators had undeniable
proof that the offering of human sacrifices formed a part of the
religious institutions of Otaheite.

One day while the navigators were in Matavia Bay, Captain
Cook, and Captain Clerke, mounted on horseback, and rode into
the country. The Otaheitans, who had never seen such animals
before, were utterly astonished, and gazed upon the gentlemen
with as much amazement, as if they had been Centaurs. Not
all the novelties, put together, which European visiters had carried amongst them, inspired them with so high an opinion of the
greatness of distant nations as this.

During this visit to Otaheite, so cordial a friendship and confi
dence were established betwixt the voyagers and the natives, that
it was not once interrupted by any unpleasant incident. From
Otaheite Captain Cook sailed on the 13th to the adjacent island
of Eimeo. At this island the transactions were, for the most part,
unpleasant. On the 11th of October the ships arrived in a harbor
on the west side of the island of Huaheine.

The grand business of Captain Cook at Huaheine was to settle
Omai there, on the very spot from which he had been taken.
On the 2nd of November 1777, Omai took his final leave of the
English in a very affectionate manner, but at the same time with

manly resolution, and the vessels sailed for Ulieta, where they arrived on the following day. The last of the Society Islands which Captain Cook visited was Bolabola. Captain Cook continued to the last his zeal for furnishing the natives of the South Sea with useful animals. The navigators finally departed from the Society Islands on the 12th of December.

Frequently as these islands had been visited, it might have been imagined that their religious, political, and domestic regulations, manners, and customs, must, by this time, have been thoroughly understood. A great accession of knowledge was undoubtedly gained in the present voyage; and yet it was confessed by Captain Cook, that his account of these was, in various respects, still imperfect; and that he still continued a stranger to many of the most important institutions which prevailed there.

In the night between the 22d and 23d of December, 1777, the ships crossed the equator, in the longitude of two hundred and three degrees fifteen minutes west. The navigators still proceeded northward; and towards the end of January, 1778, they approached a cluster of islands, which Captain Cook afterwards named the Sandwich Islands.

One of the officers was sent with the boat to search for water at an island called by the natives Atooi. On attempting to land here the inhabitants came down in such numbers, and were so violent in their endeavors to seize the oars, muskets, and, in short, every thing they could lay hold of, that he was compelled to fire upon them, and one man was killed. The rapacious disposition they at first displayed, was entirely corrected by their conviction that it could not be exercised with impunity. During the short stay of the vessels at this island, it was ascertained that the inhabitants were eaters of human flesh. It was, however, understood that their enemies slain in battle were the sole objects of so abominable a custom. This people, when Captain Cook became better acquainted with them, appeared, in general, to possess a frank and cheerful disposition, equally removed from the fickle levity which distinguishes the natives of Otaheite, and the sedate character which is discernible among many of those of the other islands of the South Sea.

Of the Archipelago, which was denominated by Captain Cook the Sandwich Islands, there were five only with which, at this time, he became acquainted. Their names, as given by the natives, were Woahoo, Atooi, Oneeheow, Oreehoua, and Tahoora. Had the Sandwich Islands been discovered by the Spaniards at an early period, that people would undoubtedly have taken advantage of so excellent a situation, and have made use of them as refreshing places to their ships, which sail annually from Acapulco for Manilla. Happy too would it have been for Anson, if he had known that there existed a group of islands half way between America and Tinian, where all his wants could

effectually have been supplied, and the different hardships to which
he was exposed have been avoided.

On the 2d of February, the navigators pursued their course
northward; in doing which the incidents they met with were almost entirely of a nautical kind. The coast of New Albion was
seen on the 7th of March, the ships being then in the latitude of
44 deg. 83 min. north, and in the longitude of 235 deg. 20 min.
east. As the vessels ranged along the west side of America,
Captain Cook gave names to several capes and headlands, which
appeared in sight. At length, on the 29th, he came to anchor in
a bay which was called by the natives Nootka, and was thence
named by Captain Cook Nootka Sound. Some of the natives
came off to the ships in canoes, but they could not be prevailed
with to venture on board. Shortly after this a regular trade was
commenced. The articles which the inhabitants offered for sale
were the skins of various animals, such as bears, wolves, foxes,
deer, raccoons, pole-cats, martins; and, in particular, of the sea-
otters. To these were added garments made of skins; another
sort of clothing, formed from the bark of a tree; and various
pieces of workmanship. The articles, which the natives took in
exchange for their commodities, were knives, chisels, pieces of
iron and tin, nails, looking-glasses, buttons, or any kind of
metal. Though commerce, in general, was carried on with mu-
tial honesty, there were some among these people, who were as
much inclined to thievery as the islanders in the Southern Ocean

In the present abstract the time will not allow of an insertion of
nore than a short account of the inhabitants. Their persons are
described to have been generally under the common stature
somewhat full or plump, though without being muscular. They
were undoubtedly eaters of human flesh, yet they had no appearance of inhumanity of character. To our navigators they seemed
a docile, courteous, and well-disposed people. The chief employments of the men were fishing and killing land or sea animals, for
the sustenance of their families; while the women were occupied
in manufacturing flaxen or woollen garments, or in other domestic
offices.

On the 26th, the repairs of the ships having been completed,
Captain Cook sailed from Nootka Sound. In the prosecution of
his voyage northward, and back again to the Sandwich Islands,
the facts that occurred were chiefly of a nautical kind.

At an inlet where the ships came to anchor on the 12th of May,
and to which Captain Cook gave the appellation of Prince William's Sound, he had an opportunity not only of prosecuting his
nautical and geographical discoveries, but of making considerable
additions to his knowledge of the inhabitants of the American
coast. The natives of this part of the coast had a near resemblance to the Esquimaux and Greenlanders. It is remarkable
concerning this people, that there were found amongst them both

beads and iron; which must have come from some civilized nation, though there was reason to suppose that our navigators were the first Europeans with whom they had ever held a direct communication.

Some days after leaving this sound, the navigators came to an inlet, from which hopes were strongly entertained, that it would be found to communicate either with the sea to the north, or with Baffin's Bay to the east; and, accordingly, it became the object of very accurate and serious examination. The Captain was soon persuaded that the expectations formed from it were groundless, yet it was requisite that this should be perfectly ascertained. A complete investigation of the inlet consequently took place, to the distance of seventy leagues from its entrance, and indubitable marks occurred of its being a river, but one of the most considerable ones that are known. It was called Cook's River.

The navigators cleared Cook's river on the 6th of June. In the prosecution of the voyage, on the 26th, there was so thick a fog, that the navigators could not see a hundred yards before them; notwithstanding which, as the weather was moderate, the Captain did not intermit his course. At length, however, being alarmed at the sound of breakers on one side of the ship, he immediately brought her to, and came to anchor; and the Discovery, by his order, did the same. A few hours afterwards, the fog having in some degree cleared away, it appeared, that both the vessels had escaped a very imminent danger. Providence, in the dark, had conducted them between rocks which the commander would not have ventured to pass through even in a clear day, and had conveyed them to an anchoring-place, as good as he could possibly have fixed upon, had the choice been entirely at his option.

On the 27th, the vessels reached an island called Oonalaska, the inhabitants of which behaved with a degree of politeness and courtesy very unusual with savage tribes. About the 10th of August Captain Cook came to anchor under a point of land, to which he gave the name of Cape Prince of Wales, and which is remarkable by being the most western extremity of America hitherto explored. This extremity is distant from the eastern Cape of Siberia only thirteen leagues: and thus our Commander had the glory of ascertaining the vicinity of the two continents, which before had only been conjectured from the reports of the neighboring Asiatic inhabitants, and the imperfect observations of the Russian navigators.

Resuming his course he crossed over to the opposite Asiatic coast, and anchored in a bay which he named the Bay of St. Lawrence, belonging to the country of the Tschutski. After this, again approaching the shore of America, he proceeded towards the north, and on the 18th, he reached the latitude of 70 deg. 44 min. The ships were now close to the edge of the ice, and un able to go any further. The ice, was as compact as a wall, and was judged to be ten or twelve feet in height. Farther to the north, it appeared much higher. Its surface was extremely rugged, and in different places there were seen upon it pools of water. A prodigious number of sea-horses lay upon the ice; and some of them, on the 19th, were procured for food, there being at this time a want of fresh provisions. They were bad eating, but the voyagers lived upon them as long as they lasted; and most of the seamen preferred them to salt meat.

Captain Cook continued until the 29th, to traverse the Icy Sea beyond Behring's Strait, in various directions, and through numberless obstructions and difficulties. Every day the ice increased, so as to preclude all hope of attaining, at least during the present year, the grand object of the voyage, the discovery of a passage northward into the Atlantic. Before Captain Cook proceeded far to the south, he employed a considerable time in examining the sea and coasts in the neighborhood of Behring's Strait, both on the side of Asia and America; and on the 3d of October he returned to the island of Oonalaska. The navigators had not been here many days, when Captain Cook and Captain Clerke each received a very singular present, of a rye loaf, or rather a pie in the form of a loaf, for it inclosed some salmon highly seasoned with pepper. And with each loaf was a note written in a language, which no one was able to read. It was imagined that the presents came from some Russians in the neighborhood, and therefore a few bottles of rum, wine, and porter, were sent to these unknown friends in return; it being rightly judged that such articles would be more acceptable than any thing besides, which it was in the power of the navigators to bestow. An intelligent man was sent with the bearer of the presents, for the purpose of obtaining further information. Two days afterwards this person returned with three Russian seamen. They had been stationed here to collect furs; and had on the island a dwelling-house, some store-houses, and a sloop of about thirty tons burden. One of them was the master or mate of the vessel, and they all appeared to be sensible and well-behaved persons. From a very intelligent Russian, who landed at Oonalaska on the 14th, Captain Cook obtained the sight of two manuscript charts of these seas, and was permitted to copy them.

All things being ready for his departure, Captain Cook left Oonalaska on the 26th, and sailed for the Sandwich Islands. On the 30th of November, he arrived at Owhyee, one of the Sandwich Islands; and one which appeared to him of greater extent and importance than any of the islands that had yet been visited in this part of the world. He occupied nearly seven weeks in sailing round, and examining its coast. On the 16th of January, 1779, canoes arrived in such numbers from all parts, that there were not fewer than a thousand about the two ships, most of them crowded with people. Among such multitudes, as, at times, were on board it will not be deemed surprising, that some should have betrayed a thievish disposition. One of them took out of the Resolution a boat's rudder; and made off with it so speedily, that it could not be recovered. Captain Cook directed two or three muskets, and as many four pounders, to be fired over the canoe in which the rudder had been carried off, but, at the report of these, the surrounding multitude of the natives appeared to be more surprised than terrified.

The ships were anchored on the 17th, in a bay which was called by the inhabitants Karakakooa. In the whole course of his voyages Captain Cook had never seen so many people assembled in one place as he saw on this occasion; for, besides the multitudes that came off in canoes, all the shore of the bay was covered with spectators, and many hundreds were swimming round the ships like shoals of fish. In the progress of the intercourse which was maintained between the voyagers and the natives, the quiet and inoffensive behavior of the latter, took away every apprehension of danger; so that the English trusted themselves among them at all times, and in all situations.

But the satisfaction that was derived from the generosity and hospitality of the inhabitants, was frequently interrupted by the propensity of many of them to stealing; and this circumstance was the more distressing, as it sometimes obliged the commander and the other officers to have recourse to acts of severity, which they would willingly have avoided, if the necessity of the case had not absolutely called for them.

Early the next day, the ships sailed out of Karakakooa bay. It was the captain's design, before he visited the other Sandwich islands, to finish the survey of Owhyee, that he had begun. His object in this was, if possible, to find a harbor better sheltered from the weather than the bay he had just left. Two days afterwards a gale of wind sprung up, in which the Resolution had the misfortune of injuring her foremast in so dangerous a manner, that he was obliged to return to Karakakooa. On the return of the ships several canoes approached, in which were many of the former acquaintance of the navigators.

The next day, February the 13th, the Resolution's foremast was landed, to be repaired, and tents were erected in their former situation on the shore. An Indian was this day detected in stealing the armorer's tongs from the forge, for which he received a severe flogging, and was sent out of the ship. Notwithstanding the example made of this man, in the afternoon another had the audacity to snatch the tongs and a chisel from the same place, with which he jumped overboard, and swam for the shore. The master and a midshipman were instantly despatched after him, in the small cutter. The Indian seeing himself pursued, made for a canoe; his countrymen took him on board, and paddled as swiftly as they could towards the shore. Several muskets were fired at them, but without effect, for they soon got out of the reach of the shots.

This was the commencement of a very fatal misunderstanding with the natives. In the night, one of the boats belonging to the Discovery was carried off; and many hostile indications on the part of the natives were remarked. These determined Captain Cook to secure, if possible, the person of the king as the most effectual step that could be taken for the recovery of the boat, and restoring amity betwixt the English and the inhabitants. Accompanied by the lieutenant of marines, a serjeant, corporal, and seven private men; having at the same time armed several men in the ship's launch and pinnace, he undauntedly proceeded to the residence of the king. At an inte. view with the king, the captain took him by the hand, in a friendly manner, and asked him to go on board the Resolution, to which he readily consented. A short time after this, several of the Indians were observed to be arming themselves with long spears, clubs, and daggers, and putting on thick mats which they used as armor. This hostile appearance increased, and became the more alarming, on the arrival of two men, with news that a chief called Kareemoo had been killed by the men in one of the Discovery's boats. Captain Cook being at this time surrounded by a great crowd, thought his situation somewhat hazardous. He therefore ordered the lieutenant of marines to march his small party to the water-side, where the boats lay, within a few yards of the shore: the Indians readily made a lane for them to pass, and did not offer to interrupt them. The distance they had to go might be about fifty or sixty yards. Captain Cook followed, having hold of the king's hand, who accompanied him very willingly: he was attended by his wife, two sons and several chiefs. His younger son went immediately into the pinnance, expecting his father to follow; but the latter had no sooner arrived at the water-side, than his wife threw her arms about his neck, and, with the assistance of two chiefs, forced him to sit down by the side of a double canoe. Captain Cook expostulated with them, but to no purpose, they would not suffer the king to proceed, telling him that he would be put to death if he went on board the ship.

While the king was in this situation, another of the chiefs was observed lurking near, with an iron dagger partly concealed under his cloak   His attention, apparently, was to stab either Captain Cook, or the lieutenant of marines. The latter proposed to fire at him, but the captain would not permit it. The chief closed upon them, on which the officer struck him with his musket, and compelled him to retire. Captain Cook seeing the tumult increase, and that the Indians grew more daring and resolute, found that it would be impossible to carry off the king by force, without sacrificing many of his people. He therefore paused a little, and was on the point of giving orders to reimbark, when a man threw a stone at him. This Captain Cook returned by a discharge of small shot. The man brandished his spear, and was about to dart it at the captain, when the latter knocked him down with his musket. He expostulated strongly with the most forward of the crowd upon their turbulent behavior; and now only sought to secure a safe embarkation for his small party, which was closely pressed by a body of several thousand people. One man was observed behind a double canoe, in the action of darting his spear at Captain Cook. He therefore was forced to fire at him in his own defence, but he happened to kill another close to him, equally forward in the tumult. The serjeant observing that the captain had missed the man he aimed at, received orders to fire at him, which he did, and killed him. By this time the impetuosity of the Indians was somewhat repressed. They fell back in a body, and seemed staggered; but being pushed on by those behind, they returned to the charge, and poured a volley of stones among the marines, who without waiting for orders, returned it with a general discharge of musketry. This was instantly followed by a fire from the boats. Captain Cook waved his hand to the boats, and called to them to cease firing, and to come nearer in to receive the marines. The officer in the pinnace immediately brought that vessel as close to the shore as he could, notwithstanding the showers of stones that fell among his people; but the lieutenant who commanded in the launch, instead of pulling in to the assistance of Captain Cook, withdrew his boat farther off, at the very moment that every thing seems to have depended upon the timely exertions of those in the boats. By his own account, he mistook the signal: but be that as it may, this circumstance appears to have decided the fatal turn of the affair, and to have removed every chance which remained with Captain Cook of escaping with his life. The marines several times fired upon the crowd, but to little purpose, for the Indians soon rushed among them, and forced them into the water where four of them were killed. Captain Cook was now the only Englishman remaining on shore. He was observed to be making towards the pinnace, holding his left hand against the back of his head, to guard it from the stones which were thrown at him, and carrying his musket under his other arm. An Indian was seen following him, but with caution and timidity; for he stopped once or twice, as if undetermined to proceed. At last he advanced upon him unawares, and with a large club, or common stake, gave him a blow on the back of the head, and then precipitately retreated. The stroke seemed to have stunned Captain Cook: he staggered a few paces, then fell on his hand and one knee, and dropped his musket. As he was rising, and before he could recover his feet, another Indian stabbed him in the back of the neck with an iron dagger. He then fell into the water, in a place where it was

about knee deep; and others immediately crowded upon him, and
endeavored to keep him under; but, struggling very stongly with
them, he got his head up, and casting his look towards the pinnance, seemed to solicit assistance. Though the boat was not
above five or six yards distant from him, yet from the crowded
and confused state of the crew, it seems it was not in their power
to save him The Indians got him under again, but in deeper
water. He was, however, able to get his head up once more;
and, being almost spent in the struggle, he naturally turned to the
rock, and was endeavoring to support himself by it, when a sav
age gave him a blow with a club, and he was seen alive no more.
They hauled him up lifeless on the rocks, where they seemed to
take a savage pleasure in using every possible barbarity to his dead
body, snatching the daggers out of each other's hands, to have the
horrid satisfaction of piercing the fallen victim of their barbarous

Death of Captain Cook.

rage; and after they had thus glutted their revenge, they carried
it off in triumph. Captain Clerke, who succeeded to the command of the expedition, made every effort to recover the remains
of Captain Cook; but his bones only could be obtained, and these
were committed to the deep, amidst the heartfelt grief of all who
had served with him.

In his manners, Captain Cook was plain, simple, and manly.
He was an excellent husband and father, a sincere and steady
friend The benevolence and humanity of his disposition were
peculiar.y remarkable. They were apparent from his treatment
of his men, through all his voyages; and from his conduct towards

the natives of all the countries which were discovered by him. The health, the convenience, and, as far as it could be admitted, the enjoyment of those under his command, were the constant objects of his attention: and he was invariably anxious to ameliorate the condition of the inhabitants of the several islands and places which he visited. With regard to their thieveries, he candidly apologized for, and overlooked many offences which others would have punished; and when he felt impelled to proceed to any acts of severity, he never exerted them without reluctance and concern.

With respect to his talents, they were undeniably of the most useful kind. He had a capacious and penetrating mind; and all his designs were accordingly bold and extensive. When these were formed, he never expressed a doubt respecting their execution; for the same perspicuity and orderly arrangement of thought which enabled him to form the designs, also enabled him to devise the most simple and effectual modes of executing them. In the execution he was equally distinguished; no difficulty perplexed, no danger appalled him. The talents and knowledge which he possessed were always completely at his command, when they were most needed. And for great designs he was also qualified by the constitution of his body, which was inured to labor, and capable of supporting the greatest fatigue and hardships. In addition to a consummate acquaintance with navigation, Captain Cook possessed a knowledge of other sciences. In this respect, the ardor of his mind rose above the disadvantages of a very confined education. His progress in the different branches of mathematics, and particularly in astronomy, became so eminent, that, at length, he was able to take the lead in making the necessary observations of this kind, in the course of his voyages. He attained, likewise, to such a degree of proficiency in general learning, and in the art of composition, as to be able to express himself with a manly clearness and propriety, and to become respectable as the narrator, as well as the performer, of great actions. Another trait, which was peculiarly conspicuous in the character of Captain Cook, was the perseverance with which he pursued the noble objects to which his life was devoted. In this he scarcely ever had an equal, and never a superior. Nothing could divert him from the points he aimed at; and he persisted in the prosecution of them, through difficulties and obstructions, which would have deterred minds even of considerable strength and firmness. In stature he is described to have been somewhat above the common size; and, though a good looking man, he was plain both in address and appearance. His head was small: his hair, which was a dark brown, he wore tied behind. His face was full of expression; his nose exceedingly well shaped; his eyes, which were small, and of a brown cast, were quick and piercing, and his eyebrows prominent; which gave to his counte nance altogether an air of austerity. In the year 1762 he had married an amiable and deserving woman. He had by her six children, but of these three sons only survived him. They were all brought up in the naval service. One of them was lost in a hurricane at sea, and the other two fell honorably in the cause of their country. On the widow a pension of two hundred pounds a year for her life, and on each of the sons a pension of twenty-five pounds a year was settled by the British government.

NARRATIVE OF EVENTS WHICH OCCURRED SUBSE QUENTLY TO THE DEATH OF CAPTAIN COOK.

After Captain Clerke, upon whom the command of the expedition devolved, had left the fatal island of Owhyhee, he considered it his duty to endeavor to execute the plans of discovery that had been laid down by his lamented predecessor. He consequently coasted several others of the Sandwich Islands; and finally left them on the 15th of March, 1779. The ships now proceeded towards Kamtschatka; and, in their course, the Resolution sprung a leak so bad, that at one time the whole space between the decks was deluged with water. On the twenty-third the mountains of Kamtschatka, covered with snow, were within view. The weather was now so severe, that the ship appeared like a complete mass of ice, and the rigging was so incrusted with it, that the different ropes were more than double their usual thickness.

Two days after the discovery of Kamtschatka, when off the entrance of Awatska Bay, the Resolution lost sight of the Discovery. The Resolution entered the bay, and soon afterwards the town of Petropaulowski was within view. It consisted of a few miserable log-houses, and some conical huts raised on poles, amounting in all to about thirty; yet here the voyagers were received and treated with feelings of humanity, joined to a greatness of mind and elevation of sentiment which would have done honor to any nation. On the 1st of May the Discovery also entered the harbor. On the 5th of July the navigators passed through Behring's Straits. They first sailed along the Asiatic coast, and then stretched over to that of America, with a view of exploring the sea between the latitudes of sixty-eight and sixty-nine degrees. But in this attempt they were disappointed; on the 7th their farther progress was stopped by a large and compact field of ice connected with the land.

At one time, in attempting to penetrate towards the north-west, the Discovery was in a very dangerous situation. She became so entangled by several large pieces of ice, that her way was stopped, and she suffered much injury. A change of wind, however taking place in the afternoon, the ice began to separate, and the navigators, setting all their sails, forced a passage through it.

On the 31st they repassed Behring's Straits Captain Clerke's health now rapidly declined. On the 17th of August, he was no longer able to rise from his bed; and five days afterwards he died of a consumption, which had commenced before he left England, and of which he had lingered during the whole voyage. The command of the expedition now devolved upon Captain Gore, who removed into the Resolution, and appointed Mr. King to the command of the Discovery. The body of Captain Clerke was interred near the town of Petropaulowski, on Sunday, the 29th, with all the solemnity and honors which the voyagers could bestow.

On the 12th of October they lost sight of Kamtschatka. In the forenoon of the 29th of November, the ships passed several Chinese fishing-boats; and the sea was covered with the wrecks of boats that had been lost, as it was conjectured, in the late boisterous weather. The navigators were now in latitude 22 deg. one min. south. On the following day, they ran along the Lema Islands, and took a Chinese pilot on board; and at 9 o'clock in the morning of the 1st of December they anchored at the distance of three leagues from Macao. Captain King was sent to Canton to obtain supplies of provisions and stores.

On account of the war between England and America, and with France and Spain as her allies, of which the navigators received intelligence at Canton, they put themselves in the best posture of defence that they were able; in the Resolution they mounted sixteen guns, and in the Discovery ten. They had reason, however, to believe, from the generosity of their enemies, that these precautions were superfluous; for they were informed that instructions had been found on board all the French ships of war captured in Europe, directing their commanders, in case of falling in with the ships that sailed under the command of Captain Cook, to suffer them to proceed without molestation; and the same orders were also said to have been given by the American Congress in the vessels employed in their service. In return for these liberal concessions, Captain Gore resolved to refrain from availing himself of any opportunities of capture, and to preserve, throughout the remainder of the voyage, the strictest neutrality.

On the 12th of January, 1780, the navigators got under sail from Macao; on the 19th, they saw Pulo Lapata, and on the 20th, descried Pulo Condore, and anchored in the harbor at the south-west end of the island. The navigators remained at Pulo Condore till the 23d of January, when they unmoored, and pro-

12 *

ceeded on their homeward passage; passing through the Straits
of Banca, and Sunda, without any occurrence worthy of particu
lar remark.   On the 18th of February they left the Straits of
Sunda.   In the night, between the 25th and 26th, they experienced a violent storm, during which almost every sail they had
bent was split to rags; and the next day they were obliged to
bend their last set of sails, and to knot and splice the rigging,
their cordage being all expended.

On the 7th of April, they saw the land of Africa; on the evening of the 12th, they dropped anchor in False Bay, and the
next morning stood into Simon's Bay, at the Cape of Good
Hope.   They sailed out of the Bay on the 9th, and on the 12th
of June, they passed the equator for the fourth time during the
voyage.   On the 12th of August they made the western coast of
Ireland, and, after a fruitless attempt to put into Port Galway,
they were obliged, by strong southerly winds, to steer northward;
and on the 26th of August, both the ships came to anchor at
Stromness in the Orkneys, whence Captain King was despatched
by Captain Gore, to acquaint the Board of Admiralty of their
arrival.   On the 1st of October, the ships arrived safe at the
Nore, after an absence of four years, two months, and twenty-
two days.

SUFFERINGS OF EPHRAIM HOW.

On the 25th of August, 1676, Mr. Ephraim How, of New
Haven, in New England, with his two eldest sons; one Mr.
Augur; Caleb Jones, son to Mr. William Jones, one of the
magistrates of New Haven; and a boy; six persons in all; set
sail from New Haven for Boston, in a small ketch, of about
seventeen tons.

Having despatched his business there, he sailed for New
Haven on the 10th of September, but was forced back to Boston
by contrary winds.   Here Mr. How was seized with a violent
flux, which continued nearly a month; many being at that time
sick, and some dying of the same.

Being in some degree restored to health, he again sailed from
Boston, October 10.   They went with a fair wind as far as Cape
Cod: but on a sudden the weather became very tempestuous, so
that they could not pass the Cape, but were driven off to sea,
where they were in great danger, experiencing terrible storms,
with outrageous winds and seas.

His eldest son fell sick and died about the 21st; soon after his
other son was taken ill and died also.   This was a bitter cup to
the poor father, for these youths were his only assistants in

working the vessel.   Soon after Caleb Jones died, so that half
the company were now no more.

Mr. How continued in a very sickly and weak state, yet was
necessitated to stand at the helm twenty-four and thirty-six hours
together.   During this time the sea was so boisterous as frequently to break over the vessel, that if he had not been lashed
fast he must have been washed overboard.   In this extremity,
he was at a loss in his own thoughts, whether he should persist
in endeavoring to make for the New England shore, or bear
away for the Southern Islands.   Upon his proposing the question
to Mr. Augur, they determined, according to the custom of some
in those times, to decide this difficult case by casting lots.   They
did so, and it fell upon New England.

Nearly about the 7th of November they lost their rudder, so
that now their only dependence was upon Providence.   In this
deplorable state they drove up and down for a fortnight longer.
During the last six weeks, the poor infirm Mr. How was hardly
ever dry, nor had he the benefit of warm food above thrice or
thereabouts.

At length, about the 21st of November, early in the morning,
the vessel was driven on the tailings of a ledge of rocks, where
the sea broke violently.   Looking out, they saw a dismal rocky
island to the leeward, upon which, if Providence had not by the
breakers given them timely warning, they had been dashed to
pieces.   They immediately let go an anchor, and got out the
boat, and the sea became calm.   The boat proving leaky, and
they being in great terror, they took but little out of the ketch,
but got on shore as they could.

Here they could discover neither man nor beast.   It was a
small, rocky, desolate island, near Cape Sable, the Southern
extremity of Nova Scotia.   They now appeared to be in great
danger of being starved to death, but the storm returning, beat
so violently upon the vessel, as it still lay at anchor, that it was
stove to pieces, and several things floated to the shore.

The following articles were all they had towards their future
support:—a cask of gunpowder, which received no damage from
the water; a barrel of wine; half a barrel of molasses; several
useful articles towards building a tent: all the above drifted from
the wreck; besides which they had, firearms and shot; a pot
for boiling; and most probably other things not mentioned in the
narrative.

Their tent was soon erected, for the cold was now getting
severe, but new and great distresses attended them, for though
they had arms and ammunition, there were seldom any fowls to
be seen, except crows, ravens, and seagulls.   These were so
few, that they could seldom shoot more than one at a time.
Many times half a fowl, with the liquor it was boiled in, served
for a meal for all three.   Once they lived five days without any

sustenance, but did not feel themselves pinched with hunger as at other times: which they esteemed a special favor of Heaven unto them.

When they had lived in this miserable condition twelve weeks, Mr. How's dear friend and companion, Mr. Augur, died, about the middle of February, 1677; so that he had none left to converse with but the lad, who likewise departed on the 2d of April

Mr. How was now the sole inhabitant of this desolate spot during April, May, and June, and saw fishing vessels, every now and then, sailing by; some of which came even nearer to the island than that which at last took him off. He used all the means in his power to make them acquainted with his distress; but they either did not see him, or were afraid to approach close to the island, lest some of those Indians should be quartered there, who were at that time in hostility against the English, viz the North-East Indians, who held out after the death of the famous Philip, king of the Wompanoags.

At length a vessel belonging to Salem, in New England, providentially passed by, and seeing this poor fellow, they sent their boat on shore, and took him away. He had been on the island more than seven months, and above a quarter of a year by himself. On the 18th of July he arrived at Salem, and at last returned to his family at New Haven. They for a twelvemonth had supposed him dead; by which it appears he did not get home till the end of August, or perhaps later

---

AN ESCAPE THROUGH THE CABIN-WINDOWS.

In the year 18—, said Capt. M——, I was bound, in a fine stout ship of about four hundred tons burden, from the port of P—— to Liverpool. The ship had a valuable cargo on board and about ninety thousand dollars in specie. I had been prevented, by other urgent business, from giving much of my attention to the vessel while loading and equipping for the voyage, but was very particular in my directions to the chief mate, in whom I had great confidence, he having sailed with me some years, to avoid entering, if possible, any but native American seamen. When we were about to sail, he informed me that he had not been able to comply with my directions entirely in this particular; but had shipped two foreigners as seamen, one a native of Guernsey, and the other a Frenchman from Brittany. I was pleased, however, with the appearance of the crew generally, and particularly with the foreigners. They were both stout and able-bodied men, and were particularly alert and attentive to orders.

The passage commenced auspiciously, and promised to be a speedy one, as we took a fine steady westerly wind soon after we lost soundings. To my great sorrow and uneasiness, I soon discovered in the foreigners a change of conduct for the worse. They became insolent to the mates and appeared to be frequently under the excitement of liquor, and had evidently acquired an undue influence with the rest of the men. Their intemperance soon became intolerable, and as it was evident that they had brought liquor on board with them, I determined upon searching the forecastle and depriving them of it. An order to this effect was given to the mates, and they were directed to go about its execution mildly and firmly, taking no arms with them as they seemed inclined to do, but to give every chest, birth and locker in the forecastle a thorough examination; and bring aft to the cabin any spirits they might find.

It was not without much anxiety that I sent them forward upon this duty. I remained upon the quarter deck myself, ready to go to their aid, should it be necessary. In a few moments, a loud and angry dispute was succeeded by a sharp scuffle around the forecastle companion-way. The steward, at my call, handed my loaded pistols from the cabin, and with them I hastened forward. The Frenchman had grappled the second mate, who was a mere lad, by the throat, thrown him across the heel of the bowsprit, and was apparently determined to strangle him to death. The chief mate was calling for assistance from below, where he was struggling with the Guernsey man. The rest of the crew were indifferent spectators, but rather encouraging the foreigners than otherwise. I presented a pistol at the head of the Frenchman, and ordered him to release the second mate, which he instantly did. I then ordered him into the foretop, and the others, who were near, into the maintop, none to come down under pain of death, until ordered. The steward had by this time brought another pair of pistols, with which I armed the second mate, directing him to remain on deck; and went below into the forecastle myself. I found that the chief mate had been slightly wounded in two places by the knife of his antagonist, who, however, ceased to resist as I made my appearance, and we immediately secured him in irons. The search was now made, and a quantity of liquor found and taken to the cabin. The rest of the men were then called down from the tops, and the Frenchman was made the companion of his coadjutor's confinement. I then expostulated, at some length, with the others upon their improper and insubordinate conduct, and upon the readiness with which they had suffered themselves to be drawn into such courses by two rascally foreigners, and expressed hopes that I should have no reason for further complaint during the rest of the voyage. This remonstrance I thought had effect, as they appeared contrite and promised amendment. They were then dismissed, and order was restored.

The next day the foreigners strongly solicited pardon with the most solemn promises of future good conduct; and as the rest of the crew joined in their request, I ordered that their irons should be taken off. For several days the duties of the ship were performed to my entire satisfaction; but I could discover in the countenances of the foreigners, expressions of deep and rancorous animosity to the chief mate, who was a prompt, energetic seaman, requiring from the sailors, at all times, ready and implicit obedience to his orders.

A week perhaps had passed over in this way, when one night, in the mid watch, all hands were called to shorten sail. Ordinarily upon occasions of this kind, the duty was conducted by the mate, but I now went upon deck myself and gave orders, sending him upon the forecastle. The night was dark and squally; but the sea was not high, and the ship was running off about nine knots, with the wind upon the starboard quarter. The weather being very unpromising, the second reef was taken in the fore and main topsails, the mizen handed and the fore and mizen top gallant yards sent down. This done, one watch was permitted to go below, and I prepared to betake myself to my birth again, directing the mate, to whom I wished to give some orders, should be sent to me. To my utter astonishment and consternation, word was brought me, after a short time, that he was no where to be found. I hastened upon deck, ordered all hands up again, and questioned every man in the ship upon the subject; but they, with one accord, declared that they had not seen the mate forward. Lanterns were then brought, and every accessible part of the vessel was unavailingly searched. I then, in the hearing of the whole crew, declared my belief that he must have fallen overboard by accident, again dismissed one watch below, and repaired to the cabin, in a state of mental agitation impossible to be described. For notwithstanding the opinion which I had expressed to the contrary, I could not but entertain strong suspicions that the unfortunate man had met a violent death.

The second mate was a protegee of mine; and, as I have before observed, was a very young man of not much experience as a seaman. I therefore felt that, under critical circumstances, my main support had fallen from me. It is needless to add, that a deep sense of forlornness and insecurity was the result of these reflections.

My first step was to load and deposit in my state room all the fire arms on board, amounting to several muskets and four pairs of pistols. The steward was a faithful mulatto man, who had sailed with me several voyages. To him I communicated my suspicions, and directed him to be constantly on the alert: and

should any further difficulty with the crew occur, to repair immediately to my state room and arm himself. His usual birth was
in the steerage, but I further directed that he should, on the following morning, clear out and occupy one in the cabin near my
own.   The second mate occupied a small state room opening into
the passage which led from the steerage to the cabin.   I called
him from the deck, gave him a pair of loaded pistols, with orders
to keep them in his birth; and, during his night watches on deck,
never to go forward of the main mast, but to continue as constant
ly as possible near the cabin companion-way, and call me upon
the slightest occasion.   After this, I laid down in my bed, ordering that I should be called at four o'clock, for the morning watch
Only a few minutes had elapsed, when I heard three or four knocks
under the counter of the ship, which is that part of the stern immediately under the cabin windows.   In a minute or two they
were distinctly repeated.   I arose—opened the cabin window and
called.   *The mate answered!*—I gave him the end of a rope to assist him up, and never shall I forget the flood of gratitude which
my delighted soul poured forth to that Being, who had restored
him to me *uninjured*.   His story was soon told.   He had gone
forward upon being ordered by me, after the calling of all hands,
and had barely reached the forecastle, when he was seized by the
two foreigners, and before he could utter more than one cry,
which was drowned in the roaring of the winds and waves, was
thrown over the bow.   He was a powerful man and an excellent
swimmer.   The topsails of the ship were clewed down to reef, and
her way, of course, considerably lessened—and in an instant, he
found the end of a rope, which was accidentally towing overboard,
within his grasp, by which he dragged in the dead water or eddy,
that is always created under the stern of a vessel while sailing,
particularly if she is full built and deeply laden, as was the case
with this.   By a desperate effort, he caught one of the rudder
chains, which was very low, and drew himself by it upon the step
or jog of the rudder, where he had sufficient presence of mind to
remain without calling out, until the light had ceased to shine
through the cabin windows, when he concluded that the search
for him was over.   He then made the signal to me.
   No being in the ship, but myself, was apprised of his safety.
for the gale had increased and completely drowned the sounds of
the knocking, opening the window, &c. before they could reach
the quarter deck; and there was no one in the cabin but ourselves, the steward having retired to his birth in the steerage.   It
was at once resolved that the second mate only should be inform.
ed of his existence.   He immediately betook himself to a large
vacant state room, and, for the remainder of the passage, all his
wants were attended to by me.   Even the steward was allowed
to enter the cabin as rarely as possible.
   Nothing of note occurred during the remainder of the voyage,

which was prosperous. It seemed that the foreigners had only been actuated by *revenge* in the violence they had committed; for nothing further was attempted by them. In due season we took a pilot in the channel, and, in a day or two, entered the port of Liverpool. As soon as the proper arrangements were made, we commenced warping the ship into dock, and while engaged in this operation, *the Mate appeared on deck, went forward, and attended to his duties as usual!* A scene occurred which is beyond description: every feature of it is as vivid in my recollection as though it occurred but yesterday, and will be to my latest breath. The warp dropped from the paralysed hands of the horror-stricken sailors, and had it not been taken up by some boatmen on board, I should have been compelled to anchor again and procure assistance from the shore. Not a word was uttered; but the two guilty wretches staggered to the mainmast, where they remained petrified with horror, until the officer, who had been sent for, approached to take them into custody. They then seemed in a measure to be recalled to a sense of their appalling predicament, and uttered the most piercing expressions of lamentation and despair.

They were soon tried, and upon the testimony of the mate, capitally convicted and *executed.*

LAMENT FOR LONG TOM.

By J. G. C BRAINARD.

Thy cruise is over now
　Thou art anchored by the shore,
And never more shalt thou
　Hear the storm around thee roar,
Death has shaken out the sands of thy glass.
　Now around thee sports the whale
　And the porpoise snuffs the gale,
　And the night winds make their wail,
　　　　As they pass.

The sea-grass round thy bier
　Shall bend beneath the tide,
Nor tell the breakers near,
　Where thy manly limbs abide;
But the granite rock thy tomb shall be
　Though the edges of thy grave
　Are the combings of the wave—
　Yet unheeded they shall rave
　　　　Over thee.

At the calling of all hands,
　When the judgment signals spread—

When the islands, and the lands,
  And the seas give up their dead,
And the south and the north shall come
  When the sinner is betrayed,
  And the just man is afraid,
  Then may Heaven be thy aid,
      Poor Tom

THE FATAL REPAST.

We had been nearly five weeks at sea, when the captain found, by a nautical observation, that we were within one hundred and thirty miles of the north side of Jamaica. Favorable winds and smooth seas had hitherto been our constant attendants, and every thing on board conspired to render the confinement and monotony of a long voyage less annoying than they usually are. The cabin passengers consisted of Major and Mrs. L——, a new-married couple; Miss P——, sister to the latter; Mr. D——, a young Irishman, and myself. Our captain was a man of pleasing manners and liberal ideas, and formed an important acquisition to our party, by joining in all its recreations, and affording every facility to the indulgence of them. Much of our time was spent in conversation, and in walking on deck; and when the dews of evening obliged us to descend to the cabin, the captain would often entertain us with a relation of the various dangers which he and other persons had encountered at sea, or detail, with great gravity, some of the prevailing superstitions of sailors.

Although he possessed more general information than usually falls to the lot of seafaring persons, his mind was tinctured with some of their weaknesses and prejudices. The ladies of our party had a great taste for natural history, and wished to obtain specimens of all the most interesting kinds of sea-birds. They had several times requested the captain to shoot one of Mother Cary's chickens, that they might take a drawing from it; however, he always declined doing so, but never gave any satisfactory reason for his unwillingness to oblige them in this respect. At last, Mr. D—— killed two of the birds, after having several times missed whole flocks of them. The captain seemed very much startled when he saw the animals drop on the waves;—"Will you have the goodness to let down the boat to pick up the game?" said Mr. D——. "Yes, sir," replied he, "if you'l. go off in her, and never return on board this vessel—Here is a serious business—Be assured we have not seen the end of it." He then walked away without offering to give any orders about lowering

13

the boat; and the seamen, who witnessed the transaction, looked as if they would not have obeyed him had he even done so.

Though we saw no land, every thing proved that we were in the West India seas. The sky had, within a few days, begun to assume a more dazzling aspect, and long ranges of conical shaped clouds floated along the horizon. Land birds, with beautiful plumage, often hovered round the vessel, and we sometimes fancied we could discover a vegetable fragrance in the breezes that swelled our sails.

One delightful clear morning, when we were in hourly expectation of making the land, some dolphin appeared astern. As the weather was very moderate, the captain proposed that we should fish for them; and a great many hooks were immediately baited for that purpose by the seamen. We caught large quantities of dolphin, and of another kind of fish, and put the whole into the hands of the steward, with orders that part should be dressed for dinner, and part distributed among the crew.

When the dinner-hour arrived, we all assembled in the cabin, in high spirits, and sat down to table. It being St. George's day, the captain, who was an Englishman, had ordered that every thing should be provided and set forth in the most sumptuous style, and the steward had done full justice to his directions. We made the wines, which were exquisite and abundant, circulate rapidly, and every glass increased our gaiety and good humor, while the influence of our mirth rendered the ladies additionally amusing and animated. The captain remarked, that as there were two clarinet players among the crew, we ought to have a dance upon the quarter-deck at sunset. This proposal was received with much delight, particularly by the females of our party; and the captain had just told the servant in waiting to bid the musicians prepare themselves, when the mate entered the cabin, and said, that the man at the helm had dropped down almost senseless, and that another of the crew was so ill that he could scarcely speak.

The captain, on receiving this information, grew very pale, and seemed at a loss what to reply. At last, he started from his chair, and hurried up the gangway. Our mirth ceased in a moment, though none of us appeared to know why; but the minds of all were evidently occupied by what they had just heard, and Major I——— remarked, with a faultering voice, that seamen were very liable to be taken suddenly ill in hot climates.

After a little time, we sent the servant to inquire what was going forward on deck. He returned immediately, and informed us that the two sailors were worse, and that a third had just been attacked in the same way. He had scarcely said these words when Mrs. I——— gave a shriek, and cried out that her sister had fainted away. This added to our confusion and alarm; and the Major and Mr. D——— trembled so, that they were hardly able to convey the young lady to her state-room.

All conversation was now at an end, and no one uttered a word till Mrs. L—— returned from her sister's apartment. While we were inquiring how the latter was, the captain entered the cabin in a state of great agitation. "This is a dreadful business," said he. "The fact is—it is my duty to tell you—I fear we are all poisoned by the fish we have ate—One of the crew died a few minutes since, and five others are dangerously ill."

"Poisoned! my God! Do you say so? Must we all die?" exclaimed Mrs. L——, dropping on her knees. "What is to be done?" cried the Major distractedly; "are there no means of counteracting it?"—"None that I know of," returned the captain. "All remedies are vain. The poison is always fatal, except—but I begin to feel its effects—support me—can this be imagination?" He staggered to one side, and would have fallen upon the floor, had not I assisted him. Mrs. L——, notwithstanding his apparent insensibility, clung to his arm, crying out, in a tone of despair, "Is there no help—no pity—no one to save us?" and then fainted away on her husband's bosom, who, turning to me, said, with quivering lips, "You are a happy man; you have nothing to imbitter your last moments—Oh, Providence! was I permitted to escape so many dangers, merely that I might suffer this misery?"

Mrs. L—— soon regained her senses, and I endeavored to calm her agitation by remarking, that we might possibly escape the fatal influence of the poison, as some constitutions were not so easily affected by it as others. "Is there then a little hope?" she exclaimed. "Oh! God grant it may be so! How dreadful to die in the midst of the ocean, far from friends and home, and then to be thrown into the deep!"—"There is one thing," said the captain, faintly, "I was going to tell you, that—but this sensation—I mean a remedy."—"Speak on," cried the major, in breathless suspense. "It may have a chance of saving you," continued the former; "you must immediately"—He gave a deep sigh, and dropped his head upon his shoulder, apparently unable to utter a word more. "Oh, this is the worst of all!" cried Mrs. L—— in agony; "he was on the point of telling us how to counteract the effects of the poison—Was it heavenly mercy that deprived him of the power of speech? Can it be called mercy?"—"Hush, hush! you rave," returned her husband. "We have only to be resigned now—Let us at least die together."

The crew had dined about an hour and a half before us, and consequently felt the effects of the poison much earlier than we did. Every one, however, now began to exhibit alarming symptoms. Mr. D—— became delirious; the major lay upon the cabin floor in a state of torpidity; and the captain had drowned all sense and recollection by drinking a large quantity of brandy Mrs. L—— watched her husband and her sister alternately, in a state of quiet despair.

I was comparatively but little affected, and therefore employee myself in assisting others until they seemed to be past all relief, and then sat down, anticipating the horrid consequences which would result from the death of the whole ship's company.

While thus occupied, I heard the steersman call out, " Taken all aback here." A voice, which I knew to be the mate's, immediately answered, " Well, and what 's that to us? Put her before the wind, and let her go where she pleases." I soon perceived, by the rushing of the water, that there was a great increase in the velocity of the ship's progress, and went upon deck to ascertain the cause.

I found the mate stretched upon the top of the companion, and addressed him, but he made no reply. The man at the helm was tying a rope round the tiller, and told me he had become so blind and dizzy, that he could neither steer, nor see the compass, and would therefore fix the rudder in such a manner, as would keep the ship's head as near the wind as possible. On going forward to the bows, I found the crew lying motionless in every direction. They were either insensible of the dangerous situation in which our vessel was, or totally indifferent to it; and all my representations on this head failed to draw forth an intelligible remark from any of them. Our ship carried a great press of canvass, the lower studding sails being set, for we had enjoyed a gentle breeze directly astern, before the wind headed us in the way already mentioned.

About an hour after sunset, almost every person on board seemed to have become worse. I alone retained my senses unimpaired The wind now blew very fresh, and we went through the water at the rate of ten knots an hour. The night looked dreary and turbulent. The sky was covered with large fleeces of broken clouds, and the stars flashed angrily through them, as they were wildly hurried along by the blast. The sea began to run high, and the masts showed, by their incessant creaking, that they carried more sail than they could well sustain

I stood alone abaft the binnacle. Nothing could be heard above or below deck, but the dashing of the surges, and the moanings of the wind. All the people on board were to me the same as dead; and I was tossed about, in the vast expanse of waters, without a companion or fellow-sufferer. I knew not what might be my fate, or where I should be carried. The vessel, as it careered along the raging deep, uncontrolled by human hands, seemed under the guidance of a relentless demon, to whose caprices its ill-fated crew had been mysteriously consigned by some superior power.

I was filled with dread lest we should strike upon rocks, or run ashore, and often imagined that the clouds which bordered the horizon were the black cliffs of some desolate coast. At last, I distinctly saw a light at some distance—I anticipated in stant destruction—I grew irresolute whether to remain upon deck, and face death, or to wait for it below. I soon discovered a ship a little way ahead—I instinctively ran to the helm, and loosed the rope that tied the tiller, which at once bounded back, and knocked me over. A horrible crashing, and loud cries, now broke upon my ear, and I saw that we had got entangled with another vessel. But the velocity with which we swept along, rendered our extrication instantaneous; and, on looking back, I saw a ship, without a bowsprit, pitching irregularly among the waves, and heard the rattling of cordage, and a tumult of voices. But, after a little time, nothing was distinguishable by the eye or by the ear. My situation appeared doubly horrible, when I reflected that I had just been within call of human creatures, who might have saved and assisted all on board, had not an evil destiny hurried us along, and made us the means of injuring those who alone were capable of affording us relief.

About midnight, our fore top-mast gave way, and fell upon deck with a tremendous noise. The ship immediately swung round, and began to labor in a terrible manner, while several waves broke over her successively.

I had just resolved to descend the gangway for shelter, when a white figure rushed past me with a wild shriek, and sprung overboard. I saw it struggling among the billows, and tossing about its arms distractedly, but had no means of affording it any assistance. I watched it for some time, and observed its convulsive motions gradually grow more feeble, but its form soon became undistinguishable amidst the foam of the bursting waves. The darkness prevented me from discovering who had thus committed himself to the deep, in a moment of madness, and I felt a strong repugnance at attempting to ascertain it, and rather wished it might have been some spectre, or the offspring of my perturbed imagination, than a human being.

As the sea continued to break over the vessel, I went down to the cabin, after having closely shut the gangway doors and companion. Total darkness prevailed below. I addressed the captain and all my fellow passengers by name, but received no reply from any of them, though I sometimes fancied I heard moans and quick breathing when the tumult of waters without happened to subside a little. But I thought that it was perhaps imagination, and that they were probably all dead. I began to catch for breath, and felt as if I had been immured in a large coffin along with a number of corpses, and was doomed to linger out life beside them. The sea beat against the vessel with a noise like that of artillery, and the crashing of the bulwarks, driven in by its violence, gave startling proof of the danger that threatened us. Having several times been dashed against the walls and transoms of the cabin by the violent pitching of the ship, I grop-

ed for my bed, and lay down in it, and, notwithstanding the horrors that surrounded me, gradually dropped asleep.

When I awaked, I perceived, by the sunbeams that shone
through the skylight, that the morning was far advanced. The
ship rolled violently at intervals, but the noise of wind and waves
had altogether ceased. I got up hastily, and almost dreaded to
look round, lest I should find my worst anticipations concerning
my companions too fatally realized.

I immediately discovered the captain lying on one side of the
cabin quite dead. Opposite him was Major I——, stretched
along the floor, and grasping firmly the handle of the door of
his wife's apartment. He looked like a dying man, and Mrs.
I——, who sat beside him, seemed to be exhausted with grief
and terror. She tried to speak several times, and at last succeeded in informing me that her sister was better. I could not
discover Mr. D—— any where, and therefore concluded that
he was the person who had leaped overboard the preceding
night.

On going upon deck, I found that every thing wore a new
aspect. The sky was dazzling and cloudless, and not the faintest breath of wind could be felt. The sea had a beautiful bright
green color, and was calm as a small lake, except when an occasional swell rolled from that quarter in which the wind had
been the preceding night; and the water was so clear, that I
saw to the bottom, and even distinguished little fishes sporting
around the keel of our vessel.

Four of the seamen were dead, but the mate and the remaining three had so far recovered, as to be able to walk across the
deck. The ship was almost in a disabled state. Part of the
wreck of the fore top-mast lay upon her bows, and the rigging
and sails of the mainmast had suffered much injury. The mate
told me, that the soundings, and almost every thing else, proved
we were on the Bahama banks, though he had not yet ascertained on what part of them we lay, and consequently could not say
whether we had much chance of soon falling in with any vessel.

The day passed gloomily. They regarded every cloud that
rose upon the horizon as the forerunner of a breeze, which we
above all things feared to encounter. Much of our time was
employed in preparing for the painful but necessary duty of in-
terring the dead. The carpenter soon got ready a sufficient
number of boards; to each of which we bound one of the corpses,
and also weights enough to make it sink to the bottom.

About ten at night, we began to commit the bodies to the
deep. A dead calm had prevailed the whole day, and not a
cloud obscured the sky. The sea reflected the stars so distinctly,
that it seemed as if we were consigning our departed companions to a heaven as resplendent as that above us. There was an
awful solemnity, alike in the scene and in our situation I read

the funeral service, and then we dropped the corpses overboard, one after another. The sea sparkled around each, as its sullen plunge announced that the waters were closing over it, and they all slowly and successively descended to the bottom, enveloped in a ghastly glimmering brightness, which enabled us to trace their progress through the motionless deep. When these last offices of respect were performed, we retired in silence to different parts of the ship.

About midnight, the mate ordered the men to cast anchor, which, till then, they had not been able to accomplish. They likewise managed to furl most of the sails, and we went to bed, under the consoling idea, that though a breeze did spring up, our moorings would enable us to weather it without any risk.

I was roused early next morning by a confused noise upon deck. When I got there, I found the men gazing intently over the side of the ship, and inquired if our anchor held fast.—" Ay, ay," returned one of them, " rather faster than we want it." On approaching the bulwarks, and looking down, I perceived, to my horror and astonishment, all the corpses lying at the bottom of the sea, as if they had just been dropped into it.

We were now exempted from the ravages and actual presence of death, but his form haunted us without intermission. We hardly dared to look over the ship's side, lest our eyes should encounter the ghastly features of some one who had formerly been a companion, and at whose funeral rights we had recently assisted. The seamen began to murmur among themselves, saying that we would never be able to leave the spot where we then were, and that our vessel would remain there and rot.

In the evening a strong breeze sprung up, and filled us with hopes that some vessel would soon come in sight, and afford us relief. At sunset, when the mate was giving directions about the watch, one of the seamen cried out, " Thank Heaven, there they are." And the other ran up to him saying, " Where, where?" He pointed to a flock of Mother Carey's chickens that had just appeared astern, and began to count how many there were of them. I inquired what was the matter, and the mate replied, " Why, only that we've seen the worst, that's all, master. I've a notion we'll fall in with a sail before twenty hours are past."—" Have you any particular reason for thinking so?" said I. " To be sure I have," returned he, " Aren't them there birds an omen of returning good fortune."—" I have always understood," said I, " that these birds indicate bad weather, or some unfortunate event, and this appears to me to be true."—" Ay, ay," replied he, " they say experience teaches fools, and I have found it so; there was a time when I did not believe that these creatures were any thing but common birds, but now I know another story—Oh I've witnessed such strange things! '

Next morning I was awakened by the joyful intelligence tha
a schooner was in sight, and that she had hoisted her flag in answer to our signals. She bore down upon us with a good wind,
and in about an hour hove to, and spoke us. When we had informed them of our unhappy situation, the captain ordered the
boat to be lowered, and came on board of our vessel, with three
of his crew. He was a thick, short, dark-complexioned man, and
his language and accent discovered him to be a native of the
southern states of America. The mate immediately proceeded to
detail minutely all that happened to us, but our visiter paid very
little attention to the narrative, and soon interrupted it, by asking
of what our cargo consisted. Having been satisfied on this point,
he said, " Seeing as how things stand, I conclude you'll be keen
for getting into some port."—" Yes, that of course is our earnest
wish," replied the mate, " and we hope to be able by your assistance to accomplish it."—" Ay, we must all assist one another,"
returned the captain—" Well, I was just calculating, that your
plan would be to run into New Providence—I'm bound for St.
Thomas's, and you can't expect that I should turn about, and go
right back with you—neither that I should let you have any of
my seamen, for I'll not be able to make a good trade unless I get
slick into port. Now I have three nigger slaves on board of me,
—curse them, they don't know much about sea-matters, and are
as lazy as h—l, but keep flogging them, *mister*,—keep flogging
them I say,—by which means, you will make them serve your
ends. Well, as I was saying, I will let you have them blacks to
help you, if you 'll buy them of me at a fair price, and pay it down
in hard cash."—" This proposal," said the mate, " sounds strange
enough to a British seaman;—and how much do you ask for your
slaves?" " I can't let them go under three hundred dollars each,"
replied the captain, " I guess they would fetch more in St.
Thomas's, for they 're prime, blow me."—" Why, there is' nt
that sum of money on board this vessel, that I know of," answered
the mate; " and though I could pay it myself, I 'm sure the owners never would agree to indemnify me. I thought you would
have afforded us every assistance without asking any thing in
return,—a true sailor would have done so at least."—" Well, I
vow you are a strange man," said the captain. " Is' nt it fair
that I should get something for my niggers, and for the chance
I 'll run of spoiling my trade at St. Thomas's, by making myself
short of men? But we shan't split about a small matter, and I 'll
lessen the price by twenty dollars a head."—" It is out of the
question, sir," cried the mate, " I ha   money,"—" Oh there's
no harm done," returned the captai. " we can 't trade, that 's
all   Get ready the boat, boys—I guess your men will soon get
smart again, and then, if the weather holds moderate, you 'll
reach port with the greatest ease."—" You surely do not mean
to leave us in this barbarous way?" cried I ; " the owners of this

vessel would, I am confident, pay any sum rather than that we should perish through your inhumanity."—" Well, mister, I 've got owners too," replied he, " and my business is to make a good voyage for them. Markets are pretty changeable just now, and it won't do to spend time talking about humanity—money 's the word with me."

Having said this, he leaped into the boat, and ordered his men to row towards his own vessel. As soon as they got on board, they squared their topsail, and bore away, and were soon out of the reach of our voices. We looked at one another for a little time with an expression of quiet despair, and then the seamen began to pour forth a torrent of invectives, and abuse, against the heartless and avaricious shipmaster who had inhumanly deserted us. Major L—— and his wife, being in the cabin below, heard all that passed. When the captain first came on board, they were filled with rapture, thinking that we would certainly be delivered from the perils and difficulties that environed us; but as the conversation proceeded, their hopes gradually diminished, and the conclusion of it made Mrs. L—— give way to a flood of tears, in which I found her indulging when I went below.

The mate now endeavored to encourage the seamen to exertion. They cleared away the wreck of the fore-top-mast which had hitherto encumbered the deck, and hoisted a sort of jury-mast in its stead, on which they rigged two sails. When these things were accomplished, we weighed anchor, and laid our course for New Providence. The mate had fortunately been upon the Bahama seas before, and was aware of the difficulties he would have to encounter in navigating them. The weather continued moderate, and after two days of agitating suspense, we made Exuma Island, and cast anchor near its shore.

CAPTAINS PORTLOCK AND DIXON.

This voyage was undertaken for the purposes of commerce; principally, indeed, for the fur-trade, on the north-west coast of America, which had been strongly recommended by Captains Cook and King in their last voyage. Two vessels were fitted out for this purpose, the King George and Queen Charlotte, by a society of merchants and others, the former commanded by Nathaniel Portlock, the latter by George Dixon, both of whom had been with Captain Cook; the King George having sixty men, the Queen Charlotte thirty.

September 20th they quitted St. Helens, and, proceeding to

Guernsey, left it on the 25th. October 16th saw the Canary
Islands, and 24th the Cape de Verde group, anchoring for a short
time in Port Praya Bay, in St. Jago. Proceeding south, they
anchored in Port Egmont, Falkland's Islands, January 5th, 1786,
where, taking in water, they made sail for States Bay, in Terra
del Fuego. Having made a good offing from Cape Horn, they
had tolerable weather; and continuing their route without touching at any place, or meeting with any thing worthy of notice,
dropped anchor 26th May in Karakooa Bay, in Owhyhee, Sandwich Islands.

The natives crowded them very much, bartering a variety of
articles; but were nevertheless extremely troublesome. It was
the general opinion, that it would be impossible to water the vessels without a strong guard, which they could not well spare;
while the people were probably jealous that these vessels were
come to revenge the death of Captain Cook. Next day they
stood out of the bay, lying-to three leagues off, to carry on trade
for hogs, plantains, taro, &c. &c. which proved so serviceable that
the sick, of whom there were several, began rapidly to recover.
June 1st anchored in a bay in Woahoo, another of the islands,
and were received very civilly by the inhabitants. They now
stood for another of the islands, named Oneehow; and, on the 8th,
anchored in yam Bay, where supplies of fruit, vegetables, and
pigs, were willingly afforded by the principal chief Abbenooe,
who seemed strongly their friend, from recollecting Captain Portlock along with Cook. They took leave of him, with regret, on
the 13th, standing for the coast of America.

July 19th made the entrance of Cook's River; and, while looking for good anchorage, were astonished by the report of a great
gun; when, soon afterwards, a party of Russians came on-board,
attended by some Indians; but none understanding the language
of either, no satisfactory information could be gained from them.
Most of the natives had fled from their huts, alarmed perhaps by
the Russians; several bears were seen, but none near enough to
fire at. Two veins of kennel-coal were found, which burned very
well, and the place was, therefore, called Coal Harbor. An elderly chief paying Captain Dixon a visit, informed him that they
h   battle with the Russians, in which the latter were worsted,
and added, that, from the difference of dress, he knew they were
of a different nation.

Quitting this place, they tried for some time to get into Prince
William's Sound; but, by a series of unfavorable winds, failed in
this pursuit. September 23rd, they stood away for the Sandwich
Islands to pass the winter, and return in the spring. November
14th saw the summit of the high mountain in Owhyhee covered with
snow, and employed two or three following days in coasting it, the
natives bringing off a variety of articles to barter for iron and
trinkets The first mate of the King George reporting, that a bay

they intended to anchor in did not admit of good anchorage, this design was dropped. During the time they lay to, hogs, fowls, wild-geese, bread-fruit, plantains, and several other things were procured in considerable quantities; the natives dealing pretty fairly, but committing a variety of thefts, even before their faces, with a dexterity almost inimitable. For several days they continued lying to off the islands of Mowee and Morotoi, procuring refreshments and receiving visits till the 30th, when both ships bore away for King George's Bay, in Whoaboo, where they anchored in safety, after experiencing a variety of winds from all points of the compass.

Here they found every thing tabooed, or forbidden, so that 't became necessary to court the king's favor; for which purpose a present was sent to him, and another to a priest, their acquaintance on the former occasion, who paid them a visit, handing up a fig and plantain, which in these islands are signs of friendship. This was soon followed by a visit from *Taheelerre*, the king, followed by all the chiefs, who took off the taboo. The priest was remarkable for drinking large quantities of the ava, or yava-juice, for which he had two men in constant attendance chewing the root, which, with their spittle, forms this singular and (to us) nauseous beverage. The yava is a root resembling liquorice in shape and color. None but the chiefs and priests have permission to use it, and these are never at the trouble of chewing it themselves; but, as above observed, employ servants; these begin with chewing a sufficient quantity, and when well masticated, it is put into a wooden bowl kept for the purpose, to which a small quantity of water is added; the whole is then strained through a cloth, and, like wine in Europe, it thus forms not merely the drink, but the delight of all parties, feasts, rejoicings, and, in short, every public assemblage of the leading people. Its effects, however, are very pernicious; it is partly intoxicating or rather stupifying; and, by its constant use, the old priest was exceedingly debilitated, and his body covered by a white scurf, resembling the leprosy, which is a common symptom throughout the South Sea islands of its frequent use.

The taboo was again put on without any explanation being given, though several canoes nevertheless came off, but without any women, as had been formerly the case. Afterwards it was understood that one of them had been detected in the King George eating Pork, which being a heinous offence, she was taken as soon as she came on shore, and offered a sacrifice to the gods: human sacrifices, it appears, are here, as in most parts of the South Sea islands, frequently presented, and it is unquestionably the most inhuman and barbarous custom among them.

December 19th weighed, and two days afterwards anchored between Attoui and Wymea, where, after paying and receiving some visits, their former friend Abbenooe came on board with two canoes loaded with provisions, and remained for two or three days, seemingly very well pleased with his new abode. The king also made his appearance; he was stout and well-made, about forty-five years of age, and possessed of more understanding and good-nature than any of his subjects. January 5th caught a shark in the King George, thirteen and a half feet long, eight and a half broad, and six feet in the liver; forty-eight young ones were in her, about eight inches each in length; two whole turtles of sixty pounds each; several small pigs, and a quantity of bones; so that the numbers and the voracity of this fish may be conceived. From this time to the 10th they were employed in purchasing wood, water, provisions, curiosities, and every thing else they wanted; and now, quitting the anchorage, proceeded to yam Bay, in Oneehow, where, after making a few excursions, they departed once more for Wymoa Bay, Attoui.

On the 3d March weighed, and made sail for the coast of America, and on the 24th April saw Montager Island, coming to anchor in the harbor, where there is sufficient shelter from the prevailing winds. The weather continued very variable, several unsuccessful attempts being made to get into Prince Williams Sound, and only a single straggling inhabitant being seen now and then, so that there was no opportunity to trade.

Captain Dixon now made an excursion in his boats up the Sound, and receiving some hints from the natives of a vessel being there, continued his search for several days, and at length got on board a vessel called the Nootka, from Bengal, commanded by Mr. Meares, which had wintered in Snug-corner Cove. The scurvy had made dreadful havoc among them, nearly all the officers and many of the crew having died of this frightful disorder, so that at length the Captain was the only person on board able to walk the deck. Along with his first mate he soon afterwards visited the ships, met with a hearty reception, and received such assistance as he wanted and as the others could afford. From him they learned that few or no furs could be procured here; that several vessels from India had been already on this coast for the purposes of trade; and that two or three were expected next month in the same pursuit, which immediately determined our voyagers to separate and push for different parts of the coast, in order to be before their expected rivals; the Queen Charlotte to proceed to King George's Sound, and Messrs. Hayward and Hill to Cook's River in the King George's long-boat, the latter o remain where she was for the present.

On the 13th May several canoes visited them, in one of which was a chief of great consequence, named Sheenaawa, whose party, like most others, were determined thieves, exerting their ingenuity and tricks for this purpose in an extraordinary degree. They danced, sung, laughed, and diverted the attention of the seamen in every possible way, while slyly their hands were seizing every thing on the decks, so that literally they were smiling in their faces and robbing them at the same time. In the meantime the Queen Charlotte and the long-boat sailed, while the King George shifted to Hinchinbroke Cove. Some of the boats were sent out to trade, which were tolerably successful; but they also suffered from continual thefts, which were sometimes accompanied by menaces, if they attempted to resist the plunderers.

June 9th the Nootka left her former anchorage, where she had been frozen in, and came close to the King George, when the crew of the latter were partly employed in rendering her assistance. Two days afterwards the long-boat returned from Cook's River with a very good cargo, and was again sent off with orders to return by the 20th of July. On the 19th the Nootka sailed. Next day the surgeon took the invalids on shore for an excursion, who, by the use of spruce-beer, which they now brewed in abundance, were rapidly recovering. In the evening observed two Indian boats and several canoes, in which were about twenty-five natives, who came alongside next morning. Their chief, named Taatucktellingnake, was paralytic on one side, had a long beard, and seemed about sixty years of age; his country was called Cheeneecock, situated towards the south-west part of the Sound. July 11th hauled the seine frequently, when not less than two thousand salmon were caught at each haul; and so great were their numbers, that ships prepared for the purpose might have obtained any quantity they wished. The long-boat returned on the 21st, though without so much success as formerly. On the 26th sailed from this place. The natives in general are short in stature, with flat faces and noses, ill-formed legs, but good teeth and eyes; they wear their hair, which is black and straight, very long, but cut it short on the death of a relation, this seeming their only method of mourning. They are attentive to their women, but jealous of them. Their thieving habits seem fixed, the most dexterous being most in esteem, and receiving the greatest applause for the exertion of his talents; he is also distinguished by a fantastical dress, which, while it excites the notice of the spectators, gives the owner additional opportunities of exerting his fingers at their expense.

By the 3d of August had made little progress, from the shifting of the wind. On the 8th, two large boats visited them, with twenty-five men, women, and children on board, who, very different from their other visiters, seemed very honest, and who were invited to dinner in the cabin, when they relished the English cookery so well, that the dishes were quickly obliged to be replenished. These departed in the evening well pleased with their entertainment, promising to return with the means of trading with their new friends.

On the 11th a new tribe visited them from the eastward, with about the same number of persons as the last; four days after, the

long boat returned, having had pretty good success, notwithstand
ing some acts of hostility which they had been compelled to re-
taliate upon the Indians. Another party, from the north-west,
were extremely addicted to thieving, nothing could escape them;
and, when detected, were very impudent, and often threatened
those they robbed. The men were of the size of Europeans, of
a fierce and savage aspect, using daggers and 'ong spears, easily
provoked and ready to indulge their anger.

August 22d weighed and made sail from this coast, having
done as much as it seemed likely they could do in the way of trade.
September 28th made Owhyhee, the principal of the Sandwich
group, when several canoes came off, with whom a brisk trade
for hogs and other refreshments was carried on. At Attoui they
found the Nootka and Queen Charlotte had been there and left
letters for the King George. After procuring what necessaries
they wanted, Captain Portlock directed his course for China
with his cargo of furs; on the 4th November saw Saypan and
Tinian, two of the Ladrone Islands; and on the 21st anchored in
Macao Roads, where Captain Dixon was found, whose transactions shall now be noticed.

After separating, the Queen Charlotte coasted it for some time,
till, seeing an appearance of an inlet, a boat was despatched which
found an excellent harbor, where she soon after anchored. Several canoes came off, from whom some skins were procured,
but by no means so many as they had at first reason to expect
The number of inhabitants was about seventy; the harbor, which
is good, was named Port Mulgrave, and is situated in 59 deg. 3°
min. north latitude; 140 deg. west longitude. The language of
these people is quite different from that of Prince William's Sound
or Cook's River, being extremely uncouth and difficult to pro
nounce. The mode in which they dispose of their dead is remarkable; the head is separated from the body, and both are
wrapped in furs, the former being put into a box, the latter into
an oblong chest which are afterwards preserved and disposed of
in a fanciful way.

June 4th quitted this place, and kept beating to the southward;
a harbor was perceived at a distance, which, upon examination
by the boats, was found to extend to a considerable distance, with
a number of coves here and there, very well calculated for anchorage; it was named Norfolk Sound. The people were at first
civil and well-behaved; but soon became troublesome and thievish, like almost all their brethren on this coast. Trade here
was not very brisk. July 1st saw an island, and were soon surrounded by Indians, who, after gratifying their curiosity in examining the vessel, began to trade, and soon parted with all their
skins. Several fresh tribes visited them almost daily, who, delighted with European articles of barter, were content to leave their furs
behind in exchange. The residence of one was strongly fortified,

resembling a nippah or fortified place, in New Zealand; and, from some circumstances which transpired, Dixon was tempted also to believe they were also like the New Zealanders, cannibals Proceeding to the eastward, eleven canoes came alongside on the 24th with one hundred and eighty persons; but curiosity was the prevailing motive, as they had nothing to sell; and, five days after, no less than two hundred men, women, and children, in eighteen canoes, came off to indulge their curiosity; a num ber that, on this coast, is rarely found in one community. Their chief had the most savage aspect of any yet seen, his whole appearance sufficiently marking him as the leader of a tribe of cannibals. His stature was above the common size, his body spare and thin, and, though seemingly lank and emaciated, his step was bold and firm, his limbs strong and muscular; his eyes, which were large and goggling, seemed ready to start from their sockets, his forehead deeply wrinkled, as well by age as an habitual frown which, joined to a long visage, hollow cheeks, high cheek-bones, and natural ferocity of temper, rendered him a most formidable figure.

August 8th, made sail for the Sandwich Islands. September 2d made Owhyhee, and, after procuring refreshments, stood on for Whahoo, being visited the next day by Abbenooe and the king by whose commands they received abundant supplies of wood, water, and provisions, of which they were in extreme want, several of the crew being nearly dead with the scurvy. Attoui was their next destination, where the chiefs inquired particularly after their friend Po-pote (Captain Portlocke,) and were desirous of contributing all in their power to the assistance of the ship, every one supplying the Captain with a liberality as unbounded as it was unexpected, but which did not go unrewarded; saws, hatchets, nails, and other iron instruments being given to the men, and buttons, beads, and a variety of ornaments to the women.

September 18th made sail for China, and anchored in Macao Roads the 9th November, where being joined as already noticed, by the King George, their meeting was extremely agreeable Captain Portlock was very much surprised in Canton with his old friend Tiaana, from the Sandwhich Islands, who was no less pleased at seeing him, embracing the Captain in the most cordial and affectionate manner.

During his stay, Tiaana was introduced to every place worthy of notice; he was usually dressed in a cloak and fine feather cap, and, to show that he was a person of consequence, carried a spear in his hand. Afterwards, at the persuasion of Mr. Ross, he wore a light satin waistcoat and a pair of trousers. He frequently attended places of public worship, behaving with the greatest decorum, and joining the congregation in the ceremonies of kneeling or standing, as if he had been all his life regularly accustomed to them. Some of the customs of the Chinese displeased him exceedingly, and, during the voyage, was nearly throwing the pilot overboard for some real or imaginary offence; he was, however, of a kind disposition, displaying frequent instances of humanity as well as generosity. Being once at an entertainment, given by one of the Captains at Macao, his compassion was strongly excited after dinner by seeing a number of poor people, in Sampans, crowding round the vessel and asking alms; he solicited his host's permission to give them some food, remarking it was a great shame to let poor people want victuals, and that in his country there were no beggars. In compliance with his importunities, the broken meat was collected under his care, and he distributed it in the most equal and impartial manner. Tiaana was six feet two inches high, exceedingly well-made, but inclined to corpulency; he had a pleasing animated countenance, fine eyes, and otherwise expressive as well as agreeable features. He was universally liked, and, previous to his departure for Attoui, the gentlemen at Canton furnished him with bulls, cows, sheep, goats, rabbits, turkeys, &c. &c. besides all kinds of seeds which could be useful in his island, with directions how to rear and propagate them. The best skins of their cargoes were disposed of to the East India Company for fifty thousand dollars, while the inferior ones were sold to the Chinese, both vessels receiving in return cargoes of tea. February, 6th, 1788, weighed and made sail down the river, quitting Macao finally a day or two afterwards. On the 20th saw the island of Pulo Sapata, four leagues distant; and, 25th, the islands of Aramba; three days afterwards Mr. Lander, surgeon of the Queen Charlotte, died, having been ill for some time, and attended by his brother surgeon, Mr. Hoggan, of the King George. On the 30th of March the ships agreed to separate, and make the best of their way to St. Helena, where the King George arrived the 13th June, and the Queen Charlotte on the 18th. The former at length reached England, without any occurrence worthy of remark, on the 22d August; and the latter the 17th September. Nor was the voyage unfortunate; for though no great gain was made, yet nothing was lost, which, in a new commercial speculation, is not an uncommon occurrence.

CURIOSITY BAFFLED.

Brook Watson was born of humble parentage, in the province of Maine, and in that part of it more appropriately known as Sagadahoc. History has not conveyed to us the incidents of his childhood. As he met with extraordinary success in life, we presume he was pretty soundly drubbed by the schoolmaster and

the older boys   He probably ran about bare-footed in summer,
and in winter, wore old woollen stockings, with the feet cut off,
under the name of leggins, to keep out snow-water.   We imagine he got on the rafts of the lumber-men, and learned to swim,
by being knocked off, as a mischief-maker, into the river.   We
think it likely he occasionally set up, of a moonshiny night, to
watch the bears, as they came down, to reconnoitre the pig-stye;
and we have little doubt that, before he was eleven years old,
he had gone cabin-boy to Jamaica, with a cargo of pine boards
and timber.   But of all this we know nothing.   It is enough for
our story, that, at the age of twenty, Brook Watson was a stout
athletic young man, sailing out of the port of New York to the
West Indies.

The Yankees knew the way to the West Indies a good while
ago; they knew more ways than one.   Their coasting vessels
knew the way, without quadrant or Practical Navigator.   Their
skippers kept their reckoning with chalk, on a shingle, which
they stowed away in the binacle; and, by way of observation,
they held up a hand to the sun.   When they got him over four
fingers, they knew they were straight for the Hole-in-the-wall;
three fingers gave them their course to the Double-headed-shot
Keys, and two carried them down to Barbadoes.   This was one
way; and when the Monsieurs and the Dons at Martinico and
the Havana heard the old New England drums, thumping away
under the very teeth of their batteries, they understood to their
cost, that the Yankees had another way of working their passage.
But Brook Watson went to the Havana in the way of trade.
He went as second mate of the Royal Consort, a fine topsail
schooner of one hundred and fifteen tons; and whether he had
any personal venture in the mules, butter, cheese, codfish, and
shooks, which she took out, is more than history has recorded.

Captain Basil Hall says the Americans are too apt to talk
about the weather.   But in the tropics, in the month of July,
aboard a small ship, without a breath stirring, captain, it is hot;
—you have been a sailor yourself, and you ought to know it.   It
was very hot on board the Royal Consort, about four o'clock in
the afternoon of the 14th of July, 1755.   There was not the
slightest movement in the air; the rays of the sun seemed to burn
down into the water.   Silence took hold of the animated creation.
It was too hot to talk, whistle, or sing; to bark, to crow, or to
bray.   Every thing crept under cover, but Sambo and Cuffee
two fine looking blacks, who sat sunning themselves on the quay,
and thought " him berry pleasant weather," and glistened like a
new Bristol bottle.

Brook Watson was fond of the water; he was not web-footed,
nor was he branchioustegous; (there's for you, see Noah Web
ster;) but were he asked whether he felt most at home on land
or in the water, he would have found it hard to tell.   He had

14*

probably swum the Kennebec, where it is as wide and deep as
the Hellespont between Sestos and Abydos, at least once a day,
for five months in the year, ever since he was eleven years old,
without Lord Byron's precaution of a boat in company, to pick
him up, in case of need.   As his Lordship seemed desirous of
imitating Leander, honesty ought, we think, to have suggested
to him, to go without the boat.   At all events, that was Brook
Watson's way; and we have no doubt, had he been in a boat,
with a head wind, he would have sprung into the river, in order
to get across the sooner.   With this taste for the water, and with
the weather so oppressive as we have described it on the present
occasion, it is not to be wondered at, that Brook Watson should
have turned his thoughts for refreshment, to a change of element;
in other words, that he should have resolved to bathe himself in
the sea.

Such was the fact.   About six o'clock in the afternoon, and
when every other being on board the vessel had crept away
into the cabin or the forecastle, to enjoy a *siesta*, Brook, who had
been sweltering, and panting, and thinking of the banks of the
Kennebec, till his stout gay heart felt like a great ball of lead
within him, tripped up on deck, dropped his loose clothing, and in
an instant was over the side of the vessel.   This was Brook's first
voyage to the West Indies, since he had grown up; and the first
day after his arrival.   He was one of that class of mankind not
bred up to books; and, consequently, in the way of learning wis-
dom only by experience.   What you learn by experience, you
learn pretty thoroughly, but at the same time, occasionally, much
to your cost.   Thus by chopping off a couple of fingers with a
broad axe, you learn, by experience, not to play with edge-tools.
Brook Watson's experience in bathing had hitherto been confined
to the Kennebec; a noble, broad, civil stream, harboring nothing
within its gentle waters more terrible than a porpoise.   The sea-
serpent had not yet appeared.   Brook Watson had certainly
heard of sharks, but at the moment of forming the resolution to
bathe, it had entirely escaped his mind, if it had ever entered it,
that the West India seas were full of them; and so over he went,
with a fearless plunge.

Sambo and Cuffee as we have said, were sitting on the quay,
enjoying the pleasant sunshine, and making their evening repast
of banana, when they heard the plunge into the water by the side
of the Royal Consort, and presently saw Brook Watson emerging
from the deep, his hands to his eyes, to free them from the brine,
balancing up and down, sputtering the water from his mouth, and
then throwing himself forward, hand over hand, as if at length he
really felt himself in his element.

"Oh, Massa Bacra," roared out Sambo, as soon as he could
recover his astonishment enough to speak, "O Senor; he white
man neber go to swim; O, de tiburon; he berry bad bite, come

tiamar—de shark; he hab berry big mouth; he eatee a Senor all up down!"

Such was the exclamation of Sambo, in the best English he had been able to pick up, in a few years service, in unlading the American vessels, that came to the Havana. It was intended to apprise the bold but inexperienced stranger, that the waters were filled with sharks, and that it was dangerous to swim in them. The words were scarcely uttered, and, even if they were heard, had not time to produce their effect, when Cuffee responded to the exclamation of his sable colleague, with—

"O, Madre de Dios, see, see, de tiburon, de shark;—ah San Salvador; ah pobre joven! matar, todo comer, he eat him all down, berry soon!"

This second cry had been drawn from the kind-hearted negro, by seeing, at a distance, in the water, a smooth shooting streak, which an inexperienced eye would not have noticed; but which Sambo and Cuffee knew full well. It was the wake of a shark. At a distance of a mile or two, the shark had perceived his prey; and with the rapidity of sound he had shot across the intervening space, scarcely disturbing the surface with a ripple. Cuffee's practised eye alone had seen a flash of his tail, at the distance of a mile and a half; and raising his voice to the utmost of his strength, he had endeavored to apprise the incautious swimmer of his danger. Brook heard the shout, and turned his eye in the direction, in which the negro pointed; and well skilled in all the appearances of the water, under which he could see almost as well as in the open air, he perceived the sharp forehead of the fearful animal rushing towards him, head on, with a rapidity which bade defiance to flight. Had he been armed with a knife, or even a stick, he would not have feared the encounter; but would have coolly waited his chance, like the negroes of the West Indies and the Spanish Main, and plunged his weapon into the opening maw of the ravenous animal. But he was wholly naked and defenceless. Every one on board the Royal Consort was asleep; and it was in vain to look for aid from that quarter. He cast a glance, in his extremity, to Sambo and Cuffee; and saw them, with prompt benevolence. throw themselves into a boat, to rescue him; but meantime the hungry enemy was rushing on.

Brook thought of the Kennebec; he thought of its green banks, and its pleasant islands. He thought of the tall trunks of the pine trees, scathed with fire, which stood the grim sentinels of the forest, over the roof where he was born. He thought of the log school-house. He thought of his little brothers and sisters, and of his mother; and there was another image that passed through his mind, and almost melted into cowardice his manly throbbing heart. He thought of Mary Atwood, and—but he had to think of himself. For though these tumultuous emotions and a thousand others rushed through his mind in a moment, crowding that one moment with a long duration of suffering; yet in the same fleet moment, the dreadful monster had shot across the entire space that separated him from Brook; and had stopped, as if its vitality had been instantly arrested, at the distance of about twelve feet from our swimmer. Brook had drawn himself up in the most pugnacious attitude possible; and was treading water with great activity. The shark, probably unused to any signs of making battle, remained, for one moment, quiet; and then, like a flash of lightning, shot sideling off, and came round in the rear. Brook, however, was as wide awake as his enemy. If he had not dealt with sharks before, he knew something of the ways of bears and catamounts; and contriving himself to get round, about as soon as the shark, he still presented a bold front to the foe.

But a human creature, after all, is out of his element in the water; and he fights with a shark, to about the same disadvantage as the shark himself, when dragged up on deck, fights with a man. He flounces and flings round, and makes formidable battle with tail and maw; but he is soon obliged to yield. The near approach to a fine plump healthy Yankee was too much for the impatience of our shark. The plashing of the oars of Sambo and Cuffee, warned the sagacious monster of gathering foes. Whirling himself over on his back, and turning up his long white belly, and opening his terrific jaws, set round with a double row of broad serrated teeth, the whole roof of his mouth paved with horrent fangs, all standing erect, sharp, and rigid, just permitting the blood-bright red to be seen between their roots, he darted toward Brook Brook's self-possession stood by him in this trying moment. He knew very well if the animal reached him in a vital part, that instant death was his fate; and with a rapid movement, either of instinct or calculation, he threw himself backward, kicking, at the same moment, at the shark. In consequence of this movement, his foot and leg passed into the horrid maw of the dreadful monster, and were severed in a moment,—muscles, sinews, and bone. In the next moment, Sambo and Cuffee were at his side; and lifted him into the boat, convulsed with pain, and fainting with loss of blood. The Royal Consort was near, and the alarm was speedily given. Brook was taken on board; the vessel's company were roused; bandages and styptics were applied; surgical advice was obtained from the shore, and in due season the hearty and sound-constitutioned youth recovered.

The place of his lost limb was supplied by a wooden one; and industry, temperance, probity, and zeal, supplied the place of a regiment of legs, when employed to prop up a lazy and dissipated frame. The manly virtues of our hero found their reward; his sufferings were crowned with a rich indemnity. He rose from one step to another of prosperity. Increased means opened a wider sphere of activity and usefulness. He was extensively engaged in public contracts, which he fulfilled to the advantage of the government as well as his own;—a thing rare enough among contracting *bipeds*. From a contractor, he became a commissary, and from commissary, Lord Mayor of London.

Behold our hero now, at the head of the magistracy of the metropolis of the British empire, displaying, in this exalted station, the virtues, which had raised him to it from humble life; and combating the monsters of vice and corruption, which infest the metropolis, as boldly as he withstood the monster of the deep, and with greater success. All classes of his majesty's subjects, who had occasion to approach him, enjoyed the benefit of his civic qualities; and his fame spread far and wide through Great Britain Nor was it confined, as may well be supposed, to the British isles. The North American colonies were proud of their fellow citizen, who, from poverty and obscurity, had reached the Lord Mayor's chair. The ambitious mother quoted him to her emulous offspring. The thrifty merchant at Boston, would send a quintal of the best Isle-of-Shoals, as a present to his worship; and once, on the annual election-day, the reverend gentleman, who officiated on the occasion, in commenting on the happy auspices of the day, (it was just after the receipt of a large sum of money from England, on account of the expenses of the colony in the old war,) included among them, that a son of New England had been entrusted with the high and responsible duties of the Chief Magistracy of the metropolis of his majesty's dominions.

It may well be supposed, that the Americans, who went *home* (as it was called, even in the case of those, who were born and bred in the colonies) were very fond of seeking the acquaintance of *Sir* Brook Watson, for knighthood had followed in the train of his other honors. Greatly to the credit of his worship, he uniformly received them with kindness and cordiality, and instead of shunning whatever recalled his humble origin, he paid particular attention to every one, that came from Sagadahoc. There was but a single point in his history and condition, on which he evinced the least sensitiveness, and this was the painful occurrence, which had deprived him of his limb. Regret at this severe loss; a vivid recollection of the agony, which had accompanied it; and probably no little annoyance at the incessant interrogatories to which it had exposed him through life, and the constant repetition, to which it had driven him of all the details of this event, had unitedly made it a very sore subject with him. He at length ceased himself to allude to it, and his friends perceived, by the brevity of his answers, that it was a topic on which he wished to be spared.

Among the Americans who obtained an introduction to his worship in London, were Asahel Ferret and Richard Teasewell, shrewd Yankees, who had found their way over to England, with a machine for dressing flax. They had obtained a letter of recommendation from a merchant in Boston to Sir Brook. They had no reason to murmur at their reception. They were invited to dine with his lordship and treated with hearty hospitality and friendship. The dinner passed rather silently away, but with no neglect of the main end of the dinner. Our Yankee visiters did full justice to his worship's bountiful fare They found his mutton fine; his turbot fine; his strong beer genuine (as they called it), and his wine most extraordinary good; and as the bottle circ lated, the slight repression of spirits, under which they commenced, passed off. They became proportionally inquisitive, and opened upon their countryman a full battery of questions. They began with the articles, that formed the dessert; and asked whether his lordship's peaches were raised in his lordship's own garden. When told they were not, they made so bold as to inquire, whether they were a present to his lordship or boughten The mayor having answered that they came from the market,—"might they presume to ask how much they had cost?" They were curious to be informed whether the silver gilt spoons were solid metal;— how many little ones his worship had; what *meeting* he went to, and whether his lordship had ever heard Mr. Whitefield preach; and if he did not think him a fine speaker. They were anxious to know, whether his lordship went to see his Majesty sociably now, as you would run in and out at a neighbor's; whether her majesty was a comely personable woman, and whether it was true, that the prince was left-handed, and the princess pock-marked. They inquired what his lordship was worth; how much he used to get, as commissary; how much he got as lord mayor; and whether her ladyship had not something handsome of her own. They were anxious to know, what his worship would turn his hand to, when he had done being lord mayor; how old he was; whether he did not mean to go back and live in America; and whether it was not very pleasant to his lordship, to meet a countryman from New England. To all these questions and a great many more, equally searching and to the point, his lordship answered good-humoredly; sometimes with a direct reply, sometimes evasively, but never impatiently. He perceived, however, that the appetite of their curiosity grew, from what it fed on; and that it would be as wise in him to hope for respite on their being satisfied, as it was in the rustic to wait for the river to run out.

These sturdy questioners had received a hint, that his lordship was rather sensitive, on the subject of his limb, and not fond of having it alluded to. This, of course, served no other purpose, than that of imparting to them an intense desire to know every thing about it. They had never heard by what accident his lordship had met this misfortune; as indeed the delicacy, which had for years been observed on the subject, in the circle of his friends, had prevented the singular circumstances, which in early youth deprived him of his leg, from being generally known. It was surmised by some, that he had broken it by a fall on the ice, in crossing the Kennebec in the winter. Others affirmed, of their certain knowledge, that he was crushed in a raft of timber; and a third had heard a brother-in-law declare, that he stood by him, when it was shot off, before Quebec. In fact, many persons, not altogether as curious as our visitants, really wished they knew how his lordship lost his leg.

This prevailing mystery, the good humor with which his worship had answered their other questions, and the keen sting of curiosity wrought upon the visiters, till they were almost in a frenzy. The volubility, with which they put their other questions, arose, in part, from the flutter of desire to probe this hidden matter. They looked at his worship's wooden leg; at each other : at the carpet; at the ceiling; and finally, one of them, by way of a feeler, asked his lordship, if he had seen the new model of a cork leg, contrived by Mr. Rivetshin and highly commended in the papers. His lordship had not heard of it. Baffled in this, they asked his lordship, whether he supposed it was very painful to lose a limb, by a cannon ball or a grape shot. His worship really could not judge, he had never had that misfortune. They then inquired whether casualties did not frequently happen to lumberers on the Kennebec river. The mayor replied that the poor fellows did sometimes slip off a rolling log, and get drowned "Were there not bad accidents in crossing the river on the ice?" His lordship had heard of a wagon of produce, that had been blown down upon the slippery surface of the ice, horses and all, as far as Merry Meeting Bay, when it was brought up by a shot from fort Charles, which struck the wagon between perch and axle-tree and knocked it over; but his lordship pleasantly added, he believed it was an exaggeration.

Finding no possibility of getting the desired information by any indirect means, they began to draw their breath hard; to throw quick glances at each other and at his lordship's limb; and in a few moments one of them, with a previous jerk of his head and compression of his lips, as much as to say, " I will know it or die," ventured to take the liberty to inquire, if he might presume so far, as to ask his lordship, by what accident he had been deprived of the valuable limb, which appeared to be wanting to his lordship's otherwise fine person.

His lordship was amused at the air and manner with which the question was put; like those of a raw lad, who shuts his eye, when taking aim with a gun. The displeasure he would otherwise have felt was turned into merriment; and he determined to sport with their unconscionable curiosity.

"Why, my friends, said he, what good would it do you to be informed? How many questions I have already answered you this morning! You now ask me how I lost my leg; if I answer you on that point, you will wish to know the when, and the wherefore; and instead of satisfying I shall only excite your curiosity."

" Oh no," they replied, " if his lordship would but condescend to answer them this one question, they would agree never to ask him another."

His lordship paused a moment, musing; and then added, with a smile, " But will you pledge yourselves to me to that effect:"

Oh, they were willing to lay themselves under any obligation; they would enter into bond not to trouble his lordship with any farther question; they would forfeit a thousand pounds, if they did not keep their word.

" Done, gentlemen," said his lordship, " I accept the condition —I will answer your question, and take your bond never to put me another."

The affected mystery, the delay, and the near prospect of satisfying their own curiosity, rendered our visiters perfectly indifferent to the conditions, on which they were to obtain the object of their desire. His lordship rang for a clerk, to whom he briefly explained the case, directing him to draw up a bond, for the signature of his inquisitive countrymen. The instrument was soon produced, and ran in the following terms.

" KNOW ALL MEN BY THESE PRESENTS,
That we, Asahel Ferret and Richard Teasewell, of the town of Gossipbridge and county of Tolland, in his majesty's colony of Connecticut, in New England, do hereby jointly and severally acknowledge ourselves firmly holden and bound to his worship, Sir Brook Watson, the present Lord Mayor of London, to his heirs, and assigns, in the sum of one thousand pounds sterling; and we do hereby, for ourselves, our heirs, and assigns, covenant and agree, to pay to his said worship, the present Lord Mayor of London, to his heirs and assigns, the aforesaid sum of one thousand pounds sterling, when the same shall become due, according to the tenor of this obligation;—

And the condition of this obligation is such, that, whereas the aforesaid Ferret and Teasewell, of the town and county, &c. and colony, &c. have signified to his aforesaid worship their strong desire, to be informed, apprised, instructed, told; made acquainted, satisfied, put at rest, and enlightened, how and in what manner his aforesaid worship became deprived, mutilated, maimed, curtailed, retrenched, damnified, abated, abscinded, amputated, or abridged in the article of his worship's right leg; and whereas his aforesaid worship, willing to gratify the laudable curiosity of the said Ferret and Teasewell; but desirous also to put some period, term, end, close, estoppel, and finish, to the numerous questions, queries, interrogatories, inquiries, demands, and examinations of the said Ferret and Teasewell, whereby his aforesaid worship hath been sorely teased, worried, wherreted, perplexed, annoyed, tormented, afflicted, soured, and discouraged; therefore, to the end aforesaid, and in consideration of the premises aforesaid, his worship aforesaid, hath covenanted, consented, agreed, promised, contracted, stipulated, bargained, and doth, &c. with the said Ferret and Teasewell, &c. &c. to answer such question, as they, the said Ferret and Teasewell, shall put and propound to his said worship, in the premises, touching the manner, &c. &c. truly, and without guile, covin, fraud, or falsehood; and the said Ferret and Teasewell, also, do on their part, covenant, consent, agree, promise, stipulate, and bargain with his aforesaid worship, and have, &c. that they will never propound, or put any farther or different question to his aforesaid worship, during the term of their natural lives;—And if the said Ferret and Teasewell, or either of them, contrary to the obligation of this bond, shall at any time hereafter, put or propound any farther, or other, or different question to his said worship, they shall jointly and severally, forfeit and pay to his said worship, the sum aforesaid, of one thousand pounds, sterling money; and if, during the term of their natural lives, they shall utterly forbear, abstain, renounce, abandon, abjure, withhold, neglect, and omit, to propound any such, other, or farther, or different question, to his aforesaid worship, then this bond shall be utterly null, void, and of no effect;—but otherwise in full force and validity.

Witness our hand and seal, this tenth day of October, in the year of our Lord, one thousand seven hundred and sixty-nine.

ASAHEL FERRET.   (Seal.)
RICHARD TEASEWELL.   (Seal.)

Signed, sealed, and delivered,
    in presence of
FRANCIS FAIRSERVICE.
SAMUEL SLYPLAY.

Middlesex, ss.   10th October, A. D. 1769.   Then personally appeared before me, the said Asahel Ferret and Richard Teaswell, and acknowledged the aforesaid obligation to be their free act and deed.

Attest   THOMAS TRUEMAN, *Justice of the Peace.*

Stamp, 3s."

The instrument was executed, handed to his worship, and deposited in his scrutoire.

"Now gentlemen," said he, "I am ready for your question."

They paused a moment, from excess of excitement and anticipation. Their feelings were like those of Columbus, when he beheld a light from the American shores; like Dr. Franklin's, when he took the electric spark from the string of his kite

15

" Your lordship then will please to inform us, how your lordship's limb was taken off."

" It was bitten off!"

They started, as if they had taken a shock from an electric
battery; the blood shot up to their temples· they stepped each a
pace nearer to his lordship, and with staring eyes, gaping mouth,
and with uplifted hands, were about to pour out a volley of questions, " by whom, by what bitten; how, why, when!"

But his lordship smilingly put his forefinger to his lip, and then
pointed to the scrutoire, where their bond was deposited.

They saw, for the first time in their lives, that they were taken
in; and departed rather embarrassed and highly dissatisfied, with
having passed an afternoon, in finding out that his lordship's leg
was bitten off. This mode of losing a limb being one of very
rare occurrence, their curiosity was rather increased than allayed
by the information; and as they went down stairs, they were heard
by the servants, muttering to each other, " Who, do you 'spose,
bit off his leg?"—*N. England Magazine.*

THE RETURN OF THE ADMIRAL.

By Barry Cornwall.

How gallantly, how merrily,
  We ride along the sea !
The morning is all sunshine,
  The wind is blowing free ;
The billows are all sparkling,
  And bounding in the light
Like creatures in whose sunny veins
  The blood is running bright
All nature knows our triumph :
  Strange birds about us sweep ;
Strange things come up to look at us,
  The masters of the deep ;
In our wake, like any servant,
  Follows even the bold shark—
Oh, proud must be our Admiral
  Of such a bonny barque !

Proud, proud must be our Admiral
  (Though he is pale to-day,)
Of twice five hundred iron men,
  Who all his nod obey ;
Who've fought for him, and conquered—
  Who've won with sweat and gore,
Nobility ! which he shall have
  Whene'er he touch the shore.
Oh ! would I were our Admiral,
  To order, with a word—
To lose a dozen drops of blood,
  And straight rise up a lord !

ı 'd shout e'en to yon shark, there,
  Who follows in our lee,
" Some day I 'll make thee carry me,
  Like lightning through the sea ! "

—The Admiral grew paler,
  And paler as we flew ;
Still talked he to his officers,
  And smiled upon his crew ;
And he looked up at the heavens,
  And he looked down en the sea,
And at last he spied the creature
  That kept following in our lee.
He shook—'t was but an instant—
  For speedily the pride
Ran crimson to his heart,
  Till all chances he defied ;
It threw boldness on his forehead ;
  Gave firmness to his breath ;
And he stood like some grim warrior
  New risen up from death.

That night, a horrid whisper
  Fell on us where we lay,
And we knew our old fine Admiral
  Was changing into clay ;
And we heard the wash of waters,
  Though nothing could we see,
And a whistle and a plunge
  Among the billows in our lee !
'Till dawn we watched the body
  In its dead and ghastly sleep,
And next evening at sunset,
  It was slung into the deep !
And never, from that moment,
  Save one shudder through the sea
Saw we (or heard) the shark
  That had followed in our lee !

SHIPWRECKED MARINERS SAVED THROUGH A DREAM.

In June, 1695, the ship Mary, commanded by Captain Jones, with a crew of twenty-two men, sailed from Spithead for the West Indies; and contrary to the remonstrances of one Adams on board, the master steered a course which brought the vessel on the Caskets, a large body of rocks, two or three leagues south east of Guernsey. It was about three o'clock in the morning, when the ship struck against the high rock, and all the bows were stove in; the water entered most rapidly, and in less than half an hour, she sunk. Those of the crew who were in the fore part of the ship, got upon the rock; but the rest, to the number of eight, who were in the hind part, sunk directly, and were seen no more. Adams and thirteen more, who were on the rock, had not time to save any thing out of the ship for their subsistence; and the place afforded them none, nor even any shelter from the heat of the sun. The first day they went down the rock, and gathered limpets, but finding that they increased their thirst, they eat no more of them. The third day they killed the dog which had swam to the rock, and eat him, or rather chewed his flesh, to allay their thirst, which was excessive. They passed nine days without any other food, and without any prospect of relief; their flesh wasted, their sinews shrunk, and their mouths parched with thirst; on the tenth day, they agreed to cast lots, that two of the company should die, in order to preserve the rest a little longer. When the two men were marked out, they were willing and ready to stab themselves, as had been agreed on with horrible ingenuity, in order that those who were living might put a tobacco pipe into the incision, and each in his turn suck so many gulphs of blood to quench his thirst! But although the necessity was so pressing, they were yet unwilling to resort to this dreadful extremity, and resolved to stay one day more in hopes of seeing a ship. The next day, no relief appearing, the two wretched victims on whom the lots had fallen, stabbed themselves, the rest sucked their blood, and were thus revived for a short time. They still continued to make signals of distress, and having hoisted a piece of a shirt on a stick, it was at length seen by a ship's crew of Guernsey, one Taskard, master, bound from that island to Southampton. They were all taken on board, when each had a glass of cider and water to drink, which refreshed them considerably; but two of them eagerly seizing a bottle, drank to excess, which caused the death of both in less than two hours.

The most remarkable circumstance connected with this shipwreck, is yet to be mentioned. It was with great reluctance that Taskard brought his ship near the Caskets, which were out of his course; but he was very much importuned by his son, who had twice dreamed that there were men in distress upon these rocks. The father refused to notice the first dream, and was angry with his son; nor would he have yielded on the second, if there had been a favorable wind to go on his own course

A POLITE SEA-ROBBER.

We often read of extremely polite and gentlemanly highwaymen, who rob with such marvellous courtesy that a man can hardly feel it in his heart to withhold his watch, his purse, or aught of goods and chattels that he may chance to have about him.—But it is quite otherwise with your sea robbers, *alias* pirates, who are represented as a most brutal and unfeeling set, who have not the least dash of politeness about them, to redeem their characters from unmitigated odium. Such being their general reputation, it is with no slight feeling of relief that we read the account of so polished and courteous a villain as the one described below. It is extracted from the "Adventures of a Wanderer." He had shipped at New Orleans, on board the Governor Griswold, bound to Havana and Liverpool, as steward:—

We got (says he) under way, and proceeded down the river until we came to a place called the English Turn, when a boat, manned by twelve or fourteen men, came off from shore, and when they had arrived within hail they called to us and asked if we wanted a pilot. The Captain answered, "No;" whereupon the man in the stern of the boat ordered one of the men to throw him à rope. The rope was handed him, and it being made fast to the boat, he came alongside. He ascended the ladder, and came on board with all his men, excepting four who remained in the boat. The captain of these desperadoes was a tall man, dark complexioned, and terrible in aspect. His eye was black and piercing, his nose slightly Roman, and he wore a huge pair of sable mustachios. His men were a ferocious looking band, hardy and sun burnt. He saluted the captain in a courteous manner, and was profuse in compliments.

His men, who wore long red Indian stockings, red caps, and were armed with pistols and knives, sauntered carelessly about the deck.

The pirate captain asked our captain where he was bound; he answered correctly, "To Liverpool via Havana."

Our captain then cut short the interrogation of the pirate, by saying, "I know your business."

The pirate then turned to our crew, and asked them what sort of usage they had received since they left Europe.

"Tolerable," they replied, "but very little grog."

The pirate then called for the steward. I made my appearance "Have you plenty of grog on board?" inquired he.

I replied in the affirmative. "Fill up that bucket," said he, "and carry it down the forecastle for the men to drink." I took up the bucket at which he pointed, carried it into the cabin, and filled it with liquor. I then took it forward to the forecastle, where the men received it and conveyed it below.

As soon as the crew had got below, and were assembled around the bucket, the pirate placed two of his men upon the scuttle to prevent any of the crew from coming on deck, while he with two of his gang stuck close to the captain and mate.—"Now, steward," said the pirate, "go down and invite all your passengers to come on deck." I did as I was ordered. Our passengers were a lady and two small children, and a gentleman who had been engaged in teaching a school in New Orleans, out having rece'ved a letter purporting that the death of a near relation had left him heir to a large fortune, had embarked for his home, which was London.

These persons came on deck. The lady was much frightened, but the pirate told her to be under no apprehension, and soothed her with language which would not have disgraced the court of Great Britain. The pirate now gave orders to bring up the gentleman's trunk. The trunk was laid at his feet.—"Now " said he, "bring up all the captain and mate's property." They also were produced.

He then proceeded to overhaul the captain's trunk, which contained " no great shakes."

'Captain, you have a very poor kit!' said he, with a scornful smile.

The pirate then examined the passenger's trunk. It contained about four hundred and forty dollars in specie. In rummaging the trunk, the pirate fell in with the letter containing the information in respect to the fortune which had been left the passenger. This letter the pirate read, and giving a significant glance at the fortunate man whose direction it bore, folded it up carefully and laid it down.

He then turned to the captain, and asked him if the man had paid his passage. ' No,' answered the captain. ' How much does his passage cost?' inquired the pirate. 'Two hundred and twenty dollars,' replied the captain. 'That you must lose,' said the pirate.

Then turning to the passenger—' You,' said he, ' I will treat fairly! You will want,' continued the pirate, 'when you arrive at Liverpool, two dollars to pay the porter for carrying your trunk;' he laid down the money; 'your passage to London will cost you £2 10s,' he counted it out and placed it with the two dollars; your dinner will come to five shillings, and you may want £2 more to treat some of your friends.' he laid down the money with the rest, ' and for fear that will not be sufficient, here are twenty-five dollars more.' He presented the amount of these several items to the passenger, gave the remainder to one of his gang, and told him to pass it into the boat. He then very courteously asked the time of day. The captain pulled out a fine watch, and answered that it was half past three. 'Your watch takes my fancy mightily,' said the pirate, and taking it from the captain, he put it into his fob with great *nonchalance*, and walked away to the forecastle. 'Come up here two of you who are sober,' said he. Two of them stumbled up, and the rest came reeling after.

"Go down into the cabin, and bring me up all the small arms you can find," said the pirate. The two first sailors went down, and soon returned with an old fowling piece and a pair of pistols

"Now," said he, turning to the sailors, "if any of you, boys, wish to change your situation for better pay and a shorter passage, I will give you a chance; for rent I am after and rent I'll have! But stop!" cried he, "this lady I had almost forgotten; come here, madam, and let me hear a little of your worldly concerns."

She immediately commenced an eloquent harangue, accompanied with tears. She had gone on for some time in this manner, when the pirate immediately cried, 'Avast! avast! there, that's enough, I'd sooner face the battery of a ninety-eight, than stem the torrent of female eloquence!"

He then ordered some brandy for himself and his men.

The liquor was brought; I poured out a glassful for him, when he said, "Stop! captain just be so good as to drink this off yourself! after you is manners. I don't know what some of you Yankee inventors may have put into this liquor. You may have thrown an onyx in the cup. The captain drank it off readily The pirate eyed the captain closely for a few moments, and then said to his followers, "Come, my boys, we may venture," and the decanter was soon drained of its contents. The pirate then pointed to the maintop, and requested the captain to take a walk up that way. "And you, Mr. Mate," said he, "begin to travel up the forerigging. But mind!" said he, "stop when I tell you!" The captain and mate had proceeded half way up the lower rigging, when he summoned them to halt. The captain was about stepping upon the next rattling, when the pirate again hailed him—"If you stir an inch backward or forward," said he, "you will come down faster than you went up." The captain looked down and saw several pistols levelled at him, ready to be discharged on the instant. He then remained stationary.

Then the pirate taking off his cap, addressed the passengers. He told them he was once poor himself, and therefore knew how to sympathize with persons in distress. He hoped they would be grateful for the lenity which he had shown them, and then wishing them a pleasant voyage, he stepped over the side into his boat, and was soon lost to our view beneath the foliage of the thick underwood which lined the shore and hung over the green wave

THE SEA-BIRD'S SONG.—BY J. G. BRAE

On the deep is the mariner's danger,
  On the deep is the mariner's death;
Who to fear of the tempest a stranger,
  Sees the last bubble burst of his breath?
        'Tis the sea-bird, sea-bird, sea-bird,
          Lone looker on despair,
        The sea-bird, sea-bird, sea-bird,
          The only witness there.

Who watches their course who so mildly,
  Career to the kiss of the breeze?
Who lists to their shrieks, who so wildly
  Are clasped in the arms of the seas!
        'Tis the sea-bird, sea-bird, sea-bird, &c.

Who hovers on high o'er the lover,
  And her who has clung to his neck?
Whose wing is the wing that can cover,
  With its shadows the foundering wreck?
        'Tis the sea-bird, sea-bird, sea-bird. &c

My eye is the light of the billow,
  My wing on the wake of the wave—
I shall take to my breast—for a pillow—
  The shroud of the fair and the brave—
        I'm the sea-bird, sea-bird, sea-bird, &c

My foot on the ice-berg has lighted
  When hoarse the wild winds veer about,
My eye when the bark is benighted
  Sees the lamp of the light-house go out.
        I'm the sea-bird, sea-bird, sea-bird,
          Lone looker on despair,
        The sea-bird, sea-bird, sea-bird,
          The only witness there.

FEELINGS EXCITED BY A LONG VOYAGE

VISIT TO A NEW CONTINENT.—BY WASHINGTON IRVING.

To an American visiting Europe, the long voyage he has to
make is an excellent preparative. From the moment you lose
sight of the land you have left, all is vacancy until you step upon
the opposite shore, and are launched at once into the bustle and
novelties of another world.

I have said that at sea all is vacancy. I should correct the expression. To one given up to day-dreaming, and fond of losing himself in reveries, a sea voyage is full of subjects for meditation; but then they are the wonders of the deep, and of the air, and rather tend to abstract the mind from worldly themes. I delighted to loll over the quarter railing, or to climb to the main top on a calm day, and to muse for hours together on the tranquil bosom of a summer's sea; or to gaze upon the piles of golden clouds just peering above the horizon, fancy them some fairy realms, and people them with a creation of my own, or to watch the gentle undulating billows rolling their silver volumes as if to die away on those happy shores.

There was a delicious sensation of mingled security and awe, with which I looked down from my giddy height on the monsters of the deep at their uncouth gambols. Shoals of porpoises tumbling about the bow of the ship; the grampus slowly heaving his huge form above the surface, or the ravenous shark, darting like a spectre through the blue waters. My imagination would conjure up all that I had heard or read of the watery world beneath me, of the finny herds that roam its fathomless valleys; of the shapeless monsters that lurk among the very foundations of the earth; and those wild phantasms which swell the tales of fishermen and sailors.

Sometimes a distant sail gliding along the edge of the ocean would be another theme for idle speculation. How interesting this fragment of a world hastening to rejoin the great mass of existence! What a glorious monument of human invention, that has thus triumphed over the wind and wave; has brought the ends of the earth to communion, has established an interchange of blessings, pouring into the steril regions of the north all the luxuries of the south; diffused the light of knowledge and the charities of cultivated life; and has thus bound together those scattered portions of the human race, between which nature seemed to have thrown an insurmountable barrier!

We one day descried some shapeless object drifting at a distance. At sea every thing that breaks the monotony of the surrounding expanse attracts the attention. It proved to be the mast of a ship that must have been completely wrecked; for there were the remains of handkerchiefs by which some of the crew had fastened themselves to this spar to prevent their being washed off by the waves. There was no trace by which the name of the ship could be ascertained. The wreck had evidently drifted about many months; clusters of shell-fish had fastened about it, and long sea weeds flaunted at its sides. But where, thought I, is the crew? Their struggle has long been over;—they have gone down amidst the roar of the tempest;—their bones lie whitening in the caverns of the deep. Silence—oblivion, like the waves have closed over them, and no one can tell the story of their end.

What sighs have been wafted after that ship! what prayers offered up at the deserted fireside of home! How often has the mistress, the wife, and the mother, pored over the daily news, to catch some casual intelligence of this rover of the deep! How has expectation darkened into anxiety—anxiety into dread—and dread into despair! Alas! not one memento shall ever return for love to cherish. All that shall ever be known is that she sailed from her port " and was never heard of more."

The sight of the wreck as usual gave rise to many dismal anecdotes. This was particularly the case in the evening when the weather which had hitherto been fair began to look wild and threatening, and gave indications of one of those sudden storms, that will sometimes break in upon the serenity of a summer voyage. As we sat around the dull light of a lamp, in the cabin, that made the gloom more ghastly, every one had his tale of ship wreck and disaster. I was particularly struck with a short one related by the captain.

" As I was once sailing," said he, " in a fine stout ship, across the banks of Newfoundland, one of the heavy fogs that prevail in those parts rendered it impossible for me to see far ahead even in the daytime; but at night the weather was so thick that we could not distinguish any object at twice the length of our ship. I kept lights at the mast head and a constant watch forward to look out for fishing-smacks, which are accustomed to lie at anchor on the banks. The wind was blowing a smacking breeze, and we were going at a great rate through the water. Suddenly the watch gave the alarm of " a sail ahead!" but it was scarcely uttered till we were upon her. She was a small schooner at anchor with her broad side towards us. The crew were all asleep, and had neglected to hoist a light. We struck her just amid-ships. The force, the size, and weight of our vessel, bore her down below the waves; we passed over her and were hurried on our course.

"As the crashing wreck was sinking beneath us, I had a glimpse of two or three half naked wretches, rushing from her cabin; they had just started from their cabins to be swallowed shrieking by the waves. I heard their drowning cry mingled with the wind. The blast that bore it to our ears swept us out of all farther hearing. I shall never forget that cry! It was some time before we could put the ship about, she was under such headway We returned as nearly as we could guess to the place where the ship was anchored. We cruised about for several hours in the dense fog. We fired several guns, and listened if we might hear the hallo of any survivors; but all was silent—we never heard nor saw any thing of them more!"

It was a fine sunny morning when the thrilling cry of land. was given from the mast-head. I question whether Columbus, when he discovered the new world, felt a more delicious throng of sensations than rush into an American's bosom when he first comes in sight of Europe. There is a volume of associations in the very name. It is that land of promise, teeming with every thing of which his childhood has heard, or on which his studious years have pondered.

From that time until the period of our arrival it was all feverish excitement. The ships of war that prowled like guardian giants round the coast; the headlands of Ireland stretching out into the channel; the Welsh mountains towering into the clouds; all were objects of intense interest. As we sailed up the Mersey, I reconnoitred the shores with a telescope. My eye dwelt with delight on neat cottages, with their trim shrubberies and green grass plots. I saw the mouldering ruins of an abbey overrun with ivy, and the taper spire of a village church rising from the brow of a neighboring hill—all were characteristic of England.

The tide and wind were so favorable, that the ship was enabled to come at once at the pier. It was thronged with people; some idle lookers-on, others eager expectants of some friends or relatives. I could distinguish the merchant to whom the ship belonged. I knew him by his calculating brow and restless air. His hands were thrust into his pockets; he was whistling thoughtfully, and walking to and fro, a small space having been accorded to him by the crowd, in deference to his temporary importance. There were repeated cheerings and salutations interchanged between the shore and the ship, as friends happened to recognise each other.

But I particularly noted one young woman of humble dress, but interesting demeanor. She was leaning forward from among the crowd, her eye hurried o'er the ship, as it neared the shore, to catch some wished for countenance. She seemed disappointed and agitated when I heard a faint voice call her name. It was from a poor sailor, who had been ill all the voyage, and had excited the sympathy of every one on board. When the weather was fine, his messmates had spread a mattrass for him on deck in the shade, but of late his illness had so increased that he had taken to his hammock, and had only breathed a wish that he might see his wife before he died.

He had been helped on deck as we came up the river, and was now leaning against the shrouds, with a countenance so wasted, so pale and so ghastly, that it is no wonder the eye of affection did not recognise him. But at the sound of his voice her eye darted on his features, it read at once the whole volume of sorrow; she clasped her hands, uttered a faint shriek, and stood wringing them in silent agony.

All was now hurry and bustle. The meeting of acquaintances —the greetings of friends—the consultations of men of business I alone was solitary and idle. I had no friend to meet, no cheering to receive. I stepped upon the land of my forefathers—but felt that I was a stranger in the land.

Captain David Harrison, who commanded a sloop of New York, called the Peggy, has left a melancholy narrative of the sufferings of himself and his crew, during a voyage from Fayal, one of the Azores, in 1769. A storm which had continued for some days, successively blew away the sails and shrouds; and on the 1st of December, one shroud on a side and the main sail alone remained. In this situation they could make very little way, and all their provisions were exhausted, except bread, of which but a small quantity was left; they came at last to an allowance of a quarter of a pound a day, with a quart of water and a pint of wine, for each man.

The ship was now become very leaky; the waves were swelled into mountains by the storm, and the thunder rolled incessantly over their heads in one dreadful almost unintermitting peal In this frightful dilemma, either of sinking with the wreck, or floating in her and perishing with hunger, two vessels came in sight; but such was the tempest that neither could approach, and they saw with sensations more bitter than death itself, the vessels that would willingly have relieved them disappear. The allowance of bread and water, though still farther contracted, soon exhausted their stores, every morsel of food was finished, and only about two gallons of water remained in the bottom of the cask. The poor fellows who, while they had any sustenance, continued obedient to the captain, were now driven by desperation to excess; they seized upon the cargo, and because wine and brandy were all they had left, they drank of both till the frenzy of hunger was increased by drunkenness, and curses and blasphemy were blended with exclamations of distress. The dregs of the water cask were abandoned to the captain, who, abstaining as much as possible from wine, husbanded them with the greatest economy.

In the midst of these horrors, this complication of want and excess, f distraction and despair, they espied another sail. Every eye was instantly turned towards it, the signal of distress was hung out, and they had the unspeakable satisfaction of being near enough to the ship to communicate their situation. Relief was promised by the captain; but this, alas! was but " the mockery of wo;" and instead of sending the relief he had promised, the unfeeling wretch crowded all sail, and left the distressed crew to all the agony of despair which misery and disappointment could occasion.

The crew once more deserted, and cut off from their last hope, were still prompted by an intuitive love of life to preserve it as long as possible. The only living creatures on board the vessel.

besides themselves, were two pigeons and a cat. The pigeons were killed immediately, and divided among them for their christmas dinner; the next day they killed the cat; and as there were nine persons to partake of the repast, they divided her into nine parts, which they disposed of by lot. The head fell to the share of Captain Harrison, and he declared that he never eat any thing that he thought so delicious in his life.

The next day the crew began to scrape the ship's bottom for barnacles; but the waves had beaten off those above water, and the men were too weak to hang long over the ship's side. During all this time, the poor wretches sought only to forget their misery in intoxication; and while they were continually heating wine in the steerage, the captain subsisted upon the dirty water at the bottom of the cask, half a pint of which, with a few drops of Turlington's Balsam, was his whole sustenance for twenty-four hours.

To add to their calamity, they had neither candle nor oil; and they were in consequence compelled to pass sixteen hours out of the twenty-four in total darkness, except the glimmering light of the fire. Still however, by the help of their only sail, they made a little way; but on the 28th of December, another storm overtook them, which blew their only sail to rags. The vessel now lay like a wreck on the water, and was wholly at the mercy of the winds and waves.

How they subsisted from this time to the 13th of January, sixteen days, does not appear, as their biscuit had been long exhausted, and the last bit of animal food which they tasted, was the cat on the 26th of December; yet on the 13th of January they were all alive, and the crew, with the mate at their head, came to the captain in the cabin, half drunk indeed, but with sufficient sensibility to express the horror of their purpose in their countenances. They said they could hold out no longer, their tobacco was exhausted; they had eaten up all the leather belonging to the pump, and even the buttons from their jackets; and that now they had no means of preventing their perishing together, but by casting lots which of them should be sacrificed for the sustenance of the rest. The Captain endeavored to divert them from their purpose until the next day, but in vain; they became outrageous, and with execrations of peculiar horror, swore that what was to be done, must be done immediately; that it was indifferent to them whether he acquiesced or dissented; and that though they had paid him the compliment of acquainting him with their resolution, yet they would compel him to take his chance with the rest, for general misfortune put an end to personal distinction.

The Captain resisted, but in vain; the men retired to decide on the fate of some victim, and in a few minutes returned, and said the lot had fallen on the negro, who was part of the cargo. The poor fellow knowing what had been determined against him, and seeing one of the crew loading a pistol to despatch him, im ω ored the Captain to save his life, but he was instantly dragged to the steerage, and shot through the head.

Having made a large fire, they began to cut the negro up almost as soon as he was dead, intending to fry his entrails for supper; but James Campbell one of the foremast men, being ravenously impatient for food, tore the liver out of the body, and devoured it raw; the remainder of the crew, however, dressed the meat, and continued their dreadful banquet until two o'clock in the morning.

The next day the crew pickled the remainder of the negro's body, except the head and fingers, which, by common consent, they threw overboard. The Captain refused to taste any part of it, and continued to subsist on the dirty water. On the third day after the death of the negro, Campbell, who had devoured the liver raw, died raving mad, and his body was thrown overboard, the crew dreading the consequences of eating it. The negro's body was husbanded with rigid economy, and lasted the crew, now consisting of six persons, from the 13th to the 26th of January, when they were again reduced to total abstinence, except their wine. This they endured until the 29th, when the mate again came to the Captain at the head of the men, and told him it was now become necessary that they should cast lots a second time. The captain endeavored again to reason them from their purpose, but without success; and therefore considering that if they managed the lot without him, he might not have fair play, consented to see it decided.

The lot now fell upon David Flat, a foremast man. The shock of the decision was so great, that the whole company remained motionless and silent for some time; when the poor victim, who appeared perfectly resigned, broke silence, and said, "My dear friends, messmates, and fellow sufferers, all I have to beg of you is, to despatch me as soon as you did the negro, and to put me to as little torture as possible." Then turning to one Doud, the man who shot the negro, he said, "It is my desire that you should shoot me." Doud reluctantly consented. The victim begged a short time to prepare himself for death, to which his companions most readily agreed. Flat was much respected by the whole ship's company, and during this awful interval, they seemed inclined to save his life; yet finding no alternative but to perish with him, and having in some measure lulled their sense of horror at the approaching scene by a few draughts of wine, they prepared for the execution, and a fire was kindled in the steerage to dress their first meal as soon as their companion should become their food.

As the dreadful moment approached, their compunction increased, and friendship and humanity at length triumphed over hunger and death. They determined that Flat should live at least until eleven o'clock the next morning, hoping, as they said that the

Divine Goodness would in the meantime open some other source
of relief. At the same time they begged the captain to read
prayers; a task which, with the utmost effort of his collected
strength, he was scarcely able to perform. As soon as prayers
were over, the company went to their unfortunate friend, Flat, and
with great earnestness and affection expressed their hopes that
God would interpose for his preservation; and assuring him that
though they never yet could catch or even see a fish, yet they
would put out all their hooks again to try if any relief could be
procured.

Poor Flat, however, could derive little comfort from the concern
they expressed; and it is not improbable, that their friendship and
affection increased the agitation of his mind; such, however, it
was, that he could not sustain it, for before midnight, he grew almost totally deaf, and by four o'clock in the morning was raving
mad. His messmates, who discovered the alteration, debated
whether it would be an act of humanity to despatch him immediately; but the first resolution, of sparing him till eleven o'clock,
prevailed.

About eight in the morning, as the captain was ruminating in
his cabin on the fate of this unhappy wretch, who had but three
hours to live, two of his people came hastily down, with uncommon ardor in their looks, and seizing both his hands, fixed their
eyes upon him without saying a word. A sail had been discovered, and the sight had so far overcome them, that they were for
some time unable to speak. The account of a vessel being in
sight of signals, struck the captain with such excessive and tumultuous joy, that he was very near expiring under it. As soon as
he could speak, he directed every possible signal of distress.
His orders were obeyed with the utmost alacrity; and as he lay
in his cabin, he had the inexpressible happiness of hearing them
jumping upon deck, and crying out, "She nighs us, she nighs
us! she is standing this way."

The approach of the ship being more and more manifest every
moment, their hopes naturally increased, and they proposed a can
to be taken immediately for joy. The captain dissuaded them all
from it, except the mate, who retired, and drank it to himself.

After continuing to observe the progress of the vessel for some
hours, with all the tumult and agitation of mind that such a suspense could not fail to produce, they had the mortification to find
the gale totally die away, so that the vessel was becalmed at only
two miles distance. They did not, however, suffer long from this
circumstance, for in a few minutes they saw a boat put out from
the ship's stern, and row towards them fully manned, and with
vigorous despatch. As they had been twice before confident of
deliverance, and disappointed, and as they still considered themselves tottering on the brink of eternity, the conflict between their
hopes and fears, during the approach of the boat, was dreadful

At length, however, she came alongside; but the appearance of the crew was so ghastly, that the men rested upon their oars, and with looks of inconceivable astonishment asked what they were?

Being at length satisfied, they came on board, and begged the people to use the utmost expedition in quitting the wreck, lest they should be overtaken by a gale of wind, that would prevent their getting back to the ship. The captain being unable to stir, was lifted out of his cabin, and lowered into the boat with ropes; his people followed him, with poor Flat still raving; and they were just putting off, when one of them observed, that the mate was still wanting. He was immediately called to, and the can of joy had just left him power to crawl to the gunnel, with a look of idiotic astonishment, having to all appearance forgot every thing that had happened. The poor drunken creature was with difficulty got into the boat, and in about an hour they all reached the ship in safety, which was the Susannah of London, commanded by Captain Thomas Evers. He received them with the greatest tenderness and humanity, and promised to lay by the wreck until the next morning, that he might, if possible, save some of Captain Harrison's property; but the wind blowing very hard before night, he was obliged to quit her, and she probably, with her cargo, went to the bottom before morning.

The crew had been without provisions *forty-five days*. The mate, James Doud, who shot the negro, and one Warner, a seaman, died on the passage. The remainder, including Flat, who continued mad during the voyage, arrived safe in the Susannah, in the Downs, in the beginning of March; whence Captain Harrison proceeded on shore, and made the proper attestation on oath of the facts related in this melancholy narrative.

THE GRECIAN MARINER'S SONG.

BY THOMAS MOORE, ESQ.

Our home is on the sea, boy,
  Our home is on the sea—
    When nature gave
    The ocean wave,
  She marked it for the free
Whatever storms befall, boy
Whatever storms befall,
    The island bark,
    is freedom's ark,
  And floats her safe through all

Behold yon sea of isles, boy,
  Behold yon sea of isles,

Where every shore,
  Is sparkling o'er,
With beauty's richest smiles.
For us hath freedom claimed, boy
  For us hath freedom claimed
    Those ocean nests
    Where valor rests
His eagle wing untamed.

And shall the Moslem dare, boy,
  And shall the Moslem dare,
    While Grecian hand
    Can wield a brand,
To plant his crescent there!
No!—by our fathers, no, boy,—
  No! by the cross we show—
    From Maina's rills
    To Thracia's hills,
All Greece reechoes " No!'

MONSIEUR DE LA PEROUSE

France becoming jealous of the renown acquired by the English circumnavigators, determined to send out an expedition, which, in its scientific equipments, should vie with them in every respect. Two ships were appointed to this service, the Boussole and Astrolabe, the former commanded by La Perouse, the latter by M. de Langle, both captains in the navy, and men of considerable attainments, besides being assisted by men of science and artists. The voyage is interesting as far as it goes; but, unfortunately, the ships, after quitting Botany Bay, in 1788, have never since been heard of, to the regret of all lovers of science and humanity, on account not only of the acquirements but the amiable character of the commander.

On the 1st of August, 1785, they quitted Brest, and, on the 13th, reached Madeira; they saw Teneriffe on the 19th, and on the 16th of October the island of Trinidada, barren, rocky, and with a violent surf breaking on the shores, where refreshments not being obtainable, the commander steered for St. Catharine's on the Brazil coast.

This island is extremely fertile, producing all sorts of fruit, vegetables, and corn, almost spontaneously. It is covered with trees of everlasting green, but they are so curiously interwoven with plants and briars, that it is impossible to pass through the forests without opening a path with a hatchet: to add to the difficulty, danger is also to be apprehended from snakes whose bite is mortal. The habitations are bordering on the sea. The woods are delightfully fragrant, occasioned by the orange-trees, and other odoriferous plants and shrubs, which form a part of them

On the 14th of January the navigators struck ground on the coast of Patagonia. On the 25th, La Perouse took bearings a league to the southward of Cape San Diego forming the west point of the straits of Lemaire. On the 9th of February, he was abreast of the Straits of Magellan. Examining the quantity of provisions he had on board, La Perouse discovered he had very little flour and bread left in store; having been obliged to leave a hundred barrels at Brest. The worms had also taken possession of the biscuits, and consumed or rendered useless a fifth part of them. Under these circumstances, La Perouse preferred Conception to the island of Juan Fernandez. The Bay of Conception in Chili is a most excellent harbor; the water is smooth, and almost without any current, though the tide rises six feet three inches.

At daybreak, on the 15th of March, La Perouse made the signal to prepare to sail. On the 17th, about noon, a light breeze sprung up, with which he got under way. On the 8th of April, about noon they saw Easter Island. The Indians were alarmed, except a few who had a kind of slight wooden club. Some of them assumed an apparent superiority over the others which induced La Perouse to consider the former as chiefs, but he soon discovered that these selected persons were the most notorious offenders. Having but a few hours to remain upon the island, and wishing to employ his time to the best advantage, La Perouse left the care of the tent, and other particulars, to his first lieutenant M. D'Escures. A division was then made of the persons engaged in the adventure; one part, under the command of M. De Langle, was to penetrate into the interior of the island to encourage and promote vegetation, by disseminating seed, &c. in a proper soil; and the other division undertook to visit the monuments, plantations, and habitations, within the compass of a league of the establishment. The largest of the rude busts upon one of the terraces is fourteen feet six inches in height, and the breadth and other particulars appeared to be proportionate.

Returning about noon to the tent, La Perouse found almost every man without either hat or handkerchief; so much had forbearance encouraged the audacity of the thieves, that he also experienced a similar depredation. An Indian, who had assisted him in descending from a terrace, rewarded himself for his trouble by taking away his hat. Some of them had dived under water, cut the small cable of the Astrolabe's boat, and taken away her grapnel. A sort of chief, to whom M. De Langle made a present of a male and female goat, received the animals with one hand, and robbed him of his handkerchief with the other.

On the 28th of May, they saw the mountains of Owhynee, covered with snow, and afterwards those of Mowee, which are less elevated. About one hundred and fifty canoes were seen putting off from the shore, laden with fruit and hogs, which the

Indians proposed to exchange for pieces of iron of the French navigators. Most of them came on board of one or the other of the vessels, but they proceeded so fast through the water that they filled along-side. The Indians were obliged to quit the ropes thrown them, and leaping into the sea swam after their hogs, when taking them in their arms, they emptied their canoes of the water, and resumed their seats.

After having visited a village, M. de Langle gave orders that six soldiers, with a sergeant, should accompany him: the others were left upon the beach, under the command of M. de Pierrevert, the lieutenant; to them was committed the protection of the ship's boats, from which not a single sailor had landed. The party re-embarked at eleven o'clock in very good order, and arrived on board about noon, where M. de Clonard had received a visit from a chief, of whom he had purchased a cloak, and a helmet adorned with red feathers; he had also purchased a hundred hogs, a quantity of potatoes and bananas, plenty of stuffs, mats, and various other articles. On their arrival on board, the two frigates dragged their anchors; it blew fresh from the south-east, and they were driving down upon the island of Morokinne, which was however at a sufficient distance to give them time to hoist in their boats. La Perouse made the signal for weighing, but before they could purchase the anchor, he was obliged to make sail, and drag it till he had passed Morokinne, to hinder him from driving past the channel.

A fair wind accompanied the navigators on their departure from the Sandwich Islands. Whales and wild-geese convinced them that they were approaching land. Early in the morning of the 23d they descried it; a sudden dispersion of the fog opened to them the view of a long chain of mountains covered with snow. They distinguished Behring's Mount St. Elias, on the north-west coast of America. Having taken in as much wood and water as was required, the navigators esteemed themselves the most fortunate of men, in having arrived at such a distance from Europe without having a sick person among them, or any one afflicted with he scurvy; but a lamentable misfortune now awaited them. At the entrance of this harbor perished twenty brave seamen, in two boats, by the surf. On the 30th of July, at four in the afternoon, La Perouse got under way. This bay or harbor, to which he gave the name of Port des Francais, is situated in 58 deg. 37 min. north-latitude and 139 deg. 50 min. west longitude. In different excursions he says, he found the high-water mark to be fifteen feet above the surface of the sea. The climate of this coast is infinitely milder than that of Hudson's Bay, in the same degree of latitude. Pines were seen of six feet in diameter, and one hundred and forty feet in height. Vegetation is vigorous during three or four months of the year. The men wear different small ornaments, pendant from the ears and nose, scarify their arms and

breasts, and file their teeth close to their gums, using, for the
last operation, a sand-stone, formed into a particular shape.
They paint the face and body with soot, ochre, and plumbago
mixed with train-oil, making themselves most horrid figures
When completely dressed, their flowing hair is powdered, and
plaited with the down of sea-birds; but, perhaps, only the chiefs
of certain distinguished families are thus decorated. Their shoulders are covered with a skin, and on the head, is generally worn a
little straw-hat, plaited with great taste and ingenuity. Sometimes, indeed, the head is decorated with two horned bonnets of
eagles' feathers. Their head-dresses are extremely various, the
grand object in view being only to render themselves terrible,
that they may keep their enemies in awe. Some Indians have
skirts of otters' skins. A great chief wore a shirt composed of a
tanned skin of the elk, bordered by a fringe of beaks of birds,
which, when dancing, imitated the noise of a bell; a common
dress among the savages of Canada, and other nations in the
eastern parts of America. The passion of these Indians for
gaming is astonishing, and they pursue it with great avidity. The
sort of play to which they are most devoted, is a certain game of
chance; out of thirty pieces of wood, each distinctly marked like
the French Dice, they hide seven: each plays in succession and
he who guesses nearest to the whole number marked upon the
seven is the winner of the stake, which is usually a hatchet or a
piece of iron.

At length, after a very long run, on the 11th of September, at
three in the afternoon, the navigators got sight of Fort Monterey,
and two three-masted vessels which lay in the road. The commander of these two ships having been informed, by the Viceroy
of Mexico, of the probable arrival of the two French frigates,
sent them pilots in the course of the night. Loretto, the only
presidency of Old California, is situated on the east coast of this
peninsula and has a garrison of fifty-four troopers, who furnish
detachments to fifteen missions; the duties of which are performed by Dominican friars. About four thousand Indians, converted and residing in these fifteen parishes, are the sole produce
of the long labors of the different religious orders which have
succeeded each other. A small navy was established by the
Spanish Government in this port, under the orders of the Viceroy
of Mexico, consisting of four corvettes of twelve guns, and one
goletta. They are destined to supply with necessaries the presidencies of North California; and they are sometimes despatched
as packets-boats to Manilla, when the orders of the court require
the utmost expedition.

The company were received with all possible politeness and respect: the president of the missions, in his sacerdotal vestment,
with the holy water in his hand, waited to receive them at the
entrance of the church, which was splendidly illuminated as on

their highest festivals: he then conducted them to the foot of the high altar, where *Te Deum* was sung in thanksgivings for their arrival. Before they entered the church they passed a range of Indians: the parish church, though covered with straw, is neat, and decorated with paintings, copied from Italian originals. The Indians, as well as the missionaries, rise with the sun, and devote an hour to prayers and mass, during which time a species of boiled food is prepared for them: it consists of barley meal, the grain of which has been roasted previous to its being boiled. It is cooked in the centre of the square, in three large kettles. This repast is called atole by the Indians, who consider it as delicious; it is destitute of salt and butter, and must consequently be insipid. The women have little more to attend to than their housewifery, their children, and the roasting and grinding of several grains, the latter operation is long and laborious, as they employ no other means than that of crushing it in pieces with a cylinder upon a stone.

The Indians of the *rancheries*, or independent villages, are accustomed to paint their bodies red and black, when they are in mourning. but the missionaries have prohibited the former, though they tolerate the latter, these people being singularly attached to their friends. The ties of family are less regarded among them than those of friendship: the children show no filial respect to the father, having been obliged to quit his cabin as soon as they were able to procure their own subsistence.

A Spanish commissary at Monterey, named M. Vincent Vassadre y Vega, brought orders to the governor to collect all the otter-skins of his missions and presidencies, government having reserved to itself the exclusive commerce of them; and M. Fages assured La Perouse that he could annually furnish twenty thousand of them. The Spaniards were ignorant of the importance of this valuable peltry till the publication of the voyages of Captain Cook; that excellent man has navigated for the general benefit of every nation; his own enjoys only the glory of the enterprise, and that of having given him birth.

New California, though extremely fertile, cannot boast of having a single settler; a few soldiers, married to Indian women, who dwell in the forts, or who are dispersed among the different missions, constituting the whole Spanish nation in this district of America. The Franciscan missionaries are principally Europeans: they have a convent in Mexico.

On the evening of the 22d every thing was on board, and leave had been taken of the Governor and missionaries. On the morning of the 24th they sailed. On the 3d of November the frigates were surrounded with noddies, terns, and man-of-war birds; and on the 4th they made an island which bore west This small island is little more than a rock of about five hundred toises in length. La Perouse named it Isle Necker. About an hour past one in the morning La Pérouse saw breakers at two cables' length ahead of the ship; the sea being so smooth, the sound of them was hardly heard; the Astrolabe perceived them at the same time, though at a greater distance than the Boussole: both frigates instantly hauled, with their heads to the south-east La Pérouse gave orders for sounding; they had nine fathoms, rocky bottom; soon after ten and twelve fathoms, and in a quarter of an hour got no ground with sixty fathoms. They just escaped the most imminent danger to which navigators can be exposed.

The Island of Assumption, to which the Jesuits have attributed six leagues of circumference, from the angles now taken, was reduced to half, and the highest point is about two hundred toises above the level of the sea. A more horrid place cannot be conceived. It was a perfect cone, as black as a coal, and very mortifying to behold, after having enjoyed, in imagination, the cocoa-nuts and turtles expected to be found in some one of the Marianne Islands. Having determined the position, he continued his course towards China; and on the 1st of January, 1787, found bottom in sixty fathoms; a number of fishing-boats surrounded him the next day. On the 2d of January our navigators made the White Rock. In the evening they anchored to the northward of Ling-sing Island, and the following day in Macao Road. Macao, situate at the mouth of the Tigris, is capable of receiving a sixty-four gun-ship into its road, at the entrance of the Typa; and in its port, below the city, ships of seven hundred tons half laden.

The climate of the road of Typa is, at this season of the year. precarious; most of the crews were afflicted with colds, accompanied with a fever; which yielded to the salutary temperature of the island of Luconia, when they approached it on the 15th of February. Wanting wood, which he knew was dear at Manilla, La Perouse came to a resolution of remaining twenty-four hours at Marivella to procure some, and early the next morning all the carpenters of the two frigates were sent on shore with the long boats; the rest of the ship's company, with the yawl, were reserved for a fishing-party; but they were unsuccessful, as they found nothing but rocks and very shallow water.

On the 28th the navigators came to an anchor in the port of Cavite, in three fathoms, at two cables' length from the town Cavite, situate three leagues to the south-west of Manilla, was formerly a place of importance. Manilla is erected on the Bay which also bears its name, and lies at the mouth of a river, being one of the finest situations in the world: all the necessaries of life may be procured there in abundance, and on reasonable terms; but the cloths, and other manufactures of Europe are extravagantly dear. La Perouse confidently asserts, that a great nation without any other colony than the Philippines, which would estab ish a proper government there, might view all the Europea

settlements in Africa and America without envy or regret.   These
islands contain about 3,000,000 of inhabitants, and that of Luconia consists of about a third of them.   These people seem not
inferior to Europeans; they cultivate the land with skill, and
among them have ingenious goldsmiths, carpenters, joiners,
masons, blacksmiths, &c.   La Perouse says he has visited them
at their villages, and found them affable, hospitable, and honest.

On the 9th of April, according to the French reckoning, and
the 10th as the Manillese reckon, our navigators sailed and got
to the northward of the island of Luconia.   On the 21st they
made the island of Formosa; and experienced, in the channel
which divides it from that of Luconia, some very violent currents.
On the 22d they set Lamy Island, at the south-west point of
Formosa, about three leagues distant.   The tack they then stood
on conveyed them upon the coast of Formosa, near the entrance
of the bay of Old Fort Zealand, where the city of Taywan, the
capital of that island is seated.

The whole of the next day a dead calm occurred, in mid-channel,
between the Bashee Islands, and those of Botol Tabacoxima.
It is probable that vessels might provide themselves in this island
with provision, wood, and water.   La Perouse preserved the
name of Kumi Island, which Father Gambil gives it in his chart.
In the night of the 25th our navigators passed the strait of Corea,
sounding very frequently, and as this coast appeared more eligible
to follow than that of Japan, they approached within two leagues
of it, and shaped a course parallel to its direction.   On the 27th
they made the signal to bear up, and steer east, and soon perceived, in the north-north-east, an Island not laid down upon any
chart, at the distance of about twenty leagues from the coast of
Corea.   He named it Isle Dagelet, from the name of the astronomer who first discovered it.   The circumference is about three
leagues.

On the 30th of May, La Perouse shaped his course east towards
Japan, and on the 2d of June saw two Japanese vessels, one of
which passed within hail of him.   It had a crew of twenty men,
all habited in blue cassocks resembling those worn by French
priests.   This vessel was about one hundred tons burden, and
had a single high mast stepped in the middle.   The Astrolabe
hailed her as she passed, but neither the question nor the answer
was comprehended.   At different times of the day seven Chinese
vessels of a smaller construction, were seen, which were better
calculated to encounter bad weather.

During the seventy-five days, since our navigators sailed from
Manilla, they had run along the coasts of Quelpert Island, Corea,
and Japan; but as these countries were inhabited by people inhospitable to strangers, they did not attempt to visit them.   They
were extremely impatient to reconnoitre this land, and it was the
only part of the globe which had escaped the activity of Captain

Cook. The geographers who had drawn the strait of Tessoy, erroneously determined the limits of Jesso, of the Company's land, and of Staten Island; it, therefore, became necessary to terminate the ancient discussions by indisputable facts. The latitude of Baie de Ternai was the same as that of Port Acqueis, though the description of it is very different. The plants which France produces, carpeted the whole of this soil. Roses, lilies, and all European meadow-flowers were beheld at every step. Pine-trees embellished the tops of the mountains; and oaks, gradually diminishing in strength and size towards the sea, adorned the less elevated parts. Traces of men were frequently perceived by the havoc they had made. By these, and many other corroborating circumstances, the navigators were clearly of opinion, that the Tartars approach the borders of the sea, when invited thither by the season for fishing and hunting; that they assemble for these purposes along the rivers, and that the mass of people reside in the interior of the country, to attend to the multiplication of their flocks and herds. M. de Langle, with several other officers who had a passion for hunting, endeavored to pursue their sport, but without success, yet they imagined that by silence, perseverance, and posting themselves in ambush in the passes of the stags and bears, they might be able to procure some of them. This plan was determined on for the next day, but, with all their address and management it proved abortive. It was therefore generally acknowledged that fishing presented the greatest prospect of success. Each of the five creeks in the Baie de Ternai afforded a proper place for hauling the seine, and was rendered more convenient by a rivulet, near which they established their kitchen. They caught plenty of trout, salmon, cod-fish, harp-fish, plaice, and herrings.

At eight in the morning of the 7th, he made an island which seemed of great extent: he supposed, at first, that this was Sega-lien Island, the south part of which some geographers had placed two degrees too far to the northward. The aspect of this land was extremely different from that of Tartary; nothing was to be seen but barren rocks, the cavities of which retained the snow. To the highest of the mountains La Perouse gave the appellation of Peak Lamanon. M. de Langle, who had come to anchor, came instantly on board his ship, having already hoisted out his long boat and small boats. He submitted to La Perouse whether it would not be proper to land before night, in order to reconnoitre the country, and gather some necessary information from the inhabitants. By the assistance of their glasses, they perceived some cabins, and two of the islanders hastening towards the woods.

Our navigators were successful in making the natives comprehend that they requested a description of their country, and that of the Mantchous; one of the old sages rose up, and, with great perspicuity pointed out the most essential and interesting particulars with the end of his staff. His sagacity in guessing the meaning of the questions proposed to him was astonishing, though, in this particular, he was surpassed by another islander of about thirty years of age. The last-mentioned native informed our navigators that they had a commercial intercourse with the people who inhabit the banks of Segalien river, and he distinctly marked, by strokes of a pencil, the number of days it required for a canoe to sail up the river to the respective places of their general traffic. The bay in which they lay at anchor was named Baie de Langle, as Captain de Langle was the first who discovered it, and first landed on its shore. They spent the remainder of the day in visiting the country and its inhabitants. They were surprised to find among a people composed of hunters and fishermen, who were strangers to the cultivation of the earth, and without flocks or herds, such gentle manners, and such a superiority of intellect. The attention of the inhabitants of the Baie de Langle was attracted by the arts and manufactures of the French, they judiciously examined them, and debated among themselves the manner of fabricating the several articles. They were not unacquainted with the weaver's shuttle. A loom of their construction was carried to France, by which it appeared that their methods of making linens was similar to that of the Europeans; but the thread of it is formed of the bark of the willow-tree. Though they do not cultivate the soil, they convert the spontaneous produce of it to the most useful and necessary purposes.

At daybreak, on the 4th of July, La Perouse made the signal for getting under way; early on the 19th, he saw the land of an island from north-east-by-north, as far as east-south-east, but so thick a fog prevailed that none of the points could be particularly discovered. The bay, which is the best in which he had anchored since his departure from Manilla, he named Baie'd 'Estaing. M. de Langle, who first landed in the island, found the islanders assembled round three or four canoes, laden with smoked fish: he was there informed that the men who composed the crews of the canoes were Mantchous, and had quitted the banks of the Segalien river to become purchasers of these fish. In the corner of the island, within a kind of circus planted with stakes, each surmounted with the head of a bear, the bones of animals lay scattered. As these people use no firearms, but engage the bears in close combat, their arrows being only capable of wounding them, this circus might probably be intended to perpetuate the memory of certain great exploits. Having entertained conjectures relative to the proximity of the Coast of Tartary, La Perouse at length discovered that his conjectures were well-founded; for when the horizon became a little more extensive, he saw it perfectly. In the evening of the 22d he came to anchor in thirty-seven fathoms, about a league from the land. He was then abreast of a small river, to the northward of which he saw a remarkable peak; its base is on the shore, and its summit on all sides preserves a regular form. La Perouse bestowed on it the title of Peak la Martiniere.

On the 28th, in the evening, our navigators were at the opening of a bay which presented a safe and convenient anchorage. M. de Langle reported to La Perouse that there was excellent shelter behind four islands; he had landed at a village of Tartars, where he was kindly received, and where he discovered a watering place abounding with the most limpid element From M. de Langle's report, La Perouse gave orders to prepare for anchoring in the bottom of the bay, which was named Baie de Castris.

In this bay the French navigators first discovered the use of the circle of lead or bone, which these people, and the inhabitants of Segalien Island, wear on the thumb like a ring; it greatly assists them in cutting and stripping the salmon with a knife, which is always hanging to their girdle Their village was built upon low marshy land, which must doubtless be uninhabitable during the winter, but on the opposite side of the gulf, another village appeared on a more elevated situation. It was seated at the entrance of a wood, and contained eight cabins, larger and better constructed than the first. Not far from these cabins, they visited three yourts, or subterranean houses. They were sufficiently capacious to accommodate the inhabitants of the whole eight cabins during the severity of the inclement season. On the borders of this village several tombs presented themselves, which were larger and more ingeniously fabricated than the houses; each of them contained three, four, or five biers, decorated with Chinese stuffs, some pieces of which were brocade. Bows, arrows, and the other most esteemed articles of these people, were suspended in the interior of these monuments, the wooden door of which was closed by a bar, supported at each end by a prop.

The women are wrapped in a large robe of nankeen, or salmon's skin, curiously tanned, descending as low as the anklebone, sometimes embellished with a border of fringe manufactured of copper, and producing sounds like those of little bells. Those salmon which furnish a covering for the fair, weigh thirty or forty pounds, and are never caught in summer; those which were taken by the French visiters did not exceed three or four pounds in weight; but that disadvantage was fully compensated by the extraordinary number, and the extreme delicacy of their flavor.

On the 2d of August, La Perouse sailed with a light breeze. On the 19th Cape Troun was perceived to the southward, and Cape Uries to the south-east-by-east; its proper direction, according to the Dutch chart: their situation could not possibly have been determined with more precision by modern navigators in the evening of the 6th, they made the entrance of Avatcha Bay, or Saint Peter and Saint Paul. The light-house, erected by the Russians on the east point of the entrance, was not kindled during the night; as an excuse for which the governor declared the next day, that all their efforts to keep it burn had been ineffectual; the wind had constantly extinguished the flame, which was only sheltered by four planks of wood very indifferently cemented.

The government of Kamtschatka had been materially changed since the departure of the English, and was now only a dependency of that of Ochotsk. These particulars were communicated to our navigators by lieutenant Kaborof, governor of the harbor of Saint Peter and Saint Paul, having a sergeant and forty soldiers under his command. M. de Lessops, who acted as interpreter, and who perfectly understood the Russian language, wrote a letter, in La Perouse's name, to the governor of Ochotsk, to whom La Perouse also wrote in French himself. He told him that the narrative of Cook's last voyage had spread abroad the fame of the hospitality of the Kamtschadale government; and he flattered himself that he should be as favorably received as the English navigators, as his voyage, like theirs, was intended for the general benefit of all maritime nations.

The Kamtschadales are of an imitative genius, and fond of adopting the customs of their conquerors. They have already abandoned the yourts, in which they were formerly accustomed to burrow like badgers, breathing foul air during the whole of the winter. The most opulent among them now build isbas, or wooden houses, like those of the Russians: they are divided into three small rooms, and are conveniently warmed by a brick-stove. The inferior people pass their winters and summers in balagans, resembling wooden pigeon-houses, covered with thatch, and placed upon the tops of posts twelve or thirteen feet high, to which the women, as well as men, find a ladder necessary for their ascension. But these latter buildings will probably soon disappear: for the Kamtschadales imitate the manners and dresses of the Russians. It is curious to see in their little cottages, a quantity of cash in circulation; and it may be considered as a still greater curiosity, because the practice exists among so small a number of inhabitants. Their consumption of the commodities of Russia and China are so few, that the balance of trade is entirely in their favor, in consequence of which it is necessary to pay them the difference in roubles. The Kamtschadales, says La Perouse, appeared to me to be the same people as those of the Bay of Castries, on the coast of Tartary; they are equally remarkable for their mildness and their probity, and their persons are not very dissimilar.

The approach of winter now warned our navigators to depart; the ground, which, on their arrival on the 7th of September, was

adorned with the most beautiful verdure, was as yellow and parched
up on the 25th of the same month, as in the environs of Paris at
the conclusion of December. La Perouse therefore gave prepar-
atory orders for their departure, and, on the 29th, got under way.
M. Kasloff came to take a final leave of him, and dined on board.
He accompanied him on shore, with M. de Langle, and several
officers, and was liberally entertained with a good supper, and
a ball.

Induced by a western gale, La Perouse attempted to reach the
parallel of Bougainville's Navigator's Islands, a discovery due to
the French, where fresh provision might probably be procured.
On the 6th of December, at three in the afternoon, he saw the
most easterly island of that Archipelago, and stood on and off during the rest of the evening and night. Meaning to anchor if he
met with a proper place, La Perouse passed through the channel
between the great and the little islands that Bougainville left to
the south; though hardly a league wide, it appeared perfectly
free from danger. He saw no canoes till he was in the channel,
yet he beheld several habitations on the windward side of the
island, and a group of Indians sitting under the shade of cocoa-nut
trees, who seemed delighted with the prospect afforded by the
frigates.

At break of day they were surprised not to see land to leeward;
nor was it to be discovered till six o'clock next morning. Charmed with the beautiful dawn of the following morning, La Perouse
resolved to reconnoitre the country, take a view of the inhabitants
at their own homes, fill water, and immediately get under way;
prudence warning him against passing a second night at that
anchorage, which M. de Langle also thought too dangerous for
a longer stay. It was therefore agreed on to sail in the afternoon,
after appropriating the morning in exchanging baubles for hogs
and fruit. At the dawn of day the islanders had surrounded the
two frigates, with two hundred different canoes laden with provision, which they would only exchange for beads, axes, and cloth;
other articles of traffic, were treated by them with contempt.
While a part of the crew was occupied in keeping them in order,
and dealing, the rest were despatching empty casks on shore to
be replenished with water. Two boats of the Boussole, armed,
and commanded by Messrs de Clonard and Colinet, and those of
the Astrolabe, commanded by Messrs. de Monti and Bellegarde,
set off with that view at five in the morning, for a bay at the distance of about a league. La Perouse followed close after Messrs
Clonard and Monti, in his pinnace, and larded when they did.
It unfortunately happened that M. de Langle had formed a resolution to make an excursion in his jolly-boat to another creek, at the
distance of about a league from their watering-place; from this
excursion a dire misfortune ensued. The creek, towards which
the long-boats steered, was large and commodious: these, and

the other boats, remained afloat at low water, within half a pistol
shot of the beach, and excellent water was easily procured.   Grea.
order was observed by Messrs. de Clonard and de Monti.   A line
of soldiers was posted between the beach and the natives, who
amounted to about two hundred, including many women and
children.   They were prevailed on to sit down under cocoa-trees
at a little distance from the boats; each of them had fowls, hogs,
pigeons, or fruit, and all of them were anxious to dispose of their
articles without delay, which created some confusion.

While matters were thus passing with perfect tranquillity, and
the casks expeditiously filling with water, La Perouse ventured
to visit a charming village, situated in the midst of a neighboring
wood, the trees of which were loaded with delicious fruit.   The
houses formed a circle of about one hundred and fifty toises in
diameter, leaving an interior open space, beautifully verdant, and
shaded with trees, which rendered the air delightfully cool and
refreshing.   Women, children, and aged men attended him, and
earnestly importuned him to enter their houses;   they even spread
their finest mats upon the floor, decorated with chosen pebbles,
and raised a convenient distance from the ground to prevent
offensive humidity.   La Perouse condescended to enter one of
the handsomest of these huts, which was probably inhabited by a
chief, and was astonished to behold a large cabinet of lattice-work,
in which as much taste and elegance were displayed as if it had
been produced in the environs of Paris.   This enchanting country, blessed with a fruitful soil without culture, and enjoying a
climate which renders clothing unnecessary, holds out to these
fortunate people an abundance of the most estimable food.   The
trees invite the natives to partake of the bread-fruit, the banana,
the cocoa-nut, and the orange; while the swine, fowls, and dogs,
which partake of the surplus of these fruits, afford them a rich
variety of viands.   The inhabitants of this enviable spot were so
rich, and entirely free from wants, that they looked with disdain
on the cloth and iron tendered by the French visiters, and only
deigned to become customers for beads.   Abounding in real blessings, they languished only for superfluities.

The boats of the Boussole now arrived loaded with water, and
La Perouse made every preparation to get under way.   M. de
Langle at the same instant returned from his excursion, and
mentioned his having landed in a noble harbor for boats, at the
foot of a delightful village, and near a cascade of transparent
water.   He spoke of this watering-place as infinitely more commodious than any other, and begged La Perouse to permit him to
take the lead of the first party, assuring him that in three hours he
would return on board with all the boats full of water.   Though
La Perouse, from the appearance of things at this time, had no
great apprehensions of danger, he was averse to sending boats on
shore without the greatest necessity, especially among an immense

numbe of people, unsupported and unperceived by the ships
The boats put off from the Astrolabe at half past twelve, and ar
rived at the watering-place soon after one; when, to their grea
astonishment, M. de Langle, and his officers, instead of finding
a large commodious bay, saw only a creek full of coral, through
which there was no other passage than a winding channel of about
twenty-five feet wide. When within, they had no more than five
feet water; the long-boats grounded, and the barges must have
been in the same situation had they not been hauled to the en·
trance of the channel at a great distance from the beach. M. de
Langle was now convinced that he had examined the bay at high-
water only, not supposing that the tide at those islands rose five or
six feet. Struck with amazement, he instantly resolved to quit
the creek, and repair to that where they had before filled water;
but the air of tranquillity and apparent good humor of the crowd
of Indians, bringing with them an immense quantity of fruit and
hogs, chased his first prudent idea from his recollection

He landed the casks on shore from the four boats without interruption, while his soldiers preserved excellent order on the
beach, forming themselves in two lines, the more effectually to
answer their purpose. Instead of about two hundred natives, including women and children, which M. de Langle found there at
about half after one, they were, at three o'clock, increased to the
alarming number of one thousand and two hundred. M. de Langle's situation became every instant more embarrassing; he found
means, however, to ship his water, but the bay was almost dry,
and he had not any hopes of getting off the long-boats till four in
the afternoon. He and his detachment, however, stepped into
them, and took post in the bow with his musket and musketeers,
forbidding any one to fire without his command; which he knew
would speedily be found necessary. Stones were now violently
thrown by the Indians, who were up to their knees in water, and
surrounded the long-boats, at the distance of about six feet;
the soldiers, who were embarked, making feeble efforts to keep
them off.

M. de Langle, still hoping to check hostilities, without effusion
of blood, gave no orders, all this time, for firing a volley of musketry and swivels; but shortly after, a shower of stones, thrown
with incredible force, struck almost every one in the long-boat.
M de Langle had only fired two shot, when he was knocked
overboard, and massacred with clubs and stones by about two
hundred Indians. The long-boat of the Boussole, commanded by
M. de Boutin, was aground near the Astrolabe, leaving between
them a channel unoccupied by the Indians. Many saved themselves by swimming, who fortunately got on board the barges,
which keeping afloat, forty-nine persons were saved out of the
sixty-one, of which the party consisted. M. Boutin was knocked
down by a stone, but fortunately fell between the two long-boats,

on board of which not a man remained in the space of abo t five minutes. Those who preserved their lives by swimming to the two barges, received several wounds; but those who unhappily fell on the other side were instantly despatched by the clubs of the remorseless Indians.

The crews of the barges, who had killed many of the islanders with their muskets, now began to make more room by throwing their water-casks overboard. They had also nearly exhausted their ammunition, and their retreat was rendered difficult, a number of wounded persons lying stretched out upon the thwarts, and impeding the working of the oars. To the prudence of M. Vaujaus, and the discipline kept up by M. Mouton, who commanded the Boussole's barge, the public are indebted for the preservation of the forty-nine persons of both crews who escaped. M. Boutin had received five wounds in the head, and one in the breast, and was kept above water by the cockswain of the long-boat, who had himself received a severe wound. M. Colinet was discovered in a state of insensibility upon the grapnel-rope of the barge, with two wounds on the head, an arm fractured, and a finger broken. M. Lavaux, surgeon of the Astrolabe, was obliged to suffer the operation of the trepan. M. de Lamanon, and M. de Langle, were cruelly massacred with Talio, master at arms of the Boussole, and nine other persons belonging to the two crews. M. le Gobien, who commanded the Astrolabe's long-boat, did not desert his post till he was left alone; when, having exhausted his ammunition, he leaped into the channel, and, notwithstanding his wounds, preserved himself on board one of the barges. A little ammunition was afterwards found, and completely exhausted on the infuriated crowd; and the boats at length extricated themselves from their lamentable situation.

At five o'clock the officers and crew of the Boussole were informed of this disastrous event; they were at that moment surrounded with about one hundred canoes, in which the natives were disposing of their provisions with security, and perfectly innocent of the catastrophe which had happened. But they were the countrymen, the brothers, the children of the infernal assassins, the thoughts of which so transported La Perouse with rage, that he could with difficulty confine himself to the limits of moderation, or hinder the crew from punishing them with death.

On the 14th of December, La Perouse stood for the Island of Oyolava, which had been observed before they had arrived at the anchorage which proved so fatal. This island is separated from that of Maouna, or of the Massacre, by a wide channel, and vies with Otaheite in beauty, extent, fertility, and population. At the distance of about three leagues from the north-east point, he was surrounded by canoes, laden with bread-fruit, bananas, cocoa-nuts, sugar-canes, pigeons, and a few hogs. The inhabitants of this island resemble those of the island of Maouna, whose treachery

had been so fatally experienced. Some exchanges were conduct
ed with these islanders with more tranquillity and honesty than at
the island of Maouna, as the smallest act of injustice received
immediate chastisement.

On the 17th they approached the island of Pola, but not a single
canoe came off; perhaps the natives had been intimidated by
hearing of the event which had taken place at Maouna. Pola is
a smaller island than that of Oyolava, but equally beautiful, and
is only separated from it by a channel four leagues across. The
natives of Maouna informed our visiters, that the Navigator's
Islands are ten in number, viz. Opoun, the most easterly, Leone,
Fanfoue, Maouna, Oyolava, Calinasse, Pola Skika, Ossamo, and
Ouera. These islands form one of the finest archipelagoes of the
South Sea, and are as interesting with respect to arts, productions,
and population, as the Society and Friendly Islands, which the
English navigators have so satisfactorily described. In favor of
their moral characters, little remains to be noticed; gratitude cannot find a residence in their ferocious minds; nothing but fear can
restrain them from outrageous and inhuman actions. The huts
of these islanders are elegantly formed: though they disdain the
fabrications of iron, they finish their work with wonderful neatness,
with tools formed of a species of basaltes in the form of an adze.
For a few glass-beads, they bartered large three-legged dishes
of wood, so well-polished as to have the appearance of being
highly varnished. They keep up a wretched kind of police; a
few, who had the appearance of chiefs, chastised the refractory
with their sticks, but their assumed power seemed generally disregarded; any regulations which they attempted to enforce and to
establish, were transgressed almost as soon as they were promul-
gated. Never were sovereigns so negligently obeyed, never were
orders enforced with such feeble shadows of authority.

Imagination cannot figure to itself more agreeable situations
than those of their villages. All the houses are built under fruit-
trees, which render them delightfully cool; they are seated on the
borders of streams, leading down from the mountains. Though
the principal object in their architecture is to protect them from
offensive heat, the islanders never abandon the idea of elegance.
Their houses are sufficiently spacious to accommodate several
families; and they are furnished with blinds, which are drawn up
to the windward to prevent the intrusion of the potent rays of the
sun. The natives repose upon fine comfortable mats, which are
cautiously preserved from all humidity. Nothing can be said, by
our travellers, of the religious rites of these natives, as no morai
was perceived belonging to them. The islands are fertile, and
their population is supposed to be considerable. Opun, Leone,
and Fanfoue, are small; but Maoune, Oyolava, and Pola, may be
classed among the largest and most beautiful in the South Sea.
Cocoa island is lofty, and formed like a sugar-loaf; it is nearly a

mile in diameter, covered with trees, and is separated from Traitors' Island by a channel about a league wide. At eight in the
morning La Perouse brought too, to the west-south-west, at two
miles from a sandy bay in the western part of the Great Island of
Traitors, where he expected to find an anchorage sheltered from
easterly winds. About twenty canoes instantly quitted the shore
and approached the frigates in order to make exchanges; several
of them were loaded with excellent cocoa-nuts, with a few yams
and bananas; one of them brought a hog, and three or four fowls.
It evidently appeared that these Indians had before some knowledge of Europeans, as they came near without fear, traded with
honesty, and never refused to part with their fruit before they were
paid for it. They spoke, however, the same language, and the
same ferocity appeared in their countenances; their manner of
tattooing, and the form of their canoes were the same, but they
had not, like them, two joints cut off from the little finger of the
left hand; two individuals had, however, suffered that operation.

On the 27th of December, Vavao was perceived, an island
which Captain Cook had never visited, but was no stranger to its
existence, as one of the archipelago of the Friendly Islands; it is
nearly equal in extent to that of Tongataboo, and is particularly
fortunate in having no deficiency of fresh water. The two small
islands of Hoongatonga are no more than two large uninhabitable
rocks, which are high enough to be seen at the distance of fifteen
leagues. Their position is ten leagues north of Tongataboo; but
that island being low, it can hardly be seen at half that distance.
On the 31st of December, at six in the morning, an appearance
like the tops of trees, which seemed to grow in the water, proved
the harbinger of Van Dieman's point. The wind being northerly,
La Perouse steered for the south coast of the island, which may,
without danger, be approached within three musket-shots. Not
the semblance of a hill is to be seen; a calm sea cannot present
a more level surface to the eye. The huts of the natives were
scattered irregularly over the fields, and not socially collected
into a conversable neighborhood. Seven or eight canoes were
launched from these habitations, and directed their course towards
the vessels; but these islanders were awkward seamen, and did
not venture to come near, though the water was smooth, and no
obstacle impeded their passage. At the distance of about eight
or ten feet, they leaped overboard and swam near the frigates,
holding in each hand a quantity of cocoa-nuts, which they were
glad to exchange for pieces of iron, nails, and hatchets; from the
honesty of their dealings a friendly intercourse ensued between
the islanders and the navigators, and they ventured to come on
board

Norfolk Island, off the coast of New South Wales, which they
saw on the 13th of January, is very steep, but does not exceed
eighty toises above the level of the sea. It is covered with pines

which appear to be of the same species as those of New Caledonia, or New Zealand. Captain Cook having declared that he saw
many cabbage-trees in this island, heightened the desire of the navigators to land on it. Perhaps the palm which produces these
cabbages, is very small, for not a single tree of that species could
be discovered. On the 26th, at nine in the morning, La Perouse
let go the anchor at a mile from the north coast of Botany Bay, in
seven fathoms water. An English lieutenant, and a midshipman,
were sent on board his ship by Captain Hunter, commander of
the Sirius. They offered him, in Captain Hunter's name, all the
services in his power; but circumstances would not permit him to
supply them with provision, ammunition, or sails. An officer was
despatched from the French to the English Captain, returning
thanks, and adding, that his wants extended only to wood and
water, of which he should find plenty in the bay. The journal of
La Perouse proceeds no further. La Perouse, according to his
last letters from Botany Bay, was to return to the Isle of France
in 1788.

They left Botany bay in March, and, in a letter which the
commodore wrote February 7, he stated his intention to continue
his researches till December, when he expected, after visiting the
Friendly islands, to arrive at the Isle of France. This was the
latest intelligence received of the fate of the expedition; and M.
d' Entrecasteaux, who was despatched by the French government,
in 1791, in search of La Perouse, was unable to trace the course
he had taken, or gain any clew to the catastrophe which had be-
fallen him and his companions.

In 1825, the attention of the public was excited towards this
mysterious affair, by a notice published by the French minister
of the marine, purporting that an Amerian captain had declared
that he had seen, in the hands of one of the natives of an island
in the tract between Louisiade and New Caledonia, a cross of the
order of St. Louis, and some medals, which appeared to have been
procured from the shipwreck of La Perouse. In consequence of
this information, the commander of a vessel which sailed from
Toulon, in April, 1826, on a voyage of discovery, received orders
to make researches in the quarter specified, in order to restore
to their country any of the shipwrecked crew who might yet remain in existence. Other intelligence, relative to the wreck of
two large vessels, on two different islands of the New Hebrides,
was obtained by captain Dillon, the commander of an English
vessel at Tucopia, in his passage from Valparaiso to Pondicherry,
in May, 1826, in consequence of which he was sent back to ascertain the truth of the matter. The facts discovered by him on
this mission, were, that the two ships struck on a reef at Mallicolo,
1° 4′ S. latitude, 169° 20′ E. longitude; one of them immediately
went down and all on board perished; some of the crew of the
other escaped, part of whom were murdered by the savages; the

remainder built a small vessel, and set sail from Mallicolo; but what became of them is not known. It is not, indeed, certain that these were the vessels of La Perouse.

MIDSHIPMAN'S PRANKS.

BY CAPTAIN HALL.

During the long winters of our slothful discontent at Bermuda, caused by the peace of Amiens, the grand resource, both of the idle and the busy, amongst all classes of the Leander's officers, was shooting—that never-ending, still-beginning amusement, which Englishmen carry to the remotest corner of the habitable globe—popping away in all countries, thinking only of game, and often but too reckless of the prejudices, or fear of the natives. This propensity is indulged even in those uninhabited regions of the earth which are visited only once in an age; and if Captain Parry had reached the pole, he would unquestionably have had a shot at the axis of the earth!

In the meantime, the officers and young gentlemen of the flag-ship at Bermuda in the beginning of 1803, I suppose to keep their hands in for the war which they saw brewing, and prayed hourly for, were constantly blazing away amongst the cedar groves and orange plantations of those fairy islands, which appeared to be more and more beautiful after every such excursion. The midshipmen were generally obliged to content themselves with knocking down the blue and red birds with the ship's pistols, charged with His Majesty's gunpowder, and, for want of small shot, with slugs formed by cutting up His Majesty's musket-bullets. The officers aimed at higher game, and were, of course, better provided with guns and ammunition. Several of these gentlemen had brought from England some fine dogs—high bred pointers, while the middies, also, not to be outdone, must needs have a dog of their own: they recked very little of what breed; but some sort of animal they said they must have.

I forget how we procured the strange-looking animal whose services we contrived to engage; but having once obtained him, we were not slow in giving him our best affections. It is true he was as ugly as anything could possibly be. His color was a dirty reddish yellow; and while a part of his hair twisted itself up in curls, a part hung down quite straight, almost to the ground. He was utterly useless for all the purposes of real sport, but quite good enough to furnish the mids with plenty of fun when they went on shore—in chasing pigs, barking at old white headed negresses

and other amusements suited to the exalted taste and habits of the
rising generation of officers.

People will differ as to the merits of dogs; but we had no doubts
as to the great superiority of ours over all others on board, though
the name we gave him certainly implied no such confidence on
our part. After a full deliberation, it was decided to call him
Shakings. Now it must be explained that shakings is a name
given to small fragments of rope yarns, odds and ends of cordage,
bits of oakum, old lanyards,—in short to any kind of refuse arising
out of the wear and tear of the ropes. This odd name was perhaps bestowed on our beautiful favorite in consequence of his
color not being very dissimilar to that of well tarred Russia hemp;
while the resemblance was increased by many a dab of pitch,
which his rough coat imbibed from the seams between the planks
of the deck in hot weather.

If old Shakings was of no great beauty, he was at least, the
most companionable of dogs; and though he dearly loved the
midshipmen and was dearly beloved by them in return, he had
enough of the animal in his composition to take a higher pleasure in the society of his own kind. So that when the high bred,
showy pointers belonging to the officers came on board, after a
shooting excursion, Mr. Shakings lost no time in applying to them
for news. The pointers who liked this sort of familiarity very
well gave poor Shakings all possible encouragement. Not so with
their masters; they could not bear to see an abominable cur, as
they called our favorite, at once so cursedly dirty and so utterly
useless, mixing with their sleek and well-fed animals. At first
their dislike was confined to such insulting expressions as these;
then it came to an occasional kick or knock on the nose with the
but-end of a fowling-piece; and lastly, to a sound cut with the
hunting whip.

Shakings, who instinctively knew his place, took all this, like a
sensible fellow, in good part; while the mids, when out of hearing
of the higher powers, uttered curses both loud and deep against
the tyranny and oppression exercised against an animal which,
in their fond fancy was declared to be worth all the dogs in the
ward room put together. They were little prepared, however,
for the stroke which soon fell upon them, perhaps in consequence
of these murmurs. To their great horror and indignation, one of
the Lieutenants, provoked at some liberty which Master Shakings
had taken with his new polished boots, called out one morning,—

" Man the jolly-boat, and land that infernal, dirty, ugly, beast
of a dog, belonging to the young gentlemen!"

" Where shall I take him to, sir?" asked the strokesman of the
boat.

" Oh, any where; pull to the nearest part of the shore, and
pitch him on the rocks. He'll shift for himself, I have no doubt '
So off went poor dear Shakings!

If a stranger had come into the midshipmen's birth at that moment, he might have thought His Majesty's naval service was about to be broken up. All allegiance, discipline, or subordination, seemed utterly cancelled by this horrible act. Many were the execrations hurled upwards at the offending "knobs," who, we thought were combining to make our lives miserable. Some of our party voted for writing a letter of remonstrance to the Admiral against this unheard of outrage; and one youth swore deeply that he would leave the service unless justice was obtained. But as he had been known to swear the same thing half a dozen times every day since he had joined the ship, no great notice was taken of his pledge. Another declared upon his word of honor, that such an act was enough to make a man turn Turk, and fly his country! At last, by general agreement, it was decided that we should not do a bit of duty, or even stir from our seats, till we obtained redress for our grievances. However, while we were in the act of vowing mutiny and disobedience, the hands were turned up to "furl sails!" upon which the whole party, totally forgetting their magnanimous resolution, scudded up the ladders, and jumped into their stations with more than usual alacrity, wisely thinking, that the moment of actual revolt had not yet arrived.

A better scheme than throwing up the service, or writing to the Admiral, or turning Mussulmen, was afterwards concocted. The midshipmen who went on shore in the next boat easily got hold of poor Shakings who was howling on the steps of the watering place. In order to conceal him, he was stuffed, neck and crop, into the captain's clothes-bag, brought safely on board, and restored once more to the bosom of his friends.

In spite of all we could do, however, to keep Master Shakings below, he presently found his way to the quarter-deck, to receive the congratulations of the other dogs. There he was soon detected by the higher powers, and very shortly afterwards trundled over the gangway and again tossed on the beach. Upon this occasion he was honored with the presence of one of his own masters, a middy, who was specially desired to land the brute, and not bring him on board again. Of course this particular youngster did not bring the dog off; but, before night, somehow or other, old Shakings was snoring away, in grand chorus with his more fashionable friends, the pointers, and dreaming no evil, before the door of the very officer's cabin whose beautiful polished boots he had brushed so rudely in the morning,—an offence which had led to his banishment.

This second return of our dog was too much. The whole posse of us were sent for on the quarter-deck, and in very distinct terms ordered not to bring Shakings on board again. These injunctions having been given, this wretched victim, as we termed him, of oppression, was once more landed amongst the cedar groves. This time he remained full a week on shore: but how or when he

13

ever found h s way off again, no one ever knew; at least no one
chose to divulge. Never was there anything like the mutual joy
felt by Shakings and his two dozen masters. He careered about
the ship, barked and yelled with delight, and, in his raptures,
actually leaped, with his dirty feet on the milk-white duck trousers
of the disgusted officers, who heartily wished him at the bottom
of the anchorage! Thus the poor beast unwittingly contributed
to accelerate his hapless fate, by this ill-timed show of confidence
in those who were then plotting his ruin. If he had kept his
paws to himself, and staid quietly in the dark recesses of the
cock-pit, wings, cable-tiers and other wild regions, the secrets of
which were known only to the inhabitants of our sub-marine world,
all might yet have been well.

We had a grand jollification on the night of Shakings restoration; and his health was in the very act of being drunk, with
three times three, when the officer of the watch, hearing an uproar
below, the sounds of which were distinctly conveyed up the wind-
sail, sent down to put our lights out, and we were forced to march
off growling to our hammocks.

Next day to our surprise and horror, old Shakings was nowhere
to be seen or heard of. We searched every where, interrogated
the cockswains of all the boats, and crossquestioned the marines,
who had been sentries during the night on the forecastle gangways
and poop, but all in vain!—no traces of Shakings could be found.

At length the opinion began to gain ground amongst us,
that the poor beast had been put to death by some diabolical
means, and our ire mounted accordingly. This suspicion seemed
the more natural, as the officers said not a word about the matter,
nor even asked us what we had done with our dog. While we
were in this state of excitement and distraction for our loss, one
of the midshipmen, who had some drollery in his composition,
gave a new turn for the expression of our thoughts.

This gentleman, who was more than twice as old as most of us,
say about thirty, had won the affections of all our class, by the
gentleness of his manners, and the generous part he always took
on our side. He bore among us the pet name of Daddy; and
certainly he was like a father to those amongst us who, like myself, were quite adrift in the ship without any one to look after
them. He was a man of talents and classical education, but he
had entered the navy far too late in life ever to take to it cordially.
His habits, indeed, had become so rigid, that they could never
be made to bend to the mortifying kind of discipline, which it appears every officer should run through, but which only the young
and light-hearted can brook. Our worthy friend, accordingly,
with all his abilities, tastes, and acquirements, never seemed at
home on board the ship, and unless a man can reach this point of
liking for the sea, he is better on the shore. At all events old
Daddy cared more about his books than about blocks, and delight-

ed more in giving us assistance in our literary pursuits, and trying to teach us to be useful, than in rendering himself a proficient in those professional mysteries, which he never hoped to practise in earnest himself.

What this very interesting person's early history was, we could never find out; nor why he entered the navy; nor how it came, that a man of his powers and accomplishments should have been kept back so long. Indeed the youngsters never inquired into these matters, being quite contented to have the advantage of his protection against the oppression of the oldsters, who occasionally bullied them. Upon all occasions of difficulty, we were in the habit of clustering around him, to tell our grievances, great and small, with the certainty of always finding in him that great desideratum in calamity—a patient and friendly listener.

It will easily be supposed, that our kind Daddy took more than usual interest in the affair of Shakings, and that he was applied to by us at every stage of the transaction. He was sadly perplexed, of course, when the dog was finally missing; and for some days, he could give us no comfort, nor suggest any mode of revenge which was not too dangerous for his young friends to put into practice. He prudently observed, that as we had no certainty to go upon, it would be foolish to get ourselves into any serious scrape for nothing at all.

" There can be no harm, however," he continued in his dry and slightly sarcastic way, which all who knew him will recollect, as well as if they saw him now, drawing his hand slowly across his chin, " There can be no harm my boys, in putting the other dogs in mourning for their departed friend Shakings; for whatever is become of him, he is lost to them, as well as to us, and his memory ought to be duly respected."

This hint was no sooner given than a cry was raised for crape, and every chest and bag ransacked, to procure badges of mourning. The pointers were speedily rigged up with a bunch of crape tied in a handsome bow, upon the left leg just above the knee. The joke took immediately. The officers could not help laughing; for, though we considered them little better than fiends, at that moment of excitement, they were in fact, except in this instance, the best natured and most indulgent men I remember to have sailed with. They of course ordered the crape to be instantly taken off from the dogs' legs: and one of the officers remarked to us seriously, that as we had now had our piece of fun out, there were to be no more such tricks.

Off we scampered to consult old Daddy what was to be done next, as we had been positively ordered not to meddle any more with the dogs.

" Put the pigs in mourning," he said.

All our crape was expended by this time, but this want was soon supplied by men whose trade it was to discover resources

in difficulty.   With a generous spirit of devotion to the cause of
public spirit one of these juvenile mutineers pulled off his black
neck-handkerchief, and, tearing it in pieces, gave a portion to each
of the circle and away we all started to put into practice this new
suggestion of our director-general of mischief.

The row which ensued in the pig-sty was prodigious—for in
those days, hogs were allowed a place on board a man-of-war,—
a custom wisely abolished of late years, since nothing can be
more out of character with any ship than such nuisances.   As these
matters of taste and cleanliness were nothing to us, we did not
intermit our noisy labor till every one of the grunters had his arm-
let of such crape as we had been able to muster.   We then watched our opportunity and opened the door so as to let out the whole
herd of swine on the main deck just at a moment when a group of
officers were standing on the fore part of the quarter deck.   Of
course the liberated pigs delighted with their freedom, passed in
review under the very noses of our superiors, each with his mourning knot displayed, grunting or squealing along, as if it was their
express object to attract attention to their domestic sorrow for the
loss of Shakings.   The officers were excessively provoked, as
they could not help seeing all this was affording entertainment, at
their expense, to the whole crew; for though the men took no
part in this piece of insubordination, they were ready enough, in
those times of the weary, weary peace, to catch at any species of
distraction or devilry, no matter what, to compensate for the loss
of pommeling their enemies.

The matter, therefore, necessarily became rather serious; and
the whole gang of us being sent for on the quarter deck, we were
ranged in a line, each with his toes at the edge of a plank according to the orthodox fashion of these gregarious scoldings, technically called ' toe-the-line matches.'   We were given to understand that our proceedings were impertinent, and after the orders
we had received, highly offensive.   It was with much difficulty
that either party could keep their countenances during this official lecture, for while it was going on, the sailors were endeavoring by the direction of the officers, to remove the bits of silk
from the legs of the pigs.   If however it be difficult—as most
difficult we found it—to put a hog in mourning, it is a job ten times
more troublesome to take him out again.   Such at least is the fair
inference from these two experiments; the only ones, perhaps, on
record,—for it cost half the morning to undo what we had done
in less than an hour; to say nothing of the unceasing and outrageous uproar which took place along the decks, especially under the guns, and even under the coppers forward in the galley,
where two or three of the youngest pigs had wedged themselves,
apparently resolved to die rather than submit to the degradation
of being deprived of their mourning.

All this was very creditable to the memory of poor Shakings

but, in the course of the day the real secret of this extraordinary difficulty of taking a pig out of mourning was discovered. Two of the mids were detected in the very act of tying a bit of black buntin to the leg of a sow, from which the seamen declared they had already cut off crape and silk enough to have made her a complete suit of black.

As soon as these new offences were reported, the whole party of us were ordered to the mast-head as a punishment. Some were sent to sit on topmast cross-trees, and some on the top-gallant yardarms, and one small gentleman being perched at the jib-boom end, was very properly balanced abaft by another little culprit at the extremity of the gaff. In this predicament we were hung out to dry for five or six hours, as old Daddy remarked to us with a grin, when we were called down as the night fell.

Our persevering friend, being rather provoked at the punishment of his young flock, now set to work to discover the real fate of Shakings. It soon occurred to him, that if the dog had really been made away with, as he shrewdly suspected, the butcher, in all probability must have had a hand in the murder; accordingly, he sent for him in the evening, when the following dialogue took place:—

" Well, butcher, will you have a glass of grog to-night? "

" Thank you, sir, thank you. Here's your honor's health! said the other, after smoothing down his hair, and pulling an immense quid of tobacco out of his mouth.

Old Daddy observed the peculiar relish with which the butcher took his glass, and mixing another, a good deal more potent, placed it before the fellow, and continued the conversation in these words:

" I tell you what it is Mr. Butcher—you are as humane as any man in the ship, I dare say; but, if required, you know well, that you must do your duty, whether it is on sheep or hogs?"

" Surely sir."

" Or upon dogs either?" suddenly inquired the inquisitor.

" I don't know about that," stammered the butcher, quite taken by surprise and thrown all aback.

" Well, well," said Daddy, " here's another glass for you—a stiff north-wester. Come! tell us all about it now. How did you get rid of the dog?—of Shakings, I mean? "

" Why, sir," said the peaching rogue, " I put him in a bag— a bread bag, sir."

" Well!—what then? "

" I tied up the mouth, and put him overboard—out of the mid ship lower-deck port, sir."

" Yes—but he would not sink?" said Daddy.

" Oh, sir," cried the butcher, now entering into the merciless spirit of his trade, " I put a four and twenty pound shot into the bag along with Shakings."

18 *

" Did you?—Then, Master Butcher, all I can say is, you are
as precious a rascal as ever went about unhanged. There—drink
your grog, and be off with you!"

Next morning when the officers were assembled at breakfast in
the ward room, the door of the captain of marines' cabin was suddenly opened and that officer half shaved, and laughing, through
a collar of soap suds, stalked out, with a paper in his hands.

" Here," he exclaimed, " is a copy of verses which I found in
my basin this morning. I can't tell how they got there or what
they are about;—but you shall judge."

So he read the two following stanzas of doggerel:—

> " When the Northern Confederacy threatened our shores,
> And roused Albion's Lion, reclining to sleep,
> Preservation was taken of all the kings stores,
> Nor so much as a *rope-yarn* was launched in the deep.

> " But now it is peace, other hopes are in view,
> And all active service as light as a feather,
> The *Stores* may be d—d, and humanity too,
> For Shakings and Shot are thrown overboard together !"

I need hardly say in what quarter of the ship this biting morsel of
cock-pit satire was concocted, nor indeed who wrote it, for there
was no one but our good Daddy who was equal to such a flight
About midnight, an urchin—who shall be nameless—was thrust
out of one of the after ports of the lower deck, from which he
clambered up to the marine officer's port, and the sash happening
to have been lowered down on the gun, the epigram, copied by
another of the youngsters was pitched into the soldier's basin.

The wisest thing would have been for the officer's to have said
nothing about the matter, and let it blow by. But angry people
are seldom judicious—so they made a formal complaint to the captain, who, to do him justice, was not a little puzzled how to settle
the affair. The reputed author was called up, and the captain
said to him—

" Pray, sir, are you the writer of these lines?"

" I am sir," he replied, after a little consideration.

" Then all I can say is," remarked the captain, " they are clever
enough, in their way—but take my advice, and write no more
such verses."

So the affair ended. The satirist took the captain's hint in good
part, and confined his pen to matters below the surface of the
water.

As in the course of a few months the war broke out, there was
no longer time for such nonsense, and our generous protector, old
Daddy, some time after the affair of Shakings took place, was
sent off to Halifax, in charge of a prize. His orders were if possible to join his own ship, the Leander, then lying at the entrance
of New York harbor, just within Sandy Hook light-house.

Our good old friend, accordingly, having completed his mission
and delivered his prize to the authorities of Halifax, took his pas-

sage in the British packet sailing from thence to the port in which we lay. As this ship sailed past us, on her way to New York, we ascertained, to our great joy, that our excellent Daddy was actually on board of her. Some hours afterwards the pilot boat was seen coming to us, and though it was in the middle of the night, all the young mids came hastily on deck to welcome their worthy messmate back again to his ship.

It was late in October, and the wind blew fresh from the north-westward, so that the ship, riding to the ebb, had her head directed towards the Narrows, between Staten island and Long island; consequently the pilot-boat,—one of those beautiful vessels so well known to every visiter of the American coast,—came flying down upon us, with the wind nearly right aft. Our joyous party were all assembled on the quarter-deck, looking anxiously at the boat as she swept past us. She then luffed round, in order to sheer alongside, at which moment the mainsail jibed, as was to be expected. It was obvious, however, that something more had taken place than the pilot had looked for, since the boat, instead of ranging up to us, was brought right round on her heel, and went off again upon a wind on the other tack. The tide carried her out of sight for a few minutes, but she was soon alongside, when we learned, to our inexpressible grief and consternation, that, on the main-boom of the pilot-boat swinging over, it had accidentally struck our poor friend and pitched him headlong overboard. Being encumbered with a great coat, the pockets of which, as we afterwards learned, were loaded with his young companions' letters, brought from England by this packet, he in vain struggled to reach the boat and then sunk to rise no more.

THE SOUND OF THE SEA.

BY MRS. HEMANS.

'Thou art sounding on, thou mighty sea,
    For ever and the same!
The ancient rocks yet ring to thee,
    Whose thunders naught can tame.

Oh! many a glorious voice is gone,
    From the rich bowers of earth,
And hushed is many a lovely tone
    Of mournfulness or mirth.

The Dorian flute that sighed of yore
    Along thy wave, is still;
The harp of Judah peals no more
    On Zion's awful hill.

And Memnon's lyre hath lost the chord
  That breathed the mystic tone,
And the songs, at Rome's high triumphs poured
  Are with her eagles flown.

And mute the Moorish horn, that rang
  O 'er stream and mountain free,
And the hymn the leagued Crusaders sang
  Hath died in Galilee

But thou art swelling on, thou deep,
  Through many an olden clime,
Thy billowy anthem, ne'er to sleep
  Until the close of time.

Thou liftest up thy solemn voice
  To every wind and sky,
And all our earth's green shores rejoice
  In that one harmony.

It fills the noontide's calm profound,
  The sunset's heaven of gold;
And the still midnight hears the sound,
  Ev'n as when first it rolled.

Let there be silence deep and strange,
  Where sceptered cities rose !
Thou speak'st of one who doth not change—
  So may our hearts repose.

ACCOUNT OF THE LOSS OF HIS MAJESTY'S SHIP

PHŒNIX,

Off Cuba, in the Year 1780.   *By Lieutenant Archer.*

The Phœnix of 44 guns, Captain Sir Hyde Parker, was lost
in a hurricane, off Cuba, in the West Indies, in the year 1780
The same hurricane destroyed the Thunderer, 74; Stirling Castle, 64; La Blanche, 42; Laurel, 28; Andromeda, 28; Deas
Castle, 24; Scarborough, 20; Beaver's Prize, 16; Barbadoes, 14;
Cameleon, 14; Endeavour, 14; and Victor, 10 guns.   Lieutenant
Archer was first-lieutenant of the Phœnix at the time she was
lost.   His narrative in a letter to his mother, contains a most
correct and animated account of one of the most awful events in
the service.   It is so simple and natural as to make the reader
feel himself as on board the Phœnix.   Every circumstance is
detailed with feeling, and powerful appeals are continually made
to the heart.   It must likewise afford considerable pleasure to

observe the devout spirit of a serman frequent y bursting forth, and imparting sublimity to the relation.

At Sea, June 30, 1781.

MY DEAR MOTHER,

I am now going to give you an account of our last cruise in the Phœnix; and must premise, that should any one see it besides yourself, they must put this construction on it—that it was originally intended for the eyes of a mother, and a mother only—as, upon that supposition, my feelings may be tolerated. You will also meet with a number of sea terms, which, if you don't understand, why, I cannot help you, as I am unable to give a sea description in any other words.

To begin then:—On the 2d of August, 1780, we weighed and sailed for Port Royal, bound for Pensacola, having two store-ships under convoy, and to see safe in; then cruise off the Havanna, and in the gulf of Mexico, for six weeks. In a few days we made the two sandy islands, that look as if they had just risen out of the sea, or fallen from the sky; inhabited, nevertheless, by upwards of three hundred English, who get their bread by catching turtle and parrots, and raising vegetables, which they exchange with ships that pass, for clothing and a few of the luxuries of life, as rum, &c.

About the 12th we arrived at Pensacola, without any thing remarkable happening, except our catching a vast quantity of fish, sharks, dolphins, and bonettos. On the 13th sailed singly, and on the 14th had a very heavy gale of wind at north, right off the land, so that we soon left the sweet place, Pensacola, a distance astern. We then looked into the Havanna, saw a number of ships there, and knowing that some of them were bound round the bay, we cruised in the track: a fortnight, however, passed, and not a single ship hove in sight to cheer our spirits. We then took a turn or two round the gulf, but not near enough to be seen from the shore. Vera Cruz we expected would have made us happy, but the same luck still continued; day followed day, and no sail. The dollar bag began to grow a little bulky, for every one had lost two or three times, and no one had won: this was a small gambling party entered into by Sir Hyde and ourselves; every one put a dollar into a bag, and fixed on a day when we shoul see a sail, but no two persons were to name the same day, and whoever guessed right first was to have the bag.

Being now tired of our situation, and glad the cruise was almost out, for we found the navigation very dangerous, owing to unaccountable currents; we shaped our course for Cape Antonio. The next day the man at the mast head, at about one o'clock in the afternoon, called out: "A sail upon the weather bow! Ha! Ha! Mr. Spaniard, I think we have you at last. Turn out all hands! make sail! All hands give chase!" There was scarcely any occasion for this order, for the sound of a sail being in sight flew like wild fire through the ship, and every sail was set in an instant, almost before the orders were given. A lieutenant at the mast head, with a spy glass, "What is she." "A large ship studding athwart right before the wind. P-o-r-t! Keep her away! set the studding sails ready!" Up comes the little doctor, rubbing his hands; "Ha! ha! I have won the bag." "The devil take you and the bag; look, what's ahead will fill all our bags." Mast-head again: "Two more sail on the larboard beam!" "Archer, go up, and see what you can make of them." "Upon deck there; I see a whole fleet of twenty sail coming right before the wind." "Confound the luck of it, this is some convoy or other, but we must try if we can pick some of them out." "Haul down the studding-sails! Luff! bring her to the wind' Let us see what we can make of them."

About five we got pretty near them, and found them to be twenty-six sail of Spanish merchantmen, under convoy of three line of battle ships, one of which chased us; but when she found we were playing with her (for the old Phœnix had heels) she left chase, and joined the convoy; which they drew up into a lump, and placed themselves at the outside; but we still kept smelling about till after dark. O, for the Hector, the Albion, and a frigate, and we should take the whole fleet and convoy, worth some millions! About eight o'clock perceived three sail at some distance from the fleet; dashed in between them, and gave chase, and were happy to find they steered from the fleet. About twelve came up with a large ship of twenty-six guns. "Archer, every man to his quarters! run the lower deck guns out, and light the ship up: show this fellow our force; it may prevent his firing into us and killing a man or two." No sooner said than done. "Hoa, the ship ahoy, lower all your sails down, and bring to instantly, or I'll sink you." Clatter, clatter, went the blocks, and away flew all their sails in proper confusion. "What ship is that?" "The Polly." "Whence came you?" "From Jamaica." "Where are you bound?" "To New York." "What ship is that?" "The Phœnix." Huzza, three times by the whole ship's company. An old grum fellow of a sailor standing close by me: "O, d—m your three cheers, we took you to be something else." Upon examination we found it to be as he reported, and that they had fallen in with the Spanish fleet that morning, and were chased the whole day, and that nothing saved them but our stepping in between; for the Spaniards, took us for three consorts, and the Polly took the Phœnix for a Spanish frigate, till we hailed them. The other vessel in company was likewise bound to New York. Thus was I, from being worth thousands in idea, reduced to the old 4s. 6d. a day again: for the little doctor made the most prize money of us all that day, by winning the bag, which contained between thirty and forty dollars; but this is nothing to what we sailors sometimes undergo.

After parting company, we steered south-south-east, to go round Antonio, and so to Jamaica, (our cruise being out) with our fingers in our mouths, and all of us as green as you please. It happened to be my middle watch, and about three o'clock, when a man upon the forecastle bawls out: "Breakers ahead, and land upon the lee-bow;" I looked out, and it was so sure enough. "Ready about! put the helm down! Helm a lee!" Sir Hyde hearing me put the ship about, jumped upon deck. "Archer what's the matter? you are putting the ship about without my orders!" "Sir, 'tis time to go about; the ship is almost ashore, there's the land." "Good God so it is! Will the ship stay?" "Yes, Sir, I believe she will, if we don't make any confusion; she's all aback—forward now?" "Well," says he, "work the ship, I will not speak a single word." The ship stayed very well. "Then, heave the lead! see what water we have!" "Three fathom." "Keep the ship away, west-north-west."—"By the mark three." "This won't do, Archer." "No, sir, we had better haul more to the northward; we came south-south-east, and had better steer north-north-west." "Steady, and a quarter three." "This may do, as we deepen a little." "By the deep four." "Very well, my lad, heave quick." "Five fathom." "That's a fine fellow! another cast nimbly." "Quarter less eight." "That will do, come, we shall get clear by and by." "Mark under water five." "What's that?" "Only five fathom, Sir." "Turn all hands up, bring the ship to an anchor, boy!" "Are the anchors clear!" "In a moment, Sir," "All clear!" "What water have you in the chains now!" "Eight, half nine." "Keep fast the anchors till I call you." "Ay, ay, Sir, all fast!" "I have no ground with this line." "How many fathoms have you out? pass along the deep-sea line!" "Ay, ay, Sir." "Come are you all ready?" "All ready, Sir." "Heave away, watch! watch! bear away, veer away, no ground, Sir, with a hundred fathom." "That's clever, come, Madam Phœnix, there is another squeak in you yet—all down but the watch; secure the anchors again; heave the main-top-sail to the mast; luff, and bring her to the wind!"

I told you, Madam, you should have a little sea-jargon: if you can understand half of what is already said, I wonder at it, though it is nothing to what is to come yet, when the old hurricane begins. As soon as the ship was a little to rights, and all quiet again, Sir Hyde came to me in the most friendly manner, the tears almost starting from his eyes—"Archer, we ought all, to be much obliged to you for the safety of the ship, and perhaps of ourselves. I am particularly so; nothing but that instantaneous presence of mind and calmness saved her: another ship's length and we should have been fast on shore; had you been the least diffident, or made the least confusion, so as to make the ship baulk in her stays, she must have been inevitably lost." " Sir, you are very good, but I have done nothing that I suppose any body else would not have done, in the same situation. I did not turn all the hands up, knowing the watch able to work the ship; besides, had it spread immediately about the ship, that she was almost ashore, it might have created a confusion that was better avoided." " Well," says he, " 't is well indeed."

At daylight we found that the current had set us between the Collarado rocks and Cape Antonio, and that we could not have got out any other way than we did; there was a chance, but Providence is the best pilot. We had sunset that day twenty leagues to the south-east of our reckoning by the current.

After getting clear of this scrape, we thought ourselves fortunate, and made sail for Jamaica, but misfortune seemed to follow misfortune. The next night, my watch upon deck too, we were overtaken by a squall, like a hurricane while it lasted; for though I saw it coming, and prepared for it, yet, when it took the ship, it roared, and laid her down so, that I thought she would never get up again. However, by keeping her away, and clewing up every thing, she righted. The remainder of the night we had very heavy squalls, and in the morning found the mainmast sprung half the way through: one hundred and twenty-three leagues to the leeward of Jamaica, the hurricane months coming on, the head of the mainmast almost off, and at short allowance; well, we must make the best of it. The mainmast was well fished, but we were obliged to be very tender of carrying sail.

Nothing remarkable happened for ten days afterwards, when we chased a Yankee man of war for six hours, but could not get near enough to her before it was dark, to keep sight of her; so that we lost her because unable to carry any sail on the mainmast. In about twelve days more made the island of Jamaica, having weathered all the squalls, and put into Montego Bay for water; so that we had a strong party for kicking up a dust on shore, having found three men of war lying there. Dancing, &c. &c. till two o'clock every morning; little thinking what was to happen in four days' time: for out of the four men of war that were there, not one was in being at the end of that time, and not a soul alive but those left of our crew. Many of the houses, where we had been so merry, were so completely destroyed, that scarcely a vestige remained to mark where they stood Thy works are wonderful, O God! praised be thy holy Name!

September the 30th weighed; bound for Port Royal, round the eastward of the island; the Barbadoes and Victor had sailed the day before, and the Scarborough was to sail the next. Moderate weather until October the 2d. Spoke to the Barbadoes off Port Antonio in the evening. At eleven at night it began to snuffle, with a monstrous heavy appearance from the eastward. Close reefed the top-sails. Sir Hyde sent for me: "What sort of weather have we, Archer!" "It blows a little, and has a very ugly look: if in any other quarter but this, I should say we were going to have a gale of wind." "Ay, it looks so very often here when there is no wind at all; however, do n't hoist the top-sails till it clears a little, there is no trusting any country." At twelve I was relieved; the weather had the same rough look: however, they made sail upon her, but had a very dirty night. At eight in the morning I came up again, found it blowing hard from the east-north-east with close-reefed top-sails upon the ship, and heavy squalls at times. Sir Hyde came upon deck: "Well, Archer, what do you think of it?" "O, Sir, 't is only a touch of the times, we shall have an observation at twelve o'clock; the clouds are beginning to break; it will clear up at noon, or else— blow very hard afterwards." "I wish it would clear up, but I doubt it much. I was once in a hurricane in the East Indies, and the beginning of it had much the same appearance as this. So take in the top-sails, we have plenty of sea-room."

At twelve, the gale still increasing, wore ship, to keep as near mid-channel, between Jamaica and Cuba, as possible; at one the gale increasing still; at two harder yet: it still blows harder! Reefed the courses, and furled them; brought to under a foul mizen stay-sail, head to the northward. In the evening no sign of the weather taking off, but every appearance of the storm in-creasing, prepared for a proper gale of wind; secured all the sails with spare gaskets; good rolling tackles upon the yards; squared the booms; saw the boats all made fast; new lashed the guns; double breeched the lower deckers; saw that the carpenters had the tarpawlings and battens all ready for hatchways; got the top-gallant-mast down upon the deck; jib-boom and sprit-sail-yard fore and aft; in fact every thing we could think of to make a snug ship.

The poor devils of birds now began to find the uproar in the elements, for numbers, both of sea and land kinds, came on board of us. I took notice of some, which happening to be to leeward, turned to windward, like a ship, tack and tack; for they could not fly against it. When they came over the ship they dashed them-selves down upon the deck, without attempting to stir till picked up, and when let go again, they would not leave the ship, but en-deavored to hide themselves from the wind.

At eight o'clock a hurricane; the sea roaring, but the wind still steady to a point; did not ship a spoonful of water. How-ever, got the hatchways all secured, expecting what would be the consequence, should the wind shift; placed the carpenters by the mainmast, with broad axes, knowing, from experience, that at the moment you may want to cut it away to save the ship, an axe may not be found. Went to supper: bread, cheese, and porter. The purser frightened out of his wits about his bread bags; the

two marine officers as white as sheets, not understanding the ship's
working so much, and the noise of the lower deck guns; which,
by this time, made a pretty screeching to people not used to it;
it seemed as if the whole ship's side was going at each roll.
Wooden, our carpenter, was all this time smoking his pipe and
laughing at the doctor; the second lieutenant upon deck, and the
third in his hammock.

At ten o'clock I thought to get a little sleep; came to look into
my cot; it was full of water; for every seam, by the straining of
the ship, had begun to leak. Stretched myself, therefore, upon
deck between two chests, and left orders to be called, should the
least thing happen. At twelve a midshipman came to me: " Mr
Archer, we are just going to wear ship, Sir!" "O, very
well, I'll be up directly, what sort of weather have you got?"
" It blows a hurricane." Went upon deck, found Sir Hyde there.
" It blows damned hard, Archer." " It does indeed, Sir." " I
don't know that I ever remember its blowing so hard before, but
the ship makes a very good weather of it upon this tack as she
bows the sea; but we must wear her, as the wind has shifted to
the south-east, and we were drawing right upon Cuba; so do you
go forward, and have some hands stand by; loose the lee yard-arm
of the fore-sail, and when she is right before the wind, whip the
clue-garnet close up, and roll up the sail." " Sir! there is no
canvass can stand against this a moment; if we attempt to loose
him he will fly into ribands in an instant, and we may lose three
or four of our people; she'll wear by manning the fore shrouds."
" No, I don't think she will." " I'll answer for it, Sir; I have
seen it tried several times on the coast of America with success."
" Well, try it; if she does not wear, we can only loose the foresail afterwards." This was a great condescension from such a
man as Sir Hyde. However, by sending about two hundred people into the fore-rigging, after a hard struggle, she wore; found
she did not make so good weather on this tack as on the other;
for as the sea began to run across, she had not time to rise from
one sea before another lashed against her. Began to think we
should lose our masts, as the ship lay very much along, by the
pressure of the wind constantly upon the yards and masts alone:
for the poor mizen-stay-sail had gone in shreds long before, and
the sails began to fly from the yards through the gaskets into
coach whips. My God! to think that the wind could have such
force!

Sir Hyde now sent me to see what was the matter between
decks, as there was a good deal of noise. As soon as I was below, one of the Marine officers calls out: " Good God! Mr.
Archer, we are sinking, the water is up to the bottom of my cot."
" Pooh, pooh! as long as it is not over your mouth, you are well
off; what the devil do you make this noise for?" I found there
was some water between decks, but nothing to be alarmed at

scuttled the deck, and let it run into the well; found she made a good deal of water through the sides and decks; turned the watch below to the pumps, though only two feet of water in the well; but expected to be kept constantly at work now, as the ship labored much, with scarcely a part of her above water but the quarter-deck, and that but seldom. "Come, pump away, my boys. Carpenters, get the weather chain-pump rigged." "All ready, Sir." "Then man it, and keep both pumps going."

At two o'clock the chain-pump was choked; set the carpenters at work to clear it; the two head pumps at work upon deck: the ship gained upon us while our chain-pumps were idle; in a quarter of an hour they were at work again, and we began to gain upon her. While I was standing at the pumps, cheering the people, the carpenter's mate came running to me with a face as long as my arm: "O, Sir! the ship has sprung a leak in the gunner's room." "Go, then, and tell the carpenter to come to me, but don't speak a word to any one else." "Mr. Goodinoh, I am told there is a leak in the gunner's room; go and see what is the matter, but don't alarm any body, and come and make your report privately to me." In a short time he returned: "Sir, there's nothing there, 'tis only the water washing up between the timbers that this booby has taken for a leak." "O, very well; go upon deck and see if you can keep any of the water from washing down below." "Sir, I have had four people constantly keeping the hatchways secure, but there is such a weight of water upon the deck that nobody can stand it when the ship rolls." The gunner soon afterwards came to me: "Mr. Archer, I should be glad if you would step this way into the magazine for a moment:" I thought some damned thing was the matter, and ran directly: "Well, what is the matter here?" "The ground-tier of powder is spoiled, and I want to show you that it is not out of carelessness in me in stowing it, for no powder in the world could be better stowed. Now, Sir, what am I to do? if you don't speak to Sir Hyde, he will be angry with me." I could not forbear smiling to see how easy he took the danger of the ship, and said to him: "Let us shake off this gale of wind first, and talk of the damaged powder afterwards."

At four we had gained upon the ship a little, and I went upon deck, it being my watch. The second lieutenant relieved me at the pumps. Who can attempt to describe the appearance of things upon deck? If I was to write for ever I could not give you an idea of it—a total darkness all above; the sea on fire, running as it were in Alps, or Peaks of Teneriffe; (mountains are too common an idea); the wind roaring louder than thunder, (absolutely no flight of imagination), the whole made more terrible, if possible, by a very uncommon kind of blue lightning; the poor ship very much pressed, yet doing what she could, shaking her sides, and groaning at every stroke. Sir Hyde upon deck lashed

to windward! I soon lashed myself alongside of him, and told him
the situation of things below, saying the ship did not make more
water than might be expected in such weather, and that I was
only afraid of a gun breaking loose. "I am not in the least
afraid of that; I have commanded her six years, and have had
many a gale of wind in her; so that her iron work, which always
gives way first, is pretty well tried. Hold fast! that was an ugly
sea; we must lower the yards, I believe, Archer; the ship is much
pressed." "If we attempt it, Sir, we shall lose them, for a man
aloft can do nothing; besides their being down would ease the
ship very little; the mainmast is a sprung mast; I wish it was
overboard without carrying any thing else along with it; but that
can soon be done, the gale cannot last for ever; 'twill soon be
daylight now." Found by the master's watch that it was five
o'clock, though but a little after four by ours; glad it was so near
daylight, and looked for it with much anxiety. Cuba, thou art
much in our way! Another ugly sea: sent a midshipman to bring
news from the pumps: the ship was gaining on them very much,
for they had broken one of their chains, but it was almost mended
again. News from the pump again. "She still gains! a heavy
lee!" Back-water from leeward, half-way up the quarter-deck,
filled one of the cutters upon the booms, and tore her all to
pieces; the ship lying almost on her beam ends, and not attempting to right again. Word from below that the ship still gained on
them, as they could not stand to the pumps, she lay so much along.
I said to Sir Hyde: "This is no time, Sir, to think of saving the
masts, shall we cut the mainmast away?" "Ay! as fast as you
can." I accordingly went into the weather chains with a pole-
ax, to cut away the lanyards; the boatswain went to leeward, and
the carpenters stood by the mast. We were all ready, when a
very violent sea broke right on board of us, carried every thing
upon deck away, filled the ship with water, the main and mizen-
masts went, the ship righted, but was in the last struggle of sinking under us.

As soon as we could shake our heads above water, Sir Hyde
exclaimed: "We are gone, at last, Archer! foundered at sea!"
"Yes, Sir, farewell, and the Lord have mercy upon us!" I then
turned about to look forward at the ship; and thought she was
struggling to get rid of some of the water; but all in vain, she was
almost full below. "Almighty God! I thank thee, that now I am
leaving this world, which I have always considered as only a passage to a better, I die with a full hope of thy mercies, through
the merits of Jesus Christ, thy son, our Saviour!"

I then felt sorry that I could swim, as by that means I might
be a quarter of an hour longer dying than a man who could not,
and it is impossible to divest ourselves of a wish to preserve life
At the end of these reflections I thought I heard the ship thump
and grinding under our feet; it was so. "Sir, the ship is ashore!"

"What do you say?" "The ship is ashore, and we may save ourselves yet!" By this time the quarter-deck was full of men who had come up from below; and 'the Lord have mercy upon us,' flying about from all quarters. The ship now made every body sensible that she was ashore, for every stroke threatened a total dissolution of her whole frame; found she was stern ashore, and the bow broke the sea a good deal, though it was washing clean over at every stroke. Sir Hyde cried out: "Keep to the quarter-deck, my lads, when she goes to pieces 't is your best chance!" Providentially got the foremast cut away, that she might not pay round broad-side. Lost five men cutting away the fore-mast, by the breaking of a sea on board just as the mast went. That was nothing; every one expected it would be his own fate next; looked for daybreak with the greatest impatience. At last it came; but what a scene did it show us! The ship upon a bed of rocks, mountains of them on one side, and Cordilleras of water on the other; our poor ship grinding and crying out at every stroke between them; going away by piece-meal. However, to show the unaccountable workings of Providence, that which often appears to be the greatest evil, proves to be the greatest good! That unmerciful sea lifted and beat us up so high among the rocks, that at last the ship scarcely moved. She was very strong, and did not go to pieces at the first thumping, though her decks tumbled in. We found afterwards that she had beat over a ledge of rocks, almost a quarter of a mile in extent beyond us, where, if she had struck, every soul of us must have perished.

I now began to think of getting on shore, so stripped off my coat and shoes for a swim, and looked for a line to carry the end with me. Luckily could not find one, which gave me time for recollection: "This wont do for me, to be the first man out of the ship, and first lieutenant; we may get to England again, and people may think I paid a great deal of attention to myself and did not care for any body else. No, that wont do; instead of being the first, I'll see every man, sick and well, out of her before me."

I now thought there was no probability of the ship's soon going to pieces, therefore had not a thought of instant death: took a look round with a kind of philosophic eye, to see how the same situation affected my companions, and was surprised to find the most swaggering, swearing bullies in fine weather, now the most pitiful wretches on earth, when death appeared before them. However, two got safe; by which means, with a line, we got a hawser on shore, and made fast to the rocks, upon which many ventured and arrived safe. There were some sick and wounded on board, who could not avail themselves of this method; we, therefore, got a spare top-sail-yard from the chains and placed one end ashore and the other on the cabin window, so that most of the sick go ashore this way.

As I had determined, so I was the last man out of the ship; this was about ten o'clock. The gale now began to break. Sir Hyde came to me, and taking me by the hand was so affected that he was scarcely able to speak. "Archer, I am happy beyond expression, to see you on shore, but look at our poor Phœnix!" I turned about, but could not say a single word, being too full: my mind had been too intensely occupied before; but every thing now rushed upon me at once, so that I could not contain myself, and I indulged for a full quarter of an hour in tears.

By twelve it was pretty moderate; got some nails on shore and made tents; found great quantities of fish driven up by the sea into holes of the rocks; knocked up a fire, and had a most comfortable dinner. In the afternoon made a stage from the cabin-windows to the rocks, and got out some provisions and water, lest the ship should go to pieces, in which case we must all have perished of hunger and thirst; for we were upon a desolate part of the coast, and under a rocky mountain, that could not supply us with a single drop of water.

Slept comfortably this night and the next day, the idea of death vanishing by degrees, the prospect of being prisoners, during the war, at the Havanna, and walking three hundred miles to it through the woods, was rather unpleasant. However, to save life for the present, we employed this day in getting more provisions and water on shore, which was not an easy matter, on account of decks, guns, and rubbish, and ten feet water that lay over them. In the evening I proposed to Sir Hyde to repair the remains of the only boat left, and to venture in her to Jamaica myself; and in case I arrived safe, to bring vessels to take them all off; a proposal worthy of consideration. It was, next day, agreed to; therefore got the cutter on shore, and set the carpenters to work on her; in two days she was ready, and at four o'clock in the afternoon I embarked with four volunteers and a fortnight's provision, hoisted English colors as we put off from the shore, and received three cheers from the lads left behind, which we returned, and set sail with a light heart; having not the least doubt, that, with God's assistance, we should come and bring them all off. Had a very squally night, and a very leaky boat, so as to keep two buckets constantly baling. Steered her myself the whole night by the stars, and in the morning saw the coast of Jamaica distant twelve leagues. At eight in the evening arrived at Montego Bay.

I must now begin to leave off, particularly as I have but half an hour to conclude; else my pretty little short letter will lose its passage, which I should not like, after being ten days, at different times, writing it, beating up with the convoy to the northward, which is a reason that this epistle will never read well; for I never sat down with a proper disposition to go on with it; but as I knew something of the kind would please you, I was resolved to finish it yet it will not bear an overhaul; so don't expose your son s nonsense.

But to proceed—I instantly sent off an express to the admiral, another to the Porcupine man of war, and went myself to Martha Bray to get vessels; for all their vessels here, as well as many of their houses, were gone to *Moco*. Got three small vessels, and set out back again to Cuba, where I arrived the fourth day after leaving my companions. I thought the ship's crew would have devoured me on my landing; they presently whisked me up on their shoulders and carried me to the tent where Sir Hyde was.

I must omit many little occurrences that happened on shore, for want of time; but I shall have a number of stories to tell when I get alongside of you; and the next time I visit you I shall not be in such a hurry to quit you as I was the last, for then I hoped my nest would have been pretty well feathered:—But my tale is forgotten.

I found the Porcupine had arrived that day, and the lads had built a boat almost ready for launching, that would hold fifty of them, which was intended for another trial, in case I had foundered. Next day embarked all our people that were left, amounting to two hundred and fifty; for some had died of their wounds they received in getting on shore; others of drinking rum, and others had straggled into the country. All our vessels were so full of people, that we could not take away the few clothes that were saved from the wreck; but that was a trifle since we had preserved our lives and liberty. To make short of my story, we all arrived safe at Montego Bay, and shortly after at Port Royal, in the Janus, which was sent on purpose for us, and were all honorably acquitted for the loss of the ship. I was made admiral's aid de camp, and a little time afterwards sent down to St. Juan's as captain of the Resource, to bring what were left of the poor devils to Blue Fields, on the Musquito shore, and then to Jamaica, where they arrived after three months absence, and without a prize, though I looked out hard off Porto Bello and Carthagena. Found in my absence that I had been appointed captain of the Tobago, where I remain his Majesty's most true and faithful servant, and my dear mother's most dutiful son,

—— ARCHER

MUTINY OF THE BOUNTY.

The merchants and planters of the West India islands, having represented to his majesty that an essential benefit might be derived by introducing the bread-fruit as an article of food for the

inhabitants of those islands: his majesty was graciously pleased
to direct the board of Admiralty to equip a ship for this purpose.
Accordingly one proper for such a voyage was purchased, and
fitted up in a most commodious manner to receive the plants. She
was named the Bounty, her burden about two hundred and fifteen
tons, and the command conferred on Lieutenant W. Bligh, who
had sailed as master with Captain James Cook, on his voyage of
discoveries. The whole crew consisted of forty-six.

On the 4th of November, 1787, the Bounty arrived at Spithead,
and on the 24th of the same month, Mr. Bligh received his final
orders from the Admiralty, which were to proceed round Cape
Horn to the Society islands, there to take on board as many of
the bread-fruit trees and plants as may be thought necessary,
from thence to proceed through Endeavour Straights, to Prince's
Island in the Straights of Sunda, or if it should be more convenient, to pass on the eastern side of Java, to some port on the
north side of that island, where any bread-fruit trees which may
have been injured, or have died, may be replaced by mangosteens,
duriens, and other fruit trees of that quarter, as well as the rice
plant which grows upon dry land. From Prince's Island, or the
island of Java, to return by the Cape of Good Hope to the West
Indies, and deposite one half of the trees and plants at his Majesty's Botanical garden at St. Vincent, for the benefit of the Windward Islands; then to go on to Jamaica, and having delivered the
remainder to Mr. East, or such person or persons as may be
authorised by the governor and council to receive them, to refresh
the people and return to England.

As the season might be too far advanced for effecting a passage
round Cape Horn, the Admiralty gave Mr. Bligh discretional
orders in this case, to go round the Cape of Good Hope.

On the 23d of December, the Bounty sailed from Spithead
On the 6th of January, 1788 she anchored in Santa Cruz road,
on the island of Teneriff. On the 10th, having taken on board
wine and other refreshments, Mr. Bligh proceeded on his voyage.
On the 20th of March the coast of Terra del Fuego was discovered; from this time they began to experience very tempestuous
weather, the winds in general blowing with great violence from
the westward, attended with frequent snow and hail-storms. Mr.
Bligh struggled with great perseverance against these troubles
for thirty days; and then came to the resolution of bearing away
for the Cape of Good Hope, where he arrived on the 23d of May.
While at the Cape Mr. Bligh procured such plants and seeds as
he thought would be valuable at Otaheite, or any other place at
which he might stop. On the 1st of July he sailed from the Cape,
and shaped his course for New Holland; the southern promontory
of which he made on the 19th of August. The next day he anchored in Adventure Bay: here the ship was refitted; the only
fresh water to be procured was what had lodged in deep pits and

gullies after tl.   .iiny season: it was found perfectly sweet and good.

This par. of the coast of New Holland abounds in large forest-trees, some running to the height of one hundred and fifty feet; one in partic dar which was seen by the Bounty's people, measured thirty-two feet in girth.   The wood of these trees is in general firm, but of two heavy and solid a nature for masts, though it might answer extremely well for ship-building.   On the trunk ot a decayed tree was observed to have been cut with a knife, the letters, " A. D. 1773,'· which is supposed to have been done by some of Captain Furneaux's people who were at this place in the March of that year.

The natives who were seen, were perfectly naked, extremely wild, but inoffensive.   Mr. Bligh held out every friendly encouragement to have an intercourse with them, but without effect.

Previous to their leaving Adventure Bay, Mr. Nelson, the botanist, planted some apple and other fruit trees, and sowed various kinds of seeds.   On the 4th of September they sailed from hence, and steering to the S. E. arrived on the 26th of October in Matavai Bay, in the island of Otaheite.

Mr. Bligh immediately set about executing the object of his voyage; for which purpose the botanists were sent on shore, in search of, and to collect the bread-fruit plants, in which they found no difficulty, receiving every assistance from the natives, with whom the greatest friendship and intimacy subsisted during their continuance at this island.

On the 31st of March, 1789, having collected as many of the trees and plants as could be conveniently stowed, they were taken on board to the number of one thousand and fifteen, contained in seven hundred and seventy-four pots, thirty-nine tubs, and twenty-six boxes; besides several other plants of various descriptions. The Bounty being now ready for sea, Mr. Bligh made the farewell presents to his friends, many of whom expressed a great desire to accompany him to England, and shewed evident signs of regret at their departure.

On the 4th of April, they took a last and affectionate leave of their hospitable Otaheiten friends, and put to sea; pursuing nearly the same tract to the Friendly Islands with former navigators; on the morning of the 10th an island and several small keys near it. were discovered; the island had a most beautiful appearance, it was covered with cocoa nut and other trees, interspersed with beau iful lawns.   The next day a canoe came off with some of tho natives, who were extremely familiar, and spoke a similar language to those of Otaheite.   They said the island was called Wytootac-kee.   Its circumference is about ten miles; latitude 18° 50,' south, longitude 200° 19 east.

Leaving this island, they proceeded for the Friendly Islands, and on the 23d anchored at Annamooka; at this place Mr. Bligh

saw an old man, who he remembered when he was here with
Captain Cook, in the year 1777, from whom he learnt that several
of the cattle which had been then left were still alive and had
bred.   Mr. Bligh had also the satisfaction to see that most of the
seeds which had been sown at that time had succeeded, especially
the pines, of which fruit the natives were very fond.

On the 27th, having completed taking on board wood and water,
and procured some bread-fruit plants to replace those which were
dead or sickly, they sailed from Annamooka.

A scene as unexpected as deplorable was now about to present
itself, which rendered the object of the voyage, after all Mr.
Bligh's exertions, ineffectual.

This individual's bearing towards his officers and crew as it
was afterwards proved, had never been of the most gentle or
conciliating kind; indeed, he had frequently indulged in the
coarsest and most brutal language towards them, and his acts
were often oppressive in the extreme.   In the afternoon of the
27th, Lieutenant Bligh came upon deck, and missing some of the
cocoa nuts which had been piled up between the guns, said they
had been stolen, and could not have been taken away without
the knowledge of the officers, all of whom were sent for and
questioned on the subject.   On their declaring that they had not
seen any of the people touch them, he exclaimed, " Then you
must have taken them yourselves;" and proceeded to inquire
of them separately how many they had purchased.   On coming
to Mr. Christian, that gentleman answered, "I do not know, sir,
but I hope you do not think me so mean as to be guilty of stealing yours   Mr. Bligh answered, " yes, you d——d hound, I
do— you must have stolen them from me, or you would be able to
give a better account of them;" then turning to the other officers,
he said, " God d—n you, you scoundrels, you are all thieves
alike and combine with the men to rob me: I suppose you will
steal my yams next; but I'll sweat you for it, you rascals—I'll
make half of you jump overboard before you get through Endeavour Straits."   This threat was followed by an order to the clerk
" to stop the villains' grog, and give them but half a pound of
yams to-morrow; if they steal them, I'll reduce them to a
quarter."

On the morning of the 28th of April, just before sun-rise, Mr.
Christian, one of the mates, (who had for some time been intrusted with the charge of the third watch), accompanied by the
master at arms, gunner's mate, and Thomas Burkett, a seaman,
entered Mr. Bligh's cabin while he was asleep, and seizing him,
bound his hands behind his back, at the same time threatening
instant death if he resisted or made the least noise.   Not intimidated by their threats, Mr. Bligh resolutely called for assistance,
but the mutineers had taken care, previously to secure all those
who were not concerned in their diabolical scheme.   They then

pulled him from his bed, and forced him upon deck, with nothing on him but his shirt, where a guard was placed over him. The boatswain was ordered to hoist the launch out, which being done, Mr. Hayward and Mr. Hallet, midshipmen, Mr. Samuel, the clerk, with some others, were directed to go into her. Mr. Bligh frequently remonstrated with his people on the impropriety and violence of their proceedings, and endeavored to persuade them to return to their duty; but all his efforts proved ineffectual: the only reply he could obtain was, "hold your tongue sir or you are dead this instant."

The officers who were confined below, were next called upon deck and forced into the boat. The mutineers were some time undecided whether they should detain the carpenter or his mate; at length, after much altercation, it was determined that the carpenter should go into the boat; and it was not without much opposition that they permitted him to take his tool-chest with him. Upon which some of them swore, that "he (meaning Mr. Bligh) would find his way home if he gets any thing with him, and that he would have a vessel built in less than a month." While others turned their miserable situation into ridicule, little expecting from the boat being so deep and crowded, that she could long keep the sea. All those now being in the boat who were intended to accompany their unfortunate commander, Christian addressed him, saying,—"Come, Captain Bligh, your officers and men are now in the boat, and you must go with them; if you attempt to make the least resistance you will instantly be put to death." He was then forced over the side, and his hands unbound. When they were putting him out of the ship, Mr. Bligh looked steadfastly at Christian, and asked him, if his treatment was a proper return for the many instances he had received of his friendship? At this question he seemed confused, and answered with much emotion,—"That, Captain Bligh,——that is the thing;——I am in hell—I am in hell."

The boat was veered astern, and soon after cast adrift, amidst the ridicule and scoffs of these deluded and unthinking men, whose general shout was, "huzza for Otaheite." The armorer and carpenter's mates called on Mr. Bligh, and begged him to remember that they had no hand in the transaction, and some others seemed to express by their manner a contrition for having joined in the mutiny.

As no complaints had been made, or dissatisfaction shown, Mr. Bligh was at a loss how to account for this sudden and unexpected change in the disposition of his people; unless it rose from the temptations held out to them by the chiefs of Otaheite, who were much attached to the English, and allured them by promises of large possessions if they would remain behind; this, in addition to the connexion which they had formed with the women, whom Mr. Bligh describes as handsome, mild and cheer

ful in their manners and conversation; possessed of great sensi
sibility, and having sufficient delicacy to make them admired and
beloved.

Although these were perhaps among the inducements which
led to the mutiny, there is no doubt but that Bligh's intemperate
language and insulting demeanor were the chief causes of the
unhappy deed. It is pretty evident, that the mutiny was not, as
Bligh in his narrative stated it to have been, the result of a conspiracy. It appears from the minutes of the court-martial, which
was afterwards instituted, that the whole affair was planned and
executed between the hours of four and eight o'clock on the
morning of the 28th April, when Christian had the watch upon
deck; that Christian, unable longer to bear the abusive language,
had meditated his own escape from the ship the day before, choosing to trust himself to fate rather than submit to the constant up-
braiding to which he had been subject; but the unfortunate business of the cocoa nuts drove him to the commission of the rash
and felonious act which ended, as such criminal acts usually do,
in his own destruction and that of a great number of others, many
of whom were wholly innocent.

The following persons were those turned adrift with Mr. Bligh
in the boat.

John Fryer, master.

Tho. Ledwood, acting surgeon;
he was never heard of after
Mr. Bligh left Batavia.

D. Nelson, botanist; died at
Batavia.

Wm Peckover, gunner.

Wm. Cole, boatswain.

Wm. Purcill, carpenter.

Wm. Elphilstone, master's
mate; died at Batavia.

T. Hayward, }
J. Hallet, }

John Norton, quarter-master
killed by the natives at Tosoa

P. Linkletter, quarter-master;
died at Batavia.

L. Lebogue, sail-maker.

John Smith, cook.

Tho. Hall, ditto; died at Batavia.

Robert Tinkler, boy.

There remained in the Bounty,

Fletcher Christian, master's
mate.

P. Heywood, }
E. Young } midshipmen.
G. Stewart, }

J. Mills, gunner's mate.

Tho. M'Intosh, of carpenter's
crew.

C. Churchill, master at arms.

Joseph Coleman, armorer.

Wm. Brown, gardiner; and 14
able seamen.

Before the boat was cast off, Mr. Bligh begged that some arms
might be handed into her; but these unfeeling wretches laughed at
him, and said " he was well acquainted with the people among
whom he was going, and therefore did not want them." They
however, threw four cutlasses into the boat

Their whole stock of provisions consisted of one hundred and fifty pound of bread, sixteen pieces of pork, six quarts of rum, with twenty-eight gallons of water; there were also four empty barrecoes in the boat. The boatswain had been allowed to collect a small quantity of twine, some canvas, lines, and cordage. Mr Samuel, the clerk, had been also permitted to take a quadrant and compass; but he was forbidden on pain of death to touch either chart, ephemeris, book of astronomical observations, sextant, time-keeper, or any of the surveys or drawings which Mr. Bligh had been collecting for fifteen years. Mr. Samuel had the good fortune to secure Mr. Bligh's journal and commission, with some other material ship papers.

At the time the boat left the ship they were about ten leagues from Tosoa. Mr. Bligh's first determination was to steer for this place, to seek a supply of bread-fruit and water, from thence to proceed to Tongataboo, and there to solicit the king to suffer him to equip the boat, and grant them such a supply of water and provisions, as might enable them to reach the East Indies. Arriving at Tosoa, they found the natives unfriendly and hostile; and availing themselves of the defenceless state of the English, attacked them violently with stones, so that the supply they got here was very scanty. It was indeed with some difficulty they escaped being entirely cut off by the natives; which most probably would have been the case, had not one of the crew (John Norton) resolutely jumped on shore and cast off the stern-fast of the boat; this brave fellow fell a sacrifice to preserve the lives of his companions; he was surrounded and inhumanly murdered by these savages.

The reception they met at Tosoa, gave them little encouragement to touch at Tongataboo; as it was evident that the former good behavior of these people proceeded more from the dread of fire arms, than a natural disposition to be friendly.

It now seemed the general wish of all in the boat, that Mr Bligh should conduct them towards home. He pointed out to them that no hopes of relief remained, excepting what might be found at New Holland, or the island of Timor, which was at the distance of full one thousand and two hundred leagues; and that it would require the greatest economy to be observed, with regard to the scanty allowance which they had to live upon for so long a voyage. It was therefore agreed by the whole crew, that only an ounce of bread, and a quarter of a pint of water should be issued to each person per day. After Mr. Bligh had recommended to them in the most solemn manner not to depart from the promise they had made; he on the 2d of May bore away, and shaped his course for New Holland, across a sea little explored, in a boat only twenty-three feet in length, six feet nine inches in breadth, and two feet nine inches deep, with eighteen persons on board, and heavy laden. The next day they encountered a violent

storm, the boat shipped such a quantity of water, that it was by
great exertions and with the utmost difficulty she could be kept
afloat The day following it moderated. On the 5th, they saw
and passed a cluster of islands, continuing their course to the
north-west. Hitherto they had not been able to keep any other
account than by guess; but had now succeeded in getting a log-
line marked, and by a little practice, some could count the seconds with a tolerable degree of exactness. The miserable and
confined state in which they were, induced Mr. Bligh to put his
crew to watch and watch, so that one half might be on the look
out, while the others lay down in the boat's bottom, or upon a
chest; even this gave but a trifling alleviation to their sufferings;
being exposed to constant wet and cold, and not having room to
stretch their limbs, they became often so dreadfully cramped, as
to be incapable of moving them.

On the 7th, another group of islands was seen, from whence
they observed two large canoes in pursuit of them, one of which
at four o'clock in the afternoon, had arrived within two miles of
the boat, when she gave over the chase and returned in shore.
Mr. Bligh imagined from their direction and vicinity to the
Friendly Islands these must have been the Fegee Islands.

On the 8th, the weather was moderate and fair, which gave
them an opportunity to dry their clothes, and clean out the boat.
Mr. Bligh also amused the people, by relating to them a description of New Guinea and New Holland, with every information in
his power, that in case any accident happened to him, the survivors might be able to pursue their course to Timor; which place
they before knew nothing of except by name.

On the 10th, the weather again began to be extremely boisterous,
with constant rain and frequent thunder and lightning; the sea
was so rough, as often to break over the boat; so that they were
forever baling, and often in imminent danger of perishing; in addition to their misfortunes, the bread was damaged by the salt
water; their clothes never being dry, they derived no refreshment
from the little rest they sometimes got; and many were so benumbed and cramped by the cold, that they were afflicted with
violent shiverings and pains in the bowels. As the weather still
continued tempestuous, Mr. Bligh, as an expedient, recommended it to every one to strip, and wring their clothes in the salt-
water, which had a good effect, and produced a warmth, that
while wet with the rain they could not have.

On the 14th they saw a number of islands, which appeared to
be a new discovery, but as they lie so near the New Hebrides,
they may be considered as a part of that group. Their latitude
from 13 deg. 16 min. to 14 deg. south, longitude 110 deg. 67 min
17 min. to 168 deg. 34 min. east from Greenwich; to these they
gave the name of Bligh's Islands.

On the 24th, it was thought necessary to reduce their already miserable pittance; it was accordingly agreed that each person should receive one 25th part of a pound of bread for breakfast, and the same quantity for dinner; so that by omitting the allowance for supper, they would have forty-three days provisions.

The next day they saw several noddies and other sea fowl, some of which they were so fortunate as to catch, and served them out as a part of the allowance. The sight of these birds indicated their being in the neighborhood of land. The weather was now more serene; but even this became distressing to them; the heat of the sun was so intense, that many of the people were seized with a langor and faintness, which made life indifferent At one in the morning on the 29th, breakers were discovered about a quarter of a mile distant under their lee; they immediately hauled off and were soon out of danger. At daylight, they again stood in and discovered the reef, over which the sea broke furiously. Steering along the edge of it, an opening was soon observed, through which the boat passed; a small island which lay within the reef of a moderate height, Mr. Bligh named Island of Direction, as it serves to show the entrance of the channel; its latitude is 12 deg. 51 min. south. As they advanced within the reef, the coast of New Holland began to show itself distinctly. They landed in a fine sandy bay on an island near the main: here they found plenty of oysters, water, and berries, which to men in their deplorable condition, were looked upon as luxuries. After a more comfortable repose than they had experienced for many nights, they were preparing the next day to depart, when about twenty natives made their appearance on the opposite shore, running and hallooing, at the same time making signs to land. Each was armed with a spear or lance; several others were seen peeping over the tops of the adjacent hills. Mr. Bligh finding that he was discovered, judged it most prudent to make the best of his way to sea. He named the island on which they landed Restoration Island; as it was not only applicable to their own situation but the anniversary of King Charles's Restoration when it was discovered; its observed latitude 12 deg. 39 min. south.

As the boat sailed along the shore, many other parties of the natives came down, waving green boughs as a token of friendship; but Mr. Bligh, suspicious of their intentions, would not venture to land. These people were naked, with black and woolly hair.

On the 31st they landed on a small island, in order to get a distinct view of the coast; from thence, after making a hearty meal on oysters, they again put to sea, steering along the shore, often touching at the different islands and keys to refresh themselves, and get such supplies as they afforded. On the evening of the 3d of June, they had passed through Endeavour Straits, and were once more launched into the open ocean, shaping their course for the island of Timor, which they were encouraged to expect they might reach in eight or ten days. A continuance of

wet and tempestuous weather, affected even the stoutest among
them to such a degree, from incessant fatigue, that many showed
evident signs of approaching dissolution. Mr. Bligh used every
effort to revive their drooping spirits, and comforted them with a
hope that they would soon arrive at a port where their distresses
would be relieved.

At three o'clock in the morning on the 12th of June, to their
inexpressible joy, the island of Timor was discovered; and on the
14th they arrived at the Dutch settlement of Coupang. Nothing
could exceed the friendly and hospitable reception they met with
from the governor, Mr. Van Este, who was lying almost at the
point of death; he regretted that his infirmity should prevent him
from officiating as a friend himself, but assured Mr. Bligh that he
would give such orders, as should procure him and his fellow sufferers every assistance in his power; he accordingly committed
them to the care of Mr. Wanjen, his son-in-law, who, with the
other principal persons of Coupang, rendered their situation comfortable during the time they staid among them.

Mr. Bligh presented the governor a formal account of the loss
of the Bounty; and a requisition in his Majesty's name, that instructions might be sent to all the Dutch settlements, to stop the
ship if she should touch at any of them; with a list and description
of the mutineers.

A short time after their arrival at Coupang, by the humane and
kind attention of the Dutch inhabitants, they had so much recovered
their health, and strength, that Mr. Bligh purchased a schooner
for one thousand rix dollars, to convey them to Batavia before the
October fleet should sail for Europe. This vessel was named the
Resource; and by the assistance and friendship of Mr. Wanjen,
(to whose liberal and hospitable treatment they were all much indebted), Mr. Bligh was able to procure four brass swivels, fourteen stand of arms, and some ammunition, which was necessary
to protect them against the pirates who infest the coast of Java.

On the 20th of July, Mr. David Nelson, the botanist died of
an inflammatory fever; he was a man much respected, and of great
scientific knowledge. This was his second voyage to the South
Seas in the capacity of botanist.

The schooner being ready for sea, on the 30th of August Mr.
Bligh and his crew took an affectionate leave of their benefactors,
and sailed from Coupang, with the launch that had preserved
their lives, in tow.

On the 1st of October they arrived in Batavia road. The next
day Mr. Bligh was taken so extremely ill, that he was obliged to
be moved into the country. Shortly after the Dutch surgeon-
general represented to him that his complaint was of such a
nature, that unless he quitted the air of Batavia, it might prove
fatal. In consequence of this, Mr. Bligh applied to the governor-
general for permission to return to Europe by the fleet which

was on the point of sailing; which being granted, he took his passage on board a Dutch packet, and sailed from Batavia on the 16th of October, 1789; the governor promising him that the remainder of his crew should be sent home by the earliest opportunity. On the 14th of March, 1790, he arrived in England. Out of the nineteen who were in the boat when she left the ship, only twelve lived to return to their native country.

The tide of public applause set as strongly in favor of Bligh, on account of his sufferings and the successful issue of his daring enterprise, as its indignation was launched against Christian and his associates, for the audacious and criminal deed they had committed. Bligh was promoted by the Admiralty to the rank of commander, and speedily sent out a second time to transport the bread-fruit to the West Indies, which he without the least obstruction, successfully accomplished; and his majesty's government was no sooner made acquainted with the atrocious act of piracy and mutiny, than it determined to adopt every possible means to apprehend and bring to condign punishment the perpetrators of so foul a deed. For this purpose, the Pandora frigate of twenty-four guns, and one hundred and sixty men, was despatched, under the command of Captain Edward Edwards, with orders to proceed in the first instance to Otaheite, and, not finding the mutineers there, to visit the different groups of the Society and Friendly Islands, and others in the neighboring parts of the Pacific, using his best endeavors to seize and bring home in confinement the whole or such part of the delinquents as he might be able to discover.

This voyage was in the sequel almost as disastrous as that of the Bounty, but from a different cause. The waste of human life was much greater, occasioned by the wreck of the ship, in returning; and the distress experienced by the crew was not much less, owing to the famine and thirst they had to suffer in a navigation of eleven hundred miles in open boats; but the captain succeeded in fulfilling a part of his instructions, by taking fourteen of the mutineers, of whom ten were brought safe to England, the other four being drowned when the ship was wrecked. Soon after their arrival, a court-martial assembled to try the prisoners, on board his majesty's ship Duke, on the 12th September, 1792. Against seven of the ten the charges of mutiny were proved, and they were adjudged worthy of death; two of them, however, Peter Heywood and James Morrison were earnestly recommended by the court to his majesty's mercy, and they were pardoned accordingly. Heywood, who at the time of the mutiny was but sixteen years of age, was very honorably and fully acquitted in public opinion of any participation in the deed, and he afterwards rose to distinction, without any invidious suspicion being attached to him. He died in the year 1831, leaving behind him a high and unblemished character in that service of which he was a most

20 *

honorable, intelligent, and distinguished member. The remaining five of the convicts were hung pursuant to sentence.

———

Twenty years had passed away, and the Bounty, and Fletcher Christian, and the piratical crew that he had carried off with him in that ship, had long ceased to occupy a thought in the public mind. It happened however, that an accidental discovery, as interesting as it was wholly unexpected, was brought to light in consequence of an American trading vessel having, by mere chance, approached one of those numerous islands in the Pacific, against whose steep and iron-bound shore the surf almost everlastingly rolls with such tremendous violence as to bid defiance to any attempts of boats to land, except at particular times and in very few places.

Captain Folger, of the American brig Topaz, of Boston, in September, 1808, landed on Pitcairn's Island in latitude 25° 2′ south, longitude 130° west, where he found an Englishman, of the name of Alexander Smith, the only person remaining of nine that had escaped in the Bounty. Smith related that, after putting Captain Bligh in the boat, Christian took command of the ship and went to Otaheite, where many of the crew left her, except Christian, Smith, and seven others, who each took wives, and six Otaheitan men-servants, and shortly after arrived at Pitcairn's Island, where they ran the ship ashore and broke her up; this event took place in the year 1790.

About four years after their arrival (a great jealousy existing), the Otaheitans secretly revolted, and killed every Englishman except Smith, whom they severely wounded in the neck with a pistol ball. The same night, the widows of the deceased Englishmen arose and put to death the whole of the Otaheitans, leaving Smith the only man alive upon the island, with eight or nine women and several small children. On his recovery, he applied himself to tilling the ground, so that it now produced plenty of yams, cocoa-nuts, bananas and plantains; hogs and poultry in abundance. There were some grown-up men and women, children of the mutineers, on the island, the whole population amounting to about thirty-five, who acknowledged Smith as father and commander of them all; they all spoke English, and had been educated by him in a moral and religious way.

It was asserted by the second mate of the Topaz, that Christian, the ringleader became insane shortly after taking up his abode on the island, and threw himself off the rocks into the sea. It is clear enough that this misguided and ill-fated young man was never happy after the rash and criminal step he had taken. He was always sullen and morose, and committed so many acts of wanton oppression as very soon incurred the hatred of his companions. According to the account of Smith, or as he was usually called, John Adams, the cause of Christian's death was his having forcibly seized on the wife of one of the Otaheite men, which so exasperated the rest that they not only sought the life of the offender, but of others also who might, as they thought, be disposed to pursue the same course. The manner of Christian's death still remains uncertain; certain it is, that however far he might escape from the reach of justice there was no escaping from

" Those rods of scorpions and those whips of steel
Which conscience shakes."

Pitcairn's Island was visited in 1814 by his majesty's frigates, the Briton and the Tagus, by which the account of Captain Folger was confirmed. From the time of this visit nothing more was heard of Adams and his family for nearly twelve years, when, in 1825, Captain Beechey, in the Blossom, bound on a voyage of discovery, touched at Pitcairn's Island. He found the descendants of the mutineers increased to sixty-six; the females were modest, handsome and pleasing, and the males added a wonderful degree of strength and agility to a beautiful symmetry of form. Adams had introduced into his little society, the most salutary laws and regulations, which he had drawn from the bible, and seemed desirous to atone for his past misconduct by training up the rising generation in piety and virtue. The death of this old patriarch took place in March, 1829, and he was sincerely lamented by the infant colony. It has recently been stated in the newspapers, that owing to a deficiency of water at Pitcairn's Island, the descendants of the mutineers had all emigrated to Otaheite: but there being disgusted with the dissolute and immoral behavior of the islanders, they had returned to the place of their birth to escape the contamination of vice and intemperance.

THE SHETLAND ISLES

These islands lie about fifteen leagues north-east of the Orkneys, between the fifty-ninth and sixty-first degrees of north latitude. They are about eighty-six in number, of which forty are inhabited, and the others are small holms or rocky islets, used only for pasturage. The small islands of Foula and Fair Isle lie in the strait between the clusters of Orkney and Shetland. The climate of these islands cannot be said to be agreeable. The weather is wet and variable, though not injurious to the health of those who have been accustomed to it.

Great numbers of horses are bred in Shetland, though they are of very small size, the ordinary height being from nine to ten hands, whilst the largest do not exceed eleven hands. The inhab-

itants are a hardy, robust and laborious race, and hospitable to
strangers. They have few manufactures, but export great quantities of stockings wrought upon wires, manufactured from the wool
of their own sheep.

The isles afford abundance of sea-fowl, which serve the inhabitants for part of their food, while the down and feathers are a
source of considerable profit to them. The several tribes of fowl
here build and hatch apart. Some of the lesser isles are so crowded with variety of sea-fowl, that they darken the air when they fly,
in great numbers. The people inhabiting the lesser isles have
plenty of eggs, and fowl, which contribute to maintain their families during the summer. The common people are generally very
dexterous in climbing the rocks in quest of the eggs and fowl;
but this exercise is attended with great danger, and sometimes
proves fatal to those who venture too far. The most remarkable
experiment of this sort is at the isle called the Noss of Brassah
and is as follows:

Bird Catching.

The Noss being about sixteen fathom distant from the side of
the opposite main; the higher and lower rocks have two stakes
fastened in each of them, and to these there are ropes tied: upon
the ropes is hung an engine which they call a cradle; and in this
a man makes his way over from the greater to the lesser rock,
where he takes a considerable quantity of eggs and fowl; but his
return being by an ascent, makes it more dangerous, though those
on the great rock have a rope tied to the cradle, by which they
draw it and the man safe over for the most part.

There are some rocks here computed to be about three hundred

fathoms high; and the way of climbing them is, to tie a rope
about a man's middle and let him down with a basket, in which
he brings up his eggs and fowl. The isle of Foula is the most
dangerous and fatal to the climbers, for many of them perish in the
attempt.

A SEA-BALLAD.

A jolly comrade in the port, a fearless mate at sea ;
When I forget thee, to my hand false may the cutlass be !
And may my gallant battle-flag be stricken down in shame,
If, when the social can goes round, I fail to pledge thy name !
Up, up, my lads ! his memory ! we'll give it with a cheer—
Ned Bolton, the commander of the Black Snake privateer !

Poor Ned ! he had a heart of steel, with neither flaw nor speck :
Firm as a rock, in strife or storm, he stood the quarter-deck ;
He was, I trow, a welcome man to many an Indian dame,
And Spanish planters crossed themselves at whisper of his name ,
But now, Jamaica girls may weep—rich Dons securely smile—
His bark will take no prize again, nor e'er touch Indian isle !

S'blood ! 'twas a sorry fate he met on his own mother wave—
The foe far off, the storm asleep, and yet to find a grave'
With store of the Peruvian gold, and spirit of the cane,
No need would he have had to cruise in tropic climes again :
But some are born to sink at sea, and some to hang on shore,
And Fortune cried, God speed ! at last, and welcomed Ned no more.

'Twas off the coast of Mexico—the tale is bitter brief—
The Black Snake, under press of sail, stuck fast upon a reef—
Upon a cutting coral-reef, scarce a good league from land,
But hundreds, both of horse and foot, were ranged upon the strand ;
His boats were lost before Cape Horn, and, with an old canoe,
Even had he numbered ten for one, what could Ned Bolton do ?

Six days and nights the vessel lay upon the coral-reef,
Nor favoring gale, nor friendly flag brought prospect of relief ;
For a land breeze, the wild one prayed, who never prayed before ,
And when it came not at his call, he bit his lip and swore.
The Spaniards shouted from the beach, but did not venture near
Too well they knew the mettle of the daring privateer !

A calm , a calm ! a hopeless calm ! the red sun burning high,
Glared blisteringly and wearily in a transparent sky ;
The grog went round the gasping crew, and loudly rose the song,
The only pastime at an hour when rest seemed far too long.
So boisterously they took their rouse upon the crowded deck—
They looked like men who had escaped, not feared, a sudden wreck

Up sprung the breeze the seventh day—away ! away ! to sea
Drifted the bark, with riven planks, over the waters free ;
Their battle-flag these rovers bold then hoisted topmast high,
And to the swarthy foe sent back a fierce defying cry.

" One last broadside !" Ned Bolton cried—deep boomed the cannon's roar
And echo's hollow growl returned an answer from the shore.

The thundering gun, the broken song, the mad, tumultuous cheer
Ceased not, so long as ocean spared the shattered privateer.
I saw her—I—she shot by me, like lightning, in the gale,
We strove to save, we tacked, and fast we slackened all our sail—
I knew the wave of Ned's right hand—farewell ! you strive in vain
And he, nor one of his ship's crew, e'er entered port again !

DANGERS OF A NOVA SCOTIA FOG.

BY CAPTAIN HALL.

There are few things more provoking than the fogs off Halifax,
for, as they happen to be companions of that very wind, the south-
east, which is the best for running in, the navigator is plagued
with the tormenting conciousness, that if he could be allowed but
a couple of hours of clear weather, his port would be gained, and
his troubles over. The clearing up, therefore, of these odious
clouds or veils is about the most delightful thing I know; and the
instantaneous effect which a clear sight of the land, or even of the
sharp horizon, when far at sea, has on the mind of every person
on board, is quite remarkable. All things look bright, fresh, and
more beautiful than ever. The stir over the whole ship at these
moments is so great that even persons sitting below can tell at
once that the fog has cleared away. The rapid clatter of the
men's feet, springing up the hatchways at the lively sound of the
boatswains call to "make sail!" soon follows. Then comes the
cheerful voice of the officer, hailing the topmen to shake out the
reefs, trice up the stay sails, and rig out the booms. That peculiar and well known kind of echo, also, by which the sound of the
voice is thrown back from the wet sails, contributes in like manner, to produce a joyous elasticity of spirits, greater, I think than
is excited by most of the ordinary occurrences of a sea life.

A year or two after the time I am speaking of, it was resolved to place a heavy gun upon the rock on which Sambro light-
house is built; and, after a good deal of trouble, a long twenty-four
pounder was hoisted up to the highest ridge of this prominent station. It was then arranged that, if, on the arrival of any ship off
the harbor, in a period of fog she chose to fire guns, these were
to be answered from the light-house, and in this way a kind of
audible though invisible telegraph might be set to work. If it
happened that the officers of the ship were sufficiently familiar
with the ground, and possessed nerves stout enough for such a groping kind of navagation, perilous at best, it was possible to run

fairly into he harbor, notwithstanding the obscurity, by watching the sound of these guns, and attending closely to the depth of water.

I never was in any ship which ventured upon this feat, but I perfectly recollect a curious circumstance, which occured, I think, to his majesty's ship Cambrian. She had run in from sea towards he coast, enveloped in one of these dense fogs. Of course they took for granted that the light-house and the adjacent land Halifax included were likewise covered with an impenetrable cloud or mist. But it so chanced, by what freak of Dame Nature, I know not, that the fog, on that day, was confined to the deep water, so that we who were in the port, could see it at the distance of several miles from the coast lying on the ocean like a huge stratum of snow, with an abrupt face fronting the shore. The Cambrian, lost in the midst of this fog bank, supposing herself to be near the land, fired a gun. To this the light-house replied; and so the ship and the light went on pelting away, gun for gun, during half the day without ever seeing one another. The people at the light-house had no means of communicating to the frigate that, if she could only stand on a little further, she would disentangle herself from the cloud, in which, like Jupiter Olympus of old she was wasting her thunder.

At last the captain, hopeless of its clearing up, gave orders to pipe to dinner; but as the weather, in all respects except this abominable haze, was quite fine, and the ship was still in deep water, he directed her to be steered towards the shore, and the lead kept constantly going. As one o'clock approached, he began to feel uneasy, from the water shoaling, and the light-house guns sounding closer and closer; but, being unwilling to disturb the men at dinner, he resolved to stand on for the remaining ten minutes of the hour. Lo and behold! however, they had not sailed half a mile further before the flying jib-boom end emerged from the wall of mist—then the bowsprit shot into day light—and, lastly the ship herself, glided out of the cloud into the full blaze of a bright and "sunshine holy day." All hands were instantly turned up to make sail; and the men, as they flew on deck, could scarcely believe their senses, when they saw behind them the fog bank, and right ahead the harbor's mouth, with the bold cliffs of Cape Sambro on the left, and, farther still, the ships at their moorings, with their ensign and pendants blowing out, light and dry in the breeze.

A far different fate, alas! attended his Majesty's ship Atalante, Captain Frederic Hickey. On the morning of the 10th of November, 1813, this ship stood in for Halifax harbor in very thick weather, carefully feeling her way with the lead, and having look-out men at the jib-boom-end, fore-yard-arms, and every where else from which a glimpse of land was likely to be obtained. After breakfast a fog signal gun was fired, in expectation of its being answered by the light-house on Cape Sambro, near which it wa known they must be. Within a few minutes, accordingly, a gun was heard in the north-north-west quarter, exactly where the light was supposed to lie. As the soundings agreed with the estimated position of the ship, and as the guns from the Atalante, fired at intervals of fifteen minutes, were regularly answered in the direction of the harbor's mouth, it was determined to stand on so as to enter the port under the guidance of these sounds alone. By a fatal coincidence of circumstances, however, these answering guns were fired not by Cape Sambro, but by his Majesty's ship Barrossa, which was likewise entangled by the fog. She, too, supposed that she was communicating with the light-house, whereas it was the guns of the unfortunate Atalante that she heard all the time.

There was certainly no inconsiderable risk incurred by running in for the harbor's mouth under such circumstances. But it will often happen that it becomes the officer's duty to put his ship as well as his life in hazard; and this appears to have been exactly one of those cases. Captain Hickey was charged with urgent despatches relative to the enemy's fleet, which it was of the greatest importance should be delivered without an hour's delay. But there was every appearance of this fog lasting a week; and as he and his officers had passed over the ground a hundred times before, and were as intimately acquainted with the spot as any pilot could be, it was resolved to try the bold experiment; and the ship was forthwith steered in the supposed direction of Halifax.

They had not, however, stood on far, before one of the lookout men exclaimed, "breakers ahead! Hard a-starboard!" But it was too late, for, before the helm could be put over, the ship was amongst those formidable reefs known by the name of the sisters' rocks, or eastern ledge of Sambro Island. The rudder and half of the sternpost, together with the greater part of the false keel, were driven off by the first blow and floated up along side. There is some reason to believe, indeed, that a portion of the bottom of the ship, loaded with one hundred and twenty tons of iron ballast, were torn from the upper works by this fearful blow, and that the ship, which instantly filled with water, was afterwards buoyed up merely by the empty casks, till the decks and sides burst through or were riven asunder by the waves.

The captain who, throughout the whole scene, continued as composed as if nothing remarkable had occurred, now ordered the guns to be thrown overboard, but before one of them could bo cast loose, or a breaching cut, the ship fell over so much that the men could not stand. It was, therefore, with great difficulty that a few guns were fired as signals of distress. In the same breath that this order was given, Captain Hickey desired the yard tackles to be hooked, in order that the pinnace might be hoisted out; but as the masts, deprived of their foundation, were tottering from

side to side, the people were called down again. The quarter
boats were then lowered into the water with some difficulty, but
the jolly boat, which happened to be on the poop undergoing repairs, in being launched overboard, struck against one of the stern
davits, bilged, and went down. The ship was now falling fast over
on her beam ends, and directions were given to cut away her fore
and main mast. Fortunately, they fell without injuring the large
boat on the booms—their grand hope. At the instant of this crash,
the ship parted in two between the main and mizen-masts; and,
within a few seconds afterwards, she again broke right across, between the fore and main-masts: so that the poor Atalante now formed a mere wreck, divided into three pieces, crumbling into smaller
fragments at every send of the swell.

By this time a considerable crowd of men had got into the pinnace on the booms in hopes that she might float off as the ship
sunk; but Captain Hickey, seeing that the boat was so loaded
that she could never swim, desired some twenty men to quit her;
and, what is particularly worthy of remark, his orders, which were
given with perfect coolness, were as promptly obeyed as ever.
Throughout the whole of these trying moments, indeed, the discipline of the ship appears to have been maintained not only without
the smallest trace of insubordination but with a degree of cheerfulness which is described as truly wonderful. Even when the
masts fell, the sound of the crashing spars were drowned in the
animating huzzars of the undaunted crew, though they were then
clinging to the weather gunwale, with the sea, from time to time,
making a clean breach over them, and when they were expecting
every instant to be carried to the bottom!

As soon as the pinnace was relieved from the pressure of the
crowd, she floated off the booms or rather was knocked off by a
sea, which turned her bottom upwards, and whelmed her into
the surf amidst the fragments of the wreck. The people however,
imitating the gallant bearing of their captain, and keeping their
eyes fixed upon him, never for one instant lost their self possession.
By dint of great exertions, they succeeded not only in righting
the boat but disentangled her from the confused heap of spars,
and the dash of the breakers, so as to place her at a little distance
from the wreck where they waited for further orders from the
captain, who with about forty men, still clung to the poor remains
of the gay Atalante once so much admired!

An attempt was next made to construct a raft, as it was feared
the three boats could not possibly carry all hands; but the
violence of the waves prevented this, and it was resolved to trust
to the boats alone, though they were already to all appearance
quite full. It was now, however absolutely necessary to take to
them, as the wreck was disappearing rapidly; and in order to
pack close, most of the men were removed to the pinnace, where
they laid flat in the bottom, like herrings in a barrel, while the small

boats returned to pick off the rest. This was no easy matter in
any case, while it was impossible in others; so that many
men had to swim for it; others were dragged through the waves
by ropes, and some were forked off by oars and other small
spars.

Amongst the crew there was one famous merry fellow, a black
fiddler, who was discovered at this critical juncture clinging to the
main chains with his beloved Cremona squeezed tightly but deli-
cately under his arm—a ludicrous picture of distress, and a subject
of some joking amongst the men even at this moment. It soon became absolutely necessary that he should lose one of the two things
his fiddle or his life. So, at last, after a painful struggle, the pro-
fessor and his violin were obliged to part company!

The pinnace now contained seventy-nine men and one woman,
the cutter forty-two and the gig eighteen, with which cargoes they
barely floated. Captain Hickey was, of course, the last man who
left the wreck; though such was the respect and affection felt for
him by his crew, that those who stood along with him on this last
vestage of the ship, evinced the greatest reluctance at leaving their
commander in such a perilous predicament. So speedy indeed
was the work of destruction, that by the time the Captain was
fairly in the boat, the wreck had almost entirely ' melted into the
yest of waves.' The crew, however, gave her three hearty cheers
as she went down, and then finally abandoned the scattered fragments, of what had been their house and home for nearly seven
years.

The fog still continued as thick as ever; the binacles had
both been washed overboard, and no compass could be procured.
As the wind was still light, there was great difficulty in steering
in a straight line. Had there been a breeze, it would perhaps
have been easier to have shaped a course. In this dilemma a resource was hit upon, which for a time answered pretty well to
guide them. It being known loosely, before leaving the wreck,
in what direction the land was situated, the three boats were placed
in a row pointing that way. The sternmost boat then quitted her
station in the rear, and pulled ahead till she came in a line with
the other two boats, but took care not to go so far as to be lost in
the fog; the boat which was now astern then rowed ahead, as the
first had done, and so on doubling along one after the other. This
tardy method of proceeding however answered only for a time;
at length they were completely at loss which way to steer. Precisely at this moment of greatest need, an old quarter-master, Samuel
Shanks by name, recollected that at the end of his watch chain
there hung a small compass seal. This precious discovery was
announced to the other boats by a joyous shout from the pinnace.

The compass being speedily handed into the gig, to the captain,
was placed on top of the chronometer, which had been nobly saved
by the clerk; and as this instrument worked on jimbles, the little

needle remained upon it sufficiently steady for stee.ing the boats within a few points.

This was enough to insure hitting land, from which they had been steering quite wide. Before reaching the shore, they fell in with an old fisherman, who piloted them to a light, called Portuguese Cove, where they all landed in safety, at a distance of twenty miles from Halifax.

THE EDDYSTONE LIGHT-HOUSE.

This most celebrated light-house is built on the Eddystone rocks These are situate nearly south-south-west from the middle of Plymouth sound, England, according to the true meridian The distance from the port of Plymouth is nearly fourteen miles; and from the promontory called Ramhead, about ten miles. They are almost in the line, but somewhat within it, which joins the Start and the Lizard points; and as they lie nearly in the direction of vessels coasting up and down the channel, they were necessarily, before the establishment of light-houses, very dangerous, and often fatal to ships under such circumstances. Their situation, likewise, with regard to the Bay of Biscay, and the Atlantic Ocean, is such, that they lie open to the swells of the bay and ocean from all south-western points of the compass, which swells are generally allowed by mariners to be very great and heavy in those seas, and particularly in the Bay of Biscay. It is to be observed that the soundings of the sea from the south-westward, toward the Eddystone, are from eighty fathoms to forty, and every where till you come near the Eddystone, the sea is full thirty fathoms in depth; so that all the heavy seas from the south-west come uncontrolled upon the Eddystone rocks, and break on them with the utmost fury.

The force and height of these seas is increased by the circumstance of the rocks stretching across the channel, in a north and south direction, to the length of above one hundred fathoms, and by their lying in a sloping manner toward the south-west quarter. This striving of the rocks, as it is technically called, does not cease at low water, but still goes on progressively; so that, at fifty fathoms westward, there are twelve fathoms water, nor do they terminate altogether at the distance of a mile. From this configuration it happens, that the seas are swelled to such a degree in storms and hard gales of wind, as to break on the rocks with the utmost violence.

The effect of this slope is likewise sensibly felt in moderate, and even in calm weather, for the liberation of the vater, cause

in the Bay of Biscay in hard gales, at south-west, continues in those
deep waters for many days, though succeeded by a calm; inso-
much, that when the sea is to all appearance smooth and even, and
its surface unruffled by the slightest breeze, yet those librations
still continuing, which are called the ground swell, and meeting
the slope of the rocks, the sea breaks upon them in a frightful
manner, so as not only to obstruct any work being done upon the
rock, but even the landing upon it, when, figuratively speaking,
you might go to sea in a walnut-shell. A circumstance which
still farther increases the difficulty of working on the rocks is
there being a sudden drop of the surface of the rock, forming a
step of about four and a half, or five feet high, so that the seas,
which in moderate weather come swelling to this part, meet so
sudden a check, that they frequently fly to the height of thirty or
forty feet

Eddystone Light-House.

Notwithstanding these difficulties, it is not surprising that the
dangers to which navigators were exposed by the Eddystone rocks,
should make a commercial nation desirous of having a light-house
on them. The wonder is, that any one should be found hardy
enough to undertake the building. Such a man was first found in
the person of Henry Winstanly, of Littlebury, in Essex, gent. who,
in the year 1696, was furnished by the master, wardens, and assistants, of the Trinity-house, of Deptford Strond, with the necessary powers to carry the design into execution. He entered upon
this undertaking in 1696, and completed it in four years. This
gentleman was so certain of the stability of his structure, that he
declared it to be his wish to be in it "during the greatest storm
that ever blew under the face of the heavens."

Mr. Winstanly was but too amply gratified in his wish, for while he was there with his workmen and light-keepers, that dreadful storm began, which raged most violently on the 26th of November 1703, in the night; and of all the accounts of the kind which history furnishes us with, we have none that has exceeded this in Great Britain, or was more injurious or extensive in its devastation. The next morning, November 27th, when the violence of the storm was so much abated that it could be seen whether the light-house had suffered by it, nothing appeared standing; but, upon a nearer inspection, some of the large irons by which the work was fixed upon the rock still remained; nor were any of the people or any of the materials of the building, ever found afterwards.

In 1709, another light-house was built of wood, on a very different construction, by Mr. John Rudyerd, then a silk mercer or Ludgate-hill. This was a very ingenious structure; after it had braved the elements for forty-six years, it was burnt to the ground in 1755. On the destruction of this light-house, that excellent mechanic and engineer Mr. Smeaton, was chosen as the fittest person to build another. It was with some difficulty that he was able to persuade the proprietors, that a stone building, properly constructed, would in all respects be preferable to one of wood, but having at last convinced them, he turned his thoughts to the shape which was most suitable to a building so critically situated. Reflecting on the structure of the former buildings, it seemed a material improvement to procure, if possible, an enlargement of the base, without increasing the size of the waist, or that part of the building which is between the top of the rock, and the top of the solid work. Hence he thought a greater degree of strength and stiffness would be gained, accompanied with less resistance to the acting power. On this occasion, the natural figure of the waist, or bole, of large spreading oak, occurred to Mr. Smeaton "Let us (says he) consider its particular figure. Connected with its roots, which lie hid below ground, it rises from the surface with a large swelling base, which at the height of one diameter is generally reduced by an elegant curve, concave to the eye, to a diameter less by at least one third, and sometimes to half its original base. From thence, its taper diminishing more slowly, its sides by degrees come into a perpendicular, and for some height form a cylinder. After that, a preparation of more circumferance becomes necessary, for the strong insertion and establishment of the principal boughs, which produces a swelling of its diameter. Now we can hardly doubt, but that every section of the tree is nearly of an equal strength in proportion to what it has to resist; and were we to lop off its principal boughs, and expose it in that state to a rapid current of water, we should find it as capable of resisting the action of the heavier fluid, when divested of the greater part of its clothing, as it was that of the lighter, when all its spreading ornaments were exposed to the fury of the

21 *

wind; and hence we may derive an idea of what the proper shape of a column of the greatest stability ought to be, to resist the action of external violence, when the quantity of matter is given of which it is to be composed."

With these views, as to the proper form of the superstructure, Mr. Smeaton began the work on the 2d of April, 1757, and finished it in August 4th, 1759. The rock, which slopes towards the south-west is cut into horizontal steps, into which are dovetailed, and united by a strong cement, Portland stone, and granite. The whole, to the height of thirty-five feet from the foundation, is a solid of stones, ingrafted into each other, and united by every means of additional strength. The building has four rooms, one over the other, and at the top a gallery and lantern. The stone floors are flat above, but concave beneath, and are kept from pressing against the sides of the building by a chain let into the walls. It is nearly eighty feet high, and since its completion has been assaulted by the fury of the elements, without suffering the smallest injury.

We regret that we cannot with propriety trace out the progress of this great work, and shew with what skill and judgment this unparalleled engineer overcame the greatest difficulties; we, however, beg to recommend to our curious readers, Mr. Smeaton's own account of the Eddystone light-house, not doubting that they will be highly gratified by the perusal. According to the requisite tables, this light-house is situated in lat. 50. 8 N., long. 4. 24. W. of Greenwich; or 4. 18. 23. W. of London.

JOHN PAUL JONES.

John Paul Jones was born at Arbingland, in Scotland, July 6, 1747. His father was a gardner, whose name was *Paul;* but the son assumed that of *Jones* in subsequent life, for what reason is not known. Young Paul early evinced a decided predilection for the sea, and, at the age of twelve, was bound apprentice to a respectable merchant of Whitehaven, in the American trade. His first voyage was to America, where his elder brother was established as a planter. He was then engaged for some time in the slave-trade, but quitted it in disgust, and returned to Scotland, in 1768, as passenger in a vessel, the captain and mate of which died on the passage. Jones assumed the command, at the request of those on board, and brought the vessel safe into port. For

this service, he was appointed by the owners master and super-
cargo. While in command of this vessel, he punished a sailor
who afterwards died of a fever at the island of Tobago—a circumstance which gave rise to an accusation against Jones, of
having caused his death, by the severity of the punishment upon
him; but this has been completely refuted. Jones was afterwards
in command of the Betsy, of London, and remained some time in
the West Indies, engaged in commercial pursuits and speculations,
by which it is said he realized a handsome fortune. In 1773, he
was residing in Virginia, arranging the affairs of his brother, who
had died intestate and childless, and about this time took the
name of *Jones*. In Virginia he continued to live until the commencement of the struggle between the colonies and mother
country. He offered his services to the former, and was appointed
first of the first lieutenants, and designated to the Alfred, on board
of which ship, to use his own language in one of his letters, " he
had the honor to hoist, with his own hands, the flag of freedom,
the first time it was displayed on the Delaware." Soon after
this, we find Jones in command of the Providence, mounting
twelve four-pounders, with a complement of seventy men, cruising
from the Bermudas to the Gut of Canso, and making sixteen
prizes in little more than six weeks. In May, 1777, he was ordered to proceed to France, where the American commissioners,
Franklin, Deane and Lee, were directed to invest him with the
command of a fine ship, as a reward of his signal services. On
his arrival in France, he was immediately summoned to Paris by
the commissioners. The object of this summons was to concert a
plan of operations for the force preparing to act against the British
in the West Indies, and on the coast of America. This plan,
which certainly did great honor to the projector, though untoward
delays and accidents prevented its immediate success, was afterwards openly claimed by Jones as his own, without acknowledging
the assistance or participation of the American commissioners or
the French ministry. The Ranger was then placed under his
orders, with discretion to cruise where he pleased, with this restriction, however, that he was not to return to France immediately
after making attempts upon the coast of England, as the French
government had not yet declared itself openly as the ally of the
U. States. April 10, 1778, he sailed on a cruise, during which
he laid open the weakness of the British coast. With a single
ship, he kept the whole coast of Scotland, and part of that of
England, for some time, in a state of alarm, and made a descent
at Whitehaven, where he surprised and took two forts, with thirty
pieces of cannon, and set fire to the shipping. In this attack upon
Whitehaven, the house of the earl of Selkirk, in whose service
the father of Jones had been gardener, was plundered, and the
family plate carried off. But the act was committed without his
knowledge, and he afterwards made the best atonement in his

power. After his return to Brest with two hundred prisoners of
war, he became involved in a variety of troubles, for want of
means to support them, pay his crew, and refit his ship. After
many delays and vexations, Jones sailed from the road of St. Croix,
August 14, 1779, with a squadron of seven sail, designing to annoy
the coasts of England and Scotland. The principal occurrence
of this cruise was the capture of the British ship of war Serapis,
after a bloody and desperate engagement, off Flamborough head,
Sept 23, 1779. The Serapis was a vessel much superior in force
to Jones's vessel, the Bon Homme Richard, which sunk not long
after the termination of the engagement. The sensation produced
by this battle was unexampled, and raised the fame of Jones to its
acme. In a letter to him, Franklin says, " For some days after
the arrival of your express, scarce any thing was talked of at Paris
and Versailles, but your cool conduct and persevering bravery
during that terrible conflict. You may believe that the impression
on my mind was not less strong than on that of the others. But
I do not choose to say, in a letter to yourself, all I think on such
an occasion." His reception at Paris, whither he went on the
invitation of Franklin, was of the most flattering kind. He was
every where caressed; the king presented him with a gold sword,
bearing the inscription, *Vindicati maris Ludovicus XVI remunera-
tur strenuo vindici*, and requested permission of congress to invest
him with the military order of merit—an honor never conferred
on any one before who had not borne arms under the commission
of France. In 1781, Jones sailed for the U. States, and arrived in
Philadelphia, February 18th, of that year, after a variety of escapes
and rencounters, where he underwent a sort of examination before
the board of admiralty, which resulted greatly to his honor. The
board gave it as their opinion, "that the conduct of Paul Jones
merits particular attention, and some distinguished mark of approbation from Congress." Congress passed a resolution, highly
complimentary to his "zeal, prudence and intrepidity." General
Washington wrote him a letter of congratulation, and he was afterwards voted a gold medal by Congress. From Philadelphia
he went to Portsmouth, New Hampshire, to superintend the
building of a ship of war, and, while there, drew up some admirable observations on the subject of the American navy. By permission of Congress, he subsequently went on board the French
leet, where he remained until the conclusion of peace, which put
a period to his naval career in the service of the U. States. He
then went to Paris, as agent for prize-money, and, while there,
joined in a plan to establish a fur-trade between the north-west
coast of America and China, in conjunction with a kindred spirit,
the celebrated John Ledyard. In Paris, he continued to be
treated with the greatest distinction. He afterwards was invited
into the Russian service, with the rank of rear-admiral, where he
was disappointed in not eceiving the command of the fleet acting

against the Turks in the Black sea.   He found fault with the conduct of the prince of Nassau, the admiral; became restless and impatient; was intrigued against at court, and calumniated by his enemies; and had permission, from the empress Catharine, to retire from the service with a pension, which was never paid.   He returned to Paris, where he gradually sunk into poverty, neglect, and ill health, until his death, which was occasioned by jaundice and dropsy, July 13, 1792.   His last public act was heading a deputation of Americans, who appeared before the national assembly to offer their congratulations on the glorious and salutary reform of their government.   This was before the flight of the king.—Jones was a man of signal talent and courage; he conducted all his operations with the most daring boldness, combined with the keenest sagacity in calculating the chances of success and the consequences of defeat.   He was, however, of an irritable, impetuous disposition, which rendered him impatient of the authority of his superiors, while he was, at the same time, harsh in the exercise of his own; and he was deficient in that modesty which adorns great qualities and distinguished actions, while it disarms envy and conciliates jealousy.   His early education was of a very limited kind.   It terminated when he went to sea, at the age of twelve; but he supplied its defects by subsequent study, so as to enable himself to write with fluency, strength and clearness, and to sustain his part respectably in the polished society into which he was thrown.   In his letters, he inculcates the necessity of knowledge for naval officers, and intimates that he had devoted " midnight studies" to the attainment of that information which he deemed requisite in his situation.   His memorials, correspondence, &c., are quite voluminous.   He also wrote poetry, and, in Paris, was a great pretender to *ton*, as a man of fashion, especially after his victory over the Serapis, which, of course, gave him great *éclat* amongst the ladies of the French capital.   At this period, he is described by an English lady then resident at Paris, as " a smart little man of thirty-six; speaks but little French, and appears to be an extraordinary genius, a poet as well as a hero."—*Am. Enc*

JAMES LAWRENCE

James Lawrence, a distinguished American naval commander, was born at Burlington, New Jersey, in 1781.   He early manifested a strong predilection for the sea; but his father, who was a lawyer was anxious that he should pursue his own professi   ; and, when only thirteen years of age, he commenced the study of the law; but after the death of his father, he entered the navy

as a midshipman, in 1798. In 1801, the Tripoli war having
commenced, he was promoted, and, in 1803, was sent out to the
Mediterranean, as the first lieutenant of the schooner Enterprise.
While there, he performed a conspicuous part in the destruction
of the frigate Philadelphia, which had been captured by the Tri
politans.   In the same year, he was invested with the temporary
command of the Enterprise, during the bombardment of Tripoli
by commodore Preble, all the ships of the squadron being employed
to cover the boats during the attack; and so well did he execute
his duty, that the commodore could not restrain the expression of
his thanks.   He remained in the Mediterranean three years, and
then returned with Preble to the U. States, having previously
been transferred to the frigate John Adams, as first lieutenant
In June, 1812, war was declared between Great Britain and the
U. States, and Lawrence, at the time in command of the Hornet,
a few days afterwards sailed with a squadron under the orders of
commodore Rogers, for the purpose of intercepting the Jamaica
fleet.   They returned, however, at the end of the following month,
to Boston, without having been able to accomplish their object.
Lawrence then accompanied commodore Bainbridge on a cruise
to the East Indies; but they separated near St. Salvador, on the
coast of Brazil, the Hornet remaining there to blockade a British
ship of war, laden with specie, till compelled to retire by the ar
rival of a seventy-four.   Feb. 24, 1813, the Hornet fell in with
the brig Peacock, captain Peake, which he took after a furious
action of fifteen minutes.   This vessel was deemed one of the
finest of her class in the British navy.   In the number of her men
and guns, she was somewhat inferior to the Hornet.   She sunk
before all the prisoners could be removed.   The latter was con
siderably damaged in the rigging and sails, but her hull was
scarcely hurt.   Lawrence returned to the U. States, where he
was welcomed with the applause due to his conduct; but the most
honorable eulogy bestowed upon it, was contained in a letter,
published by the officers of the Peacock, expressing their gratitude
for the consideration and kindness with which they had been treated.   Shortly after his return, he was ordered to repair to Boston,
and take command of the frigate Chesapeake.   This he did with
great regret, as the Chesapeake was one of the worst ships in the
navy.   He had been but a short time at Boston, when the British
frigate Shannon, captain Brooke, appeared before the harbor,
and defied the Chesapeake to combat.   Lawrence did not refuse
the challenge, although his ship was far from being in a condition
for action; and, June 1, 1813, he sailed out of the harbor, and
engaged his opponent.   After the ship had exchanged several
broadsides, and Lawrence had been wounded in the leg, he called
his boarders, when he received a musket-ball in his body.   At the
same time, the enemy boarded, and, after a desperate resistance,
succeeded in taking possession of the ship.   Almost all the officers

of the Chesapeake were either killed or wounded.   The last ex
clamation of Lawrence, as they were carrying him below, after
the fatal wound, was, " Don't give up the ship."   He lingered
for four days in intense pain, and expired on the 5th of June.
He was buried at Halifax, with every mark of honor —*Ib.*

ADDRESS TO THE OCEAN

Likeness of Heaven [1]
   Agent of power!
Man is thy victim,
   Shipwreck's thy dower!
Spices and jewels
   From valley and sea,
Armies and banners,
   Are buried in thee !

What are the riches
   Of Mexico's mines,
To the wealth that far down
   In thy deep waters shines?
The proud navies that cover
   The conquering west—
Thou fling'st them to death
   With one heave of thy breast.

From the high hills that view
   Thy wreck making shore,
When the bride of the mariner
   Shrieks at thy roar,
When like lambs in the tempest
   Or mews in the blast,
On thy ridge broken billows
   The canvass is cast

How humbling to one,
   With a heart and a soul,
To look on thy greatness
   And list to its roll ;
To think how that heart
   In cold ashes shall be,
While the voice of Eternity
   Rises from thee ?

Yes ! where are the cities
   Of Thebes and of Tyre
Swept from the nations
   Like sparks from the fire ;
The glory of Athens,
   The splendor of Rome,
Dissolved--and forever –
   Like dew in thy foam.

But thou art almighty,
  Eternal—sublime—
Unwearied—unwasted—
  Twin brother of Time !
Fleets, tempests nor nations
  Thy glory can bow ;
As the stars first beheld thee
  Still chainless art thou '

But hold ! when thy surges
  No longer shall roll,
And that firmament's length
  Is drawn back like a scroll,
Then—then shall the spirit
  That sighs by thee now,
Be more mighty, more lasting,
  More chainless than thou.

EARLY AMERICAN HEROISM.

During one of the former wars, between France and England, in which the then Colonies bore an active part, a respectable individual, a member of the society of Friends, of the name of ———, commanded a fine ship which sailed from an Eastern port, to a port in England. This vessel had a strong and effective crew, but was totally unarmed. When near her destined port, she was chased, and ultimately overhauled, by a French vessel of war. Her commander used every endeavor to escape, but seeing from the superior sailing of the Frenchman, that his capture was inevitable, he quietly retired below: he was followed into the cabin by his *cabin boy*, a youth of activity and enterprise, named Charles Wager: he asked his commander if nothing more could be done to save the ship—his commander replied that i was impossible, that every thing had been done that was practicable, there was no escape for them, and they must submit to be captured. Charles then returned upon deck and summoned the crew around him—he stated in a few words what was their captain's conclusion—then, with an elevation of mind, dictated by a soul formed for enterprise and noble daring, he observed, "if you will place yourselves under my command, and stand by me, I have conceived a plan by which the ship may be rescued, and we in turn become the conquerors." The sailors no doubt feeling the ardor, and inspired by the courage of their youthful and gallant leader, agreed to place themselves under his command His plan was communicated to them, and they awaited with firmness, the moment to carry their enterprise into effect. The suspense was of short duration, for the Frenchman was quickly alongside, and as the weather was fine, immediately grappled fast to the unoffending merchant ship. As Charles had anticipated, the exhilarated conquerors, elated beyond measure, with the acquisition of so fine a prize, poured into his vessel in crowds, cheering and huzzaing; and not foreseeing any danger, they left but few men on board their ship. Now was the moment for Charles, who, giving his men the signal, sprang at their head on board the opposing vessel, while some seized the arms which had been left in profusion on her deck, and with which they soon overpowered the few men left on board; the others, by a simultaneous movement, relieved her from the grapplings which united the two vessels. Our hero now having the command of the French vessel, seized the helm, and placing her out of boarding distance, hailed, with the voice of a conqueror, the discomfited crowd of Frenchmen who were left on board of the peaceful bark he had just quitted, and summoned them to follow close in his wake, or he would blow them out of water, (a threat they well knew he was very capable of executing, as their guns were loaded during the chase.) They sorrowfully acquiesced with his commands, while gallant Charles steered into port, followed by his prize. The exploit excited universal applause—the former master of the merchant vessel was examined by the Admiralty, when he stated the whole of the enterprise as it occurred, and declared that Charles Wager had planned and effected the gallant exploit, and that to him alone belonged the honor and credit of the achievement. Charles was immediately transferred to the British navy, appointed a midshipman, and his education carefully superintended. He soon after distinguished himself in action, and underwent a rapid promotion, until at length he was created an Admiral, and known as Sir Charles Wager. It is said, that he always held in veneration and esteem, that respectable and conscientious Friend, whose cabin boy he had been, and transmitted yearly to his OLD MASTER, as he termed him, a handsome present of Madeira, to cheer his declining days.

CAPTAIN G. VANCOUVER.

Notwithstanding the valuable discoveries of Cook, further investigation was required of some of the southern regions, with which view a voyage was planned in autumn 1789, and the command destined to Captain Henry Roberts, who had served under Captain Cook in the two last voyages, Captain Vancouver being named as his second; and for this purpose a ship of three hundred and forty tons was purchased, in a state nearly finished, and on

being launched was named the Discovery, and commissioned as
a sloop; but the disputes with Spain respecting Nootka Sound for
a short time suspended her equipment. These differences being
terminated, and the fisheries and fur-trade of China being objects
of material importance, it was deemed expedient to send an officer
to Nootka to receive from the Spaniards a formal restitution of
the territories they had seized; to survey the coast, obtain every
possible information of the natural and political state of the country. To this command Captain Vancouver was now appointed.
The same ship, the Discovery, was equipped, carrying ten four-
pounders and ten swivels, with one hundred and thirty men including officers, Captain Vancouver being Captain, Messrs. Zacha-
riah Mudge, Peter Puget, and Joseph Baker, lieutenants; and
Joseph Whidbey, master. She was to be accompanied by the
Chatham armed tender, of one hundred and thirty-five tons, four
three-pounders, six swivels, and forty-five men, commanded by
Lieutenant W. R. Broughton; James Hanson, second lieutenant;
and James Johnstone, master. Mr. Archibald Menzies, a surgeon of the navy, was also appointed for the special purpose of
botanical research.

On the 5th February, 1791, the Discovery anchored at Spithead,
on the 11th March proceeded down the chanel to Falmouth,
where she was, on the 31st, joined by the Chatham. On the 28th
April they made Teneriffe. They crossed the tropic of Capricorn
the 12th June, in 25 deg. 18 min., after which it was resolved to
proceed by the Cape of Good Hope, whither they arrived the 10th
July, and where a variety of necessary repairs employed them till
the 11th of August. After being detained by contrary winds and
calms till the 17th, they then sailed out of the Simon's Bay, bound
for the coast of New Holland, and directing their course between
the tracks of Dampier and Marion, over a space before unfrequented. On the 27th September they made land, and, in latitude
35 deg. 31 min. and longitude 160 deg. 35 min. 30 sec. passed by
a conspicuous promontory, to which Captain Vancouver gave the
name of Cape Chatham, after the Earl.

The natives along this coast appeared to be a wandering people,
who sometimes made their excursions individually; at other times
in considerable parties; this was apparent, by their habitations
being found single and alone, as well as composing tolerably large
villages. Besides the village they visited, Mr. Broughton discovered another about two miles distant from it, of nearly the same
magnitude; but it appeared to be of a much later date, as all the
huts had been recently built, and seemed to have been very lately
inhabited. The larger trees in the vicinity of both villages had
been hollowed out by fire, sufficiently to afford the shelter these
people seemed to require. Upon stones placed on the inside of
these hollow trees fires had been made, which proved that they
had been used as habitations, either for the interior of the party.

which would argu.; a degree of subordination amongst them, or for those who were too indolent to build themselves the wattled huts before described.

From this coast Captain Vancouver proceeded to New Zealand, which he reached on the 27th October, and anchored in Dusky Bay, when they encountered a heavy storm, the effects of which required considerable repair, particularly of the Discovery. Another heavy gale occurred on the 22d and 23d, after which, very unexpectedly, they made land, namely, a cluster of seven craggy islands, the largest situated in latitude 48 deg. 3 min. longitude 166 deg. 20 min., which had not been seen by Captain Cook. These sterile rocks Captain Vancouver denominated The Snares. Another new island was discovered on the 22d of December, in 215 deg. 49 min. Several canoes came off to the ship, but the natives would not go on board, while they used every solicitation to induce the English to land. One at length ventured on board.

These people were evidently of the Great South Sea nation, both from language and a similarity to the Friendly Islanders. Two or three of them remained on board nearly an hour; but so much was their attention distracted, that they could scarcely give an answer as to the name of the island, or otherwise. It appeared on the whole, that they called it Oparo, by which name it is therefore distinguished by Captain Vancouver. The tops of six of the highest hills bore the appearance of fortified places, resembling redoubts; having a sort of block-house, in the shape of an English glass-house, in the centre of each, with rows of palisadoes a considerable way down the sides of the hills, nearly at equal distances. These, overhanging, seemed intended for advanced works, and apparently capable of defending the citadel by a few against a numerous host of assailants. On all of them they noticed people, as if on duty, constantly moving about. These were the only habitations they saw.

On the 29th the Discovery reached Otaheite, where they had been expected in consequence of information by an English vessel, which turned out to be the Chatham, that had separated near Facile Harbor, and arrived before them. The Chatham, during her separation, had seen several immaterial lands, named by Mr Broughton successively, Knight's Island, (the same as The Snares of Captain Vancouver), Point Alison, Mount Patterson, The Two Sisters, and Cape Soung. An island which he named Chatham Island, and the anchorage of which, in Skirmish Bay, was 43 deg 49 min. latitude, and 183 deg. 25 min. longitude, was taken possession of. Here, having gone on shore, a number of the natives came about, held a conversation by signs and gestures, and readily received Mr Broughton's presents, but would make no exchanges. They were very anxious to have the party follow them to their habitations, but this was thought imprudent. Nothing would prevail on the islanders to give up any of their articles but they not only readily accepted, but carried off various things belonging to the party, and were particularly anxious to get Mr. Broughton's fowling-piece, which he had fired, much to their alarm. Having, in order both to get information and to procure water, at length made signs of their intention to accompany the natives, it appeared that the latter had meditated hostility, having collected large sticks, swinging them over their heads, as if with an intention of using them; several of them likewise had spears. Yet, being well armed, Mr. Broughton's party were not afraid, especially as they thought they had purchased the good opinion of the savages. They were, however, mistaken; an attack was made so violently, that both Mr. Broughton and Mr. Johnstone were reluctantly obliged to fire, as did the gentleman having the charge of the boat, which occasioned the natives to fly, but not before one of them had unfortunately perished.

On the Discovery anchoring, she was surrounded by canoes laden with the country productions. Captain Vancouver found that most of the friends he had left there in 1777 were dead. Otoo, now called Tomarrey, his father, brothers, and sisters, Potatou, and his family, were the only of their chiefs now living. Captain Vancouver and Mr. Broughton went on shore to fix on an eligible spot for tents, and to pay their respects to his Otaheitan majesty. They found Otoo, Pomarrey's son and now king, to be a boy of about nine or ten years of age. He was carried on the shoulders of a man, and was clothed in a piece of English red cloth, with ornaments of pigeons' feathers hanging over his shoulders. When they had approached within about eight paces, they were desired to stop; the present they had brought was exhibited; and although its magnitude, and the value of the articles it contained, excited the admiration of the by-standers in the highest degree, it was regarded by this young monarch with an apparently stern and cool indifference. After some other ceremonies, a ratification of peace and mutual friendship being acknowledged on both sides, the different European articles composing the present were, with some little form, presented to Otoo; and on his shaking hands with them, which he did very heartily, his countenance became immediately altered, and he received them with the greatest cheerfulness and cordiality.

On the 2d day of January, 1792, arrived Pomarrey, who was, to his great gratification, saluted with four guns. With him came Matooara Mahou, the reigning Prince of Morea, under Otoo, but who was in a deep decline. At one of the entertainments on board, Pomarrey having drank a bottle of undiluted brandy, it threw him into convulsions; after which, having slept for an hour, he was perfectly recovered. Captain Vancouver endeavored to persuade him of the bad consequence of inebriety. The chief on this accused him of being a stingy fellow, and not *tio tio*, (a jolly companion). On this it was determined to give him his own way, and orders were given to let him have as much brandy or rum as he should call for, which had completely the effect, for in a week he ceased to call for any.

Pomarrey's father, formerly called Happi, now Taou, also came to visit them, and a most affectionate interview took place between the three sons and their aged and venerable father. A very different scene was afterwards exhibited. It was announced that Otoo was approaching. On this occasion it became necessary that the grandfather should pay homage to his grandson. A pig and a plaintain-leaf were instantly procured; the good old man stripped to the waist, and when Otoo appeared in front of the marquee, the aged parent, whose limbs were tottering with the decline of life, met his grandson, and on his knees acknowledged his own inferiority, by presenting this token of submission; which, so far as could be discovered, seemed offered with a mixture of profound respect and parental regard. The ceremony seemed to have little effect on the young monarch, who appeared to notice the humiliating situation of his grandsire with the most perfect indifference and unconcern. This mode of behavior is, however, rather to be attributed to the force of education, than to a want of the proper sentiments of affection.

On the 14th a message was received of the death of Mahou, at Oparre, which district was, for some days, by a religious interdict, forbidden communication with the rest of the island. Mr. Broughton, and a party of the gentlemen belonging to the ships, having made an excursion for purchasing curiosities among the islands, landed to see the grand morai, or tapootapootatea. Mowre, the sovereign of Uleatea, who attended them, on approaching the sacred spot, desired the party would stop until he should address the Eatooa. Then, seating himself on the ground, he began praying before a watta, ornamented with a piece of wood, indifferently carved, on which was placed, for the occasion, a bundle of cloth and some red feathers. During this ejaculation the names of the party were twice mentioned. He likewise repeated the names of the several commanders who had visited the island, together with those of "Keene George" (that is, King George) and "Britarne," which were frequently expressed. When these introductory ceremonies were finished, Mowree attended them to every part of the morai, and explained every particular. He appeared to be well versed in all the ceremonials and rites appertaining to their religion, which made the party greatly lament their want of a competent knowledge of the language, as they were unable to comprehend his meaning, except in a few common instances.

The next morning they were again honored by a visit from Otoo and several of the chiefs, in their way to the morai. Soon after a canoe, covered with an awning, was seen coming from the westward, paddling in a slow and solemn manner towards the

morai, in which was the corpse of the deceased chief. On their
expressing great anxiety to see Pomarrey, for the purpose of
obtaining permission to attend the burial ceremony, they were
informed that he was gone to the morai, but would have no
objection to their being present. They proceeded; and near to
the rivulet that flows by Urripiah's house, they saw the queen-
mother, Fier-re-te, and the widow of the deceased Mahow, sitting
all in tears; and, in the paroxysms of their affliction, wounding
their heads with the sharks' teeth they had prepared the preceding
evening. The widow had a small spot shaved on the crown of
her head, which was bloody, and bore other evident marks of
having frequently undergone the cruel effect of her despair. The
body of Mahow, wrapped in English red cloth, was deposited under
an awning in a canoe, whose bow was drawn up a little way on
the beach near the morai, and was attended by one man only, at her
stern, up to his middle in water, to prevent her driving from the
spot. The priests continued chanting their prayers, frequently ex-
alting their voices, until they ended in a very shrill tone. The
address being ended, they all rose up and proceeded westward
along the shore, followed by the canoe, in which was the corpse,
to the mouth of the rivulet, where the three royal ladies still continued to indulge their excessive grief; and, on perceiving the
canoe, burst forth into a loud yell of lamentation, which was
accompanied by an accelerated application of the sharks' teeth,
until the blood, very freely following, mingled with their tears
The canoe entered the brook and proceeded towards another
morai at the foot of the mountains, where the ceremonies to be
performed on the body of the deceased required such secrecy,
that on no account could the gentlemen be permitted to attend,
although it was most earnestly requested.

In consequence of a message from Pomarrey, Captain Vancouver and Messrs. Broughton and Whidbey went to Oparre, to
assist at the mourning for the death of Mahow. The concern
here of the relatives was by no means such as might have been
expected from their tender regard to the chief when alive. The
corpse was laid on the tapapaoo, which seemed to have been erected for the express purpose, about a quarter of a mile to the eastward of the grand morai, (or, as it is called, "tapootapootatea");
and appeared to be then undergoing the latter part of the embalm-
ing process, in the same manner as described by Captain Cook
in the instance of Tee. The body was exposed to the sun, and
on their approach the covering was taken off, which exhibited the
corpse in a very advanced state of putrefaction. The skin shone
very bright with the cocoa-nut oil with which it had been anointed,
and which they understood was highly impregnated with "aehigh,"
or sweet-scented wood. One of the arms and a leg being moved,
the joints appeared perfectly flexible. The extremely offensive
exhalations that were emitted, rendered it natural to conclude

t. At the whole mass would soon be completely decomposed; but, i credit may be given to their assertions, which were indubitably confirmed by the remains of Tee, and to which the captain could bear testimony, this will not be the case. Pomarrey informed them, the corpse was to remain a month in this place; then a month was to be employed in its visiting some of the western districts; after which it was to be removed to Tiaraboo for another month whence it was to be carried to Morea, and there finally deposited with his forefathers in the morai of the family. In the course of a few months after its arrival there, it would gradually begin to moulder away, but by such very slow degrees, that several months would elapse before the body would be entirely consumed. The boat's crew were ranged before the paling that encompassed the tapapaoo; a piece of red cloth from them was given to the widow, who spread it over the dead body; some vollies were then fired, and the captain was directed to pronounce " Tera no oea Mahow," that is, For you Mahow. On some rain falling, the body was taken under cover and carefully wrapped up. They proceeded to an excellent new house of Whytooa's, where t. ey dined, and returned to Matarai with two large hogs, presented on this mournful occasion by the widow of Mahow.

A serious theft of a large quantity of linen belonging to Mr Broughton, as well as two axes, now demanded the most rigorous inquiry. An additional mortification happened on the 21st.— Towereroo, a Sandwich islander (brought out from England in the Discovery,) had, in the course of the preceeding night, found means to elope from the ship. After much trouble of investigation, and some coercion, on the 23d the three royal brothers brought back Towereroo, with a variety of expiatory presents. The linen there appeared now no prospect of recovering, without both losing time and having recourse to unpleasant measures; it was, therefore, resolved to depart without it; presents as usual were distributed, and the separation took place with the utmost harmony.

Omai, it seems, having died without children, the house which Captain Cook had built for him, the lands that were purchased, and the horse, which was still alive, together with such European commodities as remained at his death, all descended to Matuarro, as king of the island, and, when his majesty is at home, Omai's house is his constant residence. From Matuarro they learned, that Omai was much respected, and that he frequently afforded great entertainment to him, and the other chiefs, with the accounts of his travels, and describing the various countries, objects, &c. that had fallen under his observation; and that he died universally regretted and lamented. His death, as well as that of the two New Zealand boys left with him by Captain Cook, was occasioned by a disorder that is attended by a large swelling in the throat of which very few recover

On th 24th January, the Discovery and Chatham directed
their course to the northward, for the first time pointing their heads
towards the grand object of the expedition.   On the 2d February
passed Owhyhee, one of the Sandwich Islands, and were honored
by a visit from Tianna, the personage mentioned in Mr. Mears's
voyage, who, since his return from China, had taken part with
Tamaahmaah against Teamawheere, and, being victorious, these
two chiefs had agreed to share the government.   Tianna was
taken on board to go to the Leeward Islands.   Tareehooa, who
preferred the name of Jack, having been with Mr. Ingram commanding an American ship, laden with furs, from North-West
America, bound to Boston, by the way of China, was desirous of
continuing on board the Discovery, and to proceed on the voyage,
which, with consent of the chief, was complied with.   After passing some desolate islands, the Discovery anchored, on the 7th
of March, in a bay called Whykete, south of the Island of
Woahoo, on good and safe ground.   Some of the inhabitants went
.n board, and were exceedingly orderly and docile, which appeared the more remarkable, as they had formerly been represented
as the most daring and unmanageable of any in the Sandwich
Islands.

Their new ship-mate, Jack, became very useful; he took upon
him to represent them in the most formidable point of view to all
his countrymen; magnifying their powers and numbers, and pro-
claiming that they were not traders, such as they had been accustomed to see; but were belonging to King George, and were all
mighty warriors.   This being his constant discourse, it is not to
be wondered that his countrymen became much intimidated; and,
as this could be productive of no ill consequences, they permitted
Jack to proceed in his encomiums, and unanimously agreed it
would not be his fault if they were not in high repute amongst
the islanders.

The natives having failed in supplying water as expected,
Captain Vancouver set sail, on the 8th, for Attowai, where he
understood it was to be had without difficulty.   Whyhetee Bay
lies in latitude 21 deg. 16 min. 47 sec., longitude 202 deg. 9 min.
37 sec.   Next morning they made Whymea Bay, on the south
side of Attowai.   The inhabitants of this island behaved in the
same orderly manner, and with the same distant civility experienced at Woahoo, and gave the necessary assistance in watering
and other operations.   The land here was also much the same,
and similarly cultivated with the taro plant.   Here were found
Rowbottom, an Englishman, Williams, a Welshman, and Coleman, an Irishman, left for the purpose of collecting pearls and
sandal-wood for their master, John Kendrick, an American, commanding the Lady Washington, and which was to call for them in
her return from China, to take them on board with the pearls and
sandal-wood collected.   They were visited by two chiefs, No-ma

ee-he-tee and Too, announcing that Enemoh, guardian of the
young prince Ta-moo-eree, who was the eldest son of Taio, sove
-eign of this and the neighboring islands, together with the prince
himself, would be with them in a few days. They accordingly
came and behaved with the utmost propriety, although, from certain appearances of fire, as well as the circumstance of a schooner
taken by the Indians at Owyhee, and the cautions of Rowbottom,
Captain Vancouver had not been without suspicions of treachery.
Enemoh readily went on board and an exchange was made of
presents, which, though liberal on the part of Captain Vancouver,
did not give satisfaction; the great desire of the chief, as of all
of them, being to have fire-arms and ammunition, with which the
various traders touching at their islands had most improperly, and
even cruelly, supplied the inhabitants.

Wednesday, the 14th of March, the two ships sailed for the
coast of America. On the 17th of April they saw land, being
part of New Albion, and being then in 39 deg. 27 min. latitude,
236 deg. 25 min. longitude. On the 28th they spoke an American ship, Columbia, Mr. Robert Gray, commander, of Boston,
whence she had been absent eighteen months. On the 29th, anchored about eight miles within the entrance of the supposed
Straits of Juan de Fuca. Of course they made a strict investigation of this passage, and were satisfied that it did not exist.

Port Discovery, where the vessels now went to anchor, is a
perfectly safe and convenient harbor, having its outer points one
mile and three quarters asunder, and situated in latitude 48 deg.
7 min., longitude 237 deg. 20½ min. The country of New Albion,
in this neighborhood, is of a rich fertile soil. In respect to its
mineral productions no great variety was observed. Iron ore, in
its various forms, was generally found; and, from the weight and
magnetic qualities of some specimens, appeared tolerably rich,
particularly a kind that much resembled the blood-stone.

The next place of research was Admiralty Inlet, where the
ships anchored off Restoration Point. The general information
here is little. The natives were much the same, equally ill-made,
and their persons besmeared with oil and ochre, and a sort of
shining chaffy mica very ponderous, and in colors resembling
black-lead; but decked more with copper ornaments, while they
were not wanting in acts and offers of friendship and hospitality,
and behaved with perfect decorum and civility.

About a dozen of these friendly people had attended at their
dinner, one part of which was a venison pasty. Two of them,
expressing a desire to pass the line of separation drawn between
them, were permitted to do so. They sat down by the English,
and ate of the bread and fish given them without the least hesitation; but, on being offered some of the venison, they could not be
induced to taste it. They received it with great disgust, and
presented it round to the rest of the party, by whom it underwent

a very strict examination. Their conduct on this occasion left
no doubt that they believed it to be human flesh, an impression
which it was highly expedient should be done away. To satisfy
them that it was the flesh of the deer, they pointed to the skins of
the animal they had about them. In reply to this they pointed to
each other, and made signs that could not be misunderstood, that
it was the flesh of human beings, and threw it down in the dirt
with gestures of great aversion and displeasure. At length they
happily convinced them of their mistake by showing them a
haunch they had in the boat, by which means they were unde-
ceived, and some of them ate of the remainder of the pie with a
good appetite.

On Monday, the 4th of June, the ship's companies were served
a good dinner, it being the anniversary of his majesty's birth; on
which day, they designed to take formal possession of all the
countries they had lately been employed in exploring. Pursuing
the usual formalities on such occasions, and under the discharge
of a royal salute from the vessels, they took possession accordingly of the coast, from that part of New Albion, in the latitude
of 39 deg. 20 min. north, and longitude 236 deg. 26 min. east, to
the entrance of this inlet of the sea, said to be the straits of Juan
de Fuca, as likewise all the coast, islands, &c. by the name of
the Gulf of Georgia; and the continent binding the said gulf and
extending southward to the 45th degree of north latitude, with
that of New Georgia, in honor of his majesty.

On the 5th of June, the Discovery and Chatham sailed from
Possession Sound. Having anchored on the 11th in Strawberry
Bay, so named from its producing that excellent fruit in abundance, latitude 48 deg. 36 min., longitude 237 deg. 34 min., and
there being several things necessary to be done, Captain Vancouver and Mr. Puget, in the Discovery's yawl, and Mr. Whidby
in the cutter, attended by the Chatham's launch, explored the
neighborhood. As they were rowing on the 22d, for Point Grey
purposing there to land and breakfast, they discovered two vessels at anchor under the land. They were a brig and a schooner
wearing the colors of Spanish vessels of war, most probably employed in pursuits similar to their own, and this idea was confirmed. These vessels proved to be a detachment from the commission of Seignor Malaspina, who was himself employed in the
Phillippine islands. Seignor Malaspina had, the preceding
year, visited the coast, and these vessels, his Catholic majesty's
brig the Sutil, under the command of Seignor Don D. Galiano,
with the schooner Mexicana, commanded by Seignor Don C.
Valdes, both captains of frigates in the Spanish navy, had sailed
from Acapulco on the 8th of March, in order to prosecute discoveries on this coast. From these gentlemen Vancouver understood,
that Seignor Quadra, the commander-in-chief of the Spanish
marine at St. Blas and at California, was, with three frigates and

a brig, waiting his arrival at Nootka, in order to negotiate the restoration of those territories to the crown of Great Britain. Their conduct was replete with that politeness and friendship which characterize the Spanish nation; every kind of useful information they cheerfully communicated, and obligingly expressed much desire, that circumstances might so concur as to admit their respective labors being carried on together.

The 17th of August they were suddenly surprised by the arrival of a brig off the entrance of the cove, under English colors. She was the Venus, belonging to Bengal, of one hundred and ten tons burden, commanded by Mr. Shepherd, last from Nootka, and bound on a trading voyage along these shores. By him they received the pleasant tidings of the arrival of the Dædalus store-ship, laden with a supply of provisions and stores for their use; and he acquainted Mr. Baker, that Seignor Quadra was waiting with the greatest impatience to deliver up the settlement and territories at Nootka. Mr. Shepherd had brought with him a letter from Mr. Thomas Newmaster of the Dædalus, informing Vancouver of a most distressing and melancholy event. Lieutenant Hergest, the commander, Mr. William Gooch, the astronomer, with one of the seamen belonging to the Dædalus, had been murdered by the inhabitants of Woahoo, whilst on shore procuring water at that island. August 19th they proceeded from the last station, namely, Point Menzies, in latitude 52 deg. 18 min., longitude 232 deg. 55 min., and on the 28th, arrived off Nootka Sound. The Chatham, by the partial clearing of the fog, had found her way in some time before; the Dædalus store-ship, and a small merchant brig called the Three Brothers, of London, commanded by Lieutenant Alder of the navy, were also there at anchor. Seignor Quadra, with several of his officers, came on board the Discovery, on the 29th, where they breakfasted, and were saluted with thirteen guns on their arrival and departure; the day was afterwards spent in ceremonious offices of civility, with much harmony and festivity. Maquinna, the native chief of Nootka, who was present on this occasion, had early in the morning, from being unknown to them, being prevented coming on board the Discovery by the sentinels and the officer on deck, as there was not in his appearance the smallest indication of his superior rank. Of this indignity he had complained in a most angry manner to Seignor Quadra, who very obligingly found means to soothe him.

Some difficulties now occurred in respect to the particulars of the restitution, but after written and verbal correspondence, it was agreed that the objections on both sides should be referred to the respective courts. Seignor Quadra, however, having hereafter made further objections, an additional correspondence took place; but the Spanish officer insisting, and being positively resolved to adhere to certain principles proposed by him as to the restitution, to which Captain Vancouver could not accede, the latter acquainted him that he should consider Nootka as a Spanish port, and requested his permission to carry on the necessary employments on shore, which he very politely gave, with the most friendly assurance of every service and kind office in his power.

It was not till the 12th of October that the Discovery sailed from Nootka, with the Chatham and Dædalus store-ships, bound to the southward. November 15th discovered anchorage in a most excellent small bay. The herds of cattle and flocks of sheep grazing on the surrounding hills, were a sight they had long been strangers to, and brought many pleasing reflections. On hoisting the colors at sun-rise, a gun was fired, and in a little time afterwards several people were seen on horseback, coming from behind the hills down to the beach, who waved their hats, and made other signals for a boat, which was immediately sent to the shore, and on its return they were favored with the company of a priest of the order of St. Francisco, and a serjeant in the Spanish army to breakfast. The good friar, after pointing out the most convenient spot for procuring wood and water, and repeating hospitable offers, in the name of the fathers of the Franciscan order, returned to the mission of St. Francisco, which they understood was at no great distance, and to which he gave them the most pressing invitation.

Whilst engaged in allotting to the people their different employments, some saddled horses arrived from the commandant, with a very cordial invitation; which was accepted by the captain and some of the officers. They rode up to the Presidio, an appellation given to their military establishments in this country, and signifying a safe-guard. The residence of the friars is called a mission. The Spanish soldiers composing the garrison amounted to thirty-five, who, with their wives, families, and a few Indian servants, composed the whole of the inhabitants. On the left of the church is the commander's house, consisting of two rooms and a closet only, which are divided by massy walls, and communicating with each other by very small doors. Between these apartments and the outward wall was an excellent poultry-house and yard, which seemed pretty well stocked; and between the roof and ceiling of the rooms was a kind of lumber garret; these were all the conveniences the habitation seemed calculated to afford. On approaching it they found his good lady, who, like her spouse, had passed the middle age of life, decently dressed, seated cross-legged on a mat, placed on a small square wooden platform raised three or four inches from the ground, nearly in front of the door, with two daughters and a son, clean and decently dressed, sitting by her; this being the mode observed by these ladies when they receive visiters. The decorous and pleasing behavior of the children was really admirable, and exceeded any thing that could have been expected from them under the circumstances of their situation, without any other advantages than the education and example of their parents, which, however, seemed to have been studiously attended to, and did them great credit.

The next day was appointed for visiting the mission. Accompanied by Menzies and some of the officers, and Seignor Sal, the captain rode thither to dinner. The uniform, mild, and kind-hearted disposition of this religious order has never failed to attach to their interest the affections of the natives, wherever they have sat down amongst them; this is a very happy circumstance, for their situation otherwise would be excessively precarious; as they are protected only by five soldiers, who reside under the directions of a corporal, in the buildings of the mission at some distance on the other side of the church. The natives, however, seemed to have treated with the most perfect indifference the precepts, and laborious example of their truly worthy and benevolent pastors. Their persons, generally speaking, were under the middle size, and very ill made; their faces ugly, presenting a dull, heavy, and stupid countenance, devoid of sensibility or the least expression.

On the 25th, they set sail for Monterrey, where they found the Dædalus, and also Seignor Qaudra, with his broad pendant on board the brig Acteon. He, as well as the acting governor, Seignor Anquilla, both behaved in the most friendly and liberal manner. They sailed on the 14th of January, and on the 12th of February arrived off the north-east point of Owhyhee. Having, on the 21st of February, reached Tyahtatooa, Captain Vancouver was honored with a visit from Tomaahmaah, the king of the island of Owhyhee, a chief of an open, cheerful, and sensible mind, combined with great generosity and goodness of disposition He was accompanied by John Young, an English seaman, who possessed much influence with him. The queen and some of his majesty's relations also visited on board.

They were much pleased with the decorum and general conduct of this royal party. Though it consisted of many, yet not one solicited even the most inconsiderable article, nor did they appear to have any expectation of receiving presents. Being determined that nothing should be wanting to preserve the harmony and good understanding that seemed to have taken place between them, and having learned from Young, that the royal visiters did not entertain the most distant idea of accepting any thing from the captain, until they had first set the example; he considered this a good opportunity to manifest a friendly disposition towards them by presents suitable to their respective ranks and situations. Accordingly, such articles were distributed as they knew were likely to be highly acceptable to the whole party. This distribution being finished, and the whole party made very happy, the king, in addition to what he had before received, was presented with a scarlet cloak, that reached from his neck to the ground, adorned with tinsel lace, trimmed with various colored gartering tape, with blue ribbons to tie it down the front. The looking-glasses being placed opposite to each other, displayed at once the whole of his royal person; this filled him with rapture, and so delighted him, that the cabin could scarcely contain him. His ecstasy produced capering, and he soon cleared the cabin of many of their visiters whose numbers had rendered it very hot and unpleasant.

Next morning they reached Karakakooa, the residence of Tomaahmaah. Besides Young, his Owhyhean majesty's favorite before mentioned, there were here also John Smith, an Irishman, who had deserted from an American trader, and Isaac Davis, who had been captured by the islanders, in the schooner Fair American. These men behaved extremely well, and had been taken under the special patronage of Tamaahmaah, who was much irritated at the above capture; and the treatment of the people belonging to the schooner, which was atrociously taken by Tamamootoo, a powerful chief, and his people, but which Tamaahmaah caused to be delivered up to them, to be kept for the benefit of the proprietor Mr. Metcalf, who had the command of the schooner, was thrown overboard by Tamaahmootoo, who took out of her every thing he could, before the arrival of the king and Young. In this affair, Tianna had also acted a scandalous part, endeavoring, by false insinuations, to prevail on the king to kill Young and Davis, but his arts were unsuccessful on his majesty, whose sound judgment, and humane attentions, would have done credit to the sovereign of a more civilized people.

On the 4th of March, as soon as dinner was over, they were summoned to a sham-fight on shore; and as Tamaahmaah considered all ceremonies and formalities as adding to his consequence, he requested that the captain would be attended on shore by a guard. They found the warriors assembled towards the north corner of the beach, without the limits of the hallowed ground. The party consisted of about one hundred and fifty men, armed with spears; these were divided into three parties, nearly in equal numbers; two were placed at a little distance from each other; that on the right was to represent the armies of Titeeree and Taio; that on the left the army of Tamaahmaah. Their spears, on this occasion, were blunt-pointed sticks, about the length of their barbed ones, whilst, on each wing, they were to suppose a body of troops placed to annoy the enemy with stones from their slings. The combatants now advanced towards each other, seemingly without any principal leader, making speeches as they approached, which appeared to end in vaunts and threats from both parties, when the battle began, by throwing their sham spears at each other. These were parried in most instances with great dexterity; but such as were thrown with effect, produced contusions and wounds, which, though fortunately of no dangerous tendency, were yet very considerable, and it was admirable to observe the great good-humor and evenness of temper that was preserved by those who were thus injured. This battle was a mere skirmish, neither party being supported, nor advancing in any order, but such as the fancy of the individuals directed Some would advance even from the rear to the front, where they would throw their spears, and instantly retreat into the midst of their associates, or would remain picking up the spears that had fallen without effect. These they would sometimes hurl again at the foe, or hastily retreat, with two or three in their possession. Those, however, who valued themselves on military achievements, marched up towards the front of the adverse party, and in a vaunting manner bid defiance to the whole of their adversaries. In their left hand they held their spear, with which, in a contemptuous manner, they parried some of those of their opponents, whilst, with their right, they caught others in the act of flying immediately at them, and instantly returned them with great dexterity In this exercise no one seemed to excel his Owhyhean majesty who entered the lists for a short time and defended himself with the greatest dexterity, much to their surprise and admiration, in one instance particularly, against six spears, that were hurled at him nearly at the same instant; three he caught as they were flying, with one hand; two he broke, by parrying them with his spear in the other; and the sixth, by a trifling inclination of his body, passed harmless.

This part of the combat was intended to represent the king as having been suddenly discovered by the enemy, in a situation where he was least expected to be found; and the shower of darts that were instantly directed to that quarter, were intended to show that he was in the most imminent danger; until advancing a few paces, with the whole body of his army more closely connected, and throwing their spears with the utmost exertion, he caused the enemy to fall back in some little confusion, and he himself rejoined the English, without having received the slightest injury.

The consequences attendant on the first man being killed, or being so wounded as to fall on the disputed ground between the contending armies, were next exhibited. This event causes the loss of many lives, and much blood, in the conflict that takes place, in order to rescue the unfortunate individual, who, if carried off by the adverse party, dead or alive, becomes an immediate sacrifice at the morai. On this occasion, the wounded man was supposed to be one of Titeeree's soldiers, and until this unhappy period no advantage appeared on either side; but now the dispute became very serious, was well supported on all sides, and victory still seemed to hold a level scale, until, at length, the supposed armies of Taio and Titeeree fell back, whilst that of Tamaahmaah carried off in triumph several supposed dead bodies, dragging the poor fellows, (who already had been much trampled upon) by the heels, some distance through a light, loose sand; and who, notwithstanding their eyes, ears, mouth, and nostrils, were by this means filled, were no sooner permitted to use their legs, than they ran into the sea, washed themselves, and appeared as happy and as cheerful as if nothing had happened.

In this riot-like engagement, the principal chiefs were considered to bear no part; and, on its being thus concluded, each party sat quietly down on the ground, and a parley, or some other sort of conversation took place. The chiefs were now supposed to have arrived at the theatre of war, which had hitherto been carried on by the common people only of both parties; a very usual mode of proceeding among these islanders. They now on both sides came forward, guarded by a number of men armed ' with spears of great length, called *pallaloos*. These weapons are never relinquished but by death, or captivity; the former is the most common. They are not barbed, but reduced to a small point, and though not very sharp, yet are capable of giving deep and mortal wounds by the force and manner with which they are used. The missive spears are all barbed about six inches from the point, and are generally from seven to eight feet long.

The warriors armed with the *pallaloos* now advanced with a considerable degree of order, and a scene of very different exploits commenced; presenting, in comparison to what before had been exhibited, a wonderful degree of improved knowledge in military evolutions. This body of men, composing several ranks, formed in close and regular order, constituted a firm and compact phalanx, which in actual service was not easily to be broken. Having reached the spot in contest, they sat down on the ground about thirty yards asunder, and pointed their *pallaloos* at each other. After a short interval of silence, a conversation commenced, and Taio was supposed to state his opinion respecting peace and war. The arguments seemed to be argued and supported with equal energy on both sides. When peace under certain stipulations was proposed, the *pallaloos* were inclined towards the ground, and when war was announced, their points were raised to a certain degree of elevation. Both parties put on the appearance of being much upon their guard, and to watch each other with a jealous eye, whilst this negotiation was going forward, which, however, not terminating amicably, their respective claims remained to be decided by the fate of a battle. Nearly at the same instant of time they all arose, and, in close columns, met each other by slow advances. This movement they conducted with much order and regularity, frequently shifting their ground, and guarding with great circumspection against the various advantages of their opponents; whilst the inferior bands were supposed to be engaged on each wing with spears and slings. The success of the contest, however, seemed to depend entirely on those with the *pallaloos*, who firmly disputed every inch of the ground, by parrying each other's lunges with the greatest dexterity, until some to the left of Titeeree's centre fell. This greatly encouraged Tamaahmaah's party, who, rushing forward with shouts and great impetuosity, broke the ranks of their opponents, and victory was declared for the arms of Owhyhee, by the supposed death of several of the enemies; these at length retreated; and, on being more closely pressed, the war was decided by the supposed death of Titeeree and Taio; and those who had the honor of personating these chiefs, were, like those before, dragged in triumph by the heels over no small extent of loose sandy beech, to be presented to the victorious Tamaahmaah, and for the supposed purpose of being sacrificed at his morai. These poor fellows, like those before mentioned, bore their treatment with the greatest good humor.

Having sailed from Owhyhee, they arrived on the 10th of March off Mowee. On the 13th they were honored with the presence of Titeeree, who was considered as king of all the islands to the leeward of Owhyhee; and that from him Taio derived his authority. He came boldly alongside, but entered the ship with a sort of partial confidence, accompanied by several chiefs; he was greatly debilitated and emaciated; and, from the color of his skin, they judged his feebleness to have been brought on by an excessive use of the ava. Amongst the articles presented to him on this occasion, was a cloak, similar to those given Tamaahmaah, this highly delighted him; and he was also well pleased with the other presents he received.

After some further interchange of civilities, and much negotiation respecting the wished for peace, Captain Vancouver sailed from Mowee the 18th of March, having Tomohomoho on board, and on the 20th reached Whyteetee, in Woahoo. One double canoe only made its appearance. In this came James Coleman, one of the three men they found last year, left by Mr. Kendrick, at Attowai. The 21st, Coleman, with Tomohomoho and Tennavee, came on board. The two chiefs desired the captain would attend them into the cabin; where, after shutting all the doors, they informed him that the man who had murdered Mr. Hergest, with two others who had been equally active and guilty, were in the fore part of the canoe, and that no time should be lost in securing them, lest any thing should transpire, and they should again make their escape. On the 22d, a few of the natives were about the ship, but not so many as on the former days. After breakfast, Coleman, with Tomohomoho and Tennavee, came on board. The two latter demanded the immediate execution of the prisoners. This, however, was not complied with, as it was deemed right that they should again be accused by their own chiefs, in the presence of all the witnesses, of the crime with which they stood charged in order, if possible, to draw from them

23 *

a confession of their guilt, and to renew the opportunity which
before had been given them, of producing some evidence in proof
of their innocence. Nothing, however, could be extorted from
any of them, but that they were totally ignorant of any such circumstances having ever happened on the island. This very as-
sertion amounted almost to self-conviction, as it is not easy to
believe, that the execution of their comrades, by Titeeree's
orders, for the same offence with which they had been charged,
had not come to their knowledge, or that it could have escaped
their recollection. Neither the captain nor the officers discovered
any reason, from the result of this further examination, to retract
or alter their former opinion of their guilt, or of delivering them
over to their own people, to be dealt with according to the directions of their chiefs.

That the ceremony might be made as solemn and awful as possible, a guard of seamen and mariners were drawn up on that side
of the ship opposite to the shore, where, alongside of the ship,
a canoe was stationed for the execution. The rest of the crew
were in readiness at the great guns, lest any disturbance or
commotion should arise. One ceremony, however, remained yet
to be performed. One of these unfortunate men had long hair;
this it was necessary should be cut from his head before he was
executed, for the purpose of being presented, as a customary
tribute on such occasions, to the king of the island. They were
shocked at the want of feeling exhibited by the two chiefs at this
awful moment, who, in the rudest manner, not only cut off the
hair, but, in the presence of the poor suffering wretch, without
the least compassion for his situation, disputed and strove for the
honor of presenting the prize to the king. The odious contest
being at length settled, the criminals were taken one by one into
a double canoe, where they were lashed hand and foot, and put
to death by Tamavee, their own chief, who blew out their brains
with a pistol; and so dexterously was the melancholy office performed, that life fled with the report of the piece, and muscular
motion seemed almost instantly to cease.

They now bade adieu to the Sandwich Islands, and made the
best of their way for Nootka. The Discovery arrived the 20th of
May. Mr. Puget had arrived with the Chatham on the 15th of
April, and departed thence the 18th of May, according to his instructions, to proceed in the survey of the coast. In the course
of continuing the examination of the coast, they met with some
Indians of very different behavior from those they had hitherto
seen. The survey was continued sedulously till the 5th of October, when both vessels returned to Nootka. The usual ceremonies
of salutes, and other formalities having passed, accompanied by
Mr. Puget, Vancouver waited on Senr. Saavadra, the commandant of the port; who said, that he had not received any intelligence,
either from Europe, or from New Spain, since their departure

from hence in the spring; and that neither the Dædalus, nor any other ship with stores, had been there.

Having quitted Nootka, nothing of importance occurred till their arrival, on the 19th, in Port St. Francisco. They were soon hailed from the shore, upon which a boat was despatched thither, and immediately returned with their civil and attentive friend, Seignor Sal; who, in addition to the offers of his services and hospitality, gratified them by communicating the interesting intelligence of the state of Europe, up to so late a date as the preceding February. In proceeding towards Monterrey, they made so little progress, that they were still at no great distance from St. Francisco next morning, the 25th; when a vessel was descried to the north-north-west; and, on standing towards her, she proved to be the Dædalus. On the 1st of November, they reached Monterrey with the Dædalus.

Having anchored before another Spanish establishment, Vancouver sent Lieutenant Swaine to inform the commanding officer at the presidio of their arrival. The next morning, accompanied by Lieutenants Puget and Hanson, Vancouver paid his respects on shore to Seignor Don Phelipe Goycochea, the commandant of the establishment of Santa Barbara, and lieutenant in the Spanish infantry. The pleasing society of their good friends at the mission and presidio, was augmented by the arrival of Friar Vincente Sta. Maria, one of the reverend fathers of the mission of Buena Ventura; situated about seven leagues from hence, on the seacoast to the south-eastward. At eight in the evening they anchored in fifteen fathoms water, about a league to the westward of Buena Ventura. Their reverend friend expressed great satisfaction at the mode of his return to the mission; and said, that his voyage hither would probably lay the foundation for removing the absurd and deep-rooted prejudice that had ever existed amongst the several tribes of Indians in his neighborhood, who, from their earliest infancy, had invariably regarded all strangers as their enemies.

Nothing of consequence occurred till their arrival, on the 8th of January, 1794, at Owhyhee, off the Bay of Whycalea, where their return was proclaimed by shouts of joy, and they were visited by Tamaahmaah, rejoiced to meet his friends at this his favorite part of the island. Their course was now directed round the east point of the island, and as they worked into the bay of Karakakooa, many of the inhabitants were assembled on the shores, who announced their congratulations by shouts of joy; many of their former friends, particularly of the fair sex, lost no time in testifying the sincerity of the public sentiment in their favor. Young and Davis they had likewise the pleasure of finding in the exercise of those judicious principles they had so wisely adopted, and which, by their example and advice, had so uniformly been carred into effect.

On Thursday the 30th, they were favored with the company of

Terree-my-tee, Crymamahoo, Tianna, and some other chiefs
from the distant parts of the island. Their arrival had been in
consequence of a summons from the king, who had called the
grand council of the island, on the subject of its cession to the
crown of Great Britain, which was unanimously desired. These
chiefs brought intelligence, that a quantity of timber, which had
been sent for at the captain's request, was on its way hither, it
had been cut down under the direction of an Englishman, named
Boyd, formerly mate of the sloop Washington, but who had relinquished that way of life, and had entered into the service of
Tamaahmaah. He appeared in the character of a shipwright,
and had undertaken to build, with these materials, a vessel for
the king, after the European fashion; but both himself and his
comrades, Young and Davis, were fearful of encountering too
many difficulties, especially as they were all much at a loss in the
first outset, that of laying down the keel. This afforded Vancouver an opportunity of conferring on Tamaahmaah a favor that
he valued far beyond every other obligation, by permitting his
carpenters to begin the vessel, from whose example, and the assistance of these three engineers, he was in hopes that his people
would hereafter be able to build boats and small vessels for themselves. On Saturday, the 1st of February, they laid down the
keel, and began to prepare the frame-work of his Owhyhean
majesty's first man-of-war. The length of its keel was thirty-six
feet, the extreme breadth of the vessel nine feet and a quarter,
and the depth of her hold about five feet; her name was to be
The Britannia, and was intended as a protection to the royal person of Tamaahmaah; and few circumstances in his life ever afforded him more satisfaction.

Some solemn religious rites being now to take place, Captain
Vancouver had frequently expressed to Tamaahmaah a desire of
being present on some of these occasions; and he now informed
him he had obtained the consent of the priests, provided he would,
during the continuance of the interdiction, attend to all the restric-
tions which their religion demanded. The restraints imposed consisted chiefly in four particulars: first, a total seclusion from the
company of women; secondly, partaking of no food but such as
was previously consecrated; thirdly, being confined to the land,
and not being afloat or wet with sea-water; and fourthly, not receiving, or even touching, the most trivial article from any one
who had not attended the ceremonies at the morai. Their prayers
seemed to have some regularity and form, and they did not omit
to pray for the welfare of his Britannic majesty, and their safe and
happy return to their native country. The intermediate day, the
13th, and the second night, were passed in prayer, during which
they found no difficulty in complying with the prescribed regulations, and soon after the sun rose, the 14th, they were absolved
from any further attention to their sacred injunctions

The cession of Owhyhee to his Britannic majesty became now an object of serious concern. Some little delay and difficulty, however, arose from the absence of two chiefs, Commanow, who from local circumstances could not quit his government, and Tamaahmooto, chief of Coarra, the person who had captured the Fair American schooner.

At one of their evening amusements the captain was very well entertained. This was a performance by a single young woman of the name of Packoo, whose person and manners were both very agreeable. Her dress, notwithstanding the heat of the weather, consisted of an immense quantity of thin cloth, which was wound round her waist, and extended as low as her knees. This was plaited in such a manner as to give a pretty effect to the variegated pattern of the cloth; and was otherwise disposed with great taste. Her head and neck were decorated with wreaths of black, red, and yellow feathers; but, excepting these, she wore no dress from the waist upwards. Her ankles, and nearly half way up her legs, were decorated with several folds of cloth, widening upwards, so that the upper parts extended from the leg at least four inches all round, this was encompassed by a piece of net-work, wrought very close, from the meshes of which were hung the small teeth of dogs, giving this part of her dress the appearance of an ornamental funnel. On her wrists she wore bracelets made of the tusks from the largest hogs. These were highly polished and fixed close together in a ring, the concave sides of the tusks being outwards; and their ends reduced to an uniform length, curving naturally each way from the centre, were by no means destitute of ornamental effect. Thus equipped, her appearance on the stage, before she uttered a single word, excited considerable applause from the numerous spectators, who observed the greatest good order and decorum. In her performance, which was in the open air, she was accompanied by two men, who were seated on the ground in the character of musicians. Their instruments were both alike, and were made of the outsides or shells of large gourds, open at the tops; the lower ends ground perfectly flat, and as thin as possible, without endangering their splitting. These were struck on the ground, covered with a small quantity of dried grass, and in the interval between each stroke, they beat with their hands and fingers on the sides of these instruments, to accompany their vocal exertions, which, with the various motions of their hands and body, and the vivacity of their countenances, plainly demonstrated the interest they had, not only in excelling in their own parts, but also in the applause which the lady acquired by her performance advancing or retreating from the musicians a few short steps in various directions as the nature of the subject, and the numerous gestures and motions of her person demanded. Her speech, or poem, was first began in a slow, and somewhat solemn manner, and gradually became en ergetic, probably as the subject matter became interesting; until at length, like a true actress, the liveliness of her imagination produced a vociferous oration, accompanied by violent emotions. These were received with shouts of great applause; and although they were not sufficiently acquainted with the language to comprehend the subject, yet they could not help being pleased in a high degree with the performance.

On the 25th of February, Tamaahmaah, King of Owhyhee, in council with the principal chiefs of the island, assembled on board the Discovery, in Karakakooa bay, and in the presence of George Vancouver, her commander, and Lieutenant Peter Puget, commander of the armed tender the Chatham, and the other officers of the Discovery, after due consideration, unanimously ceded the island of Owhyhee to his Britannic majesty, and acknowledged themselves to be subjects of Great Britain.

Thus concluded their transactions at Owhyhee, to which they bade adieu about three in the morning of the 3d of March. They left here, however, a banditti of renegadoes, that had quitted different trading vessels in consequence of disputes with their respective commanders, who had resorted to this island since the preceding year, under American or Portuguese colors. Amongst them was one Portuguese, one Chinese, and one Genoese, but all the rest appeared to be the subjects of Great Britain, as seemed also the major part of the crew of the brig Washington, although they called themselves Americans. With Kavaheeroo also resided a person by the name of Howell, who had come to Owhyhee, in the capacity of a clerk on board the Washington; he appeared to possess a good understanding, with the advantages of an university education, and had been once a clergyman in England, but had now secluded himself from European society, so that with Young, Davis, and Boyd, there were now eleven white men on the island; but, excepting from these latter, there Owhyhean friends will have little reason to rejoice in any advantages they will receive from their new civilized companions.

After visiting some other parts of the Sandwich Islands, the ships finally bade them adieu on the 15th of March, from which period, till the end of August, the whole time was occupied in a very extensive and minute survey of the coast of North-west America. Suffice it to say, that one great object of the voyage was, namely, to ascertain the existence of a north-west passage, or any water communication navigable for shipping. The North Pacific, and the exterior of the American continent, within these limits, were completely examined, and it was proved that no such communication did exist, notwithstanding the assertions of Fuca, Fonte, and others, on that subject. On the 2d of September, the Discovery anchored in Friendly Cove, Nootka Sound, where were three of his Catholic majesty's armed vessels, and some English and American traders.

At Monterrey they arrived on the 2d of November. Having on the 2d of December quitted it, and proceeded southward, they passed the three Marias Islands, and afterwards the rich but uninhabited island of Cocos. Its produce is luxurious and abundant, as are also fowl and fish. They afterwards successively passed the Gallipagos Islands, Massafuero, and Juan Fernandes. On the 24th of March they gained a distant view of the lofty coast of Chili to the westward, in latitude 32 deg. 53 min., and at a supposed distance of forty leagues, the immense mountains of the Andes. Their destination was, however, the bay of Valparaiso, which they reached next day.

Nothing particular happened in the voyage round Cape Horn, and thence to St. Helena, where the Discovery arrived on the 2d of July, the Chatham having got thither before her. Here, in consequence of the hostilities with Holland, Captain Vancouver took a Dutch East Indiaman, the Macassar. On the 12th of September, made the western coast of Ireland; when having seen the Discovery safely moored in the Shannon, he proceeded to London, resigning the command of the ship to Lieutenant Baker, and taking with him such books, papers, and charts, as were necessary to lay before the Lords of the Admiralty, relative to the services performed. In the course of this long voyage of four years eight months and twenty-nine days, the Discovery lost by disease, out of one hundred men, only one, and five by accidents; and in the Chatham not one died from disease or otherwise

---

A VISIT TO ROCKALL

By Captain Hall.

It was a fine autumnal morning, just a week after we had sailed from Lough Swilly, to cruise off the North of Ireland, a sail was reported on the leebeam. We bore up instantly, but no one could make out what the chase was, nor which way she was standing—at least, no two of the knowing ones could be found to agree upon these matters. These various opinions, however presently settled into one, or nearly so—for there were still some of the high-spyers who had honestly confessed they were puzzled. The general opinion was, that it must be a brig with very white sails aloft, while those below were quite dark—as if the royals were made of cotton, and the courses of tarpawling,—a strange anomaly in seamanship, it is true, but still the best theory we could form to explain appearances. A short time served to dispe'

these fancies; for we discovered, on running close to our mysterious vessel, that we had been actually chasing a rock—not a ship
of oak and iron, but a solid block of granite, growing as it were,
out of the sea, at a greater distance from the main land than, I
believe any other island, or inlet, or rock of the same diminutive
size, is to be found in the world. This mere speck on the surface of the waters—for it seems to float on the sea—is only
seventy feet high, and not more than a hundred yards in circumference. The smallest point of a pencil could scarcely give it a
place on any map which should not exaggerate its proportion to
the rest of the islands in that stormy ocean. It lies at the
distance of no fewer than one hundred and eighty-four miles
very nearly due west of St. Kilda, the remotest part of the
Hebrides, two hundred and ninety from the nearest part of the
main coast of Scotland, and two hundred and sixty from the north
of Ireland. Its name is Rockall, and is well known to those Bal

Rockall.

tic traders, which go north about. The stone of which this
curious peak is composed, is a dark colored granite, but the top
being covered with a coating as white as snow, from having been
for ages the resting-place of myriads of sea-fowl, it is constantly
mistaken for a vessel under all sail. We were deceived by it
several times during the same cruise, even after we had been put
on our guard, and knew its place well. I remember boarding three
vessels in one day, each of which in reckoning the number of
vessels in sight counted Rockall as one, without detecting their
mistake till I pointed their glasses to the spot

As we had nothing better on our hands it was resolved to make an exploring expedition to visit this little islet. Two boats were accordingly manned for the purpose; and while the ship stood down to the leeward of it, the artists prepared their sketch books and the geologists their hammers, for a grand scientific field day.

When we left the ship, the sea appeared so unusually smooth, that we anticipated no difficulty in landing; but on reaching the spot, we found a swell rising and falling many feet, which made it exceedingly troublesome to accomplish our purpose. One side of the rock was perpendicular and smooth as a wall. The others though steep and slippery, were sufficiently varied in their surface to admit of our crawling up when once out of the boat.

But it required no small confidence in our footing, and a dash of that kind of faith which carries a hunter over a five-bar gate, to render the leap at all secure. A false step, or a faltering carriage, after the spring was resolved on, might have sent the explorer to investigate the secrets of the deep, in those fathomless regions where the roots of this mysterious rock connect it with the solid earth. In time, however, we all got up, hammers, sketch-books, and chronometers inclusive.

As it was considered a point of some moment to determine not only the position, but the size of the rock by actual observations made upon it, all hands were set busily at work—some to chip off specimens—others to measure the girt by means of a cord— while one of the boats was sent to make sounding in those directions where the bottom could be reached.

After we had been employed for some time in this manner, we observed a current sweeping past us, at a considerable rate, and rather wondered that the ship, which was fast drifting away from us did not fill and make a stretch, so as to preserve her distance. But as the day was quite clear, we cared less about this addition to the pull, and went on with our operations. I forget exactly at what hour a slight trace of haze first came across the field of view. This soon thickened into a fog, which felt like a drizzle, and put some awkward apprehensions into our heads. It was immediately decided to get into the boats and return to the Endymion; for, by this time, we had finished all our real work, and were only amusing ourselves by scrambling about the rock.

The swell had silently increased in the interval to such a height, that the operation of returning to the boats was rendered twice as difficult as that of disembarking; and what was a great deal worse, occupied twice as much time. It required the greater part of half an hour to tumble our whole party back again This proceeding, difficult at any season, I suppose, was now reduced to a sort of somerset or flying leap; for the adventurer, whose turn it was to spring, had to dash off the rock towards the boat, trusting more to the chance of being caught by his companions than to any skill of his own. Some of our Dutch-built gentry,

known in the cockpit by the name of heavy-sterned Christians
came floundering amongst the thwarts and oars with such a crash,
that we half expected they would make a clear breach through
the boat's bottom.

As none of these minor accidents occurred, we pushed off,
with our complement entire, towards the ship; but, to our astonishment and dismay, no Endymion could now be seen. Some
said "only a minute ago she was there!" others asserted, as
positively, that they had seen her in a totally different direction.
In short, no two of us agreed as to where the frigate had last
been seen, though all, unhappily, were of one mind as to the disagreeable fact of her being now invisible. She had evidently
drifted off to a considerable distance; and, as the first thickening
of the air had destroyed its transparency, we could see nothing in
the slightest degree, even like what is called the boom of a vessel.
The horizon was visible—indistinctly indeed; but it was certainly
not the same horizon along which we had seen the ship sailing
but half an hour before. The atmosphere had something of that
troubled look which is given to a glass of water by dropping a
little milk into it. So that, although there was no fog as yet,
properly so called, there was quite enough of moisture to serve
the unpleasant purpose of hiding the object of our search; and we
remained quite at a loss what to do. We rowed to some distance
from the rock, supposing it possible that some condensation of
vapor, incident to the spot, might have cast a veil over our eyes.
But nothing was to be seen all round.

It then occurred to some of our philosophers that as dense air,
by its very definition (as they gravely put it), is heavier than
light air, it might so happen that the humid vapors had settled
down upon the surface of the sea, and that, in fact, we were
groping about in a shallow stratum of untransparent matter.
The top of the rock, which was seventy feet higher, it was
thought, might be in the clear region, and the ship's mast heads,
if not her hull, be visible from thence. There was a sort of
pedantic plausibility about the technology of these young savans,
which induced the commanding officer of the party—a bit of a
dabbler himself in these scientific mysteries—to decide upon trying the experiment. At all events, he thought it might amuse
and occupy the party. So one of the men was landed, the most
alert of our number, who skipped up the rock like a goat.

All eyes were now turned on our look-out man, who no sooner
reached the summit, than he was asked what he saw, with an impatience that betrayed more anxiety on the part of the officers
than they probably wished should be perceived by the boats'
crews.

" I can see nothing all round," cried the man, " except something out thereabouts"—pointing with his hand.

" What does it look like?"

"I am afraid, sir, it is a fog bank coming down upon us." And so it proved.

The experienced eye of the sailor, who in his youth had been a fisherman on the banks of Newfoundland, detected a strip or extended cloud, hanging along the verge of the horizon, like the first appearance of a low coast. This gradually swept down to leeward, and, at length, enveloped rock, boats, and all, in a mantle of fog, so dense that we could not see ten yards in any direction.

Although our predicament may now be supposed as hopeless as need be, it was curious to observe the ebbs and flows in human thought as circumstances changed. Half an hour before, we had been provoked at our folly in not having left the rock sooner; but it was now a matter of rejoicing that we possessed such a fixed point to stick by, in place of throwing ourselves adrift altogether. We reckoned with certainty upon the frigate's managing, sooner or later, to regain the rock; and as that was the only mark at which she could aim, it was evidently the best for us to keep near

We had been cruising for some time off the north of Ireland, during which we observed that these fogs sometimes lasted a couple of days or even longer; and, as we had not a drop of water in the boats, nor a morsel of provisions, the most unpleasant forebodings began to beset us. The wind was gradually rising, and the waves, when driven against the rock, were divided into two parts, which, after sweeping round the sides, met again to leeward, near the spot where we lay, and dashed themselves into such a bubble of a sea, that the boats were pitched about like bits of cork in a mill-lead. Their motion was disagreeable enough, but our apprehension was, that we should be dislodged altogether from our place of refuge; while the gulls and sea-mews, as if in contempt of our helpless condition, or offended at our intrusion, wheeled about and screamed close to us, in notes most grating to our ears.

While we were waiting in this state of anxiety in the boats below, our faithful watchman perched on the peak of the rock, suddenly called out, "I see the ship!" This announcement was answered by a simultaneous shout from the two boat's crews, which sent the flocks of gannets and sea-mews screaming to the right and left, far into the bosom of the fog.

An opening or lane in the mist had occurred, along which we could now see the frigate, far off, but crowding all sail, and evidently beating to windward. We lost as little time as possible in picking our shivering scout off the rock, an operation which cost nearly a quarter of an hour. This accomplished, away we rowed, at the utmost stretch of our oars towards the ship.

We had hardly proceeded a quarter of a mile before the fog began to close behind our track, so as to shut out Rockall from our view. This we cared little about, as we not only still saw the

ship, but trusted, from her movements, that she likewise saw the
boats. Just at the moment, however, she tacked, thereby proving that she had seen neither boats nor rock, but was merely
groping about in search of her lost sheep. Had she continued
on the course she was steering when we first saw her, she might
have picked us up long before the fog came on again; but when
she went about, this hope was destroyed. In a few minutes more
we, of course, lost sight of the frigate in the fog; and there we
were, in a pretty mess, with no ship to receive us, and no island
to hang on by!

It now became necessary to take an immediate part; and we decided at once to turn back in search of the rock. It was certainly a moment of bitter disappointment when we pulled round; and
the interval between doing so and our regaining a resting-place,
was one of great anxiety. Nevertheless we made a good land-
fall, and there was a wonderful degree of happiness attendant
even upon this piece of success. Having again got hold of
Rockall, we determined to abide by our firm friend till circumstances should render our return to the ship certain. In the
meantime we amused ourselves in forming plans for a future residence on this desolate abode, in the event of the ship being blown
away during the night. If the weather should become more
stormy, and that our position to leeward was rendered unsafe, in
consequence of the divided waves running round and meeting, it
was resolved, that we should abandon the heaviest of the two
boats, and drag the other up to the brow of the rock, so as to form,
when turned keel upwards, a sort of hurricane house. These, and
various other Robinson Crusoe kind of resources, helped to occupy our thoughts, half in jest, half in earnest, till, by the increased gloom, we knew that the sun had gone down. It now became
indispensable to adopt some definite line of operations, for the
angry looking night was setting in fast.

Fortunately, we were saved from farther trials of patience or
ingenuity by the fog suddenly rising, as it is called—or dissipa-
ting itself in the air, so completely, that, to our great joy, we gained sight of the ship once again.

It appeared afterwards that they had not seen our little island
from the Endymion nearly so soon as we discovered her; and she
was, in consequence, standing almost directly away from us, evidently not knowing exactly whereabouts Rockall lay. This, I
think, was the most anxious moment during the whole adventure;
nor shall I soon forget the sensation caused by seeing the jib-sheet
let fly, accompanied by other indications that the frigate was
coming about.

I need not spin out this story any longer. It was almost dark
when we got on board. Our first question was the reproachful
one, " Why did you fire no guns to give us notice of your
position?"

" Fire guns?" said they—" why, we have done nothing bu
blaze away every ten minutes for these last five or six hours."
Yet strange to say, we had not heard a single discharge!

THE SUBTERRANEAN STREAM

BY MRS. HEMANS.

Darkly thou glidest onward
　Thou deep and hidden wave !
The laughing sunshine hath not looked
　Into thy secret cave.

Thy current makes no music—
　A hollow sound we hear,
A muffled voice of mystery,
　And know that thou art near !

No brighter line of verdure
　Follows thy lonely way !
No fairy moss, or lily's cup,
　Is freshened by thy play.

The halcyon doth not seek thee,
　Her glorious wings to lave ;
Thou know'st no tint of the summer sky
　Thou dark and hidden wave!

Yet once will day behold thee,
　When to the mighty sea,
Fresh bursting from their caverned veins
　Leap thy lone waters free.

There wilt thou greet the sunshine
　For a moment, and be lost,
With all thy melancholy sounds,
　In the Ocean's billowy host.

Oh ! art thou not, dark river !
　Like the fearful thoughts untold,
Which haply in the hush of night
　O'er many a soul have rolled ?

Those earth-born strange misgivings—
　Who hath not felt their power ?
Yet who hath breathed them to his friend
　Ev'n in his fondest hour ?

They hold no heart-communion.
　They find no voice in song,
They dimly follow far from earth
　The grave's departed throng.

24 *

Wild is their course and lonely,
  And fruitless in man's breast;
They come and go, and leave no **trace**
  Of their mysterious quest.

Yet surely must their wanderings
  At length be like thy way;
Their shadows, as thy waters lost,
  In one bright flood of day

CAPTAIN INGLEFIELD'S NARRATIVE.

The Centaur, captain Inglefield, and four ships of the line, part of a large convoy from Jamaica to England, foundered at sea, in a dreadful hurricane, in September 1782.

Captain Inglefield, and the officers and crew, did every thing possible for the preservation of their lives and ship, from the 16th to the 23d of September; when the Centaur, by repeated storms, became a wreck, and was in a sinking state. Some of the men appeared perfectly resigned to their fate, and requested to be lashed in their hammocks; others lashed themselves to gratings and small rafts, but the most prominent idea was, that of putting on their best and cleanest clothes. The booms were cleared, and the cutter, pinnace, and yawl were got over the ship's side. Captain Inglefield and eleven others made their escape in the pinnace; but their condition was nearly the same with that of those who remained in the ship; and at best appeared to be only a prolongation of a miserable existence. "They were in a leaky boat, with one of the gunwales stove, in nearly the middle of the ocean, without compass, quadrant, sail, great coat, or cloak; all very thinly clothed. in a gale of wind, with a great sea running." In half an hour they lost sight of the ship; but before dark a blanket was discovered in the boat, of which they made a sail, and scudded under it all night, expecting to be swallowed up by every wave. They were two hundred and fifty or two hundred and sixty leagues from Fayal.

Their stock consisted of "a bag of bread, a small ham a single piece of pork, two quart-bottles of water, and a few French cordials." Their situation became truly miserable, from cold and hunger. On the fifth day their bread "was nearly all spoiled by salt water; and it was necessary to go to allowance—one biscuit divided into twelve morsels, for breakfast; the same for dinner. The neck of a bottle broke off, with the cork in, served for a glass; and this filled with water, was the allowance for twenty-four hours for each man. This was done without partiality or distinction. But they must have perished ere this, had they not caught six quarts of rain-water: and this they could not have been blessed with, had they not found in the boat a pair of sheets, which by accident had been put there."

On the fifteenth day that they had been in the boat, they had only one day's bread, and one bottle of water remaining of a second supply of rain. Captain Inglefield states: " Our sufferings were now as great as human strength could bear; but we were convinced that good spirits were a better support than great bodily strength; for on this day Thomas Matthews, quarter-master, the stoutest man in the boat, perished from hunger and cold. On the day before, he had complained of want of strength in his throat, as he expressed it, to swallow his morsel; and in the night drank salt water, grew delirious, and died without a groan.

" As it became next to a certainty that we should all perish in the same manner in a day or two, it was somewhat comfortable to reflect, that dying of hunger was not so dreadful as our imagination had represented. Others had complained of the symptoms in their throats; some had drunk their own urine; and all but myself had drunk salt water."

Despair and gloom had been hitherto successfully prohibited; and the men, as the evenings closed in, had been encouraged by turns to sing a song, or relate a story, instead of a supper. This evening it was found impossible to do either. At night they were becalmed, but at midnight a breeze sprung up; but being afraid of running out of their course, they waited impatiently for the rising sun to be their compass.

On the sixteenth day their last bread and water had been served for breakfast; when John Gregory, the quarter-master, declared with much confidence, he saw land in the south-east, at a great distance. They made for it, and reached Fayal at about mid-night, having been conducted into the road by a fishing-boat: but they were not, by the regulation of the port, permitted to land till examined by the health officers.

They got some refreshments of bread, wine, and water in the boat, and in the morning of the seventeenth day landed; where they experienced every friendly attention from the English consul, whose whole employment for many days was contriving the best means of restoring them to health and strength. Some of the stoutest men were obliged to be supported through the streets; and for several days, with the best and most comfortable provisions, they rather grew worse than better.

A court-martial was held at Portsmouth on the 21st of January 1783, on the loss of the Centaur; when the court hono ably ac-quitted Captain Inglefield, as a cool, resolute, and experienced officer; and that he was well supported by his officers and ship's company; and that their united exertions appeared to have been so great and manly, as to reflect the highest honor on the whole, and to leave the deepest impression on the minds of the court, — that more could not have possibly been done to preserve the Centaur from her melancholy fate.

A MONKEY TRICK.

In 1818, a vessel that sailed between Whitehaven and Jamaica embarked on her homeward voyage, and among other passengers, carried a female, who had at the breast a child only a few weeks old. One beautiful afternoon, the captain perceived a distant sail, and after he had gratified his curiosity, he politely offered his glass to his passenger, that she might obtain a clear view of the object. Mrs. B. had the baby in her arms; she wrapped her shawl about the little innocent, and placed it on a sofa upon which she had been sitting. Scarcely had she applied her eye to the glass, when the helmsman exclaimed, " Good God! see what the mischievous monkey has done." The reader may judge of the female's feelings, when, on turning round, she beheld the animal in the act of transporting her beloved child apparently to the very top of the mast! The monkey was a very large one, and so strong and active, that while it grasped the infant firmly with the one arm, it climbed the shrouds nimbly by the other, totally unembarrassed by the weight of its burden. One look was sufficient for the terrified mother, and that look had well nigh been her last, and had it not been for the assistance of those around her, she would have fallen prostrate on the deck, where she was soon afterwards stretched apparently a lifeless corpse. The sailors could climb as well as the monkey, but the latter watched their motions narrowly; and as it ascended higher up the mast the moment they attempted to put a foot on the shrouds, the captain became afraid that it would drop the child, and endeavor to escape by leaping from one mast to another. In the meantime the little innocent was heard to cry; and though many thought it was suffering pain, their fears on this point were speedily dissipated when they observed the monkey imitating exactly the motions of a nurse, by dandling, soothing, and caressing its charge, and even endeavoring to hush it asleep. From the deck the lady was conveyed to the cabin, and gradually restored to her senses. In the meantime, the captain ordered every man to conceal himself below, and quietly took his own station on the cabin stair, where he could see all that passed without being seen. This plan happily succeeded; the monkey, on perceiving that the coast was clear, cautiously descended from his lofty perch, and replaced the infant on the sofa, cold, fretful, and perhaps frightened, but in

every other respect as free from harm as when he took it up
The humane seaman had now a most grateful task to perform,
the babe was restored to its mother's arms, amidst tears, and
thanks, and blessings.

CAPTAIN KENNEDY'S NARRATIVE.

'We sailed from Port Royal, in Jamaica, on the 21st day of
December, 1818, bound for Whitehaven; but the twenty-third
day having met with a hard gale at north, we were obliged to lay-
to under a foresail for the space of ten hours, which occasioned
the vessel to make more water than she could free with both
pumps.   Under this situation we set sail, in hopes of being able
to make the island of Jamaica again, which from our reckoning
we judged lay about ten leagues to the eastward.   But in less
than an hour's time the water overflowed the lower deck; and we
could scarcely get into the yawl (being thirteen in number) before
the vessel sank; having only with much difficulty been able to take
out a keg containing about sixteen pounds of biscuit, ten pounds
of cheese, and two bottles of wine; with which small pittance we
endeavored to make the land.   But the wind continuing to blow
hard from the north, and the sea running high, we were obliged,
after an unsuccessful attempt of three days, to bear away for
Honduras, as the wind seemed to favor us for that course, and it
being the only visible means we had of preserving our lives.
On the seventh day we made Swan's island; but being destitute
of a quadrant, and other needful helps, we were uncertain what
land it was.   However, we went on shore, under the flattering
hopes of finding some refreshments; but, to our unspeakable regret and heavy disappointment, we only found a few quarts of
brackish water in the hollow of a rock, and a few wilks.   Notwithstanding there was no human nor visible prospect of finding
water, or any other of the necessaries of life, it was with the utmost reluctance the people quitted the island; but being at length
prevailed upon, with much difficulty and through persuasive
means, we embarked in the evening, with only six quarts of water,
for the Bay of Honduras.   Between the seventh and fourteenth
days of our being in the boat, we were most miraculously supported, and at a time when nature was almost exhausted, having
nothing to eat or drink.   Yet the Almighty Author of our being
furnished us with supplies, which, when seriously considered, not
only serve to display his beneficence, but fill the mind with admiration and wonder.   Well may we cry out, with the Royal Wise
Man—'Lord, what is man, that thou art mindful of him? or the
son of man, that thou visitest him?'

" In the evening the wild sea-fowls hovered over our heads, and lighted on our hands when held up to receive them. Of these our people eat the flesh and drank the blood, declaring it to be as palatable as new milk. I eat twice of the flesh, and thought it very good.

" It may appear very remarkable, that, though I neither tasted food nor drink for *eight days*, I did not feel the sensations of hunger or thirst, but on the fourteenth, in the evening, my drought often required me to *gargle* my mouth with salt water; and on the fifteenth it increased; when, happily for us! we made land, which proved to be an island called Ambergris, lying at a small distance from the main land, and about fourteen leagues to the northward of St. George's Quay (where the white people reside) in the Bay of Honduras; though the want of a quadrant and other necessaries left us still in suspense. We slept four nights on this island, and every evening picked up wilks and conchs for next day's provision, embarking every morning, and towing along the shore to the southward. On the first evening of our arrival here we found a lake of fresh water, by which we lay all night, and near it buried one of our people.

" On walking along the shore we found a few cocoa-nuts, which were full of milk. The substance of the nuts we eat with the wilks, instead of bread, thinking it a delicious repast, although eaten raw—having no implements whereby to kindle a fire. From the great support received by this shell-fish, I shall ever revere the name.

" On the third day after our arrival at this island, we buried another of our people, which, with four who died on the passage, made six who perished through hunger and fatigue.

" On the fifth day after our arrival at Ambergris, we happily discovered a small vessel at some distance, under sail, which we made for. In the evening got on board her; and in a few hours (being the tenth of January), we arrived on St. George's Quay, in a very languid state.

" I cannot conclude without making mention of the great advantage I received from soaking my clothes twice a day in salt water, and putting them on without wringing.

" It was a considerable time before I could make the people comply with this measure; though, from seeing the good effects it produced, they afterwards, of their own accord, practised it twice a day. To this discovery I may with justice impute the preservation of my own life, and that of six other persons, who must have perished but for its being put in use.

AS FAST AND FAR O'ER WAVES WE FLY

As fast and far o'er waves we fly,
And seen beneath the distant sky
  Our native land's deep shadows fade,
We gaze upon the wave and sigh,
  And think upon the absent maid
Who sits and listens to the wind,
And turns the dark thought in her mind,
     Of what may be
     Our lot at sea,
Till the breeze freshening to a gale
Calls us aloft to shorten sail,
Then duty bids our wishes move,
And toil diverts our souls from love.

Sharply its breath the vessel feels,
Down on her groaning side she heels;
  Another reef is taken in—
Loudly the dreadful thunder peals.
  Old Ocean echoes to the din:
     Beneath the blow
     She rises slow
As smart the helmsman luffs her, then
We think no more, but feel like men,
But cheerly to our duty move,
And leave the future hour of love.

'T is past; top-gallant masts ascend,
O'er top sail yards we gaily bend;
  The loosened sail abroad we shake;
Top gallant sails aloft we send;
  No more the surges o'er us break;—
Awhile with flowing sheet we glide,
Till slow we feel the swell subside,
  And the sea slumber like a lake.
     Then thoughts of home
     Across us come,
With recollections warm and clear,
Our anxious hearts we fondly cheer;
Our duty o'er—our wishes move
Again from toil to ease and love.

TOM CRINGLE'S LOG.

We had refitted, and been four days at sea, on our voyage to Jamaica, when the gun-room officers gave our mess a blow out. The increased motion and rushing of the vessel through the water, the groaning of the masts, the howling of the gale, and the frequent trampling of the watch on deck, were prophetic of wet jackets to some of us; still, midshipman-like, we were as happy as a good dinner and some wine could make us, until the old gunner shoved his weather beaten phiz and bald pate in at the door "Beg pardon Mr. Splinter, but if you will spare Mr. Cringle or the forecastle an hour, until the moon rises"—("Spare," quotha, 'is his majesty's officer a joint stool?")—"Why, Mr. Kennedy, why? here, man, take a glass of grog." "I thank you sir." "It is coming on a roughish night, sir; the running ships should be crossing us hereabouts; indeed, more than once I thought there was a strange sail close aboard of us, the scud is flying so low and in such white flakes; and none of us have an eye like Mr Cringle, unless it be John Crow, and he is all but frozen.' "Well, Tom, I suppose you will go"—Anglice, from a first lieutenant to a mid—

Brush instanter."

Having changed my uniform for shag trousers, pea-jacket, and south-west cap, I went forward and took my station, in no pleasant humor, on the stowed jib, with my arm around the stay. I had been half an hour there, the weather was getting worse, the rain was beating in my face, and the spray from the stern was splashing over me, as it roared through the waste of sparkling and hissing waters. I turned my back to the weather for a moment to press my hands on my straining eyes. When I opened them, I saw the gunner's gaunt, high-featured visage thrust anxiously forward; his profile looked as if rubbed over with phosphorus, and his whole person as if we had been playing at snap dragon. "What has come over you Mr. Kennedy? who's burning the blue light now?" "A wiser man than I must tell you that; look forward Mr. Cringle—look there; what do your books say to that?"

I looked forth, and saw at the extreme end of the jib boom, what I have read of, certainly, but never expected to see, a pale, greenish, glow-worm colored flame, of the size and shape of the frosted glass shade over the swinging lamp in the gun-room. It drew out and flattened as the vessel pitched and rose again, and as she sheered about, it wavered round the point that seemed to attract it, like a soap suds bubble blown from a tobacco pipe, before it is shaken into the air; at the core it was comparatively bright, but faded into a halo. It shed a baleful and ominous light on the surrounding objects; the group of sailors on the forecastle looked like spectres, and they shrunk together, and whispered when it began to roll slowly along the spar where the boatswain was sitting at my feet. At this instant something slid down the stay, and a cold clammy hand passed around my neck. I was within an ace of losing my hold and tumbling overboard. "Heaven l'ave mercy on me what's that?" "It's that sky-larking son of a gun, Jem Sparkle's monkey, sir. You Jem, you'll never rest till that brute is made shark's bait of." But Jacko vanished up the stay again, chuckling and grinning in the ghastly radiance.

as if he had been 'the Spirit of the Lamp.' The light was still there, but a cloud of mist, like a burst of vapor from a steam boiler, came down upon the gale and flew past, when it disappeared. I followed the white mass as it sailed down the wind; it did not, as it appeared to me, vanish in the darkness, but seemed to remain in sight to leeward, as if checked by a sudden flaw; yet none of our sails were taken aback. A thought flashed on me. I peered still more intensely into the night. I was not certain. "A sail, broad on the lee bow." The captain answered from the quarter deck—"Thank you, Mr. Cringle. How shall we steer?" "Keep her away a couple of points, sir, steady." "Steady," sung the man at the helm; and a slow melancholy cadence, although a familiar sound to me, now moaned through the rushing wind, and smote upon my heart as if it had been the wailing of a spirit. I turned to the boatswain, who was now standing beside me, "Is that you or Davy steering, Mr. Nipper? if you had not been there bodily at my side, I could have sworn that was your voice."— When the gunner made the same remark, it started the poor fellow; he tried to take it as a joke, but could not. "There may be a laced hammock with a shot in it, for some of us ere morning."

At this moment, to my dismay, the object we were chasing shortened,—gradually fell abeam of us, and finally disappeared. "The Flying Dutchman." "I can't see her at all now." "She will be a fore and aft rigged vessel that has tacked, sir." And sure enough, after a few seconds I saw the white object lengthen and draw out again abaft our beam. "The chase has tacked, sir; put the helm down, or she will go to windward of us." We tacked also, and time it was we did so, for the rising moon now showed us a large schooner with a crowd of sail. We edged down on her, when finding her manœuvre detected, she brailed up her flat sails and bore up before the wind. This was our best point of sailing, and we cracked on, the captain rubbing his hands —"It's my turn to be the big un this time." Although blowing a strong north-wester, it was now clear moon-light, and we hammered away from our bow guns, but whenever a shot told amongst the rigging, the injury was repaired as if by magic. It was evident we had repeatedly hulled her, from the glimmering white streaks along her counter and across her stern, occasioned by the splintering of the timber, but it seemed to produce no effect.

At length we drew well upon her quarter. She continued all black hull and white sail, not a soul to be seen on deck, except a dark object which we took for the man at the helm. "What schooner is that?" No answer "Heave to, or I'll sink you." Still all silent. "Serjeant Armstrong, do you think you can pick off that chap at the wheel?" The mariner jumped on the forecastle, and levelled his piece, when a musket-shot from the schooner crushed through his skull, and he fell dead. The old skipper's blood was up. "Forecastle there! Mr. Nipper, clap a canister of grape over the round shot, in the bow gun, and give it to him." "Ay ay, sir!" gleefully rejoined the boatswain, forgetting the augury and every thing else, in the excitement of the moment. In a twinkling, the square foresail—topgallant—royal, and studding-sail haulyards, were let go by the run on board the schooner, as if they had been shot away; and he put his helm hard aport, as if to round to. "Rake him, sir, or give him the stern. He has not surrendered. I know their game. Give him your broadside, sir, or he is off to windward of you, like a shot. No, no, we have him now; heave to, Mr. Splinter, heave to!" We did so, and that so suddenly, that the studding sail booms snapped like pipe shanks short off by the irons. Notwithstanding, we had shot two hundred yards to the leeward, before we could lay our maintopsail to the mast. I ran to windward. The schooner's yards and rigging were now black with men, clustering like bees swarming, her square sails were being close furled, her fore and aft sails set, and away she was, dead to windward of us. "So much for undervaluing our American friends," grumbled Mr. Splinter.

We made all sail in chase, blazing away to little purpose; we had no chance on a bowline, and when our 'Amigo' had satisfied himself of his superiority by one or two short tacks, he deliberately took a reef in his mainsail, hawled down his flying jib and gaff topsail, triced up the bunt of his foresail, and fired his long thirty-two at us. The shot came in our third aftermost port on the starboard side, and dismounted the carronade, smashing the slide, wounding three men. The second missed, and as it was madness to remain to be peppered, probably winged, whilst every one of ours fell short, we reluctantly kept away on our course, having the gratification of hearing a clear well blown bugle on board the schooner play up "Yankee Doodle." As the brig fell off, our long gun was run out to have a parting crack at her, when the third and last shot from the schooner struck the sill of the midship port, and made the white splinters fly from the solid oak like bright silver sparks in the moonlight. A sharp, piercing cry rose in the air —my soul identified that death-shriek with the voice that I had heard, and I saw the man who was standing with the lanyard of the lock in his hand drop heavily across the breech, and discharge the gun in his fall. Thereupon a blood-red glare shot up in the cold blue sky, as if a volcano had burst forth from beneath the mighty deep, followed by a roar, and a scattering crash, and a mingling of unearthly cries and groans, and a concussion of the air and the water as if our whole broadside had been fired at once.—Then a solitary splash here, and a dip there, and short snarp yells, and low choking bubbling moans, as the hissing fragments of the noble vessel we had seen fell into the sea, and the last of her gallant crew vanished forever beneath that pale broad moon. *We were alone;* and once more all was dark, wild and stormy. Fearfully had that ball sped, fired by a dead man's hand. But what is it that clings, black and doubled, across the fatal cannon, dripping and heavy, and choking the scuppers with clotting gore, and swaying to and fro with the motion of the vessel, like a bloody fleece? " Who is it that was hit at the gun there?" " *Mr. Nipper, the boatswain, sir, the last shot has cut him in two.* '

NELSON.

Horatio, son of Edmund and Catharine Nelson, was born Sept. 29, 1758—in the parsonage house of Burnham Thorpe, a village in the county of Norfolk, England. He was never of a strong body; and at the age of twelve years, when he entered the service of his country, the ague, which at that time was one of the most common diseases in England, had greatly reduced his strength; yet he had already given proofs of a resolute heart and great nobleness of mind.

His first appointment, was on board the Raisonnable, commanded by his uncle, Capt. Maurice Suckling. The Raisonnable was lying in the Medway. He was put into the Chatham stage, and on its arrival was set down with the rest of the passengers, and left to find his way on board as he could. After wandering about in the cold, without being able to reach the ship, an officer observing the forlorn appearance of the boy, questioned him; and happening to be acquainted with his uncle, took him home, and gave him some refreshments.—When he got on board, Capt. Suckling was not in the ship, nor had any person been apprised of the boy's coming. He paced the deck the whole remainder of the day, without being noticed by any one; and it was not till the second day that somebody, as he expressed it, " took compassion on him."

The Raisonnable having been paid off shortly afterwards, he was removed to the Triumph, a seventy-four, then stationed as a guard-ship in the Thames; but this being considered too inactive a life for a boy, he was sent a voyage to the West Indies, and returned a practical seaman, but with a hatred of the king's service, and a saying then common among sailors—" aft the most honor, forward the better man." Being reconciled to the service, he was received on board his old ship, the Triumph, where he had not been many months, before his love of enterprise was excited by hearing that two ships were fitting out for a voyage of discovery towards the North Pole. By his uncle's interest, he was admitted as coxswain under Capt. Lutwidge, second in command They sailed from the Nore on the 4th of June 1773, and were away about three years, suffering many hardships and braving many dangers, in which Nelson, young as he was, displayed many of those qualities, for which he afterwards became so remarkable. After they had carefully surveyed the barrier of ice extending for more than twenty degrees between the latitudes of 80° and 81°, without the smallest appearance of any opening, they returned to England and were paid off.

Nelson was then appointed to the Seahorse, of twenty guns, then going out to the East Indies; but in about eighteen months, he experienced the effects of that climate, so perilous to European constitutions; and was carried home, with a body broken down by sickness, and spirits which had sunk with his strength. His health being somewhat improved, he was appointed acting-lieutenant in the Worcester, sixty-four, then going out with convoy to Gibraltar, and on his return, passed his examination for a lieutenancy, on the 8th of April, 1777.

The next day Nelson received his commission as second lieutenant of the Lowestoffe frigate and sailed for Jamaica. On the 8th of December, 1778, he was appointed commander of the Badger brig. While the Badger was lying in Montego Bay, Jamaica, the Glasgow, of twenty guns came in and anchored there, and in two hours was in flames, the steward having set fire to her while stealing rum out of the after-hold. Her crew were leaping into the water, when Nelson came up in his boats, made them throw their powder overboard, and point their guns upward: and, by his presence of mind and personal exertions, prevented the loss of life which would otherwise have ensued. On the 11th of June, 1779, he was made post into the Hinchinbrook, of twenty-eight guns; so that we find him, before he had attained the age of twenty-one, with that rank that brought all the honors of the service within his reach; thoroughly master of his profession, and his zeal and ability acknowledged wherever he was known. He remained in the West Indies about five years, actively employed, until he became so debilitated that he was compelled to ask leave of absence, and returned home with Capt. (afterwards Admiral Cornwallis), to whose care and kindness Nelson believed himself indebted for his life.

His health was not thoroughly established, when he was sent to the North Seas; and on his return to the Downs, in the Albemarle, while he was ashore visiting the senior officer, there came on so heavy a gale, that almost all the vessels drove, and a store ship came athwart-hawse of the Albemarle. Nelson feared she would drive on the Goodwin Sands: he ran to the beach; but even the Deal boatmen thought it impossible to get on board, such was the violence of the storm. At length, some of the most intrepid offered to make the attempt for fifteen guineas; and to the astonishment and fear of all the beholders, he embarked during the height of the tempest. With great difficulty and imminent danger, he succeeded in reaching her. She lost her bowsprit and foremast but escaped farther injury. He next sailed for Canada, and during his first cruise on that station, captured a fishing schooner, which contained, in her cargo, nearly all the property that her master possessed; and the poor fellow had a large family at home, anxiously expecting him. Nelson employed him as a pilot in Boston Bay, then restored him the schooner and cargo, and gave him a certificate to secure him against being captured by any other vessel. The man came off afterward to the Albemarle, at the hazard of his life, with a present of sheep, poultry, and fresh provisions. The certificate was preserved at Boston in memory of an act of unusual generosity; and now that the fame of Nelson has given interest to every thing connected with his name, it is regarded as a relic. On Nelson's arrival at New York, Lord Hood, on introducing him to Prince William Henry, as the Duke of Clarence was then called, told the prince, if he wished to ask any questions respecting naval tactics, Captain Nelson could give him as much information as any officer in the fleet. After cruising some time off the Spanish Main and making many captures, he received intelligence that the preliminaries of peace had been signed, and he returned to England, at the latter part of the year 1783.

"I have closed the war" said Nelson, in one of his letters. "without a fortune, but there is not a speck in my character. True honor, I hope, predominates in my mind, far above riches" He did not apply for a ship, because he was not wealthy enough to live on board in the manner which was then customary Finding it, therefore, prudent to economise, on his half pay, he went to France. In March 1784—he was appointed to the Boreas twenty-eight guns, going to the Leeward Islands on the peace establishment. On the 11th, March 1787, he was married to the widow of Dr. Nisbet, who was niece to Mr. Herbert, the President of Nevis—then in her eighteenth year; Prince William Henry, being present, gave away the bride. During his stay upon this station he had ample opportunity of observing the scandalous practices of the contractors, prize-agents, and other persons in the West Indies connected with the naval service. These accounts he sent home to the different departments which had been defrauded; but the peculators were too powerful; and they succeeded not merely in impeding inquiry but even in raising prejudices against Nelson at the board of Admiralty, which it was many years before he could subdue. He returned to England and remained principally in the country, with his family and friends.

On the 30th of January 1793, he was appointed to the Agamemnon of sixty-four guns, and ordered to the Mediterranean under Lord Hood, by whom he was sent with despatches to Sir William Hamilton, at the court of Naples. Here, that acquaintance with the Neapolitan court commenced, which led to the only blot upon Nelson's public character. Having accomplished this mission Nelson received orders to join Commodore Linzie at Tunis, and was detached with a small squadron, to cooperate with General Paoli and the Anti-Gallican party in Corsica. After a successful attack of the fort of Bastia, at the siege of Calvi, a shot struck the ground near him, and drove the sand and small gravel into one of his eyes. He spoke of it lightly at the time, but the sight was lost. Falling in with the Ca-Ira, of eighty-four guns, and Censeur, seventy-four, he engaged and captured both of them. In 1795, Nelson was made colonel of marines. Sir John Jervis had now arrived to take the command of the Mediterranean fleet. Nelson sailed from Leghorn, and joined the admiral in Fiorenzo Bay, and the manner in which he was received is said to have excited much envy. During this long course of services in the Mediterranean, the whole of his conduct had exhibited the same zeal, the same indefatigable energy, the same intuitive judgment, the same prompt and unerring decision, which characterized his after career of glory. On one occasion, and only one, Nelson was able to impede Buonaparte Six vessels, laden with cannon and ordinance-stones for the siege of Mantua, sailed from Toulon for St. Pier d' Arena. He drove them under a battery, pursued them, silenced the batteries, and captured the whole. Nelson was now ordered to hoist his broad pennant on board the Minerve frigate and proceed to Porto Ferrajo. On his way, he captured the Sabina, Spanish frigate, after an action of three hours, during which the enemy lost one hundred and sixty-four men. Another enemy's frigate coming up, compelled him to cast off the prize, and after half an hour's trial of strength, this new antagonist wore and hauled off. He sailed from Porto Ferrajo with a convoy for Gibraltar and fell in with the Spanish fleet off the Straits, on the 13th of February 1797, and communicated this intelligence to the Admiral.

He was now directed to shift his broad pennant on board the Captain, seventy-four, Captain R. W. Miller; and, before sunset, the signal was made to prepare fo action, and to keep, during the night, in close order. At daybreak the enemy were in sight. The British force consisted of two ships of one hundred guns, two of ninety-eight, two of ninety, eight of seventy-four, and one sixty-four: fifteen of the line in all; with four frigates, a sloop and a cutter. The Spaniards had one four-decker, of one hundred and thirty-six guns; six three-deckers, of one hundred and twelve; two eighty-fours; eighteen seventy-fours; in all, twenty-seven ships of the line, with ten frigates and a brig. When the morning of the 14th broke, and discovered the English fleet, a fog for some time concealed their number. Soon after daylight the Spanish fleet were seen very much scattered, while the British ships were in a compact little body. Before the enemy could form a regular order of battle, Sir J. Jervis, by carrying a press of sail, came up with them, passed through their fleet, then tacked, and thus cut off nine of their ships from the main body. These ships attempted to form on the larboard tack, either with a design of passing through the British line, or to leeward of it, and thus rejoining their friends. Only one of them succeeded in this attempt; and that only because she was so covered with smoke that her intention was not discovered till she had reached the rear: the others were so warmly received, that they put about, took to flight, and did not appear again in the action till its close. The admiral was now able to direct his attention to the enemy's main body, which was still superior in number to his whole fleet, and more so in weight of metal. He made signal to tack in succession. Nelson, whose station was in the rear of the British line, perceived that the Spaniards were bearing up before the wind, with an intention of forming their line, going large, and joining their separated ships, or else, of getting off without an engagement. To prevent either of these schemes, he disobeyed the signal without a moment's hesitation, and ordered his ship to be wore. This at once brought him into action with the Santissima Trinidad, one hundred and thirty-six, the San Joseph, one hundred and twelve, the Salvador del Mundo, one hundred and twelve, the St. Nicolas, eighty, the San Isidro, seventy-four another seventy-four, and another first-rate. Captain Trowbridge, in the Culloden, immediately joined, and most nobly supported him, and for nearly an hour did the Culloden and Captain maintain what Nelson called " this apparently, but not really, unequal contest;"—such was the advantage of skill and discipline, and the confidence which brave men derive from them.—The Blenheim then passing between them and the enemy, gave them a respite, and poured in her fire upon the Spaniards. The Salvador del Mundo and S. Isidro dropped astern, and were fired into, in a masterly style, by the Excellent Captain Collingwood. The S. Isidro struck; and Nelson thought that the Salvador struck also; " But Collingwood," says he, " disdaining the parade of taking possession of beaten enemies, most gallantly pushed up, with every sail set, to save his old friend and messmate, who was, to appearance, in a critical situation," for the Captain was at this time actually fired upon by three first-rates, by the S. Nicolas, and by a seventy-four within about pistol-shot of that vessel The Blenheim was ahead, the Culloden crippled and astern Collingwood ranged up, and hauling up his mainsail just astern, passed within ten feet of the S. Nicolas, giving her a most tremendous fire, then passed on for the Santissima Trinidad. Tho S. Nicolas luffing up, the S. Joseph fell on board her and Nelson resumed his station abreast of them, and close along-side. The Captain was now incapable of farther service either in the line or n chase: she had lost her fore-topmast; not a sail, shroud, or ope was left, and her wheel was shot away. Nelson, therefore,

directed Captain Miller to put the helm a-starboard, and, calling
for the borders, ordered them to board. Captain Berry, who had
lately been Nelson's first lieutenant, was the first man who leap
ed into the enemy's mizen-chains. Miller, when in the very act
of going, was ordered by Nelson to remain. Berry was supported from the spritsail-yard, which locked in the S. Nicolas's main
rigging. A soldier of the sixty-ninth broke the upper quarter-
gallery window, and jumped in, followed by the Commodore himself, and by others as fast as possible. The cabin-doors were
fastened, and the Spanish officers fired their pistols at them
through the window: the doors were soon forced, and the Spanish brigadier fell while retreating to the quarter-deck. Nelson
pushed on, and found Berry in possession of the poop, and the
Spanish ensign hauling down. He passed on to the forecastle,
where he met two or three Spanish officers, and received their
swords.—The English were now in full possession of every part
of the ship; and a fire of pistols and musketry opened upon them
from the admiral's stern gallery of the San Joseph. Nelson
having placed sentinels at the different ladders, and ordered Captain Miller to send more men into the prize, gave orders for
boarding that ship from the San Nicolas. Berry assisted him
into the main-chains; and at that moment a Spanish officer looked
over the quarter-deck-rail, and said they surrendered. It was
not long before he was on the quarter-deck, where the Spanish
captain presented to him his sword, and told him the admiral
was below, dying of his wounds. There, on the quarter-deck of
an enemy's first-rate, he received the swords of the officers; giving them, as they were delivered, one by one, to William Fearney,
one of his old Agamemnon's, who, with the utmost coolness, put
them under his arm; " bundling them up," in the lively expression of Collingwood, " with as much composure, as he would
have made a fagot, though twenty-two sail of their line were still
within gunshot." Twenty-four of the Captain's men were killed
and fifty-six wounded; a fourth part of the loss sustained by the
whole squadron falling upon this ship. Nelson received only a
few bruises. The Spaniards had still eighteen or nineteen ships
which had suffered little or no injury; but they declined continuing the action; and the British admiral made signal to bring
to. Nelson went on board the admiral's ship, and Sir John Jervis
received him on the quarter deck, took him in his arms, and said
he could not sufficiently thank him. For this victory, the commander-in-chief was rewarded with the title of Earl St Vincent
Nelson, who, before the action was known in England, had been
advanced to the rank of rear-admiral, had the Order of the Bath
given him.

Sir Horatio, who had now hoisted his flag as rear-admiral of
the blue in the Theseus, was employed in the command of the
inner squadron at the blockade of Cadiz. During this service,

the most perilous action occurred in which he was ever engaged
Making a night-attack upon the Spanish gunboats, his barge was
attacked by an armed launch, under their commander, D. Miguel
Tregoyen, carrying twenty-six men. Nelson had with him only
his ten bargemen, Captain Freemantle, and his coxswain, John
Sykes, an old and faithful follower, who twice saved the life of his
admiral, by parrying the blows that were aimed at him, and, at
last, actually interposed his own head to receive the blow of a
Spanish sabre, which he could not by any other means avert;—
thus dearly was Nelson beloved. Nelson always considered that
his personal courage was more conspicuous on this occasion than
on any other during his whole life. Notwithstanding the great
disproportion of numbers, eighteen of the enemy were killed, all
the rest wounded, and their launch taken.

Twelve days after this rencounter, Nelson sailed at the head
of an expedition against Teneriffe. Owing to disadvantages of
wind and tide, this expedition did not prove entirely successful.
In the act of stepping out of one of the boats, Nelson received a
shot through the right elbow, and fell. He was placed at the
bottom of the boat, and on being conveyed on board the Theseus,
exclaimed " Tell the surgeon to make haste and get his instruments. I know I must lose my right arm, so the sooner it is off
the better." Nelson made no mention of it in his official despatches. The total loss of the English, in killed, wounded and
drowned, amounted to two hundred and fifty—After his arrival
in England, his sufferings from the lost limb were long and
painful.

Early in the year 1798, Nelson hoisted his flag in the Vanguard,
and was ordered to rejoin Earl St. Vincent. Immediately on his
rejoining the fleet, he was despatched to the Mediterranean, to
ascertain, if possible, the object, of the great expedition which at
that time was fitting out, under Buonaparte, at Toulon. The armament at Toulon consisted of thirteen ships of the line, seven
forty-gun frigates, with twenty-four smaller vessels of war, and
nearly two hundred transports. Nelson sailed from Gibraltar on
the 9th of May, with three seventy-fours; four frigates; and one
sloop of war; to watch this formidable armament. On the 19th,
the fleet experienced much damage from a tempestuous gale, in
the Gulf of Lyons. While in the harbor of St. Pietro, he received a reinforcement from Earl St. Vincent of the best ships of his
fleet; the Culloden, seventy-four, Captain T. Trowbridge; Goliah,
seventy-four, Captain T. Louis; Defence, seventy-four, Captain
John Peyton; Bellerophon, seventy-four, Captain H. D. E. Darby;
Majestic, seventy-four, Captain G. B. Westcott; Zealous, seventy-
four, Captain S. Hood; Swiftrure, seventy-four, Captain B. Hal-
lowell; Theseus, seventy-four, Captain Davidge Gould. The
Leander, fifty, Captain T. B. Thompson, was afterward added
The first news of the enemy's armament was, that it had surprised

Malta, but on the 22d of June, intelligence was received that the
French had left that island on the 16th, the day after their arrival.
Nelson arrived off Alexandria on the 28th, and the enemy were
not there; he then shaped his course to the northward, but baffled
in his pursuit, returned to Sicily. Vexed, however, and disappointed as he was, Nelson, with the true spirit of a hero, was
still full of hope. On the 25th of July, he sailed from Syracuse
for the Morea. The squadron made the Gulf of Coron on the
28th, Trowbridge entered the port, and returned with intelligence
that the French had been seen about four weeks before, steering to
the south-east from Candia. The British fleet accordingly, with
every sail set, stood once more for the coast of Egypt. On the
1st of August, about ten in the morning, they came in sight
of Alexandria, the port had been vacant and solitary when they
saw it last: it was now crowded with ships; and they perceived,
with exultation, that the tricolor flag was flying upon the walls.
At four in the afternoon, Captain Hood, in the Zealous, made the
signal for the enemy's fleet. The French fleet arrived at Alexandria on the 1st of July; and Brueys, not being able to enter the
port, which time and neglect had ruined, moored his ships in
Aboukir Bay, in a strong and compact line of battle. The plan
which Nelson intended to pursue, therefore, was to keep entirely
on the outer side of the French line, and station his ships, as far
as he was able, one on the outer bow, and another on the outer
quarter, of each of the enemy's.

As the squadron advanced, they were assailed by a shower of
shot and shells from the batteries on the island, and the enemy
opened a steady fire from the starboard side of their whole line,
within half gun-shot distance, full into the bows of the van ships.
It was received in silence: the men on board every ship were
employed aloft in furling sails, and below in tending the braces,
and making ready for anchoring. Captain Foley led the way in
the Goliah, out-sailing the Zealous, which for some minutes disputed this point of honor with him. He had long conceived that
if the enemy were moored in line of battle in with the land, the
best plan of attack would be, to lead between them and the shore,
because the French guns on that side were not likely to be man
ned, nor even ready for action. Intending, therefore, to fix himself on the inner bow of the *Guerrier*, he kept as near the edge
of the bank as the depth of water would admit; but his anchor hung,
and having opened his fire, he drifted to the second ship, the *Conquerant*, before it was clear; then anchored by the stern, inside
of her, and in ten minutes shot away her mast. Hood, in the
Zealous, perceiving this, took the station which the Goliah intended to have occupied, and totally disabled the *Guerrier* in twelve
minutes. The third ship which doubled the enemy's van was the
Orion, Sir I. Saumarez; she passed to windward of the Zealous,
nd opened her larboard guns as long as she bore on the *Guerrier*,

then passing inside the Goliah, sunk a frigate which annoyed her, hauled round towards the French line, and anchoring inside, between the fifth and sixth ships from the *Guerrier*, took her station on the larboard bow of the *Franklin* and the quarter of the *Peuple Souverain*, receiving and returning the fire of both. The sun was now nearly down. The Audacious, Captain Gould, pouring a heavy fire into the *Guerrier* and the *Conquerant*, fixed herself on the larboard bow of the latter, and when that ship struck, passed on to the *Peuple Souverain*. The Theseus, Captain Miller, followed, brought down the *Guerrier's* remaining main and mizen masts, then anchored inside of the *Spartiate*, the third in the French line. While these advanced ships doubled the French line, the Vanguard was the first that anchored on the outer side of the enemy, within half-pistol-shot of their third ship, the *Spartiate*. Nelson veered half a cable, and instantly opened a tremendous fire; under cover of which the other four ships of his division, the Minotaur, Bellerophon, Defence, and Majestic, sailed on ahead of the admiral. In a few minutes every man stationed at the first six guns in the fore part of the Vanguard's deck was killed or wounded: these guns were three times cleared. Captain Louis, in the Minotaur, anchored next ahead, and took off the fire of the *Aquilon*, the fourth in the enemy's line. The Bellerophon, Captain Darby, passed ahead, and dropped his stern anchor on the starboard bow of the *Orient*, seventh in the line, Bruey's own ship, of one hundred and twenty guns, whose difference of force was in proportion of more than seven to three, and whose weight of ball, from the lower deck alone, exceeded that from the whole broadside of the Bellerophon. Captain Peyton, in the Defence, took his station ahead of the Minotaur, and engaged the *Franklin*, the sixth in the line; by which judicious movement the British line remained unbroken. The Majestic, Captain Westcot, got entangled with the main rigging of one of the French ships astern of the *Orient*, and suffered dreadfully from that three-decker's fire: but she swung clear, and closely engaging the *Heureux*, the ninth ship on the starboard bow, received also the fire of the *Tonnant*, which was the eighth in the line. The other four ships of the British squadron, having been detached previous to the discovery of the French, were at a considerable distance when the action began. It commenced at half after six; about seven, night closed, and there was no other light than that from the fire of the contending fleets. The first two ships of the French line had been dismasted within a quarter of an hour after the commencement of the action; and the others had in that time suffered so severely, that victory was already certain. The third, fourth, and fifth were taken possession of at half past eight. Meantime, Nelson received a severe wound on the head from a piece of langridge shot. When he was carried down into the cockpit, the surgeon, —with a natural and pardonable eagerness, quitted the poor fellow

then under his hands, that he might instantly attend the admiral.
" No!" said Nelson, " I will take my turn with my brave fellows.'
It was soon after nine, that a fire broke out on board the *Orient*.
Bruges was dead. The flames soon mastered his ship. By the
prodigious light of this conflagration, the situation of the two fleets
could now be perceived, the colors of both being clearly distinguishable. About ten o'clock the ship blew up, with a shock
which was felt to the very bottom of every vessel. This tremendous explosion was followed by a silence not less awful. About
seventy of the *Orient's* crew were saved by the English boats.
Four French vessels were all that escaped. The British loss, in
killed and wounded, amounted to eight hundred and ninety-five.
Three thousand one hundred and five of the French, including
the wounded, were sent on shore by cartel, and five thousand
two hundred and twenty-five perished. Nelson was now at the
summit of glory: congratulations, rewards, and honors were
showered upon him by all the states, and princes, and powers to
whom his victory gave a respite. In England he was created
Baron Nelson of the Nile, and a pension of £2000 per. annum
for his own life, and those of his two immediate successors award-
ed him. Having sent the six remaining prizes forward, under
Sir James Saumarez, Nelson left Captain Hood in the Zealous,
off Alexandria, with the Swiftsure, Goliath, Alcmene, Zealou
and Emerald, and stood out to sea himself on the seventeenth day
after the battle. On his way back to Italy he was seized with
fever. For eighteen hours his life was despaired of. On the
approach of the French to Naples, on the 21st of December 1799
—Nelson landed at night, and brought out the whole royal family
embarked them in three barges, and carried them safely, through
a tremendous sea, to the Vanguard. The next day a more violent
storm arose than Nelson had ever encountered. On the 26th, the
royal family were landed at Palermo. Nelson assisted in expel
ling the French from the Neapolitan and Roman Territories
The Sicilian Court, duly sensible of the services of Nelson—evinc
ed their gratitude by giving him the dukedom and domain of
Bronte, worth about £3000 a year. Nelson soon after arrived
in England.

In 1800, Nelson who had been made vice-admiral of the blue
was sent to the Baltic, as second in command, under Sir Hyde
Parker The fleet sailed on the 12th of March; and on the 21st
arrived in the sound. One of the fleet, the Invincible, seventy-
four, was wrecked on a sand-bank, as she was coming out of Yar-
mouth; four hundred of her men perished in her. Nelson, who
was now appointed to lead the van, shifted his flag to the Elephant.
Orders had been given to pass the Sound as soon as the wind
would permit; and in the afternoon of the 29th, the ships were
cleared for action. The signal was made, and the fleet moved on
in order of battle; Nelson's division in the van. The Sound being

the only frequented entrance to the Baltic, the great Mediterranean of the North, few parts of the sea display so frequent a navigation. Never had so splendid a scene been exhibited there as on this day, when the British fleet prepared to force that passage, where, till now, all ships had lowered their topsails to the flag of Denmark. The whole force consisted of fifty-one sail of various descriptions; of which sixteen were of the line. As soon as the Monarch, which was the leading ship, came abreast of the Danish batteries, a fire was opened from about a hundred pieces of cannon and mortars, but the shot fell full a cable's length short of its destined aim. The whole fleet passed and anchored between the island of Huen and Copenhagen. On the 1st of April, 1801, the fleet removed to an anchorage within two leagues of the town. At five minutes after ten, the next morning, the action began. The first half of the fleet was engaged in about half an hour; and, by half past eleven, the battle became general. The plan of attack had been complete: but seldom has any plan been more disconcerted by untoward accidents. Of twelve ships of the line, one was entirely useless, and two others in a situation where they could not render half the service which was required of them. The action continued along the line with unabated vigor, and with the most determined resolution on the part of the Danes. Between one and two, the fire of the Danes slackened; about two it ceased from the greater part of their line, and some of their lighter ships were adrift. By half past two the action had ceased along that part of the line which was astern of the Elephant, but not with the ships ahead and the Crown Batteries, which continued for some time longer—It was a murderous action. The British fleet lost nine hundred and fifty-three, in killed and wounded. The loss of the Danes, including prisoners, amounted to about six thousand. Nelson bore willing testimony to the valor of his foes. "The French," he said, "fought bravely; but they could not have stood for one hour the fight which the Danes had supported for four." Six line-of-battle ships and eight prames had been taken. For the battle of Copenhagen, Nelson was raised to the rank of viscount. He remained on the coast of Zealand, till despatches arrived from home, on the 5th of May, recalling Sir Hyde, and appointing Nelson commander-in-chief. Nelson visited some of the Russian ports, and then returned to England. He had not been many weeks on shore before he was called upon to undertake a service, to watch the preparations which Buonaparte was making on a great scale for the invasion of England. Having hoisted his flag in the Medusa frigate, he went to reconnoitre Boulogne, and made an unsuccessful attempt upon the flotilla, at that place. After which, he returned to England, and retired to his house at Merton, in Surrey, which he called his place of residence and rest

War was soon renewed, and Nelson departed to take the com-

mand of the Mediterranean fleet. He took his station immediately
off Toulon; and then, with incessant vigilance, waited for the
coming out of the enemy. War between Spain and England was
now declared; and, on the eighteenth of January, the Toulon
fleet, having the Spaniards to cooperate with them, put to sea.

Nelson was at anchor off the coast of Sardinia when, at three
in the afternoon, on the 19th of January, the Active and Seahorse
frigates brought this long-hoped for intelligence. Nelson beat
about the Sicilian seas for ten days, and baffled in his pursuit,
bore up for Malta. From the 21st of January the fleet had remained ready for battle, without a bulk-head up night or day.
On the 4th of April, he met the Phebe, with news that Villeneuve had put to sea on the last of March with eleven ships of the
line, seven frigates, and two brigs. When last seen, they were
steering towards the coast of Africa. After five days, a neutral
gave intelligence that the French had been seen off Cape de
Galle on the 7th. It was soon after ascertained that they had
passed the Straits of Gibraltar on the day following. Nelson
received certain knowledge that the combined Spanish and French
fleets were bound for the West Indies. May 15th, he made
Madeira, and on June 4th, reached Barbadoes, where he found
accounts that the combined fleet had been seen from St. Lucia
on the 28th, standing to the Southward, and that Tobago and
Trinidad were their object. Advices met him, that the combined
fleets, were then at Martinique. On the 9th Nelson arrived off
that island; and there learned that they had passed to leeward of
Antigua the preceding day, and taken a homeward bound convoy
That they were flying back to Europe he believed, and for Europe
he steered in pursuit on the 13th. On the 17th of July he came
in sight of Cape St. Vincent, and steered for Gibraltar where he
arrived on the 19th; " and on the 20th," says he, " I went on shore
for the first time since June 16, 1803; not having had my foot out
of the Victory, for two years, wanting ten days." On the 15th of
August, he joined Admiral Cornwallis off Ushant. No news had
yet been obtained of the enemy; and on the same evening he received orders to proceed, with the Victory and Superb, to Portsmouth. At Portsmouth, Nelson, at length, found news of the
combined fleet. Sir Robert Calder, had fallen in with them on
the 22d of July, and after an action of four hours, captured an
eighty-four and a seventy-four.

Nelson offered his services once more, which were willingly
accepted, and he was desired to choose his own officers. Unremitting exertions were made to equip the ships which he had
chosen, and especially to refit the Victory, which was once more
to bear his flag. Early on the following morning he reached
Portsmouth; and arrived off Cadiz on the 29th of September
The station which Nelson had chosen was some fifty or sixty miles
to the west of Cadiz, near Cape St. Mary's. There was now

every indication that the enemy would speedily venture out. On the 9th of October, Nelson sent Collingwood his plan of attack. The order of sailing was to be the order of battle: the fleet in two lines, with an advanced squadron of eight of the fastest sailing two-deckers. The second in command, having the entire direction of his line, was to break through the enemy, about the twelfth ship from their rear: he would lead through the centre, and the advanced squadron was to cut off three or four ahead of the centre. One of the last orders of this admirable man was, that the name and family of every officer, seaman, and marine, who might be killed or wounded in action, should be as soon as possible returned to him, in order to be transmitted to the chairman of the patriotic fund, that the case might be taken into consideration, for the benefit of the sufferer or his family.

About two in the afternoon of the 19th, the repeating ships announced, that the enemy were at sea. At daybreak on the next day the combined fleets were distinctly seen from the Victory's deck, formed in a close line of battle ahead, on the starboard tack, about twelve miles to leeward, and standing to the south. Nelson's fleet consisted of twenty-seven sail of the line, and four frigates; theirs of thirty-three, and seven large frigates. Their superiority was greater in size, and weight of metal, than in numbers. They had four thousand troops on board; and the best riflemen who could be procured. On the 21st of October, soon after daylight, Nelson came upon deck. The wind was now from the west, light breezes, with a long heavy swell. Signal was made to bear down upon the enemy in two lines; and the fleet set all sail. Collingwood, in the Royal Sovereign, led the lee line of thirteen ships; the Victory led the weather line of fourteen. Having seen that all was as it should be, Nelson retired to his cabin, and wrote the following prayer: "May the great God, whom I worship, grant to my country, and for the benefit of Europe in general, a great and glorious victory, and may no misconduct in any one tarnish it; and may humanity after victory be the predominant feature in the British fleet! For myself, individually, I commit my life to Him that made me; and may his blessing alight on my endeavors for serving my country faithfully! To him I resign myself, and the just cause which is intrusted to me to defend. Amen, Amen, Amen." About six, he appeared to be in good spirits, but very calm, with his whole attention fixed on the enemy. They tacked to the northward, and formed their line on the larboard tack, thus bringing the shoals of Trafalgar and St. Pedro under the lee of the British, and keeping the port of Cadiz open for themselves. This was judiciously done: and Nelson, aware of all the advantages which it gave them, made signal to prepare to anchor. Villeneuve was a skilful seaman. His plan of defence was as well conceived, and as original as the plan of attack. He formed the fleet in a

double line, every alternate ship being about a cable's length to
windward of her second ahead and astern.

Nelson's last signal was now made:—"ENGLAND EXPECTS
EVERY MAN TO DO HIS DUTY!" He wore that day, as usual, his
admiral's frock, bearing on the left breast four stars, of the different orders with which he was invested. It was known that
there were riflemen on board the French ships; and it could not
be doubted but that his life would be particularly aimed at. This
was a point upon which Nelson's officers knew that it was hopeless to remonstrate or reason with him; but Blackwood, and his
own captain Hardy, represented to him how advantageous to the
fleet it would be for him to keep out of action as long as possible;
and he consented at last to let the Leviathan and the Téméraire,
which were sailing abreast of the Victory, be ordered to pass
ahead. Yet even here the last infirmity of this noble mind was
indulged, for these ships could not pass ahead of the Victory who
continued to carry all her sail; and so far was Nelson from
shortening sail, that it was evident he took pleasure in pressing
on, and rendering it impossible for them to obey his own orders.
The French admiral, on beholding Nelson and Collingwood each
leading his line, is said to have exclaimed, pointing them out to
his officers, that such conduct could not fail to be successful.

At ten minutes before twelve the action commenced. Eight or
nine of the ships immediately ahead of the Victory, and across
her bows, fired single guns at her, to ascertain whether she was
yet within their range. Nelson's column was steered about two
points more to the north than Collingwood's, in order to cut off
the enemy's escape into Cadiz: the lee line, therefore, was first
engaged. The Royal Sovereign, steered right for the centre of
the enemy's line, cut through it astern of the Santa Anna, three-
decker, and engaged her at the muzzle of her guns on the starboard side. The enemy continued to fire a gun at a time at the
Victory, till they saw that a shot had passed through her main-
top-gallant-sail; then they opened their broadsides, aiming chiefly
at her rigging. The enemy showed no colors till late in the
action. For this reason, the Santissima Trinidad, was distinguished only by her four decks; and to the bow of this opponent he
ordered the Victory to be steered. Meantime an incessant raking fire was kept up upon the Victory. The Admiral's secretary
was one of the first who fell. Presently a double-headed shot
struck a party of marines, who were drawn up on the poop, and
killed eight of them. A few minutes afterwards a shot struck the
fore brace bits on the quarter deck, and passed between Nelson
and Hardy, a splinter from the bit tearing off Hardy's buckle
and bruising his foot. Nelson then smiled, and said, "This is
too warm work, Hardy, to last long."

The Victory had not yet returned a single gun; fifty of her
men had been by this time killed or wounded, and her main-top-

mast with all her studding-sails and her booms, shot away. At four minutes after twelve, she opened her fire from both sides of her deck. The master was ordered to put the helm to port, and she ran on board the Redoubtable, just as her tiller ropes were shot away. The French ship received her with a broadside; then instantly let down her lower-deck ports, for fear of being boarded through them, and never afterward fired a great gun during the action. Her tops, like those of all the enemy's ships, were filled with riflemen. Captain Harvey, in the Téméraire, fell on board the Redoubtable on the other side. Another enemy was in like manner on board the Téméraire; so that these four ships formed as compact a tier as if they had been moored together, their heads lying all the same way. The lieutenants of the Victory, seeing this, depressed their guns of the middle and lower decks, and fired with a diminished charge, lest the shot should pass through, and injure the Téméraire. An incessant fire was kept up from the Victory from both sides; her larboard guns playing upon the Bucentaur and the huge Santissima Trinidad.

It had been part of Nelson's prayer, that the British fleet might be distinguished by humanity in the victory he expected. He twice gave orders to cease firing upon the Redoubtable, supposing that she had struck. From this ship, which he had thus twice spared, he received his death. A ball fired from her mizen-top, which, in the then situation of the two vessels, was not more than fifteen yards from that part of the deck where he was standing, struck the epaulette on his left shoulder, about a quarter after one, just in the heat of the action. He fell upon his face, on the spot which was covered with his poor secretary's blood. He was taken down into the cockpit, and it was perceived, upon examination, that the wound was mortal. This, however, was concealed from all, except Captain Hardy, the chaplain, and the medical attendants. All that could be done was to fan him with paper, and frequently to give him lemonade to alleviate his intense thirst. He was in great pain, and expressed much anxiety for the event of the action, which now began to declare itself. As often as a ship struck, the crew of the Victory huzzaed, and at every huzza, a visible expression of joy gleamed in the eyes, and marked the countenance of the dying hero. Nelson desired to be turned on his right side, when his articulation became difficult, but he was distinctly heard to say, "Thank God, I have done my duty." These words he repeatedly pronounced: and they were the last words which he uttered. He expired at thirty minutes after four, three hours and a quarter after he had received his wound. The man who had given the fatal wound, was recognised, and did not live to boast of what he had done. When the Redoubtable was taken possession of, he was found dead in the mizen top, with one ball through his head and another through his breast. The Spaniards began the battle with less vivacity than their unworthy allies, but they continued it with greater firmness. Once, amid his sufferings, Nelson had expressed a wish that he were dead; but immediately the spirit subdued the pains of death, and he wished to live a little longer;—doubtless that he might hear the completion of the victory which he had seen so gloriously begun. That consolation—that joy—that triumph was afforded him. He lived to know that the victory was decisive; and the last guns which were fired at the flying enemy were heard a minute or two before he expired. The ships which were thus flying were four of the enemy's van, all French, under Rear-Admiral Dumanoir, who were afterwards captured by Sir Richard Strachan.

The total British loss in the Battle of Trafalgar amounted to one thousand five hundred and eighty-seven. Twenty of the enemy struck; but it was not possible to anchor the fleet, as Nelson had enjoined; a gale came on from the south-west; some of the prizes went down, some went on shore; one effected its escape into Cadiz; others were destroyed; four only were saved and these by the greatest exertions. The Spanish vice-admiral Alava, died of his wounds. Villeneuve was sent to England, and permitted to return to France. It is almost superfluous to add, that all the honors which a grateful country could bestow, were heaped upon the memory of Nelson. A public funeral was decreed and a public monument. The leaden coffin, in which he was carried home, was cut in pieces, which were distributed as relics of Saint Nelson,—so the gunner of the Victory called them;—and when, at his interment, his flag was about to be lowered into the grave, the sailors, who assisted at the ceremony, with one accord rent it in pieces, that each might preserve a fragment while he lived. There was reason to suppose, from the appearances upon opening the body, that, in the course of nature, he might have attained, like his father, to a good old age. Yet he cannot be said to have fallen prematurely, whose work was done; nor ought he to be lamented, who died so full of honors and at the height of human fame.

CASABIANCA.*

The boy stood on the burning deck,
   Whence all but him had fled;
The flame that lit the battle's wreck,
   Shone round him o'er the dead.

---

* Young Casabianca, a boy about thirteen years old, son to the admiral of the Orient, remained at his post (in the battle of the Nile,) after the ship had taken fire, and all the guns had been abandoned; and perished in the explosion of the vessel, when the flames had reached the powder.

Yet beautiful and bright he stood,
  As born to rule the storm ;
A creature of heroic blood,
  A proud, though childlike form.

The flames rolled on—he would not go,
  Without his father's word ;
That father, faint in death below,
  His voice no longer heard.

He called aloud—" Say, father, say
  If yet my task is done ?"
He knew not that the chieftain lay
  Unconscious of his son.

" Speak, father !" once again he cried,
  " If I may yet be gone !"
—And but the booming shots replied,
  And fast the flames rolled on.

Upon his brow he felt their breath,
  And in his waving hair ;
And looked from that lone post of death,
  In still, yet brave despair.

And shouted but once more aloud,
  " My father ! must I stay ?"
While o'er him fast, through sail and shroud
  The wreathing fires made way.

They wrapped the ship in splendor wild,
  They caught the flag on high,
And streamed above the gallant child,
  Like banners in the sky.

There came a burst of thunder sound—
  The boy—oh ! where was he ?
—Ask of the winds that far around
  With fragments strewed the sea !

With mast, and helm, and pennon fair,
  That well had borne their part—
But the noblest thing that perished there,
  Was that young faithful heart

THE CUMBERLAND PACKET

In the dreadful hurricane which took place at Antigua, on the 4th of September, 1804, several vessels were lost ; and among others, the Duke of Cumberland Packet. Every precaution had been taken, by striking the yards and masts, to secure the vessel ; and the cable had held so long, that some faint hope began to be

entertained of riding out the gale, when several of the crew were
so indiscreet, as to quit the deck for some refreshment; no sooner
had they sat down, than a loud groan from the rest of the crew
summoned them on deck. The captain ran forward, and exclaimed, "All's now over: Lord God have mercy upon us!" The
cable had parted; the ship hung about two minutes by the stream
and kedge, and then began to drive broadside on. At this mo·
ment the seamen, torn by despair, seemed for a moment to forget
themselves; lamentations for their homes, their wives, and their
children, resounded through the ship. Every man clung to a
rope, and determined to stick to it as long as the ship remained
entire. For an hour they drifted on, without knowing whither, the
men continued to hold fast by the rigging while their bodies were
beaten by the heaviest rain, and lashed by every wave. The
most dreadful silence prevailed. Every one was too intent on his
own approaching end, to be able to communicate his feelings
to another; and nothing was heard but the howling of the tempest.
The vessel drove towards the harbor of St. John's, and two alarm
guns were fired, in order that the garrison might be spectators of
their fate, for it was in vain to think of assistance. They soon
drove against a large ship, and went close under her stern. A
faint hope now appeared of being stranded on a sandy beach; and
the captain therefore ordered the carpenter to get the hatchets all
ready to cut away the masts, in order to make a raft for those who
chose to venture upon it. The vessel however drove with extreme
violence on some rocks, and the cracking of her timbers below
was distinctly heard. Every hope now vanished, and the crew
already began to consider themselves as beings of another world.
In order to ease the vessel, and if possible prevent her from
parting, the mizen-mast was suffered to remain, to steady the
vessel. The vessel had struck about two o'clock, and in half
an hour afterwards the water was up to the lower deck. Never
was daylight more anxiously wished for, than by the crew of this
vessel. After having hung so long by the shrouds, they were
forced to cling three hours longer before the dawn appeared. The
sea was making a complete breach over the ship, which was laying on her beam ends; and the crew, stiff and benumbed, could
with difficulty hold against the force of the waves, every one of
which struck and nearly drowned them.

The break of day discovered to the wretched mariners all the
horrors of their situation; the vessel was lying upon large rocks
at the foot of a craggy overhanging precipice, twice as high as
the ship's mainmast; the wind and rain beat upon the crew with
unabated violence, and the ship lay a miserable wreck. The first
thoughts of the crew in the morning were naturally directed to
the possibility of saving their lives; and they all agreed, that their
only chance of doing so, was by means of the mizen mast. The
top-mast and top-gallant-mast were launched out, and reached

within a few feet of the rock. An attempt was made by one of the crew, to throw a rope with a noose to the top of the rock; but instead of holding by the bushes, it brought them away. Another seaman, who seemed from despair to have imbibed an extraordinary degree of courage, followed the first man out on the mast, with the intention of throwing himself from the end upon the mercy of the rock; he had proceeded to the extremity of the top-gallant-mast, and was on the point of leaping among the bushes, when the pole of the mast, unable to sustain his weight, gave way, and precipitated him into the bosom of the waves, from a height of forty feet. Fortunately he had carried down with him the piece of the broken mast, and instead of being dashed to pieces, as was expected, he kept himself above water until he was hoisted up

Loss of the Cumberland Packet.

All hopes of being saved by the mizen-mast were now at an end, and while the crew were meditating in sullen silence on their situation, Mr. Doncaster, the chief mate, unknown to any one, went out on the bowsprit, and having reached the end of the jib-boom, threw himself headlong into the water. He had scarcely fallen, when a tremendous wave threw him upon the rock, and left him dry; there he remained motionless, until a second wave washed him still farther up, when clinging to some roughness in the cliff, he began to scramble up the rock; and in about half an hour, he with infinite difficulty reached the summit of the cliff. The crew anxiously watched every step he took, and prayed for his safety, conscious that their own preservation depended solely upon it. Mr. Doncaster immediately went round to that part of the precipice nearest the vessel, and received a rope thrown from the main top, which he fastened to some trees.   By means of this rope, the whole of the crew were, in the space of three hours, hoisted to the top of the cliff.

The whole of the ship's company having assembled on the rock, bent their steps towards town.   The plain before them had, in consequence of the heavy rains, become almost impassable; but after wading about three miles through fields of canes, and often plunged up to the neck in water, they reached St. John's in safety; where they would have died for want of food and necessaries, had it not been for the kind offices of a Mulatto tailor, who supplied them with clothes, beds, and provisions, and did them other kind offices of humanity

CAPTAIN D'ENTRECASTEAUX.

On September 28th, 1791, in the two sloops, La Recherche and L'Esperance, of sixteen guns, and one hundred and ten men each, they weighed from the harbor of Brest, completely equipped for a voyage of circumnavigating the globe.   The conduct of the expedition was assigned to Captain D'Entrecasteaux.   The leading object of the voyage was to endeavor to procure intelligence relative to Captain La Perouse, who had long been missing in the South Seas, and to make a complete tour of New Holland; an island, by far the largest in the world; comprehending an immense circuit of at least three thousand (French) leagues. The accomplishment of this last point was essential to the history of geography, and what had not been effected by either Cook or La Perouse.

The first port they made was Santa Cruz in Teneriffe; they arrived there on the 17th of October, and having taken in wines and provisions, proceeded on their route to the Cape of Good Hope; and while they continued there, the expedition sustained a considerable misfortune in the death of the astronomer Bertrand. February 16th, 1792, they left the Cape, and bore away for the island of New Guinea, some parts of which they explored; they reached the islands Arsacides on July the 9th, and New Ireland the 17th ditto.   They afterwards made for Amboyna, one of the Molucca islands, and arrived Sept. 6th.—October 11th, they left Amboyna, and sailed immediately for the west part of New Holland.   December 3d, 1792, they arrived at the Cape, which is at the south-west extremity of New Holland, and sailed along the southern shore, till January 3d, having by this means traced and ascertained about two-thirds of the whole extent of the southern coast   On the 11th of March, they passed very near the North cape of New Zealand, and making for the shore, several canoes came along-side. On the 16th, they discovered two little islands, at a little distance from each other. The most eastern one lies in 30 deg. 17 min. south latitude, and in 179 deg. 41 min. east longitude.—On the 17th, discovered an island about five leagues in circumference, conspicuous by its elevated situation. It lies in 29 deg. 3 min. south latitude, and in 179 deg. 54 min. east longitude.—On the 2d of March they saw Ebona, the most south westerly of the Friendly Islands. The next day anchored at Tongataboo, the largest of the Friendly Islands. Among these islanders they frequently met with men six feet high, their limbs shaped in the most comely proportion. The fertility of the soil, which exempted them from the necessity of extreme labor, may conduce not a little to the unusual perfection of their forms. Their features have a strong resemblance to those of Europeans A burning sky has impressed a slight discolor on their skins. Those, among the women, who are but little exposed to the rays of the sun, are sufficiently fair. Some of them are distinguished by a beautiful carnation, which gives a vivacity to their whole figure. A thousand nameless graces are visible in their gestures, when engaged in the slightest employments. In the dance their movements are enchanting.

The language of this people bears an analogy with the gentleness of their manners; it is well adapted to music, for which they have a peculiar taste. Their concerts wherein every one performs his part, demonstrate the just ideas which they entertain of harmony. The women, as well as the men, have their shoulders and breasts naked. A cotton cloth, or rather a piece of stuff, manufactued with the bark of mulberry-tree into paper serves them for apparel. It forms a beautiful drapery, reaching from a little above the waist down to the feet. These islands produce a species of nutmegs, which differs very little in form from those of the Moluccas. It is not, however, aromatic, and is almost twice as large. They also procured the bread-fruit tree, for the purpose of transporting it into the West India Islands. We must not confound these excellent species of bread-fruit tree with the wild species of it found in the Moluccas, and observed for a long time past in the Isle of France. In this second sort the grains do not miscarry, while in the good fruit-tree they are replaced by a food truly delicious, when baked under ashes or in the oven. In other respects it is a most wholesome viand, affording a pleasant repast during the whole time of their continuance on this island, and for which they willingly relinquished the ship's stock of baker's bread. The Molucca sort produces thirty or forty small fruits; while every tree of the Friendly Islands produces three or four hundred extremely large, of an oval form, the greatest diameter being from nine to ten inches, and the smallest from seven to eight. A tree would be oppressed with

such an enormous load, if the fruit were to ripen all at once; bu
sagacious nature has so ordered it, that the fruit succeed each
other, during eight months of the year, thus providing the natives
with a food equally salubrious and plentiful.   Every tree occupies
a circular space of about thirty feet in diameter.   A single acre
occupied by this vegetable would supply the wants of a number of
families.   Nothing in nature exhibits a similar fecundity.   As it
produces no seeds, it has a wonderful faculty of throwing out
suckers; and its roots frequently force their way up to the surface
of the earth, and there give birth to fresh plants.   It thrives exceedingly in a tropical climate, in a soil somewhat elevated above
the level of the sea; and suits very well with a marly soil, in
which a mixture of argillaceous clay preponderates.

They quitted the Friendly Islands on the 10th of April, 1793.
April 15th saw Enooan, the most eastern of the islands of the
Archipelago of the Holy Ghost, and afterwards that of Anaton
The eruptions of the volcano of Tana, presented in the night a
spectacle truly sublime.   April 27th, steering for New Caledonia; in a night darker than usual, they ran among some
islands surrounded with breakers, not noticed till then by navigators; they were only apprised of danger by an uncommon
circumstance; the flight of a flock of sea-fowl over their heads
about three in the morning.   This indication of the proximity of
land induced the officer upon watch to slacken sail, and lie-to, at
a critical juncture, when an hour's more sailing must have dashed
them to pieces against the rocks.   These new discovered islands
lie about thirty leagues north-east of New Caledonia, where they
anchored April 26th.

After the description that Cook and Forster have given of the
inhabitants of New Zealand, they expected to find realized the
advantageous portrait given of them by those celebrated voyagers.
They had reason, however, partly to suspend their belief of those
accounts, when they afterwards observed a number of human bones,
broiled, which the savages were devouring, eagerly fastening on
the smallest tendinous parts which adhere to them.   This fact at
least suffices to prove, that the New Zealanders are cannibals.
They often attacked their boat; but the good countenance exhibited prevented their assailing or massacring any of their company.
Notwithstanding these hostilities, the ship was every day visited
by numerous bodies of the islanders.   The soil being every where
barren, they perceived but few vestiges of any taste for agricul-
ture; still, however, they observed in some gardens the Colocasia,
the Caribbee cabbage, the banana-tree, and the sugar-cane.
The barbarous customs of the natives did not prevent their reiterated excursions into the interior parts of the country.   On these
occasions they kept together to the number of twenty, always
well armed.   As evening came on, they commonly took their station on some elevated post in the mountains, where they passed

the night in a situation which protected them from hostile assaults. To guard against surprise, they kept watch by turns.

May 9th, they weighed anchor, and sailed before the wind for the north. In their course, observed the eastern part of the reefs and islands, the western side of which they saw the year before. May 21st. were close on the island of St. Croix. and sent in two boats to look out for an anchoring place. While the sailors were employed in sounding, one of the natives, at the distance of upwards of eighty paces, lanced an arrow, which slightly wounded the forehead of one of them. A volley of firearms, however, soon dispersed the group of canoes which had surrounded the boats, and from which the lance proceeded. Although the wound was apparently so inconsiderable, it was attended with a tetanus, which proved mortal to the unfortunate sailor after only eight days. The arrow did not appear to have been poisoned, as it is well known that beasts pierced with the same weapons do not experience any fatal symptoms. In India, it is no uncommon thing to see the slightest puncture followed by a spasm, which is a certain forerunner of death.

July 16th and 17th, they sailed in view of the Anchoret Islands of Bougainville. On the 20th they lost D'Entrecasteaux, the captain. He died of convulsions, every fit of which was succeeded by a speechless stupor. August 16th, 1793, in 129 deg. 14 min. of east longitude, and so near the equator, that they were only half a minute to the south. Here the inhabitants brought very large sea-turtles, the soup of which they experienced to be a salutary remedy for the scurvy, which was now prevalent among them. In this island they procured a number of interesting objects, and quitted it August the 29th, and sailed for Bouao, where they anchored September the 3d, 1793. In this mountainous isle, where the productions of nature are extremely varied, they had a favorable opportunity of continuing their botanical researches, &c. Here several of the men died of a contagious bilious dysentery, contracted in the low marshy grounds of the country.

October 28, 1793, cast anchor in the road of Sourabaya, in the Isle of Java. Here divisions broke out among the crews, in consequence of gaining intelligence of the further progress of the French revolution. D'Auribeau hoisted the white flag Feb. 19th, 1794, and surrendered the two vessels to the Dutch. He also seized all the journals, charts, and memoirs, which were connected with the voyage, and arrested all those of the ship's companies that were obnoxious to his own political sentiments. One journal, however, was fortunately saved, by having been stowed in a box of tea. In this hazardous, yet important voyage, of two hundred and fifteen persons, thirty-six lost their lives; the astronomer, Pearson, died at Java; and Ventenat at the Isle of France. Riche, the naturalist, remained at Java, as well as Billadieru.

Lahay, the botanist, also stopped there; having under his care
the bread-fruit trees, brought from the Friendly Islands. Pison,
the painter, tarried with the governor of Sourabaya; but afterwards returned to Europe, and published an account of the
voyage.

THE MARINER'S ADDRESS TO HIS MISTRESS

When clouds are dark and winds blow high,
Thou'lt surely think of me—
Whose fate is in that stormy sky,
Or on the raging sea.

And oft thou'lt think at eventide,
When flowers perfume the breeze,
Of him who would be by thy side,
But still must roam the seas.

Thou'lt think, too, when the stars shine bright
Out o'er the azure sky,
Of one who views their hallowed light
And dreams that thou art nigh.

He sees thee in that one bright star,
Pure emblem of our love ;
That minds us as it beams afar,
Our vows are sealed above.

And still his wandering eye shall catch
Its loved and stilly light,
And think of thee, who too dost watch
Love's altar pure and bright.

Its incense is the sweet sea-breeze,
That bears his vows to shore,
Or visions poured on the seas,
To meet and part no more.

The merry sea-boy trolls his lay,
And lightly laughs at sadness ;
The soldier sings war's roundelay
Its notes respond his gladness.

The mariner still views his chart,
Or looks upon the pole,
Whose star will guide him to his mart
Howe'er the billows roll.

Another sighs in secret sorrow
O'er those he left behind ;
The ship rides on *to-day*. To-morrow
Their forms have left his mind

Their joys and sorrows, hopes and fears,
Are transient as the wind ;
Eyes bright in hope, or dim with fears,
Are emblems of their mind.

Ambition's lure or gainful trade
Still lead them on their way ;
Not so for me—my soul was made
To seek another stay.

My spirit turns toward that shore,
A wand'rer though I be,
And hopes to meet and part no more,
From all it loves—from thee.

CAPTAIN RILEY

There is not, perhaps, in the annals of shipwreck, a personal narrative more deeply distressing, or more painfully interesting than that of Captain Riley. Were there not the most ample testimony to his excellent moral character and unimpeachable veracity, we might be led to withhold our belief from some parts of his narrative, on the simple ground, that human nature on the one hand, was utterly incapable of inflicting, and on the other, of enduring such hardships and sufferings as this gentleman and his poor shipwrecked companions had to undergo—sufferings which, as Captain Riley truly says, have been as great and as various as ever fell to the lot of humanity.

The American Brig, Commerce, commanded by Captain Riley, with a crew of ten persons, was wrecked on the coast of Africa, on the 28th of August, 1315. With some difficulty the crew reached the shore, and secured a small quantity of provisions and tools, to repair their boat, in which they hoped to reach the Cape de Verd Island. All hopes of this were, however, soon rendered abortive by the appearance of a party of Arabs; who burnt their trunks and chests, carried off their provisions, and stove in the wine and water casks. The crew escaped to their boat, but Mr. Riley was left behind. One of the Arabs seized hold of him by the throat, and with a scimitar at his breast, gave him to understand there was money on board, and it must instantly be brought ashore.

When the ship was wrecked, Mr. Riley had divided the dollars among the crew. On being informed of the demands of the Arabs he hailed the men, and told them what the savages required; a bucket was accordingly sent on shore with about a thousand dollars. An old Arab instantly laid hold of it, and forcing Riley to accompany him, they all went behind the sand hills to divide the

spot. In this situation he felt himself very uneasy, and in order
to regain the beach, he made signs that there was still more money
remaining in the ship. The hint succeeded; and under the idea
of getting it they allowed him again to hail his people; when
instead of money, he desired them to send on shore Antonio
Michael (an old man they had taken in at New Orleans), as the
only possible means left for him of effecting his own escape. The
Arabs finding, on his reaching the shore, that he had brought no
money with him, struck him, pricked him with their sharp knives,
and stripped him of all his clothes. Mr. Riley seized this opportunity of springing from his keepers, and plunged into the sea.
On rising through the surf, he perceived the old Arab within ten
feet of him, up to his chin in water, with his spear ready to strike
him; but another surf rolling at that instant over him, saved his
life, and he reached the lee of the wreck in safety. The remorseless brutes wreaked their vengeance on poor Antonio, by
plunging a spear into his body, which laid him lifeless at their
feet.

The wreck was, by this time, going rapidly to pieces; the long
boat writhed like an old basket. The crew had neither provisions
nor water; neither oars nor a rudder to the boat; neither compass
nor quadrant to direct their course; yet, hopeless as their situation
was, and expecting to be swallowed up by the first surf, they resolved to try their fate on the ocean, rather than to encounter death
from the relentless savages on shore. By great exertion, they
succeeded in finding a water cask, out of which they filled four
gallons into a keg. One of the seamen, Porter, stole on shore
by the hawser, and brought on board two oars, with a small bag
of money which they had buried, containing about four hundred
dollars. They also contrived to get together a few pieces of salt
pork, a live pig, weighing about twenty pounds, about four pounds
of figs, a spar for the boat's mast, a jib, and a main sail. Every
thing being ready, the crew went to prayers; and the wind ceas-
ing to blow, the boat was launched through the breakers. In this
miserable boat they determined to stand out in the wide ocean
After being six days at sea, it was driven on the rocks, and com
pletely stove, but the crew again reached the shore.

On the next morning they set out from the place where they
had been cast, which, as it afterwards appeared, was Cape
Barbas, not far from Cape Blanco. They proceeded easterly
close to the water's edge, for three days, when they encountered
a large company of Arabs who were watering their camels. The
shipwrecked mariners bowed themselves to the ground with every
mark of submission, and by signs implored their compassion, but
in vain. The whole party were in an instant stripped naked to
the skin, and the Arabs began to fight most furiously for the booty,
and especially for getting possession of the prisoners. "Six or
eight of them," says Captain Riley, whose narrative we now

quote, "were about me, one hauling me one way, and one another. The one who stripped us, stuck to us as his lawful property signifying, "you may have the others, these are mine."—They cut at each other over my head, and on every side of me, with their bright weapons, which fairly whizzed through the air within an inch of my naked body, and on every side of me, now hacking each other's arms apparently to the bone; men laying their ribs bare with gashes, while their heads, hands, and thighs received a full share of cuts and wounds. The blood streaming from every gash, ran down their bodies, coloring and heightening the natural hideousness of their appearance. I had expected to be cut to pieces, in this dreadful affray, but was not injured.

"The battle over, I saw my distressed companions divided among the Arabs, and all going towards the drove of camels, though they were at some distance from me. We too were delivered into the hands of two old women, who urged us on with sticks towards the camels. Naked and barefooted, we could not go very fast, and I showed the women my mouth, which was parched white as frost, and without a sign of moisture. When we got near the well, one of the women called for another, who came to us with a wooden bowl that held, I should guess, about a gallon of water, and setting it on the ground, made myself and Dick kneel down and put our heads into it like camels. I drank, I suppose, half a gallon, though I had been very particular in cautioning the men against drinking too much at a time, in case they ever came to water. I now experienced how much easier it was to preach, than to practise aright. They then led us to the well, the water of which was nearly as black and disgusting as stale bilge water. A large bowl was now filled with it, and a little sour camel's milk poured from a goat skin into it; this tasted to me delicious, and we all drank of it till our stomachs were literally filled. We now begged for something to eat, but these Arabs had nothing for themselves, and seemed very sorry it was not in their power to give us some food. There were at and about the well, I should think, about one hundred persons, men, women, and children, and from four to five hundred camels, large and small. The sun beat fiercely upon us, and our skins seemed actually to fry like meat before the fire. These people continued to draw water for their camels, of which the animals drank enormous quantities."

The party travelled south-east over a plain covered with small sharp stones, which lacerated their feet dreadfully. About midnight they halted, and for the first time got about a pint of pure camel's milk each. The wind was chilling cold; they lay on sharp stones, perfectly naked; their bodies blistered and mangled, and the stones piercing their naked flesh to the ribs. On the morning of the 11th (September), a pint of milk was divided among four of them, and they got nothing more until midnight, when they

were allowed a little milk and water. They continued travelling
in the desert, enduring all the miseries of hunger, thirst, and
fatigue, with every addition Arab cruelty could inflict, until they
reached Wadnoon. Sidi Hamet, an African trader, who had pur
chased them of the old Arab, however, became the means of their
deliverance. He told Mr. Riley, that he must write a letter to
his friend at Suara, desiring him to pay the money for the ransom
of himself and people, when they should be free. A scrap of paper, a reed, and some black liquor, was then brought to Mr. Riley,
who briefly wrote the circumstances of the loss of the ship, his captivity, &c. adding, " worn down to the bone by the most dreadful of
all sufferings, naked, and a slave, I implore your pity, and trust that
such distress will not be suffered to plead in vain." The letter
was addressed, " To the English, French, Spanish, or American
Consuls, or any Christian merchant in Mogadore." The anxiety
of the captives may be well imagined. For seven days after Hamet's departure, they were shut up in a yard during the day, where
cows, sheep, and asses, rested; and locked up all night in a dreary
cellar.

On the evening of the eighth day, a Moor came into the inclosure,
and brought a letter from Mr. Wiltshire, the English Consul,
stating, that he had agreed to the demand of Sidi Hamet, whom
he kept as an hostage for their safe appearance, and that the
bearer would conduct them to Mogadore. He had also sent them
clothes and provisions; and thus accoutred and fortified, they set
out under their new conductor, who brought them safe to Mogadore, where they were most kindly received by Mr. Wiltshire,
who took each man by the hand, and welcomed him to life and
liberty. He conducted them to his house, had them all washed,
clothed, and fed, and spared no pains nor expense in procuring
every comfort, and in administering with his own hand, night and
day, such refreshment as their late sufferings and debility required.
Of the miserable condition to which these unfortunate men had
been reduced, one act will witness. " At the instance of Mr.
Wiltshire," says Mr. Riley, " I was weighed, and fell short of
ninety pounds, though my usual weight for the last ten years had
been over two hundred pounds; the weight of my companions was
less than I dare to mention, for I apprehended it would not be believed that the bodies of men, retaining the vital spark, should not
have weighed *forty pounds*

ADVENTURES OF CAPTAIN WOODWARD AND FIVE SEAMEN IN THE ISLAND OF CELEBES

In the year 1791, Woodward sailed from Boston for the East Indies.* On his arrival there he was employed in making country voyages until the 20th of January, when he sailed as chief ... in an American ship from Batavia bound to Manilla.

In passing through the straits of Macassar, they found the wind and current both against them, and after beating up for six weeks they fell short of provision. Captain Woodward and five seamen were sent to purchase some from a vessel about four leagues distant. They were without water, provisions, or compass,—having on board the boat only an axe, a boat hook, two penknives, a useless gun and forty dollars in cash.

They reached the ship at sunset, and were told by the captain that he had no provision to spare as he was bound to China and was victualled for only one month. He advised them to stay until morning, which they did. But when morning dawned, their own ship was out of sight even from the mast head, and with a fair wind for her to go through the straits of Macassar. Being treated coolly by the captain, they agreed with one voice to leave the ship in search of their own. On leaving the vessel, the captain gave them twelve musket cartridges and a round bottle of brandy, but neither water nor provisions of any sort.

They rowed till twelve o'clock at night, in hopes of seeing their own vessel, and then drawing near an island they thought it prudent to go there to get some fresh water. They landed and made a large fire in hopes their ship might see it. But not being able to see any thing of her in the morning and finding no water or provisions on the island, they continued their course in the middle of the straits six days longer, without going on shore or tasting of any thing but brandy. They soon had the shore of Celebes in sight, where they determined to go in search of provisions and then to proceed to Macassar.

As they approached the shore they saw two proas full of natives, who immediately put themselves in a posture of defence. The sailors made signs to them that they wanted provisions, but instead of giving it the Malays began to brandish their cresses or steel daggers. Three of the men jumped on board a proa to beg some Indian corn, and got three or four small ears. The chief seemed quite friendly and agreed to sell captain Woodward two cocoa nuts for a dollar, but as soon as he had received the money, he immediately began to strip him in search of more. Captain Woodward defended himself with a hatchet and ordered the boat to be shov-

---

* In the ship Robert Morris, Captain Hay.

ed off the chief levelled a musket at him, but fortunately it missed him.

They then stood off, went round a point of land and landed out of sight of the proas, when they found a plenty of cocoa-nut trees. Captain Woodward while engaged in cutting them down, heard the man whom he had left to take care of the boat scream out in a most bitter manner. He ran immediately to the beach where he saw his own boat off at some distance full of Malays and the poor fellow who was guarding it lying on his back with his throat cut and his body stabbed in several places.

They now fled immediately to the mountains, and finding that they had lost their boat, money, and most of their clothes, they concluded that their only chance of escape was to get to Macassar by land. Being afraid to travel in the day time, they set out in the evening taking a star for their guide bearing south. But they soon lost sight of the star and at day light found themselves within a few rods of the place, where they had set out. They had travelled on the side of a mountain, and had gone quite round it instead of going straight over it. They started again and travelled by the sea shore six nights successively, living on berries and water found in the hollows of trees.

On the sixth they arrived at a bay where they saw a party of the Maylays fishing. Here Captain Woodward found some yellowish berries which were to him quite palatable, but his men not liking them eat some of the leaves. On the next day they concluded to make a raft and go to the small island on which they first landed, thinking that they might be taken off from it by some ship passing that way. But they were obliged to abandon this project, for in the evening the men who had eaten the leaves, were attacked with violent pains and were crying out in torture during the whole night. Although they got better towards evening yet they were so weak and dejected that Captain Woodward was convinced that they could not reach the island and asked them if they were willing to surrender themselves to the Malays. On reflection they all thought this the best course which they could take; and forthwith proceeded to the bay where they had seen the Malays in the morning, in order at once either to find friends or to meet their fate. At first they saw no one, but Captain Woodward soon saw three of the natives approaching him; and ordering his men to keep quiet, he advanced alone until he had come within a short distance of them, where they stopped and drew out their cresses or knives. Captain Woodward fell on his knees and begged for mercy. The Malays looked at him for about ten minutes with their knives drawn when one of them came towards him, knelt in the same manner and offered both his hands. More natives now came up and stripped them of their hats and handkerchiefs and even the buttons on their jackets, which they took for money.

They were now taken to Travâlla and carried to the court-house

or judgment hall, accompanied by a great concourse of people,
including women and children who made a circle at some distance
from them.   The chief soon entered, looking as wild as a mad-
man, carrying in his hand a large drawn cress or knife, the blade
of which was two feet and a half long and very bright.   Captain
Woodward approached so near to him as to place the foot of the
chief on his own head, as a token that he was completely under
his power and direction.   The chief after holding a short consultation, returned to his house and brought out five pieces of betel
nut, which he gave to the sailors as a token of friendship.

They were now permitted to rest until about eight o'clock
when they were carried to the Rajah's house, where they found a
supper provided for them of sago-bread and peas, but in all
hardly enough for one man.   Their allowance afterwards was for
each man a cocoa nut and an ear of Indian corn at noon, and the
same at night.   In this manner they lived about twenty days, but
were not allowed to go out except to the water to bathe.   But the
natives soon began to relax their vigilance over them, and in
about four months, they were conveyed to the head Rajah of Parlow.   They had not been there long when the head Rajah sent to
a Dutch port called Priggia, which is at the head of a deep bay
on the east side of the island and which is under the care of a
commandant.   In a few days the commandant who was a Frenchman, and had been thirty years in the Dutch service, arrived at
Parlow and sent for Captain Woodward.   He wished him to go
with him to Priggia where he resided, but Captain Woodward refused, being apprehensive that he should be forced into the Dutch
service.   The commandant then inquired where he intended to
go.   He answered to Batavia or Macassar and thence to Bengal
He did not offer Captain Woodward or his people either money,
assistance, or clothes, but seemed quite affronted.

The Rajah now gave him the liberty of returning to Travâlla,
taking care, however, to send him in the night for fear that he
should get sight of Dungally, where there lived a Mahomedan
priest called Juan Hadgee.   This priest had been at Travâlla,
and offered a ransom for Captain Woodward and his men, but the
natives were unwilling to take it, and were fearful that their captives would try to escape to the town where the priest lived.   It
happened, however, that they were becalmed off Dungally, so that
Captain Woodward could observe its situation.   On arriving at
Travâlla, he attempted to escape alone by water, but the canoe
being leaky, he came very near losing his life.   But not discouraged, he started immediately for Dungally by land, and reached
it just as the day dawned.

Juan Hadgee received him kindly and provided him with food
and clothing.   In the course of three days the chief of Travâlla
learning that he had gone to Dungally, sent after him, but the old
priest and the Rajah of Dungally refused to let him go   They

told him that in the course of three months they would convey
him to Batavia or Macassar, and also desired him to send for the
four men he had left at Travâlla.   This he did by means of a letter which he wrote with a pen of bamboo, and sent by the captain
of a proa, who delivered it secretly.   The men made their escape from Parlow at the time of a feast, early in the evening,
and arrived at Dungally at about twelve o'clock the next day.
They were received with great rejoicing by the natives, who immediately brought them plenty of victuals.   And this fortunate
circumstance revived their hopes of reaching some European
settlement, after many narrow escapes and difficulties.

Juan Hadgee now informed Captain Woodward that he should
set off in about two months, but that he must first make a short
voyage for provisions, which he did, leaving Captain Woodward
in his house with his wife and two servants.

They soon began to suffer exceedingly for the want of provi
sions, so that the natives were obliged to convey them up the
country, there to be supplied by some of the same tribe, who
regularly went from the village into the country at a certain season to cultivate rice and Indian corn.   But the Rajah of Parlow
making war on the Rajah of Dungally, because the latter would
not deliver them up, they were soon brought back to Dungally.
There was but one engagement, and then the men of Parlow
were beaten and driven back to their own town.

Provisions again growing scarce, Juan Hadgee was bound for
another port called Sawyah, situated about two degrees north of
the line.   He gave Captain Woodward permission to accompany
him, provided the Rajah was willing, but the latter refused, saying
that he must stay there and keep guard.   Captain Woodward now
mustered his men and taking their guns they went to the house
of the Rajah and told him they would stand guard no longer for
they wished to go to Macassar.   He immediately replied that
they should not.   Being determined not to live longer in this
manner, and finding no other means of escaping, Captain Woodward came to the resolution of stealing a canoe, to which all the
men agreed.   They were lucky enough to obtain one and seemed
in a fair way to make their escape, but just as they were getting
into it they were surrounded by about twenty natives and carried
before the Rajah, who ordered them to account for their conduct.
They told him that they could get nothing to eat, and were determined to quit the place on the first opportunity that offered.
Nothing of consequence resulted from this.   Knowing the language and people they had now become fearless of danger.

The Rajah refusing to let them go with Juan Hadgee they determined to run away with him, which they were enabled to do, as
the old man set out at twelve o'clock at night, and there happened luckily to be a canoe on the beach near his own.   This they
took and followed him as well as they could, but they soon parted

from him, and in the morning discovered a proa close by them filled with Malays. They told them that they were bound with the
old man to Sawyah. The Malays took them at their word and
c, ried them there instead of to Dungally, which was a lucky
escape to them for that time. Whilst residing at Sawyah the old
priest carried Captain Woodward to an island in the bay of Sawyah, which he granted to him, and in compliment called it Steersman's island; steersman being the appellation by which Captain
Woodward was distinguished by the natives. After staying some
time in Sawyah and making sago, which they bartered for fish and
cocoa-nuts, they left the place and proceeded to Dumpolis, a little
to the southward of Sawyah. Juan Hadgee soon left his place
for Tomboo about a days' sail south, where he had business.
Here Captain Woodward and his men also followed him. The old
priest was willing to assist them to escape from here, but was evidently unable to do it, Tomboo being under the direction of the
Rajah of Dungally.

Fortunately they succeeded in stealing a canoe in the night,
and once more shoving off, they directed their course to a small
island in the bay, where they landed at daybreak. Not being able
to find water here as they expected, they landed at another point
of land, which they knew to be uninhabited. Having obtained
water and repaired their canoe, they directed their course to Macassar, which was then about five degrees to the southward.
After coasting along the island for the space of eight days, during
which time they were twice very nearly taken by the Malays,
they arrived at a part of the island of Celebes, which was very
thickly inhabited.

They passed many towns and saw many proas within the harbors. Having observed a retired place, they landed to procure
some fresh water, but they had hardly got a draught each, when two
canoes were seen coming to the very place where they were.
They immediately shoved off and kept on their course all day.
Just as the sun went down they discovered two canoes not far
from them fishing. As soon as the natives saw them they made
the best of their way to the shore. Captain Woodward wished to
inquire the distance to Macassar, but not being able to stop them
he made for one of two canoes which he saw at a distance lying
at anchor. Being told that the captain was below and asleep
he went down and awakened him. He came on deck with three
or four men all armed with spears, and inquired where they were
going. Captain Woodward told him to Macassar and inquired of
him the distance to that place. He answered that it would take
a month and a day to reach it. Captain Woodward told him it was
not true, and made the best of his way off. The Malays however
made chase, but Captain Woodward and his men by putting out to
sea and making great exertion, soon lost sight of them and were
able again to stand in towards the land.

At daylight they discovered a number of fishing canoes, two of which made towards them. They let them come alongside as there was only one man in each. One of them came on board and Captain Woodward put the same question to him respecting Macassar. He first said it would take thirty days to reach there and asked them to go on shore and see the Rajah. But they declined doing this, and he afterwards acknowledged that a proa could go there in two days.

They then left the canoe and sailed along the coast. At evening they perceived a proa full of Malay men set off from the shore. It was soon along side, and four or five of them jumping into the boat they nearly upset her, and thus Captain Woodward and his men were again prisoners of the Malays. They were carried to a town called Pamboon and then conducted to the Rajah's house. The Rajah demanded of them whence they came and whither they were going. Captain Woodward answered the same as before; he also told him that they must go immediately, and must not be stopped. They had now become so familiar with dangers and with captures, and were also so much nearer Macassar, than they could have expected after so many narrow escapes that they became more and more desperate and confident, from the persuasion that they should at last reach their destined port.

In the morning Captain Woodward again waited on the Rajah and begged to be sent to Macassar; telling him that the Governor had sent for them, who would stop all his proas at Macassar if he detained them. After thinking on it a short time, he called the captain of a proa, and delivered the prisoners to him, telling him to carry them to Macassar, and if he could get any thing for them, to take it, but if not to let them go. The proa not being ready they stayed in their canoe three days, quite overcome by their many hardships and fatigues. Captain Woodward having had no shirt, the sun had burnt his shoulder so as to lay it quite bare and produce a bad sore. Here he caught cold, and was soon attacked with a violent fever, so that by the time the proa was ready to sail he was unable to stand. He was carried and laid on the deck without a mat or any kind of clothing. The cold nights and frequent showers of rain would without doubt have killed him, had he not been kept alive by the hopes of reaching Macassar, the thoughts of which kept up all their spirits.

They landed at Macassar on the 15th of June 1795, after a voyage of about nineteen days from Tomboo, and after having been two years and five months in captivity; the reckoning which Captain Woodward kept during that time, being wrong only one day

SHIPWRECK OF THE BLINDENHALL ON THE INACCESSIBLE ISLAND.

After fortune and victory had finally abandoned Napoleon on the field of Waterloo, and it had been determined by the belligerent powers that the fortress of St. Helena should be the life prison of the fallen Emperor, the British government deemed it a measure of prudence to occupy Tristan Da Cunha, situated about twenty degrees south of St. Helena, and which, in the event of any plot for a rescue, it was apprehended might have afforded a secure rendezvous, and offered considerable facilities for combined and ulterior arrangements. In pursuance of that determination, a company of artillery was stationed on Tristan da Cunha, a temporary framed barrack was erected, a fort constructed, provisions were laid up, a few milch cows and calves were landed, and the British flag waved over the melancholy waste!

About thirty-five miles from Tristan da Cunha stands, on a base of solid rock, the Inaccessible Island.

In 1820-1, the Blindenhall, free trader, bound for Bombay, partly laden with broadcloths, was prosecuting her voyage, and being driven by adverse winds and currents, more to the westward and southward than her course required, it became desirable to make Tristan da Cunha, in order to ascertain and rectify the reckoning. It was while steering to effect this purpose, that one morning a passenger, who chanced to be on deck earlier than usual, observed great quantities of sea-weed occasionally floating alongside. This excited some alarm, and a man was immediately sent aloft to keep a good look-out. The weather was then extremely hazy, though moderate; the weeds continued—all were on the alert; they shortened sail, and the boatswain piped for breakfast. In less than ten minutes, " Breakers a-head!" startled every soul, and in a moment all were on deck. " Breakers starboard!—breakers larboard!—breakers all around!" was the ominous cry a moment afterwards, and all was confusion. The words were scarcely uttered, when—and before the helm was up—the ill-fated ship struck, and, after a few tremendous shocks against the sunken reef, she parted about midship. Ropes and stays were cut away—all rushed forward, as if instinctively, and had barely reached the forecastle, when the stern and quarter broke asunder with a violent crash, and sunk to rise no more. Two of the seamen miserably perished; the rest, including officers, passengers, and crew, held on about the head and bows;—the struggle was for life!

At this moment the Inaccessible Island, which till then had been veiled in clouds and thick mist, appeared frowning above the haze. The wreck was more than two miles from the frightful shore. The base of the Island was still buried in impenetrable gloom In this perilous extremity one was for cutting away the anchor, which had been got up to the cat-head in time of need; another was for cutting down the foremast, (the foretopmast being already by the board). The fog totally disappeared, and the black rocky island stood in all its rugged deformity before their eyes! Suddenly the sun broke out in full splendor, as if to expose more clearly to the view of the sufferers their dreadful predicament. Despair was in every bosom; death, arrayed in all its terrors, seemed to hover over the wreck. But exertion was required, and Providence inspired unhoped for fortitude;—every thing that human energy could devise was effected; and the wreck on which all eagerly clung, was miraculously drifted by the tide and wind, between ledges of sunken rocks and thundering breakers, until after the lapse of six hours, it entered *the only spot* on the island where a landing was possibly practicable, for all the other parts of the coast consisted of perpendicular cliffs of granite rising from amidst deafening surf, to the height of twenty, forty, and sixty feet. As the shore was neared, a raft was prepared, and on this a few paddled for the cove;—at last the wreck drove right in; ropes were instantly thrown out; and the crew and passengers (except two who had been crushed in the wreck,) including three ladies and a female attendant, were providentially snatched from the watery grave, which a few short hours before had appeared inevitable,—and safely landed on the beach. Evening had now set in, and every effort was made to secure whatever could be saved from the wreck: bales of cloth, cases of wine, a few boxes of cheese, some hams, the carcass of the milch cow that had been washed on shore, buckets, tubs, butts, a seaman's chest (containing a tinder-box, and needles and thread), with a number of elegant mahogany turned bed-posts, part of an investment for the India market, were got on shore. The rain poured down in torrents, all hands were busily at work to procure a shelter from the weather, and with the bed-posts and broadcloths, and part of the foresail, as many tents were soon pitched as there were individuals in the island.

Drenched with the sea and with the rain,—hungry, cold, and comfortless, thousands of miles from their native land, almost beyond expectation of human succor, hope nearly annihilated, the shipwrecked voyagers retired to their tents, some devoutly to prostrate themselves in humble thankfulness before that merciful Being who had so wonderfully delivered them from destruction, others to rest after the dreadful fatigue by which they were exhausted, and some to drown their cares in wine. In the morning the wreck had gone to pieces; and planks and spars and whatever had floated in, were eagerly dragged on shore. No sooner was the unfortunate ship broken up, than, deeming themselves freed from the bonds of authority, many began to secure whatever came to land; and the captain, officers, passengers and crew, were now reduced to the same level, and obliged to take their turn to fetch water, and explore the island for food. The work of exploring was soon over: there was not a bird, nor a quadruped, nor a single tree to be seen! All was barren and desolate. The low parts were scattered over with stones and sand, and a few stunted weeds, reeds, fern and other plants. The top of the mountain was found to consist of a fragment of original table-land, very marshy, and full of deep sloughs, intersected with small rills of water, pure and pellucid as crystal, and a profusion of wild parsley and celery. The prospect was one dreary scene of destitution, without a single ray of hope to relieve the misery of the desponding crew. After some days the dead cow, hams and cheese were consumed, and from one end of the Island to the other, not a morsel of food could be seen. Even the celery began to fail. A few bottles of wine, which, for security, had been secreted under ground, only remained. Famine now began to threaten;—every stone near the sea was examined for shell fish, but in vain.   In this extremity, as the Quarter-master's wife was sitting at her tent door, with the child crying at her breast, faint and exhausted,—a group of half starved seamen passed by, when one of them turning round exclaimed " *by — that will make a drop of broth, if nothing else turns up!*" The observation spoke daggers to the poor creature. On the return of night, as the poor hungry wretches were squatting in sullen dejection round their fires, on a sudden hundreds of birds from seaward came actually flying through the flames; many fell dead, scorched o suffocated, and thus were the sufferers again rescued for a time from the horrors which so imminently beset them. For several nights in succession, similar flocks came in, and by multiplying their fires, a considerable supply was secured.

These visits however ceased at length, and the wretched party were again exposed to the most severe privation. When their stock of wild fowl had been exhausted for more than two days, each began to fear they were now approaching that sad point of necessity, when between death and casting lots who should be sacrificed to serve for food for the rest, no alternative remains. While horror at the bare contemplation of an extremity so repulsive occupied the thoughts of all, the horizon was observed to be suddenly obscured, and presently clouds of penguins lighted on the island. The low grounds were actually covered; and before the evening was dark, the sand could not be seen for the numbers of eggs, which like a sheet of snow, lay on the surface of the earth! The penguins continued on the island four or five days, when, as if by signal, the whole took their flight, and were never seen again. A few were killed, but the flesh was so extremely rank and nauseous, that it could not be eaten. The eggs were col-

jected, and dressed in all manner of ways, and supplied abundance
of food for upwards of three weeks. At the expiration of that
period, famine once more seemed inevitable; the third morning
began to dawn upon the unfortunate company, after their stock
of eggs were exhausted; they had now been without food for
more than forty hours, and were fainting and dejected,—when, as
though this desolate rock were really a land of miracles, a man
came running up to the encampment, with the unexpected and
joyful tidings, that " millions of sea-cows had came on shore!"
The crew climbed over the ledge of rocks which flanked their
tents, and the sight of a shoal of manatees immediately beneath
them gladdened their hearts. These came in with the flood, and
were left in the puddles between the broken rocks of the cove.
This supply continued for two or three weeks. The flesh was
mere blubber and quite unfit for food, for not a man could retain
it on his stomach, but the liver was excellent, and on this they
subsisted. In the meantime, the carpenter with his gang had
constructed a boat, and four of the men had adventured in her
for Tristan da Cunha, in hopes of ultimately extricating their
fellow sufferers from their perilous situation. Unfortunately the
boat was lost, whether carried away by the violence of the currents that set in between the islands, or dashed to pieces against
the breakers, was never known, for no vestige of the boat or the
crew was ever seen. Before the manatees, however, began to
quit the shore, a second boat was launced; and in this, an officer and some seamen made a second attempt, and happily
succeeded in effecting their landing, after much labor, on the
island of Governor Glass. He received them most cordially, and
with humanity, which neither time, nor place, nor total seclusion
from the world had enfeebled or impaired; he instantly launched
his boat, and, unawed by considerations of personal danger,
hastened, at the risk of his life, to deliver his shipwrecked countrymen from the calamities they had so long endured. He made
repeated trips, surmounted all difficulties, and fortunately succeeded in safely landing them on his own island, after they had been
exposed for nearly three months to the horrors of a situation
almost unparalleled in the recorded sufferings of seafaring men

---

THE CLIFFS OF DOVER

Dover, a seaport town of England, in the county of Kent, is
situated on a small stream which falls into the harbor. It lies in
a valley almost surrounded by chalky cliffs, from the precipitation
of some of which serious accidents have ensued. Dover consists

chiefly of three long streets converging to one point; the upper part called the town, and the lower the pier. It is defended by a strong and spacious castle, including an area of about thirty-five acres; and all the neighboring heights are fortified. It occupies a lofty eminence, steep and rugged towards the town and harbor, and presents a precipitous cliff three hundred and twenty feet higher than the sea. Some antiquaries have ascribed its origin to the Romans under Julius; and it is certain that a Roman pharos, or watch-tower, whose site exhibits a modern redoubt, stood in the neighborhood. It consists of numerous edifices,

Dover Castle

among which are many towers, erected at different times, and al designated by particular names. The keep, which stands in the upper court is ninety-two feet high, is in good preservation, and is used as a magazine. Water is drawn from wells three hundred and seventy feet deep to supply the garrison.

The castle makes a distinguished figure in history, and was once deemed impregnable; but it was surprised and taken by a very small party of the parliamentary forces in the ign of Charles I. Near the edge of the cliff there is a beautiful piece of brass ordnance, twenty-four feet long, and carrying a twelve pound ball: it is finely ornamented by figures in bas relief, and was made at Utrecht in 1544. Among the recent improvements, and fortifications resulting from the apprehension of invasion by the French, are subterraneous works and casemates capable of accommodating two thousand men.

Dover is one of the Cinque Ports. The harbor can receive vessels of four hundred or five hundred tons, and is defended by strong batteries. It is the principal place of embarkation to France, and employs twenty-seven packets for that purpose. The channel is about twenty-two miles wide. There are hot and cold baths here, and the town is much resorted to in summer for sea-bathing. Samphire is still gathered from the cliffs as in the days of Shakspeare, and employed in making a fine flavored pickle.

About six miles from Dover, between Bologne and Folkstone is a narrow submarine hill, called the *Rip-raps*, about a quarter of a mile broad, and ten miles long, extending eastward, towards the Goodwin sands. Its materials are boulder-stones, adventitious to many strata. The depth of water on it, 'n very low spring tides, is only fourteen feet. The fishermen from Folkstone have often touched it with a fifteen feet oar: so that it is justly the dread of navigators. Many a tall ship has struck on it, and sunk instantly into twenty-one fathoms of water. In July, 1782, the Belleisle, of sixty-four guns, struck and lay on it during three hours; but, by starting her beer and water, got clear off. It is said that the breadth of the straits between Dover and Calais, is diminishing; and that they are two miles narrower than they were in ancient times. An accurate observer for fifty years remarks that the increased height of water, from a decrease of breadth, has been apparent, even in that space.

THE MARINER'S HYMN.

Launch thy bark, Mariner!
Christian! God speed thee—
Let loose the rudder-bands—
Good angels lead thee!
Set thy sails warily,
Tempests will come—
Steer thy bark steadily,
Christian! steer home '

Look to the weather-bow,
Breakers are round thee—
Let fall thy plummet now,
Shallows may ground thee
Reef in the foresail, there '
Hold the helm fast!—
So—let the vessel wear—
There swept the blast.

What of the night, watchman '
What of the night?
"Cloudy—all quiet—
No land yet—all's right'

Be wakeful—be vigilant—
Danger may be
At an hour when all seemest
Securest to thee.

How gains the leak so fast?
Clear out the hold—
Hoist up the merchandise—
Heave out thy gold!
There—let the ingots go!
Now the ship rights—
Huzza! the harbour's near—
Lo! the red lights!

Slacken not sail yet
At inlet or island;
Straight for the beacon steer,
Straight for the high-land:
Crowd all thy canvass on,
Cut through the foam—
Christian! Cast anchor now—
Heaven is thy home!"

AN ACCOUNT OF THE WHALE-FISHERY;

WITH ANECDOTES OF THE DANGERS &c. ATTENDING IT.

Historians, in general, have given to the Bis-cayans the credit
of having first practised the fishery for the whale; the English,
and afterwards the Dutch are supposed to have followed in
the pursuit. It was prosecuted by the Norwegians so early as
the ninth century, and by the Icelanders about the eleventh. It
was not till the seventeenth century, however, that the whale fishery was engaged in by the maritime nations of Europe as an important branch of commerce.

The crew of a whale-ship usually consists of forty to fifty men,
comprising several classes of officers, such as harpooners, boat-
steerers, line-managers, &c., together with fore-mast-men, land-
men, and apprentices. As a stimulus to the crew in the fishery,
every individual, from the master down to the boys, besides his
monthly pay, receives either a gratuity for every size fish caught
during the voyage, or a certain sum for every ton of oil which the
cargo produces. Masters and harpooners receive a small sum
before sailing, in place of monthly wages; and if they procure no
cargo whatever, they receive nothing more for their voyage; but
in the event of a successful fishing, their advantages are considerable.

The *crow's nest* is an apparatus placed on the main-top-mast, or top-gallant-mast head, as a watch tower for the officer on the look out. It is closely defended from the wind and cold, and is furnished with a speaking-trumpet, a telescope, and rifle. The most favorable opportunity for prosecuting the fishery in the Greenland seas, commonly occurs with north, north-west or west winds. At such times the sea is smooth, and the atmosphere, though cloudy and dark, is generally free from fog and snow. The fishers prefer a cloudy to a clear sky; because in very bright weather, the sea becomes illuminated, and the shadows of the whale-boats are so deeply impressed in the water by the beams of the sun that the whales are apt to take the alarm. Fogs are only so far unfavorable as being liable to endanger the boats by shutting out the sight of the ship. A well constructed whale-boat floats lightly and safely on the water,—is capable of being rowed with great speed, and readily turned round,—it is of such capacity that it carries six or seven men, seven or eight hundred weight of whale-lines, and various other materials, and yet retains the necessary properties of safety and speed. Whale-boats being very liable to receive damage, both from whales and ice, are always *carvel-built*,—a structure which is easily repaired. The instruments of general use in the capture of the whale, are the harpoon and lance. There is, moreover, a kind of harpoon which is shot from a gun, but being difficult to adjust, it is seldom used. Each boat is likewise furnished with a "jack" or flag fastened to a pole, intended to be displayed as a signal whenever a whale is harpooned. The crew of a whale-ship are separated into divisions, equal in number to the number of the boats. Each division, consisting of a harpooner, a boat-steerer, and a line manager, together with three or four rowers, constitutes a "boat's crew."

On fishing stations, when the weather is such as to render the fishery practicable, the boats are always ready for instant service. The crow's nest is generally occupied by one of the officers, who keeps an anxious watch for the appearance of a whale. The moment that a fish is seen, he gives notice to the "watch upon deck,' part of whom leap into a boat, are lowered down, and push off towards the place. If the fish be large, a second boat is despatched to the support of the other; and when the whole of the boats are sent out, the ship is said to have "a loose fall." There are several rules observed in approaching a whale to prevent the animal from taking the alarm. As the whale is dull of hearing, but quick of sight, the boat-steerer always endeavors to get behind it; and, in accomplishing this, he is sometimes justified in taking a circuitous rout. In calm weather, where guns are not used, the greatest caution is necessary before a whale can be reached; smooth careful rowing is always requisite, and sometimes sculling is practised. It is a primary consideration with the harpooner, always to place his boat as near as possible to the spot in which he expects the fish to rise, and he conceives himself successful in the attempt when the fish " comes up within a start,' that is, within the distance of about two hundred yards.

Whenever a whale lies on the surface of the water, unconcious of the approach of its enemies, the hardy fisher rows directly upon it; and an instant before the boat touches it, buries his harpoon in its back. The wounded whale, in the surprise and agony of the moment, makes a convulsive effort to escape. Then is the moment of danger. The boat is subjected to the most violent blows from its head, or its fins, but particularly from its ponderous tail, which sometimes sweeps the air with such tremendous fury, that both boat and men are exposed to one common destruction.

The head of the whale is avoided, because it cannot be penetrated with the harpoon; but any part of the body, between the head and the tail, will admit of the full length of the instrument, without danger of obstruction. · The moment that the wounded whale disappears, a flag is displayed; on sight of which, those on watch in the ship, give the alarm, by stamping on the deck, accompanied by shouts of " a fall." At the sound of this, the sleeping crew are roused, jump from their beds, rush upon deck, and crowd into the boats. The alarm of " a fall," has a singular effect on the feelings of a sleeping person, unaccustomed to hearing it. It has often been mistaken as a cry of distress. A landsman, seeing the crew, on an occasion of a fall, leap into the boats in their shirts, imagined that the ship was sinking. He therefore tried to get into a boat himself, but every one of them being fully manned, he was refused. After several fruitless endeavors to gain a place among his comrades, he cried out, in evident distress, " What shall I do?—Will none of you take me in?"

The first effort of a " fast-fish," or whale that has been struck, is to escape from the boat by sinking under water. After this, it pursues its course directly downward, or reappears at a little distance, and swims with great celerity, near the surface of the water. It sometimes returns instantly to the surface, and gives evidence of its agony by the most convulsive throes. The downward course of a whale is, however, the most common. A whale, struck near the edge of any large sheet of ice, and passing underneath it, will sometimes run the whole of the lines out of one boat. The approaching distress of a boat, for want of line, is indicated by the elevation of an oar, to which is added a second, a third, or even a fourth, in proportion to the nature of the exigence. The utmost care and attention are requisite, on the part of every person in the boat, when the lines are running out; fatal consequences having been sometimes produced by the most trifling neglect When the line happens to " run foul," and cannot be cleared on the instant, it sometimes draws the boat under water; on which, if no auxiliary boat, or convenient piece of ice, be at hand, the crew are plunged into the sea, and are obliged to trust to their oars or their skill in swimming. for supporting themselves on the surface

Captain Scoresby relates an accident of this kind, which happened on his first voyage to the whale-fishery. A thousand fathoms of line were already out, and the fast-boat was forcibly pressed against the side of a piece of ice. The harpooner, in his anxiety to retard the flight of the whale, applied too many turns of the line round the bollard, which, getting entangled, drew the boat beneath the ice. Another boat, providentially was at hand, into which the crew had just time to escape. The whale, with near two miles' length of line, was, in consequence of the accident, lost, but the boat was recovered.

The average stay under water, of a wounded whale, is about thirty minutes. When it re-appears, the assisting boats make for the place with their utmost speed, and as they reach it, each harpooner plunges his harpoon into its back, to the amount of three, four, or more, according to the size of the whale. It is then actively plied with lances, which are thrust into its body, aiming at its vitals. The sea to a great extent around is dyed with its blood, and the noise made by its tail in its dying struggle, may be heard several miles. In dying, it turns on its back or on its side; which circumstance is announced by the capturers with the striking of their flags, accompanied with three lively huzzas!

Whales are sometimes captured, with a single harpoon, in the space of fifteen minutes. Sometimes they resist forty or fifty hours, and at times they will break three or four lines at once, or tear themselves clear off the harpoons, by the violence of their struggles. Generally the capture of a whale depends on the activity of the harpooner, the state of the wind and weather, or the peculiar conduct of the animal itself. Under the most favorable circumstances, the length of time does not exceed an hour. The general average may be stated at two hours. Instances have occured where whales have been taken without being struck at all, simply by entangling themselves in the lines that had been used to destroy others, and struggling till they were drowned or died of exhaustion.

The fishery for whales, when conducted at the margin of those wonderful sheets of ice, called fields, is, when the weather is fine, and the refuge for ships secure, the most agreeable and sometimes the most productive of all other ways. When the fish can be observed " blowing " in any of the holes in a field, the men travel over the ice and attack it with lances, to turn it back. As connected with this subject, Captain Scoresby relates the following circumstance, which occurred under his own observation.

On the eighth of July 1813, the ship Esk lay by the edge of a large sheet of ice, in which there were several thin parts, and some holes. Here a whale being heard blowing, a harpoon, with a line fastened to it, was conveyed across the ice, from a boat on guard, and the harpooner succeeded in striking the whale, at the distance of three hundred and fifty yards from the verge. It dragged out ten lines, (2400 yards,) and was supposed to be seen blowing in different holes in the ice. After some time it made its appearance on the exterior, and was again struck, at the moment it was about to go under the second time. About an hundred yards from the edge, it broke the ice where it was a foot thick, with its head, and respired through the opening. It then pushed forward, breaking the ice as it advanced, in spite of the lances constantly directed against it. At last it reached a kind of basin in the field, where it floated on the surface without any incumbrance from ice. Its back being fairly exposed, the harpoon struck from the boat on the outside, was observed to be so slightly entangled, that it was ready to drop out. Some of the officers lamented this circumstance, and wished that the harpoon might be better *fast*; at the same time observing that if it should slip out, either the fish would be lost, or they would be under the necessity of flinching it where it lay, and of dragging the blubber over the ice to the ship; a kind and degree of labor every one was anxious to avoid. No sooner was the wish expressed, and its importance explained, than a young and daring sailor stepped forward, and offered to strike the harpoon deeper. Not at all intimidated by the surprise manifested on every countenance at such a bold proposal, he leaped on the back of the living whale, and cut the harpoon out with his pocket knife. Stimulated by his gallant example, one of his companions proceeded to his assistance. While one of them hauled upon the line and held it in his hands, the other set his shoulder against the end of the harpoon, and though it was without a stock, contrived to strike it again into the fish more effectually than at first! The whale was in motion before they had finished. After they got off its back, it advanced a considerable distance, breaking the ice all the way, and survived this novel treatment ten or fifteen minutes. This daring deed was of essential service. The whale fortunately sunk spontaneously after it expired; on which it was hauled out under the ice by the line and secured without farther trouble. It proved a mighty whale; a very considerable prize.

When engaged in the pursuit of a large whale, it is a necessary precaution for two boats at all times to proceed in company, that the one may be able to assist the other, on any emergency. With this principle in view, two boats from the Esk were sent out in chase of some large whales, on the 13th of June 1814. No ice was within sight. The boats had proceeded some time together, when they separated in pursuit of two whales, not far distant from each other; when, by a singular coincidence, the harpooners each struck his fish at the same moment. They were a mile from the ship. Urgent signals for assistance were displayed by each boat, and in a few minutes one of the harpooners was

obliged to slip the end of his line.   Fortunately the other fish did
not descend so deep, and the lines in the boat proved adequate
for the occasion.   One of the fish being then supposed to be lost,
five of the boats out of seven attended on the fish which yet re
mained entangled, and speedily killed it.   A short time afterwards,
the other fish supposed to be lost, was descried at a little distance
from the place where it was struck;—three boats proceeded
against it;—it was immediately struck, and in twenty minutes also
killed.   Thus were fortunately captured two whales, both of which
had been despaired of.   They produced near forty tons of oil,
value, at that time 1400l.   The lines attached to the last fish were
recovered with it.

Before a whale can be *flensed*, as the operation of taking off the
fat and whalebone is called, some preliminary measures are requisite.   These consist in securing the whale to a boat, cutting away
the attached whale-lines, lashing the fins together, and towing it
to the ship.   Some curious circumstances connected with these
operations, may be mentioned here.

In the year 1816, a fish was, to all appearance killed by the
crew of the Esk.   The fins were partly lashed, and the tail on the
point of being secured, and all the lines excepting one, were cut
away, the fish meanwhile lying as if dead.   To the alarm, however, of the sailors, it revived, began to move, and pressed forward in a convulsive agitation; soon after it sunk in the water to
some depth, and then died.   One line fortunately remained attached to it, by which it was drawn to the surface and secured.

A suspension of labor is generally allowed after the whale has
been secured aside of the ship, and before the commencement of
the operation of *flensing*.   An unlucky circumstance once occurred
in an interval of this kind.   At that period of the fishery, (forty
or fifty years ago,) when a single stout whale, together with the
bounty, was found sufficient to remunerate the owners of a ship
for the expenses of the voyage, great joy was exhibited on the
capture of a whale, by the fishers.   They were not only cheered
by a dram of spirits, but sometimes provided with some favorite
" mess," on which to regale themselves, before they commenced
the arduous task of flensing.   At such a period, the crew of an
English vessel had captured their first whale.   It was taken to
the ship, placed on the lee-side, and though the wind blew a strong
breeze, it was fastened only by a small rope attached to the fin.
In this state of supposed security, all hands retired to regale themselves, the captain himself not excepted.   The ship being at a
distance from any ice, and the fish believed to be fast, they made
no great haste in their enjoyment.   At length, the specksioneer,
or chief harpooner, having spent sufficient time in indulgence and
equipment, with an air of importance and self-confidence, proceeded on deck, and naturally turned to look on the whale.   To
his astonishment it was not to be seen.   In some alarm he looked

a-stern, a-head, on the other side, but his search was useless: the ship drifting fast, had pressed forcibly upon the whale, the rope broke, the fish sunk and was lost. The mortification of this event may be conceived, but the termination of their vexation will not easily be imagined, when it is known, that no other opportunity of procuring a whale occurred during the voyage. The ship returned home *clean.*

Flensing in a *swell* is a most difficult and dangerous undertaking: and when the swell is at all considerable, it is commonly impracticable. No ropes or blocks are capable of bearing the jerk of the sea. The harpooners are annoyed by the surge, and repeatedly drenched in water; and are likewise subject to be wounded by the breaking of ropes or hooks of tackles, and even by strokes from each other's knives. Hence accidents in this kind of flensing are not uncommon. The harpooners not unfrequently fall into the whale's mouth, when it is exposed by the removal of a surface of blubber; where they might easily be drowned, but for the prompt assistance which is always at hand.

One of the laws of the fishery universally adhered to, is, that whenever a whale is loose, whatever may be the case or circumstances, it becomes a free prize to the first person who gets hold of it. Thus, when a whale is killed, and the flensing is prevented by a storm, it is usually taken in tow; if the rope by which it is connected with the ship should happen to break, and the people of another ship should seize upon it while disengaged, it becomes their prize. The following circumstance, which occurred a good many years ago, has a tendency to illustrate the existing Greenland laws.

During a storm of wind and snow several ships were beating to windward, under easy sail, along the edge of a pack. When the storm abated and the weather cleared, the ships steered towards the ice. Two of the fleet approached it, about a mile asunder, abreast of each other, when the crews of each ship accidentally got sight of a dead fish at a little distance, within some loose ice. Each ship now made sail, to endeavor to reach the fish before the other; which fish being loose, would be a prize to the first who could get possession of it. Neither ship could out sail the other, but each contrived to press forward towards the prize. The little advantage one of them had in distance, the other compensated with velocity. On each bow of the two ships, was stationed a principal officer, armed with a harpoon in readiness to discharge. But it so happened that the ships came in contact with each other when within a few yards of the fish, and in consequence of the shock with which their bows met, they rebounded to a considerable distance. The officers at the same moment discharged their harpoons, but all of them fell short of the fish. A hardy fellow who was second mate of the leeward ship immediately leaped overboard and with great dexterity swam to the whale, se.zed it by the

fin, and proclaimed it his prize. It was, however, so swollen
that he was unable to climb upon it, but was obliged to remain
shivering in the water until assistance should be sent. His captain elated with his good luck, forgot, or at least neglected his
brave second mate; and before he thought of sending a boat to
release him from his disagreeable situation, prepared to moor his
ship to an adjoining piece of ice. Meanwhile the other ship
tacked, and the master himself stepped into a boat, pushed off
and rowed deliberately towards the dead fish. Observing the
trembling seaman still in the water holding by the fin, he addressed him with, " Well my lad, you have got a fine fish here,"—to
which after a natural reply in the affirmative, he added, " but
do'nt you find it very cold?"—" Yes," replied the shivering
sailor, " I'm almost starved. I wish you would allow me to come
into your boat until our's arrive." This favor needed no second
solicitation; the boat approached the man and he was assisted into
it. The fish being again loose and out of possession, the captain
instantly struck his harpoon into it, hoisted his flag, and claimed
his prize! Mortified and displeased as the other master felt at
this trick, for so it certainly was, he had nevertheless no redress,
but was obliged to permit the fish to be taken on board of his
competitor's ship, and to content himself with abusing the second
mate for want of discretion, and condemning himself for not
having more compassion on the poor fellow's feeling, which would
have prevented the disagreeable misadventure.

Those employed in the occupation of killing whales, are, when
actually engaged, exposed to danger from three sources, viz. from
the ice, from the climate, and from the whales themselves. The
ice is a source of danger to the fishers, from overhanging masses
falling upon them,—from the approximation of large sheets of ice
to each other, which are apt to crush or upset the boats,—from
their boats being stove and sunk by large masses of ice, agitated
by a swell,—and from the boats being enclosed and beset in a
pack of ice, and their crews thus prevented from joining their
ships.

On the commencement of a heavy gale of wind, May 11th.
1813, fourteen men put off in a boat from the Volunteer of Whitby, with the view of setting an anchor in a large piece of ice, to
which it was their intention of mooring the ship. The ship
approached on a signal being made, the sails were clewed up,
and a rope fixed to the anchor; but the ice shivering with the violence of the strain when the ship fell astern, the anchor flew out
and the ship went adrift. The sails being again set, the ship was
reached to the eastward (wind at north) the distance of about
two miles; but in attempting to wear and return, the ship, instead
of performing the evolution, scudded a considerable distance to
the leeward, and was then reaching out to sea; thus leaving fourteen of her crew to a fate most dreadful, the fulfilment of which

seemed almost inevitable. The temperature of the air was 15° or 16° of Fahr., when these poor wretches were left upon a detached piece of ice, of no considerable magnitude, without food, without shelter from the inclement storm, deprived of every means of refuge except in a single boat, which, on account of the number of men, and the violence of the storm, was incapable of conveying them to their ship. Death stared them in the face whichever way they turned, and a division in opinion ensued. Some were wishful to remain on the ice, but the ice could afford them no shelter to the piercing wind, and would probably be broken to pieces by the increasing swell: others were anxious to attempt to join their ship while she was yet in sight, but the force of the wind, the violence of the sea, the smallness of the boat in comparison to the number of men to be conveyed, were objections which would have appeared insurmountable to any person but men in a state of despair. Judging, that by remaining on the ice, death was but retarded for a few hours, as the extreme cold must eventually benumb their faculties, and invite a sleep which would overcome the remains of animation,—they determined on making the attempt of rowing to their ship. Poor souls, what must have been their sensations at that moment,—when the spark of hope yet remaining was so feeble, that a premature death even to themselves seemed inevitable. They made the daring experiment, when a few minutes' trial convinced them, that the attempt was utterly impracticable. They then with longing eyes, turned their efforts towards recovering the ice they had left, but their utmost exertions were unavailing. Every one now viewed his situation as desperate; and anticipated, as certain, the fatal event which was to put a period to his life. How great must have been their delight, and how overpowering their sensations, when at this most critical juncture a ship appeared in sight! She was advancing directly towards them; their voices were extended and their flag displayed. But although it was impossible they should be heard, it was not impossible they should be seen. Their flag was descried by the people on board the ship, their mutual courses were so directed as to form the speediest union, and in a few minutes they found themselves on the deck of the Lively of Whitby, under circumstances of safety! They received from their townsmen the warmest congratulations; and while each individual was forward in contributing his assistance towards the restoration of their benumbed bodies, each appeared sensible that their narrow escape from death was highly providential. The forbearance of God is wonderful. Perhaps these very men a few hours before, were impiously invoking their own destruction, or venting imprecations upon their fellow beings! True it is that the goodness of the Almighty extendeth over all his works, and that while ' Mercy is his darling attribute,'—' Judgment is his strange work.'

The most extensive source of danger to the whale-fisher, when actively engaged in his occupation, arises from the object of his pursuit. Excepting when it has young under its protection, the whale generally exhibits remarkable timidity of character. A bird perching on its back alarms it; hence, the greater part of the accidents which happen in the course of its capture, must be attributed to adventitious circumstances on the part of the whale, or to mismanagement or fool-hardiness on the part of the fishers.

A harpooner belonging to the Henrietta of Whitby, when engaged in lancing a whale, into which he had previously struck a harpoon, incautiously cast a little line under his feet that he had just hauled into the boat, after it had been drawn out by the fish. A painful stroke of his lance induced the whale to dart suddenly downward; his line began to run out from beneath his feet, and in an instant caught him by a turn round his body. He had but just time to cry out, " Clear away the line,"—" O dear!" when he was almost cut asunder, dragged overboard, and never seen afterwards. The line was cut at the moment, but without avail. The fish descended a considerable depth, and died; from whence it was drawn to the surface by the lines connected with it, and secured.

While the ship Resolution navigated an open lake of water, in he 81st degree of north latitude, during a keen frost and strong north wind, on the 2d of June 1806, a whale appeared, and a boat put off in pursuit. On its second visit to the surface of the sea, it was harpooned. A convulsive heave of the tail, which succeeded the wound, struck the boat at the stern; and by its reaction, projected the boat-steerer overboard. As the line in a moment dragged the boat beyond his reach, the crew threw some of their oars towards him for his support, one of which he fortunately seized. The ship and boats being at a considerable distance, and the fast-boat being rapidly drawn away from him, the harpooner cut the line, with the view of rescuing him from his dangerous situation. But no sooner was this act performed, than to their extreme mortification they discovered, that in consequence of some oars being thrown towards their floating comrade, and others being broken or unshipped by the blow from the fish, one oar only remained; with which, owing to the force of the wind, they tried in vain to approach him. A considerable period elapsed, before any boat from the ship could afford him assistance, though the men strained every nerve for the purpose. At length, when they reached him, he was found with his arms stretched over an oar, almost deprived of sensation. On his arrival at the ship, he was in a deplorable condition. His clothes were frozen like mail, and his hair constituted a helmet of ice. He was immediately conveyed into the cabin, his clothes taken off, his limbs and body dried and well rubbed, and a cordial administered to him which he drank. A dry shirt and stockings were then put upon

him, and he was laid in the captain's bed.　After a few hours,
sleep he awoke, and appeared considerably restored, but complained of a painful sensation of cold.　He was, therefore, removed to his own *birth*, and one of his messmates ordered to lie
on each side of him, whereby the diminished circulation of the
blood was accelerated, and the animal heat restored.　The shock
on his constitution, however, was greater than was anticipated
He recovered in the course of a few days, so as to be able to engage in his ordinary pursuits; but many months elapsed, before
his countenance exhibited its wonted appearance of health.

The Aimwell of Whitby, while cruising the Greenland seas,
in the year 1810, had boats in chase of whales on the 26th of
May.　One of them was harpooned.　But instead of sinking
immediately on receiving the wound, as is the most usual manner
of the whale, this individual only dived for a moment, and rose
again beneath the boat, struck it in the most vicious manner with
its fins and tail, stove it, upset it, and then disappeared.　The
crew, seven in number, got on the bottom of the boat; but the
unequal action of the lines, which for some time remained entangled with the boat, rolled it occasionally over, and thus plunged
the crew repeatedly into the water.　Four of them, after each
immersion, recovered themselves and clung to the boat; but the
other three, one of whom was the only person acquainted with
the art of swimming, were drowned before assistance could arrive.　The four men on the boat being rescued and conveyed to
the ship, the attack on the whale was continued, and two more
harpoons struck.　But the whale irritated, instead of being ener-
vated by its wounds, recommenced its furious conduct.　The sea
was in a foam.　Its tail and fins were in awful play; and in a
short time, harpoon after harpoon drew out, the fish was loosened
from its entanglements and escaped.

In the fishery of 1812, the Henrietta of Whitby suffered a
similar loss.　A fish which was struck very near the ship, by a
blow of its tail, stove a small hole in the boat's bow.　Every in
dividual shrinking from the side on which the blow was impressed,
aided the influence of the stroke, and upset the boat.　They all
clung to it while it was bottom up; but the line having got entangled among the thwarts, suddenly drew the boat under water, and
with it part of the crew.　Excessive anxiety among the people in
the ship, occasioned delay in sending assistance; so that when
the first boat arrived at the spot, two survivors only out of six
men were found.

During a fresh gale of wind in the season of 1809, one of the
Resolution's harpooners struck a sucking whale.　Its mother being near, all the other boats were disposed around, with the hope
of entangling it　The old whale pursued a circular route round
its cub, and was followed by the boats; but its velocity was so
considerable, that they were unable to keep pace with it　Being

in the capacity of harpooner on this occasion myself, I proceeded to the chase, after having carefully marked the proceedings of the fish. I selected a situation, in which I conceived the whale would make its appearance, and was in the act of directing my crew to cease rowing, when a terrible blow was struck on the boat. The whale I never saw, but the effect of the blow was too important to be overlooked. About fifteen square feet of the bottom of the boat were driven in; it filled, sunk, and upset in a moment. Assistance was providentially at hand, so that we were all taken up without injury, after being but a few minutes in the water. The whale escaped; the boat's lines fell out and were lost, but the boat was recovered.

A remarkable instance of the power which the whale possesses in its tail, was exhibited within my own observation, in the year 1807. On the 29th of May, a whale was harpooned by an officer belonging to the Resolution. It descended a considerable depth; and, on its re-appearance, evinced an uncommon degree of irritation! It made such a display of its fins and tail, that few of the crew were hardy enough to approach it. The captain, (Captain Scoresby's father,) observing their timidity, called a boat, and himself struck a second harpoon. Another boat immediately followed, and unfortunately advanced too far. The tail was again reared into the air, in a terrific attitude,—the impending blow was evident,—the harpooner, who was directly underneath, leaped overboard,—and the next moment the threatened stroke was impressed on the centre of the boat, which it buried in the water. Happily no one was injured. The harpooner who leaped overboard, escaped certain death by the act,—the tail having struck the very spot on which he stood. The effects of the blow were astonishing. The keel was broken,—the gunwales, and every plank, excepting two, were cut through,—and it was evident that the boat would have been completely divided, had not the tail struck directly upon a coil of lines. The boat was rendered useless.

Instances of disasters of this kind, occasioned by blows from the whale, could be adduced in great numbers,—cases of boats being destroyed by a single stroke of the tail, are not unknown, —instances of boats having been stove or upset, and their crews wholly or in part drowned, are not unfrequent,—and several cases of whales having made a regular attack upon every boat which came near them, dashed some in pieces, and killed or drowned some of the people in them, have occurred within a few years, even under my own observation.

The Dutch ship Gort-Moolen, commanded by Cornelius Gerard Ouwekaas, with a cargo of seven fish, was anchored in Greenland in the year 1660. The captain, perceiving a whale a-head of his ship, beckoned his attendants, and threw himself into a boat. He was the first to approach the whale; and was fortunate enough to harpoon it before the arrival of the second boat, which was on the advance. Jacques Vienkes, who had the direction of it, joined his captain immediately afterwards, and prepared to make a second attack on the fish, when it should remount again to the surface. At the moment of its ascension, the boat of Vienkes happening unfortunately to be perpendicularly above it, was so suddenly and forcibly lifted up by a stroke of the head of the whale, that it was dashed to pieces before the harpooner could discharge his weapon. Vienkes flew along with the pieces of the boat, and fell upon the back of the animal. This intrepid seaman, who still retained his weapon in his grasp, harpooned the whale on which he stood; and, by means of the harpoon and the line, which he never abandoned, he steadied himself firmly upon the fish, notwithstanding his hazardous situation, and regardless of a considerable wound that he received in his leg, in his fall along with the fragments of the boat. All the efforts of the other boats to approach the whale, and deliver the harpooner, were futile. The captain, not seeing any other method of saving his unfortunate companion, who was in some way entangled with the line, called to him to cut it with his knife, and betake himself to swimming. Vienkes, embarrassed and disconcerted as he was, tried in vain to follow this counsel. His knife was in the pocket of his drawers; and, being unable to support himself with one hand, he could not get it out. The whale, meanwhile, continued advancing along the surface of the water with great rapidity, but fortunately never attempted to dive. While his comrades despaired of his life, the harpoon by which he held, at length disengaged itself from the body of the whale. Vienkes being thus liberated, did not fail to take advantage of this circumstance; he cast himself into the sea, and, by swimming, endeavored to regain the boats which continued the pursuit of the whale. When his shipmates perceived him struggling with the waves, they redoubled their exertions. They reached him just as his strength was exhausted, and had the happiness of rescuing this adventurous harpooner from his perilous situation.

Captain Lyons of the Raith of Leith, while prosecuting the whale-fishery on the Labrador coast, in the season of 1802, discovered a large whale at a short distance from the ship. Four boats were despatched in pursuit, and two of them succeeded in approaching it so closely together, that two harpoons were struck at the same moment. The fish descended a few fathoms in the direction of another of the boats, which was on the advance, rose accidentally beneath it, struck it with its head, and threw the boat, men, and apparatus, about fifteen feet into the air. It was inverted by the stroke, and fell into the water with its keel upwards. All the people were picked up alive by the fourth boat, which was just at hand, excepting one man, who having got entangled in the boat, fell beneath it and was unfortunately drowned. The

fish was soon afterwards killed.   The following engraving is
illustrative of this remarkable accident.

Perhaps one of the most remarkable instances of the destruction of a vessel by a whale, is that of the ship Essex, which sailed
from Nantucket about the year 1820.   She was commanded by
Captain Pollard, and had entered the Pacific Ocean, where she
was employed some time in catching whales.   One day the seamen harpooned a young whale.   In this species the affection of
the mother towards its young, is very strong; as was evinced in a
remarkable manner on this occasion.   When the mother of the
young whale found that her progeny was killed, she went to some
distance from the ship, and then, rushing through the water, came
against the stern of the vessel with the greatest violence.   So
tremendous was the force of the shock, that several of the timbers
were loosened, and the vessel pitched and reeled on the water, as
if struck by a whirlwind.   Nor was the whale satisfied with this.
Again she went to the distance of more than a mile, and then,
shooting through the waves with incredible swiftness, came like a
thunderbolt upon the bow of the vessel.   The timbers were instantly beaten in, and the ship began to fill with water.   Scarcely
had the crew sufficient time to get into their boat, before she went
down.   In this sudden and frightful situation, the poor seamen
now found themselves.   They were upon the wide-heaving and
perilous ocean in an open boat, and far from any land.   If the
whale had come upon them in the condition they were now in,
they must have inevitably perished.   But they saw no more of the

monster. Captain Pollard and his men for several days suffered severe hardships from the weather, and from a want of water and food. At length the delightful vision of another ship broke upon their sight. They were all taken on board, and finally reached their native country in safety.

In 1822, two boats belonging to the ship Baffin went in pursuit of a whale. John Carr was harpooner and commander of one of them. The whale they pursued led them into a vast shoal of his own species; they were so numerous that their blowing was incessant, and they believed that they did not see fewer than an hundred. Fearful of alarming them without striking any, they remained for a while motionless. At last, one rose near Carr's boat, and he approached, and fatally for himself, harpooned it. When he struck, the fish was approaching the boat; and, passing very rapidly, jerked the line out of its place over the stern, and threw it upon the gunwale. Its pressure in this unfavorable position so careened the boat, that the side was pulled under water, and it began to fill. In this emergency, Carr, who was a brave, active man, seized the line, and endeavored to relieve the boat by restoring it to its place; but, by some circumstance which was never accounted for, a turn of the line flew over his arm, dragged him overboard in an instant, and drew him under the water, never more to rise. So sudden was the accident, that only one man, who was watching him, saw what had happened; so that when the boat righted, which it immediately did, though half full of water, the whole crew on looking round inquired what had become of Carr. It is impossible to imagine a death more awfully sudden and unexpected. The invisible bullet could not have effected more instantaneous destruction. The velocity of the whale at its first descent is from thirteen to fifteen feet per second. Now as this unfortunate man was adjusting the line at the water's very edge, where it must have been perfectly tight, owing to its obstruction in running out of the boat, the interval between the fastening the line about him and his disappearance could not have exceeded the third part of a second of time, for in one second only he must have been dragged ten or twelve feet deep. Indeed he had not time for the least exclamation; and the person who saw his removal, observed that it was so exceeding quick, that though his eye was upon him at the moment, he could scarcely distinguish his figure as he disappeared.

As soon as the crew recovered from their consternation, they applied themselves to the needful attention which the lines required. A second harpoon was struck from the accompanying boat on the raising of the whale to the surface, and some lances were applied, but this melancholy occurrence had cast such a damp on all present, that they became timid and inactive in their subsequent duties. The whale when nearly exhausted was allowed to remain some minutes unmolested, till having recovered some degree of energy, it made a violent effort and tore itself away from both harpoons. The exertions of the crews thus proved fruitless, and were attended with serious loss.

Innumerable instances might be adduced of the perils and disasters to which our whalemen are subject; of their never tiring fortitude and daring enterprise; but we believe the examples we have given alone will sufficiently convey a full and correct idea of the customs and dangers of the whale-fishery.

THE LOSS OF THE PEGGY.

On the 28th of September, 1785, the Peggy, commanded by Captain Knight, sailed from the harbor of Waterford, Ireland, for the port of New York, in America.

Here it is necessary to observe, that the Peggy was a large unwieldy Dutch-built ship, about eight hundred tons burden, and had formerly been in the Norway, and timber trade, for which, indeed, she seemed, from her immense bulk, well calculated. There being no freight in readiness for America, we were under the necessity of taking in ballast: which consisted of coarse gravel and sand, with about fifty casks of stores, fresh stock, and vegetables, sufficient to last during the voyage; having plenty of room, and having been most abundantly supplied by the hospitable neighbourhood, of which we were about to take our leave.

We weighed anchor, and with the assistance of a rapid tide and pleasant breeze, soon gained a tolerable offing: we continued under easy sail the remaining part of the day, and towards sunset lost sight of land.

Sept. 29th, made the old head of Kingsale; the weather continuing favorable, we shortly came within sight of Cape Clear, from whence we took our departure from the coast of Ireland.

Nothing material occurred for several days, during which time we traversed a vast space of the Western Ocean.

Oct. 12th, the weather now became hazy and squally;—all hands turned up to reef top-sails, and strike top-gallant-yards.—Towards night the squalls were more frequent, indicating an approaching gale:—We accordingly clued, reefed top-sails, and struck top-gallant-masts; and having made all snug aloft, the ship weathered the night very steadily.

On the 13th the crew were imployed in setting up the rigging, and occasionally pumping, the ship having made much water during the night. The gale increasing as the day advanced, occasioned the vessel to make heavy rolls, by which an accident happened, which was near doing much injury to the captain's cabin. A puncheon of rum, which was lashed on the larboard side of the cabin, broke loose, a sudden jerk having drawn asunder the cleets to which it was fastened. By its velocity it stove in the state rooms, and broke several utensils of the cabin furniture. The writer of this, with much difficulty, escaped with whole limbs: but not altogether unhurt, receiving a painful bruise on the right foot: having, however, escaped from the cabin, the people on deck were given to understand that the rum was broke loose. The word *rum* soon attracted the sailors' attention, and this cask being the ship's only stock, they were not tardy (as may be supposed) in rendering their assistance to double lash, what they anticipated —the delight, of frequently splicing the main-brace therewith during their voyage.

On the 14th the weather became moderate, and the crew were employed in making good the stowage of the stores in the hold, which had given way during the night;—shaking reefs out of the top-sails, getting up top-gallant-masts and yards, and rigging out studding-sails. All hands being now called to dinner, a bustle and confused noise took place on deck. The captain (who was below) sent the writer of this to discover the cause thereof, but before he could explain, a voice was crying out in a most piteous and vociferous tone. The captain and chief mate jumped on deck, and found the crew had got the cook laid on the windlass, and were giving him a most severe cobbing with a flat piece of his own fire wood. As soon as the captain had reached forward, he was much exasperated with them for their precipitate conduct, in punishing without his knowledge and permission, and having prohibited such proceedings in future cases, he inquired the cause of their grievance. The cook, it seems, having been served out fresh water to dress vegetables for all hands, had inadvertently used it for some other purpose, and boiled the greens in a copper of salt water, which rendered them so intolerably tough, that they were not fit for use; consequently the sailors had not their expected garnish, and a general murmur taking place, the above punishment was inflicted.

A steady breeze ensuing, all sails filled, and the ship made way, with a lofty and majestic air; and at every plunge of her bows, which were truly Dutch-built, rose a foam of no small appearance.

During four days the weather continued favorable, which flattered the seamen with a speedy sight of land.

On the 19th we encountered a very violent gale, with an unusual heavy sea:—The ship worked greatly, and took in much water through her seams;—the pumps were kept frequently going. At mid-day, while the crew were at dinner, a tremendous sea struck the ship right aft, which tore in the cabin windows, upset the whole of the dinner, and nearly drowned the captain, mate, and myself, who was at that time holding a dish on the table, while the captain was busily employed in carving a fine goose, which much to our discomfiture, was entirely drenched by the salt water. Some of the coops were washed from the quarter-deck, and several of the poultry destroyed.

In consequence of the vessel shipping so great a quantity of water, the pumps were doubly manned, and soon gained on her. The gale had not in the least abated during the night. The well was plummed, and there was found to be a sudden and alarming increase of water. The carpenter was immediately ordered to examine the ship below, in order to find the cause of the vessel's making so much water. His report was, she being a very old vessel, her seams had considerably opened by her laboring so much, therefore, could devise no means at present to prevent the evil. He also reported, the mizen-mast to be in great danger.

The heel of the mizen-mast being stepped between decks (a very unusual case, but probably it was placed there in order to make more room for stowage in the after-hold) was likely to work from its step, and thereby might do considerable damage to the ship.

The captain now held a consultation with the officers, when it was deemed expedient to cut the mast away without delay: this was accordingly put into execution the following morning, as soon as the day, made its appearance. The necessary preparations having been made, the carpenter began hewing at the mast, and quickly made a deep wound. Some of the crew were stationed ready to cut away the stays and lanyards, whilst the remaining part was anxiously watching the momentary crash which was to ensue; the word being given to cut away the weather-lanyards, as the ship gave a lee-lurch, the whole of the wreck plunged, without further injury, into the ocean.

The weather still threatening a continuance, our principal employ was at the pumps, which were kept continually going. The sea had now rose to an alarming height, and frequently struck the vessel with great violence. Towards the afternoon, part of the starboard bulwark was carried away by the shock of a heavy sea, which made the ship broach-to, and before she could answer her helm again, a sea broke through the fore-chains, and swept away the caboose and all its utensils from the deck; fortunately for the cook he was assisting at the pumps at the time, or he inevitably must have shared the same fate as his galley.

Notwithstanding the exertions of the crew, the water gained fast, and made its way into the hold, which washed a great quantity of the ballast through the timber-holes into the hull, by which the suckers of the pumps were much damaged, and thereby frequently choked. By such delays the leaks increased rapidly. We were under the necessity of repeatedly hoisting the pumps on deck, to apply different means which were devised to keep the sand from entering, but all our efforts proved ineffectual, and the pumps were deemed of no further utility. There was now no time to be lost; accordingly it was agreed that the allowance of fresh water should be lessened to a pint a man; the casks were immediately hoisted from the hold, and lashed between decks. As the water was started from two of them, they were sawed in two, and formed into buckets, there being no other casks on board fit for that purpose; the whips were soon applied, and the hands began baling at the fore and after hatchways which continued without intermission the whole of the night, each man being suffered to take one hour's rest, in rotation.

The morning of the 22d presented to our view a most dreary aspect,—a dismal horizon encircling—not the least appearance of the gale abating—on the contrary, it seemed to come with redoubled vigor—the ballast washing from side to side of the ship at each roll, and scarce a prospect of freeing her. Notwithstanding these calamities, the crew did not relax their efforts. The main hatchway was opened and fresh buckets went to work; the captain and mate alternately relieving each other at the helm. The writer's station was to supply the crew with grog, which was plentifully served to them every two hours. By the motion of the ship the buckets struck against the combings of the hatchways with great violence, and in casting them in the hold to fill, they frequently struck on the floating pieces of timber which were generally used as chocks in stowing the hold. By such accidents the buckets were repeatedly stove, and we were under the necessity of cutting more of the water casks to supply their place. Starting the fresh water overboard was reluctantly done, particularly as we now felt the loss of the caboose, and were under the necessity of eating the meat raw, which occasioned us to be very thirsty. Night coming on, the crew were not allowed to go below to sleep; each man, when it came to his turn, stretched himself on the deck.

Oct. 23. Notwithstanding the great quantity of water baled from the vessel, she gained so considerably that she had visibly settled much deeper in the water. All hands were now called aft, in order to consult on the best measures. It was now unanimously resolved to make for the island of Bermudas, it being the nearest land. Accordingly we bore away for it, but had not sailed many leagues before we found that the great quantity of water in the vessel had impeded her steerage so much that she would scarcely answer her helm; and making a very heavy lurch, the ballast shifted, which gave her a great lift to the starboard, and rendered it very difficult to keep a firm footing on deck. The anchors which were stowed on the larboard bow were ordered to be cut away, and the cables which were on the orlop deck to be hove overboard in order to right her; but all this had a very trifling effect, for the ship was now become quite a log.

The crew were still employed in baling; one of whom, in pre-

venting a bucket from being stove against the combings, let go
his hold, and fell down the hatchway; with great difficulty he
escaped being drowned or dashed against the ship's sides.   Having got into a bucket which was instantly lowered, he was providentially hoisted on deck without any injury.

During the night the weather became more moderate, and on
the following morning, (*Oct.* 25), the gale had entirely subsided,
but left a very heavy swell.   Two large whales approached close
to the ship.   They sported round the vessel the whole of the day,
and after dusk disappeared.

Having now no further use of the helm, it was lashed down,
and the captain and mate took their spell at the buckets.   My
assistance having been also required, a boy of less strength,
whose previous business was to attend the cook, now took my former station of serving the crew with refreshments.   This lad had
not long filled his new situation of drawing out rum from the cask,
before he was tempted to taste it, and which having repeatedly
done he soon became intoxicated, and was missed on deck for
some time.   I was sent to look for him.   The spigot I perceived
out of the cask, and the liquor running about, but the boy I could
not see for some time; however looking down the lazeretto (the
trap-door of which was lying open), I found him fast asleep.   He
had luckily fallen on some sails which were stowed there, or he
must have perished.

On the 26th and 27th of October the weather continued quite
clear, with light baffling winds.   A man was constantly kept aloft
to look out for a sail.   The rest of the crew were employed at
the whips.

On the 28th the weather began to lower, and appeared inclined
for rain.   This gave some uneasiness, being apprehensive of a
gale.   The captain therefore directed the carpenter to overhaul
the long-boat, caulk her, and raise a streak which orders were
immediately complied with: but when he went to his locker for
oakum, he found it plundered of nearly the whole of his stock—
all hands were therefore set to picking, by which means he was
soon supplied.

It was totally clear on the 29th, with a fresh breeze, but the
ship heeled so much that her gunwale at times was under water,
and the crew could scarcely stand on deck.   All hands were now
ordered to assemble aft, when the captain, in a short address,
pointed out the most probable manner by which they could be
saved.   All agreed in opinion with him, and it was resolved that
the long-boat should be hoisted out as speedily as possible, and
such necessaries as could be conveniently stowed, to be placed
in her.   Determined no longer to labor at the buckets, the vessel,
which could not remain above water many hours after we had
ceased baling, was now abandoned to her fate

I now began to reflect on the small chance we had of being

saved—twenty-two people in an open boat—upwards of three hundred miles from land—in a boisterous climate, and the whole crew worn out with fatigue! The palms of the crew s hands were already so flayed it could not be expected that they could do much execution with the oars—while thus reflecting on our perilous situation, one of our oldest seamen, who at this moment was standing near me, turned his head aside to wipe away a tear—I could not refrain from sympathizing with him—my heart was already full! —The captain perceiving my despondency bade me be of good cheer, and called me a young lubber.

The boat having been hoisted out, and such necessaries placed in her as were deemed requisite, one of the hands was sent aloft to lash the colors downwards to the main-top-mast shrouds; which having done, he placed himself on the cross-trees, to look around him, and almost instantly hallooed out,—" A sail."—It would be impossible to describe the ecstatic emotions of the crew: every man was aloft, in order to be satisfied; though, a minute before, not one of the crew was able to stand upright.

The sail was on our weather-bow, bearing right down on us with a smart breeze. She soon perceived us, but hauled her wind several times, in order to examine our ship. As she approached nearer she clearly perceived our calamitous situation, and hastened to our relief.

She proved to be a Philadelphia schooner, bound to Cape Francois, in St. Domingo. The captain took us all on board in the most humane and friendly manner, and after casting our boat adrift, proceeded on his voyage. When we perceived our ship from the vessel on which we were now happily on board, her appearance was truly deplorable.

The captain of the schooner congratulated us on our fortunate escape, and expressed his surprise that the ship should remain so long on her beam ends, in such a heavy sea, without capsizing. We soon began to distance the wreck, by this time very low in the water, and shortly after lost sight of her.

The evening began to approach fast, when a man loosing the main-top-sail, descried a sail directly in the same course on our quarter. We made sail for her and soon came within hail of her. She proved to be a brig from Glasgow, bound to Antigua. It was now determined, between the captains, that half of our people should remain in the schooner, and the captain, mate, eight of the crew, and myself, should get on board the brig. On our arival at Antigua we met with much kindness and humanity

THE MEDUSA.

In July, 1816, the French frigate the Medusa was wrecked on
the coast of Africa, when part of the ship's company took to their
boats; and the rest, to the number of one hundred and fifty, had
recourse to a raft hastily lashed together. In two hours after
pushing off for the shore, the people in the boats had the cruelty
to bear away and leave the raft, already laboring hard amid the
waves, and alike destitute of provisions, and instruments for navigation, to shift for itself. " From the moment," says M. Sevigne,
from whose affecting narrative this account is chiefly taken, " that
I was convinced of our being abandoned, I was strongly impressed with the crowd of dark and horrible images that presented
themselves to my imagination; the torments of hunger and thirst,
the almost positive certainty of never more seeing my country or
friends, composed the painful picture before my eyes; my knees
sunk under me, and my hands mechanically sought for something
to lay hold on; I could scarcely articulate a word. This state
soon had an end, and then all my mental faculties revived. Having silenced the tormenting dread of death, I endeavored to pour
consolation into the hearts of my unhappy companions, who were
almost in a state of stupor around me. No sooner, however, were
the soldiers and sailors roused from their consternation, than they
abandoned themselves to excessive despair, and cried furiously
out for vengeance on those who had abandoned them; each saw
his own ruin inevitable, and clamorously vociferated the dark reflections that agitated him." Some persons of a finer character
joined with M. Sevigne in his humane endeavors to tranquillize
the minds of these wretched sufferers; and they at last partially
succeeded, by persuading them that they would have an opportunity in a few days of revenging themselves on the people in the
boats. " I own," says M. Sevigne, " this spirit of vengeance animated every one of us, and we poured vollies of curses on the
boat's crew, whose fatal selfishness exposed us to so many evils
and dangers. We thought our sufferings would have been less
cruel, had they been partaken by the frigate's whole crew. Nothing
is more exasperating to the unhappy, than to think that those who
plunged them into misery, should enjoy every favor of fortune."
    After the first transports of passion had subsided, the sole efforts
of their more collected moments were directed to the means of
gaining the land, to procure provision. All that they had on board
the raft, consisted of twenty-five pounds of biscuit and some hogs-
heads of wine. The imperious desire of self-preservation silenced
every fear for a moment; they put up a sail on the raft, and every
one assisted with a sort of delerious enthusiasm; not one of them
foresaw the real extent of the peril by which they were surrounded

The day passed on quietly enough; but night at length came on; the heavens were overspread with black clouds; the winds unchained, raised the sea mountains high; terror again rode triumphant on the billow; dashed from side to side, now suspended betwixt life and death, bewailing their misfortune, and though certain of death, yet struggling with the merciless elements ready to devour them, the poor off-casts longed for the coming morn, as if it had been the sure harbinger of safety and repose. Often was the last doleful ejaculation heard of some sailor or soldier weary of the struggle, rushing into the embrace of death. A baker and two young cabin boys, after taking leave of their comrades, diliberately plunged into the deep. "*We are off*," said they, and instantly disappeared. Such was the commencement of that dreadful insanity which we shall afterwards see raging in the most cruel manner, and sweeping off a crowd of victims. In the course of the first night, twelve persons were lost from the raft.

"The day coming on," says M. Sevigne, "brought back a little calm amongst us; some unhappy persons, however, near me, were not come to their senses. A charming young man, scarcely sixteen, asked me every moment, 'When shall we eat?' He stuck to me, and followed me every where, repeating the same question. In the course of the day, Mr. Griffen threw himself into the sea, but I took him up again. His words were confused; I gave him every consolation in my power, and endeavored to persuade him to support courageously every privation we were suffering. But all my care was unavailing; I could never recall him to reason; he gave no sign of being sensible to the horror of our situation. In a few minutes he threw himself again into the sea; but by an effort of instinct, held to a piece of wood that went beyond the raft, and he was taken up a second time."

The hope of still seeing the boats come to their succour, enabled them to support the torments of hunger during this second day; but as the gloom of night returned, and every man began, as it were, to look in upon himself, the desire of food rose to an ungovernable height; and ended in a state of general delirium. The greater part of the soldiers and sailors, unable to appease the hunger that preyed upon them, and persuaded that death was now inevitable took the fatal resolution of softening their last moments by drinking of the wine, till they could drink no more. Attacking a hogshead in the centre of the raft, they drew large libations from it; the stimulating liquid soon turned their delirium into frenzy; they began to quarrel and fight with one another; and ere long, the few planks on which they were floating, between time and eternity, became the scene of a most bloody contest for momentary pre-eminence. No less than sixty-three men lost their lives on this unhappy occasion.

Shortly after, tranquillity was restored. "We fell," says M. Sevigne, "into the same state as before: this insensibility was so great, that next day I thought myself waking out of a disturbed sleep, asking the people round me if they had seen any tumult, or heard any cries of despair? Some answered, that they too had been tormented with the same visions, and did not know how to explain them. Many who had been most furious during the night, were now sullen and motionless, unable to utter a single word. Two or three plunged into the ocean, coolly bidding their companions farewell; others would say. 'Don't despair; I am going to bring you relief; you shall soon see me again.' Not a few even thought themselves on board the Medusa, amidst every thing they used to be daily surrounded with. In a conversation with one of my comrades, he said to me, 'I cannot think we are on a raft; I always suppose myself on board our frigate.' My own judgment, too, wandered on these points. M. Correard imagined himself going over the beautiful plains of Italy. M. Griflen said very seriously, 'I remember we were forsaken by the boats; but never fear, I have just written to Government, and in a few hours we shall be saved.' M. Correard asked quite as seriously, 'and have you then a pigeon to carry your orders so fast?'"

It was now the third day since they had been abandoned, and hunger began to be most sharply felt; some of the men, driven to desperation, at length tore off the flesh from the dead bodies that covered the raft, and devoured it. "The officers and passengers," says M. Sevigne, "to whom I united myself, could not overcome the repugnance inspired by such horrible food; we however tried to eat the belts of our sabres and cartouch boxes, and succeeded in swallowing some small pieces; but we were at last forced to abandon these expedients, which brought no relief to the anguish caused by total abstinence."

In the evening they were fortunate enough to take nearly two hundred flying fishes, which they shared immediately. Having found some gunpowder, they made a fire to dress them? but their portions were so small, and their hunger so great, that they added human flesh, which the cooking rendered less disgusting; the officers were at last tempted to taste of it. The horrid repast was followed with another scene of violence and confusion; a second engagement took place during the night, and in the morning only thirty persons were left alive on the fatal raft. On the fourth night, a third fit of despair swept off fifteen more; so that, finally, the number of miserable beings was reduced from one hundred and fifty, to fifteen.

"A return of reason," says M. Sevigne, "began now to enlighten our situation. I have no longer to relate the furious actions dictated by dark despair, but the unhappy state of fifteen exhausted creatures reduced to frightful misery. Our gloomy thoughts were fixed on the little wine that was left, and we contemplated with horror the ravages which despair and want had made amongst us. 'You are much altered,' said one of my

companions, seizing my hand, and melting into tears. Eight days
torments had rendered us no longer like ourselves. At length,
seeing ourselves so reduced, we summoned up all our strength,
and raised a kind of stage to rest ourselves upon. On this new
theatre we resolved to wait death in a becoming manner. We
passed some days in this situation, each concealing his despair
from his nearest companion. Misunderstanding, however, again
took place, on the tenth day after being on board the raft. After
a distribution of wine, several of our companions conceived the
idea of destroying themselves after finishing the little wine that
remained. 'When people are so wretched as we,' said they,
'they have nothing to wish for but death.' We made the
strongest remonstrances to them; but their diseased brains could
only fix on the rash project which they had conceived; a new
contest was therefore on the point of commencing, but at length
they yielded to our remonstrances. Many of us, after receiving
our small portion of wine, fell into a state of intoxication, and
then great misunderstandings arose.

"At other times we were pretty quiet, and sometimes our
natural spirits inspired a smile in spite of the horrors of our situation. Says one, 'if the brig is sent in search of us, let us pray
to God to give her the eyes of Argus,' alluding to the name of
the vessel which we supposed might come in search of us.

"The 17th in the morning, thirteen days after being forsaken,
while each was enjoying the delights of his poor portion of wine,
a captain of infantry perceived a vessel in the horizon, and announced it with a shout of joy. For some moments we were suspended between hope and fear. Some said, they saw the ship
draw nearer; others, that it was sailing away. Unfortunately,
these last were not mistaken, for the brig soon disappeared.
From excess of joy, we now sunk into despair. For my part,
I was so accustomed to the idea of death, that I saw it approach
with indifference. I had remarked many others terminate their
existence without great outward signs of pain; they first became
quite delirious, and nothing could appease them; after that, they
fell into a state of imbecility that ended their existence, like a lamp
that goes out for want of oil. A boy twelve years old, unable
to support these privations, sunk under them, after our being forsaken. All spoke of this fine boy as deserving a better fate; his
angelic face, his melodious voice, and his tender years, inspired
us with the tenderest compassion, for so young a victim devoted
to so frightful and untimely a death. Our oldest soldiers, and,
indeed, every one, eagerly assisted him as far as circumstances
permitted. But, alas! it was all in vain; neither the wine, nor
any other consolation, could save him, and he expired in M.
Coudin's arms. As long as he was able to move, he was continually running from one side of the raft to the other, calling out
for his mother, for water, and for food.

"About six o'clock, on the 17th, one of our companions looking out, on a sudden stretching his hands forwards, and scarcely able to breathe, cried out, ' *Here's the brig almost alongside;* and, in fact, she was actually very near. We threw ourselves on each other's necks with frantic transports, while tears trickled down our withered cheeks. She soon bore upon us within pistol shot, sent a boat, and presently took us all on board. We had scarcely escaped, when some of us became delirious again; a military officer was going to leap into the sea, as he said, to take up his pocket book; and would certainly have done so, but for those about him; others were affected in the same manner, but in a less degree.

"Fifteen days after our deliverance, I felt the species of mental derangement which is produced by great misfortunes; my mind was in a continual agitation, and during the night, I often awoke, thinking myself still on the raft; and many of my companions experienced the same effects. One François became deaf, and remained for a long time in a state of idiotism. Another frequently lost his recollection; and my own memory, remarkably good before this event, was weakened by it in a sensible manner.

"At the moment in which I am recalling the dreadful scenes to which I have been witness, they present themselves to my imagination like a frightful dream. All those horrible scenes from which I so miraculously escaped, seem now only as a point in my existence. Restored to health, my mind sometimes recalls those visions that tormented it, during the fever that consumed it. In those dreadful moments we were certainly attacked with a cerebral fever, in consequence of excessive mental irritation. And even now, sometimes in the night, after having met with any disappointment, and when the wind is high, my mind recalls the fatal raft I see a furious ocean ready to swallow me up; hands uplifted to strike me, and the whole train of human passions let loose; revenge, fury, hatred, treachery, and despair, surrounding me!"

THE MAIN-TRUCK, OR A LEAP FOR LIFE

"Stand still! How fearful
And dizzy 't is to cast one's eyes so low!"

"The murmuring surge,
That on th' unnumbered idle pebbles chafes,
Cannot be heard so high:—I 'll look no more;
Lest my brain turn, and the deficient sight
Topple down headlong."—*Shakspeare.*

Among the many agreeable associates whom my different cruisings and wanderings have brought me acquainted with, I can scarcely call to mind a more pleasant and companionable one than

Tom Scupper.   Poor fellow! he is dead and gone now—a victim to that code of false honor which has robbed the navy of too many of its choicest officers.   Tom and I were messmates during a short and delightful cruise, and, for a good part of the time, we belonged to the same watch.   He was a great hand to spin yarns, which, to do him justice, he sometimes told tolerably well; and many a long mid-watch has his fund of anecdotes and sea stories caused to slip pleasantly away.   We were lying, in the little schooner to which we were attached, in the open roadstead of Laguyra, at single anchor, when Tom told me the story which I am about to relate, as nearly as I can remember, in his own words.   A vessel from Baltimore had come into Laguyra that day, and by her I had received letters from home, in one of which there was a piece of intelligence that weighed very heavily on my spirits.   For some minutes after our watch commenced, Tom and I walked the deck in silence, which was soon, however, interrupted by my talkative companion, who perceiving my depression, and wishing to divert my thoughts, began as follows:

The last cruise I made in the Mediterranean was in old Iron sides, as we used to call our gallant frigate.   We had been backing and filling for several months on the western coast of Africa, from the Canaries down to Messurado, in search of slave traders; and during that time we had had some pretty heavy weather. When we reached the Straits, there was a spanking wind blowing from about west-south-west; so we squared away, and, without coming-to at the Rock, made a straight wake for old Mahon, the general rendezvous and place of refitting for our squadrons in the Mediterranean.   Immediately on arriving there, we warped in alongside the Arsenal quay, where we stripped ship to a girtline, broke out the holds, tiers, and store-rooms, and gave her a regular-built overhauling from stem to stern.   For awhile, every body was busy, and all seemed bustle and confusion.   Orders and replies, in loud and dissimilar voices, the shrill pipings of the different boatswain's mates, each attending to separate duties, and the mingled clatter and noise of various kinds of work, all going on the same time, gave something of the stir and animation of a dock-yard to the usually quiet arsenal of Mahon.   The boatswain and his crew were engaged in fitting a new gang of rigging; the gunner in repairing his breechings and gun-tackles; the fo'castle-men in calking; the top-men in sending down the yards and upper spars; the holders and waisters in whitewashing and holy stoning; and even the poor marines were kept busy, like beasts of burden, in carrying breakers of water on their backs On the quay, near the ship, the smoke of the armorer's forge which had been hoisted out and sent ashore, ascended in a thin black column through the clear blue sky; from one of the neighboring white stone warehouses the sound of saw and hammer told that the carpenters were at work; near by, a livelier rattling

drew attention to the cooper, who in the open air was tightning
the water-casks; and not far removed, under a temporary shed,
formed of spare studding-sails and tarpaulins, sat the sailmaker
and his assistants, repairing the sails, which had been rent or injured by the many storms we had encountered.

Many hands, however, make light work, and in a very few days
all was accomplished: the stays and shrouds were set up and new
rattled down; the yards crossed, the running rigging rove, and
sails bent; and the old craft, fresh painted and all a-taunt-o, looked as fine as a midshipman on liberty. In place of the storm-
stumps, which had been stowed away among the booms and other
spare spars, amidships, we had set up cap to'gallant-masts, and
royal-poles, with a sheave for skysails, and hoist enough for sky-
scrapers above them: so you may judge the old frigate looked
pretty taunt. There was a Dutch line-ship in the harbor; but
though we only carried forty-four to her eighty, her main-truck
would hardly have reached to our royal-mast-head. The side-
boys, whose duty it was to lay aloft and furl the skysails, looked
no bigger on the yard than a good-sized duff for a midshipman's
mess, and the main-truck seemed not half as large as the Turk's-
head-knot on the main-ropes of the accommodation ladder.

When we had got every thing ship-shape and man-of-war fashion, we hauled out again, and took our birth about half way
between the Arsenal and Hospital island; and a pleasant view it
gave us of the town and harbor of old Mahon, one of the safest
and most tranquil places of anchorage in the world. The water
of this beautiful inlet—which though it makes about four miles
into the land, is not much over a quarter of a mile in width—is
scarcely ever ruffled by a storm; and on the delightful afternoon
to which I now refer, it lay as still and motionless as a polished
mirror, except when broken into momentary ripples by the pad-
dles of some passing waterman. What little wind we had had in
the fore part of the day, died away at noon, and, though the first
dog-watch was almost out, and the sun was near the horizon, not
a breath of air had risen to disturb the deep serenity of the
scene. The Dutch liner, which lay not far from us, was so
clearly reflected in the glassy surface of the water, that there
was not a rope about her, from her main-stay to her signal hal-
liards, which the eye could not distinctly trace in her shadowy and
inverted image. The buoy of our best bower floated abreast our
larboard bow; and that, too, was so strongly imaged, that its entire bulk seemed to lie above the water, just resting on it, as if
upborne on a sea of molten lead; except when now and then, the
wringing of a swab, or the dashing of a bucket overboard from the
head, broke up the shadow for a moment, and showed the substance but half its former apparent size. A small polacca craft
had got underway from Mahon in the course of the forenoon, intending to stand over to Barcelona· but it fell dead calm just

before she reached the chops of the harbor; and there she lay as motionless upon the blue surface, as if she were only part of a mimic scene, from the pencil of some accomplished painter. Her broad cotton lateen-sails, as they hung drooping from the slanting and taper yards, shone with a glistening whiteness that contrasted beautifully with the dark flood in which they were reflected; and the distant sound of the guitar, which one of the sailors was listlessly playing on her deck, came sweetly over the water, and harmonized well with the quiet appearance of every thing around. The whitewashed walls of the lazaretto, on a verdant headland at the mouth of the bay, glittered like silver in the slant rays of the sun; and some of its windows were burnished so brightly by the level beams, that it seemed as if the whole interior of the edifice were in flames. On the opposite side, the romantic and pictur-esque ruins of fort St. Philip, faintly seen, acquired double beauty from being tipped with the declining light; and the clusters of ancient-looking windmills, which dot the green eminences along the bank, added, by the motionless state of their wings, to the effect of the unbroken tranquillity of the scene.

Even on board our vessel, a degree of stillness unusual for a man-of-war prevailed among the crew. It was the hour of their evening meal; and the low hum that came from the gun-deck had an indistinct and buzzing sound, which, like the tiny song of bees of a warm summer noon, rather heightened than diminished the charm of the surrounding quiet. The spar-deck was almost deserted. The quarter-master of the watch, with his spy-glass in his hand, and dressed in a frock and trowsers of snowy white-ness, stood aft upon the taffrel, erect and motionless as a statue, keeping the usual look-out. A group of some half a dozen sailors had gathered together on the fo'castle, where they were supinely ying under the shade of the bulwarks; and here and there, upon the gun-slides along the gangway, sat three or four others—one, with his clothes-bag beside him, overhauling his simple wardrobe; another working a set of clues for some favorite officer's hammock; and a third engaged, perhaps, in carving his name in rude letters upon the handle of a jack-knife, or in knotting a laniard with which to suspend it round his neck.

On the top of the boom cover, and in the full glare of the level sun, lay black Jake, the jig-maker of the ship, and a striking specimen of African peculiarities, in whose single person they were all strongly developed. His flat nose was dilated to unusual width, and his ebony cheeks fairly glistened with delight, as he looked up at the gambols of a large monkey, which, clinging to the main-stay, just above Jake's woolly head, was chattering and grinning back at the negro, as if there existed some means of mutual intelligence between them. It was my watch on deck and I had been standing several minutes leaning on the main fife-rail, amusing myself by observing the antics of the black and his congenial playmate; but at length, tiring of the rude mirth, had turned towards the taffrel, to gaze on the more agreeable features of that scene which I have feebly attempted to describe. Just at that moment a shout and a merry laugh burst upon my ear, and looking quickly round, to ascertain the cause of the unusual sound on a frigate's deck, I saw little Bob Stay (as we called our commodore's son) standing half the way up the main-hatch ladder, clapping his hands, and looking aloft at some object that seemed to inspire him with a deal of glee. A single glance to the main-yard explained the occasion of his merriment. He had been coming up from the gun-deck, when Jacko, perceiving him on the ladder, dropped suddenly down from the main-stay, and running along the boom-cover, leaped upon Bob's shoulder, seized his cap from his head, and immediately darted up the main-topsail sheet, and thence to the bunt of the mainyard where he now sat, picking threads from the tassal of his prize, and occasionally scratching his side, and chattering, as if with exultation for the success of his mischief. But Bob was a sprightly, active little fellow; and though he could not climb quite as nimble as a monkey, yet he had no mind to lose his cap without an effort to regain it. Perhaps he was the more strongly incited to make chase after Jacko, from noticing me to smile at his plight, or by the loud laugh of Jake, who seemed inexpressibly delighted at the occurrence, and endeavored to evince, by tumbling about the boom-cloth, shaking his huge misshapen head, and sundry other grotesque actions, the pleasures for which he had no words.

"Ha, you d—n rascal, Jocko, hab you no more respec' for de young officer, den to steal his cab? We bring you to de gangway, you black nigger, and gib you a dozen on de bare back for a tief."

The monkey looked down from his perch as if he understood the threat of the negro, and chattered a sort of defiance in answer.

"Ha, ha! Massa Stay, he say you mus' ketch him 'fore you flog him; and it's no so easy for a midshipman in boots to ketch a monkey barefoot."

A red spot mounted to the cheek of little Bob, as he cast one glance of offended pride at Jake, and then sprang across the deck to the Jacob's ladder. In an instant he was half-way up the rigging, running over the ratlines as lightly as if they were an easy flight of stairs, whilst the shrouds scarcely quivered beneath his elastic motion. In a second more his hand was on the futtocks.

"Massa Stay!" cried Jake, who sometimes, from being a favorite, ventured to take liberties with the younger officers, "Massa Stay, you best crawl through de lubber's hole—it take a sailor to climb a futtock shroud."

But he had scarcely time to utter his pretended caution, before

Bob was in the top. The monkey in the meanwhile had awaited his approach, until he had got nearly up the rigging, when it suddenly put the cap on its own head, and running along the yard to the opposite side of the top, sprang up a rope, and thence to the topmast backstay, up which it ran to the topmast cross-trees, where it again quietly seated itself, and resumed its work of picking the tassel to pieces. For several minutes I stood watching my little messmate follow Jacko from one piece of rig-ging to another, the monkey, all the while, seeming to exert only so much agility as was necessary to elude the pursuer, and paus-ing whenever the latter appeared to be growing weary of the chase. At last, by this kind of manoeuvring, the mischievous animal succeeded in enticing Bob as high as the royal-mast-head, when springing suddenly on the royal-stay, it ran nimbly down to the fore-to'gallant-mast head, thence down the rigging to the fore-top, when leaping on the foreyard, it ran out to the yard-arm, and hung the cap on the end of the studding-sail boom, where, taking its seat, it raised a loud and exulting chattering. Bob by this time was completely tired out, and, perhaps, unwilling to return to the deck to be laughed at for his fruitless chase, he sat down on the royal cross-trees; while those who had been attracted by the sport, returned to their usual avocations or amusements. The monkey, no longer the object of pursuit or attention, remained but a little while on the yard-arm; but soon taking up the cap, returned in towards the slings, and dropped it down upon deck.

Some little piece of duty occurred at this moment to engage me, as soon as which was performed I walked aft, and leaning my elbow on the taffrel, was quickly lost in the recollection of scenes very different from the small pantomime I had just been witnessing. Soothed by the low hum of the crew, and by the quiet loveliness of every thing around, my thoughts had travelled far away from the realities of my situation, when I was suddenly startled by a cry from black Jake, which brought me on the instant back to consciousness.

"My God! Massa Scupper," cried he, "Massa Stay is on de main-truck!"

A cold shudder ran through my veins as the word reached my ear. I cast my eyes up—it was too true! The adventurous boy, after resting on the royal cross-trees, had been seized with a wish to go still higher, and impelled by one of those impulses by which men are sometimes instigated to place themselves in situations of imminent peril without a possibility of good resulting from the exposure, he had climbed the skysail-pole, and, at the moment of my looking up, was actually standing on the main-truck! a small circular piece of wood on the very summit of the loftiest mast, and at a height so great from the deck that my brain turned dizzy as I looked up at him The reverse of Virgil's line was true in this instance. It was comparatively easy to ascend—but to de-scend—my head swam round, and my stomach felt sick at thought of the perils comprised in that one word. There was nothing above him or around him but the empty air—and beneath him, nothing but a point, a mere point—a small, unstable wheel, that seemed no bigger from the deck than the button on the end of a foil, and the taper skysail-pole itself scarcely larger than the blade. Dreadful temerity! If he should attempt to stoop, what could he take hold of to steady his descent? His feet quite covered up the small and fearful platform that he stood upon, and beneath that, a long, smooth, naked spar, which seemed to bend with his weight, was all that upheld him from destruction. An attempt to get down from "that bad eminence," would be almost certain death; he would inevitably lose his equilibrium, and be precipitated to the deck a crushed and shapeless mass. Such was the nature of the thoughts that crowded through my mind as I first raised my eye, and saw the terrible truth of Jake's excla-mation. What was to be done in the pressing and horrible exi gency? To hail him, and inform him of his danger, would be but to ensure his ruin. Indeed, I fancied that the rash boy already perceived the imminence of his peril; and I half thought that I could see his limbs begin to quiver, and his cheek turn deadly pale. Every moment I expected to see the dreadful catas-trophe. I could not bear to look at him, and yet could not with-draw my gaze. A film came over my eyes, and a faintness over my heart. The atmosphere seemed to grow thick, and to tremble and waver like the heated air around a furnace; the mast appeared to totter, and the ship to pass from under my feet. I myself had the sensations of one about to fall from a great height, and making a strong effort to recover myself, like that of a dreamer who fancies he is shoved from a precipice, I staggered up against the bulwarks.

When my eyes were once turned from the dreadful object to which they had been riveted, my sense and consciousness came back. I looked around me—the deck was already crowded with people. The intelligence of poor Bob's temerity had spread through the ship like wild-fire—as such news always will—and the officers and crew were all crowding to the deck to behold the appalling—the heart-rending spectacle. Every one, as he looked up, turned pale, and his eye became fastened in silence on the truck—like that of a spectator of an execution on the gallows—with a steadfast, unblinking and intense yet abhorrent gaze, as if momently expecting a fatal termination to the awful suspense No one made a suggestion—no one spoke. Every feeling, every faculty seemed to be absorbed and swallowed up in one deep, in tense emotion of agony. Once the first lieutenant seized the trumpet, as if to hail poor Bob, but he had scarce raised it to his lips when his arm dropped again, and sunk listlessly down beside him, as if from a sad consciousness of the utter inutility of what he had been going to say. Every soul in the ship was now on the spar-deck, and every eye was turned to the main-truck.

At this moment there was a stir among the crew about the gangway, and directly after another face was added to those on the quarter-deck—it was that of the commodore, Bob's father He had come alongside in a shore boat, without having been noticed by a single eye, so intense and universal was the interest that had fastened every gaze upon the spot where poor Bob stood trembling on the awful verge of fate. The commodore asked not a question, uttered not a syllable. He was a dark-faced, austere man, and it was thought by some of the midshipmen that he entertained but little affection for his son. However that might have been, it was certain that he treated him with precisely the same strict discipline that he did the other young officers, or if there was any difference at all, it was not in favor of Bob. Some, who pretended to have studied his character closely, affirmed that he loved his boy too well to spoil him, and that, intending him for the arduous profession in which he had himself risen to fame and eminence, he thought it would be of service to him to experience some of its privations and hardships at the outset.

The arrival of the commodore changed the direction of several eyes, which now turned on him to trace what emotions the danger of his son would occasion. But their scrutiny was foiled. By no outward sign did he show what was passing within. His eye still retained its severe expression, his brow the slight frown which it usually wore, and his lip its haughty curl. Immediately on reaching the deck, he had ordered a marine to hand him a musket, and with this stepping aft, and getting on the lookout-block, he raised it to his shoulder, and took a deliberate aim at his son, at the same time hailing him, without a trumpet, in his voice of thunder.

"Robert!" cried he, "jump! jump overboard! or I'll fire at you."

The boy seemed to hesitate, and it was plain that he was tottering, for his arms were thrown out like those of one scarcely able to retain his balance. The commodore raised his voice again, and in a quicker and more energetic tone cried,

"Jump! 't is your only chance for life."

The words were scarcely out of his mouth, before the body was seen to leave the truck and spring out into the air. A sound, between a shriek and groan burst from many lips. The father spoke not—sighed not—indeed he did not seem to breathe. For a moment of intense agony a pin might have been heard to drop on deck. With a rush like that of a cannon ball, the body descended to the water, and before the waves closed over it, twenty stout fellows, among them several officers, had dived from

the bulwarks. Another short period of bitter suspense ensued.
It rose—he was alive! his arms were seen to move!—he struck
out towards the ship!—and despite the discipline of a man-of-war
three loud huzzas, an outburst of unfeigned and unrestrainable.
joy from the hearts of our crew of five hundred men, pealed
through the air, and made the welkin ring. Till this moment,
the old commodore had stood unmoved. The eyes, that glistening with pleasure, now sought his face, saw that it was ashy pale.
He attempted to descend the horse-block, but his knees bent
under him; he seemed to gasp for breath, and put up his hand, as
if to tear open his vest; but before he accomplished his object,
he staggered forward, and would have fallen on the deck, had he
not been caught by old Black Jake. He was borne into his
cabin, where the surgeon attended him, whose utmost skill was
required to restore his mind to its usual equability and self-command, in which he at last happily succeeded. As soon as he
recovered from the dreadful shock, he sent for Bob, and had a
long confidential conference with him; and it was noticed when
the little fellow left the cabin that he was in tears. The next day
we sent down our taunt and dashy poles, and replaced them with
the stump-to'gallant-masts; and on the third, we weighed anchor,
and made sail for Gibraltar.

THE HARPOONER TRANSPORT.

The hired transport Harpooner, was lost near Newfoundland,
in November, 1818; she had on board three hundred and eighty
five men, women, and children, including the ship's company.
The passengers consisted of detachments of several regiments,
with their families, who were on their way to Quebec. On Saturday evening, November 10th, a few minutes after nine o'clock,
the second mate on watch called out, " the ship's aground;" at
which she slightly struck on the outermost rock of St. Shotts, in
the Island of Newfoundland. She beat over, and proceeded a
short distance, when she struck again, and filled; encircled among
rocks, the wind blowing strong, the night dark, and a very heavy
sea rolling, she soon fell over on her larboard beam end; and, to
heighten the terror and alarm, a lighted candle communicated
fire to some spirits in the master's cabin, which, in the confusion,
was with difficulty extinguished.

The ship still driving over the rocks, her masts were cut away,
by which some men were carried overboard. The vessel drifted
over, near the high rocks, towards the main. In this situation
every one became terrified: the suddenness of the sea rushing in,

carried away the births and stauncheons between decks, when
men, women, and children, were drowned, and many were killed
by the force with which they were driven against the lose baggage, casks, and staves, which floated below. All that possibly
could, got upon deck, but from the crowd and confusion that
prevailed, the orders of the officers and master to the soldiers
and seamen were unavailing; death staring every one in the face;
the ship striking on the rocks, as though she would instantly
upset. The shrieking and pressing of the people to the starboard
side was so violent, that several were much hurt. About eleven
o'clock, the boats on the deck were washed overboard by a heavy
sea: but even from the commencement of the disaster, the hopes
of any individual being saved were but very small.

From this time, until four o'clock the next morning, all on the
wreck were anxiously praying for the light to break upon them.
The boat from the stern was in the meanwhile lowered down,
when the first mate and four seamen, at the risk of their lives,
pushed off to the shore. They with difficulty effected a landing
upon the main land, behind a high rock, nearest to where the
stern of the vessel had been driven. The log-line was thrown
from the wreck, with a hope that they might lay hold of it; but
darkness, and the tremendous surf that beat, rendered it impracticable. During this awful time of suspense, the possibility of
sending a line to them by a dog occurred to the master: the animal was brought aft, and thrown into the sea with a line tied round
his middle, and with it he swam towards the rock upon which the
mate and seamen were standing. It is impossible to describe
the sensations which were excited at seeing this faithful dog struggling with the waves; and on reaching the summit of the rock
repeatedly dashed back again by the surf into the sea; until at
length, by unceasing exertions, he effected a landing. One end
of the line being on board, a stronger rope was hauled and fastened
to the rock.

At about six o'clock in the morning of the 11th, the first person
was landed by this means; and afterwards, by an improvement in
rigging the rope, and placing each individual in slings, they were
with greater facility extricated from the wreck; but during this
passage, it was with the utmost difficulty that the unfortunate
sufferers could maintain their hold, as the sea beat over them and
some were dragged to the shore in a state of insensibility. Lieutenant Wilson was lost, being unable to hold on the rope with
his hands; he was twice struck by the sea, fell backwards out of
the slings, and after swimming for a considerable time amongst
the floating wreck, by which he was struck on the head, he perished. Many who threw themselves overboard, trusting for their
safety to swimming, were lost: they were dashed to pieces by the
surf on the rocks, or by the floating pieces of the wreck

The rope at length, by constant working, and by swinging

3 .

across the sharp rock, was cut in two; and there being no means
of replacing it, the spectacle became more than ever terrific; the
sea beating over the wreck with great violence, washed numbers
overboard; and at last the wreck, breaking up at the stern from
midships and forecastle, precipitated all that remained into one
common destruction.

The parting of the ship was noticed by those on shore, and
signified with the most dreadful cry of " Go FORWARD!"—It is
difficult to paint the horror of the scene;—children clinging to
their parents for help; parents themselves struggling with death,
and stretching out their feeble arms to save their children, dying
within their grasp.

The total number of persons lost was two hundred and eight,
and one hundred and seventy-seven were saved.

Lieutenant Mylrea, of the 4th Veteran Battalion, one of the
oldest subalterns in the service, and then upwards of seventy
years of age, was the last person who quitted the wreck; when
he had seen every other person either safe, or beyond the power
of assistance, he threw himself on to a rock, from which he was
afterwards rescued.

Among the severest sufferers, was the daughter of Surgeon
Armstrong, who lost on this fatal night her father, mother, brother,
and two sisters!

The rock which the survivors were landed upon, was about one
hundred feet above the water, surrounded at the flowing of the
tide.   On the top of this rock they were obliged to remain during
the whole of the night, without shelter, food, or nourishment, exposed to wind and rain, and many without shoes.   The only
comfort that presented itself was a fire, which was made from
pieces of the wreck that had been washed ashore.

At daylight on the morning of the 12th, at low water, their
removal to the opposite land was effected, some being let down by
a rope, others slipping down a ladder to the bottom.   After they
crossed over, they directed their course to a house or fisherman's
shed, distant about a mile and a half from the wreck, where they
remained until the next day; the proprietor of this miserable shed
not having the means of supplying relief to so considerable a number as took refuge, a party went over land to Trepassy, about
fourteen miles distant, through a marshy country, not inhabited
by any human creature.   This party arrived at Trepassy, and reported the event to Messrs. Jackson, Burke, Sims, and the Rev.
Mr. Brown, who immediately took measures for alleviating the
distressed, by despatching men with provisions and spirits, and
to assist in bringing all those forward to Trepassy who could
walk.

On the 13th, in the evening, the major part of the survivors
(assisted by the inhabitants, who, during the journey carried
the weak and feeble upon their backs) arrived at Trepassy where

they were billeted, by order of the magistrate, proportionably upon each house.

There still remained at St. Shotts, the wife of a serjeant of the Veteran Battalion; with a child, of which she was delivered on the top of the rocks shortly after she was saved. A private, whose leg was broken, and a woman severely bruised by the wreck, were also necessarily left there.

Immediately after the arrival at Trepassy, measures were adopted for the comfort and refreshment of the detachments, and boats were provided for their removal to St. John's, where they ultimately arrived in safety.

COMMODORE BARNEY.

" The old Commodore,
The fighting old Commodore he."

No old Triton who has passed his calms under the bows of the long boat could say of Joshua Barney that he came into a master's berth through the cabin windows. He began at the rudiments, and well he understood the science. All his predilections were for the sea. Having deserted the counting room, young Barney, at the age of twelve, was placed for nautical instruction in a pilot boat at Baltimore, till he was apprenticed to his brother-in-law. At the age of fourteen, he was appointed second mate, with the approbation of the owners, and before he was sixteen he was called upon to take charge of his ship at sea, in which the master died. This was on a voyage to Nice. The ship was in such a state that it was barely possible to make Gibraltar, where for necessary repairs he pledged her for £700, to be repaid by the consignee at Nice, who however declined, and called in the aid of the Governor to compel Barney to deliver the cargo, which he had refused to do. He was imprisoned, but set at large on some intimation that he would do as desired, but when he came on board, he struck his flag, and removed his crew, choosing to consider his vessel as captured. He then set out for Milan, to solicit the aid of the British Ambassador there, in which he succeeded so well, that the authorities of Nice met him on his return to apologize for their conduct. The assignees paid the bond, and Barney sailed for Alicant, where his vessel was detained for the use of the great armada, then fitting out against Algiers, the fate of which was total and shameful defeat. On his return home, his employer was so well satisfied with his conduct, that he became his firm friend ever after. He soon offered himself as second in command on board the sloop Hornet, of ten guns, one of two ves

sels then preparing for a cruise under Commodore Hopkins, for
this was in the early part of the revolution. The sloop fell in
with a British tender, which she might have captured, but for
the timidity of the American captain. The tender, mistaking her
enemy, ran alongside and exposed herself to much danger. Barney, stood by one of the guns as the enemy came near, and was
about to apply the match, when the bold commander commanded
him to desist. Barney, whose spirit revolted at such a cause,
threw his match-stick at the captain, with such force that the iron
point stuck in the door of the round-house. This, in a youth not
seventeen, argued well for the pugnacity of the man. At the end
of this cruise, he volunteered on board the schooner Wasp, in
which he soon had a brush with the Roebuck and another frigate,
and with the aid of some galleys in which he had a command, the
enemy was forced to retreat, with more loss than honor. Barney,
for his good conduct in this affair, was appointed to the command
of the sloop Sachem, with the commission of Lieutenant, before
he was seventeen. Before the cruise, however, Captain Robinson took command of the Sachem, which soon had an action with
a letter-of-marque of superior force and numbers. It was well contested, and nearly half the crew of the brig were killed or wounded. In about two hours the letter-of-marque struck. The captors
secured a valuable prize, in a cargo of rum, and also a magnificent
turtle, intended as a present to Lord North, whose name was
marked on the shell. This acceptable West-Indian, Lieutenant
Barney presented to a better man than it had been designed for,
for he gave it to the Hon. R. Morris. On the return of the Sachem, both officers were transferred to a fine brig of fourteen
guns, the Andrew Doria, which forthwith captured the Racehorse,
of twelve guns, and a picked crew. This vessel was of the Royal
Navy, and had been detached by the Admiral purposely to take
the Doria; but, saith the proverb, if two men ride the same horse,
one must ride behind.

On this voyage a snow was captured, in which the Lieutenant
went as prize master, making up his crew partly of the prisoners.
Being hard by an enemy's ship, he discovered signs of mutiny
among his crew, and shot the ringleader in the shoulder; a proceeding that offered so little encouragement to his comrades, that
they obeyed orders, and made sail, but it was too late to escape
The purser of the frigate which captured him, was, on a subsequent occasion, so much excited as to strike Barney, who knocked
him down, and went further in his resentment than fair fighting
permits, for he kicked him down the gangway.—The commander
obliged the purser to apologize to Barney. Having been cap-
ured in the Virginia frigate, which ran aground at the Capes,
and was deserted by her commander, Barney, with five hundred
other prisoners, was sent round, in the St. Albans frigate, to New
York. As the prisoners were double in number to the crew

Barney formed a plan of taking the ship, which was defeated or prevented, by the treachery of a Frenchman.

"O for a curse to kill the slave,
    Whose treason, like a deadly blight,
Comes o'er the councils of the brave,
    To blast them in the hour of might."

Barney was a prisoner at New York, for five months, after which he took the command of a schooner of two guns, and eight men, with a cargo of tobacco for St. Eustatia, for he was better pleased to do a little than to do nothing. He was, however, taken, after a running fight, by boarding, by a privateer of four large guns and sixty men. His next cruise was with his friend Robinson, in a private ship of ten guns and thirty-five men, in which they encountered the British privateer Rosebud of sixteen guns and one hundred and twenty men. On the return, a letter-of-marque of sixteen guns and seventy men was captured. The Lieutenant had now prize money enough to be converted, on his return, into a large bundle of continental bills, which he stowed away in a chaise box, on taking a journey, but which he could not find when he arrived at his destination. He kept his own secret, however, and "went to sea again," second in command of the United States' ship Saratoga, of sixteen nine-pounders. The first prize was a ship of twelve guns, captured after an action of a few minutes. On the next day, the Saratoga hoisted English colors, and came along side a ship which had two brigs in company; then running up the American ensign, she poured in a broad side, while Lieutenant Barney, with fifty men, boarded the enemy. The immediate result was, the conquest of a ship of thirty two guns and ninety men. The two brigs, one of fourteen, and the other of four guns, were also captured. The division of prize money would have made the officers rich, but no division took place, for all but the Saratoga were captured by a seventy-four and several frigates. Lieutenant Barney was furnished with bed and board, on deck, and, with him, bed and board were synonymous terms, but he was allowed to choose the softest plank he could find. In England he was confined in prison, from which he escaped, and, after various adventures, arrived at Beverly, Massachusetts, and, as soon as he landed, was offered the command of a privateer of twenty guns. On his arrival at Philadelphia, he accepted the command of one of several vessels, cruising against the enemies' barges, and the refugee boats, that infested the Delaware River and Bay. His ship was the Hyder Ally, a small vessel of sixteen six-pounders. As a superior vessel of the enemy was approaching, Barney directed his steersman to interpret his command by the *rule of contraries.*

When the enemy were ranging alongside, Barney cried out, ' Hard a-port." The helmsman clapped his helm the other way, and the enemy's jib-boom caught in the fore rigging, and held her

in a position to be raked, and never was the operation of raking
more suddenly or effectually performed. The British flag came
down in less than half an hour, and the captors made little delay
for compliments, for a frigate from the enemy was rapidly approaching. The prize was the general Marle, of the Royal Navy,
with twenty nine pounders, and one hundred and thirty-six men;
nearly double the force and metal of the captors. After the peace,
Commodore Barney made a partial settlement in Kentucky, and
became a favorite with the old hunters of that pleasant land. He
was appointed Clerk of the District Court of Maryland, and also
an auctioneer. He also engaged in commerce, when his business
led him to Cape François during the insurrection, and where he
armed his crew, and fought his way, to carry off some specie
which he had secreted in barrels of coffee.

On his return he was captured by a pirate, which called herself
an English privateer. Barney, however, was a bad prisoner, and
with a couple of his hands rose upon the buccaneers and captured
their ship. In this situation it was no time for Argus himself to
sleep, with more than an eye at a time. The Commodore slept
only by day in an armed chair on deck, with his sword between his
legs, and pistols in his belt, while his cook and boatswain, well
armed, stood the watch at his side. On another occasion, he was
captured in the West Indies, by an English frigate, where he received the usual British courtesies, and he was tried in Jamaica
for piracy, &c. It is needless to say that, though in an enemy's
country, he was acquitted by acclamation. This accusation originated with the commander of the frigate, who, however, prudently
kept out of sight; though an officer in the same frigate, expressed
at a Coffee House, a desire to meet Barney, without knowing
that he was present, that he might have an opportunity to settle
accounts with the *rascal.* The rascal bestowed upon the officer
the compliments that were usual on such occasions, and tweaked
that part of his head that is so prominent in an elephant.

We cannot follow the Commodore through his subsequent fortunes and adventures, but refer to the book for a more interesting
account of them. In France he received the *hug fraternal* of the
President of the Convention, and the commission of Captain of
the highest grade in the Navy. He fitted out several vessels of
his own to harass the British trade, in which he was very successful. He received the command of two frigates, which were almost totally wrecked in a storm, though he succeeded in saving
them   In the last war, his services are more immediately in our
memories. The Memoir of Commodore Barney, from which
these particulars are taken, is just published by Gray and Bowen,
and it is a valuable addition to our naval biography.—*Boston
Courier.*

NAVAL BATTLES

OF THE UNITED STATES.

The depradations committed on American commerce in the Mediterranean, by the piratical corsairs of the Barbary powers, induced Congress, in 1794, to authorise the formation of a naval force for its protection. Four ships of forty-four guns each and two of thirty-six were ordered to be built. Captain THOMAS TRUXTON was one of the first six captains appointed by the President, at the organization of the naval establishment, in 1794. He was appointed to the command of the Constellation of thirty-six guns, and ordered to protect the commerce of the United States in the West Indies from the ravages of the French. On the ninth of February, 1799, he captured the French frigate Insurgente, of which twenty-nine of the crew were killed and forty-four wounded. The Constellation had but one man killed and two wounded.

In 1800, the Constellation engaged with the French frigate Vengeance of fifty-four guns, near Guadaloupe; but owing to the darkness of the night the latter escaped, after having thrice struck her colors and lost one hundred and sixty men.

The same year, the United States frigate Boston captured the French national corvette Le Berceau.

In the month of August, 1801, Captain Sterrett of the United States schooner Enterprize, of twelve guns, and ninety men, fell in, off Malta, with a Tripolitan cruiser of fourteen guns, and eighty-five men. In this action the Tripolitans thrice hauled down her colors, and thrice perfidiously renewed the conflict. Fifty of her men were killed and wounded. The Enterprize did not lose a man. Captain Sterrett's instructions not permitting him to make a prize of the cruiser, he ordered her crew to throw overboard all their guns and powder, &c, and to go and tell their countrymen the treatment they might expect from a nation, determined to pay tribute only in powder and ball. On her arrival at Tripoli, so great was the terror produced, that the sailors abandoned the cruisers then fitting out, and not a man could be procured to navigate them.

The Tripolitan cruisers continuing to harass the vessels of the U. States, Congress determined, in 1803, to fit out a fleet that should chastise their insolence. The squadron consisted of the Constitution, 44 guns; the Philadelphia, 44; the Argus, 18; the Siren, 16; the Nautilus, 16; the Vixen, 16; and the Enterprize, 14. Commodore Preble was appointed to the command of this squadron, in May, 1803, and on the 13th of August, sailed in he Constitution for the Mediterranean. Having adjusted the difficulties which had sprung up with the emperor of Morocco he turned his whole attention to Tripoli. The season was, however, too far advanced for active operations.

On the 31st of October, the Philadelphia, being, at nine o'clock in the morning, about five leagues to the westward of Tripoli, discovered a sail in shore, standing before the wind to the eastward. The Philadelphia immediately gave chase. The sail hoisted Tripolitan colors, and continued her course near the shore. The Philadelphia opened a fire upon her, and continued it, till half past eleven; when, being in seven fathoms water, and finding her fire could not prevent the vessel entering Tripoli, she gave up the pursuit. In beating off, she ran on a rock, not laid down in any chart, distant four and a half miles from the town. A boat was immediately lowered to sound. The greatest depth of water was found to be astern. In order to back her off, all sails were then laid aback; the top-gallant-sails loosened; three anchors thrown away from the bows; the water in the hold started; and all the guns thrown overboard, excepting a few abaft to defend the ship against the attacks of the Tripolitan gun-boats, then firing at her. All this, however, proved ineffectual; as did also the attempt to lighten her forward by cutting away her foremast. The Philadelphia had already withstood the attack of the numerous gun-boats for four hours, when a large reinforcement coming out of Tripoli, and being herself deprived of every means of resistance, and defence, she was forced to strike, about sunset The Tripolitans immediately took possession of her, and made prisoners of the officers and men, in number three hundred. Forty-eight hours afterwards, the wind blowing in shore, the Tripolitans got the frigate off, and towed her into the harbor.

On the 14th of December, commodore Preble sailed from Malta, in company with the Enterprize, commanded by lieutenant Stephen Decatur. When the latter was informed of the loss of the Philadelphia, he immediately formed a plan of recapturing and destroying her, which he proposed to commodore Preble. At first the commodore thought the projected enterprise too hazardous; but at length granted his consent. Lieutenant Decatur then selected for the enterprise the ketch Intrepid, lately captured by him. This vessel he manned with seventy volunteers, chiefly of his own crew; and on the 3d of February sailed from Syracuse, accompanied by the brig Siren, lieutenant Stewart.

After a tempestuous passage of fifteen days, the two vessels arrived off the harbor of Tripoli, towards the close of day. It was determined that at ten o'clock in the evening the Intrepid should enter the harbor, accompanied by the boats of the Siren. But a change of wind had separated the two vessels six or eight miles. As delay might prove fatal, lieutenant Decatur entered the harbor alone about eight o'clock. The Philadelphia lay within half gun shot of the Bashaw's castle and principal battery. On her starboard quarter lay two Tripolitan cruisers within two cable length; and on the starboard bow a number of gun-boats within half gun-shot. All her guns were mounted and loaded. Three hours were, in consequence of the lightness of the wind, consumed in passing three miles, when, being within two hundred yards of the Philadelphia, they were hailed from her, and ordered to anchor on peril of being fired into. The pilot on board the Intrepid was ordered to reply, that all their anchors were lost The Americans had advanced within fifty yards of the frigate, when the wind died away into a calm. Lieutenant Decatur ordered a rope to be taken out and fastened to the fore chains of the frigate, which was done, and the Intrepid warped alongside. It was not till then the Tripolitans suspected them to be an enemy; and their confusion in consequence was great. As soon as the vessels were sufficiently near, lieutenant Decatur sprang on board the frigate, and was followed by midshipman Morris. It was a minute before the remainder of the crew succeeded in mounting after them. But the Turks, crowded together on the quarter deck, were in too great consternation to take advantage of this delay. As soon as a sufficient number of Americans gained the deck they rushed upon the Tripolitans; who were soon overpowered; and about twenty of them were killed. After taking possession of the ship, a firing commenced from the Tripolitan batteries and castle, and from two corsairs near the frigate; a number of launches were also seen rowing about in the harbor; whereupon lieutenant Decatur resolved to remain in the frigate, for there he would be enabled to make the best defence. But perceiving that the launches kept at a distance, he ordered the frigate to be set on fire, which was immediately done, and so effectually, that with difficulty was the Intrepid preserved. A favorable breeze at this moment sprang up, which soon carried them out of the harbor. None of the Americans were killed, and only four wounded. For this heroic achievement lieutenant Decatur was promoted to the rank of post captain. His commission was dated on the day he destroyed the Philadelphia.

After the destruction of the Philadelphia frigate, commodore Preble was, during the spring and early part of the summer, employed in keeping up the blockade of the harbor of Tripoli, in preparing for an attack upon the town, and in cruising. A prize that had been taken was put in commission, and called the Scourge A loan of six gun-boats and two bomb-vessels, completely fitted for service, was obtained from the king of Naples. Permission was also given to take twelve or fifteen Neapolitans on board each boat, to serve under the American flag.

With this addition to his force, the commodore, on the 21st of July, joined the vessels off Tripoli. The number of men engaged in the service amounted to one thousand and sixty.

On the Tripolitan castle and batteries, one hundred and fifteen guns were mounted; fifty-five of which were pieces of heavy ordnance; the others long eighteen and twelve pounders. In the harbor were nineteen gun-boats, carrying each a long brass eighteen or twenty-four pounder in the bow, and two howitzers abaft; also two schooners of eight guns each, a brig of ten, and two galleys, of four guns each. In addition to the ordinary Turkish garrison, and the crews of the armed vessels, estimated at three thousand, upwards of twenty thousand Arabs had been assembled for the defence of the city.

The weather prevented the squadron from approaching the city until the 28th, when it anchored within two miles and a half of the fortifications; but the wind suddenly shifting, and increasing to a gale, the commodore was compelled to return. On the 3d of August, he again approached to within two or three miles of the batteries. Having observed that several of the enemy's boats were stationed without the reef of rocks, covering the entrance of the harbor, he resolved to take advantage of this circumstance. He made signal for the squadron to come within speaking distance, to communicate to the several commanders his intention of attacking the shipping and batteries. The gun-boats and bomb-ketches were immediately manned, and prepared for action. The former were arranged in two divisions of three each. At half past one, the squadron stood in for the batteries. At two, the gun-boats were cast off. At half past two, signal was made for the bomb-ketches and gun-boats to advance and attack. At three quarters past two, the signal was given for a general action. It commenced by the bomb-ketches throwing shells into the town. A tremendous fire immediately commenced from the enemy's batteries and vessels, of at least two hundred guns. It was immediately returned by the American squadron, now within musket-shot of the principal batteries.

At this moment, captain Decatur, with the three gun-boats under his command, attacked the enemy's eastern division, consisting of nine gun-boats. He was soon in the midst of them. The fire of the cannon and musketry was immediately changed to a desperate attack with bayonet, spear, sabre, &c. Captain Decatur having grappled a Tripolitan boat, and boarded her with only fifteen Americans; in ten minutes her decks were cleared, and she was captured. Three Americans were wounded. At this moment captain Decatur was informed that the gun-boat commanded by his brother, had engaged and captured a boat belonging to the enemy; but that his brother, as he was stepping on board, was treacherously shot by the Tripolitan commander, who made off with his boat. Captain Decatur immediately pursued the murderer, who was retreating within the lines; having succeeded in coming along side, he boarded with only eleven men. A doubtful contest of twenty minutes ensued. Decatur immediately attacked the Tripolitan commander, who was armed with a spear and cut-ass. In parrying the Turk's spear, Decatur broke his sword close to the hilt, and received a slight wound in the right arm and breast; but having seized the spear he closed; and, after a violent struggle, both fell, Decatur uppermost. The Turk then drew a dagger from his belt; but Decatur caught hold of his arm, drew a pistol from his pocket, and shot him. While they were struggling, the crew of both vessels rushed to the assistance of their commanders. And so desperate had the contest around them been, that it was with difficulty Decatur could extricate himself from the killed and wounded that had fallen around him. In this affair an American manifested the most heroic courage and attachment to his commander. Decatur, in the struggle, was attacked in the rear by a Tripolitan; who had aimed a blow at his head, which must have proved fatal, had not this generous-minded tar, then dangerously wounded and deprived of the use of both his hands, rushed between him and the sabre, the stroke of which he received in his head whereby his scull was fractured. This hero, however survived, and afterwards received a pension from his grateful country. All the Americans but four were wounded Captain Decatur brought both his prizes safe to the American squadron.

Two successive attacks were afterwards made upon Tripoli; and the batteries effectually silenced. The humiliation of this barbarous power was of advantage to all nations. The Pope made a public declaration, that, "the United States, though in their infancy, had, in this affair, done more to humble the anti-christian barbarians on that coast, than all the European States had done for a long series of time." Sir Alexander Ball, a distinguished commander in the British navy, addressed his congratulations to commodore Preble.

After the junction of the two squadrons, commodore Preble obtained leave to return home. This he did with the greater pleasure, as it would give the command of a frigate to captain Decatur. On his return to the United States, he was received and treated every where with that distinguished attention, which he had so fully merited. Congress voted him their thanks, and requested the President to present him with an emblematical medal.

Our limits will only allow us to glance briefly at a few of the remaining victories of the American navy. A formal declaration of war against Great Britain was passed by Congress on the 18th of June, 1812. On the 19th of August the memorable capture of the British frigate Guerriere by the Constitution under captain Hull, took place. On the 18th of October the British sloop of war Frolic was taken by the Wasp, commanded by captain Jacob Jones; before the latter could escape, however, with her prize, being in a very disabled state, she was captured by the British seventy-four, Poictiers. On the 25th of October, the United States under commodore Decatur, fell in with and captured, off

the Western Isles the British frigate Macedonian, mounting
forty-nine guns and carrying three hundred and six men. The
Macedonian had one hundred and six men killed and wounded:
the United States five killed and seven wounded. The victory
of the Constitution over the Java followed; and was succeeded
by that of the Hornet, commanded by Captain Lawrence, over
the Peacock. The loss of that brave officer in the subsequent
engagement between the Chesapeake and the Shannon, has been
mentioned in a previous notice of his life. On the 1st of September, 1813, the British brig Boxer of fourteen guns, was cap
tured by the United States brig Enterprize, commanded by
lieutenant William Burrows, who fell in the engagement. We
must close our notice of American naval history, by a brief sketch
of some of the most interesting cruises and engagements.

CRUISE OF THE WASP

On the 1st of May 1814, the United States sloop of war Wasp,
of eighteen guns and one hundred and seventy-three men, captain Blakely commander, sailed from Portsmouth, N. H. on a
cruise, and on the 28th of June, in latitude 48. 36, longitude
11. 15, after having made several captures, she fell in with, engaged, and after an action of nineteen minutes, captured his Britanic majesty's sloop of war Reindeer, William Manners, esquire,
commander. The Reindeer mounted sixteen twenty-four pound
carronades, two long six or nine pounders, and a shifting twelve
pound carronade, with a complement on board of one hundred
and eighteen men. She was literally cut to pieces in a line with
her ports; her upper works, boats and spare spars were one
complete wreck, and a breeze springing up the day after the action,
her foremast went by the board; when the prisoners having been
taken on board the Wasp, she was set on fire and soon blew up.
The loss on board the Reindeer was twenty-three killed and
forty-two wounded, her captain being among the former. On
board the Wasp five were killed and twenty-one wounded
More than one half of the wounded enemy were, in consequence
of the severity and extent of their wounds, put on board a Portuguese brig and sent to England.—The loss of the Americans,
although not as severe as that of the British, was owing, in a
degree, to the proximity of the two vessels during the action, and
the extreme smoothness of the sea, but chiefly in repelling
boarders.
On the 8th of July, the Wasp put into L'Orient, France, after
capturing an additional number of prizes, where she remained
until the 27th of August, when she again sailed on a cruise. On
the 1st of September she fell in with the British sloop of war
Avon, of twenty guns, commanded by captain Abuthnot, and
after an action of forty-five minutes, compelled her to surrender,

her crew being nearly all killed and wounded. The guns were then ordered to be secured, and a boat lowered from the Wasp in order to take possession of the prize. In the act of lowering the boat, a second enemy's vessel was discovered astern and standing towards the Wasp. Captain Blakely immediately ordered his crew to their quarters, prepared every thing for action, and awaited her coming up. In a few minutes after, two additional sail were discovered bearing down upon the Wasp. Captain Blakely stood off with the expectation of drawing the first from its companions; but in this he was disappointed. She continued to approach until she came close to the stern of the Wasp, when she hauled by the wind, fired her broadside, (which injured the Wasp but trifling,) and retraced her steps to join her consorts. Captain Blakely was now necessitated to abandon the Avon, which had by this time become a total wreck, and which soon after sunk, the surviving part of her crew having barely time to escape to the other enemy's vessels.

On board the Avon forty were killed and sixty wounded. The loss sustained by the Wasp was two killed and one wounded.

The Wasp afterwards continued her cruise, making great havock among English merchant vessels and privateers, destroying an immense amount of the enemy's property. From the first of May until the 20th of September, she had captured fifteen vessels, most of which she destroyed.

HORNET AND PENGUIN.

On the 23d of March, 1815, as the Hornet, commanded by captain Biddle, was about to anchor off the north end of the island of Tristan d'Acuna, a sail was seen to the southward; which, at forty minutes past one, hoisted English colors, and fired a gun. The Hornet immediately luffed to, hoisted an ensign, and gave the enemy a broadside. A quick and well directed fire was kept up from the Hornet, the enemy gradually drifting nearer, with an intention, as captain Biddle supposed, to board. The enemy's bowsprit came in between the main and mizen rigging on the starboard side of the Hornet, giving him an opportunity to board, if he had wished, but no attempt was made. There was a considerable swell, and as the sea lifted the Hornet ahead, the enemy's bowsprit carried away her mizzen shrouds, stern davits, and spanker booms, and hung upon her larboard quarter. At this moment an officer called out that they had surrendered Captain Biddle directed the marines to stop firing, and, while asking if they had surrendered, received a wound in the neck. The enemy just then got clear of the Hornet; and his foremast and bowsprit being both gone, and perceiving preparations to give him another broadside, he again called out that he had surrendered. It was with great difficulty that Captain Biddle could

restain his crew from firing into him again, as it was certain that
he had fired into the Hornet after having surrendered.   From the
firing of the first gun to the last time the enemy cried out that he
had surrendered, was exactly twenty-two minutes.   The vessel
proved to be the British brig Penguin, of twenty guns, a remarkably fine vessel of her class, and one hundred and thirty-two men;
twelve of them supernumeraries from the Medway seventy-four,
received on board in consequence of their being ordered to cruise
for the privateer Young Wasp.

The Penguin had fourteen killed and twenty-eight wounded.
Among the killed was captain Dickenson, who fell at the close
of the action.   As she was completely riddled, and so crippled as
to be incapable of being secured, and being at a great distance
from the United States, Captain Biddle ordered her to be scuttled
and sunk.

The Hornet did not receive a single round shot in her hull;
and though much cut in her sails and rigging, was soon made
ready for further service.   Her loss was one killed and eleven
wounded.

ALGERINE WAR.

Immediately after the ratification of peace with great Britain,
in February 1815, Congress, in consequence of the hostile conduct of the regency of Algiers, declared war against that power.
A squadron was immediately fitted out, under the command of
commodore Decatur, consisting of the Guerriere, Constellation,
and Macedonian frigates, the Ontario and Epervier sloops of war,
and the schooners Spark, Spitfire, Torch, and Flambeau.   Another squadron, under commodore Bainbridge, was to follow this
armament, on the arrival of which, it was understood, commodore
Decatur would return to the United States in a single vessel,
leaving the command of the whole combined force to commodore
Bainbridge.

The force under commodore Decatur rendezvoused at New
York, from which port they sailed the 20th day of May, 1815,
and arrived in the Bay of Gibraltar in twenty-five days, after
having previously communicated with Cadiz and Tangier.   In
the passage, the Spitfire, Torch, Firefly, and Ontario, separated
at different times from the squadron in gales, but all joined again
at Gibraltar, with the exception of the Firefly, which sprung her
masts, and put back to New York to refit.   Having learned at
Gibraltar that the Algerine squadron, which had been out into the
Atlantic, had undoubtedly passed up the straits, and that information of the arrival of the American force had been sent to Algiers
by persons in Gibraltar, commodore Decatur determined to proceed without delay up the Mediterranean, in the hope of intercepting the enemy before he could return to Algiers, or gain a
neutral port.

The 17th of June, off Cape de Gatt, he fell in with and captured the Algerine frigate Mazouda, in a running fight of twenty-five minutes. After two broadsides the Algerines ran below. The Guerriere had four men wounded by musketry—the Algerines about thirty killed, according to the statement of the prisoners, who amounted to four hundred and six. In this affair the famous Algerine admiral, or Rais, Hammida, who had long been the terror of this sea, was cut in two by a cannon shot. On the 19th of June, off cape Palos, the squadron fell in with and captured an Algerine brig of twenty-two guns. The brig was chased close to the shore, where she was followed by the Epervier, Spark, Torch, and Spitfire, to whom she surrendered, after losing twenty-three men. No Americans were either killed or wounded. The captured brig, with most of the prisoners on beard, was sent into Carthagena. From cape Palos, the American squadron proceeded to Algiers, where it arrived the 28th of June.

The treaty which captain Decatur finally succeeded in negotiating with the Dey, was highly favorable. The principal articles were, that no tribute under any pretext or in any form whatever, should ever be required by Algiers from the United States of America—that all Americans in slavery should be given up without ransom—that compensation should be made for American vessels captured, or property seized or detained at Algiers—that the persons and property of American citizens found on board an enemy's vessel should be sacred—that vessels of either party putting into port should be supplied with provisions at market price, and, if necessary to be repaired, should land their cargoes without paying duty—that if a vessel belonging to either party should be cast on shore, she should not be given up to plunder—or if attacked by an enemy within cannon shot of a fort, should be protected, and no enemy be permitted to follow her when she went to sea within twenty-four hours. In general, the rights of Americans on the ocean and land, were fully provided for in every instance, and it was particularly stipulated that all citizens of the United States taken in war, should be treated as prisoners of war are treated by other nations, and not as slaves, but held subject to an exchange without ransom. After concluding this treaty, so highly honorable and advantageous to this country, the commissioners gave up the captured frigate and brig, to their former owners.

Commodore Decatur despatched captain Lewis in the Epervier, bearing the treaty to the United States, and leaving Mr Shaler at Algiers, as consul-general to the Barbary states, proceeded with the rest of the squadron to Tunis, with the exception of two schooners under captain Gamble, sent to convoy the Algerine vessels home from Carthagena. Having obtained from the bashaw of Tunis a full restoration in money, for certain outrages which had been sustained by American citizens the squad-

ron proceeded to Tripoli, where commodore Decatur made a
similar demand for a similar violation of the treaty subsisting
between the United States and the bashaw, who had permitted
two American vessels to be taken from under the guns of his
castle by a British sloop of war, and refused protection to an
American cruiser lying within his jurisdiction. Restitution of the
full value of these vessels was demanded, and the money
amounting to twenty-five thousand dollars, paid by the bashaw
into the hands of the American consul. After the conclusion of
this affair, the American consular flag, which Mr. Jones, the
consul, had struck, in consequence of the violation of neutrality
above mentioned, was hoisted in the presence of the foreign
agents, and saluted from the castle with thirty-one guns. In addition to the satisfaction thus obtained, for unprovoked aggres-
sions, the commodore had the pleasure of obtaining the release
of ten captives, two Danes, and eight Neapolitans, the latter of
whom he landed at Messina

View of Boston.

After touching at Messina and Naples, the squadron sailed for
Carthagena on the 31st of August, where commodore Decatur
was in expectation of meeting the relief squadron, under commodore Bainbridge. On joining that officer at Gibraltar, he relinquished his command, and sailed in the Guerriere for the United
States, where he arrived on the 12th of November, 1815. Every
thing being done previous to the arrival of the second division of
the squadron, under commodore Bainbridge, that gallant officer
had no opportunity of distinguishing himself. Pursuant to his

instructions he exhibited this additional force before Algiers, Tunis, and Tripoli, where they were somewhat surprised at the appearance of the Independence seventy-four. Commodore Bainbridge sailed from Gibraltar thirty-six hours before the Guerriere, and arrived at Boston the 15th of November

---

THE AMERICAN FLAG.

When Freedom from her mountain height,
    Unfurled her standard to the air,
She tore the azure robe of night,
    And set the stars of glory there ;
She mingled with the gorgeous dyes
The milky baldric of the skies,
And striped its pure celestial white,
With streakings of the morning light,
Then, from his mansion in the sun,
She called her eagle-bearer down,
And gave into his mighty hand
The symbol of her chosen land.

    Majestic monarch of the cloud,
        Who rearest aloft thy regal form
    To hear the tempest trumping loud,
    And see the lightning lances driven,
        When stride the warriors of the storm
    And rolls the thunder drum of heaven,—
    Child of the Sun, to thee 't is given,
        To guard the banner of the free
    To hover in the sulphur smoke,
    To ward away the battle stroke,
    And bid its blendings shine afar,
    Like rainbows on the cloud of war,
        The harbinger of victory.

Flag of the brave, thy folds shall fly,
'.he sign of hope and triumph, high.
When speaks the signal trumpet-tone,
And the long line comes gleaming on,
(Ere yet the life-blood, warm and wet,
Has dimmed the glistening bayonet,)
Each soldier's eye shall brightly turn
To where thy meteor-glories burn,
And, as his springing steps advance
Catch war and vengeance from the glance '
And, when the cannon-mouthings loud
Heave, in wild wreaths, the battle shroud,
And gory sabres rise and fall,
Like shoots of flame on midnight's pall !
There shall thy victor glances glow,
    And cowering foes shall sink beneath
Each gallant arm that strikes below
    That lovely messenger of death.

Flag of the seas, on ocean's wave
Thy stars shall glitter o'er the brave,
When death, careering on the gale,
Sweeps darkly round the bellied sail,
And frightened waves rush wildly back
Before the broad-side's reeling rack,
The dying wanderer of the sea
Shall look at once to heaven and thee,
And smile to see thy splendors fly,
In triumph, o'er his closing eye.

Flag of the free hearts' only home,
    By angel-hands to valor given,
Thy stars have lit the welkin dome,
    And all thy hues were born in heaven.
Forever float that standard sheet!
    Where breathes the foe, but falls before us,
With freedom's soil beneath our feet,
    And Freedom's banner streaming o'er us?

CAPTAIN PARRY'S FIRST VOYAGE OF DISCOVERY.

On the 16th of January, 1819, Lieutenant Parry was appointed to the command of his Majesty's ship Hecla, a bomb of three hundred and seventy-five tons; and the Griper, gun brig, one hundred and eighty tons, commissioned by Lieutenant Matthew Liddon, was at the same time directed to put herself under his orders. The object of the expedition was to discover a north west passage into the Pacific. Every individual engaged in the expedition was to receive double pay. They took in provisions for two years, and also a supply of fresh meats and soups preserved in tin cases, essence of malt and hops, and other stores adapted to cold climates and a long voyage. The ships were ballasted entirely with coals, and the men were supplied with an abundance of warm clothing.

Captain Parry was to pass, if possible, through Lancaster's Sound to Behring's Strait. If he succeeded, he was to proceed to Kamtschatka and return to England round Cape Horn. Other instructions were given, but much was left to his own discretion. He sailed in the beginning of May, and proceeded up the straits of Davis, where he found the ice close packed. As he was making his way towards the western shore, on the 25th of June, the ice closed round the ships and arrested their progress. Here the ice was so close, that the whales could not descend in the usual way, but were obliged to go down tail first, much to the amusement of he Greenland sailors. Their situation during the 28th was very unpleasant, and would have been dangerous to ships built in the ordinary way. Each roll of the sea forced the heavy masses of ice against the rudder and counter with great violence; but being so well strengthened, they escaped without damage. While in this state, a large white bear approached the Griper, attracted by the smell of some red herrings, which the men were frying at the time. They killed him, but he sunk between the pieces of ice, and they were unable to obtain him. On the 30th, the ice began to slacken a little about the ships, and after two hour's heaving, they succeeded in moving the Hecla about her own length to the eastward; and the ice continuing open after eight hours' incessant labor, they hauled both ships into open water.

Captain Parry having failed in his first attempt to approach the western shore, came to the determination of trying to effect this object, about the latitude of mount Raleigh, which forms one side of the narrowest part of Davis's Strait. They kept on during the 1st and 2d of July, without finding any opening. On the third day, the wind having shifted to the south-west, another large chain of icebergs was seen to the northward. They could find no bottom near these icebergs with one hundred and ten fathom of line. At four A. M. on the 4th, they came to a quantity of loose ice floating among the bergs. The breeze blew lightly from the southward, and wishing to avoid going to the eastward, they pushed the Hecla into the ice, in hopes of being able to make way through it. But it immediately fell calm and the ship becoming perfectly unmanageable, was for some time at the mercy of the swell, which drifted her fast towards the bergs. The Griper's signal was made not to enter the ice, and after two hours' hard pulling, they succeeded in getting the Hecla clear of the icebergs, which it is very dangerous to approach whenever there is a swell.

The ice was now so close that they found it impossible to proceed further westward; and they made the best way they could, by beating to the northward, until the 10th, when a thick fog came on, which made it necessary to use great caution in sailing to avoid the icebergs. The reflection of light, however, is so strong from these vast bodies of ice, that in the thickest fog they can be seen at a sufficient distance to enable the navigator, if in smooth water, to keep clear of them. The people succeeded in killing a large bear, which was seen near them on a piece of ice and towed it on board. These animals sink immediately on being wounded, and to secure them, it is necessary to throw a rope over the neck, at which the Greenland seamen are very expert. After encountering many difficulties from the tenacity of the ice, on the 21st Captain Parry reached latitude 73°. As he was unwilling to increase his distance from Lancaster's Sound, he determined to enter the ice here. He accordingly ran in among the floes, and on the evening of the 22d, the ships were so beset, that no open water could be seen from the mast-head. The weather being clear on the next day, and a few narrow lanes of water appearing to the westward, they proceeded to warp the ships through the ice. At eight P. M., they had advanced four miles to westward, and having come to the end of clear water, they secured the ships in a deep bight, or bay in a floe, called by the sailors, natural dock! On the next day, a boat was sent to try to find a lane of clear water leading to the westward. She returned without success, and the weather was so foggy, that it was with difficulty she found her way back to the ships by means of muskets and other signals.

On Tuesday 27th, the clear water had made so much to the westward, that a narrow neck of ice was all that separated the ships from a large open space in that quarter. The men were just ordered out to saw off the neck, when the floes suddenly opened, and allowed the Griper to push through under all sail. Although they lost no time in attempting to get the Hecla through after her, yet before they could effect it, the passage was completely blocked up by a piece of floating ice, which was drawn after the Griper, by the eddy produced in her motion. Before they could haul it out of the channel, the floes pressed together and wedged it immoveably, and although the saws were used with great effect, it was not until after seven hours' labor, that they succeeded in getting the Hecla into the lanes of clear water, which opened towards the westward. They now perceived with pleasure, a pitching motion of the vessel, which, from the closeness of the ice, does not often occur in those regions, as a sure indication of an open sea. The wind breezing up by one o'clock P. M., the ice had all disappeared, and the sea was free from obstructions of any kind. Here they found the whales so numerous, that no less than eighty-two are mentioned in this day's log. It is commonly thought by the Greenland fishermen, that the presence of ice is necessary to insure the finding of whales; but no ice was seen this day, when they were most numerous. At half past five P. M., the high land about Possession bay came in sight. Lancaster's Sound was now open to the westward, and the experience of a former voyage had given Captain Parry reason to believe that the two best months for the navigation of those seas were yet to come. This, together with the magnificent view of the lofty Byaur Martin Mountains, which recalled forcibly to his mind the events of the preceding year, animated him with expectation and hope. On the 31st, they anchored in Possession bay, and discovered a flag staff which had been erected on the former expedition. The only animals found here were a fox, a raven, some ring plovers, snow-buntings, and a wild bee. Several tracks of bears and reindeers were also seen upon the moist ground. Three black whales were seen in the bay, and the crown bones of several others were lying near the beach. The tide rises here about eight feet, and the flood seems to come from the northwest.

On the first of August, Captain Parry finding that the Griper could not keep up with the Hecla, determined to leave her. He appointed the middle of Lancaster Sound as a place of rendezvous, and crowding all sail on the Hecla, he came towards evening in sight of the northern shore of the sound; and the next day had a clear view of both sides of it

Having run due west nearly out of sight of the Griper, the Hecla hove to for her to come up in longitude 83° 12' west from Greenwich, there being not the slightest appearance of land to the westward. The only ice met consisted of a few large bergs, much worn by the washing of the sea. Whales were seen, and the wind increased so that the top-gallant-yards were taken in On the 4th, Lieutenant Beechy discovered, from the crow's nest, breakers to the northward They sounded, and found bottom with forty-five fathoms of line. The Griper coming up, the vessels bore away to the westward. The sea was here so clear of ice, that they began to flatter themselves, that they had indeed entered the Polar Sea. Their vexation was therefore extreme, when, towards evening, land was seen ahead. At eight P. M., they came to a stream of ice extending several miles in a direction parallel to their course; and after sailing for two hours along the edge of the ice, they found it proceeded from a compact body of floes, which completely cut off their passage. The weather here was calm and foggy, and the men amused themselves in pursuing white whales, which were swimming about the ships in great numbers. But these animals were so wary, that they seldom suffered the boats to approach within thirty or forty yards of them, without diving. They also saw for the first time, one or two shoals of nar-whales, called by the sailors sea-unicorns. Finding that the sound or strait was closed, excepting in one place to the southward, to this opening they directed their course. They had sailed but a few hours, however, when it fell calm; and the Griper, having spread both her top-masts, advantage was taken of the calm weather to shift them. The Hecla's boats were at the same time employed in bringing aboard ice to be used as water. Berge-ice is preferred for this purpose, but that of floes which is in fact the ice of sea water, is also used. One of the boats was upset by the fall of a mass of ice, but fortunately no injury was sustained. A breeze springing up from the north-north-west, they made sail and stood to the southward. After sailing a short time they discovered that they were entering a large inlet about ten leagues wide at its mouth, and n the centre of which, no land could be distinguished. The western shore was so encumbered with ice, that it was impossible to sail near it. They therefore ran along between the ice and the eastern shore, where there was a broad channel, with the intention of seeking a lower latitude or a clearer passage to the westward. Since they had first entered Lancaster's Sound, the sluggishness of the compasses, and the irregularity produced by the attraction of the ship's iron, had been

found to increase rapidly as they proceeded to the westward.
The irregularity increased as they advanced to the southward,
which rendered it not improbable that they were approaching the
magnetic pole. The compasses therefore were no longer fit for
the purposes of navigation, and the binacles were removed as
useless lumber into the carpenter's store-room, where they remained during the rest of the season. Being desirous of obtaining all
the magnetic observations they were able, on a spot which appeared so full of interest in this department of science, two boats were
dispatched from each ship to the nearest eastern shore, under
the command of Lieutenant Beechy and Hoppner, who, together
with Captain Sabine, were directed to make the necessary observations. As soon as the boats returned, the ships hove to the
southward, along the edge of the ice, and by midnight the channel
was narrowed to about five miles. They could find no soundings;
the weather was serene and the sun for the second time that season just dipped below the northern horizon, and reappeared a few
moments after. They had hoped to find a passage to the south
of the ice, especially as the inlet widened considerably as they
advanced in that direction; but on the morning of the 8tn, they
perceived that the ice ran close in with a point of land, which
seemed to form the southern extremity of the eastern shore. The
prospect from the crow's nest began to assume a very unpromising
appearance. The whole western horizon from north round to
south by east, being completely covered with ice, beyond which
no indication of water was visible. Captain Parry therefore determined, as the season was fast advancing, to return immediately to the northward, in the hope of finding the channel between
Prince Leopold's Isles and Maxwell Bay, more open than when
they left it, in which there could be little doubt of effecting a
passage to the westward. They had sailed to the southward in
this inlet about one hundred and twenty miles, Cape Kater
being by the observations in latitude 71° 53′ 30″ longitude 90° 03′
45″. They returned to the northward with a light but favorable
breeze. On the 10th, the weather was thick with snow, which
was succeeded by rain and fog. The ships moored to a floe, but
when the weather cleared, they found themselves drifting with the
floe upon another body of ice to leeward. They therefore cast
off and beat to the northward, which was very difficult to do, on
account of the drift ice with which the whole inlet was now covered. Although several days were thus passed in contending with
fogs, head winds, and all the difficulties of arctic navigation, yet
neither officers nor crews lost health or spirits. They repined
not at the dangers and difficulties of their situation, but because
the accomplishment of their hopes was delayed.

A light southern breeze enabled them to steer towards Prince
Leopold's Isles, which they found more encumbered with ice than
before. Here they saw a great number of nar-whales, lying with

their backs above the water in the same manner as the whale, and frequently with their horns erect and quite stationary for several minutes together. Three or four miles to the northward, they discovered an opening, having every appearance of a harbor, with an island near the entrance. It was named Jackson's Bay. The whole of the 14th was consumed in the attempt to find an opening in the ice, but as it remained perfectly close and compact, on the 15th Captain Parry went on shore to make observations. He landed in one of the numerous valleys, which occur on this part of the coast, very much resembling bays, being bounded by high hills, which appear like bluff head-lands. He ascended the hill on the south side of the ravine, which is very steep, and covered with detached blocks of lime-stone, some of which are constantly rolling down, and which afford a very insecure footing. From the top of the hill no water could be seen over the ice to the northwest; and the whole space comprised between the islands and the northern shore, was covered with a bright dazzling blink.

It was a satisfaction, however, to find that no land appeared and Captain Parry was too well aware of the suddenness with which obstructions, occasioned by the ice, are often removed, to be at all discouraged by present appearances. On the top of this hill, he deposited a bottle containing a short notice of his visit, and raised over it a small mound of stones. The wind was light the next day, and the ice being close, the ships scarcely changed their position. Despairing of being able to penetrate westward, in the neighborhood of Prince Leopold isles, Captain Parry determined to stand towards the northern shore again, and after beating for some hours among the drift ice, the ships got into clear water near the coast. They had just light enough at midnight, to see to read and write in the cabin. Passing along the shore, they left the ice behind them, and on the 21st they had nothing to hinder their passage westward, but want of wind. But the wind freshening soon after, all sail was made to the westward, where the prospect began to wear a more and more interesting appearance. It was soon perceived that the land along which they were sailing, and which had appeared to be continuous from Baffin's Bay, began now to trend much to the northward, leaving an open space between that coast, and a distant land to the westward, which appeared like an island, of which the extremes to the north and south were distinctly visible. The latter was a remarkable headland, and was named Cape Hotham. They discovered also several headlands on the eastern land; between the northernmost of which and the island to the westward, there was a channel of more than eight leagues in width, in which neither land nor ice could be seen from the mast head. The arrival off this noble channel, to which Captain Parry gave the name of Wellington, was an event for which they had all been anxiously looking; for the continuity of land to the northward, had always been a source

of uneasiness to them, from the possibility that it might take a
turn to the southward, and unite with the coast of America.
Every one thought that they were now finally disentangled from
the land, which forms the western side of Baffin's Bay; and that
in fact they had actually entered the Polar Sea. Fully impressed
with this idea, Captan Parry gave to this opening the name of
Barrow's Strait.

Two thirds of the month of August had now elapsed, and they
expected the sea would remain navigable six weeks more. The
ships had suffered no injury, they had a plenty of provisions, the
crews were in high health and spirits, and the sea before them,
if not open, was at least navigable. On the 23d, a fresh breeze
sprung up, and although Wellington channel was open to the northward, Captain Parry judged it best to try a large opening south of
Cornwallis's Island. But their disappointment was extreme, when
it was suddenly reported from the crow's nest, that their passage
was obstructed by a body of ice. Lieutenant Beechy discovered,
however, that one part of the barrier consisted of loose pieces of
ice, and the Hecla being immediately pushed into this part of it,
succeeded, after a quarter of an hour's 'boring,' in forcing her
way through the neck. The Griper followed, and they continued
their course to the westward, having once more a navigable sea
before them. At two P. M. having reached longitude 95° 67 min.,
they came to two extensive floes, which obliged the ships to tack,
as there was no passage between them. They then beat to the
northward in search of a passage, but none was found. After
several unsuccessful attempts to force a passage, they at last
succeeded by 'boring' through several heavy streams, and at
midnight were enabled to pursue their course to the westward.

The ships made very little way this night, but in the morning
they advanced with more speed, and more land was seen to the
westward. The space to westward was now so broad, that Captain
Parry thought best to appoint a place where the Griper could
find the Hecla in case of separation. But about seven P. M.,
this precaution was found to have been needless, for the ice
stretched across the strait, and barred the passage. Captain
Parry now resolved to seek a passage along the northern shore
As the vessels were rounding the eastern side of the island, Captain Sabine was despatched to make observations, and examine
the natural productions of the shore. He reported that he had
found the island much more interesting than any other parts of
the shores of the Polar Regions they had yet visited. The remains of Esquimaux habitations were found in four different places.
Some of them are described by Captain Sabine, as consisting of
stones rudely placed in an elliptical form. They were from seven
to ten feet in diameter, the flat sides of the stones standing vertically, and the whole structure being similar to that of the summer
huts of the Esquimaux, which had been seen the preceding year

Attached to each were smaller circles of about four or five fret in diameter, and from the moss and sand which covered some of the lower stones, the whole encampment appeared to have been deserted for several years. The fogs now froze hard upon the rigging, which made it difficult to work the ship as each rope was increased to twice or three times its proper diameter.

On the evening of the 29th, a very thick fog came on, and they sailed under such circumstances as have seldom occurred 'n navigation. Observing that the wind always blew some hours steadily from one quarter, the quarter masters steered by the vane at the mast head, instead of the compass, which was here utterly useless. At night the ships made fast to a floe, about six or seven feet thick, which was covered with numerous pools of water, all hard frozen. The officers amused themselves in skating upon the pools, and the men in sliding, foot-ball and other games. Thus the ships remained until the 31st, when a new expedient for sailing was adopted.

Before the fog commenced, and while they were sailing on a course, which they knew to be the right one, the Griper was exactly astern of the Hecla, at the distance of about a quarter of a mile. The quarter master stood aft, near the taffrail, and kept her constantly astern, by which means they were enabled to steer a tolerably straight course to the westward. The Griper, on the other hand, kept the Hecla right ahead, and thus they steered one ship by the other, for the distance of ten miles out of sixteen and a half, which they traversed between one and eleven P. M. The morning of the first of September brought a breeze, and with it a snow storm, so that they were unable to shape their course that afternoon. At one on the 2d, a star was seen, the first that had been visible for more than two months. The fog came on again, and there was not wind enough to enable them to keep the ships under command. On the morning of the third, a northern breeze enabled them to make considerable progress, and on the 4th, at nine P. M., they crossed the meridian of 110° west from Greenwich, in latitude 74°. 44 min. 20 sec., by which the ship's company became entitled to a reward of 5000 pounds, offered by the king's order in council "to such British subjects as might penetrate so far west within the Arctic circle." On the 5th, they found the passage blocked up again, and as no change seemed likely to take place, they came to anchor in a tolerable roadstead, a mile and a half from the northern shore. In the evening, Captain Sabine and some of the other officers landed on an island, to which they gave the name of Melville island. Here they saw several flocks of ducks and gulls; tracks of the deer and musk ox were also observed, and some addition made by the gentlemen to their collection of marine insects. The bay of the Hecla and Griper, as they called the roadstead, where the ships lay, was the first place in which they had dropped anchor since leaving Eng-

land. The flags were hoisted in honor of the epoch; the first time
that the eye of civilized man had looked on that barren and inhospitable region. In the afternoon the ice was observed to be in
motion; and the ship got under way and sailed a short distance.
But finding no opening, the ships were secured to a floe, which it
was necessary to do every night, the weather being too dark to
allow them to keep under way. Captain Parry, fearing that the
floes might change their position, determined to remove nearer
the shore. Two large masses lay aground, and the vessels were
secured between them and the shore. Parties went out and returned with a white hare, some fine ptarmigans, a few snow-buntings, skulls of the musk ox, and several reindeer's horns; but they
were unable to meet with either of the two latter animals. Several lumps of coal were also picked up, and were found to burn
with a clear lively flame, like canalcoal, but without splitting
and crackling in the same manner. At five A. M., on the 10th,
a floe ran against the berg, within which the Hecla was secured
and turned it round as on a pivot.

They were now so surrounded with ice, that all they could do
was to attend carefully to the safety of the ships. On the 11th,
one of the officers killed the first musk ox, that they had yet been
able to approach.

The packed ice remained immoveable, and the 'young ice'
rapidly forming, farther progress was considered impracticable
that season. Captain Parry thought it best to run back to the
bay of Hecla and Griper and to pass the winter there. The signal for weighing anchor was given on the 22d, but the cables had
become so stiff with frost, that it was five P. M. before the anchors
were brought on board; and they did not reach the anchorage till
the evening of the next day. A proper place being found, the
ships dropped anchor on the edge of the bay of ice in the evening
of the 24th; and on the next day, they commenced cutting a canal. Two parallel lines were marked out a little more than the
breadth of the ships apart; along these lines, a cut was then made
with an ice saw, and others again at right-angles with them, at
intervals of from ten to twenty feet. The pieces thus cut, were
again divided diagonally, in order to give room for their being
floated out of the canal. The seamen, who are fond of doing
things in their own way, took advantage of a fresh northerly
breeze, by setting some boat's sails on the pieces of ice, a contrivance which saved both time and labor.

At half past seven P. M., they weighed anchor, and began to
warp up the canal; but the wind blew so fresh, and the people
were so much fatigued, that it was midnight before they reached
the termination of their first day's labor. All hands were again
set to work on the morning of the 25th, when it was proposed to
sink the pieces of ice under the floe instead of floating them out.
To effect this it was necessary for some to stand on the end of the

piece of ice, which it was intended to sink, while others hauling upon ropes attached to the opposite end, dragged the block under that part of the floe, on which the people stood. The officers took the lead in this employ, and were frequently up to their knees in water during the day, with the thermometer generally at 12° and never higher than 16°. At six P. M. the Griper was made fast astern of the Hecla, and the two ships' companies, being divided on each bank of the canal, soon drew the ships to the end of their second day's work. The next day at noon, the whole canal was completed a length of four thousand and eighty-two yards through ice seven inches thick. The wintering ground was called winter harbor, and the group, of which the island formed a part, was denominated Georgian Islands, in honor of the reigning soveriegn of Great Britain.

Having reached the place, where they were probably to pass nine months, and three of them in the absence of the sun, Captain Parry was called upon to act in circumstances, in which no British naval officer had ever before been placed. The security of the ships, the preservation of the stores, a regular system for the maintenance of good order, cleanliness, and consequently good health, amusement and employment for the men were all to be attended to. Scientific observations were also to be made, and Captain Sabine employed himself immediately in selecting a place for an observatory, which was erected in a convenient spot, about seven hundred yards to the westward of the ships. The whole of the masts were dismantled, except the lower ones and the Hecla's main-top-mast; the lower yards were lashed fore and a't amidships, to support the planks of the housing intended to be erected over the ships; and the whole of this frame work was afterwards roofed over with a cloth. This done, Captain Parry's whole attention was directed to the health and comfort of the officers and men. The surgeon reported that not the slightest disposition to scurvy had shown itself in either ship. In order to preserve this healthy state of the crew, arrangements were made for the warmth and dryness of the berths and bedplaces; and finding that when the temperature had fallen considerably below zero, the steam from the coppers began to condense into drops on the beams and the sides, they were obliged to adopt such means for producing a sufficient warmth, combined with due ventilation, as might carry off the vapor and thus prevent its settling on any part of the ship. For this purpose, a large stone oven, cased with cast iron, in which all their bread was baked in the winter, was placed on the main-hatch-way, and the stove pipe led fore and aft on one side of the lower deck, the smoke being thus carried up the fore hatchway. On the opposite side of the deck, an apparatus had been attached to the galley-range for conveying a current of heated air between decks For the preservation of health, a few alterations were made in the quantity and quality of the provisions issued. The allowance of bread was reduced to two-thirds. A pound of preserved meat, together with a pint of vegetable or concentrated soup per man, was substituted for one pound of salt beef weekly; and a small quantity of sour krout and pickles, with as much vinegar as could be used, was issued at regular intervals. They were obliged to institute the most rigid economy, with regard to their coals, as they were unable to find any on the island, excepting a few lumps; and the moss which grew in abundance was found totally unfit for the purposes of fuel.

Great attention was paid to the clothing of the men, and one day in the week was appointed for the examination of the men's shins and gums by the medical gentlemen, in order that any slight appearance of the scurvy might be at once detected and checked by timely and adequate means.

Under circumstances of leisure and inactivity, such as they were now placed in, and with every prospect of its continuance, Captain Parry was desirous of finding some amusement for the men during this long and tedious interval. He proposed, therefore, to get up a play occasionally on board the Hecla; and his proposal being readily seconded by the officers, Lieutenant Beechy having been chosen manager, the performance was fixed for the 5th of November, to the great delight of the ships' companies. In order still further to promote good humor, and to afford amusing occupation during the hours of constant darkness, they set on foot a weekly newspaper, which was to be called the North Georgia Gazette and Winter Chronicle, and of which Captain Sabine undertook to be the editor, under the promise of being supported by original contributions from the officers of the two ships. The meridian altitude of the sun was observed, for the last time, on the 16th of October.

On the 26th the light was sufficient to allow of reading and writing in the cabins, from half past nine till half past two. The rest of the hours were spent by lamp light. It now became rather a painful experiment to touch any metallic substance in the open air, with the naked hand; the feeling produced by it exactly resembling that occasioned by the opposite extreme of intense heat; and taking off the skin from the part affected. They found it necessary, therefore, to use great caution in handling the sextants and other instruments; particularly the eye-pieces of the telescopes, which, if suffered to touch the face, occasioned an intense burning pain; but this was easily remedied by covering them over with soft leather. The month of November set in with mild weather. The 4th was the last day that the sun, independently of refraction, would be seen above the horizon for ninety-six days; but the weather was too thick for making any observations. On the 5th, their theatre was opened, with the representation of Miss in her teens; which afforded the men a great fund of amusement Even fitting up the theatre and taking it to pieces

again, was a matter of no small importance; as it kept the men
employed a day or two before and after each performance, which
was a considerable object gained.

On the 11th, the thermometer fell to 26½ for the second time.
The wolves began to approach the ships boldly, howling most
piteously on the beach near, and sometimes coming along side
the ships, when every thing was quiet at night; but they seldom
saw more than one or two together, and therefore could form no
idea of their number. The white foxes used also to visit the
ships at night, and one of these was caught in a trap, set under
the Griper's bows.

The stars of the second magnitude in Ursa Major were perceptible to the naked eye, a little after noon on the 11th of December, and the Aurora Borealis appeared faintly in the southwest
at night. The cold continued to increase. About the middle of
the month, a serious loss took place in the bursting of the bottles
of lemon juice; in some boxes of which, two thirds of the contents
were found to be destroyed. The vinegar also froze in the same
manner, and lost much of its acidity, when thawed. A few gallons of highly concentrated vinegar, congealed into a consistence
like honey.

Theatrical entertainments took place regularly once a fortnight,
and continued to prove a source of infinite amusement to the
men; and more than one or two plays were performed, with the
thermometer below zero, on the stage on board the Hecla.

The *North Georgia Gazette*, which we have already mentioned,
was a source of great amusement, not only to the contributors,
but to those who, from diffidence of their own talents, or other
reasons, could not be prevailed on to add their mite to the little
stock of literary composition, which was weekly demanded; for
those who declined to write were not unwilling to read, and more
ready to criticise than those who wielded the pen; but it was
that good-humored sort of criticism that could not give offence.

On Christmas day the weather was raw and cold, with a con
siderable snow drift, although the wind was only moderate from
northwest. Divine service was performed on board. The men's
usual proportion of fresh meat was increased, as also their allowance of grog, and the day passed with much of the same kind of
festivity by which it is usually distinguished at home.

On the first of January scurvy made its appearance among
them. Mr. Scallon, gunner of the Hecla, had complained for
some days, and the symptoms were now decidedly scorbutic. It
was found to be owing to the dampness of his bedding, and proper
measures were taken to prevent an increase of the malady. By
raising mustard and cress in small boxes near the cabin stove,
they were able to give Mr. Scallon and one or two more patients
nearly an ounce of sallad per day. The vegetables thus raised
were necessarily colorless from the privation of light; but they

had the same taste as if raised in ordinary circumstances. So
effectual were they in the case of Mr. Scallon, that he recovered
in less than a fortnight.

Toward the end of the month they began to look out for he
sun from the mast head. On the morning of the third of February, the weather being clear, a cross, consisting of the usual
vertical and horizontal rays, was seen about the moon. At twenty
minutes before noon, the sun was seen from the Hecla's maintop,
at the height of fifty-one feet above the sea, being the first time
it had been seen for eighty-four days, twelve days less than its
actual stay below the horizon. There was now, from eight
o'clock till four, sufficient light for any kind of work, and on the
seventh they began to collect ballast for the Hecla, to make up
for the expenditure of stores.

The coldest part of the year was now approaching; yet the sun
had sufficient power to affect the thermometer, which rose from—
46° to 35° when exposed to its rays. The distance at which
sounds were heard in the open air during the continuance of this
intense cold was truly surprising. Conversation carried on a mile
off could be distinctly heard. The smoke from the ships, too,
owing to the difficulty it has to rise in a low temperature, was
carried horizontally to a great distance. On the 15th, the mercury sunk to 55° below zero, which was the most intense degree
of cold observed during the winter. Mercury was malleable in
this state of the atmosphere.

From this time the temperature gradually rose. The length
of the days had so much increased by the 26th of February, that
a very sensible twilight was visible in the north.

For the last three or four days of April, the snow on the black
cloth of the housing had begun to thaw a little during a few
hours in the middle of the day, and on the 30th so rapid a change
took place in the temperature of the atmosphere, that the thermometer stood at the freezing, or, as it may more properly be
termed in this climate, the thawing point, being the first time that
such an event had occurred for nearly eight months, or since the
9th of the preceding September.

This rapid change in the weather revived their hopes of a
speedy departure from Melville Island; and they all had sanguine
expectations of leaving their winter quarters before July. On
the 1st of May, however it blew a gale, and the sun was seen at
midnight for the first time that season. On the 6th, the people
began the operation of cutting the ships out of the harbor; and
on the 17th, the ships were once more afloat. On the 21st, some
of the officers took a walk inland, and were able to fill a pint bottle with water from a pool of melted snow, which was the first
they had seen; a proof of the extreme severity of the climate.

A perceptible change had now taken place in the ice. The
upper surface was covered with innumerable pools of brackish

water, so that the liberation of the sea might be daily expected Being desirous of obtaining as much game as possible during the remainder of the time that must be passed in Winter Harbor, Captain Parry sent out hunting parties to remain ten or twelve miles inland, with orders to send whatever game they might procure, to the ships, and also to observe the ice from the hill tops, and report any change that might take place.

The dissolution of the ice continued daily, and on the 22d, it was observed to be in motion in the offing; setting to the east ward at the rate of a mile an hour. The dissolution of the ice of the harbor went on so rapidly, in the early part of July, that they were greatly surprised, on the 6th, in finding that in several of the pools of water, on its upper surface, holes were washed quite through to the sea beneath.

On the morning of the 26th, there being a space of clear water for three quarters of a mile to the southward, they took advantage of a northern breeze to run as far as the opening would permit, and then dropped anchor at the edge of the ice, intending to advance step by step as it separated. The ice across the entrance of the harbor in this spot, as well as that in the offing, appeared from the crow's nest quite continuous and unbroken, with the same appearance of solidity as at midwinter.

On the 30th, the whole body of the ice was in motion toward the southeast, breaking away, for the first time, from the points at the entrance of the harbor. This rendering it probable that the ships would soon be released, Captain Parry furnished Lieutenant Liddon with instructions for his guidance during the coming season of operations, and appointed places of rendezvous in case of separation.

On the first of August, the harbor was clear of ice, and there appeared to be water in the direction of their intended course. At one P. M., every thing having been brought on board, they weighed anchor and ran out of Winter Harbor, in which they had passed ten entire months of the year, and a part of the two remaining ones, September and August.

After a few tacks, they had the mortification to perceive that the Griper sailed much worse than before, though great pains had been taken during her re-equipment to improve her qualities. By midnight the Hecla had gained eight miles to windward of her, and was obliged to heave to, to avoid parting company.

A southerly wind springing up the next day, made it probable that the ice would close in upon the ships, and they therefore began to look out for a situation where they might be secured inshore, behind some of the heavy grounded ice. At one o'clock they perceived that a heavy floe had already closed completely in with the land at a point a little to the westward of them. A proper place having been found for their purpose, the ships were hauled in and secured, the Griper's bow resting on the beach, in order to allow the Hecla to lie in security without her. This place was so completely sheltered from the accession of the main ice, that Captain Parry began to think of taking the Griper's crew on board the Hecla, and pursuing the voyage in that ship alone.

Every moment's delay confirmed Captain Parry in the opinion that it was expedient to attempt to penetrate to the southward, as soon as the ice would allow the ships to move at all, rather than persevere in pushing directly westward. He therefore ordered Lieutenant Liddon to run back a certain distance eastward as soon as he could, without waiting for the Hecla, should that ship still be detained, and to look out for any opening to the southward, which might seem favorable to the object in view, and then wait for the Hecla.

On the 15th, Lieutenant Liddon was enabled to sail, in the execution of his orders. Captain Parry, however, observing that the Griper made little or no way, hoisted the signal of recall, with the intention of making one more attempt to penetrate westward. The ice had so far separated as to allow him to sail a mile and a half along shore, when he was again stopped. He was fortunate in finding a tolerably secure situation for the Hecla within the grounded ice; but the Griper was left by the wind in a place where, should the ice press upon her, there could be no hope of safety. For fear of the worst, Captain Parry made preparations to send parties to assist the Griper's company, if the wreck should become unavoidable; but they were shortly after relieved from all anxiety on this account, by the recession of the ice from the shore, whereby the Griper was enabled to gain a station near the Hecla.

The ice to the west and southwest, as seen from their present station, gave them no reason to expect a speedy opening in the desired direction. It appeared as solid and compact as so much land; to which the inequalities of the surface gave it no small resemblance. Captain Parry, therefore, determined to defer the attempt to try a more southern latitude no longer.

The point at which the ships were now lying, and which is the westernmost to which Arctic navigation has ever been carried, is in latitude 74° 26 min. 25 sec., and longitude 113° 64 min. 43 sec. Cape Dundas seen yet farther west, is in longitude 113° 57 min. 35 sec., by which the length of Melville island appears to be abou an hundred and thirty-five miles, and its breadth, at the meridian of Winter Harbor, from forty to fifty miles.

At nine P. M., they were abreast of the place where they had landed on the 5th, and here perceived that the ice closed with the land a little to the eastward. There was no safety for the ships, unless they could get past one of the small points at the embouchure of a ravine, against which a floe was setting the smaller pieces of ice, and had blocked up the passage before they arriv ed. After heaving two hours at the halsers, they succeeded in getting through, and moored the ships to some very heavy grounded ice near the beach. Hares were observed here, feeding on the sides of the cliffs, and a few ptarmigans were seen. The place where the Hecla was now secured, being the only one of the kind which could be found, was a little harbor, formed, as usual, by the grounded ice, some of which was fixed to the bottom in ten or twelve fathoms. One side of the entrance to this harbor consisted of masses of floes, very regular in their shape, placed quite horizontally, and broken off so exactly perpendicular, as to resemble a handsome, well-built wharf. On the opposite side, however, the masses to which they looked for security were themselves rather terrific objects, as they leaned over so much towards the ship, as to give the appearance of their being in the act of falling upon her deck; and as a very trifling concussion often produces the fall of much heavier masses of ice, when in appearance very firmly fixed to the ground, Captain Parry gave orders that no guns should be fired near the ship during her continuance in this situation. The Griper was of necessity made fast near the beach, in rather an exposed situation, and her rudder unshipped, in readiness for the ice coming in; it remained quiet, however, though quite close, during the day, the weather being calm and fine.

In the evening of the 18th, some heavy pieces of grounded ice to which the bow halser of the Hecla was fastened, fell off into the water, snapping the rope without injuring the ship. Nevertheless, as every alteration of this kind must materially change the centre of gravity of the whole mass, it was thought prudent to move the Hecla out of her harbor to the place where the Griper was lying, lest some of the bergs should fall upon her deck and crush or sink her.

On the 20th and 21st, the young ice formed to such a degree, as to cement together all the loose ice about the ships; nor did it thaw on either of those days, though the sun shone clearly upon it for several hours. The main body remained close and firm in every direction. The same state of things obtained on the 22d, and in the morning of the 23d, the young ice was an inch and a half thick. A breeze springing up from the westward put it in motion, so that by noon the ships were able to warp out and proceed eastward. In a short time, however, the ice closed so firmly around them that they became wholly unmanageable, and received many blows, more severe than any they had experienced before. After having drifted with the ice six miles, they were made fast to some grounded ice

The situation in which the ships were now placed, and the shortness of the remaining part of the navigable season, caused great anxiety. Judging from the experience of 1819, it was reasonable to conclude that about the 7th of September, was the

limit beyond which the ships could not keep the sea with any degree o. safety or prospect of success; but being strongly impressed wi..i the idea that it was incumbent on him to make every
possible effort, Captain Parry determined to extend this limit to
the 14th of September, before which date the winter would have
set in. The prospect was not very encouraging, even with this
extension; they had only advanced sixty miles this season, and
the distance to Icy Cape was yet between eight and nine hundred
miles, supposing them to find a clear passage. The provisions
too, were so far reduced in quantity, that by no means could they
be made to hold out longer than till April, 1822, and the deficiency of fuel was even more apparent. These and other minor
considerations, induced Captain Parry to ask the advice and
opinions of his officers relative to the expediency of returning to
England. They all agreed that any attempt to penetrate farther
westward in their present parallel, would be fruitless, and attended
with loss of time that might be more profitably employed else-
where. They advised that the vessel should run back along the
edge of the ice, in order to look for an opening that might lead
toward the American continent, and after a reasonable time spent
in the search, to return to England. This advice agreeing with
his own opinions, Captain Parry resolved to comply with it.

On the twenty-fourth the ships moved again, and found less ice
as they advanced, so that when, on the morning of the 27th, they
cleared the east end of Melville Island, the navigable channel
was not less than ten miles wide. A constant look-out was kept
from the crow's nest for an opening to the south, but none occurred. The weather was hazy, so much so that they were again
obliged to steer the ships the one by the other. As they proceeded, several islands hitherto unknown, were discovered, but no
opening was seen in the ice, and when they had, on the 30th,
reached longitude 90°, they became satisfied that there was no
possibility of effecting their object, and Captain Parry, therefore,
conceived it to be his duty to return forthwith to England, in
order that no time might be lost in following up his discoveries,
if his government should deem fit to do so.

The Hecla arrived at the Orkney Islands on the 28th of
October; and the Griper on the first of November. Thus did
they return from a voyage of eighteen months duration, in good
health and spirits, with the loss of only one man.

CAPTAIN PARRY'S SECOND VOYAGE OF DISCOVERY.

The discoveries made by the expedition under Captain Parry in 1819-20, being believed to afford a strong presumption of the existence of a Northwest Passage to the Pacific Ocean, the British government commanded that another attempt should be made to discover it. The Hecla having been found well adapted to this kind of service, the Fury, a ship of precisely the same class, was selected to accompany her. Captain George F. Lyon was appointed to command the Hecla, and Captain Parry, whose efforts had made him justly celebrated, was commissioned to command the expedition.

Some alterations in the interior arrangements of the vessels, such as were suggested by the experience of Captain Parry, were made. Among these was an apparatus for melting snow, which was found very useful, and was so little in the way, that it could not even be seen. Cots and hammocks were substituted for the former bed places, and some improvements were made in the manner of victualling the ships.

In his official instructions, Captain Parry was directed to proceed into Hudson's Strait, till he should meet the ice, when the Nautilus Transport, which was placed at his disposal, was to be cleared of its provisions and stores. He was then to penetrate westward, till he should reach some land which he should be convinced was a part of the American *continent*, at some point north of Wager River. If he reached the Pacific, he was to proceed to Kamschatka; thence to Canton or the Sandwich Islands, and thence to England, by whatever route he might deem most convenient.

Accordingly, in the beginning of April, 1821, the three vessels sailed from England. Nothing worthy of note occurred till they met with the ice in Davis' Strait, where the vessels were moored to an iceberg, and the Nautilus was unladen. This done, she parted company on the 1st of July, and sailed for England, while the Fury and Hecla stood toward the ice, which they reached a little before noon, and ran along its edge, keeping as much to the westward as possible.

On the 24th, they reached the Savage Islands, and landed on one of them. They are many—all exhibiting the same appearance of utter sterility. That on which they landed was from six to eight hundred feet above the level of the sea. Here they noticed the same appearances of an Esquimaux camp as had been seen at Melville Island, with a few pieces of fir, which proved that the savages, in these parts, were not in want of wood, since they could afford to leave it behind 'icm. Hares and several species of birds were seen on this islar 1.

As soon as the exploring party retur ed on board, all sail was made to the westward, the sea being ow nearly free from ice The next day the hills on the coast of Labrador were seen. Thus they kept on till the 31st, discov ring islands as they proceeded. On the afternoon of this day, an Esquimaux *oomiak* was seen coming from the shore of Sali bury Island, under sail, accompanied by eight kayaks. In this boat were sixteen persons, of which two were men, and the rest women and children. In dress and personal appearance, these pe ple did not differ from the Esquimaux last seen, but their behavio was far less offensive.

On the first of August, the ships kept on westward between Nottingham Island and the north she e, which is fringed with small islands. This channel is about twelve miles wide. In the course of the morning, some Esquimaux came to the ships from the main land, bringing oil, skin dresses, and walrus's tusks, which they exchanged for any trifle that was offered. They also offered toys for sale, such as models of canoes, weapons, &c. Here, for the first time, the navigators saw the dresses of the savages lined with the skins of birds, having the feathers inside.

Having run forty miles in the night without seeing any ice, they came the next morning to a pack so close as to prevent their farther progress. The ships received very heavy blows, and with considerable difficulty got clear of it. They ran along the edge several miles to the northward, in search of an opening; but finding none, they stood back to the southward, to try what could be done in that quarter.

The expedition being now about to enter upon ground hitherto unexplored, it became necessary for Captain Parry to decide on the route he should pursue with most advantage, and after mature deliberation, he came to the resolution to attempt a direct passage of the Frozen Strait, though he greatly feared the loss of time that would be the consequence of a failure.

After contending with the ice for several days, c. the 11th, the ship succeeded in getting to the northern land, and a party of the officers landed upon a small rock, or islet, a mile and a half from the shore.

Soon after the party returned on board, a fresh gale from the north compelled them to make the ships fast to the largest floe near, in order not to lose much ground. The gale moderated about noon, and they cast off from the floe and made sail. They made considerable progress till evening, when the ice closed round them again. After sunset on the 13th, they descried land to the westward, which they believed to be a part of the continent. Yet they continued closely beset, and on the 15th the Hecla drifted back with the ice, out of sight of her consort. This was partly owing to the extraordinary refraction upon the horizon.

which apparently diminished and distorted objects, at no great distance, in a wonderful manner. On the next day, however, the Hecla hove in sight, and upon which the Fury set sail and beat through the channel. On the morning of the 17th, the weather being too foggy to move, parties from both ships went on shore, to examine the country, and to procure specimens of its natural productions.

As soon as the weather cleared up, they returned on board, and sailed to the northeast, where alone they had any chance of finding an outlet. Having ascertained the continuity of land round this inlet, they gave it the name of Duke of York's Bay. It was now certain that the object of the expedition could not be effected in that direction; and they therefore sailed back, through the narrow channel by which they had entered, with the intention of seeking an opening farther north, without delay.

It would be tedious to tell of every obstacle, that hindered or delayed the ships. They pursued their intended course along the shore, when the wind and weather permitted; and when unavoidably detained, they landed. Among other places, they landed at Repulse Bay, in latitude 66° 30 min. and longitude 86° 30 min. From all indications, the water through which they had been sailing, was the imperfectly known Frozen Strait; and Captain Parry resolved to keep along the land to the northward, and examine every bend or inlet, which might appear likely to afford a practicable passage to the westward.

Sailing on the 23d along the northern shore of Frozen Strait, it was observed that the land appeared in one place to consist of islands only, behind which no land was visible. This part of the coast appeared to Captain Parry so favorable to the accomplishment of his enterprise, that he resolved to examine it more closely. Having beat up to the mouth of an opening that seemed practicable, he found the greater part of the channel filled with a body of ice, rendering examination in ships or boats impossible. The only means, therefore, of exploring it were, to despatch a party by land. Captain Lyon undertook this service, accompanied by five persons, furnished with a tent and four days' provision. The ships were anchored to await his return a mile from the shore. The flood tide came *out* of this inlet, a circumstance that materially strengthened their hopes of success.

Captain Lyon first landed on an island, and then crossed a strait to a steep point. Thence proceeding northward to a high hill, he found the strait continuous, and returned to the ships. On this short journey, he passed the remains of a great many Esquimaux habitations. The result of Captain Lyon's excursion was to convince all concerned, that a communication existed here between Frozen Strait and a sea to the northward and eastward of it, and Captain Parry determined to explore it as far as possible

After drifting about some time in the ice, and more than once narrowly escaping shipwreck, measures were taken to survey this part of the Frozen Strait; but little knowledge was gained by all their efforts. On the 1st of September, the prospect of getting northward, was by no means encouraging; and they were, from time to time, beset with ice, and drifted back. On the 3d, they found that after a laborious investigation, which had occupied a whole month, they had returned to nearly the same spot where they had been on the 6th of August, near Southampton Island.

On the 1st of October, rain fell, which immediately freezing, made the decks and ropes as smooth as glass. For several days the thermometer had been below the freezing point, and sometimes as low as 20° at night, which change, together with the altered aspect of the land, and the rapid formation of young ice near the shores, gave notice of the approach of winter. The commencement of this dreary season in these regions may, indeed, be dated from the time when the earth no longer receives and radiates heat enough to melt the snow which falls upon it.

On the 8th, the young ice on the surface began to give them warning that the navigation of those seas was nearly ended .or the season. When the young ice has acquired the thickness of half an inch, and is of considerable extent, a ship must be stopped by it, unless favored by a strong and fair wind; and even when making progress, is not under control of the helmsman, depending mostly on the thickness of the ice on one bow or the other. Boats cannot be employed in such situations with much effect.

When to these difficulties were added the disadvantage of a temperature near zero, and twelve hours of daily darkness, Captain Parry became convinced that it was expedient to place the ships in the most secure situation that could be found, rather than run the risk of being permanently detached from the land by attempting to gain the continent. Accordingly, a canal was sawed into a harbor on the south side of a small island, to which the name of Winter Island was given, and the ships were warped to their winter stations. Thus ended their operations for the season, after having explored a portion of coast six hundred miles in extent, one half of which belonged to the continent of America.

The arrangements for passing the winter comfortably were pretty much the same as those which had been made at Melville Island, with some improvements, suggested by former experience. The theatre was better fitted than before, and a school was established for the benefit of such of the crews as might wish to learn to read and write. The lower deck of the Fury was fitted for a church, and the companies of both ships attended during the winter. The men were sent to walk on shore for exercise, whenever the weather was favorable; and finger-posts were erected in various parts of the island, to prevent them from losing their way

On the 11th of December, the weather being tolerably clear, stars of the third magnitude were visible to the naked eye at forty minutes past eight, and those of the second magnitude till a quarter past nine, which may give some idea of the degree of light at this period. The twilight was, of course, very long, and the redness of the sun's rays might be seen more than three hours after its setting.

On the 13th, the thermometer fell to—31°, being the lowest temperature yet experienced. Rising on the 17th to—5°, the play of The Poor Gentleman was performed. On Christmas eve the theatre was again put in requisition, and the next day was celebrated to the utmost extent their means would allow. Among the luxuries of the Christmas dinner were a few joints of English roast beef, which had been preserved expressly for the occasion, the first and last ever eaten in Frozen Strait.

The same occupations, that had employed them at Melville Island served to beguile the time this winter. Nothing material occurred till the first of February, unless the circumstance of seeing a white bear may be accounted so.

On the 1st of February, a number of Esquimaux were seen coming toward the ships over the ice, and the appearance of huts was discovered on the shore with a telescope. Captains Parry and Lyon, with three or four others, set out to meet the natives who were slowly advancing, to the number of twenty-five. As the officers advanced, they stood still, awaiting their approach. They had no arms, but carried only a few strips of whalebone, which they had brought for a peace-offering, and which the gentlemen immediately purchased for a few small nails and beads. There were several women and children with the party, and the behavior of all was quite peaceable and orderly. They were all handsomely dressed in deerskins, and some had double suits.

However quiet these savages were, they did not exhibit the slightest signs of apprehension or distrust. As soon as some understanding was established, the officers expressed a wish to visit their huts, and the Esquimaux readily complying, they all set out together. The savages were greatly astonished on the way to see a large dog, belonging to the whites, fetch and carry; and the children could scarcely contain their joy when Captain Lyon gave them a stick to throw, and the dog brought it back to them. An infirm old man, who supported himself with a staff, which he much needed, was left behind by his companions, who took no notice of his infirmities, but left him to find his way as he might, without reluctance or scruple.

An intercourse was kept up between the ships and the Esquimaux, as long as the latter remained there, which was until the 23d of May, when they set off with all their goods and chattels, including a parting gift from Captain Parry.

The caulking of the bows being now completed, the ships were released from the ice by sawing round them; an operation which made them rise in the water six inches and a half, in consequence of the buoyancy occasioned by the winter's expenditure.

An increased extent of open water appearing in the offing, Captain Lyon again departed, accompanied by nine persons, with a tent, fuel, and provisions for twenty days. Each individual was furnished with a light sledge, to draw his provision and baggage, which might weigh about an hundred pounds. Their instructions were, after gaining the continent to proceed along the coast and examine it, and to make observations respecting the tides and the natural productions of the country.

He set out on the 8th of May, and rested on the 9th at a low, rocky point, which he called Point Belford. Proceeding northward, he had given the following names successively to different parts of the coast, viz. Blake's Bay, Adderly's Bluff, Palmer Bay, Point Elizabeth, and Cape William; when, finding his provision and fuel half expended, he judged it prudent to return.

Flocks of birds now began to give token of returning summer, and, on the 25th, some Esquimaux, who came from an encampment to the westward, reported having seen a great many reindeer. Yet at the close of May it was matter of general regret that there was little prospect of the departure of the ice, and that few indications of a thaw had been observed. The navigators could not fail to remember that at Melville Island, though so much farther north, the season had, on the same day two years before, advanced full as far as now at Winter Island. The parts of the land which were most bare were the smooth, round tops of the hills, on some of which were little pools of water. There were also, on the low lands, a few dark, uncovered patches, looking, in the snow, like islets in the sea. Vegetation seemed striving to commence, and a few tufts of saxifrage oppositifolia, when closely examined, discovered some signs of life. Such was the state of things on shore: upon the ice appearances were as unpromising. Except in the immediate vicinity of the ships where from incessant trampling, and the deposit of various stores upon the ice, some heat had been absorbed artificially, there was no perceptible sign of dissolution on the upper surface, where six or seven inches of snow yet remained on every part. In these circumstances, Captain Parry resolved to try what could be done to release the ships by cutting and sawing. Arrangements were, therefore, made for getting everything on board, and for commencing this laborious work.

The operation began on the 3d of June, and was completed in sixteen days, by severe and persevering labor. In the meanwhile, Nature seemed unwilling to lend our mariners any aid: the dissolution of the ice was so slow as scarcely to be perceptible. However, it was so weakened by the cut made, that the first pressure from without effected a rupture so that a favorable breeze only was needed, to enable the ships to put to sea. On the 2d of July, the wind, for the first time, became fair, and the ships sailed.

Winter Island is ten miles and a half in length, from north-west by north, to south-east by south, and its average breadth from eight to ten miles. It is what seamen call rather low land; the height of the south-east point, which was named Cape Fisher, out of respect to the chaplain and astronomer, being seventy-six feet, and none of the hills above three times that height. The outline of the land is smooth, and in the summer, when free from snow, presents a brown appearance. Several miles of the north-west end of the island are so low and level, that, when the snow lay thick upon it, our travellers could only distinguish it from the sea by the absence of hummocks of ice.

The basis of the island is gneiss rock, much of which is of a gray color, but in many places also the feldspar is so predominant as to give a bright and red appearance to the rocks, especially about Cape Fisher, where also some broad veins of quartz are seen intersecting the gneiss; and both this and the feldspar are very commonly accompanied by a green substance, which appeared to be pistacite, and which usually occurs as a thin lamina adhering strongly to the others. In many specimens these three are united, the feldspar and quartz displaying tolerably perfect crystals. In some of the gneiss small red garnets are abundant, as also in mica-slate. In lumps of granite, which are found detached upon the surface, the mica sometimes occurs in white plates, and in other specimens is of a dirty brown color. There are several varieties of mica-slate, and some of these have a brilliant metallic appearance, like silver; those which are most so, crumble very easily to pieces. The most common stone next to those already mentioned is lime, which is principally schistose, and of a white color. Many pieces of this substance, on being broken, present impressions of fossil-shells, and some have also brown waved lines running quite through them. Nodules of flint occur in some masses of lime, but they are not common. Iron pyrites is found in large lumps of black stone, tinged externally with the oxyde of iron: it is here and there met with in small perfect cubes.

Sailing northward along the coast, the ships were soon stopped by the ice. While they remained stationary, a party of natives were discovered on shore, who proved to be their neighbors of Winter Island. They were cordially greeted by the officers and seamen as old acquaintances, and loaded with presents. On leaving the ships, one of them sent Captain Parry a piece of seal skin as a present, without the least prospect or expectation of a return. We mention this trifling incident, merely because it was the first and only undeniable proof of gratitude observed among these people

Slowly and painfully our navigators pursued their course north-ward, always with difficulty and often with great danger. On the 12th of the month, they discovered the mouth of a considerable river, and Captain Parry went on shore to examine it. The water was fresh, and the stream varied in breadth from four hundred yards to the third of a mile. After ascending a mile and a half, the Captain heard the roar of a waterfall. At the mouth, the banks of the river were about two hundred feet high, but here they rose much higher, and the water ran on a more elevated level. As Captain Parry proceeded inland, he found the stream rushing with great fury over two small cataracts. Then turning a right angle of the river, he perceived a greater spray, occasion-ed by a very magnificent fall. Where the stream begins its de-scent it is contracted to the breadth of one hundred and fifty feet, the channel being worn in a solid bed of gneiss rock. After fall-ing about fifteen feet, at an angle of thirty degrees, the river is again narrowed to forty yards, and, as if collecting its strength for a great effort, is precipitated ninety feet, in one unbroken mass. A cloud of spray rises from the cataract, surmounted by an uncommonly vivid rainbow. The basin which receives the fall is circular and about four hundred yards in diameter, rather wider than the river immediately below. Above the cataract, the stream winds in the most romantic manner imaginable among the hills, with a smooth and unruffled surface. To this beautiful water-course Captain Parry gave the name of Barrow's River. Its entrance is in latitude 67° 18′ 05″, and longitude 81° 25′ 20′.

The next day large herds of walrusses were seen upon the drift ice, and the boats were sent to kill some for the sake of the oil. The sportsmen found them lying huddled together, piled upon one another. They waited quietly to be shot, and were not greatly alarmed even after one or two volleys. They suffered the people to debark on the ice near them, but on their near approach displayed a somewhat pugnacious purpose. After they got into the water three were struck with harpoons and killed. When first wounded, they were quite furious: one of them resolutely attacked Captain Lyon's boat, and injured it with his tusks. Those which remained uninjured surrounded the wounded animals, and struck them with their tusks; whether to assist their escape, or with a hostile intention, cannot be ascertained. Two of the animals killed were females, and one weighed over fifteen hundred pounds, which was not considerd an uncommon bulk. The strength of the walrus is very great. One of them being touched with an oar, seized it with his flippers, and snapped it with the utmost ease. Many of these animals had young ones, which, when assailed, they carried off, either between their flippers or on their backs. They were most easily killed with musket-balls, even after being struck with the harpoon, as their skins are so tough as to resist a whaling lance

On the 15th, the ships reached Igloolik, fo the situation of which we refer our readers to the map. Here t iey found a new band of Esquimaux, who proved to be the acquaintances and relatives of those of Winter Island. These people dwelt not in snow huts, but in tents, made of the skins of the walrus and seal, the former shaved thin enough to allow the transmission of light. They were clumsily made, and supported by a kind of tent-pole, constructed by tying bones or deer's horns together. The edges of the tents were kept down by placing stones upon them. To keep the whole fabric erect, a thong was extended from the top to a large stone at the distance of a few yards. These abiding places had little appearance of affording comfort or convenience.

From these people Captain Parry learned that he had unquestionably been coasting the *continent*. He then determined to attempt to penetrate a large inlet, stretching w stward from Igloolik, which, at the time of his arrival, was closed by a fixed barrier of ice, and which he named The Strait of the Fury and Hecla. We shall not follow the navigators in their arduous but unsuccessful efforts to penetrate westward at this point, as we have already alloted more space to their adventures than consists with our intended limits. Suffice it to say, that after persevering in the attempt till the 30th of September, they found themselves as far from the attainment of their object as at first. The cold weather then setting in, they were compelled to lay the ships up at Igloolik.

One important point was settled, however, beyond the possibility of doubt. Finding his researches ineffectual by water, Captain Parry undertook to explore the Strait of the Fury and Hecla by land. He found it continuous, and pursued his journey far enough to see the open sea beyond, thus proving the existence of a passage at this point, though it was then, and probably ever will be, closed by an insurmountable barrier of ice. Beside this result of his endeavors, the position of Cockburn Island, and indeed of all the lands adjacent to Igloolik, was ascertained, and correctly laid down on the map.

Beside the Esquimaux found at Igloolik, our friends had the society of the savages of Winter Island, who rejoined them shortly after their arrival. We are sorry that we cannot relate the adventures and observations of this winter, as they are extremely entertaining; but as they are not important in their nature, we trust to be excused for omitting them.

Igloolik is a low island, ten miles long and six broad, and exhibits the same appearance of sterility as the adjacent continent, excepting in places which have been inhabited by the natives. There, the accumulation of animal substances has produced a luxuriant vegetation. In some parts there are spots several hundred yards in extent, covered with bright green moss. The whole land seems to be composed of innumerable fragments

of thin schistose limestone, some of which contain the impressions
of fossil remains, while others present the cellular structure
usually found in madreporite. The interior is almost an entire
swamp; but there are rising grounds, which, with the remains of
Esquimaux habitations upon them, are excellent landmarks.

East of Igloolik is a group of small islands called by Captain
Parry Calthorpe Islands. Like almost all the land in this vicinity,
they are low, but their geology differs from that of Igloolik, and
in every respect resembles that of Winter Island, being composed
of gneiss. Two of this group, however, are high and rugged
From the top of one of these there is a good view of the adjacen
shores.

The entrance of the Strait of the Fury and Hecla is about
three miles wide, and is formed by two projecting headlands
between which the tide rushes with great velocity. The south
shore is high, but of gradual ascent, perfectly smooth, and com
posed of beautifully variegated sand-stone. Beyond the entrance
the land is bold and mountainous. Captain Parry, who it will be
remembered explored the southern shore of the strait, states the
hills to consist of gray gneiss and red granite, rising, in some instances, a thousand feet above the level of the sea. In some
places he saw slate, and in others sand-stone. He has left no
positive data, by which we may determine the length of this
strait; but as he was rather more than a day in accomplishing the
distance on foot, by a circuitous route, we may conclude that it
does not exceed fifteen or twenty miles. From the point where
his journey terminated he saw a continuous sea to the westward,
open and unobstructed save by ice and by one small island

There are several islands in the Strait of the Fury and Hecla.
On one of these (Liddon Island) abundance of beautifully veined
clay iron stone was found. The other minerals were asbestos,
crystals of carbonate of lime, and a great variety of sand-stone,
of which the island is formed.

Amherst Island is flat, and the northern part is formed of black
slate, with strong indications of coal. This part of the island is
utterly bare of vegetation. In a low cliff of black and rugged
slate there is a beautiful and romantic grotto. The water, oozing
through the sides and roof, has formed the most brilliant stalac-
tites, which form a splendid contrast with the shady part of the
ebon grotto behind. The other part of the island is of clay and
limesto e, on which there is a very scanty covering of shrivelled
grass and moss.

The winter in Igloolik was spent like the preceding one,
in amusements on board ship, and intercourse with the Esquimaux.

On the 9th of August the ships ran out of their harbor, where
they had been detained three hundred and nineteen days. They
were so embarrassed by the ice, that little use could be made of

their sails; nevertheless, by the 30th of the month they passed Winter Island, having been carried three degrees by the drift in which they were beset. On the 9th of October, they made the Orkney Islands, and on the 10th reached Lerwick in Shetland, where they were received with many congratulations on their safe return.

CAPTAIN PARRY'S THIRD VOYAGE OF DISCOVERY.

The British Government having resolved to fit out a third expedition, under Captain Parry, the Hecla and Fury were made ready for sea, the latter under the command of Captain Hoppnet, and sailed from England on the 16th of May 1824. They were to attempt the northwest passage at Prince Regent's Inlet. Having crossed the Atlantic without any material adventure, they made the bay of Lievely in Disko Island on the 5th of July.

Sailing up Baffin's Bay, on the 17th the ships came to the ice, and after many obstructions, only penetrated seventy miles to the westward. Here they encountered a hard gale, and sustained several shocks that would have crushed any ship of ordinary strength. They reached Lancaster's Sound on the 10th of September. The winds not being favorable, the ships made small progress, and on the 13th the crews had the mortification to perceive the sea ahead covered with ice, in attempting to penetrate which they were soon immovably beset. Nevertheless, the exertions of Captain Parry and his coadjutor were unremitting.

The officers landed at one place, a little east of Admiralty Inlet. The vegetation was, as usual in those regions, very scanty. With great exertion and extreme difficulty, the expedition reached Port Bowen in Prince Regent's Inlet, on the 27th, where, by the middle of October, Captain Parry deemed it advisable to lay up the ships for the winter. Several journeys inland proved the country to be exceedingly broken and rugged; so much so that the researches of the explorers were of necessity confined to a very limited extent.

About midnight on the 27th of January, a brilliant display of the Aurora Borealis was observed. It broke out in a single compact mass of yellow light, appearing but a short distance above the land. This light, notwithstanding its general continuity, sometimes appeared to be composed of numerous groups of rays, compressed laterally, as it were, into one, its limits to right and left being well defined and nearly vertical. Though always very brillant, it constantly varied in intensity; and this appeared to be

produced by one volume of light overlaying another, as we see the
darkness of smoke increase when cloud rolls over cloud. While
some of the officers were admiring the exceeding beauty of the
phenomenon, they were suddenly astonished at seeing a brilliant
ray shoot down from the general mass *between them and the land,*
thence distant three thousand yards.

The principal animals seen were bears, foxes, hares and mice,
but no deer or wolves. These animals appeared but rarely, and
the same may be said of the feathered creation. In July, a canal
was sawed in the ice, and the ships were towed to sea. Captain
Parry hoped to sail over to the western shore of the inlet, but he
had only made eight miles in the intended direction, when he was
stopped by the ice. As no opening appeared in that quarter, he
determined to try to cross more to the northward. The most he
gained was some knowledge of the character of the shores.

On the 30th of July, the ships being beset close to the land,
a hard gale brought the ice close upon them. The Hecla received no damage but the breaking of two or three hawsers; but
the Fury was forced on shore. She was heaved off again, with
little injury, but this was but the commencement of her misfortunes. On the 1st of July, she was again nipped, and so
severely strained as to leak a great deal. As the tide fell, her
stern, which was aground, was lifted several feet, and the Hecla
also remained aground. No place was found where the Fury
might be hove down to repair the damage, as the shore was everywhere lined with masses of grounded ice. The ships were again
made to float, but it was found, notwithstanding incessant labor
on board the Fury, that four pumps constantly going could hardly
keep the water under. In these circumstances the only harbor
that could be found was formed by three grounded masses of ice,
within which the water was from three to four fathoms deep at
low tide.

On the night of the 2d, the ice came in with great violence,
and again forced the Fury on shore. The strength and number
of the Hecla's hawsers only saved her from sharing the same
fate. In the meanwhile the crew of the Fury were completely
exhausted by labor, and their hands had become so sore by the
constant friction of the ropes that they could no longer handle
them without mittens. In this situation it was determined to land
the stores and provisions of the vessel, in order that she might
undergo a complete repair.

Accordingly anchors were carried to the beach, by which the
grounded icebergs that formed the harbor were secured in their
position, thus enclosing a space just sufficient to admit both ships
In this position a great part of the Fury's stores were landed
The injury was found to be more severe than had at first been
supposed; indeed, it appeared that the compactness of her fabric
had alone saved her from sinking. Nevertheless, no exertion

was spared to render her seaworthy again, though the daily pressure of the ice was another, and a very great disadvantage.

In spite of every effort, it was found impossible to save the Fury, and the Hecla was greatly endangered in the attempt. She was compelled to leave the land and drift about among the ice, to avoid being forced on shore.   On returning, Captain Parry found that the Fury had been driven farther on the beach than before, and nine feet of water were in her hold.   Her keel and bottom were more injured than ever.   The first glance satisfied Captain Parry that the vessel could never return to England. By and with the advice of a council of his officers, therefore, he decided to leave her to her fate, and as his provisions would barely suffice for another twelvemonth, to return home.   In pursuance of this resolution the Hecla reached Sheerness on the 21st of October.   On the eastern shore of Prince Regent's Inlet is Cape Kater, the most southern point attained by the ships in this expedition.   It is in latitude 71°, 53′ 30,″ and longitude 90° 03′ 45″

NARRATIVE OF THE LOSS OF THE ALCESTE.

The Alceste sailed from Whampoa on the 21st of January, 1817; exchanged friendly salutes with the guardians of the Bocca Tigris; touched at Macao and Manilla; rounded the numerous clusters of rocks and shoals lying to the westward of the Phillippines, and to the northwest of Borneo; and then shaped a course for the Straits of Gaspar, which she entered soon after daylight on the 18th of February.

The morning was fine, the wind fresh and favorable, and the Alceste moving rapidly through the water; every appearance promised a rapid passage into the Java sea, for which Captain Maxwell, who had been on board the whole of the preceding night, was steering the course laid down in the most approved charts, and recommended by the sailing directions in his possession, when the ship struck against a sunken rock, three miles distant from Pulo Leat, or Middle Island, and having grated over it for a few seconds, took a slight heel to starboard, and became immovable.   The rapidity of her motion, at the instant of striking, rendered it highly probable that she had received serious injury; and every doubt on this subject was soon removed by the appearance of her false keel floating along side, and the report of the carpenter, who stated that the water in the hold had increased from two and a half to seven feet, and that it was gaining rapidly on the pumps.

The sails, which had at first been thrown aback, were now furled, and the best-bower anchor was dropped, to keep her fast, from the apprehension, if she went off the rock, of her instantly sinking. At this alarming crisis, not the slightest confusion or irregularity occurred; every necessary order was as coolly given, and as steadily obeyed, as if nothing unusual had happened; every one did his duty calmly, diligently, and effectually.

The boats being hoisted out, Lord Amherst and the gentlemen of his suite, within half an hour of the striking of the ship, were in the barge, and making for the nearest part of the above mentioned desert island. After leaving the Alceste, they saw more accurately the dangerous nature of her situation. The rock on which she had struck was distinctly seen from the boat, extending only a few yards from her. Beyond, the water was dark and deep for nearly half a mile; it then became so shallow that the beautiful but fatal coral was continually seen as they approached the shore. When about a mile from Pulo Leat, rocks, covered by not more than from one to three feet water, surrounded them on all sides. The barge struck several times, but was saved from any serious accident by the skill of Lieutenant Hoppner, who commanded her. After sailing or rowing for about an hour, they gained what had appeared from the ship to be land covered with wood—but, to their mortification, discovered nothing but insulated masses of granite, interspersed with mangrove trees growing in the water. Being now joined by a cutter, with the servants of the embassy, and a part of the guard, they proceeded along shore in quest of a more convenient place for debarkation. Several creeks, which seemed to penetrate inland, were in vain explored; they all terminated in deep swamps. Similar attempts were reiterated, till anxiety to send back the boats determined his Excellency to land on the first rocks which should be found sufficiently large or numerous for the reception of the party. This intention was at length effected in a small bay, where the rocks were so mingled with the trees as to afford firm hand-hold. The boats were then immediately despatched to assist in bringing on shore whatever could be saved from the wreck. A more convenient landing-place being subsequently discovered near an eminence on which an encampment might be formed, the whole party removed thither, leaving a marine behind to communicate with the boats as they successively approached the shore.

The heat of the day as it advanced, and the exertions of the men in clearing the ground, for the reception of persons and baggage, produced great thirst, and rendered it necessary to look for water, of which none had been brought on shore, except a very small quantity collected from the dripstones on deck. A search for this purpose was conducted in several directions without success; and, night coming on, it was relinquished in hopes of better fortune on the morrow. During the whole day, and till a late hour in the evening, the boats were constantly employed conveying articles from the wreck, and towing ashore a raft on which had been placed the baggage, stores, and a small supply of provisions rescued with much labor and difficulty, under the superintendence of Captain Maxwell, whose exertions and self-possession were most highly spoken of by all his fellow sufferers.

Towards midnight, as the tide rose, the swell of the sea lifted the ship from the rock, and dashed her on it again with such violence as to render it necessary for the topmast to be cut away In doing this, two men were very severely bruised.

The following morning Captain Maxwell landed; and, after consulting with Lord Amherst, it was determined that his Excellency, and the gentlemen of the embassy, should proceed without delay to Batavia in the barge, with a picked crew, commanded by the Junior Lieutenant, (Mr. Hoppner;) one of the cutters was also prepared to accompany them, for the purpose of assisting in case of attack or accident. The master of the Alceste was sent on board the latter to navigate the boats. At this season there was no probability of the passage to Batavia exceeding sixty hours, the distance being only one hundred and ninety seven miles; the inconvenience to which his Excellency would be subjected was, consequently, very limited in duration; and much additional expedition in the despatch of relief might be expected from his personal exertions at Batavia. The stock of liquors and provisions furnished to the boats was necessarily very small, and only sufficient on very short allowance to support existence for four or five days; only seven gallons of water could be spared for the whole party, consisting of forty-seven persons; but they were fortunately visited by a heavy fall of rain on the day after their departure, which more than supplied the place of what had already been expended.

The number left behind was two hundred men and boys and one woman. The first measure of Captain Maxwell, after fixing a party to dig a well in a spot which was judged, from a combination of circumstances, the most likely to find water, was to remove our bivouac to the top of the hill, where we could breathe a cooler and purer air, a place, in all respects, not only better adapted to the preservation of our health, but to our defence in case of attack. A path was cut upwards, and a party employed in clearing away and setting fire to the underwood on the summit. This last operation tended much to free us from myriads of ants, and of snakes, scorpions, centipedes, and other reptiles, which, in such a place and climate, generally abound. Others were employed in removing upwards our small stock of provisions, which were deposited, under a strict guard, in a sort of natural magazine, formed by the tumbling together of some huge masses of rock on the highest part of this eminence. On board the wreck a party was stationed, endeavoring to gain any accession they could to

our stock of provisions and arms, and to save any public stores
that could be found.   There was a communication for this purpose
between the shore and the ship whenever the tide permitted
For the last two days every one had experienced much misery
from thirst; a small cask of water (the only one which could be
obtained from the ship) was scarcely equal to a pint each in the
course of that period; and perhaps no question was ever so anxiously repeated as, "What hope from the well?"   About eleven
at night the diggers had got, by rather a tortuous direction,) on
account of large stones,) as far down as twenty feet, when they
came to a clayey or marly soil, that above it being a red earth,
which seemed rather moist, and had nothing saline in the taste.
At a little past midnight, a bottle of muddy water was brought the
captain as a specimen; and, the moment it was understood to be
fresh, the rush to the well was such as to impede the workmen;
therefore it became necessary to plant sentries to enable them to
complete their task, and permit the water to settle a little.   Fortunately, about this time a heavy shower of rain fell, and, by
spreading sheets, tablecloths, &c., and wringing them, some relief
was afforded.   There are few situations in which men, exposed
without shelter, to a torrent of rain would, as in the present instance, hail that circumstance as a blessing; bathing in the sea
was also resorted to by many in order *to drink by absorption*, and
they fancied it afforded relief.

   "Thursday, 20th.   This morning the Captain, ordering all
hands together, stated to them in a few words, that every man,
by the regulations of the navy, was as liable to answer for his
conduct on the present as on any other occasion; that, as long
as he lived, the same discipline should be exerted, and, if necessary, with greater rigor than on board; a discipline for the general welfare, which he trusted every sensible man of the party must
see the necessity of maintaining; assuring them, at the same time,
he would have much pleasure in recommending those who distinguished themselves by the regularity and propriety of their
conduct; that the provisions we had been able to save should be
served out, although necessarily with a very sparing hand, yet
with the most rigid equality to all ranks, until we obtained that
relief which he trusted would soon follow the arrival of Lord
Amherst at Java.

   "During this day the well afforded a pint of water for each
man; it had a sweetish milk-and-water taste, something like the
juice of the cocoa-nut, but nobody found fault with it; on the
contrary, it diffused that sort of happiness which only they can
feel who have felt the horrible sensation of thirst under a vertical
sun, subject at the same time to a harassing and fatiguing duty.
This day was employed in getting up every thing from the foot
of the hill; boats passing to the ship; but, unfortunately, almost
every thing of real value to us in our present case, was under

water. We were in hopes, however, that, as no bad weather was likely to happen, we might be enabled, by scuttling at low water, or by burning her upper works, to acquire many useful articles.

"On Friday (21st) the party stationed at the ship found themselves, soon after daylight, surrounded by a number of Malay proas, apparently well armed, and full of men. Without a single sword or musket for defence, they had just time to throw themselves into the boat alongside, and push for the shore, chased by the pirates, who, finding two of our other boats push out to their assistance, returned to the ship and took possession of her. Soon afterwards it was reported, from the look-out rock, that the savages, armed with spears, were landing at a point about two miles off. Under all the depressing circumstances attending shipwreck —of hunger, thirst, and fatigue, and menaced by a ruthless foe, it was glorious to see the British spirit stanch and unsubdued. The order was given for every man to arm himself in the best way he could; and it was obeyed with the utmost promptitude and alacrity. Rude pike-staves were formed, by cutting down young trees; small swords, dirks, knives, chisels, and even large spike nails sharpened, were firmly affixed to the ends of these poles; and those who could find nothing better, hardened the end of the wood in the fire, and bringing it to a sharp point, formed a tolerable weapon. There were, perhaps, a dozen cutlasses; the marines had about thirty muskets and bayonets, but could muster no more than seventy-five ball cartridges among the whole party. We had fortunately preserved some loose powder drawn from the upper deck guns after the ship had struck, (for the magazine was under water in five minutes,) and the marines, by hammering their buttons round, and by rolling up pieces of broken bottles in cartridges, did their best to supply themselves with a sort of langrage which would have some effect at close quarters; and strict orders were given not to throw away a single shot until sure of their aim. Mr. Cheffy, the carpenter, and his crew, under the direction of the Captain, were busied in forming a sort of abattis, by felling trees, and enclosing in a circular shape the ground we occupied; and, by interweaving loose branches with the stakes driven in among these, a breastwork was constructed, which afforded us some cover, and must naturally impede the progress of any enemy unsupplied with artillery. That part of the island we had landed on was a narrow ridge, not above a musket shot across, bounded on one side by the sea, and on the other by a creek, extending upwards of a mile inland, and nearly communicating with the sea at its head. Our hill was the outer point of this tongue, and its shape might be very well represented by an inverted punch bowl; the circle on which the bowl stands would then show the fortification, and the space within it our citadel.

" It appeared by the report of scouts, a short time after the first account, that the Malays had not actually landed, but had taken possession of some rocks near this point, on which they deposited a quantity of plunder brought from the ship; and during the day they continued making these predatory trips.

" In the evening all hands were mustered under arms, and a motley group they presented; it was gratifying, however, to observe, that, rude as were their implements of defence, there seemed to be no want of spirit to use them, if occasion offered. The officers and men were now marshalled regularly into different divisions and companies, their various posts assigned, and other arrangements made. An officer and party were ordered to take charge of the boats for the night; and they were hauled closer into the landing place. An alarm which occurred during the night showed the benefit of these regulations; for, on a sentry challenging a noise among the bushes, every one was at his post in an instant, and without the least confusion.

"On Saturday morning, (22d,) some of the Malay boats approached the place where ours were moored; and, with the view of ascertaining whether they had any inclination to communicate on friendly terms, the gig, with an officer and four hands, pulled gently towards them, waving the bough of a tree, (a general symbol of peace every where,) showing the usual demonstrations of friendship, and of a desire to speak to them; but all was vain, for they were merely reconnoitring our position, and immediately pulled back to their rock.

" The second Lieutenant (Mr. Hay) was now ordered, with the barge, cutter, and gig, armed in the best way we could, to proceed to the ship, and regain possession of her, either by fair means or by force; the pirates not appearing at this time to have more than eighty men. Those on the rocks, seeing our boats approach, threw all their plunder into their vessels and made off.

" Two of their largest proas were now at work on the ship; but, on observing their comrades abandon the rock, and the advance of the boats, they also made sail away, having previously set fire to the ship; which they did so effectually, that in a few minutes the flames burst from every port, and she was enveloped in a cloud of smoke. The boats were unable to board her, and therefore returned.

" Here was a period to every hope of accommodation with these people—if, indeed, any reasonable hope could ever have been entertained on that head. The Malays, more especially those wandering and piratical tribes who roam about the coasts of Borneo, Billiton, and the wilder parts of Sumatra, are a race of savages, perhaps the most merciless and inhuman to be found in any part of the world. The Battas are literally cannibals. In setting fire to the ship, they gave a decided proof of their disposition towards us; but, although certainly with no good intention, they did merely what we intended to do; for, by burning her upper works and decks, every thing buoyant could float up from below, and be more easily laid hold of.

"The ship continued burning during the whole of the night; and the flames, which could be seen through the openings of the trees, shed a melancholy glare around, and excited the most mournful ideas. This night, also, all hands were suddenly under arms again, from a marine firing his musket at what he very properly considered a suspicious character near his post, who appeared advancing upon him, and refused to answer after being repeatedly hailed. It turned out afterwards that the branch of a tree, half cut through the day before, had given away, under one of a race of large baboons, which we found about this time disputed the possession of the island with us. At the well, where there generally was kept a good fire at night, on account of the mosquitoes, the sentries had more than once been alarmed by these gentlemen showing their black faces from behind the trees. They became so exceedingly troublesome to some ducks we had saved from the wreck, (seizing and carrying them up the trees, and letting them fall down again when alarmed,) that on several occasions they left their little yard, and came up among the people, when the monkeys got among them; thus instinctively preferring the society of man for protection.

"On Sunday morning, (23d,) the boats were sent to the still smoking wreck; and some flour, a few cases of wine, and a cask of beer, had floated up. This last God-send was announced just at the conclusion of divine service, which was this morning held in the mess-tent; and a pint was ordered to be immediately served out to each man, which called forth three cheers. This seems to be the only style in which a British seaman can give vent to the warmer feelings of his heart. It is his mode of thanksgiving for benefits received; and it equally serves him to honor his friend, to defy his enemy, or to proclaim victory. This day we continued improving our fence, and clearing away a glacis immediately around it, that we might see and have fair play with these barbarians, should they approach. They had retired behind a little islet, called Pulo Chalacca, or Misfortune's Isle, about two miles from us, and seemed waiting there for reinforcements; for some of their party had made sail towards Billiton.

"Monday morning, (24,) the boats, as yesterday, went to the wreck, and returned with some casks of flour, only partially damaged; a few cases of wine, and about forty boarding pikes, with eighteen muskets, were also laid hold of. With the loose powder secured out of the great guns in the first instance, Mr. Holman, the gunner, had been actively employed forming musket-cartridges; and by melting down some pewter basins and jugs, with a small quantity of lead lately obtained from the wreck, balls were cast in clay moulds, increasing not a little our confidence and security. A quart of water each had been our daily allowance from the well hitherto; and on this day a second was completed near the foot of the hill in another direction, which not only supplied clearer water, but in greater plenty; and we could now, without restriction, indulge in the luxury of a long drink—not caring even to excite thirst, in order to enjoy that luxury in a higher perfection.

"On Tuesday, (25th,) the boats made their usual trip; some more cases of wine, and a few boarding-pikes, were obtained, both excellent articles in their way, in the hands of men who are inclined to entertain either their friends or their foes. On shore we were employed completing the paths to the wells, and felling trees which intercepted our view of the sea.

"Wednesday (26th,) at daylight, two of the pirate proas, with each a canoe astern, were discovered close in with the cove where our boats were moored. Lieutenant Hay, (a straight-forward sort of a fellow,) who had the guard that night at the boats, and of course slept in them, immediately dashed at the Malays with the barge, cutter, and gig. On perceiving this, they cut adrift their canoes, and made all sail, chased by our boats. They rather distanced the cutter and gig, but the barge gained upon them. On closing, the Malays evinced every sign of defiance, placing themselves in the most threatening attitudes, and firing their swivels at the barge. This was returned by Mr. Hay with the only musket he had in the boat; and, as they closed nearer, the Malays commenced throwing their javelins and darts, several falling into the barge, but without wounding any of the men. Soon after they were grappled by our fellows, when three of them having been shot, and a fourth knocked down with the but-end of the musket, five more jumped overboard and drowned themselves, (evidently disdaining quarter,) and two were taken prisoners, one of whom was severely wounded. This close style of fighting is termed by seamen *man-handling* an enemy.

"The Malays had taken some measures to sink their proa, for she went down almost immediately. Nothing could exceed the desperate ferocity of these people. One who had been shot through the body, but who was not quite dead, on being removed into the barge, with a view of saving him, (as his own vessel was sinking,) furiously grasped a cutlass which came within his reach; and it was not without a struggle wrenched from his hand; he died in a few minutes. The consort of this proa, firing a parting shot, bore up round the north end of the island and escaped. Their canoes* (which we found very useful to us,) were also brought on

---

* "During the time the boats were absent in chase, Mr. Fisher, anxious to secure one of the canoes, which was drifting past with the current, swam out towards it. When within a short distance of his object, an enormous shark was seen hovering near him, crossing and recrossing, as they are sometimes observed to do before making a seizure. To have called out might probably have unnerved him, (for he was unconscious of his situation;) and it was resolved to let him proceed without remark to the canoe, which was the nearest point of security. Happily he succeeded in getting safely into it; whilst the shark, by his too long delay, lost a very wholesome breakfast."

shore, containing several articles of plunder from the ship. They appeared to be the two identical proas which set fire to her. The prisoners, (the one rather elderly, the other young,) when brought on shore, seemed to have no hope of being permitted to live, and sullenly awaited their fate; but, on the wounds of the younger being dressed, the hands of the other untied, and food offered to them, with other marks of kindness, they became more cheerful, and appeared especially gratified at seeing one of their dead companions, who had been brought on shore, decently buried.

"The Malays are a people of very unprepossessing aspect; their bodies of a deep bronze color; their black teeth and reddened lips, (from chewing the beetle-nut and siri,) their gaping nostrils, and lank clotted hair hanging about their shoulders and over their scowling countenances, give them altogether a fiendlike and murderous look. They are likewise an unjoyous race, and seldom smile.

"The state of one of the wounds received by the Malay, (his knee joint being penetrated, and the bones much injured,) would have justified, more particularly in this kind of field practice, amputation; but, on consideration that it would be impossible to convince him of this being done with the intention of benefitting him, and might have the appearance of torture, which it was not improbable might suggest the idea of amputation and other operations to them, in the event of any or all of us falling into their hands, it was determined to try the effect of a good constitution, and careful attention. A little wigwam was built, and a blanket and other comforts given to him, his comrade being appointed his cook and attendant. They refused at first the provisions we offered them; but, on giving them some rice to prepare in their own way, they seemed satisfied. Never expecting quarter when overpowered in their piratical attempts, and having been generally tortured when taken alive, may account for the others drowning themselves.

'In the forenoon, immediately after this rencounter, fourteen proas and smaller boats appeared standing across from the Banca side; and soon after they anchored behind Pulo Chalacca. Several of their people landed, and carrying up some bundles on their shoulders, left them in the wood, and returned for more. We had some hope from the direction in which they first appeared, as well as their anchoring at that spot, (the rendezvous agreed upon at the departure of Lord Amherst,) that they might have been sent from Batavia to our relief.

"The small flag, belonging to the embassy, was brought down and displayed on the look-out rock; the strangers each immediately hoisted some flag at their mast-heads. Anxious to know still more about them, Mr. Sykes was allowed to advance with the union-jack, accompanied by some more of the young gentlemen, along the strand, to a considerable distance; and soon after some

of their party, with a flag, set off to meet them.   As they mutually
approached, the Malays dropped a little in the rear of their flag-
bearer, and laid down their arms; ours also fell astern, and the
two ancients, (or color men,) wading into a creek which separated them, cautiously met each other.   The Malay *salamed* a good
deal; many fine Yorkshire bows were made on the other side;
shaking hands was the next ceremony, and then, joining flags,
they walked up arm and arm to the place where the Captain and
several others were stationed.   Satisfied now that they must be
friends sent to our assistance, they were welcomed with cheers, and
every countenance was gladdened.   But our joy was of short
duration; for although their flag was laid submissively at the
Captain's feet, and all were sufficiently civil in their deportment,
yet they turned out to be mere wanderers, employed in gathering
a sort of seaweed, found on the coast of these (but in still greater
abundance among the Pelew) islands, said by some to be an article
of commerce with the Chinese epicures, who use it like the bird-
nests in their soups.   All this was made out chiefly by signs, added to a few Malay words which some understood.

  " Mr. Hay, with his division armed, proceeded down to their
anchorage, himself and some other officers going on board with
their Rajah, as they styled him, who expressed a great desire to
see the Captain on board, and sent him a present of a piece of
fish and some cocoa-nut milk.   During the night many schemes
were proposed as to the best mode of negotiating with these people.   Some thought that, by the hope of reward, they might be
induced to carry part of us to Java, and our four remaining boats
would then be equal to the conveyance of the rest.   Others, ad-
verting to the treacherous conduct of the Malays, and the great
temptation to murder us when in their power, from that sort of
property still in our possession, and to them of great value, considered it safest to seize upon and disarm them, carrying ourselves
to Batavia and then most amply to remunerate them for any inconvenience they might have sustained from being pressed into
the service.

  " The morning of Thursday, the 27th, however, perfectly relieved us from any further discussion on the subject, the Rajah and
his suite having proceeded to plunder the wreck, which by this
time they had espied.   It is probable they were not certain of our
real situation on the first evening, but might have supposed, from
seeing the uniforms, colors, and other military appearance, that
some settlement, as at Minto, in the island of Banca, had
been established there; and this may also account for their civility
in the first instance; for, from the moment their harpy-like spirit
was excited by the wreck, and they saw our real condition, there
were no more offerings of fish or of cocoa-nut milk.

  " To have sent the boats openly to attack them was judged im-
politic; i would only have driven them off for a moment, and put

them on their guard against surprise by night, should it be thought necessary in a day or two to do so. They could deprive us of little; for the copper bolts and iron work, which they were now most interested about, were not to us of material importance.

" We had the day before moved the boats into another cove, more out of sight, from the overspreading branches of the trees, and safer in case of attack, being commanded by two strong little forts, one having a rude draw-bridge, erected on the rocks immediately above it, and wattled in, where an officer and piquet were nightly placed; and a new serpentine path was cut down to this inlet, communicating with our main position aloft.

" On Friday, the 28th, the Malays were still employed on the wreck. A boat approached us in the forenoon; but, on the gig going out to meet it, they refused to correspond, and returned to their party. No relief having appeared from Batavia, and the period being elapsed at which, as was now thought, we had reason to expect it, measures were taken, by repairing the launch and constructing a fine raft, to give us additional powers of transporting ourselves from our present abode, before our stock of provisions was entirely exhausted.

" On Saturday, the first of March, the Malays acquired a great accession of strength, by the arrival of fourteen more proas from the northward, probably of the old party, who joined in breaking up the remains of the wreck.

" At daylight, on Sunday the 2d, still greater force having joined them during the night, the pirates, leaving a number at work on the wreck, advanced with upwards of twenty of their heaviest vessels towards our landing place; fired one of their patereroes; beat their gongs, and, making a hideous yelling noise, they anchored in a line about a cable's length from our cove. We were instantly under arms, the party covering the boats strengthened, and scouts sent out to watch their motions, as some of their boats had gone up the creek, at the back of our position, and to beat about, lest any should be lying in ambush from the land. About this time the old Malay prisoner, who was under charge of sentries at the well, and who had been incautiously trusted by them to cut some wood for the fire, hearing the howling of his tribe, left his wounded comrade to shift for himself, ran off into the wood, and escaped, carrying with him his hatchet. Finding, after waiting a short time in this state of preparation, that they made no attempt to land, an officer was sent a little outside the cove in a canoe, waving in a friendly manner, to try how they would act. After some deliberation, one of their boats, with several men armed with creeses, or their crooked daggers, approached; here, as usual, little could be made out, except a display of their marauding spirit, by taking a fancy to the shirt and trousers of one of the young gentlemen in the canoe; but, on his refusing to give them up, they used no force.

" A letter was now written, and addressed to the chief authority
at Minto, a small settlement on the north-west point of Banca,
stating the situation in which we were placed, and requesting him
to forward, if in his power, one or two small vessels to us, with a
little bread and salt provisions, and some ammunition. Again the
officer went out in the canoe, and was again met by the Malay
boat. This letter was given to them, the word Minto repeatedly
pronounced, which they seemed to understand, the direction
pointed out, and signs made that on their return with an answer
they should be rewarded with abundance of dollars, showing them
one as a specimen. This was done more to try them, than with
any hope of their performing the service; for, although a boat
went down to Pulo Chalacca, where they appeared to have somebody in superior authority, yet none took the direction of Banca.
Meantime their force rapidly increased, their proas and boats of
different sizes amounting to fifty. The larger had from sixteen to
twenty men, the smaller about seven or eight; so that, averaging
them at the lowest, ten each, they had fully five hundred men.
The wreck seemed now nearly exhausted, and appeared to be a
very secondary object, knowing the chief booty must be in our
possession; and they blockaded us with increased rigor, drawing
closer into the cove, more especially at high water, fearful lest our
boats, being afloat at that period, should push out and escape
them. In the afternoon some of the Rajah's people, whom we at
first considered our friends, made their appearance, as if seeking
a parley; and on communicating with them, gave us to understand by signs, and as many words as could be made out, that all
the Malays, except their party, were extremely hostile to us; that
it was their determination to attack us that night, and urging also
that some of their people should sleep up the hill, in order to protect us. Their former conduct and present connexions displayed
so evidently the treachery of this offer, that it is needless to say
that it was rejected; giving them to understand we could trust to
ourselves. They immediately returned to their gang, who certainly assumed a most menacing attitude. In the evening, when
the officers and men were assembled as usual under arms, in order
to inspect them, and settle the watches for the night, the Captain
spoke to them with much animation, almost verbatim as follows;

" ' My lads, you must all have observed this day, as well as myself, the great increase of the enemy's force—for enemies we must
now consider them—and the threatening posture they have assumed. I have, on various grounds, strong reason to believe they will
attack us this night. I do not wish to conceal our real state, because I think there is not a man here who is afraid to face any
sort of danger. We are now strongly fenced in, and our position
is in all respects so good, that, armed as we are, we ought to
make a formidable defence against even regular troops; what, then,
would be thought of us if we allowed ourselves to be surprised

by a set of naked savages, with their spears and creeses? It is true they have swivels in their boats, but they cannot act here; I have not observed that they have any matchlocks or muskets; but if they have, so have we. I do not wish to deceive you as to the means of resistance in our power. When we were first thrown together on shore, we were almost defenceless; only seventy-five ball cartridges could be mustered; we have now sixteen hundred. They cannot, I believe, send up more than five hundred men; but with two hundred such as now stand around me, I do not fear a thousand, nay, fifteen hundred of them. I have the fullest confidence we shall beat them; the pikemen standing firm, we can give them such a volley of musketry as they will be little prepared for; and when we find they are thrown into confusion, we will sally out among them, chase them into the water, and ten to one but we secure their vessels. Let every man, therefore, be on the alert, with his arms in his hands, and should these barbarians this night attempt our hill, I trust we shall convince them that they are dealing with Britons.'

"Perhaps three jollier hurrahs were never given than at the conclusion of this short but well-timed address. The woods fairly echoed again; whilst the piquet at the cove, and those stationed at the wells, the instant it caught their ear, instinctively joined their sympathetic cheers to the general chorus.

"There was something like unity, and concord in such a sound, (one neither resembling the feeble shout nor savage yell,) which, rung in the ears of these gentlemen, no doubt had its effect; for about this time (8 P. M.) they were observed making signals with lights to some of their tribe behind the islet. If ever seamen or marines had a strong inducement to fight, it was on the present occasion, for every thing conduced to animate them. The feeling excited by a savage, cruel, and inhospitable aggression on the part of the Malays—an aggression adding calamity to misfortune —roused every mind to a spirit of just revenge; and the appeal now made to them on the score of national character was not likely to let that feeling cool. That they might come, seemed to be the anxious wish of every heart. After a slender but cheerful repast, the men laid down as usual on their arms, whilst the Captain remained with those on guard to superintend his arrangements. An alarm during the night showed the effect of preparation on the people's minds, for all, like lightning, were at their posts, and returned growling and disappointed because the alarm was false.

"Daylight, on Monday the 3d, discovered the pirates exactly in the same position in front of us; ten more vessels having joined them during the night, making their number now at least six hundred men. The plot began to thicken, and our situation became hourly more critical. Their force rapidly accumulating, and our little stock of provisions daily shortening, rendered some desperate measure immediately necessary.

"'That which seemed most feasible was, by a sudden night attack, with our four boats well armed, to carry by boarding some of their vessels; and, by manning them, repeat our attack with increased force, taking more, or dispersing them. The possession of some of their proas, in addition to our own boats, taking into consideration that our numbers would be thinned on the occasion, might enable us to shove off for Java, in defiance of them. Any attempt to move on a raft, with their vessels playing round it armed with swivels, was evidently impossible. Awful as our situation now was, and every hour becoming more so, starvation staring us in the face on one hand, and without a hope of mercy from the savages on the other, yet were there no symptoms of depression, or gloomy despair; every mind seemed buoyant; and, if any estimate of the general feeling could be collected from countenances, from the manner and expressions of all, there appeared to be formed in every breast a calm determination to dash at them, and be successful; or to fall, as became men, in the attempt to be free

"About noon on this day, whilst schemes and proposals were lying about, as to the mode of executing the measures in view, Mr. Johnstone, ever on the alert, who had mounted the look-out-tree, one of the loftiest on the summit of our hill, descried a sail at a great distance to the southward, which he thought larger than a Malay vessel. The buzz of conversation was in a moment hushed, and every eye fixed anxiously on the tree for the next report; a signal-man and telescope being instantly sent up. She was now lost sight of from a dark squall overspreading that part of the horizon; but, in about twenty minutes, she emerged from the cloud, and was decidedly announced to be a square-rigged vessel. 'Are you quite sure of that?' was eagerly inquired. 'Quite certain,' was the reply; 'it is either a ship or a brig, standing towards the island under all sail.' The joy this happy sight infused, and the gratitude of every heart at this prospect of deliverance, may be more easily conceived than described. It occasioned a sudden transition of the mind from one train of thinking to another; as if waking from a disagreeable dream. We immediately displayed our colors on the highest branch of the tree, to attract attention, lest she should only be a passing stranger.

"The pirates soon after this discovered the ship, (a signal having been made with a gun by those anchored behind Pulo Chalacca,) which occasioned an evident stir among them. As the water was ebbing fast, it was thought possible, by an unexpected rush out to the edge of the reef, to get some of them under fire, and secure them. They seemed, however, to have suspected our purpose; for the moment the seamen and marines appeared from under the mangroves, the nearest proa let fly her swivel among a party of the officers, who had been previously wading outwards: and the whole instantly getting under weigh, made sail off, fired at by our people; but unfortunately without effect; for, in addi tion to the dexterous management of their boats, the wind enabled them to weather the rocks. It was fortunate, however, this attack on them took place, and that it had the effect of driving them away; for, had they stood their ground, we were as much in their power as ever—the ship being obliged to anchor eight miles to leeward of the island, and eleven or twelve from our position, on account of the wind and current; and, as this wind and current continued the same for some time afterwards, they might most easily, with their force, have cut off all communication between us. Indeed, it was a providential and most extraordinary circumstance, during this monsoon that the ship was able to fetch up as far as she did. The blockade being now raised, the gig, with Messrs. Sykes and Abbot, was despatched to the ship, which proved to be the Ter nate, one of the Company's cruisers, sent by Lord Amherst to our assistance, having on board Messrs. Ellis and Hoppner, who embarked on the day of their arrival at Batavia, and pushed back to the island."

"OLD IRONSIDES."*

Ay ! pull her tattered ensign down,
   Long has it waved on high,
And many a heart has danced to see
   That banner in the sky ;
Beneath it rung the battle shout,
   And burst the cannon's roar—
The meteor of the ocean air
   Shall sweep the clouds no more.

Her deck, once red with heroes' blood,
   Where knelt the vanquished foe,
When winds were hurrying o'er the flood
   And waves were white below,
No more shall feel the conqueror's tread
   Or know the conquered knee ;
The harpies of the shore shall pluck
   The eagle of the sea !

Oh better that her shattered hulk
   Should sink beneath the wave ;
Her thunders shook the mighty deep
   And there should be her grave.
Nail to the mast her holy flag,
   Set every threadbare sail,
And give her to the god of storms—
   The lightning and the gale '

* Vide Frontispiece.

KOTZEBUE.

Captain Kotzebue sailed from Cronstadt in a frigate of considerable size, with a cargo for Kamschatka. His orders were to proceed from thence to the north-west coast of America, for the protection of the Russian company at Ross—to remain on that station a year, and then to return to Cronstadt. In going and returning he was left wholly to his own discretion, and he turned the liberty allowed him, to the prosecution of geographical discovery. Starting from Cronstadt, in the summer of 1823, he first landed at Portsmouth, and next at Rio Janeiro, where he met with Lord Cochrane, and made his acquaintance. Lord Cochrane had recently quitted Chili, and was then in the Brazil service, and longing to enter the Russian, for the purpose of assisting the Greeks and fighting the Turks. "War seems to him," says Captain Kotzebue, "as indispensable, and struggle in defence of a good cause the highest enjoyment." The captain, however, is puzzled how to reconcile this, which he calls enthusiasm, with the noble lord's passion for money. Doubling Cape Horn, with scarcely a gale to ripple the waters, he stopped next on the coast of Chili, where though he was welcomed with apparent cordiality, suspicions were excited—the natives were full of alarms about the Spaniards, and he found it prudent to hasten his departure From the port of Talcuquanha, he struck into the south-east trade wind, and three thousand or four thousand miles swept over in three weeks, took him to O Tahaita (for the O, it seems, is only the article), where he spent some time—long enough to ascertain the degenerating condition of the island. The advance so rapidly made by the activity and energy of Pomareh, is fast retrograding. The navy, of which so much was said a few years ago, has almost wholly vanished. Three or four missionaries, themselves ignorant men, rule despotically; and praying and preaching, Captain Kotzebue found substituted for more active pursuits. So completely cowed are the natives, by the theocratic discipline of these men, that they allow themselves to be driven to prayers by the cudgel. The religion of the islanders, Captain Kotzebue affirms, is mere formality. The missionaries, it is true, have abolished some superstitions, but only to make way for others scarcely less gross. Thieving and concubinage are under some restraint, but bigotry and hypocrisy flourish vigorously, and the Tahaitians are now any thing but the open and benevolent beings they appeared to their first discoverers. If human sacrifices are abandoned, it nas been at the expense of a large majority of the population They were once estimated at one hundred and fifty thousand; and do not now exceed eight thousand—the effect of the chief's

(Taio) *conversion*, who butchered right and left, and almost cleared the island. There must be some exaggeration here, for the massacre took place in 1797, and Pomareh could never have accomplished what he did with a population of eight thousand. A son of Taio, whom Pomareh destroyed, is still living,—he has, it seems, a party in the island, and Captain Kotzebue anticipated an explosion, and a violent end to the present dynasty and the missionary power.

At O Tahaita, he met with one of Adams's seraglio, lately returned to her native home from Pitcairn's Island. From information received from her, and an American captain who had recently visited the island, M. Kotzebue learned the now well-known story of the settlement of the mutineers of the Bounty. The Mal du pays had brought the old lady home, but she soon changed her mind again. She found O Tahaita sadly degenerated —it was no longer like the Paradise she had left; nobody could be compared, she said, with her Adams. Missionaries, it seems, are likely to extend their dominion to that peaceful and gentle family. "May Adams's paternal government," says Kotzebue, "never be exchanged for despotism, nor his practical lessons of piety be forgotten in empty forms of prayer."

From O Tahaita Kotzebue steered westerly to Navigator's Islands, and beyond—ascertaining the geographical positions of several contested spots, and discovering new lands. Proceeding then northward he reached the Radack Islands, a group, in about ten degrees north and one hundred and seventy east from Greenwich, which he himself discovered in 1816. Landing at Otdia, he was joyfully recognised by many of the natives, and the name of Totabu (their articulation of Kotzebue) was echoed with delight. The natives of these beautiful islands are represented as gentle and well disposed—very much, indeed, as the O Tahaitians were originally They have not yet got the missionaries among them.

On the captain's arrival at the Russian company's settlement, at Ross, on the north-west coast of America, he found his services not required for some months, and he filled up the interval by an excursion to California and the Sandwich islands. In a few months after his return to Ross, he prepared to return home by the sea of China, and the Cape of Good Hope. In his way, he a second time called at O Wahi (Owhyee). He found a considerable change. Queen Nomahanna—who stands six feet two, without shoes or stockings, (for none from Europe can she get on, and none, of course, are made at home,) and two ells round, s governed by the missionaries, and the island, like O Tahaita, s rapidly going backwards. The chief charm of religion seemed to the women to be—that they might now eat pork as much as they liked, and not be confined solely to dogs' flesh. He met an old man with a book—the captain inquired if he was learning

to read—No, he was only making believe, to please the Queen
What is the use of B, A, Ba? Will it make yams and potatoes
grow? Another old man was imploring the Queen's assistance
—" If you won't learn to read," says she, " you may go and
drown yourself." Captain Kotzebue in his passage to the Ladrones and Philippines, made some new discoveries, and visited
St. Helena in his way home.

WRECK OF THE ROTHSAY CASTLE STEAMER

The Rothsay Castle was a steam packet which formerly traded
on the Clyde. She belonged to the line of steamers which sailed
from Liverpool to Beaumaris and Bangor, and was furnished with
one engine only. She was commanded by Lieutenant Atkinson
At ten o'clock on the — of August, 1831,—the vessel was appointed to sail from the usual place, George's Pierhead, but a casual
delay took place in starting, and it was eleven o'clock before she
had got every thing in readiness. Whilst taking passengers on
board, a carriage arrived at the Pierhead for embarkation. It belonged to M. W. Foster, Esq. of Regent's park, London, who,
with his wife and servant, were conveyed in it to the packet, and
took their passage at the same time. They were all subsequently
drowned, a little dog which accompanied them being the only sur-
vivor of this unfortunate group. When the steamer left the Pier
head her deck was thronged with passengers. The captain, crew,
musicians, &c. amounted to fifteen, in addition to whom, it was
supposed by persons who saw the vessel sail that one hundred
and ten or one hundred and twenty souls were on board. The
majority of the passengers consisted of holyday and family parties,
chiefly from country places; and in one of these companies, who
came on a journey of pleasure from Bury, the hand of death committed a merciless devastation. It consisted of twenty-six persons; in the morning, joyous with health and hilarity, they sat
out upon the waves, and when the shades of that evening approach
ed, every soul but two saw his last of suns go down.

The weather was not particularly boisterous at the time she
sailed. A severe storm however, had raged in the morning and
must have agitated the water on the Banks more than usual.
The wind too, blew strongly from the north-west, and the vessel
had to contend with the tide, which began to flow soon after she
passed the rock. When the steamer arrived off the Floating-light,
which is stationed about fifteen miles from Liverpool, the rough
ness of the sea alarmed many of the passengers.—One of the survivors stated, that Mr. Tarry, of Bury, who, with his family, con-

sisting of himself, his wife, their five children, and servant, was on board, being, in common with others, greatly alarmed for his own safety and the safety of those dear to him, went down to the cabin, where the captain was at dinner, and requested him to put back. His reply was, " I think there is a great deal of fear on board, and very little danger. If we were to turn back with passengers, it would never do—we should have no profit." To another gentleman who urged him to put back, he is reported to have said very angrily, " I'm not one of those that turn back." He remained in the cabin two whole hours, and peremptorily refused to comply with the repeated requests made to him by the more timid of his passengers to return to Liverpool; observing that if they knew him, they would not make the request. Before dinner, his behavior had been perfectly unexceptionable; but, after he had dined, a very striking difference was observed in his conduct. He became violent in his manner, and abusive in his language to the men. When anxiously questioned by the passengers, as to the progress the vessel was making, and the time at which she was likely to reach her destination, he returned trifling, and frequently very contradictory answers. During the early part of the voyage, he had spoken confidently of being able to reach Beaumaris by seven o'clock; but the evening wore away, night came on, and the vessel was still a considerable distance from the termination of her voyage. It was near twelve o'clock when they arrived at the mouth of the Menai Strait, which is about five miles from Beaumaris. The tide, which had been running out of the strait, and which had, consequently, for some time previous retarded the steamer's progress towards her destination, was just on the turn. The vessel, according to the statement of two of the seamen and one of the firemen saved, had got round the buoy on the north end of the Dutchman's Bank, and had proceeded up the river as far as the tower on Puffin Island; when suddenly the steam got so low that the engine would not keep her on her proper course. When asked, why there was not steam on, the fireman said, that a deal of water had been finding its way into the vessel all day, and that sometime before she got into the strait, the bilge-pumps were choked. The water in the hold then overflowed the coals; so that, in renewing the fires, a deal of water went in with the coals, slackened the fires, and made it impossible to keep the steam up. It was clearly the duty of the fireman to give notice of this occurrence; but he seems not to have mentioned it to the captain. The vessel, which had evidently come fair into the channel, though there was no light on the coast to guide her, now drifted, with the ebb tide and north-west wind, towards the Dutchman's Bank, on the north point of which she struck, her bows sticking fast in the sand. Lieutenant Atkinson immediately ordered the man at the helm to put the helm a starboard. The man refused to do so; but put it to port. The mate, perceiving this, ran aft,

took the helm from the man, and put it to starboard again.—In the
meantime, the captain and some of the passengers got the jib up
No doubt he did this intending to wear her round and bring her
head to the northward; but in the opinion of nautical men, it
could not make the least difference which way her head was turned, as she was on a lee shore, and there was no steam to work
her off. The captain also ordered the passengers first to run aft,
in the hope, by removing the pressure from the vessel's stem, to
make her float: this failing to produce the desired effect, he then
ordered them to run forward. All the exertions of the captain,
the crew and the passengers united were unavailing. The ill-
fated vessel stuck still faster in the sands, and all gave themselves up for lost. The terror of the passengers became excessive.
Several of them urged the captain to hoist lights, and make other
signals of distress; but he positively refused to do so, assuring
the passengers that there was no danger, and telling them several
times, that the packet was afloat, and doing well, and on her way;
when the passengers knew perfectly well that she was sticking
fast in the sand, and her cabins rapidly filling with water. Doubtless the unfortunate man was perfectly aware of the imminence of
the danger; but we may charitably suppose, that he held such
language for the purpose of preventing alarm which might be fatal.
The alarm bell was now rung with so much violence that the clap-
per broke, and some of the passengers continued to strike it for
some time with a stone. The bell was heard, it is said, at Beaumaris, but, as there was no light hoisted on the mast of the steamer,
(a fatal neglect!) those who heard the signal were, of course, ignorant whence it proceeded. The weather, at this awful moment,
was boisterous, but perfectly clear. The moon, though slightly
overcast, threw considerable light on the surrounding objects.—But
a strong breeze blew from the north-west, the tide began to set in
with great strength, and a heavy sea beat over the bank on which
the steam packet was now firmly and immovably fixed.

We cannot describe the scene which followed. Certain death
seemed now to present itself to all on board, and the most affecting
scenes were exhibited. The females, in particular, uttered the
most piercing shrieks; some locked themselves in each others
arms, while others, losing all self-command, tore off their caps
and bonnets, in the wildness of despair. A Liverpool pilot, who
happened to be in the packet, now raised his voice and exclaimed,
" It is all over—we are all lost !" At these words there was a
universal despairing shriek. The women and children collected
in a knot together, and kept embracing each other, keeping up,
all the time, the most dismal lamentations. When tired with
crying they lay against each other, with their heads reclined, like
inanimate bodies. The steward of the vessel and his wife, who
was on board, lashed themselves to the mast, determined to spend
their last moments in each other's arms. Several husbands and

wives also met their fate locked in each other's arms; whilst parents clung to their beloved children,—several mothers it is said, having perished with their dear little ones firmly clasped in their arms. A party of the passengers, about fifteen or twenty, lowered the boat and crowded into it. It was impossible for any open boat to live in such a sea, even though not overloaded, and she immediately swamped and went to the bottom, with all who had made this last hopeless effort for self-preservation.

For some time the vessel, though now irrecoverably lost, continued to resist the action of the waves, and the despairing souls on board still struggled with their doom. But hope had forever fled; the packet was beaten and tossed about by the tumultuous waters with a violence which threatened to dash her into fragments at every shock, and the sea now made a continual breach over her. The decks were repeatedly swept by the boiling ocean, and each billow snatched its victims to a watery grave. The unfortunate captain and his mate were among the first that perished About thirty or forty passengers were standing upon the poop clinging to each other in hopeless agony, and occasionally uttering the most piteous ejaculations. Whilst trembling thus upon the brink of destruction, and expecting every moment to share the fate which had already overtaken so many of their companions in misery, the poop was discovered to give way; another wave rolled on with impetuous fury, and the hinder part of the luckless vessel, with all who sought safety in its frail support, was burst away from its shattered counterpart, and about forty wretched beings hurried through the foaming flood into an eternal world

" Then rose from sea to sky the wild farewell,
Then shrieked the timid, and stood still the brave."

Those who retained any degree of sensibility endeavored to catch at whatever was floating within their reach, with the vain hope of prolonging their lives, though it was certain that life could only lengthen their sufferings. Many grasped with frantic despair, at the slightest object they could find, but were either too weak to retain their hold, or were forced to relinquish their grasp by the raging of the surge. The rudder was seized by eight of the sinking creatures at the same time, and some of them, were ultimately preserved. The number of those who clung to the portion of the wreck which remained upon the bank gradually grew thinner and thinner, as they sunk under their fatigues, or were hurled into the deep by the remorseless waves. At length, about an hour and a half from the time when she struck, the remnant of the Rothsay Castle disappeared from the bosom of the ocean, and the remainder of her passengers and crew were precipitated into the foaming abyss.

NARRATIVE OF CAPTAIN W. L. CAZNEAU.

The Brig Polly, of one hundred and thirty tons burden, sailed from Boston, with a cargo of lumber and provisions, on a voyage to Santa Croix, on the 12th of December 1811, under the command of captain W. L. Cazneau—with a mate, four seamen and a cook; Mr. I. S. Hunt and a negro girl of nine years of age, passengers. Nothing material happened until the 15th, when they had cleared cape Cod, the shoal of Georges, and nearly, as they supposed, crossed the gulf stream, when there came on a violent gale from the south-east, in which the brig labored very hard, which produced a leak that so gained on the pumps as to sound nearly six feet,—when about midnight she was upset, and Mr. Hunt washed overboard! Not having any reason to hope for her righting, by much exertion the weather lanyards were cut away, the deck load having been before thrown over and the lashings all gone; in about half an hour the mainmast went by the board, and soon after the foremast, when she righted, though full of water, a dreadful sea making a fair breach over her from stem to stern. In this situation the night wore away, and daylight found all alive except the passenger, and upon close search the little girl was found clinging to the skylight, and so saved from drowning in the cabin. The glass and grating of the skylight having gone away, while on her beam ends, the little girl was drawn through the openings, but so much chilled that she survived but a few hours. In this situation they remained, without fire, as near as the captain can recollect, twelve days, when the cook, an Indian from Canton, near Boston, suggested the operation of rubbing two sticks together, which succeeded. Very fortunately the cambose did not go overboard with the deck load: this was got to windward, a fire kindled and some provisions cooked, which was the first they had tasted, except raw pork, for the whole time.—They now got up a barrel of pork, part of a barrel of beef, and one half barrel of beef. A small pig had been saved alive, which they now dressed, not having any thing to feed it with. But at this time no apprehension was entertained of suffering for meat, there being several barrels stowed in the run, and upwards of one hundred under deck. With this impression, the people used the provisions very imprudently, till they discovered that the stern post was gone, and the gale continuing for a long time, the barrels had stove, and their contents were all lost forever.

There happened to be a cask of water lashed on the quarter deck, which was saved, containing about thirty gallons, all the rest was lost. This lasted about eighteen days, when the crew were reduced to the necessity of catching what rain they could, and having no more. At the end of forty days the meat was all gone, and absolute famine stared them in the face. The first victim to this destroyer was Mr. Paddock, the mate, whose exquisite distress seemed to redouble the sufferings of his companions. He was a man of a robust constitution, who had spent his life in the Bank fishing, had suffered many hardships and appeared the most capable of standing the shocks of misfortune of any of the crew. In the meridian of life, being about thirty-five years old, it was reasonable to suppose that, instead of the first, he would have been the last to have fallen a sacrifice to cold and hunger: but Heaven ordered it otherwise—he became delirious, and death relieved him from his sufferings the fiftieth day of his shipwreck. During all this time, the storms continued, and would often overwhelm them so as to keep them always drenched with seawater, having nothing to screen them, except a temporary kind of cabin which they had built up of boards between the windlass and nighthead on the larboard side of the forecastle. The next who sunk under this horrid press of disasters was Howes, a young man of about thirty, who likewise was a fisherman, by profession, and tall, spare, and as smart and active a seaman as any aboard. He likewise died delirious and in dreadful distress, six days after Paddock, being the fifty-sixth day of the wreck. It was soon perceived that this must evidently be the fate of all the survivors in a short time, if something was not done to procure water. About this time good luck, or, more probably, kind Providence, enabled them to fish up the tea-kettle and one of the captain's pistols; and necessity, the mother of invention, suggested the plan of distillation. Accordingly, a piece of board was very nicely fitted to the mouth of the boiler, a small hole made in it, and the tea-kettle, bottom upwards, fixed to the upper side of the board, the pistol barrel was fixed to the nose of the kettle and kept cool by the constant application of cold water. This completely succeeded, and the survivors, without a doubt, owe their preservation to this simple experiment. But all that could be obtained by this very imperfect distillation, was a scanty allowance of water for five men; yet it would sustain life and that was all. The impression that there was meat enough under the deck, induced them to use every exertion to obtain it; but by getting up pieces of bone, entirely bare of meat and in a putrid state, they found that nothing was left for them but to rely on Heaven for food, and be contented with whatever came to hand, till relief should come. Their only sustenance now was barnacles gathered from the sides of the vessel which were ate raw that the distilling might not be interrupted, which would give them no more than four wine glasses of water each, per day. The next food which they obtained was a large shark, caught by means of a running bowline. This was a very great relief and lasted some time. Two advantages arose from this signal interposition of kind Providence; for while they lived upon their shark, the barnacles were growing larger and more nutritive. They likewise found many small crabs among the sea-weed which often floated around the wreck, which were very pleasant food. But from the necessity of chewing them raw and sucking out the nourishment, they brought on an obstinate costiveness, which became extremely painful and probably much exasperated by the want of water.

On the 15th of March, according to their computation, poor Moho, the cook, expired, evidently from want of water, though with much less distress than the others and in the full exercise of his reason: he very devoutly prayed and appeared perfectly resigned to the will of the God who afflicted him. Their constant study was directed to the improvement of their still, which was made much better by the addition of the other pistol barrel, which was found by fishing with the grain they made by fixing nails into a piece of a stave. With this barrel they so far perfected the still as to obtain eight junk bottles full of water in twenty four hours. But from the death of Moho to the death of Johnson, which happened about the middle of April, they seemed to be denied every kind of food. The barnacles were all gone, and no friendly gale wafted to their side the sea-weed from which they could obtain crabs or insects—It seemed as if all hope was gone forever, and they had nothing before them but death, or the horrid alternative of eating the flesh of their dead companion. One expedient was left, that was to try to decoy a shark, if happily there might be one about the wreck, by part of the corpse of their shipmate! This succeeded, and they caught a large shark, and from that time had many fish till their happy deliverance. Very fortunately, a cask of nails which was on deck, lodged in the lea scuppers while on their beam ends: with these they were enabled to fasten the shingles on their cabin, which by constant improvement, had become much more commodious, and when reduced to two only, they had a better supply of water.

They had now drifted above two thousand miles and were in latitude 23 North and longitude 13 West, when to their unspeakable joy they saw three ships bearing down upon them. The ships came as near as was convenient, and then hailed, which Captain Cazneau answered with all the force of his lungs. The ship which hailed proved to be the Fame of Hull, Captain Featherstone bound from Rio Janeiro home. It so happened that the three Captains had dined together that day and were all on board the Fame. Humanity immediately sent a boat, which put an end to the dreadful thraldom of Captain Cazneau and Samuel Badger, the only surviving persons, who were received by these humane Englishmen with exalted sensibility. Thus was ended the most shocking catastrophe which our naval history has recorded for many years, after a series of distresses from December 15th to

the 20th of June, a period of one hundred and ninety one days!
Every attention was paid to the sufferers that generosity warmed
with pity and fellow feeling could dictate, on board the Fame.
They were cherished, comforted, fed, clothed and nursed until
the 9th of July, when they fell in with Captain Perkins, of the
brig Dromo, in the chops of the channel of England, who gene
rously took them on board and carefully perfected the work of
goodness begun by the generous Englishmen, and safely landed
them in Kennebunk.

It is natural to inquire how they could float such a vast distance upon the most frequented part of the Atlantic and not be
discovered all this time? They were passed by more than a
dozen sail, one of which came so nigh them that they could
distinctly see the people on deck and on the rigging looking at
them: but to the inexpressible disappointment of the starving and
freezing men, they stifled the dictates of compassion, hoisted sail
and cruelly abandoned them to their fate.

NEW YORK AND ITS ENVIRONS.

There are few spectacles at once more grateful and more
magnificent to the weary wanderer over the ocean, than that
which rises up before him, like a lovely dream, as he passes the
Narrows, and is wafted by fair breezes towards the city of New
York. The green shores of Long and Staten Islands, within less
than a quarter of a mile of each other, slope down to the water's
edge, and form the gates of the harbor. When "radiant summer
opens all her pride," they are clothed with the luxuriant harvest,
and dotted with dwellings of peace and plenty. A vast city with
its bristling forest of masts and spires, rises suddenly in the distance, sending forth the hum of more than two hundred thousand
inhabitants. He inhales the mingled perfumes which the wind
bears from wood and field, from valleys of clover, and gardens of
flowers. Immense steamboats, superior to any other in the world,
plough the waters around him, and shape their steady course in
different directions; and ships, with white sails spread, are returning, storm-beaten, from their perilous voyages, or hurrying forth,
through the narrow outlet, to distant quarters of the globe. Forts
command the prominent stations, and vessels of war, like castles,
are resting on the wave.

Perhaps no situation could be chosen for a more advantageous
survey of the city, with its surrounding scenery, than that part
of the Bay adjoining Governor's Island, and near the fort, a por-

tion of which appears on the extreme left of the picture, and
whence the present view was taken.

The opening discernible on the right, is the passage termed
the East River, leading from the Bay into the Sound, between
Long and York Islands, and thence along the shores of Connecticut and Rhode Island, into the Atlantic. The eye can almost
pierce to that point of the strait entitled Hurl Gate, but, by the
lovers of the marvellous, dignified with an appellation which
would seem to conduct the traveller into a region of a very
different description from the pleasant hills and orchards, the
costly dwellings, and the humble but bright looking cottages, that
make the banks of this stream a succession of charming pictures

View of New-York.

The small promontory jutting out on the eastern side, represents that part of Long Island occupied by the village of Brooklyn
and the Navy Yard.

On the left, the eye seeks to explore the windings of the Hudson or North River. In many respects this stream may be
considered one of the most important in the world. It is affected
by the tide more than a hundred and sixty miles towards its source.
Its steamboat navigation is unobstructed, and it presents facilities
for commerce of an extraordinary and tempting nature. The
magnificent canal, which strikes it at Albany, connects the city
of New York with Lake Erie, and thence with the interior and
most western portion of the Union. This stupendous work,
which directly augments the prosperity of more than two millions
of people, is but a single branch in the vast plan of internal im

provement, of which Dewitt Clinton was the most influential promoter, and which equally associates his name with the glory of the state, and the increasing importance of the city.

At all times the view of the metropolis of the State is imposing; but should the stranger approach it at the close of a pleasant summer day, he would find the scene yet more enchanting. At this period the bustle of business is superseded by the voice of pleasure. As he draws near the Battery, he perceives that the fort has changed its martial character, and been metamorphosed into a garden and pleasant promenade. The stillness of the evening is sometimes broken by the sound of the rushing rocket, as it darts into the spangled heaven, illuminating the scene with a glare of temporary radiance, and sometimes by bursts of music, softened by the distance, as it floats over the placid water. Now you may hear the drum from Governor's Island, and now the song of the sailor from the distant ship, which is preparing again to encounter the perils of the deep; while the regular dash of the oar, as some occasional boat glides by, adds to the charm of the music, and increases the interest of the scene

---

NARRATIVE OF CAPTAIN LINCOLN.

I have reluctantly yielded to the urgent solicitation of friends, to give a short narrative of the capture, sufferings and escape of myself and crew, after having been taken by a piratical schooner, called the Mexican, December, 1821. The peculiar circumstances attending our situation, gave us ample opportunity for learning the character of those cruisers which have lately infested our southern coasts, destroying the lives and plundering the property of so many peaceable traders. If this narrative should effect any good, or urge our government to still more vigorous measures for the protection of our commerce, my object will be attained.

I sailed from Boston bound for Trinidad, in the island of Cuba, on the 13th November, 1821, in the schooner Exertion, burden one hundred and seven tons, owned by Messrs. Joseph Ballister and Henry Farnam, with a crew consisting of the following persons:—

Joshua Bracket,	mate,	Bristol,
David Warren,	cook,	Saco,

---

* The reader will probably recollect the alarming number of piracies, which took place in the West Indian seas during the years 1824–1825. Captain Lincoln's narrative will be found to convey a full and correct idea of the nature and extent of these depredations ; and the striking interest of his account will be considered a sufficient apology for the space we have afforded it

Thomas Goodall,   seaman,   Baltimore,
Thomas Young,   "   Orangetown,
Francis de Suze,   "   St. John's,
George Reed.   "   Greenock, Scotland.

The cargo consisted of flour, beef, pork, lard, butter, fish beans, onions, potatoes, apples, hams, furniture, sugar box shooks, &c. invoiced at about eight thousand dollars. Nothing remarkable occurred during the passage, except much bad weather, until my capture, which was as follows:—

Monday, December 17th, 1821, commenced with fine breezes from the eastward. At daybreak saw some of the islands northward of Cape Cruz, called Keys—stood along northwest; every thing now seemed favorable for a happy termination of our voyage. At three o'clock, P. M. saw a sail coming round one of the Keys, into a channel called Boca de Cavolone by the chart, nearly in latitude 20° 55′ north, longitude 79° 55′ west, she made directly for us with all sail set, sweeps on both sides (the wind being light) and was soon near enough for us to discover about forty men on her deck, armed with muskets, blunderbusses, cutlasses, long knives, dirks, &c. two carronades, one a twelve, the other a six pounder; she was a schooner, wearing the Patriot flag, (blue, white and blue) of the Republic of Mexico. I thought it not prudent to resist them, should they be pirates, with a crew of seven men, and only five muskets; accordingly ordered the arms and ammunition to be immediately stowed away in as secret a place as possible, and suffer her to speak us, hoping and believing that a republican flag indicated both honor and friendship from those who wore it, and which we might expect even from Spaniards. But how great was my astonishment, when the schooner having approached very near us, hailed in English, and ordered me to heave my boat out immediately and come on board of her with my papers.—Accordingly my boat was hove out, but filled before I could get into her.—I was then ordered to tack ship and lay by for the pirates' boat to board me; which was done by Bolidar, their first lieutenant, with six or eight Spaniards armed with as many of the before mentioned weapons as they could well sling about their bodies. They drove me into the boat and two of them rowed me to their privateer, (as they called their vessel,) where I shook hands with her commander, Captain Jonnia, a Spaniard, who before looking at my papers, ordered Bolidar, his lieutenant, to follow the Mexican in, back of the Key they had left, which was done. At six o'clock, P. M. the Exertion was anchored in eleven feet water, near their vessel, and an island, which they called Twelve League Key, (called by the chart Key Largo,) about thirty or thirty-five leagues from Trinidad. After this strange conduct they began examining my papers by a Scotch man who went by the name of Nickola, their sailing master.— He spoke good English, had a countenance rather pleasing

although his beard and mustachios had a frightful appearance—
his face, apparently full of anxiety, indicated something in my
favor; he gave me my papers saying "take good care of them,
for I am afraid that you have fallen into bad hands." The pirate's
boat was then sent to the Exertion with more men and arms;
a part of them left on board her; the rest returning with three of
my crew to their vessel; viz. Thomas Young, Thomas Goodall,
and George Reed—they treated them with something to drink,
and offered them equal shares with themselves, and some money,
if they would enlist, but they could not prevail on them. I then
requested permission to go on board my vessel which was granted,
and further requested Nickola should go with me, but was refused by the captain, who vociferated in a harsh manner, "No,
No, No," accompanied with a heavy stamp upon the deck.
When I got on board, I was invited below by Bolidar, where I
found they had emptied the case of liquors, and broken a cheese
to pieces and crumbled it on the table and cabin floor; the pirates
elated with their prize, (as they called it,) had drank so much as
to make them desperately abusive. I was permitted to lie down
in my birth; but reader, if you have ever been awakened by a
gang of armed desperadoes, who have taken possession of your
habitation in the midnight hour, you can imagine my feelings.—
Sleep was a stranger to me, and anxiety was my guest. Bolidar,
however, pretended friendship, and flattered me with the prospect
of being soon set at liberty. But I found him, as I suspected, a
consummate hypocrite; indeed, his very looks indicated it. He
was a stout and well built man, of a dark, swarthy complexion, with
keen, ferocious eyes, huge whiskers, and beard under his chin
and on his lips four or five inches long; he was a Portuguese by
birth, but had become a naturalized Frenchman—had a wife, if
not children, (as I was told) in France, and was well known
there as commander of a first rate privateer. His appearance
was truly terrific; he could talk some in English, and had a most
lion-like voice.

Tuesday, 18th.—Early this morning the captain of the pirates
came on board the Exertion; took a look at the cabin-stores,
and cargo in the state rooms, and then ordered me back with him
to his vessel, where he, with his crew, held a consultation for
some time, respecting the cargo. After which, the interpreter,
Nickola, told me that "the captain had or *pretended to have* a
commission under General Traspelascus, commander in chief of
the republic of Mexico, authorizing him to take all cargoes whatever of provisions, bound to any Spanish royalist port—that my
cargo being bound to an enemy's port, must be condemned; but
that the vessel should be given up and he put into a fair channel
for Trinidad where I was bound." I requested him to examine
the papers thoroughly, and perhaps he would be convinced to
the contrary and told him my cargo was all American property

taken in at Boston and consigned to an American gentleman
agent at Trinidad. But the captain would not take this trouble,
but ordered both vessels under way immediately, and commenced
beating up amongst the Keys through most of the day, the
wind being very light. They now sent their boats on board
the Exertion for stores, and commenced plundering her of bread,
butter, lard, onions, potatoes, fish, beans, &c. took up some
sugar box shooks that were on deck, and found the barrels
of apples; selected the best of them, and threw the rest overboard. They inquired for spirits, wine, cider, &c. and were told
"they had already taken all that was on board." But not satisfied they proceeded to search the state rooms and forecastle,
ripped up the floor of the latter and found some boxes of bottled
cider, which they carried to their vessel, gave three cheers, in an
exulting manner to me, and then began drinking it with such
freedom, that a violent quarrel arose between officers and men,
which came very near ending in bloodshed. I was accused of
falsehood, for saying they had already got all the liquors that
were on board, and I thought they had; the truth was, I never
had any bill of lading of the cider, and consequently had no recollection of its being on board; yet it served them as an excuse
for being insolent. In the evening peace was restored and they
sung songs. I was suffered to go below for the night, and they
placed a guard over me, stationed at the companion way.

Wednesday, 19th, commenced with moderate easterly winds,
beating towards the northeast, the pirate's boats frequently
going on board the Exertion for potatoes, fish, beans, butter,
&c. which were used with great waste, and extravagance. They
gave me food and drink, but of bad quality, more particularly the
victuals, which was wretchedly cooked. The place assigned
me to eat was covered with dirt and vermin. It appeared that
their great object was to hurt my feelings with threats and observations, and to make my situation as unpleasant as circumstances
would admit. We came to anchor near a Key, called by them
Brigantine, where myself and mate were permitted to go on
shore, but were guarded by several armed pirates. I soon returned to the Mexican and my mate to the Exertion, with George
Reed one of my crew; the other two being kept on board the
Mexican. In the course of this day I had considerable conversation with Nickola, who appeared well disposed towards me. He
lamented most deeply his own situation, for he was one of those
men, whose early good impressions were not entirely effaced, although confederated with guilt. He told me "those who had
taken me, were no better than pirates, and their end would be the
halter; but," he added, with peculiar emotion, " I will never
be hung as a pirate," showing me a bottle of laudanum which he
had found in my medicine chest, saying, " If we are taken, *that*
shall cheat the hangman, before we are condemned." I endeav-

ored to get it from him, but did not succeed. I then asked him
how he came to be in such company, as he appeared to be dissatisfied. He stated, "that he was at New Orleans last summer
out of employment, and became acquainted with one Captain
August Orgamar, a Frenchman, who had bought a small schooner of about fifteen tons, and was going down to the bay of Mexico
to get a commission, under General Traspelaseus, in order to go
a privateering under the patriot flag. Captain Orgamar made
him liberal offers respecting shares, and promised him a sailing
master's birth, which he accepted and embarked on board the
schooner, without sufficiently reflecting on the danger of such
an undertaking. Soon after she sailed from Mexico; where they
got a commission, and the vessel was called Mexican. They
made up a complement of twenty men, and after rendering the
general some little service, in transporting his troops to a place
called —————— proceeded on a cruise; took some small prizes off
Campeachy; afterwards came on the south coast of Cuba, where
they took other small prizes and the one which we were now on
board of. By this time the crew were increased to about forty,
nearly one half Spaniards, the others Frenchmen and Portuguese.
Several of them had sailed out of ports in the United States, with
American protections; but, I confidently believe, none are natives,
especially of the northern states. I was careful in examining the
men, being desirous of knowing if any of my countrymen were
among this wretched crew; but am satisfied there were none, and
my Scotch friend concurred in the opinion.* And now with a
new vessel, which was the prize of these plunderers, they sailed
up Manganeil Bay; previously, however, they fell in with an
American schooner from which they bought four barrels of beef,
and paid in tobacco. At the Bay was an English brig belonging
to Jamaica, owned by Mr. John Louden of that place. On board
of this vessel the Spanish part of the crew commenced their
depredations as pirates, although Captain Orgamar and Nickola
protested against it, and refused any participation; but they persisted, and like so many ferocious blood-hounds, boarded the brig,
plundered the cabin stores, furniture, captain's trunk, &c. took a
hogshead of rum, one twelve pound carronade, some rigging and
sails. One of them plundered the chest of a sailor, who made
some resistance, so that the Spaniard took his cutlass and beat
and wounded him without mercy. Nickola asked him " why he
did it?" the fellow answered " I will let you know," and took up
the cook's axe and gave him a cut on the head, which nearly deprived him of life.† Then they ordered Captain Orgamar to
leave his vessel, allowing him his trunk and turned him ashore,
to seek for himself. Nickola begged them to dismiss him with

* The Spaniards at Havanna have been in the habit of saying to those who arrive there,
after suffering the horrid abuse of cutting, beating, hanging, robbing, &c. " it is your countrymen that do this."

† He showed me th i wound, which was quite large, and not then healed

his captain, but *no, no*, was the answer; for they had no complete navigator but him. After Captain Orgamar was gone, they put in his stead the present brave (or as I should call him cowardly) Captain Jonnia, who headed them in plundering the before mentioned brig, and made Bolidar their first lieutenant, and then proceeded down among those Keys or Islands, where I was captured. This is the amount of what my friend Nickola told me of their history.

Thursday, 20th, continued beating up, wind being light, the pirate's boats were sent to the Exertion for more stores, such as bread, lard, &c. I this day discovered on board the Mexican three black girls, of whom it is well to say no more. It is impossible to give an account of the filthiness of this crew, and were it possible it would not be expedient. In their appearance they were terrific, wearing black whiskers and long beards, the receptacles of dirt and vermin. They used continually the most profane language; had frequent quarrels; and so great was their love of gambling that the captain would play cards with the meanest man on board. All these things rendered them to me objects of total disgust (with a few exceptions, as will hereafter appear.)—I was told they had a stabbing match, but a few days before I was taken, and one man came near being killed; they put him ashore at a fisherman's hut and there left him to perish. I saw the wound of another who had his nose split open.

Friday, 21st.—After laying at anchor through the night in ten fathoms water, made sail and stood to the eastward—by this time I was out of my reckoning, having no quadrant, charts or books. The pirate's boats were again sent for stores. The captain for the second time demanded of me where my wine, brandy, &c. were, I again told him, they had already got the whole. They took the deep sea line and some cordage from the Exertion and at night came to anchor.   •

Saturday, 22d.—Both vessels under way standing to the eastward, they ran the Exertion aground on a bar, but after throwing overboard most of her deck load of shooks, she floated off; a pilot was sent to her, and she was run into a narrow creek between two keys, where they moored her head and stern along side the mangrove trees, sent down her yards and topmasts, and covered her mast heads and shrouds with bushes to prevent her being seen by vessels which might pass that way. I was then suffered to go on board my own vessel, and found her in a very filthy condition; sails torn, rigging cut to pieces, and every thing in the cabin in waste and confusion. The swarms of moschetoes and sand-flies made it impossible to get any sleep or rest. The pirate's large boat was armed and manned under Bolidar, and sent off with letters to a merchant (as they called him) by the name of Dominico, residing in a town called Principe, on the main island of Cuba. I was told by one of them who could speak English, that Principe was a very large and populous town, situated at the head of St. Maria, which was about twenty miles north east from where we lay, and the Keys lying around us were called Cotton Keys.—The captain pressed into his service Francis de Suze, one of my crew, saying that he was one of his countrymen. Francis was very reluctant in going, and said to me, with tears in his eyes, "I shall do nothing but what I am obliged to do, and will not aid in the least to hurt you or the vessel; I am very sorry to leave you." He was immediately put on duty and Thomas Goodall sent back to the Exertion.

Sunday, 23d.—Early this morning a large number of the pirates came on board of the Exertion, threw out the long boat, broke open the hatches and took out considerable of the cargo, in search of rum, gin, &c. still telling me "I had some and that they would find it," uttering the most awful profaneness. In the afternoon their boat returned with a perough,* having on board the captain, his first lieutenant and seven men of a patriot or piratical vessel that was chased ashore at Cape Cruz by a Spanish armed brig These seven men made their escape in said boat and, after four days, found our pirates and joined them; the remainder of the crew being killed or taken prisoners.

Monday, 24th—Their boat was manned and sent to the before mentioned town.—I was informed by a line from Nickola, that the pirates had a man on board, a native of Principe, who in the garb of a sailor was a partner with Dominico, but I could not get sight of him. This lets us a little into the plans by which this atrocious system of piracy has been carried on. Merchants having partners on board of these pirates ! thus pirates at sea and robbers on land are associated to destroy the peaceable trader. The willingness exhibited by the seven above-mentioned men, to join our gang of pirates, seems to look like a general understanding among them; and from there being merchants on shore so base as to encourage the plunder and vend the goods, I am persuaded there has been a systematic confederacy on the part of these unprincipled desperadoes, under cover of the patriot flag; and those on land are no better than those on the sea. If the governments to whom they belong know of the atrocities committed (and I have but little doubt they do) they deserve the execration of all mankind.

Tuesday, 25th.—Still on board the Exertion—weather very calm and warm. The pirate's boat returned from St. Maria, and came for candles, cheese, potatoes, &c. they saying they must have them, and forbid my keeping any light on board at night—took a case of trunks for the captain's use and departed. Their irritating conduct at this time can hardly be imagined

Wednesday, 26th.—I was told by Bolidar that three Spanish

---

* A boat built of two halves of a large tree hollowed out and so put together as to carry about thirty barrels.

cruisers were in search of them, that they could fight two of them at once, (which by the way I believe was not true) and were disappointed at not finding them. Same evening they took both of my boats, and their own men, towed their vessel out of the creek, and anchored at its mouth, to get rid of sand-flies ; while they obliged us to stay on deck under an awning, exposed to all the violence of these flies; we relieved ourselves in some measure by the burning of tobacco, which lasted but for a short time.

Thursday, 27th.—A gang of the pirates came and stripped our masts of the green bushes, saying, "she appeared more like a sail than trees"—took one barrel of bread and one of potatoes, using about one of each every day. I understood they were waiting for boats to take the cargo; for the principal merchant had gone to Trinidad.

Friday, 28th.—Nothing remarkable occurred this day—were frequently called upon for tar and butter, and junk to make oakum. Captain Jonnia brought on board with him his new captain and officer before mentioned. Again they asked for wine, and were told as before, they had gotten the whole.

Saturday, 29th.—Same insulting conduct continued.—Took off a barrel of crackers.

Sunday, 30th.—The begining of trouble! This day which peculiarly reminds Christians of the high duties of compassion and benevolence, was never observed by these pirates. This, of course, we might expect, as they did not often know when the day came, and if they knew it, it was spent in gambling. The old saying among seamen, "no Sunday off soundings," was not thought of; and even this poor plea was not theirs, for they were on soundings and often at anchor.—Early this morning the merchant, as they called him, came with a large boat for the cargo. I was immediately ordered into the boat with my crew, not allowed any breakfast, and carried about three miles to a small island out of sight of the Exertion and left there by the side of a little pond of thick, muddy water, which proved to be very brackish, with nothing to eat but a few biscuit. One of the boat's men told us the merchant was afraid of being recognised, and when he had gone the boat would return for us; but we had great reason to apprehend they would deceive us, and therefore passed the day in the utmost anxiety. At night, however, the boats came and took us again on board the Exertion; when, to our surprise and astonishment we found they had broken open the trunks and chests and taken all our wearing apparel, not even leaving a shirt or pair of pantaloons, nor sparing a small miniature of my wife which was in my trunk. The little money I and my mate had, with some belonging to the owners, my mate had previously distributed about the cabin in three or four parcels, while I was on board the pirate, for we dare not keep it about us; one parcel in a butter pot they did not discover —Amidst the hurry with which I was obliged to leave my vessel to go to the before mentioned island, I fortunately snatched my vessel's papers, and hid them in my bosom, which the reader will find was a happy circumstance for me. My writing desk, with papers, accounts, &c. all Mr. Lord's letters (the gentleman to whom my cargo was consigned) and several others were taken and maliciously destroyed. My medicine chest, which I so much wanted, was kept for their own use. What their motive could be to take my papers I could not imagine, except they had hopes of finding bills of lading for some Spaniards, to clear them from piracy. Mr. Bracket had some notes and papers of consequence to him, which shared the same fate. My quadrant, charts, books and some bedding were not yet taken, but I found it impossible to hide them, and they were soon gone from my sight.

Monday, 31st.—We complained to them, expressing the necessity of having clothes to cover us—but, as well might we have appealed to the winds, and rather better, for they would not have upbraided us in return. The captain, however, sent word he would see to it, and ordered their clothes bags to be searched, where he found some of our things, but took good care to put them in his own cabin. I urgently requested him to give me the miniature, but, *no* was all I could get.

Tuesday, January 1st, 1822.—A sad new year's day to me Before breakfast orders came for me to cut down the Exertion's railing and bulwarks on one side, for their vessel to heave out by, and clean her bottom. On my hesitating a little they observed with anger, " very well captain, suppose you no do it quick, we do it for you."—Directly afterwards another boat full of armed men came along side; they jumped on deck with swords drawn and ordered all of us into her immediately; I stepped below, in hopes of getting something which would be of service to us; but the captain hallooed, "Go in the boat directly or I will fire upon you."—Thus compelled to obey, we were carried, together with four Spanish prisoners, to a small, low island or key of sand in the shape of a half moon and partly covered with mangrove trees; which was about one mile from and in sight of my vessel. There they left nine of us, with a little bread, flour, fish, lard, a little coffee and molasses; two or three kegs of water, which was brackish; an old sail for a covering, and a pot and some other small articles no way fit to cook in. Leaving us these, which were much less than they appear in the enumeration, they pushed off, saying, " we will come to see you in a day or two."—Selecting the best place, we spread the old sail for an awning; but no place was free from flies, moschetoes, snakes, the venomous stinged scorpion and the more venomous santipee Sometimes they were found crawling inside of our pantaloons, but fortunately no injury was received. This afternoon the pirates hove their vessel out by the Exertion and cleaned one side, using her paints, oil, &c for that purpose.—To see my vessel in that situation and to think of our prospects was a source of the deepest distress. At nigh we retired to our tent; but having nothing but the cold damp ground for a bed, and the heavy dew of night penetrating the old canvass—the situation of the island being fifty miles from the usual track of friendly vessels, and one hundred and thirty-five from Trinidad—seeing my owner's property so unjustly and wantonly destroyed—considering my condition, the hands at whose mercy I was, and deprived of all hopes, rendered sleep or rest a stranger to me.

Wednesday, 2d. The pirates hove out and cleaned the other side. She then commenced loading with the Exertion's cargo, which appeared to be flour and lard. In the afternoon their boat came and took two of the Spaniards with them to another island for water, and soon after returned with four kegs of poor, un-wholesome water, and left us, saying they should not bring us provisions again for some time; as they were going away with goods from the prize, to be gone two or three days." According-ly they brought a present supply of beef, pork, and a few potatoes, with some bedding for myself and mate. The mangrove wood afforded us a good fire, as one of the Spanish prisoners happened to have fire-works; and others had tobacco and paper with which we made cigars. About this time one of my men began to be unwell; his legs and body swelled considerably, but having no medicine I could not do much to relieve him.

Thursday, 3d. The pirates had dropped off from the Exertion, but kept their boats employed in bringing the cargo from her; I supposed it to be kegs of lard to make stowage. They then got under way with a perough in tow, both deeply laden, ran out of the harbor, hauled on the wind to the eastward till out of sight behind the Keys; leaving a guard on board the Exertion.

Friday, 4th.—Commenced with light winds and hot sun, saw a boat coming from the Exertion, apparently loaded; she passed between two small Keys to northward, supposed to be bound for Cuba. At sunset a boat came and inquired if we wanted any thing, but instead of adding to our provisions, took away our molasses, and pushed off. We found one of the Exertion's water casks, and several pieces of plank, which we carefully laid up, in hopes of getting enough to make a raft.

Saturday, 5th.—Pirates again in sight coming from the east-ward; they beat up along side their prize, and commenced load-ing. In the afternoon Nickola came to us, bringing with him two more prisoners, which they had taken in a small sail boat coming from Trinidad to Manganeil, one a Frenchman, the other a Scotchman, with two Spaniards, who remained on board the pirate, and who afterwards joined them. The back of one of these poor fellows was extremely sore, having just suffered a cruel beating from Bolidar, with the broad side of a cutlass. It appeared, that when the officer asked him " where their money was, and how much," he answered, "he was not certain but believed they had only two ounces of gold"—Bolidar furiously swore he said "ten," and not finding any more, gave him the beating. Nickola now related to me a singular fact; which was, that the Spanish part of their crew were determined to shoot him; that they tied him to the mast, and a man was appointed for the purpose; but Lyon, a Frenchman, his particular friend, stepped up and told them, if they shot him, they must shoot several more; some of the Spaniards sided with him, and he was released. Nickola told me, the reason for such treatment was, that he continually objected to their conduct towards me, and their opinion was if he should escape they would be discovered, as he declared he would take no prize money. While with us, he gave me a letter written in great haste, which contains some particulars respecting the cargo;—as follows:—

January 4, 1822.

Sir—We arrived here this morning, and before we came to anchor, had five canoes alongside ready to take your cargo, part of which we had in; and as I heard you express a wish, to know what they took out of her, to this moment, you may depend on this account of *Jamieson*,* for quality and quantity; if I have the same opportunity you will have an account of the whole. The villain who bought your cargo is from the town of *Principe*, his name is Dominico, as to that it is all that I can learn; they have taken your charts on board the schooner Mexican and I suppose mean to keep them, as the other captain has agreed to act the same infamous part in the tragedy of his life. Your clothes are here on board, but do not let me flatter you, that you will get them back; it may be so, and it may not. Perhaps in your old age, when you recline with ease in a corner of your *cottage*, you will have the goodness to drop a tear of pleasure to the memory of him, whose highest ambition should have been to subscribe himself, though devoted to the gallows, your friend,

Excuse haste.   NICKOLA MONACRE.

P. S   Your answer in writing when I come again.

Sunday, 6th.—The pirates were under way at sunrise, with a full load of the Exertion's cargo, going to Principe again, to sell a second freight, which was done readily for cash. I afterwards heard that the flour brought only five dollars per barrel, when it was worth at Trinidad thirteen; so that the villain who bought my cargo at Principe, made very large profits by it.

Monday, 7th.—The pirates brought more water, but being very brackish, it was unfit for use. We were now greatly alarmed at Thomas' ill health, being suddenly attacked with a pain in the head, and swelling of the right eye, attended with derangement

* This is the real name of Nickola.

He however soon became better; but his eye remained swollen several days without much pain. In the evening we had some heavy showers of rain, and having no secure cabin, no sheltered retreat, our exposure made us pass a very uncomfortable night.

Tuesday, 8th.—Early this morning the pirates in sight again, with fore top sail and top gallant sail set; beat up along side of the Exertion and commenced loading; having, as I supposed, sold and discharged her last freight among some of the inhabitants of Cuba. They appeared to load in great haste; and the song "O he oh," which echoed from one vessel to the other, was distinctly heard by us. How wounding was this to me! How different was this sound from what it would have been, had I been permitted to pass unmolested by these lawless plunderers, and been favored with a safe arrival at the port of my destination, where my cargo would have found an excellent sale. Then would the "O he ho," on its discharging, have been a delightful sound to me. In the afternoon she sailed with the perough in tow, both with a full load; having chairs, which was part of the cargo, slung at her quarters.

Wednesday, 9th.—Very calm and warm. The swarms of moschetoes and flies made us pass a very uncomfortable day. We dug in the sand for water, but were disappointed at finding none so good as they left us. In walking round among the bushes, I accidentally discovered a hole in the sand, and saw something run into it; curiosity led me to dig about it. With the help of Mr. Bracket I found at the distance of seven feet from its mouth, and one from the surface, a large solitary rat, apparently several years old; he had collected a large nest of grass and leaves; but there was not the least appearance of any other being on the island.

Thursday, 10th.—No pirates in sight. The day was passed in anxious suspense; David Warren being quite sick.

Friday, 11th.—They came and hauled along-side of the Exertion, but I think took out none of her cargo: but had, as I supposed, a vendue on board, wherein was sold among themselves, all our clothing, books, quadrants, charts, spy-glasses, and every thing belonging to us and our fellow prisoners. I was afterwards told they brought a good price; but what they could want of the Bible, Prayer-Book and many other books in English, was matter of astonishment to me.

Saturday, 12th.—They remained along side the Exertion; took her paints, oil, brushes, &c. and gave their vessel a new coat of paint all round, and a white boot top—took the perough to another key and caulked her—there was no appearance of their taking any cargo out; the Exertion however appeared considerably high out of water. About sunset the pirates went out of the harbor on a cruise.—Here we had been staying day after day, and exposed night after night—apprehensions for our safety were much increased; what was to become of us, seemed now to rush into every one's mind.

Sunday, 13th.—Deprived of our good books, deprived in fact of every thing, save life, and our ideas respecting our fate so gloomy, all tended to render time, especially the Lord's day, burdensome to us. In the afternoon a boat came for cargo, from, as I supposed, that villain Dominico.

Monday, 14th.—They again hove in sight, and beat up, as usual, along-side their prize. While passing our solitary island they laughed at our misery which was almost insupportable—looking upon us as though we had committed some heinous crime, and they had not sufficiently punished us; they hallooed to us, crying out, "Captain, Captain," accompanied with obscene motions and words, with which I shall not blacken these pages—yet I heard no check upon such conduct, nor could I expect it among such a gang, who have no idea of subordination on board, except when in chase of vessels, and even then but very little. My resentment was excited at such a malicious outrage, and I felt a disposition to revenge myself, should fortune ever favor me with an opportunity. It was beyond human nature not to feel and express some indignation at such treatment.—Soon after, Bolidar, with five men, well armed, came to us; he having a blunderbuss, cutlass, a long knife and pair of pistols—but for what purpose did he come? He took me by the hand saying, "Captain, me speak with you, walk this way." I obeyed, and when we were at some distance from my fellow prisoners, (his men following) he said, "the captain send me for your *wash*." I pretended not to understand what he meant and replied "I have no clothes, nor any soap to wash with—you have taken them all"—for I had kept my watch about me, hoping they would not discover it. He demanded it again as before; and was answered, "I have nothing to wash;" this raised his anger, and lifting his blunderbuss he roared out, "what the d—l you call him that make clock? give it me"—I considered it imprudent to contend any longer and submitted to his unlawful demand.—As he was going off, he gave me a small bundle in which was a pair of linen drawers, sent to me by Nickola, and also the Rev. Mr. Brooks' "Family Prayer Book." This gave me great satisfaction.—Soon after, he returned with his captain who had one arm slung up, yet with as many implements of war, as his diminutive wicked self could conveniently carry; he told me (through an interpreter who was a prisoner) "that on his cruise, he had fallen in with two Spanish privateers, and beat them off; but had three of his men killed and himself wounded in the arm" —Bolidar turned to me and said, "it is a d—n lie"—which words proved to be correct, for his arm was not wounded, and when I saw him again, which was soon afterwards, he forgot to sling it up. He further told me, "after to-morrow you shall go with your vessel and we will accompany you towards Trinidad.' This gave me some new hopes, and why I could not tell. They then left us without rendering any assistance.—This night we got some rest.

Tuesday, 15th.—The words "go after to-morrow," were used among our Spanish fellow prisoners, as though that happy to-morrow would never come—in what manner it came will soon be noticed.

Wednesday, 16th.—One of their boats came to inquire if we had seen a boat pass by last night, for their small sloop sail boat was gone and two men deserted: I told them " no"—at heart I could not but rejoice at the escape, and approve the deserters—I said nothing, however, of this kind to the pirates. On their return, they manned three of their boats and sent them in different directions to search, but at night came back without finding boat or men. They now took our old sail, which hitherto had somewhat sheltered us, to make, as I supposed, some small sail for their vessel. This rendered our night more uncomfortable than before, for in those islands the night dews are very heavy.

Thursday, 17th, was passed with great impatience.—The Exertion having been unmoored and swung to her anchor, gave some hopes of being restored to her; but was disappointed.

Friday, 18th, commenced with brighter prospects of liberty than ever—the pirates were employed in setting up our devoted schooner's shrouds, stays, &c. My condition now reminded me of the hungry man, chained in one corner of a room, while at another part was a table loaded with delicious food and fruits, the smell and sight of which he was continually to experience, but, alas! his chains were never to be loosed that he might go and partake—at almost the same moment they were thus employed, the axe was applied with the greatest dexterity to both her masts, and I saw them fall over the side! Here fell my hopes—I looked at my condition, and then thought of home.—Our Spanish fellow prisoners were so disappointed and alarmed, that they recommended hiding ourselves, if possible, among the mangrove trees, believing, as they said, we should now certainly be put to death; or, what was worse, compelled to serve on board the Mexican as pirates. Little else it is true seemed left for us; however, we kept a bright look out for them during the day, and at night " an anchor watch" as we called it, determined if we discovered their boats coming towards us, to adopt the plan of hiding, although starvation stared us in the face; yet preferred that to instant death. This night was passed in sufficient anxiety—I took the first watch.

Saturday, 19th.—The pirate's large boat came for us—it being daylight, and supposing they could see us, determined to stand our ground and wait the result. They ordered us all into the boat, but left every thing else; they rowed towards the Exertion —I noticed a dejection of spirits in one of the pirates, and in-

quired of him where they were going to carry us? He shook
his head and replied " I do not know." I now had some hopes
of visiting my vessel again—but the pirates made sail, run down,
took us in tow and stood out of the harbor. •Bolidar afterwards
took me, my mate and two of my men on board and gave us some
coffee.   On examination I found they had several additional light
sails, made of the Exertion's.   Almost every man, a pair of canvass trousers; and my colors cut up and made into belts to carry
their money about them.—My jolly boat was on deck, and I was
informed, all my rigging was disposed of.   Several of the pirates
had on some of my clothes, and the captain one of my best shirts,
a cleaner one, than I had ever seen him have on before.—He
kept at a good distance from me, and forbid my friend Nickola's
speaking to me.—I saw from the companion way in the captain's
cabin my quadrant, spy glass and other things which belonged to
us, and observed by the compass, that the course steered was
about west by south,—distance nearly twenty miles, which brought
them up with a cluster of islands called by some " Cayman
Keys."   Here they anchored and caught some fish, (one of
which was named *guard fish*) of which we had a taste.   I observed that my friend Mr. Bracket was somewhat dejected, and asked
him in a low voice, what his opinion was with respect to our fate?
He answered, " I cannot tell you, but it appears to me the worst
is to come," I told him that I hoped not, but thought they would
give us our small boat and liberate the prisoners.   But mercy
even in this shape was not left for us.   Soon after, saw the captain and officers whispering for some time in private conference.
When over, their boat was manned under the command of Bolidar,
and went to one of those Islands or Keys before mentioned.*
On their return, another conference took place—whether it was
a jury upon our lives we could not tell—I did not think conscience
could be entirely extinguished in the human breast, or that men
could become fiends.   In the afternoon while we knew not the
doom which had been fixed for us, the captain was engaged with
several of his men in gambling, in hopes to get back some of the
five hundred dollars, they said, he lost but a few nights before;
which had made him unusually fractious.   A little before sunset
he ordered all the prisoners into the large boat with a supply of
provisions and water, and to be put on shore.   While we were
getting into her, one of my fellow prisoners, a Spaniard, attempted with tears in his eyes to speak to the captain, but was refused,
with the answer—" I'll have nothing to say to any prisoner, go
into the boat "   In the mean time Nickola said to me, " My
friend, I will give you your book," (being Mr. Colman's Ser-
mons,) " it is the only thing of yours that is in my possession, I

---

* This Key was full of mangrove trees, whose tops turn down and take root, forming a
kind of umbrella. The tide at high water flows two feet deep under them ; it is therefore
impossible for human beings to live long among them, even with food and water.

dare not attempt any thing more." But the captain forbid his giving it to me, and I stepped into the boat—at that moment Nickola said in a low voice, " never mind, I may see you again before I die." The small boat was well armed and manned, and both set off together for the island, where they had agreed to leave us to perish! The scene to us was a funeral scene. There were no arms in the prisoners' boat, and, of course, all attempts to relieve ourselves would have been throwing our lives away, as Bolidar was near us, well armed. We were rowed about two miles northeasterly from the pirates, to a small low island, lonely and desolate. We arrived about sunset; and for the support of us eleven prisoners, they only left a ten gallon keg of water, and perhaps a few quarts, in another small vessel, which was very poor; part of a barrel of flour, a small keg of lard, one ham and some salt fish; a small kettle and an old broken pot; an old sail for a covering, and a small mattrass and blanket, which was thrown out as the boats hastened away. One of the prisoners happened to have a little coffee in his pocket, and these comprehended all our means of sustaining life, and for what length of time we knew not. We now felt the need of water, and our supply was comparatively nothing.—A man may live nearly twice as long without food, as without water.—Look at us now, my friends, left benighted on a little spot of sand in the midst of the ocean, far from the usual track of vessels, and every appearance of a violent thunder tempest, and a boisterous night. Judge of my feelings, and the circumstances which our band of sufferers now witnessed.—Perhaps you can and have pitied us—I assure you, we were very wretched; and to paint the scene, is not within my power. When the boats were moving from the shore, on recovering myself a little, I asked Bolidar, " If he was going to leave us so?"—he answered, " no, only two days—we go for water and wood, then come back, take you." I requested him to give us bread and other stores, for they had plenty in the boat, and at least one hundred barrels of flour in the Mexican " no, no, suppose to-morrow morning me come, me give you bread," and hurried off to their vessel. This was the last time I saw him. We then turned our attention upon finding a spot most convenient for our comfort, and soon discovered a little roof supported by stakes driven into the sand;* it was thatched with leaves of the cocoa-nut tree, considerable part of which was torn or blown off. After spreading the old sail over this roof, we placed our little stock of provisions under it. Soon after came on a heavy shower of rain which penetrated the canvass, and made it nearly as uncomfortable inside, as it would have been out. We were not prepared to catch water, having nothing to put it in. Our next object was to get fire, and after gathering some of the driest fuel to be found,

* This was probably erected by the turtle men or fishers, who visit these islands in June for the purposes of their trade.

and having a small piece of cotton wick-yarn, with flint and steel,
we kindled a fire, which was never afterwards suffered to be extinguished. The night was very dark, but we found a piece of
old rope, which when well lighted served for a candle. On examining the ground under the roof, we found perhaps thousands of
creeping insects, scorpions, lizards, crickets, &c. After scraping
them out as well as we could, the most of us having nothing but
the damp earth for a bed, laid ourselves down in hopes of some
rest; but it being so wet, gave many of us severe colds, and one
of the Spaniards was quite sick for several days.

Sunday, 20th.—As soon as daylight came on, we proceeded to
take a view of our little island, and found it to measure only one
acre, of coarse, white sand; about two feet, and in some spots
perhaps three feet above the surface of the ocean. On the highest part were growing some bushes and small mangroves, (the
dry part of which was our fuel) and the wild caster oil beans.
We were greatly disappointed in not finding the latter suitable
food; likewise some of the prickly pear bushes, which gave us
only a few pears about the size of our small button pear; the
outside has thorns, which if applied to the fingers or lips, will
remain there, and cause a severe smarting similar to the nettle;
the inside a spungy substance full of juice and seeds, which are
red and a little tartish—had they been there in abundance, we
should not have suffered so much for water—but alas! even this
substitute was not for us. On the northerly side of the island
was a hollow, where the tide penetrated the sand, leaving stag-
nant water. We presumed, in hurricanes the island was nearly
overflowed. According to the best calculations I could make,
we were about thirty five miles from any part of Cuba, one hundred from Trinidad and forty from the usual track of American
vessels, or others which might pass that way. No vessel of any
considerable size, can safely pass among these Keys or "Queen's
Gardens," (as the Spaniards call them) being a large number
extending from Cape Cruz to Trinidad, one hundred and fifty
miles distance; and many more than the charts have laid down,
most of them very low and some covered at high water, which
makes it very dangerous for navigators without a skilful pilot.
After taking this view of our condition, which was very gloomy,
we began to suspect we were left on this desolate island by those
merciless plunderers to perish. Of this I am now fully convinced;
still we looked anxiously for the pirate's boat to come according
to promise with more water and provisions, but looked in vain.
We saw them soon after get under way with all sail set and run
directly from us until out of our sight, and *we never saw them again!*
one may partially imagine our feelings, but they cannot be put
into words. Before they were entirely out of sight of us, we
raised the white blanket upon a pole, waving it in the air, in
hopes, that at two miles distance they would see it and be moved

to pity. But pity in such monsters was not to be found. It was not their interest to save us from the lingering death, which we now saw before us. We tried to compose ourselves, trusting that God, who had witnessed our sufferings, would yet make use of some one, as the instrument of his mercy towards us. Our next care, now, was to try for water. We dug several holes in the sand and found it, but quite too salt for use. The tide penetrates probably through the island.—We now came on short allowance for water. Having no means of securing what we had by lock and key, some one in the night would slyly drink, and it was soon gone. The next was to bake some bread, which we did by mixing flour with salt water and frying it in lard, allowing ourselves eight quite small pancakes to begin with. The ham was reserved for some more important occasion, and the salt fish was lost for want of fresh water. The remainder of this day was passed in the most serious conversation and reflection.—At night, I read prayers from the " Prayer Book," before mentioned, which I most carefully concealed while last on board the pirates. This plan was pursued morning and evening, during our stay there.—Then retired for rest and sleep, but realized little of either.

Monday, 21st.—In the morning we walked round the beach, in expectation of finding something useful. On our way picked up a paddle about three feet long, very similar to the Indian canoe paddle, except the handle, which was like that of a shovel, the top part being split off; we laid it by for the present. We likewise found some konchs and roasted them; they were a pretty good shell fish, though rather tough. We discovered at low water, a bar or spit of sand extending northeasterly from us, about three miles distant, to a cluster of Keys, which were covered with mangrove trees, perhaps as high as our quince tree. My friend Mr. Bracket and George attempted to wade across, being at that time of tide only up to their armpits; but were pursued by a shark and returned without success. The tide rises about four feet.

Tuesday, 22d.—We found several pieces of the palmetto or cabbage tree, and some pieces of boards, put them together in the form of a raft, and endeavored to cross, but that proved ineffectual. Being disappointed, we set down to reflect upon other means of relief, intending to do all in our power for our safety while our strength continued. While setting here, the sun was so powerful and oppressive, reflecting its rays upon the sea, which was then calm, and the white sand which dazzled the eye, was so painful, that we retired under the awning; there the moschetoes and flies were so numerous, that good rest could not be found. We were, however, a little cheered, when, in scraping out the top of the ground to clear out, I may say thousands of crickets and bugs, we found a hatchet, which was to us peculiarly serviceable. At night the strong northeasterly wind, which p e-

vails there at all seasons, was so cold as to make it equally uncomfortable with the day.—Thus day after day, our sufferings
and apprehensions multiplying, we were very generally alarmed

Wednesday, 23d.—Early this morning one of our Spanish
fellow prisoners crossed the bar, having taken with him a pole
sharpened at one end; this he said "was to kill sharks"—but he
saw none to trouble him.   While he was gone, we tried for water
in several places, but still it was very salt; but not having any
other, we drank of it, and found it had a similar effect, to that of
glauber salts.   We now concluded to reduce the allowance of
bread or rather pancakes, being too sensible that our little stock
of provisions could last but a few days longer; we had the faintest
hope of any supplies, or escape, before it would be too late to save
life.   Towards night the Spaniard returned, but almost famished
for want of water and food.   He reported that he found some
plank on one of the islands, (but they proved to be sugar-box
shooks) which revived us a little; but *no water.*—He said he had
great difficulty to make his way through the mangrove trees, it
being very swampy; so that we should not better ourselves by
going there, although the key was rather larger than ours.   This,
I understood through Joseph, the English prisoner who could
speak Spanish.   After prayers, laid ourselves down upon our bed
of sand, and being nearly exhausted we obtained some sleep.

Thursday, 24th.—This morning, after taking a little coffee,
made of the water which we thought least salt, and two or three of
the little cakes, we felt somewhat refreshed, and concluded to make
another visit to those Keys in hopes of finding something more,
which might make a raft for us to escape the pirates, and avoid
perishing by thirst.   Accordingly seven of us set off, waded
across the bar and searched all the Keys thereabouts.—On one
we found a number of sugar-box shooks, two lashing plank and
some pieces of old spars, which were a part of the Exertion's
deck load, that was thrown overboard when she grounded on the
bar, spoken of in the first part of the narrative.—It seems they
had drifted fifteen miles, and had accidentally lodged on these
very Keys within our reach.   Had the pirates known this, they
would undoubtedly have placed us in another direction.   They
no   thought that they could not put us on a worse place.
     and at this time was blowing so strong on shore, as to pre-
vent rafting our stuff round to our island, and we were obliged to
haul it upon the beach for the present; then dug for water in the
highest place, but found it as salt as ever, and then returned to
our habitation.—But hunger and thirst began to prey upon us, and
our comforts were as few as our hopes.

Friday, 25th.—Again passed over to those Keys to windward in
order to raft our stuff to our island, it being most convenient for
building.   But the surf on the beach was so very rough, that we
were again compelled to postpone it.   Our courage however did

not fail where there was the slightest hopes of life—Returning without it, we found on our way an old top timber of some vessel; it had several spikes in it, which we afterwards found very serviceable. In the hollow of an old tree, we found two guarnas of small size, one male, the other female.—One only was caught After taking off the skin, we judged it weighed a pound and a half With some flour and lard, (the only things we had except salt water,) it made us a fine little mess. We thought it a rare dish though a small one for eleven half starved persons.—At the same time a small vessel hove in sight; we made a signal to her with the blanket tied to a pole and placed it on the highest tree—some took off their white clothes and waved them in the air, hoping they would come to us; should they be pirates, they could do no more than kill us, and perhaps would give us some water for which we began to suffer most excessively; but, notwithstanding all our efforts, she took no notice of us.

Saturday, 26th.—This day commenced with moderate weather and smooth sea; at low tide found some cockles, boiled and eat them, but they were very painful to the stomach. David Warren had a fit of strangling with swelling of the bowels; but soon recovered, and said, "something like salt, rose in his throat and choked him" Most of us then set off for the Keys, where the plank and shooks were put together in a raft, which we with pieces of boards paddled over to our island; when we consulted the best plan, either to build a raft large enough for us all to go on, or a boat; but the shooks having three or four nails in each, and having a piece of large reed or bamboo, previously found, of which we made pins, concluded to make a boat.

Sunday, 27th.—Commenced our labor, for which I know we need offer no apology. We took the two planks, which were about fourteen feet long, and two and a half wide, and fixed them together for the bottom of the boat; then with moulds made of palmetto bark, cut timber and knees from mangrove trees which spread so much as to make the boat four feet wide at the top, placed them exactly the distance apart of an Havanna sugar box. —Her stern was square and the bows tapered to a peak, making her form resemble a flat-iron. We proceeded thus far and retired to rest for the night—but Mr. Bracket was too unwell to get much sleep.

Monday, 28th.—Went on with the work as fast as possible.— Some of the Spaniards had long knives about them, which proved very useful in fitting timbers, and a gimlet of mine, accidentally found on board the pirates, enabled us to use the wooden pins.— And now our spirits began to revive, though *water, water,* was continually in our minds. We now feared the pirates might possibly come, find out our plan and put us to death, (although before we had wished to see them, being so much in want of water.) Our labor was extremely burdensome, and the Spaniards considerably peevish—but they would often say to me "never mind capitan, by and by, Americana or Spanyola catch them, me go see um hung." We quitted work for the day, cooked some cakes but found it necessary to reduce the quantity again, however small before. We found some herbs on a windward Key, which the Spaniards called Spanish tea.—This when well boiled we found somewhat palatable, although the water was very salt. This herb resembles pennyroyal in look and taste, though not so pungent. In the evening when we were setting round the fire to keep off the moschetoes, I observed David Warren's eyes shone like glass. The mate said to him—"David I think you will die before morning—I think you are struck with death now." I thought so too, and told him, " I thought it most likely we should all die here soon; but as some one of us may survive to carry the tidings to our friends, if you have any thing to say respecting your family, now is the time."—He then said, " I have a mother in Saco where I belong—she is a second time a widow—to-morrow if you can spare a scrap of paper and pencil I will write something." But no to-morrow came to him.—In the course of the night he had another spell of strangling, and soon after expired, without much pain and without a groan. He was about twenty-six years old. —How solemn was this scene to us! Here we beheld the ravages of death commenced upon us. More than one of us considered death a happy release. For myself I thought of my wife and children; and wished to live if God should so order it, though extreme thirst, hunger and exhaustion had well nigh prostrated my fondest hopes.

Tuesday, 29th.—Part of us recommenced labor on the boat, while myself and Mr. Bracket went and selected the highest clear spot of sand on the northern side of the island, where we dug Warren's grave and boxed it up with shooks, thinking it would be the most suitable spot for the rest of us—whose turn would come next, we knew not. At about ten o'clock, A. M. conveyed the corpse to the grave, followed by us survivers—a scene, whose awful solemnity can never be painted. We stood around the grave, and there I read the funeral prayer from the Rev. Mr. Brooks's Family Prayer Book; and committed the body to the earth; covered it with some pieces of board and sand, and returned to our labor.—One of the Spaniards an old man, named Manuel, who was partial to me, and I to him, made a cross and placed at the head of the grave saying, " Jesus Christ hath him now." Although I did not believe in any mysterious influence of this cross, yet I was perfectly willing it should stand there. The middle part of the day being very warm, our mouths parched with thirst, and our spirits so depressed, that we made but little progress during the remainder of this day, but in the evening were employed in picking oakum out of the bolt rope taken from the old sail

Wednesday, 30th.—Returned to labor on the boat with as

much vigor as our weak and debilitated state would admit; but it was a day of trial to us all; for the Spaniards and we Americans could not well understand each other's plans, and they being naturally petulant would not work, nor listen with any patience for Joseph our English fellow prisoner to explain our views—they would sometimes undo what they had done and in a few minutes replace it again; however before night we began to calk her seams, by means of pieces of hard mangrove, made in form of a calking-iron, and had the satisfaction of seeing her in a form something like a boat.

Thursday, 31st.—Went on with the work, some at calking, others at battening the seams with strips of canvass, and pieces of pine nailed over, to keep the oakum in. Having found a suitable pole for a mast, the rest went about making a sail from the one we had used for a covering, also fitting oars of short pieces of boards, in form of a paddle, tied on a pole, we having a piece of fishing line brought by one of the prisoners. Thus, at three P. M the boat was completed and put afloat.—We had all this time confidently hoped, that she would be sufficiently large and strong to carry us all—we made a trial and were disappointed! This was indeed a severe trial, and the emotions it called up were not easy to be suppressed. She proved leaky, for we had no carpenter's yard, or smith's shop to go to.—And now the question was, "who should go, and how many?" I found it necessary for six; four to row, one to steer and one to bale. Three of the Spaniards and the Frenchman claimed the right, as being best acquainted with the nearest inhabitants; likewise, they had when taken, two boats left at St. Maria (about forty miles distant) which they were confident of finding. They promised to return within two or three days for the rest of us—I thought it best to consent—Mr. Bracket it was agreed should go in my stead, because my papers must accompany me as a necessary protection, and my men apprehended danger if they were lost. Joseph Baxter (I think was his name) they wished should go, because he could speak both languages—leaving Manuel, George, Thomas and myself, to wait their return. Having thus made all arrangements, and putting up a keg of the least salt water, with a few pancakes and salt fish, they set off a little before sunset with our best wishes and prayers for their safety and return to our relief.—To launch off into the wide ocean, with strength almost exhausted, and in such a frail boat as this, you will say was very hazardous, and in truth it was; but what else was left to us?—Their intention was to touch at the Key where the Exertion was, and if no boat was to be found there, to proceed on to St. Maria and if none there, to go to Trinidad and send us relief.—But alas! it was the last time I ever saw them!—Our suffering this day was most acute.

Tuesday, February 1st.—This day we rose early and traversed the beach in search of cockles, &c. but found very few—I struck my foot against something in the sand, which proved to be a curious shell, and soon found two others of a different kind; but they were to me like Crusoe's lump of gold, of no value. I could not drink them; so laid them by.—I returned to our tent and we made some skillygolee, or flour and salt water boiled together, which we found better than clear salt water. We passed the day very uncomfortably, and my people were dissatisfied at not having an equal chance, as they called it, with the others in the boat—but it is not always, that we know what is for our good.

Saturday, 2d.—Thomas and George made another visit to the windward Keys, where they found some more shooks and two pieces of spars; towed them round as before. We now had some hopes of finding enough to make us a raft, which would carry us to some place of relief, in case the boat should not return.

Sunday, 3d.—A calm warm day, but a very gloomy one to us, it being more difficult to support life—our provisions nearly expended, no appearance of rain since the night we first landed, our thirst increasing, our strength wasting, our few clothes hanging in rags, our beards of great length and almost turned white, nothing like relief before us, no boat in sight.—Think, compassionate reader, our situation. We had marked out for each one the place for his grave. I looked at mine, and thought of my wife and family.—Again we reduced the allowance of bread; but even the little which now fell to my share, I could scarcely swallow—I never seemed to feel the sensation of hunger, the extreme of thirst was so overpowering.—Perhaps never shall I be more reconciled to death, but my home made me want to live, although every breath seemed to increase thirst.

Monday, 4th.—Having seriously reflected on our situation, concluded to put all the shooks, &c. together and form a raft, and ascertain what weight it would carry; but here again we were disappointed, for we had not enough to carry two of us.

Tuesday, 5th.—About ten o'clock, A. M. discovered a boat drifting by on the southeast side of the island about a mile distant. I deemed it a providential thing to us, and urged Thomas and George trying the raft for her. They reluctantly consented and set off, but it was nearly three P. M. when they came up with her.—It was the same boat we had built! Where then was my friend Bracket and those who went with him? Every appearance was unfavorable.—I hoped that a good Providence had yet preserved him—The two men who went for the boat, found it full of water, without oars, paddle, or sail; being in this condition, and about three miles to the leeward, the men found it impossible to tow her up, so left her, and were till eleven o'clock at night getting back with the raft. They were so exhausted, that had it not been nearly calm, they could never have returned.

Wednesday, 6th.—This morning was indeed the most gloomy I had ever experienced.—There appeared hardly a ray of hope

that my friend Bracket could return, seeing the boat was lost.—
Our provisions nearly gone; our mouths parched extremely with
thirst; our strength wasted; our spirits broken, and our hopes
imprisoned within the circumference of this desolate island in the
midst of an unfrequented ocean; all these things gave to the scene
around us the hue of death. In the midst of this dreadful despon-
dence, a sail hove in sight, bearing the white flag. Our hopes
were raised, of course—but no sooner raised than darkened, by
hearing a gun fired. Here then was another gang of pirates.—
She soon, however, came near enough to anchor, and her boat
pushed off towards us with three men in her.—Thinking it
no worse now to die by sword than famine I walked down immediately to meet them. I knew them not.—A moment before the
boat touched the ground, a man leaped from her bows and caught
me in his arms! *It was Nickola!*!—saying, " Do you now believe
Nickola is your friend? yes, said he, *Jamieson* will yet prove himself so."—No words can express my emotions at this moment.—
This was a friend indeed. The reason of my not recognising
them before, was that they had cut off their beards and whiskers.
Turning to my fellow-sufferers, Nickola asked—" Are these all
that are left of you? where are the others?"—At this moment
seeing David's grave—" Are they dead then? ah I suspected it,
I know what you were put here for." As soon as I could recover
myself, gave him an account of Mr. Bracket and the others.—
" How unfortunate, he said, they must be lost or some pirates
have taken them "—" but, he continued, we have no time to lose;
you had better embark immediately with us, and go where you
please, we are at your service." The other two in the boat with
him were Frenchmen, one named Lyon, the other Parrikete.
They affectionately embraced each of us; then holding to my
mouth the nose of a teakettle, filled with wine, said " Drink plenty,
no hurt you." I drank as much as I judged prudent. They then
gave it to my fellow sufferers.—I experienced almost immediate
relief, not feeling it in my head; they had also brought in the
boat for us, a dish of salt beef and potatoes, of which we took a
little. Then sent the boat on board for the other two men, being
five in all; who came ashore, and rejoiced enough was I to see
among them Thomas Young, one of my crew, who was detained
on board the Mexican, but had escaped through Nickola's means;
the other a Frenchman, named John Cadedt. I now thought,
again and again, with troubled emotion of my friend Bracket's
fate.- I took the last piece of paper I had, and wrote with pencil
a few lines, informing him (should he come there,) that " I and
the rest were safe; that I was not mistaken in the friend in whom
I had placed so much confidence, that he had accomplished my
highest expectations; and that I should go immediately to Trinidad, and requested him to go there also, and apply to Mr. Isaac W.
Lord, my consignee, for assistance." I put the paper into a junk

bottle, previously found on the beach, put in a stopper, and left it, together with what little flour remained, a keg of water brought from Nickola's vessel, and a few other things which I thought might be of service to him. We then repaired with our friends on board, where we were kindly treated. She was a sloop from Jamaica, of about twelve tons, with a cargo of rum and wine, bound to Trinidad. I asked "which way they intended to go?" they said "to Jamaica if agreeable to me." As I preferred Trinidad, I told them, "if they would give me the Exertion's boat which was along-side (beside their own) some water and provisions, we would take chance in her," "for perhaps, said I, you will fare better at Jamaica, than at Trinidad." After a few minutes consultation, they said "you are too much exhausted to row the distance of one hundred miles, therefore we will go and carry you—we consider ourselves at your service." I expressed a wish to take a look at the Exertion, possibly we might hear something of Mr. Bracket. Nickola said "very well," so got under way, and run for her, having a light westerly wind. He then related to me the manner of their desertion from the pirates; as nearly as I can recollect his own words, he said, "A few days since, the pirates took four small vessels, I believe Spaniards; they having but two officers for the two first, the third fell to me as prize master, and having an understanding with the three Frenchmen and Thomas, selected them for my crew, and went on board with orders to follow the Mexican; which I obeyed. The fourth, the pirates took out all but one man and bade him also follow their vessel. Now our schooner leaked so bad, that we left her and in her stead agreed to take this little sloop, (which we are now in) together with the one man. The night being very dark we all agreed to desert the pirates—altered our course and touched at St. Maria, where we landed the one man—saw no boats there, could hear nothing from you, and agreed one and all at the risk of our lives to come and liberate you if you were alive; knowing, as we did, that you were put on this Key to perish. On our way we boarded the Exertion, thinking possibly you might have been there. On board her we found a sail and paddle.[*] We took one of the pirate's boats which they had left along-side of her, which proves how we come by two boats. My friend, the circumstance I am now about to relate, will somewhat astonish you. When the pirate's boat with Bolidar was sent to the before mentioned Key, on the 19th of January, it was their intention to leave you prisoners there, where was nothing but salt water and mangroves, and no possibility of escape. This was the plan of Baltizar, their abandoned pilot; but Bolidar's heart failed him, and he objected to it; then, after a conference, Captain Jonnia ordered you to be put on the little island from whence we have

---

[*] This proved to me that Mr Bracket had been there, these being the ones which he took from the island

now taken you. But after this was done, that night the French
and Portuguese part of the Mexican's crew protested against it;
so that Captain Jonnia to satisfy them, sent his large boat to take
you and your fellow prisoners back again, taking care to select his
confidential Spaniards for this errand. And will you believe me,
they set off from the Mexican and after spending about as much time
as would really have taken them to come to you, they returned, and
reported they had been to your island, and landed, and that none of
you were there; somebody having taken you off! This, all my
companions here know to be true.—I knew it was impossible you
could have been liberated, and therefore we determined among
ourselves, that should an opportunity occur we would come and
save your lives, as we now have." He then expressed, as he
hitherto had done, (and I believe with sincerity) his disgust with
the bad company which he had been in, and looked forward with
anxiety to the day when he might return to his native country.
I advised him to get on board an American vessel, whenever an
opportunity offered, and come to the United States; and on his
arrival direct a letter to me: repeating my earnest desire to make
some return for the disinterested friendship which he had shown
toward me. With the Frenchman I had but little conversation,
being unacquainted with the language.

Here ended Nickola's account. "And now" said the Frenchmen, "our hearts be easy." Nickola observed he had left all
and found us. I gave them my warmest tribute of gratitude,
saying, I looked upon them under God as the preservers of our
lives, and promised them all the assistance which my situation
might ever enable me to afford.—This brings me to

Thursday evening, 7th, when, at eleven o'clock, we anchored
at the creek's mouth, near the Exertion. I was anxious to board
her; accordingly took with me Nickola, Thomas, George and two
others, well armed, each with a musket and cutlass. I jumped
on her deck, saw a fire in the camboose, but no person there: I
called aloud Mr. Bracket's name several times, saying "it is
Captain Lincoln, don't be afraid, but show yourself;" but no answer was given. She had no masts, spars, rigging, furniture,
provisions or any thing left, except her bowsprit, and a few barrels of salt provisions of her cargo. Her sealing had holes cut
in it, no doubt in their foolish search for money. I left her with
peculiar emotions, such as I hope never again to experience; and
returned to the little sloop where we remained till—

Friday, 8th—When I had a disposition to visit the island on
which we were first imprisoned.—Found nothing there—saw a
boat among the mangroves, near the Exertion. Returned, and
got under way immediately for Trinidad. In the night, while
under full sail, run aground on a sunken Key, having rocks above
the water, resembling old stumps of trees; we, however, soon
got off and anchored. Most of those Keys have similar rocks
about them, which navigators must carefully guard against.

Saturday, 9th.—Got under way again, and stood along close in for the main island of Cuba, in order, that if we should see the pirates, to take our boats and go on shore.

Sunday, 10th.—Saw the highlands of Trinidad. At night came to anchor in sight of the town, near a small Key; next morning—

Monday, 11th—Got under way—saw a brig at anchor about five miles below the mouth of the harbor; we hoped to avoid her speaking us; but when we opened in sight of her, discovered a boat making towards us, with a number of armed men in her. This alarmed my friends, and as we did not see the brig's ensign hoisted, they declared the boat was a pirate, and looking through the spy-glass, thought they knew some of them to be the Mexican's men! This state of things was quite alarming. They said, "we will not be taken alive by them." Immediately the boat fired a musket; the ball passed through our mainsail. My friends insisted on beating them off: I endeavored to dissuade them, believing, as I did, that the brig was a Spanish man of war, who had sent her boat to ascertain who we were. I thought we had better heave too. Immediately another shot came. Then they insisted on fighting and said, "if I would not help them, I was no friend." I reluctantly acquiesced, and handed up the guns—commenced firing upon them and they upon us. We received several shot through the sails, but no one was hurt on either side. Our two boats had been cast adrift to make us go the faster, and we gained upon them—continued firing until they turned from us, and went for our boats, which they took in tow for the brig. Soon after this, it became calm: then I saw that the brig had us in her power.—She manned and armed two more boats for us. We now concluded, since we had scarcely any ammunition, to surrender; and were towed down along-side the brig, taken on board, and was asked by the captain, who could speak English, "what for you fire on the boat?" I told him "we thought her a pirate, and did not like to be taken by them again, having already suffered too much;" showing my papers. He said, "Captain Americana, never mind, go and take some dinner—which are your men?" I pointed them out to him, and he ordered them the liberty of the decks; but my friend Nickola and his three associates were immediately put in irons. They were, however, afterwards taken out of irons and examined; and I understood the Frenchmen agreed to enlist, as they judged it the surest way to better their condition. Whether Nickola enlisted, I do not know, but think that he did, as I understood that offer was made to him: I however endeavored to explain more distinctly to the captain, the benevolent efforts of these four men by whom my life had been saved, and used every argument in my power to procure their discharge. I also applied to the governor, and exerted myself with peculiar interest, dictated as I trust with heartfelt gratitude—and I ardently hope ere this, that Nickola is on his way to this country, where I may have an opportunity of convincing him that such an act of benevolence will not go unrewarded. Previous to my leaving Trinidad, I made all the arrangements in my power with my influential friends, and doubt not, that their laudable efforts will be accomplished. —The sloop's cargo was taken on board the brig; after which the captain requested a certificate that I was politely treated by him, saying his name was Captain Candama, of the privateer brig Prudentee of eighteen guns. This request I complied with. His first lieutenant told me he had sailed out of Boston, as commander for T. C Amory, Esq. during the last war. In the course of the evening my friends were taken out of irons and examined separately, then put back again. The captain invited me to supper in his cabin, and a birth for the night, which was truly acceptable. The next morning after breakfast, I with my people were set on shore with the few things we had, with the promise of the Exertion's small boat in a day or two. But it was never sent me—the reason, let the reader imagine. On landing at the wharf Casildar, we were immediately taken by soldiers to the guard house, which was a very filthy place; thinking I suppose, and even calling us pirates. Soon some friends came to see me. Mr. Cotton, who resides there brought us in some soup. Mr. Isaac W. Lord, of Boston, my merchant, came with Captain Tate, who sent immediately to the governor; for I would not show my papers to any one else. He came about sunset, and after examining Manuel my Spanish fellow prisoner, and my papers, said to me, giving me the papers, "Captain, you are at liberty." I was kindly invited by Captain Matthew Rice, of schooner Galaxy, of Boston, to go on board his vessel, and live with him during my stay there. This generous offer I accepted, and was treated by him with the greatest hospitality; for I was an hungered and he gave me meat, I was athirst and he gave me drink, I was naked and he clothed me, a stranger and he took me in. He likewise took Manuel and my three men for that night. Next day Mr. Lord rendered me all necessary assistance in making my protest. He had heard nothing from me until my arrival. I was greatly disappointed in not finding Mr. Bracket, and requested Mr. Lord to give him all needful aid if he should come there. To Captain Carnes, of the schooner Hannah, of Boston, I would tender my sincere thanks, for his kindness in giving me a passage to Boston, which I gladly accepted. To those gentlemen of Trinidad, and many captains of American vessels, who gave me sea clothing, &c. I offer my cordial gratitude.

Captain Carnes sailed from Trinidad on the 20th February. Fearing the pirates, we kept a long distance from the land and two degrees to westward of Cape Antonia. On our passage experienced several gales of wind, in one of which, while lying to, shipped a sea, which did considerable injury, and swept a young man overboard from the pump, named Nelson. We never saw him again. We arrived at Boston, March 25th, and when I stepped upon the wharf, though much emaciated, I felt truly happy.

I am fully of the opinion that these ferocious pirates are linked in with many inhabitants of Cuba; and the government in many respects appears covertly to encourage them.

It is with heartfelt delight, that, since the above narrative was written, I have learned that Mr. Bracket and his companions are safe; he arrived at Port d'Esprit, about forty leagues east of Trinidad. A letter has been received from him, stating that he should proceed to Trinidad the first opportunity.—It appears that after reaching the wreck, they found a boat from the shore, taking on board some of the Exertion's cargo, in which they proceeded to the above place. Why it was not in his power to come to our relief will no doubt be satisfactorily disclosed when he may be so fortunate as once more to return to his native country and friends.

For many months, I remained without any certain information respecting the fate of Mr. Bracket and his companions. But in the course of the ensuing Autumn, if I recollect right, Mr. Bracket very unexpectedly paid me a visit, at Hingham, the place of my residence. We were mutually rejoiced to see each other once more among the living, as for a time at least, each had regarded the other as dead. He gave me an account of his adventures, and of the reasons, why he did not return to us. He told me that when they left us, and put to sea, in the miserable boat, which we had constructed, they went to the Exertion, and fortunately found a better boat, of which they took possession, and suffered the old one to float away, and it accordingly passed our solitary island, in its random course, causing us a great deal of alarm. From the wreck, they steered among the keys to the main-land of Cuba, and reached Principe, the town where my cargo was sold. Here Mr. Bracket related his tale of suffering, and requested assistance, to rescue the remaining prisoners, on the key. The authorities furnished him with several soldiers, with whom he again put to sea, with the humane intention of coming to relieve us. They had gone but a short distance, however, when the soldiers positively refused to go any farther, and forced him to return with them to Principe; thus all his hopes of being able to rescue us, were entirely extinguished. A stranger, and helpless as he was, it was out of his power to do any thing more, and he could only hope that we might have been saved in some other way. Friendless, without money, and debilitated by recent suffering, he hardly knew which way to turn. He was desirous of reaching home, and finally resolved to travel to the north side of Cuba. After a long and tedious journey, during which he

suffered dreadfully, from the hard travelling, and want of necessaries and comforts, he at length arrived at Havannah, from
which port he took passage home to Boston. Thus the reasons
of his conduct were satisfactorily explained, and my uncertainty
respecting his fate, happily terminated.

I felt great anxiety to learn what became of Jamieson, who,
my readers will recollect, was detained on board the Spanish Brig
Prudentee near Trinidad. I heard nothing from him, until I
believe about eighteen months after I reached home, when I received a letter from him, from Montego Bay Jamaica, informing
me that he was then residing in that island. I immediately wrote
to him, and invited him to come on to the United States. He
accordingly came on passenger with Captain Wilson of Cohas-
set, and arrived in Boston, in August 1824. Our meeting was very
affecting. Trying scenes were brought up before us; scenes
gone forever, through which we had passed together, where our
acquaintance was formed, and since which time, we had never
met. I beheld once more the Preserver of my life; the instrument, under Providence, of restoring me to my home, my family
and my friends, and I regarded him with no ordinary emotion.
My family were delighted to see him, and cordially united in
giving him a warm reception. He told me that after we separated
in Trinidad, he remained on board the Spanish Brig. The Commander asked him and his companions if they would enlist; the
Frenchmen replied that they would, but he said nothing, being
determined to make his escape, the very first opportunity which
should present. The Spanish Brig afterwards fell in with a
Columbian Patriot, an armed Brig of eighteen guns. Being of
about equal force, they gave battle, and fought between three
and four hours. Both parties were very much injured; and, without any considerable advantage on either side, both drew off to
make repairs. The Spanish Brig Prudentee, put into St. Jago
de Cuba. Jamieson was wounded in the action, by a musket
ball, through his arm, and was taken on shore, with the other
wounded, and placed in the hospital at St. Jago. Here he remained for a considerable time, until he had nearly recovered,
when he found an opportunity of escaping, and embarked for
Jamaica. He arrived in safety at Kingston, and from there,
travelled barefoot over the mountains, until very much exhausted,
he reached Montego Bay, where he had friends, and where one
of his brothers possessed some property. From this place, he
afterwards wrote to me. He told me that before he came to
Massachusetts, he saw the villainous pilot of the Mexican, the
infamous Baltizar, with several other pirates, brought into Montego Bay, from whence they were to be conveyed to Kingston, to
be executed. Whether the others were part of the Mexican's
crew, or not, I do not know. Baltizar was an old man, and as
Jamieson said, it was a melancholy and heart-rending sight, to see

him borne to execution with those gray hairs, which might have been venerable in virtuous old age, now a shame and reproach to this hoary villain, for he was full of years, and old in iniquity. When Jamieson received the letter which I wrote him, he immediately embarked with Captain Wilson, and came to Boston, as I have before observed.

According to his own account he was of a very respectable family in Greenoch, Scotland. His father when living was a rich cloth merchant, but both his father, and mother, had been dead many years. He was the youngest of thirteen children, and being as he said of a roving disposition, had always followed the seas. He had received a polite education, and was of a very gentlemanly deportment. He spoke several living languages, and was skilled in drawing and painting. He had travelled extensively in different countries, and acquired in consequence, an excellent knowledge of their manners and customs. His varied information (for hardly any subject escaped him,) rendered him a very entertaining companion. His observations on the character of different nations were very liberal; marking their various traits, their virtues and vices, with playful humorousness, quite free from bigotry, or narrow prejudice.

He was in France, during the disturbance between France and England, when all British subjects whatever in France were detained prisoners of war. He was one who was thus compelled to remain a prisoner to Napoleon. He was there, at the time of Napoleon's memorable expedition to Russia; and saw the splendid troops of the Emperor when they left delightful France to commence their toilsome, and fatal journey; and also the remnant when they returned, broken down, dispirited, haggard, and wan, their garments hanging about them in tatters, and hardly life enough in them to keep soul and body together. The particulars respecting this period, he could communicate with the minuteness of an eye-witness, which consequently rendered them very interesting. During the first part of his residence in France, he was supported by remittances from his father, and allowed the liberty of the city of Valenciennes; a gentleman there, being bound for his good behavior. He thus had an opportunity of visiting and becoming acquainted with the inhabitants. He lived in this manner several years. At length aroused, as he said, by the consciousness that he was spending the best days of his life in idleness, he formed the determination to try and make his escape from the country. He honorably released the gentleman who was bound for him, from his obligation, frankly telling him that he should run away the first opportunity. From this time he was alternately arrested and imprisoned, and by various stratagems effected his escape, until he had been placed in ninety-three different prisons. During his wanderings, he climbed the

Alps, and visited the famous passage, cut through the solid rock, by Hannibal, which as he said, was of sufficient magnitude to admit a large loaded wagon to pass through. From his long residence in France, he had learned to speak the French language with a facility, almost equal to a native. The charm of his conversation and manners drew people around him, they hardly knew how, or why.

I was in trade, between Boston and Philadelphia, at the time he came to Massachusetts, and he sailed with me several trips as my mate. He afterwards went to Cuba, and was subsequently engaged in the mackerel fishery, out of the port of Hingham, during the warm season, and in the winter frequently employed himself in teaching navigation to young men, for which he was eminently qualified. He remained with us, until his death, which took place in 1829. At this time he had been out at sea two or three days, when he was taken sick, and was carried into Cape Cod, where he died, on the first day of May 1829, and there his remains lie buried. Peace be to his ashes! They rest in a strange land, far from his kindred, and his native country.

Since his death I have met with Mr. Stewart in Philadelphia, who was Commercial Agent in Trinidad at the time of my capture. He informed me, that the piratical schooner Mexican, was afterwards chased by an English government vessel, from Jamaica, which was cruising in search of it. Being hotly pursued the pirates deserted their vessel, and fled to the Mangrove bushes, on an island similar to that on which they had placed me and my crew to die. The English surrounded them, and thus they were cut off from all hope of escape. They remained there, I think fourteen days, when being almost entirely subdued by famine, eleven surrendered themselves, and were taken. The others probably perished among the mangroves. The few who were taken were carried by the government vessel into Trinidad Mr. Stewart said that he saw them himself, and such miserable objects that had life he never before beheld. They were in a state of starvation; their beards had grown to a frightful length, their bodies were covered with filth and vermin, and their countenances were hideous. From Trinidad they were taken to Kingston, Jamaica, and there hung. Thus there is every reason to believe that this horde of monsters was at last broken up, and dispersed

GREENWICH HOSPITAL.

Greenwich, which was formerly a distinct town, but is now an appendage to the British metropolis, is seated on the south bank of the Thames, five miles below London bridge. It is celebrated for its hospital for wounded and decayed seamen of the nationa.

Greenwich Hospital.

marine, which is one of the finest architectural edifices in the world. The buildings consist of four distinct piles, two along the bank of the river, with a noble terrace in front, eight hundred and sixty feet in length; between these two piles is a lawn two hundred and seventy feet wide; the two other piles are built behind, projecting into the square or lawn, so as to form a quadrangle with an opening in the centre, which is terminated by an elegant building more recently erected for a naval school; behind this, on the summit of a hill, is the royal observatory, from whence the English and American mariners reckon their longitude. The hill at this point, if the atmosphere happens by rare good fortune to be clear, commands a grand view of London and the space intervening. It projects so boldly, that the tops of the trees appear at the feet of the spectator—the hospital, with its domes, appears embosomed in a wooded amphitheatre—and the river in its serpentine course, thicker and thicker covered with boats, barges, and large vessels.

Greenwich hospital is decorated by several colossal statues and beautiful pieces of sculpture. One is an emblematical representation of the death of Nelson.

The pensioners to be received into the hospital must be aged and maimed seamen of the navy, or of the merchant service, if wounded in battle, and marines and foreigners who have served two years in the navy. The total expense of the establishment is sixty-nine thousand pounds per annum, which is appropriated to the support of about three thousand seamen on the premises, and fifty-four hundred out-pensioners.

LOSS OF THE SHIP BOSTON.

An unusual degree of sensation was excited in Boston, on the first of June, by the melancholy tidings of the loss of the packet ship Boston. This strong and elegant ship—one of the finest packets that belong to this country—was struck by lightning in the Gulf Stream, six days out from Charleston, and burnt to the water's edge. We present the details below, as furnished by Captain Mackay. "On Tuesday, the 25th May, lat 39, 31, long. 63, 46, commenced with fresh breeze and squally weather —at 2 P. M. heavy rain which continued until sunset—at 8 P. M. forked lightning in the southwest, and dark and heavy clouds rising from the westward—at 9, the wind hauled to the westward— at 10, P. M. a heavy cloud began to rise in the southwest—at 10½, sharp lightning, clued up the topgallant-sails, and hauled the mainsail up—at 11, heavy thunder and sharp lightning; the second flash struck the ship, burst the main-royal from the gaskets and burnt it; knocked down the steward and Isaac Hopkins a sailor, and filled the ship full of electric fluid. We examined the ship immediately to ascertain if the masts were injured, or the lightning had passed through the deck; but the mast appeared uninjured, a bright *complaisance* resting on each royal-mast head. We single reefed the maintop-sail, and were about to haul the mainsail, when we ascertained that the ship was on fire. We immediately cleared the main and after hatchways, to get at the fire, heaving the cotton overboard and cutting holes in the deck, plying water in every direction—but all in vain; the cotton in the main hold was on fire, fore and aft, on both sides, burning like tinder. Our only alternative was to clear away the boats and get them out, part of the crew and passengers at work keeping the fire down as much as possible by drawing and heaving water, the scuppers being stopped up; we stove water casks over holes cut in the deck and in the main hatchway; starting the water but all to no good purpose, for before we could get the long boat over the ship's side, the fire had burst through the deck and out the larboard side of the ship. The flames raged with such violence and consumed the vessel so quick, that nothing could be saved from the wreck. We got about forty gallons of water and provisions sufficient, on a short allowance, to keep the passengers and crew alive for three weeks—almost every thing else was burnt up in the ship, even the money, watches, and clothes—all destroyed. At 3, A. M. the main and mizen masts were burnt off below deck, and the masts fell in the water at half-past 3, the passengers and crew were all in the boats; the flames had then reached the forecastle, and the ship was one complete flame of fire, fore and aft. The passengers had exerted themselves to the utmost to assist us. The officers had with unwearied exertion, coolness, and persevering activity done all that men could do. The ship's crew worked like horses and behaved like men; but all would not do.—About three hours time had changed one of the best ships that ever swam to a complete volcano, and twenty three persons cast adrift on the open ocean. The cabin passengers were Admiral Sir Isaac Coffin and servant, Dr. William Boag, and his sister Miss Ansella Boag, Mr. Niel McNeil, and Mr. Samuel S. Osgood. It was then raining and the sea was running high, and every person drenched through with water; in this situation the constitution of Miss Boag, the only lady passenger, soon gave way. This amiable young lady's firmness of conduct at the first alarm of fire, and during the whole scene, is worthy of the highest praise. To the divine will of her God she submitted without a murmur, and at 11 o'clock on Wednesday, in the boat, she died in the arms of her brother, thanking him in the most affectionate manner for his kindness, giving her blessing to us all. On the following day, she was buried with the church service, our situation not admitting of the corpse being kept longer in the boat. We remained in the boats near the fire or the wreck, two days, and at three o'clock P. M. on Thursday, were taken on board the brig Idas, of Liverpool, N. S. from Demarara, bound to Halifax, Captain Joseph Barnaby, who with his officers and crew treated us with every kindness and attention. We remained on board the brig two days, when Sunday morning, May 30th, falling in with the brig Camilla, Captain Robert B. Edes, he was good enough to offer us a passage to Boston, and received us on board his vessel."

Admiral sir Isaac Coffin, after landing from the brig Camilla, authorized his agent to present Captain Mackay with a check for five hundred dollars; and subsequently sent him an elegant gold watch, to replace one which he had lost by the destruction of the ship.

THE LOSS OF THE KENT

COMMUNICATED BY AN EYE WITNESS.

The *Kent*, Captain Henry Cobb, a fine new ship of one thou-sand three hundred and fifty tons, bound to Bengal and China, left the Downs on the 19th of February, with twenty officers, three hundred and forty-four soldiers, forty-three women, and sixty-six children, belonging to the thirty-first regiment; with twenty private passengers, and a crew (including officers) of one hundred and forty-eight men on board.

On the night of Monday, the 28th of February 1827, when the Kent was in lat. 47 degrees 30 minutes, lon. 10 degrees, a violent gale blew from the west, and gradually increased during the follow ing morning. The rolling of the vessel became tremendous about midnight, so that the best fastened articles of furniture in the principal cabins were dashed about with violence, and the main chains were thrown at every lurch under water.

It was a little before this period, that one of the officers of the ship, with the well-meant intention of ascertaining that all was fast below, descended with two of the sailors into the hold, where they carried with them, for safety, a light in the patent lantern; and seeing that the lamp burned dimly, the officer took the precaution to hand it up to the orlop-deck to be trimmed. Having after-wards discovered one of the spirit casks to be adrift, he sent the sailors for some billets of wood to secure it; but the ship in their absence having made a heavy lurch, the officer unfortunately dropped the light; and letting go his hold of the cask in his eager-ness to recover the lantern, it suddenly stove, and the spirits com-municating with the lamp, the whole place was instantly in a blaze.

It so happened that the author, went into the *cuddy* to observe the state of the barometer, when he received from Captain Spence, the captain of the day, the alarming information that the ship was on fire in the after hold.

As long as the devouring element appeared to be confined to the spot where the fire originated, and which we were assured was surrounded on all sides by water casks, we ventured to cherish hopes that it might be subdued; but no sooner was the light blue vapor that at first arose succeeded by volumes of thick dingy smoke, which speedily ascended through all the four hatchways, rolling over every part of the ship, than all farther concealment became impossible, and almost all hope of preserving the vessel was abandoned. "The flames have reached the cable tier," was exclaimed by some individuals, and the strong pitchy smell that pervaded the deck confirmed the truth of the exclamation.

In these awful circumstances Captain Cobb, with an ability

and decision of character that seemed to increase with the imminence of the danger, resorted to the only alternative now left him,
of ordering the lower deck to be scuttled, the combing of the
hatches to be cut, and the lower ports to be opened, for the free
admission of the waves.

These instructions were speedily executed by the united efforts
of the troops and seamen: but not before some of the sick soldiers,
one woman, and several children, unable to gain the upper deck,
had perished.   On descending to the gun-deck with colonel Fearon, Captain Bray, and one or two other officers of the 31st regiment to assist in opening the ports, I met, staggering towards the
hatchway, in an exhausted and nearly senseless state, one of the
mates, who informed us that he had just stumbled over the dead
bodies of some individuals who must have died from suffocation
to which it was evident that he himself had almost fallen a victim
So dense and oppressive was the smoke, that it was with the ut
most difficulty we could remain long enough below to fulfil Captain Cobb's wishes; which were no sooner accomplished than the
sea rushed in with extraordinary force, carrying away in its resist-
less progress to the hold, the largest chests, bulk-heads, &c.

On the one hand stood death by fire, on the other death by water; the dilemma was dreadful.   Preferring always the more remote alternative, the unfortunate crew were at one moment attempting to check the fire by means of water; and when the
water became the most threatening enemy, their efforts were
turned to the exclusion of the waves, and the fire was permitted
to rage with all its fury.

The scene of horror that now presented itself, baffles all description—The upper deck was covered with between six and
seven hundred human beings, many of whom, from previous sea
sickness, were forced on the first alarm to flee from below in a
state of absolute nakedness, and were now running about in quest
of husbands, children or parents.

While some were standing in silent resignation, or in stupid
insensibility to their impending fate, others were yielding themselves up to the most frantic despair.   Some on their knees were
earnestly imploring, with significant gesticulations and in noisy
supplications, the mercy of Him, whose arm they exclaimed, was
at length outstretched to smite them; others were to be seen
hastily crossing themselves, and performing the various external
acts required by their peculiar persuasion, while a number of the
older and more stout-hearted sailors suddenly took their seats
directly over the magazine, hoping as they stated, that by means
of the explosion, which they every instant expected, a speedier
termination might thereby be put to their sufferings.*

* Captain Cobb, with great forethought, ordered the deck to be scuttled forward, with a
view to draw the fire in that direction, knowing that between it and the magazine was
several tiers of water casks, while he hoped that the wet sails, &c. thrown into the ad-
vold, would prevent it from communicating with the spirit-room abaft.

Several of the soldiers' wives and children, who had fled for temporary shelter into the after cabins on the upper deck, were engaged in praying and in reading the scriptures with the ladies, some of whom were enabled with wonderful self-possession, to offer to others those spiritual consolations, which a firm and intelligent trust in the Redeemer of the world appeared at this awful hour to impart to their own breasts.

All hope had departed! the employment of the different individuals indicated utter despair of rescue—one was removing a lock of hair from his writing desk to his bosom—others were awaiting their fate in stupor—some with manly fortitude—others bewailing it with loud and bitter lamentation—and part were occupied in prayer and mutual encouragement.

It was at this appalling instant, when "all hope that we should be saved was taken away," that it occurred to Mr. Thompson, the fourth mate, to send a man to the foretop, rather with the ardent wish than the expectation, that some friendly sail might be discovered on the face of the waters. The sailor, on mounting, threw his eyes round the horizon for a moment—a moment of unutterable suspense—and waving his hat, exclaimed, "A sail on the lee-bow!" The joyful announcement was received with acep-felt thanksgiving, and with three cheers upon deck. Our flags of distress were instantly hoisted, and our minute guns fired; and we endeavored to bear down under our three-topsails and foresail upon the stranger, which afterwards proved to be the Cambria, a small brig of two hundred tons burden, — Cook, bound to Vera Cruz, having on board twenty or thirty Cornish miners, and other agents of the Anglo-Mexican company.

While Captain Cobb, colonel Fearon, and major Macgregor of the 31st regiment, were consulting together, as the brig was approaching us, on the necessary preparations for getting out the boats, &c. one of the officers asked major M. in what order it was intended the officers should move off? to which the other replied, "of course the funeral order;" which injunction was instantly confirmed by Colonel Fearon, who said, "Most undoubtedly the juniors first—but see that any man is cut down who presumes to enter the boats before the means of escape are presented to the women and children."

Arrangements having been considerately made by Captain Cobb for placing in the first boat, previous to letting it down, all the ladies, and as many of the soldiers' wives as it could safely contain, they hurriedly wrapt themselves up in whatever article of clothing could be most conveniently found; and I think about two, or half past two o'clock, a most mournful procession advanced from the after cabins to the star-board cuddy port, outside of which the cutter was suspended. Scarcely a word was heard—not a scream was uttered—even the infants ceased to cry, as if conscious of the unspoken and unspeakable anguish that was at this instant rending the hearts of the parting parents—nor was the silence of voices in any way broken, except in one or two cases, where the ladies plaintively entreated to be left behind with their husbands. But on being assured that every moment's delay might occasion the sacrifice of a human life, they successively suffered themselves to be torn from the tender embrace, and with a fortitude which never fails to characterize and adorn their sex on occasions of overwhelming trial, were placed, without a murmur, in the boat, which was immediately lowered into a sea so tempestuous, as to leave us only " to hope against hope " that it should live in it for a single moment. Twice the cry was heard from those on the chains that the boat was swamping. But he who enabled the Apostle Peter to walk on the face of the deep, and was graciously attending to the silent but earnest aspirations of those on board, had decreed its safety.

After one or two unsuccessful attempts to place the little frail bark fairly upon the surface of the water, the command was at length given to unhook; the tackle at the stern was in consequence, immediately cleared; but the ropes at the bow having got foul, the sailor there found it impossible to obey the order. In vain was the axe applied to the entangled tackle. The moment was inconceivably critical; as the boat, which necessarily followed the motion of the ship, was gradually rising out of the water, and must, in another instant have been hanging perpendicularly by the bow, and its helpless passengers launched into the deep, had not a most providential wave suddenly struck and lifted up the stern, so as to enable the seaman to disengage the tackle; and the boat being dexterously cleared from the ship, was seen after a little while, battling with the billows: now raised, in its progress to the brig, like a speck on their summit, and then disappearing for several seconds, as if engulphed " in the horrid vale " between them.

Two or three soldiers, to relieve their wives of a part of their families, sprang into the water with their children, and perished in their endeavors to save them. One young lady, who had resolutely refused to quit her father, whose sense of duty kept him at his post, was near falling a sacrifice to her filial devotion, not having been picked up by those in the boats, until she had sunk five or six times. Another individual, who was reduced to the frightful alternative of losing his wife, or his children, hastily decided in favor of his duty to the former. His wife was accordingly saved, but his four children, alas! were left to perish. A fine fellow, a soldier, who had neither wife nor child of his own, but who evinced the greatest solicitude for the safety of those of others, insisted on having three children lashed to him, with whom he plunged into the water; not being able to reach the boat, he was drawn again into the ship with his charge, but not before two of the children had expired. One man fell down the hatchway

into the flames, and another had his back so completely broken
as to have been observed quite doubled falling overboard. The
numerous spectacles of individual loss and suffering were not confined to the entrance upon the perilous voyage between the two
ships. One man who fell beneath the boat and brig, had his
head literally crushed fine—and some others were lost in their attempts to ascend the sides of the Cambria.

When the greater part of the men had been disposed of, the
gradual removal of the officers commenced, and was marked by
a discipline the most rigid, and an intrepidity the most exemplary:
none appearing to be influenced by a vain and ostentatious bravery,
which in cases of extreme peril, affords rather a presumptive proof
of secret timidity than of fortitude; nor any betraying an unmanly
or unsoldier-like impatience to quit the ship; but with the becoming deportment of men neither paralysed by, nor profanely insensible to, the accumulating dangers that encompassed them, they
progressively departed in the different boats with their soldiers;
—they who happened to proceed first leaving behind them an
example of coolness that could not be unprofitable to those who
followed.

Every individual was desired to tie a rope round his waist.

While the people were busily occupied in adopting this recommendation, I was surprised, I had almost said amused, by the
singular delicacy of one of the Irish recruits, who in searching
for a rope in one of the cabins, called out to me that he could
find none except the cordage belonging to an officer's cot, and
wished to know whether there would be any harm in his appropriating it to his own use.

Again: As an agreeable proof too, of the subordination and good
feeling that governed the poor soldiers in the midst of their sufferings, I ought to state that toward evening, when the melancholy
groupe who were passively seated on the poop, exhausted by previous fatigue, anxiety and fasting, were beginning to experience
the pain of intolerable thirst, a box of oranges was accidentally discovered by some of the men, who with a degree of mingled consideration, respect, and affection, that could hardly have been
expected at such a moment, refused to partake of the grateful
beverage, until they had afforded a share of it to their officers.

The spanker-boom of so large a ship as the Kent, which projects, I should think, sixteen or eighteen feet over the stern, rests
on ordinary occasions about nineteen or twenty feet above the
water; but in the position in which we were placed, from the
great height of the sea, and consequent pitching of the ship, it
was frequently lifted to a height of not less than thirty or forty
feet from the surface.

To reach the rope, therefore, that hung from its extremity, was
an operation that seemed to require the aid of as much dexterity
of hand as steadiness of head. For it was not only the nervous-

ness of creeping along the boom itself, or the extreme difficulty
of afterwards seizing on and sliding down by the rope, that we
had to dread, and that occasioned the loss of some valuable
lives, by deterring the men from adopting this mode of escape:
but as the boat, which one moment was probably under the boom,
might be carried the next, by the force of the waves, fifteen or
twenty yards away from it, the unhappy individual, whose best
calculations were thus defeated, was generally left swinging for
some time in mid-air, if he was not repeatedly plunged several
feet under water, or dashed with dangerous violence against the
sides of the returning boat—or, what not unfrequently happened,
was forced to let go his hold of the rope altogether. As there
seemed, however no alternative, I did not hesitate, notwithstanding my comparative inexperience and awkwardness in such a
situation, to throw my leg across the perilous stick; and with
a heart extremely grateful that such means of deliverance, dangerous as they appeared, were still extended to me; and more
grateful still that I had been enabled, in common with others, to
discharge my honest duty to my sovereign and to my fellow-
soldiers; I proceeded after confidently committing my spirit, the
great object of my solicitude, into the keeping of Him who had
formed and redeemed it, to creep slowly forward, feeling at every
step the increased difficulty of my situation. On getting nearly
to the end of the boom, the young officer whom I followed and
myself were met with a squall of wind and rain, so violent as to
make us fain to embrace closely the slippery stick, without attempting for some minutes to make any progress, and to excite
our apprehension that we must relinquish all hope of reaching
the rope. But our fears were disappointed, and after resting for
awhile at the boom end, while my companion was descending to
the boat, which he did not find until he had been plunged once or
twice over head in the water. I prepared to follow; and instead
of lowering myself, as many had imprudently done at the moment
when the boat was inclining towards us—and consequently being
unable to descend the whole distance before it again receded—I
calculated that while the boat was retiring, I ought to commence
my descent, which would probably be completed by the time the
returning wave brought it underneath; by which means I was, I
believe, almost the only officer or soldier who reached the boat
without being either severely bruised or immersed in the water.
But my friend Colonel Fearon had not been so fortunate; for
after swimming for some time, and being repeatedly struck against
the side of the boat, and at one time drawn completely under it,
he was at last so utterly exhausted, that he must instantly have
let go his hold of the rope and perished, had not one in the boat
seized him by the hair of the head and dragged him into it, almost
senseless and alarmingly bruised.

Captain Cobb, in his immovable resolutions to be the last, if possible, to quit his ship, and in his generous anxiety for the preservation of every life entrusted to his charge, refused to seek the boat, until he again endeavored to urge onward the few still around him, who seemed struck dumb and powerless with dismay. But finding all his entreaties fruitless and hearing the guns, whose tackle was burst asunder by the advancing flames, successively exploding in the hold into which they had fallen—this gallant officer, after having nobly pursued, for the preservation of others, a course of exertion that has been rarely equalled either in its duration or difficulty, at last felt it right to provide for his own safety, by laying hold on the topping lift, or rope that connects the driver-boom with the mizen-top, and thereby getting over the heads of the infatuated men who occupied the boom, unable to go either backward or forward, and ultimately dropping himself into the water.

PROPERTIES OF THE SEA, &c.

THE sea seems not less necessary to the existence of man himself, than the solid earth upon which he treads. It absorbs and decomposes the noxious particles of the atmosphere; and if it were dried up, the earth would become as arid and unfruitful as a desert. Its various basins—which, with the exception of the Caspian, all stand in connexion with each other—facilitate the transactions of commerce, and the intercourse of nations; and its productions form a valuable branch of industry in every maritime country.

The bed or basin of the ocean, being only a continuation of the land, exhibits the same inequalities of surface which continents present. Were the sea dried up, it would present a scene of mountains, valleys, rocks, and plains, covered in some instances with their own peculiar vegetation, and the abode of various species of animals. The depth of the sea varies greatly in different places. The greatest depth ever measured was that ascertained by Mr. Scoresby, the captain of a Greenland whaler, who sunk a very heavy lead in the Greenland Sea, to the depth of nearly 4,700 feet, without finding ground. According to the laws of gravitation, by which in all connected bodies of water, the higher parts must flow towards the lower, till they attain the same level, the level of the ocean is, generally speaking, the same everywhere. The only exception to this position may perhaps be found in gulfs and inland seas, which have only a slight communication with the ocean.

The color of the ocean is generally of a deep bluish green particularly in the deeper seas; as the depth diminishes towards

.he coasts, the water assumes a lighter shade This apparent color of the sea may be explained upon the same principle as that of the azure blue of the atmosphere. Both fluids are colorless when in a glass; the air reflects chiefly the most refrangible rays of light, viz. the violet, indigo, and blue, and therefore usually appears of an azure color, the result of a mixture of these: but the sea, from its density and depth, is able to reflect not only many blue and violet, but also some of the less refrangible rays in sufficient proportion to compose a greenish blue. The other shades in the color of seawater depend on illusory or local causes. The green and yellow shades of the sea arise from marine plants; a distinct shade is often communicated to its surface by the presence of myriads of minute insects: and in shallow water, the light reflected from the sand at the bottom often gives a reddish hue to the surface. In the West Indies, where

> " The floor is of sand like the mountain-drift;
> And the pearl-shells spangle the flinty snow,"

the waters of the ocean are often so beautifully transparent, as to exhibit the minutest object they contain or cover at the depth of several fathoms. In the Gulf of Guinea the sea is white; and around the Maldive islands it is black.

A very curious and magnificent spectacle is often presented at night by the luminous appearance of the sea,—a phenomenon which seamen generally regard as the precursor of blowing weather. It is of most frequent occurrence in summer and autumn. Three species are generally distinguished. The first is generally seen close to a ship when sailing before a fresh wind and forms a tail of light in the wake of the ship; at other times during stormy weather, it spreads over the whole surface of the sea, clothing it apparently in a sheet of fire. This species is ascribed to electricity. The second kind of marine phosphorescence, penetrates beneath the surface; and when a quantity of the illuminated water is put into a vessel, it retains the brilliance as long as it is kept agitated, but loses it as soon as the agitation subsides. This species occurs during dead calms or in very hot weather, and seems to be a true phosphoric light, emanating from particles of putrid animal matter suspended in the water. The third species exceeds the two former in intensity of brilliance; and it is supposed that the appearance is occasioned by innumerable minute animals of a round shape, moving rapidly through the water in all directions, like so many luminous sparks.

The sea is subject to various motions, arising from different causes. Even when unruffled by the winds, it is agitated by the rotation of the earth, and the attraction of the moon and the sun. These three causes produce a threefold motion, viz. the motion of the *waves*, that of the *currents*, and that of the *tides*.

The most wonderful and important motion of the sea is that of *high* and *low tide*, or that regular ebb and flow of he sea whicr occur every day at a certain interval. The sea rises to its greatest height in about 6 hours, and remains stationary for about 6 minutes; after which it recedes for other 6 hours, and having remained stationary at its lowest tide for a few minutes, begins to rise again. In the Baltic and the Black Sea there is no tide; and almost none in the Mediterranean.

Besides these motions of the ocean, there is another not so easily accounted for. There is felt in the open sea between the Tropics, and as far as the 30th degree of latitude, a constant motion from east to west, which manifests itself in the quick sailing of vessels moving in that direction. The most celebrated of these currents is the *Gulf-stream*, which rises in the Gulf of Mexico, between Florida and the Bahama islands, and sets in a bended and expanded flow north-easterly, along the coasts of North America, till it reaches Norway, whence repulsed by the Scandinavian coasts, it turns N. W. towards Greenland. The current is known by the beautiful blue color of its waters.

When two or several currents meet each other, or cross at angles, violent circular motions of the sea are produced, which attract every thing coming within their vortex, and whirling it round in decreasing gyrations, finally ingulf it in their bosoms. These motions of the sea are called *whirlpools*. Some naturalists believe that they mark the situation of profound abysses in the bottom of the sea, into which the water precipitating itself produces this dangerous suction. Among the most remarkable whirlpools is that of Chalcis in the Euripus, near the coast of Smreee, which alternately absorbs and rejects the water seven times every twenty-four hours. Charybdis, near the Strait of Sicily, rejects and absorbs the water thrice in twenty-four hours. The largest known whirlpool is the *Maelstrom* in the Norwegian sea, the circumference of which exceeds 20 leagues.

CLASSIFICATION OF CLOUDS.

The clouds are aqueous vapors, which hover at a considerable height above the surface of the earth. They differ from fogs only by their height and less degree of transparency. The distance of the clouds from the surface of the earth is very different. Thin and light clouds are higher than the highest mountains; thick and heavy clouds on the contrary, touch low mountains, steeples, and even trees. The average height of the clouds is calculated to be two miles and a half. Innumerable as the forms of clouds may appear to be, correct observers have stated that they may be all comprised in seven modifications.

These following modifications are arranged in the order of their ordinary elevation, but which is very frequently deranged We give the names both in Latin and English; the former are perhaps most generally used. The figures refer to the above engraving.

Fig. 1, Cirrus . . . . . Curl-Cloud.
2, Cirrocumulus . . Sonder-Cloud.

41

Fig. 3, 4, 5, 6, 7, Cirrostratus   .   .   .   *Wane-Cloud*
          9, Cumulostratus   .   .   .   *Twain-Cloud*
          9, Cumulus   .   .   .   .   *Stacken-Cloud*
         11, Nimbus   .   .   .   .   *Rain-Cloud*
         11, Stratus   .   .   .   .   *Fall-Cloud*

Fig. 1   The *curling* and flexuous forms of this cloud constitute
its most obvious external character, and from these it derives its
name.   It may be distinguished from all others by the lightness
of its appearance, its fibrous texture, and the great and perpetually
changing variety of figures which it presents to the eye.   It is
generally the most elevated, occupying the highest regions of
the atmosphere.   The *comoid cirrus cloud*, vulgarly called the
mare's tail, is the proper cirrus.   It has, as represented in the
engraving, somewhat the appearance of a distended lock of white
hair, or of a bunch of wool pulled out into fine pointed ends.
This variety is an accompaniment of a variable state of weather,
and forebodes wind and rain.

Fig. 2.   This consists of extensive beds of a number of little,
well defined, orbicular masses of clouds, or small *cumuli*, in close
horizontal opposition; but at the same time lying quite asunder
(*sonder-cloud*), or separate from one another.   Their picturesque
appearance in summer often presents, as Bloomfield expresses it,

The beauteous semblance of a flock at rest.

This variety is commonly a forerunner of storms, and has been
remarked as such by the poets.

Fig. 3, 4, 5, 6, 7.   This cloud is distinguishable by its flatness,
and great horizontal extension in proportion to its perpendicular
height.   Under all its various forms, it preserves this character
istic.   As it is generally changing its figure, and slowly subsiding,
it has received the name of *wane-cloud*.   Sometimes this cloud is
disposed in wavy bars or streaks, in close horizontal opposition,
and these bars vary infinitely in size and color, generally blended
in the middle, but distinct towards its edges, *fig.* 4.   A variety
not unlike this, is the *mackerel-back sky* of summer evenings.   It
is often very high in the atmosphere.   Another common variety
appears like a long streak, thickest in the middle, and wasting
away at its edges.   This, when viewed in the horizon, has the
appearance of *fig.* 7.   Another principal variety of the cirrostratus
is one which consists of small rows of little clouds, curved in a
peculiar manner; it is from this curvature called *cymoid, fig.* 5
This cloud is a sure indication of stormy weather.   *Fig.* 6 is the
representation of a similar one, less perfectly formed, having more
of the character of the cirrocumulus, and is often produced when
a large cumulus passes under the variety marked *fig.* 7.   Another
remarkable developement of this varying genus is, that extensive
and shallow sort of cloud, which occurs particularly in the evening
and during night, through which the sun and moon but faintly

appear. It is in this cloud that those peculiar refractions of the light of those bodies, called halos, mock suns, &c. usually appear This variety is the surest prognostic we are acquainted with, of an impending fall of rain or snow.

Fig. 9. The base of this modification is generally flat, and lies on the surface of an atmospheric stratum, the superstructure resembling a bulky cumulus overhanging its base in large fleecy protuberances, or rising into the forms of rocky mountains. Considerable masses of these frequently are grouped upon a common stratum or base, from which it has been named *cumulostratus*. It derives the other appellation, *twain-cloud*, from the frequently visible coalescence of two other modifications, as, for example, the cirrus and the cumulus. Cumulostratus often evaporates, sometimes changes to cumulus, but, in general, it ends in nimbus, and falls in rain. In long ranges of these clouds it has been observed that part has changed into nimbus, and the rest remained unchanged.

Fig. 9. This cloud is easily known by its irregular hemispherical or heaped superstructure, hence its name *cumulus, a heap or pile*. It has usually a flattened base. The mode of its formation is by the gathering together of detached clouds, which then appear *stacked* into one large and elevated mass, or *stacken-cloud*. The best time for viewing its progressive formation is in fine settled weather. It may be called *the cloud of day*, as it usually exists only during that period.

Fig. 11. This is not a modification depending upon a distinct change of form, but rather from increase of density and deepening of shade in the cumulostratus, indicating a change of structure, which is always followed by the fall of rain. This has been, therefore, called *nimbus*, (*a rainy black cloud.*) Any one of the preceding six modifications may increase so much as to obscure the sky, and, without falling in rain, "dissolve," and "leave not a rack behind." But when cumulostratus has been formed, it sometimes goes on to increase in density, and assume a black and portentous darkness. Shortly afterwards the intensity of this blackness yields to a more gray obscurity, which is an evidence that a new arrangement has taken place in the aqueous particles of the cloud; the nimbus is formed, and rain begins to fall.

Fig. 11. This kind of cloud rests upon the surface of the globe. It is of variable extent and thickness, and is called *stratus, a bed or covering*. It is generally formed by the subsidence of vapor in the atmosphere, and has, therefore, been denominated *fall-cloud*. This genus includes all fogs, and those creeping mists, which in summer evenings fill the valleys, remain during the night, and disappear in the morning. This cloud arrives at its density about midnight, or between that time and morning, and it generally disappears about sunrise. It is, for this reason, called by some, *the cloud of night*.

LITERARY PURSUITS OF SAILORS.

There are many cases on record of individuals who, even with scarcely any other education than what they contrived to give themselves while serving in subordinate and laborious situations in the camp or on shipboard, have attained to great familiarity with books, and sometimes risen to considerable literary or scientific distinction. The celebrated English navigator, *Dampier*, although he had been some time at school before he left his native country, yet went to sea at so early an age that, considering he for a long time led a vagabond and lawless life, he must have very soon forgotten every thing he had been taught, if he had not, in the midst of all his wild adventures, taken great pains both to retain and extend his knowledge. That he must have done so is evident from the accounts of his different voyages, which he afterwards published. We have few works of the kind more vigorously or graphically written than these volumes; and they contain abundant evidences of a scientific and philosophical knowledge of no ordinary extent and exactness. Along with Dampier's, we may mention an older name, that of *John Davis*, the discoverer of the well-known strait leading into Baffin's Bay. Davis also went to sea when quite a boy, and must have acquired all his knowledge both of science and of the art of composition, while engaged among the duties of his profession. Yet we not only have from his pen accounts of several of his voyages, but also a treatise on the general hydrography of the earth. He was the inventor, besides, of a quadrant for taking the sun's altitude at sea. *Robert Drury*, too, who wrote an account of the Island of Madagascar, and of his strange adventures there, deserves to be remembered when we are making mention of authors bred at sea Drury was only fourteen when he set out on his voyage in a vessel proceeding to India, and he was shipwrecked in returning home on the island we have mentioned, where he remained in a species of captivity for fifteen years; so that when he at last contrived to make his escape, he had almost forgotten his native language. He afterwards, however, set about writing an account of his life—a task which he accomplished whilst acting in the humble capacity of a porter at the India House. The work is composed in a plain but sensible style, and contains many interesting details respecting the manners of the natives of Madagascar It is perhaps somewhat better for having been compressed by one of the friends of the author, whose original manuscript is said to have extended to eight hundred large folio pages.

Falconer, the author of " The Shipwreck," as is generally known, spent his life, from childhood, at sea. He was probably born in one of the small towns in the county of Fife, which border the Frith of Forth; but nothing is very certainly ascertained either as to his native place or his parentage. Nor has any account been given of how he acquired the elements of education, with the exception of a report that he found an instructer in a person of the name of Campbell, a man of some literary taste and acquirements, who happened to be purser in one of the vessels in which young Falconer sailed. However this may be, Falconer appeared as an author at a very early age, having been only, it is said, in his twenty-first year when he gave to the world his first production, a poem on the death of Frederick, Prince of Wales, the father of his late Majesty, George III. He was ten or twelve years older when he published his " Shipwreck," which is said to be founded in a great measure on the personal adventures of the author. Falconer did not permit the success of his poetical efforts to withdraw him from his profession, in which, having now transferred himself from the merchant service to the navy, he continued to rise steadily till he was appointed purser of a man-of-war. Sometime after attaining this promotion, he published the other work by which he is chiefly known, his " Universal Marine Dictionary," which was very favorably received, and is still a standard work. He had previously to this written several other poetical pieces on temporary subjects, which have long been forgotten. Shortly after the publication of his dictionary, he sailed for Bengal as purser of the frigate Aurora. This vessel, however, was never heard of, after she passed the Cape of Good Hope, having in all probability foundered at sea.

Giordani, an Italian engineer and mathematician of the seventeenth century, was originally a common soldier on board one of the Pope's gallies. In this situation his capacity and good conduct attracted the attention of his admiral; and as a reward he was promoted to the post of purser of one of the vessels. It was his appointment to this situation which first formed his mind to study. Having accounts to keep, he soon found how necessary it was that he should know something of arithmetic, of which he was till then quite ignorant; and he determined therefore to teach himself the science, which it is said he did without assistance. By pursuing his studies from this commencement, he eventually acquired considerable reputation as a mathematician; and, having published several able works, was appointed at last to a professorship in the Sapienza College at Rome. Giordani died in the year 1711.

The late *Mr. John Fransham*, who died at Norwich in 1810 was altogether one of the most eccentric characters to be found in the list of self-educated persons. His name suggests itself to us here from the circumstance of his having passed part of his early life as a common soldier. He had been originally apprenticed to a cooper, with whom he remained for about two years

and it was in this situation that he taught himself mathematics
But although he obtained the situation of clerk to an attorney,
his restless disposition would not allow him to remain at his desk;
and after wandering for some time about the country, he enlisted
in the army, where, however they did not keep him long, finding
him quite unfit for service. Indeed, it was by this time become
pretty evident that his mind was not a little deranged,—a matter
which he shortly after put beyond doubt by renouncing christiani-
ty, and making a formal profession of paganism. Although he
published several works, however, in support of his peculiar the-
ology, and in other respects conducted himself with great eccen-
tricity, he contrived to maintain himself by teaching mathematics,
in which occupation he is said to have displayed very considerable ability. He resided and took pupils for some years in
London. Somewhat similar to Fransham's history is that of
Mr. John Oswald, who is said to have taught himself Greek, Latin,
and Arabic, while holding a lieutenant's commission in a regiment
of infantry in India. He afterwards returned to England, where
he published a succession of poetical and political pamphlets,
making himself remarkable at the same time by various singular-
ities of behavior and opinions, and especially by a rigid abstinence from animal food, and a professional predilection for the religious doctrines of the Brahmins. When the revolution broke
out in France, Oswald went over to that country, and entered the
service of the republic, in which he obtained the rank of colonel.
He was at length killed in battle.

Columbus himself, one of the greatest men that ever lived, if it
be grand ideas grandly realized that constitute greatness, while
leading the life of a seaman, not only pursued assiduously the
studies more particularly relating to his profession, rendering
himself the most accomplished geographer and astronomer of his
time, but kept up that acquaintance which he had begun at
school with the different branches of elegant literature. We are
told that he was even wont to amuse himself by the composition
of Latin verses. It was at sea, too, that *Cook* acquired for himself those high, scientific, and we may even add literary accomplishments, of which he showed himself to be possessed. The
parents of the celebrated navigator were poor peasants. and all
the school education he ever had was a little reading, writing, and
arithmetic, for which he was indebted to the liberality of a gentleman in the neighborhood. He was apprenticed, at the age of
thirteen, to a shopkeeper in the small town of Snaith, near New-
castle; and it was while in this situation that he was first seized
with a passion for the sea. After some time, he prevailed upon
his master to give up his indentures, and entered as one of the
crew of a coasting vessel engaged in the coal trade. He continued in this service till he had reached his twenty-seventh year,
when he exchanged it for that of the navy. in which he soon dis-

tinguished himself so greatly, that he was three or four years
after appointed master of the Mercury, which belonged to a
squadron then proceeding to attack Quebec. Here he first
showed the proficiency he had already made in the scientific part
of his profession, by an admirable chart which he constructed
and published of the river St. Lawrence. He felt, however, the
disadvantages of his ignorance of mathematics; and, while still
assisting in the hostile operations carrying on against the French
on the coast of North America, he applied himself to the study
of Euclid's Elements, which he soon mastered, and then began
that of astronomy. A year or two after this, while again stationed in the same quarter, he communicated to the Royal Society
an account of a solar eclipse which took place on the 5th of August, 1766: deducing from it, with great exactness and skill, the
longitude of the place of observation; and his paper was printed
in the Philosophical Transactions. He had now completely established his reputation as an able and scientific seaman; and it
having been determined by government, at the request of the
Royal Society, to send out qualified persons to the South Sea to
observe the approaching transit of the planet Venus over the
sun's disc—a phenomenon which promised several interesting re-
sults to astronomy,—Cook was appointed to the command of the
Endeavour, the vessel fitted out for that purpose. He conducted
this expedition, which, in addition to the accomplishment of its
principal purpose, was productive of a large accession of important geographical discoveries, with the most consummate skill
and ability; and was, the year after he returned home, appointed
to the command of a second vessel destined for the same regions,
but having in view more particularly the determination of the
question as to the existence of a southern polar continent. He
was nearly three years absent upon this voyage; but so admirable
were the methods he adopted for preserving the health of his seamen, that he reached home with the loss of only one man from
his whole crew. Having addressed a paper to the Royal Society
upon this subject, he was not only chosen a member of that
learned body, but was farther rewarded by having the Copley
gold medal voted to him for his experiments. Of this second voyage he drew up the account himself, and it has been universally
esteemed a model in that species of writing.

All our readers know the termination of Cook's distinguished
career. His third voyage, undertaken for the discovery of a
passage from the Atlantic to the Pacific along the north coast of
America, although unsuccessful in reference to this object, was
fertile in geographical discoveries, and equally honorable with
those by which it had been preceded, to the sagacity, good management, and scientific skill of its unfortunate commander. The
death of Captain Cook took place at Owyhee, in a sudden tumult
of the natives of that island, on the 14th of February, 1779

The news of the event was received with general lamentation, not only in his own country but throughout Europe. Pensions were bestowed on his widow and three sons by the government, the Royal Society ordered a medal to be struck in commemoration of him; his eulogy was pronounced in the Florentine Academy; and various other honors were paid to his memory, both by public bodies and individuals. Thus, by his own persevering efforts, did this great man raise himself from the lowest obscurity to a reputation wide as the world itself, and certain to last as long as the age in which he flourished shall be remembered by history But better still than even all this fame—than either the honors he received while living, or those which, when he was no more, his country and mankind bestowed upon his memory,—he had exalted himself in the scale of moral and intellectual being; had won for himself, by his unwearied striving, a new and nobler nature, and taken a high place among the instructers and benefactors of mankind. This alone is true happiness—the one worthy end of human exertion or ambition—the only satisfying reward of all labor, and study, and virtuous activity or endurance. Among the shipmates with whom Cook mixed when he first went to sea, there was, perhaps, no one who ever either raised himself above the condition to which he then belonged in point of outward circumstances, or enlarged in any considerable degree the knowledge or mental resources he then possessed. And some will perhaps say that this was little to be regretted, at least, on their own account; that the many who spent their lives in their original sphere were probably as happy as the one who succeeded in rising above it; but this is, indeed, to cast a hasty glance on human life and human nature. That man was never truly happy—happy upon reflection, and while looking to the past or the future—who could not say to himself that he had made something of the faculties God gave him, and had not lived altogether without progression, like one of the inferior animals. We do not speak of mere wealth or station; these are comparatively nothing; are as often missed as attained, even by those who best merit them; and do not of themselves constitute happiness when they are possessed. But there must be some consciousness of an intellectual or moral progress, or there can be no satisfaction—no self-congratulation on reviewing what of life may be already gone—no hope in the prospect of what is yet to come. All men feel this, and feel it strongly; and if they could secure for themselves the source of happiness in question by a wish, would avail themselves of the privilege with sufficient alacrity. Nobody would pass his life in ignorance, if knowledge might be had by merely looking up to the clouds for it; it is the labor necessary for its acquirement that scares them; and this labor they have not resolution to encounter. Yet it is, in truth, from the exertion by which it must be obtained, that knowledge derives at least half its value; for to this entirely we owe the sense of merit in ourselves which the acquisition brings along with it; and hence no little of the happiness of which we have just described its possession to be the source, besides that, the labor itself soon becomes an enjoyment.

To the example of Cook, if it were necessary, we might add those of others of his countrymen, who, since his time, have shown, in like manner, the possibility of uniting the cultivation of literature and science to the most zealous performance of the duties of the same laborious profession. For instance, *Vancouver* was a sailor formed under Cook; and to him we owe an interesting and ably written account of the voyage which he made round the world, in 1790, and the four following years. Lieutenant *Flinders* commanded the expedition sent out in 1801, to survey the coast of New Holland, and afterwards published an account of his voyage, accompanied by a volume of charts, which are considered as placing the author in the highest rank of modern hydrographers. Nor ought we here to forget the late Lord *Collingwood*, second in command to Nelson at Trafalgar, and, in all respects, a man of first-rate merit, who, although he never sent any production to the press, has been proved by his correspondence, published since his death, to have been in reality one of the best of writers. Yet he was only thirteen when he first entered the navy, and during the remainder of his life he was scarcely ever ashore—circumstances which used to make his acquaintances wonder not a little where he got his style. He had always, however, been fond of reading and the study of elegant literature; and he found that even a life at sea afforded him many opportunities of indulging his taste for these enjoyments.

It does not belong to the plan of this work to notice any living examples: but the names of a crowd of naval officers of our own times, who have distinguished themselves as men of science and learning, as well as skilful commanders, will present themselves at once to the memory.

ABSTRACT OF AMERICAN NAUTICAL LAWS.

Shipping articles are required to be signed by every mariner, declaring the voyage and the term of time for which the seamen are shipped, and when they are to render themselves on board. Seamen are liable to imprisonment for desertion. But if the master sails and leaves a seaman in imprisonment abroad, he will be entitled to his wages till his return to the United States, deducting the time of imprisonment. Provision is made for the prompt recovery of seamen's wages, by admiralty process against the ship, if the wages be not paid within ten days.

It is the duty of the American consuls and commercial agents, to relieve American seamen who may be found destitute in foreign ports, and to provide for their passage to some port in the United States, at the expense of the United States. American vessels are bound to take them, not exceeding two for every hundred tons, at a rate not exceeding ten dollars per man.

If an American vessel be sold in a foreign port, or a seaman discharged with the master's consent, the master is obliged to pay the consul three months' wages besides the amount then due, two months to be paid to the seamen when they engage again, and one month's pay to the fund for the return of American Seamen.

The master has the right to discharge a seaman for just cause in a foreign port, but is responsible in damages if he does it without just cause. The master must be supreme in the ship. The French law affords peculiar protection to seamen, and prohibits the master from discharging a seaman for any cause, in a foreign country.

The expense of curing a sick seaman in the course of the voyage is a charge upon the ship; and this rule recommends itself as much by its intrinsic equity and sound policy, as by the sanction of general authority. Such an expense is in the nature of additional wages during sickness, and it constitutes a material ingredient in the just remuneration of seamen for their labor and services. This claim, equally with a claim for wages, may be enforced in a court of admiralty.

Every seaman engaged to serve on board a ship, is bound, from the nature and terms of the contract, to do his duty to the utmost of his ability, and therefore, a promise made by the master when the ship is in distress, or when some of the crew are sick or the like, to pay extra wages, as an inducement to extraordinary exertion, is illegal and void. It requires some service not within the scope of the original contract, as by becoming a hostage or the like, to create a valid claim for extra wages. No wages can be recovered for an illegal voyage, for the law will not countenance such a contract, nor permit any one to claim the wages of iniquity.

A seaman is entitled to his wages for the whole voyage, even though he is unable to render his service by sickness, or bodily injury, happening in the course of the voyage, and while in the performance of his duty; or if wrongfully discharged by the master in the course of the voyage, or forced to quit the ship by the cruelty of the master. In this case the voyage is ended as to him, and he is immediately entitled to his wages for the whole voyage.

The general principle of the marine law is, that freight is the mother of wages, and if no freight be earned, no wages are due If the ship perish by the perils of the sea, as tempest, fire, enemies, &c. the mariners lose their wages. Otherwise they might not use their endeavors to save the ship. But the seamen do not lose their wages, if the freight is lost by the misconduct of the master.

When a seaman dies on the voyage, his wages are due to his representatives, up to the time of his death. The seaman's wages on the outward voyage are due when the ship delivers her outward cargo. And if the owners and the charterer agree to consider the voyages out and home as one entire voyage, they cannot, by this, deprive the seamen, without their consent, of the rights belonging to them by the general principles of the marine law Capture by an enemy extinguishes the seamen's contract for wages, but if by recapture, the owner recovers his freight, the seamen recover their wages, for freight is the parent of wages And this holds for those seamen who remain prisoners, and render no assistance in the recapture or afterwards, because they are suffering in the service. And in case of shipwreck, if any portion of freight is paid for the cargo saved, the wages of the seamen are due in the same proportion.

Every agreement that goes to separate the demand for wages, from the fact of freight being earned, is viewed with distrust by the court, as an encroachment on the rights of seamen. "The courts of maritime law extend to them a peculiar protecting favor, and treat them as wards of the admiralty; and though they are not incapable of making valid contracts, they are treated by the courts in the same manner that courts of equity are accustomed to treat young heirs dealing with their expectancies, wards with their guardians, &c. They are considered as placed under the influence of men who have naturally acquired a mastery over them. Every deviation from the terms of the common shipping paper is rigidly inspected, and if additional burdens are imposed upon the seamen without adequate remuneration, the courts will interfere, and moderate or annul the stipulation."

Mariners are bound to contribute out of their wages for embezzlements of the cargo, or injuries produced by the misconduct of any of the crew. But the individual criminal must be unknown, and circumstances must be such as clearly to fix and prove the wrong upon some of the crew; and then those of the crew upon whom the presumption of guilt rests, must stand sureties for each other, and contribute rateably to the loss. If an individual can free himself from suspicion, he does not contribute. And if no reasonable presumption lies against any of the crew, the loss falls upon the owner or master.

In case of shipwreck, and there are materials of the ship saved, the seamen by whose exertions they are saved, are entitled to their wages out of the proceeds of the fragments, even although no freight was earned to the owners. Chancellor Kent, however thinks that in such a case, the allowance to seamen out of the wreck ought to be called salvage. "Wages, in such cases, would be contrary to the great principle in marine law, that freight is the mother of wages, and the safety of the ship the mother of freight."

The wages of seamen constitute a lien upon the ship, which does not, like other liens, depend on possession. Seamen's wages are hardly earned, and liable to many contingencies, by which they may be entirely lost, without any fault on their part. Few claims are so highly favored by law, and when due, the vessel, owners, and master, are all liable for them. Their demand takes precedence of all bottomry bonds, and is good against even a subsequent *bona fide* purchaser. It is a sacred claim, and as long as a single plank of the ship remains, the sailor is entitled, as against all other persons, to the proceeds, as security for his wages. The wages of seamen do not contribute to the general average, when a loss of goods, masts, or the like, is voluntarily incurred at sea for the common safety, except in the single instance of the ransom of the ship. They are exempted here, lest the fear of personal loss should restrain them from making the requisite sacrifice. And the hardships and perils they endure, well entitle them to an exemption from farther distress.

Desertion from a ship without just cause, or the justifiable discharge of a seaman by the master for bad conduct, will work a forfeiture of the wages previously earned. This is the rule of justice and of policy. But if the seaman quits the vessel involuntarily, or is driven ashore by reason of cruel usage, and for personal safety, the wages are not forfeited. On the other hand, it is the duty of the seamen to abide by the vessel as long as reasonable hope remains; and if they desert the ship in the perils of the sea, when they might have prevented damage, or saved the vessel, they forfeit their wages and are answerable in damages.

So liberal and kind is the care which our laws have taken for the interests of seamen in the merchant service. It would seem that nothing more is wanting for *their* benefit, excepting a more effectual security for the *kind* of provision which is to be made for them when they fall into sickness or distress in a foreign port, and some arrangement for their comfortable support, when worn out and decrepit at home

www.ingramcontent.com/pod-product-compliance
Lightning Source LLC
Chambersburg PA
CBHW032016110726

47901CB00004B/1106